# As Time Goes By

OcEA,

Hope you

enjoy—

MYloven 4/22/00

# As Time Goes By

by
**Michael W. Glover, M. D.**

**Writer's Showcase**
New York   San Jose   Lincoln   Shanghai

# As Time Goes By

Published by Writer's Showcase,
an imprint of iUniverse.com, Inc.

For information address:
iUniverse.com, Inc.
620 North 48th Street
Suite 201
Lincoln, NE 68504-3467
www.iuniverse.com

ISBN: 0-595-00016-9

*To my wife, Cathy, who has persevered
the hours of my work, the absence of my
physical being, and the wanderings of
my heart. For these things, she has been,
and always will be my one true love.*

# Prologue

**April, 1978; Vienna, Austria; Conference of the Organization of Petroleum Exporting Countries (OPEC):**

"Gentlemen! Gentlemen, please!" Jofur Abdul Armani, the newly elected Chairman of the Board of Governors of O.P.E.C., rapped the bottom of the firmly grasped water glass on the gleaming surface of the horseshoe shaped table before him. Although his demeanor usually forbade such action, Jofur had stood from his seat and leaned forward onto the table surface supporting himself with his left hand while he applied a gavel like action with the base of the glass. "Please come to order so we can discuss the next item on our agenda." Armani, the Saudi Arabian representative, perceived that he had finally attained the attention of the other cartel members and released his strangle hold on the water glass. He straightened the sleeves of his tailored suit, adjusted his tie and while giving his best Oxford smile to the rest of the group sat down. "Now," he continued with more composure, "we must proceed without further outbursts or we shall never complete today's agenda."

"This is ridiculous, Jofur." Igor Rafstani, the grizzled looking, thick-chest Iranian representative stood from his seat at the left tip of the table. "How can we proceed to any other items when we haven't settled what you have just proposed? And, how can you propose price reductions and production quotas to the rest of this group while you enjoy the luxury of overproduction for the past three years?" Igor motioned his hands across the other seated members. "You're proposal would strangle the rest of us while you sit back and live on the surplus you have accumulated over that time. Jofur, my friend, we don't have any surplus, and we don't have the time or patience to wait for you to decide what we should charge for our oil." Igor, well known for his past acts of terrorism, was well trained in the art of killing, and some even said his smile could kill. If that were so, Jofur was as good as dead. Igor relaxed his full-toothed smile and looked once again around at a selected group of representatives. "Unlike Saudi Arabia, the rest of us depend on producing as much crude oil as possible. We don't bask in the luxury of having the time to do as we wish with our oil. We have great needs for the new revenues the price increases have afforded. Our people are hungry. Our towns still need fresh water and electricity. I'm sure the rest of the smaller producers will agree with my feelings. So, why do you plague us with these humorous diversions?" Igor was rein-forced by affirmative nods from those representatives that had previously agreed to ally themselves with Iran if ever an attempt were made to place further quotas on production.

Further individual, uncontrolled discussions broke out among the other representatives, but before anyone tried to formally speak, Jofur slammed the glass onto the walnut surface splashing its remaining con-tents onto the table top. The loud report of the glass on wood caused all heads to turn to the Chairman. Jofur smiled and slowly stood. "Excuse my outburst, but it seems my intentions have been misconstrued. My friends," Jofur looked around the table at each member making sure to make eye contact as he spoke, "the items I have suggested are not intended as mandates. We all know that policy change requires a unanimous vote by the membership. My thoughts are only presented for discussion, and much to the disbelief of others, they are not influenced by outside interests. My interests and my loyalties are represented at this table. However, each of us has a responsibility to our own country, and that responsibility is for not only now but the future." Jofur gathered his thin five foot eight inch frame and held upturned hands out to the group. "You have elected me as chairman of this Organization. As chairman, I feel it my duty to convey to the organization any item that I have discovered that would be of value to the group as a whole. We all have that responsibility." Jofur especially focused on Igor Rafstani for a few emphatic moments and then continued. "We have all felt the recent decreasing petroleum needs of the West. Even the gluttonous United States has reduced its purchases by ten percent. They are developing alternative fuels even as we quibble over prices. They have increased their own production, and they are even buying a poorer but cheaper product from their southern neighbor Mexico. Recently, it has been learned that they are also preparing to strike deals with their long time enemy, the Soviet Union. The need for OPEC oil will always be present, but we must not price ourselves out of the market. And, we must not overly produce because that would only cause a further price reduction. Doesn't anyone else see the writing on the wall? If this pattern continues, when we do request further price increases, our customers will only smile and live on other producers until our prices come back on line. It is for these reasons, and these reasons alone, that I have made these proposals. I welcome any other suggestions, preferably those that make good business sense."

"Good business sense for who, Jofur?" Jaresh Hassani, the Iraqi representative, jumped up from his position at the right tip of the table. "Saudi Arabia can withstand a lull in production. Your plus has been your volume. But for the rest of us, to cut production is to starve. But, perhaps that is what you want." Other members aligned with Iraq and Iran murmured their agreement with Jaresh.

"I personally resent that line of thought, Jaresh. But neither your nor my thoughts mean anything. The facts are as I have stated. We can use these facts for profit, or we can disregard the facts, put our heads in the sand, and eventually see how our blindness causes the collapse of our prices and perhaps even this organization."

"Whose facts are these, Jofur? Who has such a crystal ball?" Khartum Addafi, the Libyan representative seated next to Igor Rafstani spoke. "Why have you now changed your position on prices and quotas? Perhaps it has something to do with your recent trip to the United States." Khartum looked around the table at the astonished faces. "Yes, my brothers. Jofur has been to the lion's den. Have we been sold out, Jofur?"

"I travel where I wish, Khartum. My visit to the U.S. has nothing to do with these suggestions. If you must know, I have been to Las Vegas." Jofur smiled as he thought about all the wonderful lights and the all the beautiful women, but he also made sure not to be supplicative in his rebuttal.

"Regardless, Jofur. I must agree with Igor." Khartum motioned to Rafstani. "We must sustain our production and our prices. If the West continues on their quest for alternative fuels, I'm sure there are ways we can convince them to stop. Or, we will have to convince those that supply the West with new oil to stop. We all know that there are ways to tame the beasts." Khartum smiled and looked at Igor.

Igor Rafstani nodded agreement without looking at Khartum. Their contrived plan to undermine the conference was snowballing. It was the goal of Iran's newly formed Khomeni government and the military leadership of Libya and Iraq to stall the meetings, keep the prices at the present levels, and remove all quotas.

Jofur uncomfortably dismissed the comment from Khartum with a hand pass and recognized the man sitting next to his left. "The chair recognizes the representative from Qatar, Benjamin Arudi, and then, we must proceed with our scheduled agenda."

Ben Arudi, the "Abe Lincoln of Qatar", as he was called by Jofur, stood and looked around the table. "Gentlemen, my country also has great need for oil profits, and we would like to pump the largest amount our facilities will permit. But, as Jofur has commented, we must not let a quick fortune overshadow the long term needs of the future. Truly the United States is a slow study, but, as witnessed by the past, it has the capacity and ingenuity to open oil fields in other countries as it did in our own. At this time, the Americans are opening huge fields on the Northern Slopes of Alaska. They are preparing to help Mexico explore and open new oil fields. And, as our Chairman has all ready mentioned, the United States has begun a practice of detente with the Soviets. My country has discovered, but through questionable intelligence, that part of that package is to include oil purchases from the Baku region. That area in the Soviet Union, for those that aren't aware, has the capability of producing as much oil as all of us, save for Kuwait and Saudi Arabia. Also, the U.S. is developing safe nuclear energy for production of electricity, and over the past three years, they have increased their overall automotive fleet fuel efficiency by fifty percent. We must not ignore these signs, and we must cease our mindless aggravation of their government." Arudi glared at Igor. "Igor, this needless harassment of American tankers as they move through the Gulf must end immediately. What must your leader be thinking?"

"This is no place to discuss my country's policy on the way we treat American ships." Rafstani stood. "I am insulted, and I blame our Chairman for allowing this meeting to get out of hand. I will not continue this meeting so long as he sits at the center of the table." As Igor stood, he slung his chair up against the adjacent wall. "From this day onward, Iran will do what it wishes with its oil. We will charge what we wish, and we will produce what we wish. No longer will the wishes of this group govern the way my country does business. And, as for you, Arudi, beware. My jackals will eat on your flesh, along with you neighbor's, if you stand in our way." Igor puffed his chest to its full extent and stomped out of the room. Close on his heels were the representatives from Iraq, Libya, Algeria, and Venezuela.

Armani shook his head in amazement. The meeting had quickly turned into a disaster. He turned to his aide and whispered. "Hafar, summon my car. Then call the members of our personal council. We will meet in my hotel room in one hour." Jofur waited for the room to quieten. "Gentlemen, in the face of loosing our quorum, we must adjourn. I will contact each of you tonight after talking with the Iranian and Iraqi representatives. Let us hope we can salvage this conference. While awaiting my call, I urge the rest of you to think long and hard about what you have heard and seen here today. Realize who is looking out for your best interest. Thank you." Jofur slowly lifted from his chair, assembled his papers and neatly filed them into his briefcase. Then, he straightened his suit, smoothed out his beard and mustache, and briskly covered the distance to the front of the building where his black Mercedes limousine awaited. He slid into the back seat, motioned the driver to proceed, and breathed deeply for the first time in the past two hours. After composing his thoughts, he picked up the car phone and dialed a frequently used number. Two rings and the other end responded. After a brief conversation, the tension of the meeting seemed to leave Jofur's body as he relaxed into the plush leather seat.

* * *

## IRANIAN SPECIAL ENVOY'S COUNCIL ROOM

"Okay, Igor. I have helped you disrupt the meeting. Now, it is your turn to help me." Jaresh Hassani leaned over the desk of the Iranian representative and glared into Igor's riveting dark eyes. "We're on very shaky ground here, Igor. And, there are many tensions growing, even between our own countries. How are you going to help the rest of us?" Jaresh motioned to the other representatives in the room.

"In due time, Jaresh, In due time, when it's needed. We're a patient people. Things will eventually come our way."

"We don't have that kind of time, Igor." Jaresh slammed his fists onto Igor's desk. "My country must have the profits brought it by our oil sales. We can't wait two, three, or four months before we generate any income."

Igor looked at Jaresh's clenched fists and slowly lifted his gaze to the angered face. "Relax, my brother. A plan is beginning to unfold that will remove a major oil supplier from the market place. When that happens, you can sell all the oil you can produce." Igor grinned, rubbed his chin and leaned back in his chair. He thought momentarily, motioned for his aide, and whispered quietly into Cali Bijani's ear, "Cali, get me Yassar Akazian on the scrambled phone. We have another job for him."

# 1

CHRISTMAS EVE 1978, MOBJACK BAY, VIRGINIA'S EASTERN SHORE

John Chadwick hunkered his six foot two inch, two hundred pound frame deeper into the concrete pit. The hissing of the catalytic heater struggled to warm the cold air as it stealthily slipped into the hunting pit which he and Larry Goodenau had occupied since thirty minutes before dawn. Regardless of how well he dressed, John was always cold until the first flight of geese arrived from the protective waters of Mobjack Bay. From the corner of his right eye, he could see Larry Goodenau, his long time hunting partner, college buddy, medical school partner, and now pediatrician, attempting to steal some of the radiant heat escaping from the heater before it slipped between the corn stalks that lay across their access to the outside world. The remnants of a good corn harvest made excellent camouflage for the opening of their goose pit, but, for insulation, their efficiency was nil. John caught Larry's stare and smiled between shivers.

"Are we having fun yet?" John whispered between the chattering of his teeth.

Larry grimaced and inched closer to the *Coleman.*

Just before dawn the rain they had fought while driving into the bottom became a mixture of snow and sleet, and each gust of wind pushed the cold, ice-filled air deeper into their lair. With each pulse of air, the catalytic heater groaned its attempt to keep up with the drop in temperature.

"If that thing goes out, I'm outta here!" Larry said with sincerity. He tried to act happy about the situation, but the bite in the air reminded him that he could be home in bed snuggled up to his wife's warm behind. "You know, I could be home with Janie instead of in this cold-assed pit." Larry wiped the ice from his mustache, reached for his cup of coffee, took a long warming drink and set the cup on the wooden bench between him and John. "She even likes to make love in the morning!" Larry's attempted wink at John turned suddenly into an uncontrollable shiver. "Damn! It's Christmas Eve. I'm off until midnight, and here I sit in a hole in the ground freezing my ass off. Why do I let you talk me into this every year?"

"Because you can't kill geese from your bedroom. That's why. And, if you'd admit it, you like this as much as I do." John's chill shook the bench.

Larry handed John his cup of coffee. John wrapped his gloved hand around the cup and put it up to his mouth. He turned up the cup, but no liquid issued forth. He looked into the cup and then he looked at Larry.

"What's wrong?" Larry puzzled at John's stare.

John turned up the cup and shook the chunk of coffee ice out of the bottom of the cup onto the floor of the pit.

They both watched the ice hit the floor and bounce once on the slatted bottom before it danced its way into the water that had accumulated beneath their bench. As if they were in a trance for a moment, it was several seconds before they looked at each other and laughed. "Shit, it is cold!" they chimed in unison.

"Are we sure we need to be here?" Larry was ready to hang it up for the morning, but he would persevere in the face of adversity if John wanted to stay.

"Of course, we want to be here. There's no better place to be than here...now...today. When those geese start talking, you'll warm up. They'll come up off the bay, fly over those trees," John pointed to the eastern line of oak trees that declared the perimeter of his land, " and then, they'll..."

"They'll take off for Abernathy's just as they always do."

"Not this year, Lar. Those fellows at the hunt club will have to take seconds from us this year. That's why we spent thirty minutes putting out all those decoys. When the sun comes up, you'll see why we're going to have better luck. You'll see."

John's determined voice helped Larry somewhat, but Larry also knew all hunters, particularly goose hunters, were overly optimistic before the first sunrise of their first hunt. "Well, I hope this secret you've been keeping is a good one. I'm still freezing." Larry embraced the heater. He removed his right glove and felt over the face of the burner. Yep, it was working, but it sure didn't seem like it in the pit. "I wonder why good old Cecil didn't pick a warmer climate to move to when he left Tangier Island?"

John smiled as he reminisced about his Grandfather. Cecil Chadwick had transplanted from Tangier Island to Severn, Virginia, just after the first World War. Through his own frugal ways, and as a result of the Depression, Cecil had acquired just over one thousand acres of land around the Severn area. His own son Matthew, John's father, never acquired a love for farming, but as John grew and spent more and more time on the farm, Cecil recognized the gleam in John's eye whenever the farm was discussed. On a morning just as this, as John remembered, Cecil pledged the farm to John.

"Oh, I don't know why he came here, but I'm sure glad he did. Otherwise, how would I have ever met a bum like you?" John grinned and winked at Larry.

"Yeah, we've had some good times right in this field. I killed my first goose out of this pit while hunting with you and Cecil."

"Yeah, I remember…lucky shot!"

"Lucky, my ass!"

"Well, you won't need luck today. When the sun comes up, look into the bottom. Even Janie's body would have a hard time competing with what you're about to see."

"I beg your pardon. I don't like an Ob-Gyn man, particularly one who's seen my wife's body, commenting on it's appearance. And I particularly don't like him comparing it to a piece of Virginia bottom land." Larry grinned with his comment. "Anyway, speaking of "pieces", when are you going to get serious with Maggie? You wouldn't have to talk about women's bodies all the time if you had one at home."

John squirmed on his cushion. "You never know. I might consider popping the question tonight after the party."

Larry's head jerked toward John. "Really? Are you really thinking about asking her? Hell, I was kidding. I never thought you would get married."

John grinned. "Just what is that supposed to mean?"

"Oh, you know. You've told me a thousand times you would never get married. You're too busy with the hospital. You're too busy with the farm. You're too busy with your research. You're just too busy!" Larry took off his gloves, put them on top of the heater, and poured another cup of coffee. He set the coffee down after closing his thermos and slipped the gloves back onto his chilled hands. "Mmm, feels good after being over the heater. So, am I going to get a response out of you, or are you going to clam up as usual?"

"I know what I've said in the past, but Maggie's different. She's no quick roll in the hay. She's someone I've gotten serious about."

"Well, listen to John Chadwick. Is this the same man I grew up with? Is he actually going to open up about his feelings?"

"Shut up! You especially should know what a good woman brings out in a man."

"Well, if I know Maggie, you won't have to ask twice."

"What do…" John tweaked his ears up to the edge of the pit. "What was that?" John tuned his ears to the new squawking sounds from the direction of the bay.

"What's what?" Larry was impervious to the sound. He liked to shoot geese, but the intricacies of the hunt didn't excite him as they did John.

John didn't answer Larry's query. Instead, he reached down and stroked the head of his black Labrador retriever. "Easy, Jute. I hear them." He looked into the Lab's dark brown eyes. "We won't let you down today. Will we, Larry?"

"Not if I get off a couple of luck…," Larry stopped mid sentence as he looked over the edge of the pit into the bottom. "Damn! When did you have time to do that?"

The stream that ran through the bottom and terminated into Mobjack Bay had been meticulously widened and dammed close to its outlet. Behind the dam, a six to seven acre lake had formed. The jagged shore line was frozen for a distance of two or three feet into the lake before the choppy water prevented ice formation. The central portion was open, and in the choppy water tossed at least a hundred decoys. "Man! This is going to be great." Larry reached over and patted John on the shoulder.

"Quiet!" The cacophony of the geese had increased. John edged to the brim of the pit and looked between the dried leaves of the corn stalks. Out over the bay he could see large flights of geese heading inland, searching for familiar landmarks to their feeding grounds. He set his *Ithaca* ten gauge, automatic safely against the front edge of the pit within easy reach and began mouth calling the geese. With each expulsion of air, his buttocks rose two or three inches from where he was crouched on the wooden slats.

"I wish Maggie could see you now, " Larry mused. "She'd probably die laughing."

"You better quit talking and get that pea shooter ready," John gasped for air between calls. "I've got a group interested."

"That'll be the day." Larry set his coffee on the bench. He had to pee, badly, but just as sure as he got out of the pit, the damn geese would land and walk around his feet. It always seemed to happen that way. Instead, he suppressed the urge, picked up his *Browning Superposed*, and prepared to heed John's command. "Okay, I'm ready. Where are the geese?"

John didn't comment. He just pointed in the general direction of the approaching flight and continued to call fervidly.

The lead goose had eyed the new situation in Chadwick's Bottom and seemed to like what he had seen. The rain and sleet had kept the nictatating membrane over the old goose's eyes, so that the decoys looked enough like his kind to bring him over to the field. First he led the flock downwind one hundred yards over the field. Then, they dropped fifty yards and turned into the wind to land among the tempting corn. After making his approach, the lead goose scooped his wing and allowed another ten yards of drop, but suddenly, he pulled his head closer to his body, performed a quick ninety degree turn and led the group crosswind out of the field.

"Damn! He must have seen us! I guess they'll head for Abernathy's now." Larry set his gun against the front wall of the pit with a frustrated clank. "Freeze my ass off for nothin…"

"Keep ready. They're coming back." John quit calling.

The lead goose had flown downwind, turned, and was coming back into the field over their decoys. The flock was only forty yards off the ground, one hundred yards in front of the pit. A group of fifteen or twenty birds had set their wings in preparation for landing.

"They're going to land about twenty or thirty yards in front of the pit." John looked quickly at Larry and smiled. "Get them just as they put their flaps down."

"Okay, okay." Larry whispered. "I know when to shoot." Larry watched the flock break up into smaller groups of six or eight. They were flying into the wind heading directly at the open side of the pit. They glided into a position about twenty yards off the ground and gulled their wings, or as

John said, "dropped their flaps" to land. They were committed, and it would take four or five seconds to convert to regular flight from this mode. Now was the time!

"Now!" John shouted as he shoved the corn stalks to his left and stood up with gun ready. He quickly grasped the fore piece of the Ithaca with his left hand and zeroed in on the left group of geese. His aim went instinctively to the closest member of the group. The sight covered up the great bird and without his thinking…BOOOMMMM! The Ithaca belched it full load. The shot riveted the lead goose, tearing through feathers, down, skin, and thick flight pectorals, through to the chest cavity finally piercing the heart. The goose folded in mid-air, thumped onto the ground and rolled to a stop among the corn stobs, its last migration along the Eastern Flyway terminated in Chadwick's Bottom.

The geese were confused. The goose next to its fallen comrade broke right and pumped its wings attempting to reach for the low cloud cover. John swung onto the goose, led it about three feet, and touched the trigger. BOOOMMM! The shot sped after the goose, but the bird made an instinctive hard right turn for the water, and the pattern whistled by its head causing it to pull its great black beak and neck closer to its body. However, its partner failed to sense the danger and continued on a flight straight toward the tree line. John saw the goose remain low and to his left. He calculated it would be a safe area to shoot, swung the *Ithaca's* muzzle through the flight path of the goose and past its head six feet or so. WHAMMM!!! The Ithaca responded while leaving the chamber open, since John had expended his last shell in the magazine. The last brown Federal three and one-half inch shell had answered John's command and spit its black death into the path of the big bird. The goose buckled under the impact and plummeted fifty feet into the lake's choppy water.

Larry reacted as quickly as John to the approaching geese. He had kept his Browning in his left hand and threw the shocks to his right. He shifted the grip of the gun to his right hand and nestled the fore stock into the notch formed by his thumb and first finger of his left hand, as was his style for pass shooting. As soon as he emerged from the pit, he singled out a big honker that had bolted from the group. The goose was gaining altitude, but kept heading for the pit. Larry kept the bead on the head of the goose for a split second, touched the trigger, and the Browning reported with a kick. The left wing of the goose buckled near the tip. The goose veered left, began squawking, and started loosing altitude. Larry, not wanting to loose a wounded goose, put the bead on the birds tail. He instinctively calculated his lead for a quartering shot and touched the trigger. The bottom barrel of the "over-and-under " responded and sent its messengers of death down the thirty inch barrel, through the full choke, and out over a circular pattern toward the fleeing bird. As it passed though the big Canada's location, one of the pattern's members shattered the head of the ten pound goose. The limp carcass thudded to the ice covered earth, exploding tiny ice droplets off the corn stubble.

Larry kept his eye on the group, reloaded his weapon, and searched for any remaining birds. By now, most of the geese had identified the location of the danger and were exiting the field downwind. However, one lone goose, perhaps a mate of a fallen bird, had landed among the field decoys during the furor. Larry spotted the goose as it rose and flew toward the water's shimmering safety. As the goose descended the hill toward the lake, it set its wings to glide onto the beckoning water. When it was fifteen yards off the ground, Larry touched the gold trigger of the Browning. The muzzle of the upper barrel belched fire and sent its lethal lead shot toward the goose. Four or five of the pellets found their target felling the prey. Larry placed his gun on safety and looked at John. The entire scene had taken a brief twenty seconds. "Damn! That was exciting! And I've really got to pee!" The adrenaline rush had quickly reminded Larry of his need to urinate.

"I knew you would like the surprise." John grinned at Larry not expecting an answer. He then looked down at Jute. The dog's muscular back legs were like springs ready to uncoil. The shooting had prepared Jute to do his work. He was ready to explode, but his training had kept him at "STAY" until John commanded otherwise. Jute's eyes were on John. His eagerness was accentuated in his whine. "Jute, birds!" John waved his hand in a casting motion, and Jute launched himself from the pit, tearing corn shocks before him. As soon as his feet hit the cold earth, he tore around the pit area with his nose to the ground. He ventured out about twenty yards, sniffed around, emptied his bladder and looked back at John for directions.

"Come on, Larry. Grab some coffee and watch this. Here's the fun part of bird hunting." Both quickly poured a cup of coffee and climbed from the pit. John reloaded and took his *Ithaca*, but Larry removed the unspent shell from the *Browning's* chamber and left his gun in the pit. John stood erect, stretched, looked at Jute, and waved his hand in the direction of the first fallen bird. "Bird, Jute, Bird!"

Jute jumped to his left and danced among the cut corn stalks. First he smelled the game; then, he saw it. He circled the bird and pounced on it from the rear. He sunk his teeth into the carcass up to the skin at the base of the bird's neck. Then, he proudly carried it to his master. He kept his head high so the body of the goose wouldn't drag the ground. As he pranced back toward John, he appeared satisfied with his performance. This is what he was bred for. To Jute, this was living. He dropped the goose at John's feet, came around behind him and sat at John's heels.

"Good dog! Good boy!" John firmly stroked Jute's head, knelt down, patted the dog's neck, and then stood up to direct Jute to the other two birds that had fallen on dry land. The Lab promptly retrieved the other birds and placed them at John's feet. "We'll have the other bird in no time." John said to Larry as he stroked Jute's head.

"No hurry. I've emptied my bladder and had some warm coffee. I'm ready for an instant replay." Larry watched Jute plant himself beside John's feet. "Jute's a great dog. I love Labs. If Janie would let me, I'd have a yellow, not that I don't like black, Jute, but I've always been partial to those big ole sad eyes of a yellow Lab. But, hell-o, we hardly have enough room for the kids."

"I've told you a thousand times to move out here. I'd give you the land just to have a close neighbor." John walked toward the water's edge with Jute circling him like an Indian galloping around a wagon train.

"I appreciate the offer, John, but Janie has to make five thousand trips a day around town with the kids. She would have to drive all day if we lived out here." Larry looked around the field and sighed. "Maybe someday."

"Well, the offer is always good. You know that." They both walked silently to the edge of the lake and searched the surface for the downed fowl. Jute took his position along John's left side and sat down as if a lead weight were on his tail. The wind had played with the floating body of the goose until it was about fifty feet from shore, and the bird's back barely visible from where John stood, bobbed aimlessly up, down, left and right among the waves. John looked down at the anxious dog. "Bird, Jute, Bird." John waved his hand over the water's edge.

Jute took two leaps, ran along the ice until it began breaking under his weight and jumped into the chilly water. He swam twenty or thirty feet into the lake, his webbed feet making the task easy, and turned looking for instructions from John. John didn't speak. Instead, he pointed to the goose's location, and Jute followed his prompts. Shortly, Jute spied the goose, swam up behind the carcass, and grasped it by the base of the neck. The muscular Lab broke through the shore ice, walked out of the water, and marched proudly to John. He set the goose down, shook from head to tail, and looked up at John with sad eyes, sensing the hunt was over, at least for today.

"Okay, Jute. Good dog. Kennel, Jute, Kennel." Jute broke into a run for the four wheel drive Blazer. John had left the tailgate down and door to Jute's box open. Jute reached the concealed truck long before his hunting partners. He jumped onto the tailgate, crawled into his box, reversed directions, lay down, and hung his head out the door. He was tired, but his tail beat a tattoo onto the cage floor.

John and Larry collected the geese, cased their guns, gathered their belongings, and headed for the truck. Their big hunt was over long before most of the inhabitants of the area rose for work. They arranged their gear in the back of the truck, and John poured Jute a small bowl of dry food, which was devoured before John finished closing the sack and slamming the back tailgate. John started the motor, adjusted the heat to high, and closed the tailgate window. "I love this life. I just love it!" John didn't look at Larry for affirmation of his feelings, but his comment was directed to him.

"Yeah, and I'm damned glad I'm your friend because I love it, too. Aren't you glad you were born rich?" Larry laughed intending his remark as a joke.

John usually didn't take that joke particularly well. He had been born into a wealthy family. His Grandfather had worked hard farming this area of Tidewater Virginia, and the Chadwick Estate was a family tradition. In addition to hunting and farming, and for reasons unknown to himself, John had developed a love for medicine. After high school, John had attended Princeton University and then Johns Hopkins Medical School. His Grandfather had lived to see him graduate from medical school, and , to have heard Cecil tell it, one would have thought John was the only person to ever make it through. After John had completed his training, his professors at Hopkins attempted to recruit him into the Obstetrical program as a assistant professor, but John knew he would return home, close to the farm.

When the hospital in Clifton Forge, a large community near Severn, had advertised for a Chief of Obstetrics to help establish an outlying residency program for the Medical College of Virginia, John was on their doorstep the next day. It took the Administrator thirty minutes to decide to hire John. Life was ideal at Greene Memorial. John lived on the farm in a house his parents had built but rarely used because of their work with the State Department. He was usually a thirty minute drive from the hospital, but with owning a 928 S Porsche, it rarely took him more than fifteen minutes to get to his parking place outside the hospital Emergency entrance. And for the most part, the residents took "call" for the obstetrical patients, giving John ample time to get to the delivery suite. So, his lifestyle did appear easy to those uneducated about his life. He knew Larry was joking; so, he shrugged off the comment along with his heavy coat. "Yeah, I'm glad. Real glad. That's why I get up at all hours to deliver babies. That's why I work every day of the week. That's why…"

"Whoa, big fella! I was only fooling."

"I know, but I get sick and tired of hearing, behind my back mind you, about how rich and how spoiled I am. It's as if they didn't think I work for what I have."

"Well, John. Not everyone knows you as I do, and you're not the most open individual. They think everything was handed you on a silver platter."

"Since when do they sell medical degrees?"

"People think money can buy everything. You know that. Forget it! I was only ribbing you. You know how I feel. Besides, get us out of here. I'd kill for one of Marie's biscuits." Larry waved directions out of their parking place.

John put the truck in gear and grinned. "I know how you feel. Sorry I'm so thin skinned. I wasn't jumping down YOUR throat. Let's go get these birds plucked. Travis has bought a new electric picker from *Cabela's*, and he's dying to try it out."

"Now, you're talking. How is Travis anyway? Didn't he have some heart problems two or three months ago?"

"Yeah, but he's much better. I had him see Jorge last month. He diagnosed him as having atypical angina and put him on Nitro patches making Travis a new man. Says he's going to get Marie pregnant three or four more times."

Larry laughed. "Did Travis put in the lake? I love it."

"Yep. Drove the dozer himself. One heck of a job!" John looked out over the shimmering lake, grinned, and eased out of the woods. He hit the tractor path where it crossed the corn field and worked the four-wheel drive through the pot holes back to the gravel road. He made a left turn onto the paved main road and headed for Travis's tenant house. He pulled into the yard and honked.

Travis Longworth, along with his sons Jeff and Mack walked out the front door of the neat white one story house. His wife, Marie, stood behind the glass storm door. Sue and Julia, Travis' two daughters peered out from behind their mother's shoulders and grinned.

"Did ya get any?" Travis drawled as he walked across the yard toward the truck.

John opened his door and walked to the back of the truck. He opened the tailgate and Jute jumped to the ground. "Jute, heel." Jute sat down beside John as if his rear had been crazy glued.

"Oh, let him play," Travis pointed to Jute. "The boys have made a practice decoy for him. Its got real goose feathers."

John looked down at Jute. Jute, his rear legs twitching and his tail rattling the frozen grass with each wag, was eyeing the sixteen and seventeen year old boys like long lost friends. "Okay, Jute. Hunt." Jute sprang for the boys, and the three raced for the back of the house. John reached into the confines of the back of the truck and pulled out a Santa sized sack of presents for Travis' family. He handed the bundle to Larry. "Take these to Marie. Please!"

"Well, now, I know why I was invited." Larry threw the sack over his shoulder and started for the house. He stopped and looked over his shoulder at John. "I really don't mind. I can smell Marie's biscuits and coffee all the way out here. While you're plucking, I'll be eating."

"Get on in the house, you bum." John waved Larry on his way and leaned back into the truck. "Travis, you can help me with these." John handed Travis two of the geese.

"Whew, them's nice 'uns. I guess the new lake was the ticket." Travis took the geese and held them by the neck, one in each hand.

"The corn was the drawing card, and the lake our trump, Travis. It was beautiful. Just after dawn a huge flock of geese lifted off the bay, and I was able to call a group of thirty into our decoys. You and I will be there day after tomorrow."

"You're right, there." Travis nodded his head in agreement as they headed for the workshed. Larry joined them in the back yard, coffee in one hand and a biscuit in the other.

The electric picker made short work of the geese. Travis manipulated the bodies across the rubber fingers of the circulating wheel, and each goose was naked in three or four minutes. "Marie and I have made about three hundred dollars with this thing. The hunters have done pretty good this year. Seems like everyone has been getting their limit." Travis whistled as he cleaned the last goose.

John busied himself with the removal of the pin feathers and began removing the entrails while Larry perched himself atop an old John Deere tractor and watched the men prepare the geese for the traditional Chadwick Christmas Eve party. "Funny how we can sit here, enjoying the season while one of our own countrymen is held hostage in a foreign land." Larry said almost to himself as he thought about the recent news articles concerning the American pilot being held hostage along with a group of Saudi oil sheiks in Rasht, Iran.

"Whadya say?" Travis queried as the plucker wound down. "I didn't hear ya."

"Oh, nothing. I was just talking about the hostage situation in Iran." Larry took another bite of biscuit and swallowed some warm coffee. "I wonder how long it has been since he had a good cup of coffee?" Larry looked at the white porcelain mug and took another drink.

"Well, I tell you what I'd do," Travis said as he cut into the body of the goose he was cleaning. "I'd march my butt in there and take 'em back. And, I'd kill every damned Iranian that got in my way, I tell you. You can't pussy foot around with those kind. They only understand the sword, jest like it says in the Bible. You turn your back on 'em, and they'll always come back and haunt you." Travis jabbed his knife in the air punctuating his speech while the goose dangled from his other hand.

"Hey," John called from his position over the sink. "Let's get these geese cleaned, and then we can cure the world's political problems. Anyway, you know we're not going to make any military moves. They've all ready screwed up one attempt, and now, the President's not sure what he's going to do. Plus, it would be too out of character to jump in and be militarily active this close to Christmas."

"Well, maybe this is a perfect time," Larry chimed from his perch. "And, by the way, John, you missed some pin feathers on that goose you're cleaning."

John turned and looked up at the perched pediatrician. "Which one?" John pointed to the goose he had just finished cleaning. "This one?"

"Yeah, see those pin feathers." Larry pointed his biscuit-filled right cuff at the goose. "Those won't be too tasty at the party tonight. You had better get them off." Larry turned to continue his discussion of the hostage situation with Travis, but before he could speak he felt the impact of something wet on his shoulder. He looked at the point of impact just as a second piece of goose liver hit him on the sleeve spraying bloody water over his coat and shirt collar. "Okay, okay. I surrender. I guess I deserved that."

"Guess?" John laughed.

"All right! I deserved it, but Janie is going to be pissed. She just washed these clothes."

"Ain't supposed to wash them hunting clothes. It's bad luck. Them animals can smell fresh duds." Travis commented dryly and sincerely.

"Well, if those geese can smell me from fifty yards in the air, more power to them. I've given up hunting about everything else."

Travis smiled. "You come on down some time in season, and I'll show you some real hunting...deer. Now, that's hunting, not just shooting."

"Lordy, if I killed a deer, my wife would disown me, and my little girl would swear I'd killed Bambi. I'll stick to geese." Larry tilted back his coffee mug and finished the brown liquid. "Shoot! This goose hunting is hard enough for me." He smiled sheepishly at John.

They sacked the geese in plastic bags, and Travis packed them in a Styrofoam cooler with ice. John carried the cooler to the truck, put it in the back, and called Jute.

The dog and the two boys raced around the edge of the house. Jute's purple tongue hung limp from the side of his mouth. He dashed across the yard, skidded to a semi-stop five feet from the truck and bounded onto the tailgate. He turned around and waited for the expected hugs and pats from the boys. They didn't disappoint him.

"Kennel, Jute." John waved toward his box.

Jute slid into his box and lay down still panting. A few downy feathers clinging to his mouth moved to and fro as he breathed.

"Thanks, fellas. I'm sure Jute loved his workout."

"So did we, Dr. Chadwick." The two boys patted Jute on the head and backed away as John shut the tailgate.

"I've got you fellas something for Christmas. Thanks for everything. I couldn't keep this place like it is without your help. Just wanted you to know I appreciate your work."

"Aw, it's our pleasure, John," Travis drawled. "I promised your Granddaddy I wouldn't let you go astray, and I aim to keep that promise to the grave." Travis shook John's outstretched hand. "We'll see ya, tonight."

"Thanks, Travis. I'm looking forward to this evening." John rolled up his window and pulled the truck onto the main road heading for home.

# 2

Margaret Quince sat in front of her bedroom dressing-chest mirror combing her long black hair. Her low cut bra revealed her ample cleavage as she stroked her hair, and her lace bikini underwear shifted positions with each movement. "I can't believe you agreed to work tonight. I just can't believe it," she commented to her reflection as she slipped the white uniform over her head. She sat back down and fixed her hair in a tight bun on the back of her head knowing that she would have a headache before her shift was over. However, she had to wear it in this fashion to keep it out of her way. Perhaps she could find a particular doctor to take care of her headache before she signed off her shift in the morning, Christmas morning. "I'm going to kill Betty before the night is up. I know I will." Maggie finished putting on her makeup, picked up her purse, turned out the lights, and headed out the door to start a twelve hour shift on Obstetrics at Greene Memorial. It was 7:15 P.M., plenty of time to take report and start her 8:00 P.M. shift. As Maggie eased her car from the her apartment's parking structure, the freezing rain that had been a threat all day began to fall once again. She looked up through the bare trees and watched intently as the low clouds slipped silently across the sky. "Looks like the same weather as when I first came to Greene," she thought as she pulled into traffic.

The trip into the hospital took about twenty minutes, and Maggie's little yellow Beetle seemed to know its own way. Unfortunately, the drive in tonight wouldn't be as interesting as her first trip to Greene Memorial. It had all started with what Maggie had regarded as a tragedy. She all to well remembered her disappointment at the closing of the Birthing Center in Richmond just six months ago. She had worked so hard to become a Nurse Midwife. The years at the University of Kentucky, the training with the Mountain Maternal Health League, and finally realizing her dream by taking a joint interest in the Birthing Center. The two years the clinic was open had been wonderful. Everything she had wanted Midwifery to be seemed to have culminated within the walls of the Center. However, the clinic had been forced to close because their physician coverage had been lost because of the medical liability crunch.

Maggie smiled at her thoughts as she eased the Volkswagen away from the stoplight. She imagined the party she was missing tonight at John's was a bit more elaborate than the small get together the nurses had had on the closing of the center. The utter depression she had felt that day had been overwhelming. She hadn't had a clue as to what she was going to do after she left the clinic, but as things occasionally work out, Maggie had read an interesting job advertisement in one of the Richmond newspapers the day of the closing. Impulsively, she had picked up the phone, and the next day she had an appointment to be interviewed for the position of Obstetrical Nurse Coordinator at Greene Memorial Hospital in Clifton Forge, Virginia.

Maggie pulled into the Convenient Market located one mile from the hospital. She ran into the store and purchased a bag of M&M peanuts. "Energy for the long night," she thought as she restarted the Beetle and chugged back into traffic easing through the gears as she aimed the VW toward the hospital. "This thing is running a heck of a lot smoother than the day I first arrived," Maggie grinned. Her car had made it fine to the Cifton Forge exit off the Interstate from Richmond on the day of her scheduled interview. But, no sooner than she had exited the car began making a terrible sound and had begun to jerk. She had eased into the now familiar Convenient and rolled the car to a stop. As she had pondered her fate knowing she would have been late for her appointment, a tall, blonde-haired man had approached her asking if she had needed help. She finally had choked out an affirmative answer, and the man had promptly gone to the back of her Beetle and opened the "hood".

"I've found your problem," he had replied all too soon to Maggie's liking because the view of his rear end had been pleasing. "Try it now," he had said as he closed the "hood". Maggie had started the car and immediately knew the problem had been rectified. "A spark plug wire had worked its way loose. Nothing major." The stranger had smiled as he leaned in her window. "You'll be fine."

His smile had left Maggie at a loss for words, but she finally had been able to thank him. He had turned to walk away before Maggie had the strength to muster, "Excuse me! "

"Yes?" The stranger had turned and responded.

"I didn't catch your name. Mine's Margaret, Margaret Quince, but my friends call me Maggie."

"Nice to meet you, Maggie. My name's John, John Chadwick."

Maggie eased the VW Beetle into her parking place inside the hospital's parking garage.

The first meeting with John Chadwick had not been her last on that fateful day. She remembered the meeting with the hospital administrator. As they had completed their conversation, the administrator had informed Maggie that she had the job as far as he had been concerned. But, the final decision would have to come from Dr. Chadwick. When Maggie had heard the name she had thought the doctor must be the father of the man she had just met at the Convenient Market. However, when John had arrived, it was indeed him; too young and way too handsome. John had not felt awkward at the coincidence of their earlier meeting and had immediately put Maggie at ease. After they had discussed her credentials, John had stood, shaken her hand, and welcomed her to Greene Memorial.

Maggie slid her trim five foot four inch frame out of the door and headed for the Emergency Room entrance. Usually, Maggie was a happy person, but tonight, the anger she had for her ignorance in agreeing to work while missing John's party was causing her to reach her boiling point. Betty Sims, her head supervisor, had pleaded until Maggie finally agreed to work. But Maggie was still angry, more so at herself than anybody else. The only saving grace would be if John had admitted a labor patient. "I'd hate to take him away from his party," she lied to herself, "but I sure would like to see him," she thought as she covered the short distance to the electric doors.

Over the past eighteen months, Maggie had fallen in love with John. But John had a difficult time taking their relationship seriously. He was still a big little boy, at heart, and his loves were the farm, obstetrics, cars, and hunting, in that order. Maggie wondered where women, especially Maggie Quince, fit into the scheme. She and John had become romantically involved over the past few months, and she knew John loved her. His touch, his mannerisms when he was with her, and his attentiveness were too real, but John found it difficult to put his feelings into words. She hoped he was the strong silent type, but occasionally she needed the verbal feedback of his emotions. Until now, all she knew about his life was what she had heard from the hospital grapevine, but she knew better than to put too much credence in those stories. Larry Goodenau, one of the pediatricians, would speak with her openly about John; furthermore, he seemed to know things no one else knew. But out of respect for John, Dr. Goodenau wouldn't go too deeply into John's personal life. Maggie would have to find out about that herself.

Maggie breezed through the E. R. entrance, and the swoosh of the electric doors had barely quieted when she saw Betty. "I'm here, I'm here! Not in spirit, but in mind and body."

Betty walked her lanky, but well endowed five foot, seven inch redheaded frame over to Maggie and sighed. "I'm glad to see you. This place has gone crazy, and I'm not ready for it! Not tonight. I've got two cardiacs in here already and Dr. Redmond is at John's par..."

"Don't mention the party. Just don't mention it." Maggie held her loose hand defensively. "If I pretend it's not happening, then it's not happening."

"All right. I'll try not to mention it again."

"Fine. Now, what else is going on? It doesn't sound bad so far."

"Hold on, Maggie. I've saved the best for last."

"What? Don't keep me in suspense. You know how I hate that."

"You have a labor patient. It's..."

"John's?"

"No, not John's. Dr. Chesley's."

"Oh, damn!"

"Yes, damn!" Betty grinned. "I know you've had trouble with Chesley in the past, but I think this lady will be delivering soon, and you won't have to be bothered with him for long."

"You know he doesn't come in until they're crowing. I hate that. Betty, you really know how to hurt a gal."

"Well, you shouldn't have been so agreeable as to come in to work. Anyway, Chesley is already here."

"Agreeable? If I were agreeable, I'd hate to see someone that wasn't. I'll keep that in mind for future requests." Maggie slipped past Betty and headed for the elevator. "Merry Christmas, Betty."

"Merry Christmas, and thanks for coming in tonight."

"Anytime. Except this time next year!" Maggie's turn put emphasis on the "next year" portion of her reply.

"All right, but you won't have to worry about it next year." Betty winked.

"What's that supposed to mean?" Maggie smiled inquisitively.

"Why, you and John will be married by next year. I'm not blind. You won't have to work then. He's loaded."

"Well, I'm not sure about either. Goodnight." Maggie's smile melted. She turned and darted for the opened elevator door. She didn't want to hear about how rich John was, and how she could quit work if they married. Tonight wasn't the night for a disquieting discussion.

As the elevator opened onto the labor floor, Maggie was confronted by the anxious gaze of Rachel Toombs, the labor hall nurse presently on duty. "Thanks for the welcome, Rachel, but you really didn't have to." Maggie smiled as she stepped from the car.

"Maggie, you've got to do something about Dr. Chesley." Rachel took Maggie by the hand. "Usually, I don't make a big deal about him because we have the residents around, but tonight they're off. The man shouldn't be doing Ob. Come on. Let me show you something." Rachel led Maggie down the hall.

"Easy, Rachel." Maggie pulled her hand from Rachel's grasp. "I've been jerked around by all the wrong people tonight."

Rachel turned, not understanding what Maggie meant.

"Lead on. I'm right behind you."

Rachel headed down the hall, through the labor hall doors, and they both sat down in front of the central monitoring unit. "Just look at that…" Rachel pointed to the monitor strip on the present labor patient.

Maggie took one look at the strip and recognized the deep variable decelerations of the baby's heart beat every time the patient had a contraction, the type of dip seen when compression on the umbilical cord diminishes blood flow to the fetus. "It should be okay. How close is she to delivery?"

"That's just it, Maggie. She could have been delivered thirty minutes ago. Dr. Chesley's in the doctor's lounge watching the news or something. He could break her water and deliver the baby, but he says he wants nature to run its own course. I'm not qualified to rupture membranes without physician observation, and I'm having trouble explaining all this to the patient. What would you do?" Rachel was anxious for Maggie to take over the situation so she could avoid a confrontation with Dr. Chesley.

Maggie began rocking back and forth in the chair; her eyes squinted at the monitor and then shifted to the door to the doctor's lounge. The fetal heart tracing continued to have the periodic dips. "Well, this won't usually be a problem," Maggie said as she traced the decelerations on the monitor screen with her finger, "but there's no reason not to at least rupture the membranes and get a better quality tracing particularly if the baby is near delivery." Maggie picked up the patient's chart and read Rachel's notes. "You've been too kind to Dr. Chesley in your record." She tossed the chart back onto the counter with a bang, got up, and bounded toward the patient's labor room.

Rachel jumped with the report of the aluminum chart hitting the gray Formica counter top. She watched as Maggie entered the Labor-Delivery Room, and inconspicuously she caught the chair that was about to fall backward from Maggie's hasty departure. Rachel set the chair behind the counter and tracked Maggie into the room.

"Hello, Mrs. Markey, I'm Maggie Quince, the Labor Hall nurse coming on duty. It appears that you are about ready to have a baby."

The patient reached up and grabbed Maggie's arm. "Is my baby all right? Why does the heartbeat keep dropping when I have a contraction? It didn't happen with my first child. Where's Dr. Chesley? I...oooh, I'm starting another pain." Julia Markey began panting with her contraction.

Maggie watched as the heartbeat dropped into the seventies. She took sterile gloves and examined the patient. The cervix was completely dilated, and the membranes were bulging almost to the vaginal opening. The baby was deliverable. "Excuse me, Mrs. Markey. Your baby will be fine. I'm going to get Dr. Chesley. You're ready for delivery."

"Thank, God!" Julia mustered as good a smile as possible for Maggie.

"Rachel, where's Mr. Markey? I'm sure he would like to be present for the delivery." Maggie knew that Dr. Chesley didn't allow the husband in the delivery room, but since it was Christmas Eve, what the heck!

Before Rachel could speak, Julia Markey winced with he contraction but was able to assure Maggie that her husband didn't want to be in the delivery room. "He faints," she grinned sheepishly as the contraction completed. "I'm feeling some pressure."

"I'm sure you are," Maggie reassured Julia and headed for the doctor's lounge. She knocked at the door and waited.

"Yes," Dr. Raymond Chesley had come to the door and was peering down at Maggie with his crystal blue eyes over top his reading glasses.

"Doctor Chesley," Maggie sternly gazed into Chesley's fifty year old face. His full head of gray hair gave him a distinguished ethereal appearance, but Maggie wasn't reverential. "Your patient is having deep variable decelerations indicative of a tight nuchal cord or occult prolapse of the cord, and I think she's ready for delivery. Could you scrub, please?" Maggie began to walk away from the door.

"Excuse me, Ms. Quince, but is she crowning?"

Maggie turned and glared at Dr. Chesley. "No sir, but in the baby's best interest, I think…"

"Well, you don't have to think. Call me when she's crowning. I'll be the one to decide when she's ready to deliver."

"But, doctor. She's a gravida three, fully dilated, and at plus two station with the membranes bulging to the perineum. The fetal heart tracing is exhibiting deep variable decelerations, and…"

Raymond Chesley flung the door open and walked to within inches of Maggie. His six feet two inches elevated his gray hair over her frame. "Look here, Ms. Quince! I don't know who the hell you think you are, but your antics won't hold water with me like they do with Dr. Chadwick or the snotnosed residents he's brought here. Why, I've been delivering babies long before either of you knew where they came from, and I'll be damned if I'm going to let you tell me when it's time to deliver one. Call me when she's crowning! Is that understood?" Chesley turned and reentered the lounge. If the pneumatic controller had not been attached, the door might have crashed off its hinges.

"Yes, Doctor Chesley," Maggie said to his back as it went through the doorway. "You old shit!" she added after the door closed.

Rachel had melted from the scene as Dr. Chesley chewed out Maggie. "See! See what I mean. He's an old fart." Rachel snickered at Maggie's comment, but not so loud that the doors could hear.

Maggie grinned at Rachel, shook her head, and reentered the patient's room.

Julia watched as Maggie came through the door. "Are we ready?"

"Yes, we're ready. I just have to do a few things before Dr. Chesley comes in. All right?"

"Anything. I just want my baby to be all right. I'm afraid."

"Don't be frightened, Julia. Everything should be fine." Maggie removed an *amnihook*, a device for sterily rupturing the membranes, from the bedside drawer and picked up an exam glove.

"What are you going to do?" Rachel asked as she grabbed Maggie's arm.

Maggie gently helped Rachel release her grasp. "Sometimes, we have to do what we know is right. Okay, Julia roll onto your back and bring your legs up toward your chest." Maggie reexamined Julia and ruptured the membranes while Julia was having a contraction. The fluid was slightly meconium tinged indicating that the baby was in some distress. "Julia, push with your next contraction. Rachel, give me an internal heart lead, get the DeLee suction, start some oxygen on Julia, and tell the nursery they are about to have a new customer." Maggie smiled at Julia. "Push when you feel the pressure."

Julia shook her head in agreement.

"Should we get Dr. Chesley?" Rachel asked as she hooked the oxygen up to the mask and placed it over Julia's nose.

"Heavens no," Maggie said through her clenched teeth. "She's not crowning."

Julia began a contraction and pushed. The baby's head quickly rotated and began to deliver.

Maggie eased Julia's legs into the stirrups of the birthing bed, prepped the perineum with an iodine solution, and draped the delivery area. She put on a cap, mask, gown and gloves.

"Should I call Dr. Chesley, now?" Rachel was dancing around as if she had to urinate.

"No, not yet! She' not crowning, and I want it charted as such!" Maggie glared at Rachel. "Okay, Julia, push. Your contraction is starting."

Julia held her breath and pushed. Maggie ironed the perineum, and the baby's head emerged through the opening. Maggie checked for a nuchal cord and identified it looped three times. The cord was loose enough that it could be easily reduced. The baby then quickly delivered, screaming at the top of its lungs. "It's a boy, Julia! It's a boy! Rachel, perhaps you should call Dr. Chesley and tell him the baby just CROWNED.

"Okay, but I'm leaving immediately afterwards. All right?"

"Sure, that's fine. Julia has everything under control. Don't you Julia?"

Maggie placed the baby on Julia's abdomen, and Julia quickly took him into her arms. "Can I breast feed now?"

"Sure. That's why I rolled the warmer over. The baby looks fine." Maggie took a quick peek at the baby, and both his color and breathing seemed good.

Raymond Chesley opened the door with his rear end. As he turned to put on his gown, he was greeted by the delivery scene. He walked over to the delivery table, dried his dripping hands, and put on his gown and gloves. "Looks like you had that one quick, Julia."

"Yes, I did. As soon as my water broke, the baby came. I'm sorry you didn't make it, but the nurse was great." Julia smiled at Maggie.

"It was you that did the great job, Julia. She pushed that baby right out of there. No problem." Maggie grinned behind her mask.

"I can see that she did." Chesley picked the baby up from Julia's abdomen. "Now, Julia, I told you we would put the baby in the warmer for a while, then you can breast feed."

"But Maggie said…"

"Well, Ms. Quince doesn't make this decision. I do!"

"Yes, Doctor." Julia frowned and watched intently as Dr. Chesley placed the baby in the basinette.

"You may go about your charting duties now, Ms. Quince. I'll finish here."

"Yes, Doctor." Maggie removed her gown and gloves and began charting the event exactly as it had happened.

"Oh, Ms. Quince? I'd like to talk to you after we take the patient to her room. I would personally like to thank you for your endeavors." "That won't be necessary, Doctor."

"I insist, Ms. Quince."

"Yes, sir." Maggie knew what Dr. Chesley had in mind, but she was ready for ass chewing number two. It made no difference because Maggie knew she had done what was right for her patient and the baby. After all, that was the name of the game in obstetrics.

Maggie gave Raymond Chesley plenty of room after he completed the remainder of the delivery duties. And after he had finished with Julia, Maggie walked over to the bed and began fluffing the sheets around the patient.

Julia softly grasped Maggie by the wrist and looked into her eyes. "I won't tell Dr. Chesley what you did, because it would get you into trouble. I appreciate everything you did for little Daniel and me."

"Don't worry, Julia. Hearing your baby cry was thanks enough. Anyway, Dr. Chesley knows what I did." Maggie began to move away from the bed.

Julia held Maggie's wrist firmer for a moment. "Well, we still appreciate it. I hope you don't have any trouble."

Maggie patted the young hand around her wrist. A small tear formed in Maggie's right eye. "I'll be fine. I've got friends at the top." Maggie winked. "I'll go get your husband now, and we'll see if we can keep him from fainting this time."

Julia snickered.

"Now, get a little rest, and I'll be right back." Maggie exited the labor room and was immediately confronted by Raymond Chesley who was dressed and waiting for her in the hall. "I know what you're going to say, and I don't want to hear it," Maggie started to walk around him.

"What the hell are you trying to do, Ms. Quince? I think you want to be fired. That was the most irresponsible thing I have ever seen a nurse do."

Maggie glared at Dr. Chesley. "And I don't suppose sitting on your butt while that baby was trying to tell you it was in trouble wasn't irresponsible."

"And how is the baby, Ms. High and Mighty?"

"The baby is fine, and you might reconcile things in your mind because of it. But that still doesn't mean you were right by not acting appropriately. How did you know her water wouldn't break and the cord slip down? Or, how did you know the cord wouldn't tighten around the baby's neck and cause more severe problems?"

"That's what experience tells us, Ms. Quince."

"That's bullshit, Dr. Chesley, and you know it. Every situation has to be evaluated on its own merit."

"Well, I'm not going to discuss this any further with you tonight. I will take action on this. I assure you. You have overstepped your boundaries."

"Fine. Do what you have to do, but you'd better be ready for the consequences."

"Consequences? What on earth are you babbling about?"

"I'm not babbling. When we discuss this matter before the obstetrical committee, I'll bring up the number of instances you have delayed care or given inappropriate care during the past year. You know your rear end has been saved on a number of occasions by the residents and my nurses. I keep excellent notes. Remember? You complimented me on that very fact just a few months ago. Goodnight, Dr. Chesley."

"Ms. Quince!" Raymond Chesley softened his position. He knew he was behind times in Obstetrics. His frustration increased during each encounter with the residents, but instead of using the exposure as a learning experience, he simply denied his ineptness. "I will have to discuss this matter with Dr. Chadwick. Then, we'll decide what should be done. Until then, we'll just keep it between the two of us. Correct?"

"Correct! Just the two of us and the chart." Maggie turned and smiled knowing she would probably never hear about the situation again.

After transporting Julia to the postpartum floor, Maggie returned to the labor hall and began the busy work of cleaning equipment. In her frustration, she clanged the pans around the sink and threw papers on the floor. After her anger was partially vented on the stainless steel sink, she sat down and made her final charting entries. However, before she could complete the paper work, she had to stop and call John. She had to tell him her version of the story before Chesley arrived at John's party. "Damn! Why did I agree to work tonight?"

# 3

As the guests entered the gate to the Chadwick Farm and drove the winding two mile asphalt road to the main house, they admired John's Christmas traditions. The field rock gate posts were decked with pine bough roping, and the vertical balusters of the wrought iron gate were wrapped in white and red paper to look like peppermint candy sticks. The road passed through a second set of gates, decorated like the first, before circling in front of the house. As the guests arrived, Jeff and Mack Longworth dressed in Santa suits greeted them as they exited their cars. The house was aglow with flood lamps, and each window adorned with a huge evergreen wreath bespeckled with mistletoe, holly and a red bow. Fruit and magnolia leaves decorated the arch above the main entrance, and the multitude of small white lights on the twelve foot Frazier fir danced in the beveled glass panes of the side lights. The main entry hall opened on either side into a huge living room and dining area, and the heartwood, yellow pine random width floor reflected the lights of the season everywhere they weren't smothered by Persian rugs. Sue and Julia Longworth, dressed in red velvet with white lace trim, flitted about the rooms like nervous cardinals delivering drinks, cookies, homemade candies and sundry other delectables. The butler pantry and kitchen, adjacent to the dining room, teemed with caterer's activities, and the guests, bedecked in holiday attire, migrated between the various sources of food and drink. Christmas music played in the background, but the sweetest sound was the buzz of friendly, cheerful, seasonal conversation.

John had found an empty spot on the bench seat of the Steinway Grand Piano. Beside him sat petite, brown haired Janie Goodenau. Her small features seemed lost against the black shiny sea of the Steinway, but her thin fingers seemed to command the rich sound produced by the instrument. Larry stood at the edge of the keyboard, sipping punch while talking to Travis Longworth and admiring Janie's touch on the keys.

"So, John. I understand you and Larry were discussing my body's similarity to a piece of Virginia bottom land this morning." Janie continued to play an abbreviated version of "The Christmas Song" without missing a note.

John frowned and looked up at Larry.

Larry shrugged his shoulders and smiled in an apologetic fashion. He placed his right hand on Janie's shoulder. "Janie, you're not supposed to divulge information learned in the heat of passion." Larry took another drink of punch and looked at Travis. "Now, what were you saying you would do about that pilot the Iranians have?"

"Actually, Janie, the comparison was between the sight of your body and the sight of the new lake Travis put in the bottom this fall. We didn't compare any notes, but I gave your body admirable reviews." John tried to overcome the blush that had come to his cheeks.

Janie leaned over and pecked John on the cheek. Then she looked back up at Larry. "See, Larry. At least John doesn't think I'm fat."

Travis grinned. "I believe my mug is empty. I think I'll go get me some more of that there punch while you three decide just who is going to work on that woman's body. Janie, if this feller don't want to take you home, I'd be willing to give it a go. I got my ticker reworked, and I sure wouldn't throw you out of my bed for eatin' crackers." Travis winked at Larry.

"I might have to take you up on that, Travis." Janie blew Travis a kiss.

"Now, Honey," Larry sat down on the edge of the bench and lightly touched Janie's shoulder. "I didn't say you were fat."

"Did so." Janie stopped playing and pointed at Larry with her right index finger. "You said I was developing handles."

Larry smiled. "Yes, I did. But I also said I liked holding on, didn't I?"

Janie blushed. "Hush! Quit talking like that in public."

"You started it." Larry smirked as he took a long drink from his punch glass. He set the glass down and gave Janie a big hug. He whispered in her ear, and she giggled.

"Not now, big boy. I have to play the piano."

Larry stood and peered out the window that was adjacent to the piano bench. As he squinted to see through the mist forming on the window pane, he spied Raymond Chesley's silver Cadillac pulling up the driveway and turning in front of the entry door. "Uh oh, John, Chesley's here. It's a good thing Maggie called and gave you some warning that he was on the warpath. At least you'll know why he's having a blue veiner." Larry smiled and winked at John. Larry had coined the term for Chesley's temper tantrums as "blue veiners" after one of the more heated arguments that occurred during a staff meeting just after he and John's arrival at Greene. When Chesley became angry, his neck veins over distended and his face turned deathly blue. Larry just knew one of them would pop during staff meeting someday.

"I'm sure sorry Maggie missed this party. I miss intelligent conversation." Janie tried to derail Larry's chain of thought. She didn't like it when he became upset over things at the hospital. It made their home-life difficult.

"Well, thanks a lot," John said as he rose and started for the door.

"Just joking." Janie smiled and continued to play.

"I know." John bent over and kissed Janie on the head. "Well, I might as well get this over with." John straightened his bright red plaid Pendleton jacket and unruffled his deep green slacks. He walked to the entry hall and waited a turn at the punch bowl, which was set up in front of the Christmas tree. He picked up a small cup of the virgin punch for himself because he was on call as of midnight, and he poured a larger cup, heavily spiked for Chesley.

"Ray! Merry Christmas and welcome! I'm glad to see you could make it. Have some punch." John thrust the punch into Ray Chesley's right hand as he entered the door.

Chesley took a long drink of punch and looked into the glass. "Very good. Very good indeed." He took another sip of punch and looked back at John. "John, I need to talk with you in private if I could?"

Sure, Ray, sure. Follow me." John led him down a side hall and into the study. The dark oak paneling absorbed even the brightness of the outside decorations. John flipped on his desk lamp and pointed toward the over-sized green leather chair. "Care to sit down?"

"No, I'd rather say this standing up."

"Shoot. We're both big boys. Speak your mind."

"Now, John." Ray took another drink of punch. "I don't mean to step on any toes, and I know Ms. Quince is a close friend of yours." Chesley raised his eyebrows toward John attempting to inflect a provocative tone. "But I thought you might want to know about something that happened tonight at the hospital. Now, I'm not going to mention it to anyone but you, but I just thought you, as head of the Ob department, needed to know."

"Okay, Ray. Quit beating around the bush. I've got guests."

"Well, John. Ms. Quince deliberately delivered one of my patients tonight. And, if that wasn't bad enough, she had the audacity to infer I wasn't giving good care to my Labor patients. John, I've been here a long time. Why, I was the first doctor to do deliveries in Greene, but don't let that influence you. I think we need to put some reins on that woman. She is going to get some of us in trouble, if we're not careful."

"Well, Ray. Those are powerful words. What exactly happened to make Maggie want to deliver the baby? Weren't you in the hospital? Was there fetal distress?"

"John, I was in the doctor's lounge when the baby was born. I'd been there since five o'clock this evening. I wasn't contacted until that baby was already in the warmer. I don't believe there was any distress, but you know I don't believe in those new monitors. The baby's heartbeat was fine each time it was checked by the external Doppler, but Ms. Quince thought there was distress. I think the woman just wants to make me look bad. She's determined to get me off the Labor Hall, and I'll be damned if I'll let any woman push me around no matter who she's in love with."

"Wait a minute, Ray." John's face lost all conviviality. "My connection with Maggie has nothing to do with this, and I'd appreciate it if you didn't make those inferences. Anyway, Maggie usually keeps her cool about these things, and if she thinks something is amiss, she will always inform the physician and wait for his response. I've never known her deliberately to interfere with patient care unless she deemed it potentially life threatening."

"Well, she had absolutely no indication to interfere tonight." Ray slammed his fist on the desk, shaking the glass he had just set down. He gathered his composure remembering Maggie's threats. "Well, I think we need to inform her she shouldn't interfere with my patients. That's all. I'm going out to enjoy the party." Ray turned and started out the room.

John walked in front of him and closed the door. He turned and faced the shocked Ray Chesley. "Ray, I know what happened tonight. Maggie called twenty minutes ago. What I should do is call a special committee meeting and discuss your care of this patient with the potential of disciplinary action."

Ray backed away from John and sat down in the leather chair. "John, you got anything else to drink in here?"

John turned to the cabinet behind his desk, opened the upper drawer, and pulled out a quart bottle of Wild Turkey. He held it up to Ray. "Will this do?"

Ray smiled sheepishly. "Yeah, give me about two fingers in that punch glass."

John poured the bourbon into Ray's glass and returned it to its spot in the drawer. As he turned to face Ray, he noticed the glass was already empty. "Ray, you better slow down, or I'll have to get you a driver for your trip back into town."

"No, I'll be fine. Just needed a little more spine to confess."

"Confess?" John had been prepared to have a lengthy battle with Ray over this evening's confrontation, but he saw a chink in Ray's armor.

"Yeah, confess. I was wrong tonight, John. Dead wrong. Fortunately no one was hurt. Maggie was dead right in doing what she did, but I wasn't thinking about that at the time." Ray looked down at the floor and sighed. "You know, John, I'm losing my drive for Obstetrics. I love Gyn, and I love the new technology that appears to be coming into that field, but, John, I just don't believe in all that new stuff in Ob."

"Well, Ray, times have changed, and along with the times, Obstetrics has changed. We no longer have the understanding of the patient when something, even something uncontrollable, goes wrong. Acts of God aren't acceptable any longer. Every baby is supposed to be perfect, and you and I know that's not possible. We practice defensively and occasionally interfere if there is any doubt of fetal jeopardy. Sometimes, what we do is unnecessary, but we don't know that until we've done it. All Maggie was trying to do was to get you to practice the best brand of Obstetrics that we know."

"Yes, I realize that now, but hell, we did just as good a job twenty years ago as we do now, and we did a hell of a lot less sections."

"That may be true, but you still have to remain current in care standards. It's required by your college, the hospital, and, most of all, your own ethics." John walked over to Ray and put his hand on Ray's shoulder.

"Hell, Ray. Why do you want to put up with all that crap anyway? You've done your time. You've got an enviable Gyn practice, and you keep current in your brand of gynecology. You're one hell of a surgeon. I've been witness to that. Why don't you give up Ob?"

"You're right, John. I am a damned good surgeon." Ray leaned back in the chair and rubbed his temples while allowing the Wild Turkey to take effect. He mulled Maggie's threats over in his mind, considered his past and present call schedule, and saw a way out of something he had wanted to stop doing for the past three years. "I'll think about it, and you know, I could do you a favor by quitting."

"How's that, Ray?" John watched Ray's wheels turn.

"Well, I wouldn't be putting you in the uncomfortable situation of having to review all of my cases for the past year. You know it would be a tough battle to get my Obstetrical privileges rescinded, and if you decided to do so, I would have to fight."

"I figured nothing less." John smiled.

"And, John," Ray leaned forward in the green chair and pointed his finger at John. "...if I agree to stop doing Obstetrics, none of this will be brought before the board. Right?"

"That's right, Ray. Nothing."

Ray leaned back, folded his arms, closed his eyes and tilted his head against the high back. He yielded to the effects of the bourbon and slowly relaxed deeper into the supple leather. "John, if I quit, I would want to quit immediately. Would you accept my present patients?"

"I could arrange that."

"Well, by golly, John. I think I'll do it, but give me until Monday to make up my mind definitely. Fair?"

"Fair." John smiled and extended his right hand to Ray. "I'll expect to hear your answer Monday?"

Ray rose from his chair and extended his hand to John. "Sure thing, John. You'll probably have my written request to drop Ob privileges by the middle of the week."

"I think you're doing the right thing, Ray, and I appreciate your frankness about these matters."

"Good! And John, this discussion didn't happen, right?"

"What discussion?" John shrugged his shoulders and grinned.

Ray smiled and licked his lips. "I'm getting thirsty again. I think I'll have some more punch. Shall we get back to the party?"

"You go ahead. I'll be back in a moment."

After Ray left the study, John picked up the phone and called the labor hall.

"Labor and Delivery, Margaret Quince speaking."

"Maggie, you doing okay?"

"Oh, hello, John. Yes, I'm doing all right. Why?"

"I've just finished speaking with Chesley, and…"

"What's he want to do? Call a special meeting of the board and fire me?"

"No. He quit practicing obstetrics."

"He what?"

"You heard me. He quit obstetrics. I couldn't believe it. He confessed that you did the right thing tonight and that he wasn't up to practicing Ob with all its present constraints."

"Wait a minute." Maggie couldn't believe what she was hearing. "Are we talking about the same Raymond Chesley?"

"Yeah," John laughed. "I know it sounds out of character, but I think he was ready for this move and looking for the right situation to give him an excuse to quit."

"And he told you he thought I had done the right thing?"

"That's right."

"Well, I'll be. Maybe he's not such an old shit after all." Maggie chuckled to herself.

John laughed.

Maggie was tired of talking about Dr. Chesley. "I sure miss being at the party, John. I wish I had never agreed to work. I wish I were there, and I wish we were spending the night together."

"I miss you, too, Maggie. Don't worry. I've got a special day planned for us as soon as I make rounds and you're off duty."

"Mmmm sounds delicious. I think I'll be able to rustle you up a great breakfast." Maggie twisted the phone cord with her index finger as she spoke.

"You know I don't like to eat much in the mornings."

"Who's talking about eating?"

"Whew!" John whistled. "You better quit talking. I'm not sure I can stand much more."

"Oh, you'll be able to stand it. I look forward to tomorrow. Merry Christmas. I love you."

"Merry Christmas, Maggie. I love you, too. Goodnight."

"Goodnight." Maggie softly slipped the handset onto the cradle and leaned back in her chair. A soft smile grew across her face as she thought about Christmas morning.

John hung up the phone and walked over to the window. His life had been missing something for a long time, and he now knew that something was Maggie. He knew this was the last Christmas he would be giving his party as a bachelor. He would ask Maggie to marry him tomorrow, and his Christmas would be complete.

"Hey," Larry's voice broke the silence. "You coming back to the party, or what? Janie sent me to rescue you. All the geese have been eaten, and she wants to know what else you have to eat."

"Yeah, I'm coming. Tell her there's a five pound roll of bologna in the fridge." John pointed to the developing shower. "It looks like tomorrow morning would be a fine day for hunting."

"You bet, but I'd have a hell of a time getting out of the house on Christmas morning. Whew, if you could hear those kids."

"I look forward to the possibility. Come on let's get back. It's almost eleven thirty."

\* \* \*

Later John felt as if he had just closed his eyes and drifted off to sleep when he was aroused by a beep. He had finally relaxed from the party-goer's departures, the storage of the remaining foodstuffs, the wait for the caterers to clean up the mess, and the final deep felt thanks to Travis' family. He was literally Merry Christmased out, when sleep had finally wrapped its arms about him. Yet, the tone persisted. John slapped every item he could reach on his bedside table until the noise subsided, and he drifted back to sleep. However, after a few moments, a much louder sound split the silence of his bedroom. John knew it was the telephone, and he knew he would have to answer. He lifted the receiver from the cradle and started to answer. However, before he could unglue his tongue from the roof of his mouth, the other end of the line came to life.

"John, are you awake? I paged you, but I guess you were too tired to hear your beeper."

"Hello," John managed to answer in spite of his dry mouth. "Who is this?" John looked at his digital clock...2:30..."Geez, it's only two thirty in the morning."

"John, wake up! This is Maggie. I need you to come in to the hospital. I have a service patient in labor, and you're on call."

"Let the resident see her and call me."

"John, wake up! We don't have a resident. It's Christmas."

"Oh, yeah. Is there a problem?"

"Yes, there is a problem. I need your help. So, get up and come on in."

John sat on the edge of the bed and rubbed the sleep from his eyes. "What's her history?"

"She's twenty five years old and having her first child. The due date is today. She has been seeing Dr. Robert Vance of Norfolk, but while on her way home from Washington, she started into labor. She was afraid she wouldn't make it back to Norfolk because her contractions were getting closer, and she feared the baby was about to deliver."

"Well, is it?"

"No. She's four centimeters dilated."

"Good." John yawned. "Man, it's too early in the morning. I think you called me before Santa Claus came." John heard Maggie laugh. "What else do we know about her?"

"Oh, we know quite a bit. She just happened to be carrying a copy of her entire prenatal record. Seems convenient, don't you think?"

"Yeah. Almost as if it were planned." John rubbed his head. "Well, no difference. She's at our hospital and needs our help. What else is going on with our version of Mary?"

"She has a history of Rheumatic Fever and has been treated for heart failure on one occasion during this pregnancy. She's on 0.25 milligrams of Digoxin daily."

"You're just full of good news. What do her lungs sound like?" "Her blood pressure is 130/60, and her pulse is 100. Temp 99.2. She has slight distention of her neck veins, and her lungs are congested in the bases. The baby is vertex, but measures small for dates. The history indicates a diagnosis of Fetal Growth Retardation. She has two plus edema of the legs, and her reflexes are normal. Her urine is negative for sugar and protein."

"Sounds like she might have some mild failure. Go ahead and start an I.V. with an eighteen Jelco. Run five percent dextrose and 1/2 normal saline at 75 cc's per hour. Get the routine lab, but add an E.K.G., blood gases, and portable chest x-ray. Notify the anesthesiologist on call that we have a candidate for an epidural and will possibly need a CVP line. I'll be there in thirty minutes."

"John?"

"Yes, Maggie."

"Don't drive too crazy. It's been raining, and the roads are slick."

"Don't worry. I never drive crazy, just fast." John placed the phone back on the hooks wishing he could slip back between the sheets. He pried himself off the mattress and stumbled into the shower. The pelting from the shower head drove the rest of any remaining thoughts of sleep from his body, and he quickly toweled off and dressed. He left the house through the kitchen, activated the house alarm, and walked across the portico leading to the garage.

John opened the garage door and walked over to the cloth covered automobile in the number one slot of five in the garage. As he touched the automatic garage door button beside the stall, and the opener cranked the door up along its track, he pulled the gray cloth from the black 928S Porsche. John knew he shouldn't get such a hype from fast driving. Heaven knew he had lectured enough against it when he serviced the Emergency Room during his medical training. He walked to the driver's side of the car and inserted the oversized key: first, counter-clockwise to deactivate the alarm, then, clockwise to unlock the door. He eased into the black leather, power-adjustable seat and buckled the safety belt. Just the smell of the car infused a false sense of power.

It was nineteen miles from the Chadwick Farm to Greene, and John knew the road like the back of his hand. After all, he had been driving it since he was sixteen. First came the two miles to the entrance gate. He had to key the electronic gate opener at the proper time as he passed the tennis courts, or the gate would still be closed when he arrived. Then, there was six miles of straight road to the Interstate. John had received multiple introductions to some of the fine members of the Virginia Highway Patrol on that section of road. Next, the eight miles of Interstate took him to the hospital exit, and, finally, a straight run of three miles to the E. R. entrance. On a good night, he could be there in eleven minutes, but, if he had to hold his speed under one hundred on the Interstate, he might have a problem maintaining his record.

Herr Ferdinand Porsche had made the 928S to do better than one hundred and fifty miles per hour, and John knew it could bury the needle. He turned the ignition switch, and the fuel injected, V-8 purred to life. It was 2:46 A.M. John eased the stick into reverse, and his personal race began. He was going over 100 MPH as he passed the tennis courts. He timed the gate perfectly and grinned as the Porsche slipped through the gate, for he had taken the right hand gate off its hinges, several times, when he hadn't timed his exit correctly. He negotiated the hard right turn out the gate, slipped the transmission back down to third, and floored the accelerator through the straight-away, shifting quickly through fourth and into fifth gear. The speedometer was a blur in his peripheral vision, but John knew he was doing at least 145 MPH. The Interstate entrance was coming up quickly. He downshifted through the gears to second, floated through the right turning on ramp, and merged with the meager traffic flow. He accelerated through the gears, and within seconds, he was cruising an effortless 150 MPH. The black projectile ate up the eight miles of Interstate in less than four minutes. The hospital exit loomed ahead. John smoothly downshifted to third, touched the brakes lightly, and made the 270 degree, one-quarter cloverleaf exit at sixty miles per hour. Counter control was required to keep the ass end from moving around, but the lateral acceleration of the car was so good, John had no problem keeping the nose pointed in the right direction. He put the center line of the highway between the bulbous raised headlights and rapidly accelerated through the gears. The hospital appeared rapidly in his windscreen, and John eased off the accelerator. He eased the car into his appointed slot, and a quick look at the stopwatch mode of his Seiko confirmed a ten minute forty-six second elapsed time.

"Not bad," he said while looking at the watch. As he entered the Emergency Room, he noted the time on the wall clock. Three A.M. "Just where I wanted to be on Christmas Day."

"Good morning and Merry Christmas, Dr. Chadwick." Betty Sims walked over and greeted John.

"Good morning, Betty. What brings the head nurse in on a holiday?"

"Same thing that brought in Maggie. Stupidity."

"Oh, the penalties of leadership, eh Betty?" John half-heartedly spoke to Betty. He knew her as one of the major sources of gossip in the hospital.

"I saw your new Ob patient as she came through the E. R. She certainly isn't one of our routine service patients." Betty said as she tried to match John's stride.

"Oh, why is that?"

"Well, for one thing, she was dressed in a full length dark blue cashmere coat that would cost a month of my salary."

"Now, Betty. You know some of our patients can afford to dress well. Besides, I didn't know you were prejudiced against the more affluent."

"Oh, I'm not. Otherwise I wouldn't have anything to do with you, would I?"

"I guess not." John didn't care to continue the conversation. He stepped into the elevator and waved to Betty as the door closed. "See you later, Betty. Merry Christmas."

"Merry Christmas to you, Doctor. Hope everything goes well upstairs."

"The elevator eased to a stop, and the door reopened. Maggie was waiting. "It's about time."

"About time?" John smiled at Maggie. "I made it here in record time."

"Your fascination with that car scares me. You know I worry every time I call you to come in. Especially at night."

John leaned over and gave Maggie a kiss. "I love you, too."

"And I love you." Maggie brushed John's lackadaisical kiss aside. "That's why I worry."

"Oh, Maggie. Don't worry. I can handle that car a lot better than I can handle you. Come on. Let's go do some doctoring and nursing." John followed Maggie back to the labor hall. "What's the patient's name?"

"Sabrina MacKenzie. She's in labor room five. I'll introduce you."

Maggie walked through the door to the labor room, and John followed. "Sabrina, this is Doctor Chadwick. Doctor Chadwick, Sabrina MacKenzie.

"Good morning, Doctor Chadwick. It's a ple...asure to meet you. Please call me Sabrina." Sabrina winced through a contraction but extended her arm to shake John's hand.

John walked slowly over to the labor bed and took Sabrina's hand. As he held her soft skin in his right hand, he was taken aback by her beauty even under these dire conditions. Her jet black hair had the same sheen as Maggie's, and her skin had been spared any effects of the pregnancy. "It's my pleasure, Sabrina." John held Sabrina's hand for a moment longer and then released his hold. "It seems you've drawn the short straw and gotten me for your obstetrician on this Christmas morning."

"It wasn't all by chance," Sabrina grinned and then coughed. "Sorry, I seem to be a little short of breath."

John picked up the stethoscope that hung on the blood pressure apparatus and listened to Sabrina's chest. He could hear the tell tale signs of pulmonary congestion indicating borderline heart failure. "Maggie, give 40 mg Lasix I.V. push, and let's get the anesthesiologist up here. I think Sabrina would benefit from an epidural…Now, Sabrina, why is it you say our meeting is not all by chance?"

"Well, Dr. Chadwick, I already know a lot about you. Initially, you were one of my choices for an obstetrician." Sabrina winced as another contraction began.

John held her hand during the pain and noticed that Sabrina was trying to concentrate through the contraction by fixing her gaze on his hand. "I see you're trying to practice Lamaze. Have you and your husband been to classes?"

"I'm not married, Dr. Chadwick, and, no, I haven't been to classes. I've read quite a bit about labor techniques. No, that's not quite true. Actually, I've had the techniques drilled into me nightly by a close friend." Sabrina smiled as she thought about her daily lectures from her roommate, Cathy Winston.

John was somewhat shocked by Sabrina's statement about her marital status. Rarely did John see someone of Sabrina's apparent social status, pregnant and unmarried. "I'm sorry about the question, Sabrina. I didn't know…"

"Don't be sorry. My fiancé is presently out of the country. It's not a problem for me." Sabrina smiled.

Wanting to change the subject, John picked up Sabrina's chart and began to leaf through the pages. "Well, you seem to have come prepared. It's not often someone carries her obstetrical history around with her."

"Oh, I'm a good Girl Scout, Dr. Chadwick. You know…Be Prepared and all that."

John laughed. "You have quite a sense of humor, considering…" John pointed to Sabrina's pregnant abdomen.

"Might as well make the best of it, I always say. Oh, damn!" Sabrina arched her back and held onto her abdomen as the next contraction hit.

After the contraction had subsided, John turned to a clean page in Sabrina's chart, took out a pen, and looked back at Sabrina. "Well, since you have me at a disadvantage, why don't I ask some questions about you. There's no reason you should know all about me and I shouldn't know anything about you. I'm sure there's more to Sabrina MacKenzie than what is in these records."

"Well, Dr. Chadwick, it's a long story. I'm not sure you have the time."

"Sabrina, I have all night, and I can't think of a nicer person I would like to talk to."

"All right, get comfortable." Sabrina wriggled herself up in the bed and began to tell John about what had brought her to Greene Memorial on Christmas morning 1978.

# 4

## JUNE, 1978; MACKENZIE ISLAND

Sabrina nervously sat on the edge of the white, slatted wooden bench encircling the interior of the octagonal, Victorian gazebo. Besides the screened back porch of her beach house, Gull Haven, this was her favorite place on MacKenzie Island. She had asked Kent to meet her here tonight because it was a place where she was comfortable, and Sabrina needed familiar surroundings to break the news she had kept inside her for the past two weeks. She had hoped for plenty of time to prepare her fiancé for what she had to say, but Kent's impending departure with the Navy had put a wrench in her plans. And now that she knew what she was going to say, Kent wasn't being cooperative because he was late, real late for tonight's meeting. The longer Sabrina waited, the more she feared the outcome of their meeting.

Sabrina's thoughts kept her unaware of the approaching clouds and impending rainstorm rapidly materializing over the Chesapeake on this hot June night. The wind preceding the storm front gusted up the hill from the yacht basin and surprised her as it whistled through the gazebo's ornate balusters, tossing her long, silky dark brown hair into the air. Usually, her fastidiousness impelled her to fidget with her hair's arrangement, but tonight her thoughts were on more important matters. Tonight, it would take more than the weather to divert her attention from the business at hand. There could be no further procrastination, a trait she had leaned toward when there were possible adverse results. Tonight, she must formulate the most acceptable method for announcing her, no, *their* unplanned pregnancy. Even though Kent, a Navy fighter pilot, was engrossed in his preparation to ship out on the nuclear aircraft carrier, *U.S.S. Carl Vinson*, for Mediterranean maneuvers, Sabrina had to tell him the news. She had to know how he was going to react before she could make future plans.

Sabrina cringed, anticipating Kent's reaction. She hadn't wanted to become pregnant. She had attempted to use birth control pills, as Kent had desired...it was easier for him. But the risks imposed by her past Rheumatic Heart Disease made it an impossibility. Besides, they had made her deathly sick. She had used a contraceptive suppository, but she assumed it had failed, or, she hadn't used it correctly. Regardless, she was pregnant, and she knew it WAS a bad time. Kent would be gone for the next six months. As he put it when they had talked about marriage, he didn't need the worry of a commitment. *His* thoughts needed to be one hundred percent channeled into *his* duties. Sabrina smiled as she considered the stereotypical, arrogant clichés she expected from Kent. Usually, she could argue with the best, but if Kent used those excuses tonight, she mustn't seem cynical. She did not want to alienate him. If she had to wait for six months to get married and provide her child a father, she would do it. However, there was another negative factor looming on the horizon- Kent's mother. Because Sabrina's recent encounters with Beth Pooley had placed a definite crimp in any long term plans, she knew she had to cement the chinks in their relationship. She WAS having the baby, and the baby WOULD have a father. Regardless of the sacrifices she might have to endure, even to the point of pretending she liked Kent's mother, Sabrina was determined, without compromise, to assure her child a father and family.

* * *

Kent Pooley leaned his svelte body against the hood of his midnight blue 420 SL Mercedes. The churn of the ferry's diesel engines slowed as the boat maneuvered toward the off ramp on the lee side of MacKenzie Island. The eight mile trip from Yorktown to the Western side of the Island had taken its usual forty five minutes. Why Sabrina, or anyone, wanted to live in near seclusion had always bewildered Kent. If it weren't for Soames, a private coed college, MacKenzie Island held absolutely nothing of interest. Besides Sabrina, the only interest it had to Kent was providing a reference point when he flew combat exercises from Oceana Naval Air Station. Kent needed action, and the island was the exact opposite prescription to fill his need.

It was two miles from the ferry's off ramp to Sabrina's office complex where she had wanted to meet. For some reason, Sabrina always wanted to meet at the gazebo. However, Kent didn't mind not going by Sabrina's home, for he was always thankful to avoid contact with Cathy, Sabrina's housemate and business partner. Their dislike for one another was not a secret. However, tonight, Kent could take anything. His thoughts weren't on his date with Sabrina. Tonight, his thoughts were on his first carrier duty aboard the *Vinson*.

All his life, Kent had wanted to be a fighter pilot. To fly a jet off the deck of an aircraft carrier was his dream…his only dream. Everything he had done to this point in his life had been keyed to that one goal. Now, he was on the brink of making his dream a reality. Nothing, or no one, was going to keep him from grasping the moment. No one! His mother had recently warned him Sabrina might try to trap him. After all, she had convinced Kent how good a "catch" he would be for some young woman. She had advised Kent to break off his relationship with Sabrina because she would "ruin his chances of realizing his dream." Her seeds of doubt had convinced Kent that Sabrina would go to no ends to disrupt his career. Because of the misgivings nurtured by his mother, Kent had tried to terminate the relationship, but Sabrina's beauty and his desire for her kept him from taking the final step. But, even though Sabrina had never pushed him into anything, Kent knew he would eventually make the break. He seemed to be unable to resist his mother's wishes. She had a power to subliminally make his decisions. She had done it before, and she was doing it now.

Kent had grown up on the West Coast. His father, Brian Pooley, was a real estate entrepreneur. Entrepreneur? Yes, by using his mother's inheritance as capital. The only way his father had ever made it was with his mother's money, or at least that was what his mother had told him. Brian's frequent absences during Kent's childhood had left his mother the responsible party for his rearing, and she had always been available, too available according to Brian, to bail Kent out of any problems that arose. If Kent and Brian had had one argument about lack of responsibility and immaturity, they had had a thousand. Responsibility, accountability, honesty, faithfulness—Kent had heard those words over, and over, and over again, until he was literally sick of their syllables.

The jolt of the ferry's abutment to the off ramp shook Kent from his thoughts. A storm seemed to be approaching from the east, so Kent raised the brown canvas top, made the appropriate attachments, and eased the Mercedes off the ferry onto dry land. He stopped the car at the entrance to the ferry and rolled down his window. "Hey!" Kent called to the ferry captain who was busy making sure his boat's lines were attached to the ramp.

The ferry captain turned and walked over to Kent's car. "Yeah-up. What can I do for you?"

Kent passed the captain a fifty dollar bill. "Take a good look at this car, and don't leave this island on your last trip without it being on board and me being in it."

The captain slipped the fifty into his pocket and looked at Kent's car. "Don't see as how I could forget it. Last ferry leaves at 11:00 P.M. Thank you, now."

Kent eased the Mercedes away from the gate and negotiated the circuitous route to the parking lot adjacent to Sabrina's gazebo. Finally, he turned his thoughts to Sabrina and wondered what could be so damned important to pull him away from his duties.

Kent turned off the ignition, opened the door, stepped out of the car, and straightened his khaki's. As he peered in the direction of the gazebo, he could see Sabrina's outline against the low lying clouds that were partially illuminated by the full moon. The wind was blowing her hair at a ninety degree angle behind her. As he watched, Sabrina slowly walked around the edge of the structure, hesitated for a moment, and sat on the far side. She appeared deep in thought. Kent slowly made his way up the flagstone walk and onto the gazebo steps. Sabrina was unaware of Kent's approach as she kept her watch of the yacht basin's vessels as they bobbed in their slips.

"Okay, Sabrina. I'm here. What's so important that it had to be discussed tonight?"

Sabrina looked up from her thoughts, smiled when she saw Kent, and walked over toward him. "Hi, honey. I didn't see you drive up." Sabrina tiptoed and gave Kent a kiss on his cheek. "Come over and sit down." Sabrina felt the tension emanate from Kent. This wasn't going to be easy.

Kent didn't move. "Come on, Sabrina. What did you need to talk about? I've got a million things I need to do before we ship out Sunday. Four days isn't going to be enough, especially if Mom and Dad expect to be entertained when they arrive Saturday."

"Oh? Your Mother and Father are coming in this weekend. I didn't know they were coming. We could have had them come to my house

Saturday night. It might give your mother and me a chance to bury the hatchet." Sabrina grinned and beckoned for Kent to come and sit down next to her on the bench.

"I was trying to tell you they were coming when you called tonight, but you wouldn't let me get a word in edgewise." Kent lied, but he hoped Sabrina wouldn't notice. "Now, come on, Sabrina. What do you want?"

Sabrina's tolerance was usually short, particularly when someone was being exceptionally rude. But, she had vowed to herself to remain in control. "Okay, Kent. I wanted to do this in a special way, but since you're in such a hurry, I'll come right out with it." She clasped her hands, looked down at the slatted floor of the gazebo, and took a deep breath.

Kent sighed and threw his arms open in exasperation. "Well?"

Sabrina looked up and thought, "you ass!", but smiled and replied, "Kent, I love you."

"Yeah, yeah. Go on."

Sabrina frowned. "What's wrong? Have I done something to make you angry."

Kent was reaching the limits of his patience. He didn't appreciate Sabrina's tactics. "Sabrina, you called me! I've got a thousand things to do in preparation for sea duty."

"At least it's down from a million," Sabrina joked.

Kent paid no attention to her attempt at levity. "Come on, Sabrina. You're acting like a high school girl wanting to make out or something. What's so damned important that I had to stop everything and…"

"Kent, I'm pregnant!" Sabrina blurted out her news at a tactical moment.

Words and thoughts stopped in mid sentence, as Kent reeled with the announcement, looked at Sabrina, and turned from her sight. "Shit!" He walked to the steps, sat down on the floor of the gazebo resting his feet on the top one, leaned forward and put his head in his hands. "Shit, shit, shit!!!" Kent banged his fist against the wooden floor. "How in the hell could you be pregnant?"

"What do you mean? You know how!"

"Of course, I know how. But how? You were taking the pill, weren't you?"

"I was, but I guess they didn't work." Sabrina covered up the truth for the sake of furthering the argument.

"Guess? You mean you're not sure." Kent stood and turned to Sabrina. "Maybe you're not pregnant. Maybe you've missed your period for some other reason."

Sabrina smiled. "Nope. There's no doubt. The blood test is positive. I'm six to seven weeks pregnant. You're going to be a daddy." Sabrina affectionately patted her abdomen.

"Sabrina! For God's sake! How in the hell can you be so damned happy? This is a disaster!"

Sabrina's face turned to stone. "Disaster?" Sabrina rose from her seat and walked toward Kent. She lightly touched his arm.

Kent jumped as if he had been touched by the devil.

"How can this be a disaster, Kent? We love each other. It's not as if we're still in high school and can't take care of a baby. I know it will be difficult, but we can handle it."

"Handle it? You make it sound as if this is no problem at all. We're not even married, Sabrina. We can't think about having a baby. Not now!"

"But we're going to be married, aren't we, Kent? Kent? Aren't we going to be married?" Sabrina waited for a reply, but when Kent hesitated, Sabrina knew something was wrong. Cathy's prognostications were coming true. Kent really was a son-of-a-bitch. "Kent, I would have never let you make love to me if I didn't think we were eventually going to get married."

"Oh, Sabrina, hell! Don't be so damned Victorian. We made love because we cared for each other, not because we wanted to have a baby or get married. You can't stay pregnant, and that's all there is to it."

Sabrina glared at Kent. "What do you mean by that statement, Kent Pooley. I am having a baby…your baby, and there's not one thing you can do to prevent it."

"Sabrina, you can't have a baby. I won't permit it. Not now! Not yet! Think about it. I'm ready to leave for six months. I can't be worrying about a pregnant wife. This could knock me out of carrier duty."

"Well! Would that be so bad?" Sabrina smiled. "You could stay home and be with the baby and me."

Kent grabbed Sabrina's shoulders tightly. He wanted to shake some sense into her but refrained.

"Kent, you're hurting me." Sabrina's smile was replaced by a look of apprehension.

"Sabrina! Listen to me!" Kent shook Sabrina with each word.

Sabrina broke Kent's hold and began to walk over to the bench.

Kent whirled Sabrina around and looked her in the eye. "Sabrina, I'm not sacrificing my life's dream for you or any damned baby. I've worked too hard for this, and you'll not keep me from it." Kent's anger made him shake. He turned and looked out over the parking area from his position in the entrance of the gazebo. Kent wanted out. This couldn't be happening. He was being trapped, exactly as his mother had warned.

Sabrina sat down on the bench closest to where Kent stood. She melted back against the rail and began to cry. "How can you treat me this way?"

Kent turned , looked at her, and grinned. "You can put those tears away right now! They won't work."

Sabrina sniffed and gathered an inner strength she kept for such situations. "Kent," Sabrina's voice did not quiver as Kent might have expected. "these tears aren't for your benefit. But, you have a choice in this matter. I don't! The decision for marriage and family is for both of us to make. I thought by our actions, we had made that decision.."

Kent quickly pointed a finger at Sabrina. "Just a damned minute. We hadn't made any such commitment. I…"

Sabrina jumped up and stomped toward Kent stopping a few feet short of where he stood. "No, Kent. You wait! I'm not finished. I don't care if the words were never said, but you and I both know we were headed in the direction of marriage. We were, at least until your mother's last visit. Has she changed things between us?"

"My mother doesn't control my relationships," Kent quickly replied, defensive about his inability to break his mother's power over him.

Sabrina sarcastically grinned and shrugged her shoulders. "You and I both know better than that, but that's not the issue. Is it? Whether she has soured you towards me is not important. The issue is, I'm pregnant. That's a fact. Now. Do you want to be part of it? Yes or no?" Sabrina reached out for Kent's hand.

Kent rejected her advance and walked around her into the center of the gazebo. "Sabrina, I think we should consider alternatives."

"Kent, there are no alternatives. I'm having the baby. That decision has been made."

"HOW IN THE HELL…" Kent attempted to calm down before proceeding. "Sabrina, how can you say that? Why can't we both make the decision. After all, it belongs to us."

"Kent, there is no us. There is only me. I'm one person. I'm pregnant. We're not married. The decision about this baby is up to me. Not us!"

"I don't believe you. I fuckin' don't believe you. Look, goddammit, you can play around with the words all you want, but you know what I'm talking about. Why can't you abort the pregnancy? You're trying to force me into something I'm not ready for. You've had this planned all along, haven't you? Mother said you would do something like this."

"Do something like what, Kent?"

"Something to trap me! That's what! I don't like to be forced into anything, Sabrina."

Sabrina sat back down on the wooden seat. She slumped down feeling exhausted. Kent had made his decision. She would have to abort the pregnancy, or he was walking. She thought for a few moments, then looked at Kent. She forced a smile though her misery. "Kent, I'm not forcing you to do anything."

Kent threw his hands in the air and laughed. "How in the hell can you sit there and say that? You're pregnant!" Kent thought for a moment. "Wait a damned minute. Am I the father of this child?"

Sabrina's face turned beet red. She jumped from her seat and marched to within inches of Kent's face. "What do you mean by that?"

"How do I know it's mine? You could be seeing another man. Hell, maybe you're back together with Steve. Yeah! How do I know you haven't been fuckin' around with him, and this is his baby? How do I know you're not using his baby to trap me?"

Without warning, Sabrina forcefully slapped Kent as hard as she could manage.

Kent reeled backward, clutching his right hand into a fist and brought it to his side posing to strike.

"Touch me, Mr. Pooley, and you won't have to worry about a career. Believe me! I have the power to make it happen, and you know it." Sabrina gritted her teeth and stood her ground.

Kent dropped his hand and began rubbing his assaulted cheek.

"You deserved that slap, and you know it. I wish it had knocked some sense into you. You know good and well I'm not seeing any other man, and you know I haven't seen Steve since you and I met. God knows I wish it were his child. He wouldn't be worming out of his responsibility." Sabrina stopped. She had said enough about Steve Hardesty, a person she reserved a special spot for in her heart. She glanced at Kent's bemused expression. "You can wipe those deviant thoughts from your mind." Sabrina walked a few feet from Kent and slowly turned back to face him, a sense of resolve coming into her speech. "Kent, you don't have to be vengeful, and you don't have to look for excuses. If you don't want to be part of this, say so." Sabrina paused, stiffened her jaw and continued. "But Kent, this is your child, and I'm not having an abortion. You can forget that right now!"

Kent had hurt Sabrina. He knew it and, at the time, had wanted to do so. But as she walked away from him, he felt guilty. If he did want to get married, it would be to a woman such as Sabrina. If he wanted a child, it would be with someone like Sabrina. Something inside made him walk to Sabrina and take her hand. He led her to the bench, and they sat side by side. Kent intended to become apologetic, but his underlying desire to be rid of the situation wouldn't permit him to make a sincere effort. "Sabrina, I'm sorry about what I said. I know you've been faithful, but think for a moment. Don't let your heart take over. Be practical. You have a flourishing career here. You're a major stockholder in one of the biggest bank chains in New England, and you have inherited a fortune. You have it made! Why do you want to endanger your life and future with a pregnancy?"

"None of that's important, and my doctor said I would probably be able to have a bab…"

"Not important!" Kent released his hold on Sabrina's hands and jumped from his seat. He paced around the gazebo for a moment and then stood directly over her. "Not important? Maybe it's not important to you because you didn't have to work for it, but it is important. Do you want to ruin it? Do you want to wreck a great situation and maybe ruin your health by having a baby? How the hell can you do that?"

Sabrina rose, avoiding Kent, and walked back to the gazebo's entrance. She watched as small droplets of rain danced across the walk up the steps and halted where the steps were protected by the roof. She turned, gathered herself, and looked at Kent. "Whose career are we talking about, mine or yours? I don't see how having a baby could harm my career. As for my health, my cardiologist thinks I can have a baby as long as I take proper care of myself. Kent, let's be truthful, shall we?"

Kent walked toward Sabrina, lightly grasped her shoulders, and turned her toward the ocean. "Look out there, Sabrina. What do you see?"

"I see the ocean, Kent. Only the ocean."

"You're wrong, Sabrina. Out there is my life's dream…my future. Just as much as your future rests here on this island, my future rests out there."

"Your future or your death, you mean."

"So be it. If I die doing what I love, then it has been my decision. It's the same as the decision you're making. Don't you see?"

"No, Kent. I don't see. How can the two be compared?"

"Sabrina, if I die flying a jet off an aircraft carrier, I'll be doing something I have dreamed of all my life. If my life ends doing what I love, then I'll have at least made some meaning to my existence. If I don't at least try after coming this far, I'll never be able to live with myself. It's the same for you. If you die having this baby, it obviously makes no difference to you. But, at least you'll have done something with meaning. Right?"

Sabrina looked at Kent in a way she had never seen him before. She tip-toed and kissed him on the forehead. "You know, Kent, those four years at Annapolis didn't brainwash you completely."

"I appreciate your understanding."

"I didn't say I understand. I don't and never will understand the macho, balls to the wall attitude you fighter jocks have, but I can appreciate your never say die attitude. I guess you have to have it to survive, but what does that say for our child? I'm pregnant with YOUR child, Kent. Doesn't that mean anything?"

"Sabrina!" Kent turned from Sabrina and walked back to the gazebo entrance. He turned and looked her square in the eye. "Sabrina, I'm going to fulfill my dream, and nothing is going to stop me. Understand? Nothing. If you want me to help you make arrangements to terminate the pregnancy, I will do so. But, if you're determined to have the baby, I'm sorry, but I'll have nothing to do with it."

"Sabrina turned and growled, "I told you, Kent. I won't terminate the pregnancy."

"Then the decision is made, isn't it?"

"I guess it is." Sabrina looked down at the floor, and then she looked back at Kent. She had a strange smile on her face. "Kent, someday you'll realize that it takes a lot more people than Kent Pooley to make this world go around. I hope you don't find that out too late." Sabrina walked over to Kent and took his hands into hers. "I guess you've made your decision, haven't you?"

"Yes, I have."

Sabrina could feel the tension in Kent's body relax. "Kent, would you answer me one question?"

"What's that?"

"Did you love me?"

"What do you mean?"

"It's a simple question. Did you love me? Did you love me when this baby was conceived?" Sabrina thought for a few moments, and before Kent could answer, she placed her fingers over his mouth. "No, don't answer. I don't want to know." Sabrina smiled. "Let me just believe that you loved me, and I'll be fine." Sabrina dropped her hand from Kent's face and sighed. "There is one other thing."

"What?" Kent couldn't tell if he felt guilt or relief in what he was about to do.

"Be sure you don't want me or this baby, because after tonight, there will be no turning back. I mean it, Kent."

"I'm sure of what I have to do, Sabrina. The Navy is my wife, and that Tomcat is my baby. There's no way I can separate myself from them. Please try to see it my way."

"No, Kent. I'll never see it your way. Ever." Sabrina gave Kent another kiss on the cheek. "Good-by, Kent. I hope your career is a great one. I mean it. Because it will take a great life to justify giving away what you could have had right here."

Kent smiled, but didn't respond. He turned his back to Sabrina and, without hesitation, headed for the parking lot. However, he stopped after opening the door to the Mercedes. "Sabrina!"

Sabrina turned and peered through the rain. "Yes, Kent?"

"I do love you. I love you now. I loved you when the baby was conceived. I'll always love you. I just wanted you to know that!" Kent got into the car without waiting for a response from Sabrina. He wiped a tear from his eye, started the Mercedes, and drove mindlessly to the ferry.

Sabrina watched as Kent drove out of the parking lot. She sat down on the steps of the gazebo and stomped her feet. "Damn, damn, damn!!! Why did he have to say that and drive away?" Sabrina waited for her anger to subside before she began assessing her situation. "How could I have been so stupid? How could a twenty five year old Harvard graduate have been so stupid? Well…" Sabrina patted her stomach and dried her tears. "don't worry little one. Everything will be okay. Cathy and I will think of something."

* * *

Sabrina loved MacKenzie Island. Memories of the better times in her life brought her back to the Island again and again. Pleasant memories of her mother and father were here-times she wished she could relive. It had been eight years since her parents had been killed in the flying accident. They might have been alive if her father hadn't loved skiing so much, or if they hadn't decided to take the private jet all the way to Austria, or if Steve had not been in Vietnam and could have been their pilot. It had taken the past six years for Sabrina to accept the way things were.

Her parent's untimely death had left Sabrina an instant multi-millionaire. With her cash inheritance came a fifty-one percent stock ownership in Planter's Bank of New York, a responsibility she delegated to her Godfather and parental surrogate, Taggat Delaney. Sabrina, only seventeen at the time of her parents' deaths, had lived with Taggat in New York City while finishing High School. She had received her M.B.A. from Harvard, and, after leaving Harvard, she returned to MacKenzie Island. There, she and Cathy Winston, a long time friend, and business partner, had built a home and opened the investment trust advisory firm, MacKenzie & Winston, Inc. Their offices were located in a complex adjacent to the Commons of Soames College.

Sabrina's gazebo was adjacent to the office building and in direct eyesight of her private office's bay window. Their house, Gull Haven, was a two mile road walk from the gazebo, but only a mile stroll along the beach. Tonight the distance didn't disturb Sabrina. It would give her time to think and hopefully resolve her dilemma.

"Why did Kent have to bring Steve into this?" Sabrina scoffed as she kicked a shell along the beach. She had been trying hard not to think of Steve. She thought she was in love with Kent, but now, she would have to admit to what Cathy had said all along. Kent was her substitute for Steve's lost love. Steve had been a twenty four year old dashingly handsome Naval aviator when Sabrina first met him. His six foot one inch muscular frame was embedded in her mind forever. But it wasn't his body that had kept her interested. Oh, it attracted her at first, yes, but, as she grew to know Steve, she was impressed by his quiet and gentle nature. She had never understood how such a gentle man could think about blasting people out of the air or killing them on the ground. Steve's dark side, a trait Taggat had mentioned frequently, had never been revealed to Sabrina, but she did know of Steve's anger and strength when aroused.

Sabrina had first met Steve close to the time of her seventeenth birthday. He had accompanied her father home after a business party. Seth MacKenzie and Steve had hit it off from their first introduction at a party given by Planter's Bank for Government Military Contractors. Sabrina had attributed their compatibility to duplicate personalities. Over the months, Steve had adopted Seth as second father, and Seth had given no opposition.

Sabrina became deeply infatuated with Steve, and because Sabrina was both physically and mentally mature beyond her years, Steve shared an interest. However, because of their age difference, her parents discouraged a dating relationship, and Steve respected their wishes. Eventually, by some difficult persuasion and a few mild threats, Sabrina gained her parent's permission to date Steve. But before their chance materialized, Steve was called for active duty in Vietnam, and Sabrina carried the scars of an unfulfilled first love.

After Steve completed his obligation with the Navy, he accepted an invitation from Taggat Delaney, prompted by a bequest from Seth, to establish a private flying service based at Kennedy International Airport. Because of their busy schedules, Sabrina's and Steve's relationship never matured, a fact Sabrina regretted. Taggat had frequently tried to bring them back together, but it just never seemed to work out. After Sabrina became involved with Kent, a sore spot with Taggat, she didn't hear from Steve. Even the usual cards stopped. Sabrina hadn't realized, until lately, how much she missed Steve's attention and physical presence. Being with Steve was always a thrill.

Sabrina kicked the shell further along the sandy path. "I wonder what Cathy's going to say? She's seen through Kent from the beginning. She always told me Kent couldn't take it when the chips were down. I guess she's right, again. She never did like him, but she doesn't like any man." Sabrina laughed.

The wind rustled through the sea oats, bending their heads towards the West. The waves began to smack the sand a little harder, and larger drops of rain hit Sabrina's face, bringing her out of her thoughts. She looked up and, between the dunes, saw the lights of the back of the house. She followed the zig-zagged wooden walkway from the beach, climbed the circular back steps, stomped the sand from her shoes, took a deep breath, and opened the door. "Well, here goes nothing." Sabrina prepared to answer Cathy's attack.

* * *

Cathy Winston was Sabrina's alter ego. That's why they were so compatible. Her blonde hair, bright blue eyes, and fair complexion were but a fancy facade for her sharp, tactless tongue and unbridled, occasionally bawdy, wit. Men were attracted to her five foot six inch body because she had all the outward appearance of a beauty contest winner. But unless

Cathy had an immediate attraction to an admirer, she could terminate the acquaintance with a flow of cutting rhetoric that would put a longshoreman to shame. However, Cathy's devotion to those she loved was incomparable. She loved with all her heart and gave of herself completely. She expected the same in return.

Cathy and Sabrina's friendship had grown out of adversity, making it the strongest bond of all. The seed of their relationship was planted in their junior year of high school. Sabrina, still hurt and bitter from the loss of her parents, was living with Taggat Delaney and attending a new high school. Her paucity of friends did not disturb her, but the loneliness was overwhelming. She spent solitary hours on the bleachers of the football field trying to bring some meaning to the events of the past few months-the loss of Steve to the Navy and Vietnam and the loss of her parents to the plane accident.

Cathy, attending the high school to which Sabrina had transferred, being vibrant and loving, had given herself to a boy, Jeff Marks, and found herself pregnant. She confronted Jeff but was rejected. Alone and afraid, she couldn't tell her parents, and she couldn't tell any of her friends. To Cathy, the romantic, the only escape was death. Her intricate, analytical mind planned the entire scenario. The next time she was to have her mother's sleeping pill prescription filled, a monthly ritual, she would forge a double dose. Then, she would take the medicine to school, leave a note for Jeff to meet her behind the bleachers on the football field, and take the drugs. Jeff would be the one to find her limp dead body. It would serve him right...the cad!

Cathy's solution was simple, but she hadn't thought about the effects it might have on her parents or others. And Cathy hadn't calculated, in her master plan, on meeting Sabrina MacKenzie that day on those bleachers. Their meeting and ensuing conversation had made Cathy realize her problems were insignificant beside Sabrina's recent losses. Sabrina's straightforward approach promised Cathy support in resolving her dilemma with Jeff. The relationship established that afternoon cemented a bond that would last a lifetime.

When things didn't work out as anticipated for Cathy, Sabrina went against her own morals and entertained the abortion possibility. The arrangements had been difficult, particularly with no parental consent, but in the first of many subsequent MacKenzie-Winston schemes, Sabrina and Cathy managed to bluff their way through one of the Inner City clinics. Sabrina stood by Cathy throughout the procedure, and the hand holding that took place during Cathy's anesthetic bonded their life-long sisterhood.

Cathy had a difficult time, at first, accepting the reality of the abortion. But now, with success behind her that she never would have accomplished otherwise, she shuddered to think of the life she would have had with Jeff. Her heart occasionally panged at the lost child, but there would be other opportunities for children. She owed herself and her future children the best life she could offer. With Sabrina's friendship and her own initiative, she had grown toward attaining that goal.

\* \* \*

"Hey, I thought you were swearing off those M & M's," Sabrina remarked as she entered the back door and found Cathy mining the candy drawer.

Cathy turned from her position over the drawer. She was unable to immediately respond because the first handful of the candy was still in her mouth, and she had her hand inside the pound bag of candy extracting her next helping. She removed her hand from the bag but kept the multi-colored treasures in her palm. She quickly swallowed her mouth's contents and looked at Sabrina. "This is just my first handful." Her bright blue eyes searched for belief or at least understanding.

"Right! And I guess you didn't have your Hershey earlier?" Sabrina smiled as she walked over to the refrigerator. "I need a drink." Sabrina reached inside and removed the orange juice container.

"I ran two miles earlier this evening. I need some carbs," Cathy grinned. A green candy shell clung to her right front tooth.

"Oh? Making up for the energy loss?" Sabrina reached and attempted to flick the shell from Cathy's tooth.

Cathy flinched from Sabrina's reach, picked the shell from her tooth and consumed it along with another handful of candy. "Get your own, and yes, I am trying to catch up on what I've burned. Anyway, when did you become my conscience?" Cathy turned back to the refrigerator. She opened the door, removed the milk from the top shelf, poured a small glass, and returned the carton. "Want to talk about it?"

"You were right. That's all I'm going to say. I don't want to dwell on the subject any longer." Sabrina headed for the living room.

"Okay, but you'll be sorry."

"How do you figure?"

"Well, it will just swell up inside until you'll have to tell someone. Who else is there? Huh?" Cathy poked the rest of the candy into her mouth. She looked at her palm. "See, they really don't melt in your hand." Cathy looked at Sabrina and gave a ten year olds smile.

"Cute. That's real cute."

"Oh, come on, Sabrina. Tell me all about what happened tonight. I'm going to get it out of you somehow. You know that."

"You're probably right." Sabrina's smile dissolved. "Cathy, you were right about Kent. He dropped me like a ton of bricks. He doesn't care about the baby. He doesn't care about what happens to me. What am I going to do?" Sabrina stretched her arms open and searched for Cathy's help.

Cathy's smile quickly faded. She rushed to Sabrina, reached out, and embraced her. "Easy, Sabrina. We'll figure out something. Tell me about it."

Sabrina sniffed back a few tears. She leaned back and looked into Cathy's reassuring eyes. "Well, I told Kent I was pregnant, and all he could talk about was having the pregnancy aborted so he could get on with his naval career." Sabrina broke loose from Cathy's hug and walked to the sink. She banged a few of the dishes around in the water, picked up a butcher knife that was lying in the bottom of the sink, turned, and pointed it at Cathy. "He wanted me to terminate the pregnancy so he could have a clear conscious. He said he didn't want any responsibility other than his damned airplanes." She turned and sunk the blade a quarter of an inch into the chopping block. Sabrina walked to the outside door. The rain had started in torrential sheets, and the lightning danced across the sky. "When I gave him a choice, he jumped at the chance to get away." Sabrina continued to circle the kitchen, opening and banging closed the cabinet doors.

"Well, Sabrina, I really hoped it wouldn't turn out this way, but it was predictable. And sit down. You're making me dizzy."

"Why do you have to be right all the time?"

"I'm not. Just most of the time. Hell, Sabrina, I've told you. Men are all alike. I believe they take an oath as they pass through puberty: Find 'em, fuck 'em, forget 'em."

"Cathy!"

"Oh, don't be such a prude. I don't believe any of them ever grow up. We should invent a way to get along without them. It would be a much nicer place to live." Cathy laughed. "Don't you agree?"

"Tonight, yes!"

"Come on. Let's go sit on the couch. You're making me nervous. You can tell me every sticky detail. Don't leave anything out." They passed through the double wide arched kitchen entrance, walked through the dining room, and settled on the oversized couch in the living area. Cathy was wearing her most comfortable pink, terri cloth robe and nothing else. Her blonde hair was networked into a French braid. She sat cross legged and patted the spot next to her. "Now. Everything." Her blue eyes were ready to "listen" to Sabrina's story. The dark bag of candy was nestled in her lap.

Cathy "watched" Sabrina's story of the confrontation with interest. She listened without interruption, a feat in itself for Cathy. "Sabrina, I know what you're feeling. Remember, I lived through this in high school. That little twerp, Jeff, did the same thing to me after he got me pregnant. He acted as if it were all my fault and treated me like I was a little whore. Then, when you and I went to his parents, they tried to buy me off. What's worse, Jeff wouldn't even come out of his room and face us. Remember? They offered to pay for the abortion, and, remember, we told them to stick the money where the sun didn't shine. I still can't believe you did that , Sabrina."

"Me?"

"Yes, you. Don't you remember?"

"I remember quite well, and you've got a sugar buzz going. Please let me finish. I'm tired."

"Can't stop now. I'm on a roll. Have to tell you this, then I'll shut up."

"Promise?"

"No!" Cathy grinned. "What I want to say is." Cathy took a deep breath. "After the abortion, I really got down. If it hadn't been for you, I don't know what I would have done. You convinced me what I did was the right thing for me at the time, and you were right."

"What's the point to all this, Cathy?"

"The point is…I know we can work our way through this. I know we can come to some solution, and I'm sure you'll make the right decision. We need to think it out. Got any thoughts?" Cathy childishly smiled, put her hand into the M & M bag, pulled out another handful of candies and put them in her mouth. Her eyebrows raised in anticipation of Sabrina's reply.

"Oh, I've thought of a real doozy. I thought about it walking back from the gazebo, but I'm not sure it's so smart."

"Well, run it by me. I'll see how it fits."

"Okay, but bear with me."

"Hell, I've been doing that for years." Cathy winked.

"All right, enough comments from your dark side."

"Okay, I'll listen."

"That'll be the day."

"Sabrina!"

Sabrina grabbed a handful of chocolates and downed them quickly. "First of all, I can't have an abortion. There is no way I could let that happen. I'm not making judgments of those who do, but I won't do that. I'm not sure I would ever recover. I've lost too much that's close to me already."

"I understand. What's right for one isn't always right for another. It's usually a matter of timing when it comes to these things, anyway. And it depends on who's involved. Right?" The words came quickly from Cathy's chocolate hype.

"Right!" Sabrina smiled at Cathy's energetic speech.

"All right. You're going to have the baby. I think we've established that. Now, do you think that's wise with your heart condition?" Cathy picked through the M & M's and popped a few more into her mouth.

"I'm not sure, but the last time I saw my cardiologist, she gave me a clean bill of health."

"Provided you took things easy!"

"I was about to say that."

"Well, don't forget it."

"Thanks, mother."

"Oh, shut up."

"I'll see the doctor soon. I promise."

"Good. What's your big idea?"

"Well..." Sabrina was hesitant to answer.

"Oh, go on. It's me, remember?"

"What do you think about my going to California and filling Kent's parents in on the details." Sabrina sheepishly looked at Cathy as if she should be guilty of such thoughts.

Cathy jumped from the couch, throwing the candy bag into the floor. The candies scattered across the hardwood, and Cathy almost choked on the half-melted pieces she had just placed in her mouth. She stood in front of Sabrina with her hands outstretched. "All right! Now I've got you thinking like a business woman. Hit him where it hurts. But, are you sure you can accept the consequences of such a trip?"

"What do you mean?"

"Well, you have to be ready for both possibilities."

"What are you talking about?"

"If they agree to help, you'll have to be ready to accept Kent." Cathy stuck her finger into her mouth. "YUCK."

Sabrina laughed.

"But if Kent's parents shun you like Kent did, be ready to stick it to them."

"How could I possibly do that? Kent's mother could give a big damn if I were alive or dead. I'm sure she will love it when she finds out Kent and I are no longer together."

"Oh, you can get to them. Tell them they'll never see their ONLY grandchild as long as they are alive. Believe me. That will get more results than you might want, if they're human."

"Do you really think so? You don't know Kent's mother."

"No, I don't. But I know people, and you have within you the most powerful leverage known to human kind. Blood! They will want to see the baby. They will want to know it's healthy and taken care of."

"They know I can take care of a child. They're aware of my financial status."

"It wouldn't make any difference if you were Malcolm Forbes, himself. No grandparent believes a parent can take care of a grandchild. It's inherent. You've got to be ready to hit them with both barrels. You can't hesitate. Can you do that?"

"I'm not sure. You know I usually let you handle the strong arm stuff at meetings. I'm afraid I might back off and leave. Oh, I could tell them, all right. That's no problem. But I'm not sure I could hit them when they're down."

"Then, it's settled."

"What's settled?"

"I'm going with you."

"I thought you were scheduled to be in North Carolina this weekend. The Chesworth account is potentially one of our biggest."

"Don't worry. I'll make the meeting. We'll be back by then."

"Be back? When do you suggest we leave?"

"Why, tomorrow, or course. Strike while the iron is hot."

"Tomorrow! I thought I could talk to them this weekend and save a trip to California. I just remembered they're coming to see Kent before he ships out Sunday."

"All the better for us. Sabrina, this is perfect. We'll leave tomorrow for the West Coast, see Kent's parents, break the news, and boy, will Kent's send off be a hot one. I can see the scene on the pier now. This is perfect."

"Wait, Cathy. I don't know if they're home."

Cathy handed Sabrina the telephone. "Easy way to find out. Let your fingers do the walking." Cathy kneeled down and began to gather the scattered chocolates.

"You watch too many movies and way too much television."

"Oh, hush! If you're not careful I'll start my Bogart impressions."

"Please, not that. You're terrible."

Cathy pointed her cocked thumb and straight forefinger at Sabrina. "Dial it, schweetheart!"

"Okay, okay! My, God, what we women will do!"

# 5

Approximately one hundred miles down the coast from San Francisco, the flowing California shoreline is marred by an anomalous projection of earth and stone. Anomalous because, if one were to follow the natural curvature of the coast, this warty lump should have been chiseled off and discarded by The Hand sculpting this magnificent meeting of land and sea. Fortunately, it was not cast aside. Instead it was treated as a gifted child and given characteristics unlike any other. While its sheer beauty and its memorable golf courses are the major attraction, its most consistent characteristic is its unusual weather. Even so, as inclement as the weather can be, the inhabitants of the region, at least those who can afford the life style, consider the Monterey Peninsula special.

Brian Pooley, one of the inhabitants, recognized the value of this area when his real estate syndicate purchased a section of Pescadero Point overlooking Carmel Bay. The syndicate held the land for two years and resold the property to a major hotel chain. Instead of taking his share of the profit in cash, Brian requested five select acres on the Point. The buyers reneged at first, fearing competitive development, but, when Brian assured with legal documentation that he wanted the property for a personal dwelling, the corporate attorneys were instructed to agree.

Brian chose to construct his little bit of heaven on a site just pass the acme of the point. The view to the east of his property was of the rugged shoreline and Pebble Beach golf links while, out to the west, the waters of the Pacific stretch to the horizon. From an exit on Seventeen Mile Drive, his home's entrance road meanders through a myriad of towering pine trees. The road then circles in front of the house and falls back to the main highway through another network of landscaped pines. The seven thousand square foot, Mexican style ranch home was sited with the living areas overlooking Carmel Bay while the sleeping areas were partially cantilevered over a precipice viewing the expanse of the Pacific. Brian found serenity on this spot. It possessed the solitude he sometimes needed to resolve the dilemmas life occasionally presented. His study, the spot for formulating resolutions, included an oversized, dark oak desk set atop the Bokhara rug covered hardwood floor, and when he sat in his black leather, swivel desk chair, he could turn and look over the expanse of Carmel Bay and the distant erratic shoreline of the golf links.

Physically, Brian didn't reveal his forty nine years. His six foot, two inch frame carried its lean one hundred eighty five pounds well. His skin was drawn from the combined years of his native Texan and adopted Californian sun, but his sandy blonde hair and bright blue eyes gave no hint of the number of days they had seen come and go. His complexion was marked with the tattle-tale lines etched by many emotions, but his commanding presence and outgoing personality caused those around him to see nothing but his bright smile and self-confidence.

Brian had been orphaned at birth, literally left on a church step. He had never known his mother or father, and he didn't care to find out about them now. He been raised in foster homes until adulthood, and by necessity, he had become self-sufficient and had acquired the traits of a responsible individual. After high school, Brian had attended a small business college in Houston, and upon graduation, he had remained in the Houston area working his way to a full partnership in a major real estate agency. During a presentation of one of his investment properties, he had met Beth Sparks, the daughter of a deceased San Francisco newspaper magnate. Beth was five years older than Brian, but they seemed attracted to one another from their first introduction. After the sale, Brian continued to see Beth, and they had been married two years later. After the honeymoon, he and Beth had made their home on the West Coast.

Brian's interest in money didn't bother Beth. She had gladly relinquished the responsibility of her inheritance because, after their marriage, she had been interested in only one thing, having a child. Within eighteen months of their marriage, a son, Kent, had been born. Beth had devoted all her time and energy. Brian, on the other hand, wasn't able to "enjoy" Kent's childhood because of travel requirements associated with his business. Through the years, Beth's obsession with her son bled her attention from her husband. Consequently, Brian had become more and more alienated. Eventually, he began having affairs. At first, his activities had been clandestine. But, as the years passed, and Beth proved obviously aware of his philandering, he had become openly involved with his ladies. Their marriage had persevered because of their son. However, now that Kent was questionably ready to assume the responsibilities of maturity, Brian was closer and closer to leaving Beth and finding the happiness he desired.

* * *

Brian watched through his study's mist covered windows the breakers beating upon the rocks along the distant shoreline. The surf exploded as high as some of the cliffs, and the gnarly roots of the ancient cypress clung to the craggy outcroppings for existence. Their branches were swept into swirling configurations by the uncountable years of attack by the relentless ocean winds. Through the haze, one could imagine them as sentinels guarding the coast for years past and years to come.

Thoughts of the previous evening's phone call distracted Brian's attention from the scene. Why had she called? Why did she feel it necessary to come to California? Why did she want to see them? After all, Kent had called and said that he and Sabrina had broken up, a fact not surprising to Brian because Beth's jealousy and possessive nature made it impossible for any woman to have a lasting relationship with their son.

"Do you want anything to drink?" Beth Pooley asked from the entrance to the study.

"No, not now." Brian spun from his view to see Beth standing in the doorway. Beth had changed since Kent's departure over the past seven years. Her increase in alcohol intake degenerated her once well proportioned body into thin arms and legs attached to a paunchy middle. Her once well managed brown hair was now streaked with gray and poorly kept. Her once immaculate detail in dress had become daily sweat pants and loose fitting sweatshirt. Even though she no longer sough his opinion, Brian thought Beth should attempt some pride in her appearance. However, without the stimulus of desire, Beth seemed no longer to care for anything, thus making her fifty-four years look like ten more. "It's a little early to start drinking. Isn't it?"

"I need some support this morning. I don't seem to get any from you. I don't know why you agreed to see Sabrina, anyway."

"Curiosity, my dear. Besides, we owe her our hospitality since she was almost engaged to our son."

"We don't owe her a damned thing, Brian. As far as I'm concerned, she's a stranger now that she's no longer seeing Kent."

"Beth, you know better than that. Sabrina was always willing to open her house to us when we visited Kent, and I think we can give her a little of our time since she's flying out specifically to talk to us. Why? I'm sure I don't know."

Beth looked away from Brian. "Neither do I."

"Are you sure you don't know why Sabrina's coming?"

"What's that supposed to mean?" Beth's exasperation showing in the form of childish frustration. She turned back to face Brian and put her clenched fists on her hips.

"You know what it means. You and Kent are alike. You keep things to yourself until the truth is known. Then, you lie your way out of the situation by manipulating your story to fit the facts."

"Dammit, Brian. Why can't you believe your own son? Kent said he and Sabrina had broken up. He didn't mention anything else, did he?"

"I don't know, Beth. Did he? Remember, you spoke to Kent. Not me."

"Well, that's all he said. Why can't you be supportive of our son?"

"Beth! Kent has my support, but he's had your protection for so long, he has difficulty facing facts. Hopefully, the Navy has instilled some honor into his fiber, but I'd still like to hear Sabrina's side of the story concerning their break up. Besides, I liked her. She would have been good for Kent."

"She most certainly would not! Sabrina wasn't the right girl for Kent."

Brian laughed, "You wouldn't like any one wanting to marry Kent."

Beth appeared startled. "Married? They weren't getting married."

"Well, you and I both knew they were heading that way."

"It would have never happened. Kent would have finally seen the truth about Sabrina."

"The truth about Sabrina? What's that supposed to mean?"

"Sabrina is a manipulative, conniving, devilish female. Kent would have finally realized that and left her. Evidently, something happened to bring about that revelation much sooner than I had anticipated."

"You didn't help Kent make that revelation, did you Beth?"

"No!" Beth stomped on the floor. "How could you think such a thing?"

"Because, I don't think you want Kent to be devoted to anyone else in his life. It's killing you that he loves that aircraft carrier so much."

"I don't have to listen to this. You always get so damned sarcastic when we talk about Kent." Beth started to leave the room, but abruptly stopped and turned back toward Brian. "Just remember. He's your son and deserves your support regardless of what Sabrina has to say."

"Beth, I'll support Kent, but you better not be hiding anything from me."

"Well, I'll tell you one thing, if that little bitch comes in here and starts making up lies about my Kent, I'll have her out of this house before she knows what hit her."

Brian looked at his watch. 11 A.M. "Sabrina said she would be here by noon. We won't have to wait much longer to hear what she has to say."

"Brian, please try being a father, for once. Not a board chairman, not a hard-hearted Texas business man, just a father. See things from your son's standpoint. See what he has had to contend with all his life. Try to understand his feelings, and maybe for once in your life you'll understand why he is like he is."

"He's like he is because you've conditioned him to be so."

"You'll never understand." Beth spun on her heels and huffed toward the kitchen. "I need a drink."

Brian attributed Beth's attitude to her alcohol level, spun around in his chair and continued to absorb the effects of the view from his study.

"Meester Pooley, there iz two ladeez at the door. They say they iz expected." Maria Sanchez, the Mexican house servant, announced the guests from the entryway of Brian's study.

Brian spun in his chair to greet Maria. "There ARE, Maria, there ARE."

"Yes, there iz, I promise."

Brian grinned. "Thank you. Show them to the living room, and tell Mrs. Pooley they're here. I'll be there in a moment. Offer them a drink, if you would, and fix me a double bourbon. Open a new bottle of wine for Mrs. Pooley. It could be a long afternoon."

\* \* \*

The outermost entrance to the Pooley's home was through a six foot high redwood gate opening into an enclosed rock garden. Light filtering through the slatted wood ceiling cast erratic shadows across the intricately placed patterns of multicolored pebbles. An elevated redwood walk meandered from the gate across a small bridge to the front door. The arched oriental bridge spanned a small nephroid pond. Koi languidly drifted among the water lilies and leisurely swam under the bridge.

Maria Sanchez greeted Sabrina and Cathy at the main entrance and escorted them into a twenty foot square vaulted foyer. Sunshine pouring through the overhead skylights was broken into divergent rays by the rustic brass and wood spoked chandelier. From the foyer, they could look down a long hall, through swinging doors, and into the kitchen. They followed Maria down the brown tiled hallway until she stopped in the middle of a large arched entrance and directed them into the living room.

"Please have a seat. Meester and Meesees Pooley will be in shortly." Maria turned and disappeared down the hall.

The wall opposite the arched entrance was one long six foot high picture window allowing the expanse of Carmel Bay to spread out before them. A large tan leather couch faced the room's entrance, and on either side of the couch stood a matching chair. Glass topped iron end tables and a matching coffee table completed the group. Two deep brown and red flame stitched wing backed chairs faced the couch with a matching end table between them. The tables were graced with Kovaks lamps, and a Frederick Remington sculpture of a bronco buster sat on the coffee table.

As Sabrina and Cathy sat on the couch, they could see that the wall on both sides of the entrance was covered with family photographic memorabilia. As the leather warmed to their presence, they squinted at the photos and looked nervously at one another without talking.

Cathy crossed her legs, patted her foot, and rocked to and fro. She looked again at Sabrina and grinned. "I feel like I'm waiting for the principal."

"You've certainly had plenty of practice." Sabrina somberly returned.

"Don't remind me." Cathy raised both eyebrows and smiled.

They both laughed nervously.

Cathy straightened her legs and adjusted her skirt as Maria reentered the room.

"Could I get you ladies sometheeng to drink?"

Cathy looked at her watch. "Hmm, eleven fifty. It is a little early. Oh, what the hell! I'll have a scotch and soda."

"Cathy!" Sabrina chided.

"Well? It's almost noon. It's past noon back home!" Cathy looked at Maria. "Scotch and soda."

"Yes, senorita. Anything for you?" Maria looked at Sabrina.

"Do you have lemonade?"

"Yes, Mam. Fresh."

"Mmm. I'll have a small glass, por favor."

"Si," Maria turned and left the room.

"Better watch out, Sabrina. Those California lemons pack a kick."

"I'm not drinking anything alcoholic until the baby arrives. I've told you that."

"I know, I know. Just trying to break the ice."

Sabrina smiled, bent over and picked up her briefcase. She placed it on the coffee table, opened the top, and began shuffling through a stack of papers.

Cathy watched with interest, but became frustrated when Sabrina didn't show her any of the satchel's contents. "I can see I'm not going to get a lot out of you."

Sabrina slowly lifted her head, but didn't look at Cathy. "What? What did you say? I'm sorry, I wasn't listening."

"Never mind. It wasn't important." Cathy stood, walked to the family pictures, and scrutinized the photos. "Sabrina," Cathy waved to Sabrina, but kept her eyes on the photos. "Come over here a sec."

"What do you want?" Sabrina replied with frustration.

"Come here! I want you to see this. It won't take you away from your precious papers for very long."

Sabrina put the papers into the briefcase, sighed, and slowly beckoned to Cathy's call. "What is it?" Sabrina settled beside Cathy and scrutinized the photos more closely.

"Notice anything strange?"

"No, I don't believe so. Just photographs of Kent and his mother."

"Exactly! Kent and his mother. Not Kent and his father...not Kent's father and mother...not Kent's father. If Kent and his mother weren't apart in these two pictures, you'd think they were joined at the hip. No wonder the boy has problems with women. No one is as good as his mommy."

"Cathy!" Sabrina gently slapped Cathy's forearm and looked around the room. "Someone might hear. His mother is very sensitive."

"Hell, I don't care! She probably needs to hear."

"You're hopeless. You know that?" Sabrina grinned, pinched Cathy on the fleshy part of her exposed left arm, and walked back to the couch.

Cathy followed and looked down into the papers Sabrina continued to shuffle. "What you got in there?"

"Stuff." Sabrina smiled.

"Oh? What kind of stuff?"

"Just stuff." Sabrina looked into Cathy's prying eyes and grinned.

"All right. I can take a hint. I'll leave you to your STUFF." Cathy strolled to the picture window and watched as the surf pelted the rocks below her. "This is a beautiful place."

"It sure is." Sabrina said as Maria escorted Beth and Brian into the room and set a serving platter full of drinks onto the coffee table.

"Thank you! We like it. That's all for now, Maria. Thanks." Brian walked over and grasped Sabrina's hand. "It's good to see you, Sabrina. I wish we could be meeting under different circumstances."

"So do I, Brian. It's good to see both of you again." Sabrina accepted a small peck on her cheek from Brian and then backed away. "I would like to introduce you both to my business partner and close friend Cathy Winston. Cathy, Beth and Brian Pooley."

Brian clasped Cathy's right hand with both his. "It's always a pleasure to meet a good looking woman."

"Why, thank you! I'm flattered. I'm sure I look like the devil after such a long flight."

"Flattery intended." Brian released Cathy's hand. "And you look just fine."

Cathy extended her hand to Beth.

Beth looked at Cathy's hand, huffed, turned her back, and sat down on one of the wing backed chairs.

"Yes. Well, I'm glad to meet you, too." Cathy turned to Sabrina, shrugged her shoulders, and grinned. She picked her drink off the tray and sat in the other wingback.

Sabrina reassumed her prior position on the couch, and Brian sat in one of the adjacent leather chairs.

Brian looked from Sabrina to Cathy and back to Sabrina. "It's been a long time since two such pretty women graced this living room."

Cathy smiled and tipped her drink to Brian. "You certainly know how to impress a lady. Don't you?"

"I'll say he does." Beth scoffed.

Cathy turned and scowled at Beth. "I knew you weren't mute. See Sabrina, she can speak."

"Cathy!" Sabrina's mouth fell open.

Cathy looked at Brian and then to Beth. "I'm sorry. Sometimes my mouth begins to work before my brain has checked out the content." Cathy sunk back into the chair.

"Apology accepted, Ms. Winston." Brian attempted to keep a straight face.

"Please call me "Cathy". No one has called me Ms. Winston since I can remember."

"Okay, Cathy." Brian turned in his chair to Sabrina. "Sabrina, your visit intrigues me. Kent called us last evening and told us of your breakup. Personally, I was quite sorry to hear this has happened, but what will be, will be. Then, we receive a call from you asking to speak to us. Once again, I'm bewildered. What brings you to California?"

"Yes, Sabrina. Tell us." Beth leaned forward in her chair. "What lies do you wish to spread about my Kent."

Brian's head jerked toward Beth. "Beth, please! Let's try and keep this civil."

Beth poured another glass of wine and leaned back into the chair. She cocked her right heel onto the edge of her seat, leaned forward on her thigh, and fixed her stare on Sabrina.

Sabrina watched Brian's response with interest. She knew she would never win Beth's support, but she felt an alliance with Brian might be attainable. "Before I begin, I want it understood that what I am about to tell you is not a lie. Mrs. Pooley, I never lie! Lies only delay the inevitable." Sabrina's stare and words were directed toward Beth, but as soon as she finished, she turned to Brian. "The reason I came to California is to discuss a child, MY CHILD, and its right to have a mother and father. I'm pregnant! Pregnant with your son's child, YOUR grandchild."

"No, you're not! It's not Kent's child. He told me so!" Beth leaned forward in her chair. As she spoke, she changed her focus from Sabrina to Brian. "It's not Kent's child, Brian. You must believe us."

"What the hell are you talking about, Beth? "Us?" Who the hell is "us"? Did Kent tell you Sabrina was pregnant?"

"Yes," Beth hung her head and eased back into the seat.

"Then, why in the hell didn't you tell me?"

"I didn't think you needed to know. It wasn't important."

"Not important! It sounds pretty damned important to me. At least, it explains why Sabrina was so intent on seeing us."

"It's not an issue. The baby isn't Kent's. So, it's not important. She's here to spread lies about Kent. I knew it!"

Sabrina looked at Beth and glared. "If Kent isn't my baby's father, who is? I would like to know what Kent told you."

Brian looked at Beth. "Yes, I would like to know myself."

Beth thought for a moment. She had been drinking when Kent called, and she wasn't sure if she would get all the names correct. Then, as if a light came on in her dark mind, she remembered. "Kent said it was your other boyfriend's baby. Uh...I think he said his name was, um...Steve!

Yes. His name is Steve. Kent said you and he had quarreled over some-thing a couple of months ago, and you had dated Steve for a while. After you got back together, Kent had forgiven your indiscretion with your old boyfriend until last night when you told him you were pregnant."

Brian stood up from his chair and took a deep breath. "Whoa! Just a damned minute. Let's clear some of this muddy water." He looked at Sabrina. "Sabrina, are you truly pregnant?"

"Yes, I'm pregnant."

"I suppose you brought proof." Brian looked down his nose at Sabrina.

"Now, you wait just a damned minute." Cathy jumped from her chair and walked to within a foot of Brian. "Sabrina doesn't have to prove any-thing. We're not here to threaten you."

Brian didn't back away from Cathy's assault. He slowly looked Cathy over and peered into her blue eyes. "Oh, I think she owes us some proof, especially, if she plans to claim Kent in any paternity action."

"Whoa, yourself!" Sabrina stood quickly, walked around the coffee table, and stood beside Brian and Cathy. "I don't want anything from you or Kent, but I assure you, I have all the proof I need." Sabrina turned, bent over, and began shuffling the papers.

Brian watched intently. Suddenly a slight smile crossed his face. "I hope there aren't any bombs in there, Sabrina. The first one you dropped will be sufficient."

Cathy giggled, but she immediately stopped when Sabrina gave her a cold stare.

"Why are we doing this?" Beth announced from her spot away from the trio. She flipped her hands into the air discarding the conversation to this point. "It doesn't make one bit of difference is she's pregnant or not. Does it, Brian?"

"Shut up, Beth!" Brian looked at Beth in exasperation. "You've only heard Kent's side of this story. I'd like to hear the truth."

Beth bolted from her chair. "I don't believe you said that! You're doing exactly what I thought you would. You're taking her side instead of helping your son."

"Dammit, Beth! I'm doing this because I want to know the facts. I've heard some of what Kent told you, but how can I believe it?"

"You can believe it, because your son told you."

"No, he told you! You told me, and I'm not sure what to believe. You and Kent can be deceitful, especially if you have something to gain."

"Brian, you son-of-a-bitch." Beth started toward Brian. "I'll show you deceit." Beth stopped short of Brian and Sabrina, grabbed a handful of papers from the confines of the briefcase, and pitched them into the air. As they haphazardly fell about her, she looked at Brian and pointed her finger at Sabrina. "There's deceit standing before you! Deceit packaged in a she devil's body. Deceit trying to turn us against our son."

Brian grabbed Beth's arms. "Beth, please sit down."

Beth shook her arms free of Brian's grip. "I don't want to sit. I don't want to hear anymore of this. And if you're any kind of father, you'll get rid of this woman and her friend. Now!" Beth turned, picked up her wine glass, took the bottle off the coffee table, and left the room.

Brian watched Beth march through the living room entrance and turn left down the hall to her bedroom. He was dumbfounded. "I'm sorry, but I'm afraid I'll have to ask you both to go. I don't believe we'll be able to continue. Maybe we can discuss this further this evening or in the morning after I have a chance to talk over the problem with Beth. Then, I'll try to contact Kent. We're supposed to fly to Norfolk tomorrow, but I don't think this can wait."

"Brian, I'm sorry, but I must complete this today." Sabrina seemed unshaken by Beth's show of emotion. "What I have to say won't take but a few more minutes. Cathy and I are scheduled to fly back this evening."

Brian shrugged his shoulders and sat down. "Very well, but I'm afraid I won't be a very good audience."

Sabrina, realizing she was destined to raise her child on her own, took a deep breath and sat back down on the couch. She knew there would be no reconciliation with the Pooley's. She picked up the papers Cathy had placed back into her briefcase and began to speak.

Brian reached over and lightly grasped her hands. "Sabrina, I don't need proof if that's what you're about to show me. All I want to know is when did Kent find out you were pregnant?"

Sabrina quizzically looked at Brian. "We discussed it last night just before I called and spoke to Beth. Why?"

"How did he react to the news?"

"I don't understand, Brian. What makes the difference how he…"

"Please!" Brian squeezed Sabrina's hands tighter, "Just answer my question. It's important to me."

"Okay, Brian." Sabrina slowly relocated her hands from inside Brian's to the outside of his. She held them lightly as she spoke. "At first, Kent was outraged because I had become pregnant. Then, he seemed to resolve matters in his own mind and asked me to abort the pregnancy because it was inconvenient."

"And how do you feel about that now? Now that you know Kent will take no responsibility for you or the baby."

"I won't terminate this pregnancy. This baby's a part of me, and I won't have it removed from by body just because it's inconvenient for Kent, or Beth, or you."

"Wait a minute. Don't include me in their little game. I would have hoped for a better response from my son. I'm sorry if I implied that I was in their little game of denial and deception."

Sabrina patted Brian's hands and then released them. "Thank you for being so candid, Brian, and I'm glad you're not involved in their little game of denial. Knowing that makes my trip worthwhile."

"Thank you." Brian smiled at Sabrina. "So, what shall you do?"

"I have to keep on living. I have a business to run, and I'm going to have a baby. I also know I must erase what I can of Kent's memory.

Therefore, Kent and his family must be eliminated from my life because my child will never be a part of it."

"Including me?"

"That's the only way I can see it. It's the only way I can assure myself of the freedom to find the love I need for myself and my child. It will be hard, but as time goes by, I will find that love, I promise you."

"I'm sure you will, but I wish you would not act hastily and exclude me from seeing my grandchild. I was an orphan, Sabrina, and family is very important to me. Children need ties. They need anchors so strong that no storm can rock them from their harbors. Believe me! I know this from experience. I assure you that within the next six months I'll no longer be a part of this, and I would like to at least foresee a day when I too will find the same love you seek. So, please reconsider your decision, or at least think about it."

"I will think about it, Brian. I promise." Sabrina looked over at Cathy. "You ready to go?"

Cathy had watched Brian and Sabrina's discussion with interest. She felt empathy for Brian, but even more, she felt excitement. Cathy had done her homework. She knew the financial power Brian Pooley possessed. Perhaps the excitement she felt was underscored with this knowledge. Perhaps it wasn't. "I'm ready." Cathy stood, straightened her skirt, and smiled at Brian. "Well, if you're ever in Virginia, look me up." She extended her hand to Brian.

Brian walked closer to Cathy, held her hand with both of his, and looked into her eyes. "I'll plan on it, Cathy. I would like to get to know you better."

Cathy blushed and extracted her hand from his grip. "I look forward to your call, I think." Cathy tried to laugh off the seriousness of Brian's approach. She looked past Brian's shoulders and focused on Sabrina. "I'll get the car." Cathy turned and started from the room.

"Cathy, I'll be in New York in a few weeks," Brian smiled.

Cathy turned back to Brian and looked into his seriously set eyes. "Yeah? Well, okay. If I'm not busy, maybe we can work something out." Cathy spun on her heels, made the quickest exit possible, and closed the entry door behind her. She leaned back on the door and sighed, grateful to be out of Brian Pooley's presence. Her heart was racing, and she had felt a few beads of perspiration form under her arms. She took a deep breath and gathered her composure. "Damn! I haven't let a man bother me like that since college."

Sabrina gathered her papers and began stuffing them into the briefcase. Brian peered over her shoulder. "What else had you brought?"

"It's not important. It can wait."

"You sure?"

"I'm certain. What I have in here will keep." Sabrina closed her briefcase, straightened up, and looked at Brian. "You put on quite a little show with Cathy."

Brian turned, looked down the hall and then back to Sabrina. "She's a beautiful woman. Her wit intrigues me, but her fangs bother me a little."

Sabrina laughed. "Me, too. But Cathy's my dearest friend, and I don't want her hurt. When she hurts, she hurts deeply."

"Believe me, Sabrina. If I ever had anything to do with Cathy, it wouldn't be to hurt her. I imagine any dealings with that lady would have to be strictly business." Brian rubbed his chin and smiled. "However, I would hope it wouldn't have to stay that way forever. Come on. I'll walk you to the car."

"That's not necessary."

"I know. That's why I want to do it. Brian took Sabrina's briefcase, and they walked into the garden. Brian stopped inside the gate and handed Sabrina the satchel. "Why did you come, Sabrina? Really? You knew how Beth would react. At least you knew she would never go along with any coercion of Kent."

Sabrina looked at Brian and thought for a moment. "I guess I knew how she would react, but I hoped she would see through Kent's story and grant my child its father. However, now, I see exactly the way things are to be, and you know, Brian, maybe that's why I came."

"I don't follow you, Sabrina."

"I guess I needed to hear it in person. I needed to know that Kent's family didn't want any part of this baby. Now, I know I'm free to find the life my baby deserves."

"I'll miss the opportunity of being your father-in-law, Sabrina." Brian leaned down and kissed Sabrina on the forehead. "Remember, I want to do what I can for you and the baby."

Sabrina turned and grasped the gate handle, but she released the latch and turned back to face Brian. She saw a tear in his right eye. Stepping closer, she opened her arms and hugged him tightly. "I understand your feelings, Brian. I've lost too much not to know what you've been through. I'll find a way to keep you in my child's life. I swear."

"That's all I need to hear. You'll never regret your decision."

"I know." Sabrina stepped back and looked into Brian's misted eyes. "You're right, Brian. You're not part of this. You're too good a person to be associated with Beth. I'm sorry, but that's how I see it."

"That's all right. I understand. I don't know who Beth is any longer. Our marriage is close to being over, but you don't need to hear my problems. If you permit me to take part in your child's life, I promise I'll never jeopardize its relationship with you. The child will never know who the real father was."

"I believe you, Brian. Now, I really must go. Good-by." Sabrina quickly turned, lifted the latch, and walked to the awaiting Lincoln Continental. She slid into the driver's seat, latched her belt, and headed down the drive. Before loosing site of the house, she stopped, looked over her shoulder, and wondered about the life her child could have had with Brian as a grandfather and Kent as a father. Her child would never know the beauty of Pescadero Point. For this, she was sorry.

"What's wrong? Forget something?" Cathy squirmed in her seat and looked back to the house.

"No, just thinking."

"That can be dangerous to your health." Cathy turned back to the front of the car and waved down the drive. "Let's go, I'm hungry, and you're going to feed me before we get back on the plane. I'm having one good meal while we're in California."

"What did you think of Brian?" Sabrina asked as she turned onto the main highway.

"He's good looking, but he makes me nervous."

"He makes you nervous?"

"Yes. Do you find that strange?"

"Yes, I do." Sabrina grinned.

"He must be younger than ole pruneface."

"Who?"

"You know,…Beth."

"Oh, yes he is. Five or six years, I think."

"Really? They won't be together much longer. Too much tension. Too many secrets."

"You're quite perceptive."

"What! What do you know?"

"Oh, probably nothing, but when Brian visits the East Coast, I don't think he'll be returning to California for a long while."

"I knew it! I bet he hasn't screwed her in the past five years."

"How can you tell? I didn't see any horns." Sabrina laughed.

"You're bad," Cathy smiled and picked up the *Cosmopolitan* she had been reading from its position on the seat beside her.

* * *

As Brian walked back into the house, the serenity of Sabrina's resolution was soon melted by the rage he felt against Beth. He walked briskly down the hall, turned to Beth's bedroom door, and grasped the knob only to find the entrance locked. "Okay, Beth. Open this damned door. We need to talk."

"I have nothing to say to you." The voice was shaky but stern.

"Beth, open this goddamned door, or I'll kick it down."

"No! Not while you're in this kind of mood."

Brian raised his right foot and kicked the door opened.

Beth quickly jumped from her bed, ran to bathroom, and locked the door.

Brian saw Beth close the door, and without breaking stride, kicked the door open breaking the door jam into a multitude of chunks and slivers of white pine. He stormed into the bathroom and stood among the door's remains. "All right, Beth. I want some answers, and I want them now."

From her cornered position against the sink, Beth attempted to hide her fear, but the shakiness of her voice revealed her anxiety. "Get out of here! You haven't been in this bedroom for two years, and I don't see any reason for you to be here now. Besides, I have nothing to say to you....you....you traitor."

"Traitor! How can you call me a traitor when you're the one that knew Sabrina was telling the truth? How could you say all those things? You know Kent's the father of that child?"

"No I most certainly do not!" Beth walked around Brian and into the bedroom. Even though she had no prior reason to fear Brian, she wanted running room in case Brian's temper flared.

Brian watched as Beth sat on the edge of her bed and reached for the wine bottle she had brought from the living room. He quickly covered the ground between himself and Beth and snatched the bottle from her hands. "No more! Not now. I want your mind clear so you can hear what I have to say."

Beth quickly grabbed the bottle from Brian's hands. "What are you going to say that I don't know already? You're leaving me. Hell, you left me five years ago. You're disappointed in Kent. When haven't you been disappointed in our son? Brian, why don't you finish what you never had the guts to start. Get out of my goddamned house and out of my life." Beth filled her glass and took a long drink. "Good, goddamned riddance." She waved the glass toward her broken bedroom door.

Brian laughed. "I'll leave, but I'll see you in Norfolk. Kent and I have a few things to discuss before he leaves on his precious aircraft carrier."

"Don't you ruin this for him, you son-of-a-bitch. He's worked all his life to get where he is."

"Yeah, and look where he's gotten himself." Brian laughed, turned and walked out the door and into the kitchen. He looked around and found Maria washing the glasses from the earlier meeting. As she worked, she hummed a Mexican tune. "You don't have to pretend you didn't hear us, Maria." Brian walked to Maria, reached into his pocket and gave her a one hundred dollar bill. "Take care of her, Maria. I won't be around for awhile." He leaned over and kissed Maria on her cheek.

Maria turned to Brian. "I will see that she is okay, Meester Pooley, but I theenks you should do whatever you have to do and hurry home. Meeses Pooley, she's very lonely, no?"

"She's very lonely, yes, Maria. But I'm afraid I'm not the one to console her. She'll be fine after she makes her trip to Norfolk. She'll be in her own little world for a few days. It's after she returns home that I worry. So, keep an eye out for her. Okay?"

Maria wondered how she could watch Mrs. Pooley with an eye out of her head, but she confirmed Brian's wishes. She knew what he really meant. "Yes, Sir. I will make sure she is okay."

Brian patted Maria on the back and went into his study. He picked up the phone and dialed a familiar number.

"Kevin Peterson Detective Agency, the other end quickly responded."

"Hello, Jacque. This is Brian Pooley."

"Oh, hello, Mr. Pooley. Kevin's not here. May I take a message?"

"Yes. Tell Kevin to contact me tomorrow at my New York number. He has it on file. I have some work for him to do."

"Yes, Sir. I'll see that he gets the message."

"Thank you, Jacque."

"Yes, Sir. Good-by."

"Good-by." Brian hung up the phone and headed to his bedroom to pack for his departure from Pescadero Point.

* * *

Sabrina braced for the takeoff from San Francisco International. The massive size of the Boeing 747 took some of the exhilaration from the rapid acceleration of takeoff, but lifting off from the runway and watching the earth fall beneath her was one of Sabrina's favorite moments of air travel. As the jet rose, turned east, and flew toward the darkness, Sabrina watched the billowy clouds fall beneath them. At moments like this, Sabrina felt she could communicate with her mother and father. It was as if they were walking among the clouds waiting for Sabrina to join them. *Why did you subject yourself to this trip?* She thought. *Brian was very perceptive in his question. You did* know *the eventual outcome.* Sabrina grinned at her own image in the window. The setting sun's bright reflection from the trailing edge of the wing caused her to blink. *Because I had* to *give my baby a chance to have a father. It's that easy.* Sabrina's composure became more thoughtful. *And why am I thinking more about you, Steve Hardesty? You haven't* spoken to *me since Taggat told you about my relationship with Kent. Maybe a man and a woman* can't be *friends.* Sabrina shook her head hoping Steve would fall out. *I have to get you out of* my *mind, and think about what I can do for my daughter. But, I can't. Damn you, Steve. Why do I still love you? I don't know why, but I do…*

*Quit, Sabrina. Quit blubbering over Steve like some teenager. You're pregnant with another man's child.*

*So? I can still love Steve, can't I?*

*Perhaps you can, but what good will it do you? You can't possibly see him. Not like this.*

*Why can't I see him? Yes, that's it! I will see him and maybe I can wash all these nightmares out of my head. Yes, I will see him. I'll call Taggat. He'll know how to arrange it." Sabrina had won the conversation with herself. If anyone could help her with her problem, Taggat could.*

\* \* \*

The 747 touched down at Dulles four and one-half hours after leaving San Francisco, but seven and one-half hours had elapsed on the clock. Sabrina retrieved the luggage while Cathy found the car. They were halfway to Richmond before Sabrina spoke. "Whew, it'll be nice to get home."

"It certainly will." Cathy took a side glance at Sabrina. "Why so quiet?"

Sabrina shrugged. "I've been thinking. That's all."

"Yeah, me too. Thinking about taking my clothes off and taking a run into the ocean. Want to come along?"

"No! There's creepies out there. They might get somewhere they don't belong." Sabrina reached over to pinch Cathy's arm.

"Hey, I'm driving." Cathy drew away from the tease. "Who cares! Someone needs to be in there. I'm getting horny."

"Cathy!"

"Just kidding. I wanted to see if your brain was back on track."

"Cathy, what do you know about hearts?" Sabrina fidgeted in her seat belt.

"I know how to break 'em, honey." Cathy winked at Sabrina and grinned.

"No, I mean it. What do you know about hearts? Your heart, my heart, anyone's heart."

"Seriously?"

"Yes, seriously." Sabrina kept looking straight out the window.

"Well, I've had my share of anatomy and physiology in high school and college. I know they have four chambers, valves, electrical circuits and other stuff. Why? Need one? You can have mine."

"No way. I'd have trouble getting the black out of it." Sabrina didn't crack a smile.

"Oh, that's cruel. Very cruel."

"Enough kidding. Serious now. Okay?" Sabrina swung around in her seat and looked at the side of Cathy's head as she drove the Interstate around Richmond and took the exit road to the Yorktown Ferry.

"Okay, serious." Cathy waited. "Well, I'm as serious as I'm going to get."

"The reason I never had to take Phys Ed in high school was because when I was six years old, I got sick…real sick. It started out as a sore throat, and I got better. But about six weeks later I became so tired my mom and dad took me to the hospital. I thought everything was okay until I saw my parents cry when the doctor spoke to them. I spent four weeks in the hospital, and after I was released, I was never permitted to play sports."

"And I just thought you were always having your period or something." Cathy tried to make light of the serious tone Sabrina was using.

Sabrina smiled, but she didn't laugh. "I was excused because the infection partially destroyed two valves in my heart. The doctor says one of them might need to be replaced some day."

"What are you telling me, Sabrina? Are you doing something crazy by trying to have this baby?"

"I don't know, Cathy, but I want this baby more than anything else in my life. You have to promise me that you'll stick by me no matter what happens."

"Of course I will. You know that."

"And if I died, you would take care of my baby? Right?"

Cathy skidded the car to a halt and rammed the transmission into park. Sabrina's BMW rocked on its springs as Cathy abruptly turned to Sabrina. "Wait just a damned minute, Sabrina. If you're telling me this pregnancy is going to kill you, I want to discuss alternatives. Right now! Don't give me any hypothetical crap. I want the facts."

"I don't have any facts, Cathy. That's just it." Sabrina's eyes got bigger, and a look of horror took over her face. "I just don't know. I'm frightened." Sabrina began to shake as Cathy tried to comfort her.

"Look, Sabrina. You'll just have to see your cardiologist and find out. It's that simple. We can make an appointment…"

"I don't want to make an appointment. Doesn't that sound silly?" Sabrina tried to grin, but her sobs kept her from an honest effort.

"Why? Why don't you want to make an appointment?"

"Because I'm afraid the Doctor will tell me I have to abort my baby, and I won't do it!"

"Not even if it's going to kill you?"

"No!" Sabrina stopped shaking and looked Cathy in the eye. "I won't let them take this baby from me, and you have to promise me that you won't let anyone talk you into making me do it."

"I couldn't talk you into anything!"

"You could. You know you could. So, you have to promise me that you won't try."

Cathy thought for a moment. "Sabrina, I'll promise you that I will protect you and your pregnancy for as long as it is possible. But, I won't stand by and watch you get sick and possibly die if you can be saved by terminating the pregnancy. Don't ask me to do that. It's not fair."

"All right. I'll accept those conditions, but only if I get so sick I can't make the decision for myself."

Cathy started the car and prepared to pull back into traffic. "Do you think we'll need a contract?" She giggled.

"Cathy, I'm serious!"

Cathy kept her foot on the brake and turned looking Sabrina squarely in the eye. She gave Sabrina an icy stare as she yelled. "Don't you think I know that! Damn!"

Sabrina allowed Cathy to calm down for a few moments. "Cathy, I'm naming you as my child's guardian in my will. I'm going to New York tomorrow and have Taggat draw up the necessary papers if that's okay."

"It's okay, but there's two prerequisites."

"What?"

"One: You see your cardiologist while you're in New York. Two: You understand I have no plans for marriage."

"Deal. I don't care if you're married or not. You're the only person I can trust to properly raise my daughter."

"Daughter? You keep saying "daughter". How do you know it's going to be a girl?"

"It wouldn't dare be anything else."

They both laughed as Cathy pulled back onto the Ferry's access road.

\* \* \*

BZZZZZZZZ....Sabrina quickly shut off her alarm. She put on her robe and went into the living room. She picked up the phone and dialed Taggat's home phone number.

Six rings later a sleepy voice answered. "Hello, Taggat Delaney."

"Taggat, I need to see you."

"Well, Sabrina. Fancy hearing from you at...Damn, it's two fifteen in the morning. What's so important?"

"I have to see you. Tomorrow. And I need a ride into the city."

"All right. I'll send a plane down in the morning. Say, around eleven?"

"Eleven's fine. Who's coming?"

"I think Steve's the only one available. Is that all right, or will the engagement plans interfere?" Taggat disliked Kent, but he knew better than to interfere with Sabrina's affairs.

"Steve's fine. I'm looking forward to seeing him, and there is no engagement. Good-by."

"Sabrina. Wait! What do you mean..." Taggat scratched his head. "What the hell did all that mean?"

# 6

Steve Hardesty had just lathered his face in preparation for shaving when the telephone rang out from its new position next to the shower stall. "Damn! I knew I should have never let them install that thing in here," Steve lamented as he wiped the lather from his face and threw it against the shower wall with a splat. He opened the door, allowing a large rush of steam to escape into the bathroom and reached around the corner of the shower stall to pick up the phone. He pulled the coiled cord to its extent and closed the door not so gently on his communication link. "I hope that cut the damn thing off! Hello!"

"Steve! Glad I caught you before you got into something." Taggat Delaney grinned on the other end of the line and held the phone away from his head in preparation for Steve's reply.

"Got into something? Hell, Taggat! I just got INTO the shower. I've only had three hours of sleep." Steve looked at his watch. "It's just seven-thirty. What in the hell could you possibly need at this hour? Surely Armani doesn't want to go back to Vegas."

Taggat chuckled. "No, no. But, hey, those Arabs can party when they loosen up, can't they?"

"I'll say. I don't think the Lear will ever recover. You know, Jof and his buddies brought three women back with them, and those ladies weren't hookers."

"Yeah, money talks, eh buddy?"

"That it does. But I'm sure you didn't call to talk about the Arabs, did you, Taggat?"

"Yes and no. Do you think the Shiek and his friends had a good time? Were there any problems?"

"None that I couldn't handle. You might have to bail me out of a few charges for assault, but otherwise no difficulties."

"I don't want to hear about it. I've seen your temper. Do you think they enjoyed their trip?"

"Oh, yeah. They enjoyed themselves immensely. Just how good of a time did they need to have?"

"That job was very important, Steve. Mac tells me that if we pull off this arrangement between the Saudi's and Egyptians, we'll be famous."

"Infamous is probably the more correct word, knowing you and the illustrious Secretary of State. How did you get on such friendly terms with Mr. Orberson, anyway?"

"It's a long story. Mac and I were law partners at one time, and I owe him some favors. Someday, I'll have to tell you about it, but, for now, I have a more pleasant task for you."

"I'll bet! Okay, surprise me."

"I need you to fly to MacKenzie Island and pick up Sabrina. She called this morning."

"What about? Did she want to discuss wedding plans?" Steve sneered at the phone.

"No! I didn't hear everything she had to say, but I think she mentioned the engagement was off. I'm not sure. It was early, and she was talking too fast."

"Did you tell her I would be the one coming after her?"

"Yes."

"What did she say about that?"

"She seemed excited."

"Oh, hell, Taggat. That doesn't make sense. I haven't heard from her for six months. What's going on?"

"How the devil do I know? I never know what she's thinking. All I do know is that she has business to discuss, and she needs a flight into New York. I can arrange for another pilot to pick her up if you prefer, but she did ask for you."

"Asked for me?" Steve scratched his head with his free hand. "Of course I'll go, Taggat. But I can't figure this out."

"Well, you can sort it out later, but I'm glad you're going. I think Sabrina may have seen the light about this Pooley fellow. She sounded strange over the phone, but she seemed genuinely happy that I thought you would be the one to bring her to New York. Understand?"

"Yeah, I understand. What time do I need to be there?"

"Eleven A.M. I'll expect you at the helipad by 4:00 P.M. Sound about right to you?"

"Five hours? Sure. I'll have time to spare."

"Steve?"

"Yes, Taggat?"

"Sabrina has loved you since she met you. Now, once and for all, why in the hell don't you do something about it?"

"I've told you a million times, Taggat. What would a rich college graduate want with a beat up old pilot like me?"

"Hell, Steve! You're not old, and you're for damned sure far from beat up. Sabrina's just seven years younger than you, and she doesn't give a damn about what you are. It's who you are. She fell in love with you a long time ago, and she's in love with you now. I think that says it all. Take a chance. Tell her you love her and see what happens. I'll see both of you this afternoon."

"I guess I should have told her how I feel, but, hey, look who's talking. You've been pining away over your secretary for years, and won't say anything."

"We're not talking about me. We're talking about you and Sabrina. Let me take care of my own lovelife. Okay?"

"Okay. Maybe I still have another chance with Sabrina. I've sure as hell missed her."

"Steve, as far as Sabrina's concerned, you don't need another chance. She's never given up on you since she was seventeen. This past ordeal was all your fault any way."

"Well, I'll be damned. How the hell do you figure that?"

"Well, if you had come back from 'Nam and told her how much you loved her, you two would already be married and having kids. Instead..."

"All right, already. I'll think about what you've said. Taggat, I have to get out of the shower. I'm getting waterlogged. I'll see you this afternoon."

"Shouldn't have a phone in the bathroom anyway. That's the only place you ever get peace and quiet."

"I'm beginning to find that out. Goodbye."

"Goodbye, and good luck! Bring me back some good news. I'm dying to be a grandfather even if it is a surrogate role."

Steve depressed the headpiece holder for a dial tone. He touched in 319, and after two rings the other end came to life.

"Hanger Nineteen, Stokes." Charlie Stokes, Delaney and Hardesty's chief mechanic, held the phone between his chin and left shoulder as he cleaned grease from his hands with an nearby rag.

"Charlie, my main man. How you doing?" Steve winced at the thought of asking Charlie to preflight the Lear.

"Okay, Steve. What do you need and how quick?"

"Charlie, you read me like a book. How is that?"

"I'm never your main man unless you need something fast."

"Guilty as charged, Charlie. I need the Lear by zero-nine hundred."

"O-nine hundred! That aircraft was a mess. What did you do in there?"

"It was a non-stop party from Vegas to New York. I can't say what happened in the back. I only flew the plane. What do you think? Can she be ready?"

"She's ready now. What do you need her for?"

"Ready? How long have you been working?"

"Ever since you got in this morning. Where are you heading? Back to Washington?"

"No. Short hop to MacKenzie Island."

"You're going to see Sabrina. Good! You've been too damned mean since the two of you broke up."

"Wait a minute. How many people are following my love life? I didn't know Sabrina and I were a matter of public record."

"Now, Steve. You know everyone expected you and Sabrina to be married a long time ago. I still can't believe you never tied the knot. She is one good looking lady, and if you don't put your claim on her, someone else will be slipping into bed…"

"Whoa, Charlie. Watch how you're talking about MY lady."

"Ex-lady, Boss. She's pretty heavy with another younger pilot, now. She might be getting married, I hear."

"Taggat's not so sure anymore. He suspects she's split with the dude. He's not sure, but…Hey! What do you mean, 'younger'?"

"Sorry, Boss. No offense. Well, if you find out she's available, you better not let her loose this time."

"What's this? Advice to the lovelorn from my head mechanic?"

"Listen, Steve. I've known Sabrina as long as you have. She and I have had some good talks. She loves you and always has. I don't care if she was talking marriage. That girl loves you. Don't let her go. That's all I have to say. I've said too much already."

"You're right about that." Steve grinned into the phone.

"I'll have the plane fueled and checked out by oh-eight-fifty."

"See you at oh-eight-thirty. Thanks, Charlie." Steve stepped out of the shower, hung up the telephone, and dried off. He pulled on a pair of underwear, shaved, and entered the living room of his hanger apartment where he picked up his direct line to Kennedy's ground controller to file his flight plan to MacKenzie Island. Living in a renovated hanger at one of the world's largest airports had its drawbacks, but for his business with Taggat, it had many more advantages. His flight plan was quickly approved. He was scheduled for takeoff at o-nine-fifteen from Runway 22 R. He began to review the flight in his mind, but soon his thoughts rushed back to his first encounter with the beautiful, black haired daughter of Seth MacKenzie.

Steve had always wanted to fly airplanes. He had lived and dreamed about flight, but his educational performance hadn't been adequate for enrollment into a military academy. However, through persistence, he had qualified for Naval Aviation School at the U.S. Naval Reservation on Puget Sound. With hard work, he had qualified for jet fighter training and accelerated to the rank of captain. At one of the frequent parties held on the base, Steve befriended a visiting Boston businessman, Seth MacKenzie. Over a period of time, they had become friends through a number of common interests: flying, flying, and flying. After Steve had been reassigned to Oceana Naval Air Station, he visited Seth and his wife Linda many times. It was on one of these visits that he had met Sabrina. She was beautiful. Her wit, charm and intelligence seemed beyond her years, and Steve, not letting their age differences affect his feelings, immediately fell in love. Unfortunately, the Vietnam conflict escalated causing Steve to be assigned duty on the *U.S.S. Enterprise* in the Tonkin Gulf. He had flown the F-4 Phantom during his tour of duty becoming one of the war's few aces. While still "on station", Steve had learned of Seth and Linda's death. However, it wasn't until after his return that he had learned of Seth's bequest leaving him, along with Taggat Delaney, a share of the flying service. Delaney was Seth's attorney and Sabrina's godfather. With all the activity of the newly acquired business, he had never seemed to have adequate time for Sabrina. He had hoped to pursue the matter many times, but Taggat had him globe hopping at a steady pace. After Sabrina had completed college, Steve began to avoid her. He feared she had "outgrown" him. When he had heard of her involvement with Kent Pooley, he shied away from any contact. If she loved someone else, it hadn't been his place to mar the relationship with belated love confessions. Now, he would see her again. Had fate dealt him another chance? If so, he wouldn't let it slip away. He was revived by the anticipation, but he would have to be careful and see exactly what Sabrina's situation was.

Steve put the phone down, went into the bedroom, slid into a pair of snug Levis, and pulled a short sleeved white Polo shirt over his head. He walked over to his safe, dialed in the combination and opened the door. He extracted a small black felt box from the back of the safe and placed it into his well-stocked flight bag. Then, after closing the safe, he pulled on his flight boots and picked up his Nomex jacket. Putting on his dark Ray-Bans he stepped outside onto the tarmac of the Hanger complex. He looked into the blue sky. The day was beautiful; ceiling and possibilities were unlimited.

Steve quickly covered the distance to Hanger Nineteen. The hive of activity around the Lear was so thick it took a moment to pick Charlie out of the swarm. "Charlie! She looks great!" Steve scanned the length of the Gates Learjet C-21A. Her full forty-eight feet gleamed. The fuselage and wings were painted light beige. A maroon pinstripe ran down the lower side of the fuselage, continued along the leading edge of the wing, and spread out to envelop the wing tanks. A black band edged with gold encircled the vertical stabilizer, and above the five passenger windows, maroon letters spelled Delaney and Hardesty Flight Service. The call letters "DHJ-003" stood out on the rudder assembly beneath the black band. The twin jet engines attached to the aft fuselage were the same beige color, but the intake and exhaust remained unfinished brushed steel. The Lear was a magnificent performer. She could almost do Mach One when empty, and she cruised effortlessly at 400 knots.

"See," Charlie remarked, "you're in a better mood already."

"What do you mean by that?" Steve reluctantly smiled.

"Any other day, you'd come busting in here, walk over to the plane, look around for a few moments, and start yelling about how bad things look."

"I haven't been that bad, have I?"

The entire ground crew looked up and in unison yelled, "Yes!"

Steve held up both hands. "Sorry. I'll try to do better. We ready to go? I've got to pick up an angel."

"The tanks are topped off. All systems check out, but keep and eye on the Nav Computer. It acted up a little before it came on line. I don't think it will be a problem. Otherwise, she's ready. I fixed you a Thermos of coffee. It's in the cockpit."

"Thanks. I'll need it."

Steve stepped up the passenger ladderway and locked the airlock after Charlie pushed the door closed. He stepped forward into the cockpit, slid his flight case into it's appropriate slot beside the pilot's seat, and eased down into the familiar chair. He fastened the harness, adjusted the headphones, and settled comfortably into the foam padding. Steve systematically rechecked all flight controls with Charlie's outside observation. Meanwhile, Charlie disconnected his intercom and closed the access door. He stepped back from the Lear, held up his right index finger, and gave Steve the wind up signal. Steve eased the throttle forward until the Lear broke ground resistance, and the 13,000 calculated pounds of jet rolled out of Hanger Nineteen.

"Kennedy Tower. Lear DHJ-003. Request taxi and clearance 22R, Over."

"Roger, DHJ-003. Kennedy Tower. Read you 5 by 5. Clear to taxi 22R."

"Understood, Tower." Steve saluted Charlie who was giving him the thumbs up after his walk around inspection. He pushed the throttle forward and slowly taxied to the entrance of 22R.

"Kennedy Tower. DHJ-003. Ready for takeoff. Over"

"Roger, DHJ-003. Hold position. United 334-Heavy landing 22R. You are clear to enter runway after touchdown and runout. Over."

"Roger, Tower. Understood. Over." Steve watched as the 747 lumbered down from the heavens. She was at full flaps and seemed to float in like a butterfly. "Damn, they're big mothers!" he thought. "Kinda like bumblebees. To look at them, there's no way they can fly, but they do."

"DHJ-003, Kennedy Tower. Cleared for take off. Hold runway heading. Maintain 3000. Further instructions from Kennedy Traffic at 121.75. Over."

"Roger, Tower. 220 degrees. 3000. 121.75. DHJ-003, out."

Steve eased the throttle forward and turned onto the runway. He steered the jet onto center line and quickly did a visual check of his instruments: both jets operating at proper temps and pressures, flaps at full. He gently pushed the throttles to full, and the Lear quickly responded. She settled on her wheels and began the roll down the runway. Steve watched the groundspeed build to 180 knots and eased back on the yoke. The jet's nose gently lifted off the ground, and the back two gear quickly followed. Steve retraced the landing gear and continued his climb. The Lear built up additional airspeed, and he retracted the flaps.

"DHJ-003, Kennedy Traffic. Turn right to 270. Flight level 130."

"Understood, Tower. 270 degrees, 13,000 feet. Over." Steve eased the rudder and yoke to the right until he was flying on a heading of 270 degrees. He leveled off at the assigned altitude.

"DHJ-003, Kennedy Traffic. Turn left 090. Flight level 230."

"Roger. zero niner zero, 23,000. DHJ-003, Out."

"Lear DHJ-003. You have cleared our controlled space. Further communication will be with Logan Central at 133.5. Out."

"Roger, Kennedy. Thanks and good day." Steve remained at 23,000 feet. He switched to his second Com radio already preset for Logan. He reset Com One for McKenzie and checked his Nav Computer for his vectors to McKenzie Island. E.T.A. 1045 hours. Steve engaged the autopilot and picked up the Thermos from its secured position on the left side of the cockpit. He poured some of the steaming brown liquid into the cup hoping Charlie's coffee was as strong as usual.

\* \* \*

Sabrina's eyes opened slowly. She gazed at the face of her clock radio and squinted. How could it be seven thirty already? After showering she searched her closet for a dress appropriate for greeting Steve. She put on white lace bikini underpants and a low cut, white lace French bra. With her recent increase in breast size, everytime she leaned forward her breasts bulged out the top revealing her areola. "Oh well", she thought, "I have nothing to hide today." She selected a yellow linen dress piped in black trim with a low V-cut neck. She elected not to wear stockings. It was too hot, and besides, her tan made stockings unnecessary. She left her hair down, like Steve liked, and she applied touches of Shalimar behind her ears and other pulse points. Steve always commented how he thought Shalimar smelled like candy, and today, Sabrina hoped he would try to take a bite. She slipped on a pair of black leather shoes, grabbed her brief-case, and headed out the door. She stopped in the kitchen, scribbled Cathy a note, and stuck it to the refrigerator door where she knew she would see it. As she left the house, she looked at her Rolex-8:30 A.M. She drove to the local bank, got the necessary papers for her meeting with Taggat from her safe deposit box, and stopped by "The Bakery" for a cup of decaf coffee and a pastry. After finishing her Danish, she purchased two creme filled chocolate covered eclairs. "I hope Steve still likes these," she thought as the clerk wrapped them in the waxed tissue and placed them in a sack.

"These were just made, honey," The hefty clerk remarked. "The chocolate's still warm." A wide smile appeared between two rosy red cheeks.

"Thank you. That's how he likes them."

"So do I," the two hundred pound woman said from behind the counter. She patted her belly. "Unfortunately," she laughed. "I wasn't like this until I had three babies."

Sabrina choked on her coffee. Her eyes got wide, and she set down the sack before she dropped it. She continued to stare at the woman's protruding abdomen.

"You okay, honey?"

"Yes, Mam. Sorry, but your comment about pregnancy threw me for a loop. I'm pregnant."

"Really? Why, you'd never know. You have such a good figure. Here. Wait just a minute."

The clerk handed her another cup of coffee. "You sure you're okay?"

"Yes, thank you. I'm fine."

"Hope your husband enjoys his eclairs. Don't you eat them before you get home. Sometimes that baby can make you open those sacks without your even knowing it. Why, I could eat a whole sack of doughnuts before I got home at night and swear I hadn't bought any at the grocery. That's what those babies did to me." The clerk continued to laugh in such a way that Sabrina couldn't help but laugh with her.

"Don't worry. You've taught me a lesson. I'll keep this," Sabrina held up the sack, "...tightly closed. This baby will just have to do without." Sabrina patted her tummy.

"You come back and see Rosa anytime. Bye now."

Sabrina drove to the airport and arranged for one of the ground crew to drive her BMW back to the house. She paid him for his trouble and gave him extra money to cover taxi fare back to the airfield. As she entered the terminal, she noted the wall clock-10:15. Sabrina walked over to the young man behind the counter. "Have you had any contact with a plane from New York?"

The young college student looked up from his reading. When he saw Sabrina, he quickly stood, straightening his hair and attempting to square his shoulders. "Yes, Mam." He continued to stare up and down at Sabrina.

"Well?" Sabrina was amused by his fixation on her cleavage.

"Well, what?" The thin blonde haired young man continued to gawk.

"Well, when do you expect the plane to arrive?" Sabrina smiled. "Are you all right?"

"Me? I'm fine. I've never seen a woman as beautiful as you...except in the movies. Are you a student? I hope." The boy quickly became embarassed by his frankness. "I'm sorry. I didn't mean..."

"That's quite okay." Sabrina held up her hand. "I'm flattered. Is the plane due soon?"

"Yes. The pilot's asked for clearance and has been given a direct approach to Runway 32. You'll be able to see the plane come in if you look through that window." He pointed to the southeasterly exposed window overlooking the tarmac and threshold of Runway 32. "The plane will settle in over the flagpole."

"Thank you for everything, and I'm not a student." Sabrina winked and walked over to a small couch. She was nervous and excited about Steve's arrival. The admiration she received from the young man at the desk had increased her confidence, but the student wasn't Steve. As she peered though the window, she wondered how many women Steve had been with since they had last seen each other. "I hope Taggat heard me when I told him I wasn't seeing Kent any longer. If he didn't, this could be just another job to Steve." She fidgeted in her seat. "Why am I so nervous?"

"Excuse me, Miss?"

Sabrina jumped.

"Sorry. Didn't mean to startle you, but the Lear is on final."

Sabrina stood and straightened her dress. "Thank you." She walked to the window, slipped on her Ray-Bans, and strained to see the jet as it settled onto the runway. The beige and maroon Lear taxied to the front of the closest hanger, and two of the ground crew chocked the wheels. As the engines whined down to idle, the door swung open while the stairs appeared. Steve stepped onto the top platform, stretched, and descended the ladder. He talked briefly to the ground crew members before heading for the terminal. Sabrina adjusted her dress at the hips and nervously smoothed her hair. "Here goes nothing," she thought as she stepped out onto the tarmac. She walked about twenty paces before stopping when she spied Steve approaching her location. "Whew, he looks good. What can I say? How shall I act? What is he thinking? I don't know what to do! Well, when in doubt, do nothing. I'll wait for him to act first." Even with her sunglasses on, Sabrina squinted against the sun's brightness in order to see Steve, but she could see him well enough to note his tight Levis showed the firmness of his legs, and his knit shirt revealed his shoulders were as broad as ever. Her heart raced. "Okay, okay! Don't get so nervous. After all, it's only been six months, and I don't want him to think I've been dying to see him."

Steve headed straight to Sabrina as soon as he saw her come out of the terminal door. She was wearing a yellow dress with the front V-cut full of breast. She was as beautiful as ever. At that moment he decided how he was going to break the ice of their first encounter after six months. He rapidly increased his pace, and before Sabrina knew what he was doing, Steve walked up, grabbed her by the shoulders, and gave her a kiss square on the lips. "Good morning, you good looking, long haired devil." He kissed her again.

Not wanting to look too anxious, Sabrina backed away and promptly gave Steve a half-hearted slap on the shoulder. "Just what gave you the idea you could take these liberties with me, you old bum?"

Steve smiled and took Sabrina by the arm. "Come on, Sabrina. You can buy me a good cup of coffee while they're topping the tanks. Charlie's coffee leaves a lot to be desired. We should be able to take off in forty-five minutes."

Sabrina couldn't talk at first. She didn't know how it could happen so quickly, but the fire was rekindled. "I brought you some of your favorite pastries," she managed to stammer as she held the bag toward Steve.

"Really? Sweets for the sweet? Aren't you thoughtful? I missed breakfast."

They walked inside and sat down at one of the three serving tables. "Anything for you, Brina?"

"Something cool will be nice. I've already eaten." Sabrina was taken back by Steve's calling her the name he had used before he left for Vietnam. He hadn't called her that in years.

Steve went to the pilot's service table where he poured a large cup of coffee and fixed Sabrina a glass of iced tea. He looked back at Sabrina, thought how beautiful she was, and wondered why he had let her slip away. He was determined not to let it happen again. Walking back to the table, he set down his coffee, handed Sabrina her tea, and sat down. He opened the pastry sack and grabbed one of the eclairs devouring the entire pastry before drinking some of his coffee.

"Sabrina, that was delicious. I'm glad you remembered I liked them." Steve leaned back in his chair. "So, I understand you're about to get engaged. Is that right?"

Sabrina looked quizzically at Steve. Obviously, Taggat had not understood her. "Why are you interested? I haven't heard from you for six months."

"Just making conversation." Steve was disappointed, but he didn't want it to show. Perhaps Taggat's intuition was wrong. "I wanted to wish you good luck. That's all."

Sabrina watched Steve's expression with interest. She couldn't detect any emotion, but Steve always had a good poker face. She eyed Steve closely as she dropped the next bomb. "No need to bother with the well wishes. That arrangement didn't work out, fortunately." She saw Steve's eyebrows raise. "I'm a free woman."

"Really? Sorry to hear that." Steve's expression remained flat while his heart leaped.

"What part are you sorry about? That I'm not getting married or that I'm a loose woman?"

"You've always been a loose woman." Steve took the second eclair out of the sack and held it toward Sabrina. "Want a bite?"

"No thanks. Don't tempt me. I wouldn't want to ruin my figure." Sabrina leaned toward Steve, "How would you know if I was a loose woman? You've never tested my virtues."

Steve looked Sabrina over from head to waist. "You certainly don't have to worry about your figure, and my lack of testing your virtues was out of respect for you and your parents. Believe me. It wasn't because I didn't want to. I've missed you, Sabrina." Steve reached over and touched Sabrina's clasped hands.

"Ah, the iceman breaketh," she thought. Sabrina leaned close to Steve's face. Her dress fell open slightly to reveal the smooth skin of her cleavage and the white lace trim of her low cut bra. The brownish tint of her areolae was visible above the fabric of her bra. "I've missed you, too. Maybe we can correct that tonight after I see Taggat." She gave Steve a kiss on the tip of his nose, leaned back in her chair and adjusted the position of her breasts by putting her right index finger inside the cups and slowly unrolling the lace of the bra.

"Don't do that. I'm enjoying the view."

"Oh, shut up! It's no different than a bikini."

Steve smiled. "I've always liked you in them, too. But I think I would like you better out of one."

"Steve!"

"What?" Steve smiled provocatively.

"You're embarrassing me."

"Okay, I'll quit, for now, but there is some catching up I'd like for us to do." Steve turned and looked outside to see if the refueling was complete. He noted a small bald headed man dressed in a off-white grease-speckled maintenance suit coming through the door and approaching their table.

"They must be finished, Sabrina. Do you need to go to the restroom?"

"I will. I hate airplane toilets." Sabrina slowly walked to the ladies room feeling Steve's eyes on her all the way.

The ground crewman walked over to Steve. "Excuse me. Is that your Lear?"

"Yes, it is. Is there a problem?"

"Your Nav computer has gone out. I'm going to need to replace it."

Steve looked at the stocky, round faced man and wondered who was passing judgment on his jet. "Who are you?"

"Oh, excuse me. I'm Jerry Mongrove, chief ground mechanic and engineer here at the field."

"The computer seemed fine on the way down, but my mechanic warned me it might be a problem."

"I'm afraid it must have caught a current surge. I was checking out your instruments, and the Nav computer kept kicking the selected coordinates. I can't get it to accept any new coordinates now. It won't even load the test program. I think we should replace it with a new one."

"Where did you get your knowledge of avionics? Sorry. I thought that would sound terrible. I didn't mean it as an insult."

"I understand. Actually, I get to work on quite a few private jets. You wouldn't believe some of the aircraft flown into this field, but my sophisticated training was on the *Enterprise* during the Vietnam War."

"Really? I flew F-4's off the Big E in '70. We lost a few people learning not to replace components in our ground avoidance radar units when problems like this happened. This solid state stuff is best tossed when it acts up."

"Right. I pulled two tours of duty, '68 and '71."

"Well, Jerry, do your 'thing'. She's in your qualified hands. Order what you need. What do you think it will take? Two or three days?"

"Oh, no. I have a supplier who can drop ship the unit today. I'll have it here tonight. I'll install it in the morning and have you out by noon tomorrow."

Sabrina was emerging from the bathroom toward them. Steve motioned toward her, thought for a moment, and winked at Jerry. "I need a favor, Jerry."

"Sure, anything. What can I do?"

"Follow my lead." Steve waited until Sabrina approached. He drew her close and put his right arm around her shoulders. "Sabrina, we have a problem."

"Oh? "

"The Nav computer on the Lear is broken. It can't be fixed for…" Steve looked at Jerry. "…three days? Is that right, Jerry? Oh…excuse me. Sabrina MacKenzie, Jerry Mongrove. Jerry and I served on the same carrier in 'Nam, but at different times. We've been talking about the repair work. Three days? Right?"

"That's right. Three days. Pleased to meet you Miss MacKenzie."

Sabrina reached out to shake Jerry's hand but he refused because of the grime on his palms. "My pleasure, Jerry."

"So, Brina. We're grounded until Thursday. Isn't that a bitch?" Steve smiled, looked at Jerry, and silently mouthed, 'Thanks' "Okay, Jerry. Order the part and we'll see you Thursday."

"Fine, I'll get right on it." Jerry walked back toward the hanger. He enjoyed working with people instead of for them. Some of the people flying into the Island treated him like dirt under their feet. If he had a better offer, he would leave this place, but it appeared that he was destined to work on the toys of the rich forever.

"So, what should we do?" Sabrina questioned. "Taggat expects me at four."

"I guess you're stuck with me until Thursday. We'll have to call Taggat and cancel today's meeting. Can you think of anything to do until then?"

"Oh, I can think of plenty to do, but they all involve work. I really need to see Taggat. It's important."

"But…" Steve moved his Ray-Bans down to tip of his nose and looked over the rims with his innocent, but provocative, blue eyes. "…not so important that it can't wait until Thursday. Right, Brina?"

Sabrina pushed Steve's face away with her hand. "No, not when you put it like that. Oh well, I'll go call Taggat and tell him we won't be there until Thursday. I'll call Cathy and have her come and pick us up. I sent my car home since I wasn't going to need it, or so I thought." She turned and headed for the phone.

"Wait, Sabrina."

Sabrina turned and looked at Steve. "Yes?"

"Can I rent a car here?"

"I guess so. Why?"

"I like to have my own wheels while enjoying the local color."

"We can use mine."

"No, I'd prefer my own. I'm peculiar that way. I'll get a car. You call Taggat."

Steve went to the attendant's desk and checked for a rental car. Three were available; one was a new Corvette. "We keep a few available for the students' families when they fly into the Island," the attendant said. Steve rented the Corvette, retrieved his flight bag from the Lear, and brought the car around to the front of the terminal. He walked back into the building and went over to the pay phone Sabrina was using. He had left the car running with the air conditioner on full.

Sabrina completed her phone call and turned giving Steve a curious look as he approached. "I've just told Taggat our predicament, and he asked me if you were up to your old tricks. It seems he's had phone calls like this before. Is that right?"

"Not from me, Brina. Never." Steve crossed his heart with his right hand.

Sabrina smiled and picked up her briefcase. "Right. Where's the car?"

"Out front. Let's go. This place is getting hot." Steve grinned at Sabrina. "In more ways than one."

"You're a rat, but you're right about the temperature. It gets extremely hot this time of day. That's why I love my house. Even at this hour, the ocean breeze keeps the porch cool. I love having lunch on the porch. I can take off my clothes, lean back, and watch the waves while the ceiling fan cools me."

"I'd like to see that! May we go?"

Sabrina smiled, grabbed Steve's arm, and followed him out the door.

Steve helped Sabrina in, closed the door, walked to the driver's side, and slid into the leather seat. Putting his foot on the brake, he shifted the transmission into drive. "Point the way. I've never been to your place from this direction."

"Straight out the entrance and to the right." Sabrina leaned forward and let one of the air conditioner vents direct its cool air down the front of her dress. "Take a left at the first intersection, then it's three miles to the house. You can't miss it. It's the only one out there."

"I do remember that." Steve pushed on the accelerator and sprinted for the exit.

Sabrina rocked back with the acceleration. She put her hands behind her head and lifted the hair off her neck. She leaned forward, tilted her head down and directed the cool air over her neck and down her back. "Whew. It must be ninety today. The air is awfully humid."

"Yes, it is." Steve watched the road and thought for a few more moments. He made the turn to Sabrina's house, eased to the shoulder of the road, and put the car in "Park". He turned to Sabrina.

She returned his stare with confusion. "Why are we stopping?" She reached over and touched his neck with her index finger. "We don't have to park on the side of the road. We're big boys and girls now."

Steve smiled at her innuendo. "Sabrina, I want you to think about something if you would."

"What's that, Steve?" Sabrina leaned back in her seat.

"If it's possible, I want us to pick up from where we left off. Not six months ago, but seven years ago. I want a chance to become part of your life, again. There are some things I need to clear up in my own mind, but in order to do that I need some time alone with you..."

Sabrina opened her mouth preparing to speak.

"Don't say anything. I want us to go somewhere for the next three days. Somewhere we can be alone. Somewhere I can devote my attention and energy to showing you I love you. Do you think it would be possible?"

Sabrina was at a loss for an immediate answer. This couldn't be happening. Not already. What could she say without looking anxious? She had dreamed of such opportunities, but they had never happened. She loved him! But how would the pregnancy figure into the scheme of things? She was frightened. How could it ever work? She was pregnant with another man's child, yet her love for Steve was greater now than it had ever been. Slowly, her love for Steve overcame her fears and reasoning. She immediately knew the answer to her questions, but she wasn't sure it would work out. However, she had to give it a chance.

"Well? Will you think about it?"

"Sabrina blinked back to reality. "I don't know, Steve. I have a lot of work to do. I was out of town the first part of this week."

"Come on, Sabrina. Cathy can watch the store. You were going to be gone for a couple of days, anyway. Surely, a few more won't matter. Think about it. You can give me an answer tonight. Okay?"

"Okay." Sabrina gasped. She the knew the answer already.

"Okay, you'll go?" Steve said in anticipation.

"No! Okay, I'll think about it. Can we go home now? I'm burning up."

"Okay, I'll accept that for now, but you know I have a hard time taking no for an answer."

"Don't worry. I doubt if you'll be disappointed."

Steve put the Corvette back into gear and eased onto the highway. All he could think about was he and Sabrina being together…again."

# 7

Gull Haven was located on the eastern most tip of MacKenzie Island. It was Sabrina and Cathy's answer to the insane pace of their business world. Here they gathered their strength to face the anxieties and challenges of each day. Sabrina had always liked Gull Haven's location. She had been there many times both in reality and in her dreams. In years past her father and mother had brought her down for weekends of sand castling, kite flying, and surf fishing. After her parents died, Taggat sold the townhouse in Boston because there Sabrina recalled only the hectic times of her life, times when her mother and father were too busy in their world to enjoy hers. She had found herself asking Taggat more and more to bring her to this spot on the Island where she could sit on the sand, watch the waves, and imagine the happier days of those peaceful weekends. Even during college, Sabrina was drawn to this spot when she needed to recharge her inner strength. After she graduated, she knew MacKenzie Island would be her home.

The Island had been in Sabrina's family since the 1700's. Her ancestors had made their homes on this four square mile island located at the mouth of the James River in the Chesapeake. It filled all their needs. Here they could hunt, fish, and cultivate small areas for the prosperity and propagation of their families. Here they found the religious freedom they sought. The population on the Island remained relatively stable as had the cultural advances until the early 1900's. Through the insistence of his wife Maria, Sabrina's grandfather Blake MacKenzie, one of the earliest inhabitants, set aside enough land for the establishment of Soames College. Maria Soames MacKenzie had been educated in England and was determined to bring a diciplined style of education to her world. The college grew rapidly in size and reputation. When it appeared the college was to be the only business on the island and many of the families moved to the mainland, the directors of the MacKenzie Trust, with agreement of the beneficiaries, had donated all the uninhabited areas of the island to the college.

After Sabrina and Cathy had finished Harvard Business College and come to the island, they created MacKenzie & Winston Inc., a trust management firm specializing in corporate retirement plans. First, they acquired small, seemingly insignificant accounts. However, success bred success, and, eventually, the news of their accomplishments spread throughout the banking world of the Tidewater. Their most recent acquisition was an account for Dynacorp Industrials, a company producing small electric motors for the auto industry. And now, Chesworth Motors, a new automotive manufacturer, whose home office was in Raleigh, North Carolina, was interested in the trust expertise touted by their firm.

When Sabrina and Cathy brought their business from New York to MacKenzie Island, and offered $750,000.00 for the ten acres of saltmarsh and sand dunes of Gull Haven, the board of directors of the college quickly accepted. They built the first house one hundred yards from high tide's wateredge. The second house, Cathy's home, would be built when either of them married. The house was strategically placed so none of the dunes were destroyed, and the second floor living level was elevated so they could appreciate the seabreeze. Each of the four bedrooms enjoyed a full view of the ocean through glass walls. Functioning French doors exited from each bedroom onto the covered porch surrounding the house, and the part adjacent to the kitchen was screened. Here Sabrina and Cathy could bask in the soothing ocean rhythms without insect invasion.

\* \* \*

Steve eased the Corvette into the garage of Sabrina's haven. He looked around and then looked at Sabrina. "I thought you sent your car home?"

"I did. I guess Cathy must have used it to go to work. Strange though. She usually likes to walk."

"Must have been too hot for her today."

Sabrina fanned her dress open and directed the air conditioned coolness down her cleavage. "I can appreciate that."

"I'm glad she's not here." Steve turned in his seat to face Sabrina.

"Oh? Why?"

"It gives us time to discuss a few things."

"Such as?"

"Sabrina, you're making this difficult."

Sabrina grinned. "I know. I mean to."

"Why?" Steve seemed surprised.

"Well, who's been avoiding whom? I tried calling you, but all I got was silence. You never returned any of my phone calls."

"So? Who was engaged? Me or you?"

"I was, but we're still friends. Aren't we?"

"I guess…well, no. We're not friends in the way you think of friends."

"Just what does that mean?"

"We were beyond friends. You know that. Besides, I was hurt and I was jealous. You were mine."

"I was yours! I'll have you know that I don't belong to anybody, Mr. Hardesty."

"Wait a minute. Let me back up. You know what I'm trying to say. Sabrina, when I found out about you and Pooley, I was livid. Not at you, at myself for letting you get away. I couldn't believe I was so stupid. And I was hurt."

"Hurt! So, what if you were hurt? How do you think I felt? I've loved you since I met you, and you knew it. I thought we had something special. I waited for you to come back from Vietnam. My parents died before you came back, and I didn't even hear from you then. I wrote you. I wrote you many times, but I never received that first letter."

"We've been through this before, Sabrina, and that's no longer the point. I admit I was a real ass, and I should have let you know then."

"Let me know what? Steve, what should you have let me known?"

Steve reached over and grabbed Sabrina's shoulders. He pulled her close and looked into her eyes. He kissed Sabrina passionately on the lips. She offered no resistance. Steve slowly pulled away from the embrace. "I should have told you then how much I love you. How much I've always loved you, and I always will. I'll do anything to keep from losing you again."

Sabrina reeled from Steve's second confirmation of his love. She was thrilled, but his passion frightened her. True, this was what she wanted, but things were happening way too quickly. She hadn't calculated this into her plans for today. "Maybe we should go upstairs." Without waiting for a reply, Sabrina retrieved her briefcase from the storage area and exited the car. "You coming?" She asked as she leaned down and looked into the door.

Steve shrugged his shoulders. "I'll be damned." He turned off the car, grabbed his flight bag, and locked the doors. As he approached Sabrina, he waved his hand up the stairs. "After you."

The steps from the garage to the first floor opened into the kitchen. Sabrina set her briefcase on the counter and went to the refrigerator. "You want something to drink? There's…" She saw the folded note stuck to the door. She pulled it off and read Cathy's message.

"I'll have a beer," Steve said as he set his bag down and noticed Sabrina reading. "Anything important?"

Sabrina tossed the note down on the counter, leaned forward placing her chin on her palms. "It seems we have the house all to ourselves. Cathy's gone to North Carolina. She's taken my car and won't be back until next week. So, what would you rather do? Stay here, or go someplace else?"

"I'd rather stay here."

"Good. Me too." Sabrina opened the refrigerator and handed Steve a Lite beer. "If we're going to eat, we'll have to go to the grocery. The cupboard is bare."

"I'll go. I know exactly what I want for supper. We're going to have a cookout on the beach."

"Mmm, that sounds teriffic. " Sabrina wiped her forehead with a moistened paper towel. "Whew it's hot." A small trickle of perspiration from Sabrina's neck ran down her chest stopping shy of her cleavage. "I think I'll change clothes and get into something more suitable for beach wear."

"Need any help?"

"No, I think I can manage." Sabrina grinned at Steve's suggestion. "But you can unzip my dress for me."

"Always glad to be of assistance." Steve walked behind Sabrina and unzipped her dress to her waist as she held her hair to one side. "You know, I'm glad Cathy had to go to North Carolina."

Sabrina turned to Steve, holding the top of her dress so as not to let it fall. "You don't care much for Cathy, do you?"

Steve put his hands on the counter and pushed himself up to a sitting position on the top. "It's not that I don't care for her, but when she's around I feel as if I should be covering my crotch."

Sabrina almost choked on the Perrier she had just drunk. "You don't mean you're threatened by Cathy?"

"Not threatened, just," Steve thought for a tactful reply. "...emasculated. I don't think Cathy wants a man to be a man."

"She's been hurt. Cathy's very careful with her feelings."

"Well, if she remains that protective, she'll have a hard time getting any one near her. Cathy's a good looking woman, and she's going to have men making advances. But when she cuts them down like only she can do, they won't stay around long waiting for seconds."

Sabrina laughed and leaned against Steve's knees. She kissed him on the cheek. "You're cute. Let's let Cathy take care of Cathy, and let's let Steve go get supper. We'll sit out and count the stars."

Steve smiled, looked at Sabrina, kissed her on the cheek, and slid down from the counter top. "I'm on my way. Be back in an hour. You better get ready for the best meal you've had in years."

* * *

Twinkling snow white stars poked holes through the dark summer sky. Steve and Sabrina sat next to each other on a plaid blanket they had spread on the sand. Steve peered into the darkness of the bay and watched as small waves rolled into the beach and slipped gently back into the depths from which they came. The relentless rhythm was hypnotic and soothing. Sabrina snuggled closer as the wind whipped through the dunes. She shivered pulling the blanket up around her and leaning her head on Steve's shoulder.

"Cold?" Steve placed his arm around Sabrina's waist.

"A little, but I feel better now." She looked at Steve and smiled.

"Sabrina? What did you ever see in Kent?" Steve hesitated wishing he hadn't asked. "Sorry. I'm not usually the nosy type, but I was wondering."

Sabrina looked up and gave Steve a surprised look.

"You don't have to answer. It's none of my business. What's important is you're here with me."

"I don't mind answering." Sabrina shivered slightly.

"You all right? We can go in if you would like. I didn't mean to make you feel uneasy."

"I'm okay." Sabrina thought for a moment and snuggled closer to Steve. "Before you left for Vietnam, I was head over heels in love with you.

I had ongoing fantasies about you, but I didn't want to ruin what we had. If you and I had made love and if I had become pregnant, it would have destroyed my mother and father."

"I wouldn't have let that happen. You know that."

"I know. You were quite the officer and gentleman. But after you left, I had a difficult time. I missed you terribly, and I thought the worst. I was afraid you didn't care for me because we hadn't made love. I was sorry. Sorry because we might have missed our only chance, especially if something happened to you. Then I thought about the women you would be with whenever your carrier put into port."

"Sabrina, we've talked about this. You know I've never seriously looked at another woman. I was in love with you, and I was in love with the war."

Sabrina jerked her head back and looked at Steve. "The war?"

"Yes. I loved the war. I thrived on the intensity, the anxieties, the adrenaline highs. I love flying combat jets. They consumed me. I didn't have room for anyone else. But I kept you with me everywhere I went. Actually I hated leaving for Vietnam."

"You hated leaving? You said you loved war?"

"I did love it and still do." Steve turned and looked at Sabrina. "But I still hated leaving you. I needed you then, and I need you now. You're part of my life. I'm lost without you." Steve turned from Sabrina and looked back into the comfort of the darkness. "I was afraid that when I left you, you would find someone else. Our age difference was too great, and you were…are so beautiful." Steve knew Charlie and the rest of the crew had been correct in their accusation. He hadn't been the same since he had "lost" Sabrina. Sabrina was his anchor to reality. He had never met a woman that could soothe his tensions while igniting his romantic fires. He didn't want her to get away again because he didn't like what he had become since she had been out of his life.

"And I'm not too young for you now?" Sabrina grinned.

"You don't seem to be. What do you think?"

"I never have been." Sabrina tried to snuggle closer into the crook of Steve's arm. "This is where I belong. I know now what Cathy knew all along."

"What's that?"

Sabrina held on tightly to Steve's hand. The tighter she held, the more she hoped he would understand. "I realize I was never in love with Kent. I was hoping he could be like you." Sabrina hugged Steve's waist. "He wasn't."

Steve felt Sabrina shudder, "Sabrina, stop thinking about that. I'm sorry I brought it up. It doesn't make any difference. It's over. All I need is your love. That's all I've ever needed."

Sabrina buried her head into Steve's shoulder and began to cry.

"What's wrong? Did I say something to hurt you?"

"Hurt me?" Sabrina dried a tear from her eye. "I love what you said. I love you more now than ever. I just feel so guilty."

"Guilty?"

"Yes. Steve, please understand. There are times with Kent I regret. Things happen when you think you're in…"

Steve placed his hand over Sabrina's mouth. "Don't say it. I understand." He kissed Sabrina. "I love you."

"I'm sorry, Steve. I'm truly sorry." Sabrina leaned her head onto Steve's shoulder and looked into the dark serenity of the bay.

"Don't be sorry. It's all my fault. Enough people have told me."

Sabrina sniffed. "What do you mean?"

"Charlie and Taggat have already given me reprimands about loosing you. I've had orders from both to grab on to you and never let you go."

"Oh? You're doing this under orders?" Sabrina shivered laughing nervously.

"You know what I mean."

"I know. Let's go in. I am getting cold."

"Go in? I thought we'd take a midnight swim."

"You don't have a bathing suit."

"So?"

"Funny! Let's go. If you want to take a swim, be my guest." Sabrina waved her arm toward the ocean. "There's plenty of room."

"Alone?"

"Most definitely!"

"No, thanks. I'll go inside. You go ahead. I'll straighten up our mess and brings things indoors."

\* \* \*

They made their way back to the house along the zigzagged walk. Steve put away the dinner paraphernalia and found Sabrina wrapped in a blanket sitting in front of the television. She had left a comfortable place for him next to her.

"I'm going to change. I'll be right back." Steve smiled at Sabrina's wrapping.

"I'm warm in this, thank you, and I didn't think you had any other clothes."

"Oh, I brought a change. They're in my flight bag."

"You devil! Taggat was right, wasn't he?"

"What do you mean?"

"Well, he said he had received calls about the plane needing repairs before."

"Not from me, 'Brina. I've never pulled that stunt."

"Uh-huh. Go change. I've saved you a spot." Sabrina patted the space next to her. "This should be interesting. Not much could fit in that bag."

"You have no room to talk." Steve motioned to Sabrina's blanket. "What are you wearing under the blanket?"

"What do you think?" Sabrina raised her eyebrows and tilted her head.

"I know what I wish," Steve grinned.

"Wanna see, big boy?" Sabrina stood and walked closer to Steve.

"I'm not sure I could stand it, but how about a little peek?"

"Okay. Stand right there and prepare to see something you've never seen before." Sabrina quickly opened the blanket. "I have nothing to hide." Her full length flannel nightgown fell privy to Steve's eyesight.

"Well, hell's bells. That's like the six-o'clock news."

Sabrina closed the blanket, and stared quizzically at Steve. "Six o'clock news?"

"You know. Full coverage."

Sabrina laughed and threw a pillow at Steve, hitting him in the abdomen. "Go change!"

Steve picked up the pillow and tossed it back. He went into the bedroom, opened the flight bag, and pulled out a pair of gray sweatpants. He removed the small felt box and slid it into one of the inner pockets. He left his shirt off, returned to the living room, and sat beside Sabrina.

Sabrina had tuned to a movie on one of the satellite channels. She looked at Steve and then at his lap. "Do you mind?"

"Be my guest."

Sabrina laid her head in Steve's lap. As she watched the introduction to "Casablanca", she thought how natural being with Steve felt. "This is nice."

"I agree," Steve said as he stroked Sabrina's hair. He could smell faint traces of Shalimar floating up from her neck.

"So, I've told you all my secrets. Do you have anything you'd wish to expose?" Sabrina circled her fingers on Steve's left knee. "By the way, you still look good for an old man."

Steve laughed. "Nice, Sabrina. You really know how to inflate an ego."

Sabrina laughed, but she didn't look at Steve. "Well, do you?"

"Sabrina, I'm a man who has had control of everything in his life. I knew exactly what I wanted and how I was going to get it. I've accomplished that by not allowing anyone to control me." Steve took a deep breath.

Sabrina sat up and looked at Steve. "Are you afraid I'll control your life?"

"I'd rather you would lie back down."

"Oh, no. I want to see you answer this one."

Steve grinned. "No, I'm not afraid you're going to control my life." He hesitated. "This is hard to admit, but I was afraid I couldn't fulfill your hopes of what a husband should be."

Sabrina tilted her head and squinted her eyes. "Just a minute. Who was talking about marriage?"

"Sabrina, you know I would never let us become lovers if marriage weren't in the immediate future?"

"Okay, I understand and I love you for those convictions, but let me get this straight. A Vietnam war ace who had been decorated with the Navy Cross and the Air Medal was…is afraid he can't measure up to my ideal of a lover?"

"I believe I said husband."

"Oh, so you did." Sabrina blushed. She regained her composure and slyly grinned at Steve. "So, what are you asking me? Are you wanting to know what I want in a husband? Or, are you wanting to know how I would want you to be, if you were my husband? Or, are you wanting to know if I want you for my husband?"

Steve laughed. "Run that by me one more time."

"Not a chance."

"Sabrina, I've never been to college. Hell, I barely got out of high school. I worked hard to get where I am today, and, if it weren't for your father, I don't know what I'd be doing now."

"What does this have to do with us?"

"I'm afraid my lack of a college education might make a difference in our relationship. I can't change that, not now. Sabrina, I am what I am."

Sabrina snuggled close to Steve laying her head on his shoulder and twirling her finger in his chest hair. "I've never wanted anything different. Steve, we both have different goals and ideals. I would be proud to show you off as my husband. All the women would be green with envy."

"How do you do it, Sabrina?"

"Do what?"

"Make me feel so good when I'm around you?"

Sabrina looked up into Steve's eyes. "I guess that's what love is all about. At least, that's what my mom and dad said whenever I'd ask them the same question."

"So, what shall we do about this?" Steve put a worried look on his face and held Sabrina away from his chest. "Do you know any solution?"

"Do about what? We're doing fine, I thought. Aren't we?"

"No! We're not! I mean, yes we're doing fine, but we're not finding a solution."

Sabrina snickered. "What in the world are you trying to say? You look like you're in pain."

"Sabrina, I know you have been through a trying relationship, and I don't want to put any pressure on you, but I don't want to live through the possibility of ever losing you again."

Sabrina put her arms around Steve's neck and pulled him close. She kissed him passionately on the mouth slowly drawing away. Then, she placed her lips beside his ear and whispered, "Steve, I'm yours forever. Nothing will change that."

Steve slowly pushed Sabrina away from their embrace. He reached inside his sweatpants and removed the felt box from the pocket.

"What's wrong?" Sabrina queried. "You got a gun in your pocket, or are you just happy to see me?"

Steve chuckled. "Both…No, I've got something that belongs to you."

"What is it?" Sabrina tried to pry into Steve's clasped hand.

"Oh, no. I've waited a long time to do this, and I'm doing it right." Steve opened the felt box and removed the ring he had bought a year ago. He had made a special flight to New York and had Tiffany's make the engagement ring he was about to give Sabrina.

He picked up Sabrina's left hand and slowly slipped the ring on her third finger. "Sabrina MacKenzie, will you marry me?"

Sabrina looked at the ring and then Steve. She held the ring up to her heart, then to her cheek, and then in front of her. Tears welled up in her eyes, and her throat swelled. She tried to speak, but nothing came out.

"Well? I've never known you to be at a loss for words. I'll get down on my knees, if you want."

"When?"

"When, what? When will I get down on my knees?"

"No, silly. When…when" Sabrina pointed to the ring. "You know."

"Oh! When do I want to get married?"

"Yes…" Sabrina swallowed. "That when…married when?"

"Well, I haven't heard anybody say yes."

Sabrina jumped for Steve's neck and hugged as hard as she could. She kissed him until he begged for air. "Yes, yes, yes! I'll marry you."

"Whew, I'm glad I finally got that out. I guess we'll get married as soon as possible."

"As soon as possible? I'm not ready. I have to tell Taggat. I've got to make plans."

"Whoa…Okay, as soon as you're ready."

"Whew.." Sabrina sat back on the couch. She looked at the ring and then grasped her locket. "You remember when you gave me this?"

Steve looked at the gold locket. "Before I left for Vietnam. Your mom and dad gave me the pictures I had put in it."

"I've cherished it ever since. It hasn't been off my neck, and this ring will never leave my finger." Sabrina looked at Steve and smiled. "I don't believe this is happening. I thought I had lost you forever. I thought I'd never see you again. Now, this has happened." Sabrina leaned against Steve's chest for a moment. Slowly she gazed up into his eyes with hers. Then, she stood, took Steve's hand, and motioned for him to follow.

"Sabrina?"

"Don't talk, Steve. I want you to make love to me. Now."

"But???"

Sabrina placed her hand over his mouth. "Shhh…" She led him to her bedroom. She stopped at the foot of her bed and kissed him on the lips searching his mouth with her moist tongue. As she felt Steve's firmness against her thigh, she stepped back, pulled off her gown and stepped back close to Steve's body. When she pressed her breasts against Steve's muscular chest, it was more than she could stand. "Take me to bed," she whispered.

Steve picked Sabrina up in his arms and carried her to the bed. He laid her on the bedspread removed his clothing, and stretched out on his side beside her supporting his weight on his left arm. "Sabrina, you're beautiful."

"This body is for you only...tonight, tomorrow, whenever...forever." Sabrina raised up and met Steve's embrace.

Steve traced the outline of Sabrina's thigh with the fingers of his right hand. He softly ran his fingers across her smooth thigh and steadily worked up her torso until he danced his fingers between her breasts. Sabrina was on her back and the weight of her breasts has caused them to gravitate toward her sides. However, their firmness kept them taut and the nipples were hard. Steve traced the outline of each breast and teased the nipples gently between his thumb and index finger.

Sabrina arched her back and pulled Steve's head harder against her flesh. "Oh, God, Steve. I can't stand this. Make love to me. I can't wait. This is how I always dreamed it would be. Now, Steve, Now." She tugged for Steve to cover her with his body.

Steve kissed Sabrina deeply. He supported his body with his hands placing his knees between her receptive legs.

She moved her legs wider, opened her eyes, and looked into Steve's. "I love you. I've always loved you."

Steve eased into Sabrina's warmth.

"Oh, God. You feel wonderful." Sabrina moaned.

They melted into each other until they became one. Later, they slept.

\* \* \*

The sun rose above the horizon and spread its golden glow across the calm waters of the Chesapeake. Its reflection cut across the surface and seemed to arc directly into the stone atop Sabrina's ring. The sun danced inside the facets and jumped toward her face in the many colors of the spectrum. She had not stopped looking at the large diamond since she walked out onto the beach. Her body still stirred from the warmth of Steve's love, but the joy of the sensation was blunted by the guilt from the stirrings within her of another man's child. The dilemma gnawed at her moral fiber. She knew she had to deal with the fact, but how? How would Steve handle the situation? She looked for answers, but none came. She needed a clue.

From the first time Steve came into her life, he had been a dilemma. She had loved him from the moment she met him. At first, her parents refused to let her date Steve, but eventually she bribed them. She had used bribery in many of her dealings with her parents, not unpleasant bribery, but a benign daughter-parent bribery. It had worked. She had planned evenings like last night a thousand times in her head. And last night had been everything she had ever wished. So, why was she sitting here on the beach and not still beside Steve? How could she accept the love of the man she had always wanted when she was pregnant with another's child? It hurt to make her decision, and she wasn't sure it would work, but it was the only way she would ever be happy. She loved Steve with all her heart, and she would be with him forever. She had to be. Fate hadn't brought them back together for any other purpose, and she hoped Steve would forgive her if he ever found out.

Sabrina continued to watch the bay come to life. As her eyes followed a shrimp boat churning its way out into the Chesapeake, she felt a presence behind her. She turned and saw Steve standing over her. He was wearing his sweatpants and nothing else. Sabrina stood silently and wrapped her arm around his waist. "Mmm...Good morning."

"Morning. Still love me?"

"More than ever," she said as she leaned against his side.

"Something wrong?"

"No, something's very right."

"You're not having second thoughts about my proposal, are you?" Steve asked in a less than serious fashion. Inside he wondered if Sabrina might be disenchanted now they had consummated the desire they had both suppressed for years. "I didn't mean to take advantage of you at a weak moment."

Sabrina silenced Steve with a kiss. "Now listen to me, Steve Hardesty. I love you. I've always wanted you to make love to me. I wanted you last night. Every time you're around me, I want you. You aren't safe around me. I've resolved my previous relationship. My love for you is greater now than ever, so I don't want to hear any more of your insecurity."

"I'll never mention it again."

"Good!" Sabrina stretched. "I'm going to take a shower. Want to join me?"

Steve smiled. "I'd love to, but I'm going to run first. Gotta keep this old body in shape for you."

Sabrina fingered the outline of Steve's pectoral muscles and winked. "Your shape is just fine."

He put his arm around Sabrina's waist, and they walked slowly back to the house. Sabrina stopped in the kitchen and poured a glass of orange juice. Steve came back from the bedroom wearing gym shorts and running shoes.

"What all do you keep in that bag?"

"Only things I need in an emergency." Steve winked. He gave Sabrina a kiss on the cheek. "See you later." He left through the back porch and headed for the beach.

Sabrina watched him walk down to the hard packed sand. She admired his body as he loosened up and headed down the long stretch of beachfront. Instead of waiting for Steve, Sabrina decided to shower and surprise him with breakfast. She checked their provisions and found that Steve had been a proficient shopper. She had everything she needed for pancakes. She went to the bedroom to undress and got into the shower. Closing the door, she stood in the pelting flow of warm water. Sabrina could still smell Steve's presence in her hair and on her skin. She dwelt on the reality of his love, and was determined not to do anything to lose it. She closed her eyes, tilted her head back, and began massaging shampoo into her hair.

Suddenly, she felt a sharp pain in her chest, once..., twice..., three times. She became hot, then dizzy and then slightly disoriented. As she reached for the wall, perspiration sprung from her forehead. She leaned into the wall and slid slowly to the floor. All she felt as the darkness closed in around her was the shower hitting her in the face. Then she felt nothing.

\* \* \*

Summertime on the Island filled Sabrina with joy, and today was no disappointment. They had already had their picnic, and her father had put out his surf fishing line waiting for the monster of the Bay to latch on to the baited hook and create a struggle like the one he had read to her in *The Old Man And The Sea*. Sabrina liked the story. Her Dad said it was about the struggle of one man going against the elements and winning but not being able to keep the reward of conquest. However, winning was enough for the fisherman. Sabrina preferred to think the story was just about fishing. No matter, because today her father had sworn to go looking for buried treasure with her...alone. She didn't get to spend as much time as she wanted with her dad, but today promised to be different.

"Come on, Daddy. Let's go." Sabrina tugged on Seth's shirt tail.

"Hold your horses, Cookie. The treasure isn't going anywhere. We'll find it." Seth MacKenzie set his reel drag, checked the anchoring device, and turned toward Sabrina. He approached her with hands over head and a Frankenstein-ish look on his face. "Ve vouldn't vant ze Monster of ze Bay to get avay, vould ve?"

"I don't care! Come on! Please?"

"All right, all ready. Linda, you want to join us on this hunt?"

"No, Daddy! You promised." Sabrina tugged at Seth's pant leg. "Just the two of us."

Linda MacKenzie looked up from her reading. "No. I don't think I'm invited. I'll just relax and read." Linda put her sunglasses back down on her nose and resumed her novel.

Seth knelt down and closed one eye. "Well, Jim 'awkins, 'ave ye ever seen such a delectable wench?"

"Oh, Daddy, hush. It's just Mother."

"Nay, me laddie. It be Ol' Mawgret from yonder pub. Be said she can kiss the patch right off a one-eyed man. Maybe ole Long John ere, should hobble over and see if it be true."

"No! Come on! Let's go! I swear, you and your voices."

"Just getting into the mood, Cookie." Seth swung Sabrina up on his shoulders. "Which way, Captain?"

"Let's try down the beach where the stream runs into the ocean. If I were a pirate, that's where I'd hide my treasure." Sabrina jumped up and down on his neck. "Giddy-up!"

Seth headed down the beach with Sabrina pointing the way. "And why's yonder stream a good place to look, me hardie?"

"Cause I would always know where it was later."

"Good point!"

They spent the next few hours looking for buried treasure, but, alas, none was found. However, Sabrina's treasure was the solitary hours she spent with her father. As they returned to the beach, they could see the Bay monster had foiled them once again. As Seth reeled in his line, Sabrina hung onto his pant leg. Even though they were in two feet of water, and the waves bounced her around like a cork, Sabrina grasped her Father's leg as if she would never get the opportunity again.

"Sabrina, come on! Let's get our things together. Time to go." Linda stood at the waters edge and called.

Sabrina turned and looked at her Mother. "Not yet. Daddy hasn't reeled in the line all the way. We have to see if we caught anything."

"Now, Sabrina!" Linda yelled emphatically. We have to get back to the airport."

"Go on, Cookie. I'll bring the rod in."

"Not until you promise we'll do this again…real soon!"

"Okay, I promise."

Sabrina released her grasp on Seth's pants, turned, and fought the outgoing tide toward shore. Suddenly, a large breaker caught her by surprise from behind throwing her headlong onto the sandy bottom. Sabrina disappeared from sight just as Linda screamed.

Seth turned quickly, threw his rod into the water and headed for Sabrina. He saw her rolling in the surf with her face down.

As Sabrina recovered from the slam of the first wave, a second inundated her. She rolled over, sat up, and sputtered salt water. She was able to take two or three breaths just before the third wave hit. Sabrina saw it coming and closed her eyes to take its force. However, prior to the smack of the crest, two strong hands picked her up and began wiping water from her face.

\* \* \*

"Sabrina! Sabrina! Are you all right?"

The voice seemed to call out from the far end of a dark tunnel.

"Sabrina!"

She heard it, but she couldn't speak. A pungent odor filled the tunnel, and Sabrina jerked her head from side to side trying to find its source. Suddenly, the tunnel illuminated, and she saw a face rushing toward her. "I'm okay, Daddy."

"Daddy?"

Steve continued to pass the ammonia capsule beneath Sabrina's nose.

Sabrina opened her eyes and recognized Steve. "Oh, it's you. What happened?"

"I don't know. I was hoping you could tell me."

"Whew, what is that stuff?" Sabrina brushed Steve's hand away.

"Ammonia. It's used for fainting."

"Where in heaven's name did you get it?"

"Flight bag."

Sabrina opened one eye and grinned. "You must have been a Boy Scout."

"Why?" Steve smiled as he tossed the capsule into the trash.

"You definitely came prepared." They both laughed.

Sabrina looked around and realized she was lying on her bed, naked. She looked up at Steve. "Enjoying the view?" She pulled the bedspread over her.

"Yes." He grinned as he took another look over her wet body. "Sorry, but I didn't have much time to dress you. I found you slumped down in the corner of the shower. The water was hitting you square in the face, and I was afraid you weren't able to breathe. I grabbed you by the shoulders and carried you to the bed. If I hadn't heard the water running, I might not have found you so quick. Are you sure you're all right?"

Sabrina sat up slowly on the edge of the bed, put on her robe, and looked at Steve. "I'll be fine. Must have had the water too hot." She stood, wobbling a little, and stopped where she stood. She didn't want to tell Steve about the chest pain. She knew it would worry him, and he might force her to go to the infirmary. And she certainly didn't want him finding out about the pregnancy. Not yet!

"Why don't you lie down and rest. I'll take my shower in here. If you need anything, you can just whistle."

"I think I will." Sabrina lay back on the bed and put her feet on a pillow.

Steve slipped out of his running shorts, shoes, and underwear. He was about to step into the shower when he heard Sabrina call his name. He stuck his head around the edge of the door. "Need something?"

"How about getting me some orange juice?"

"Sure." Steve went to the kitchen and quickly returned with a cold glass of juice. Sabrina took the glass while eyeing Steve's naked body and whistled.

"What?"

"Well, you said if I needed anything, just whistle."

"That's right."

"I need something, and from the look of things, something needs me." Sabrina winked and motioned to Steve's erection with a nod.

"Sabrina, you've just recovered from a faint!"

"So, I've recovered. I feel fine." Sabrina looked at him again. "Well, not fine…" She removed her robe, arched her body forward giving Steve full view of her breasts, and fanned her hair behind her shoulders. "I am a little hot." She motioned for Steve to join her on the bed. "Wanna come and cool me off?"

"I'm sweaty, Brina, and you're killing me."

"You want to make love to me, or not?"

"I do." Steve eased into the bed next to Sabrina's inviting body. They made love to the sounds of the ocean and rested in each others arms.

# 8

Mac Orberson squinted at his reflection in the mirror of his State Department office bathroom. He had arrived in Washington the night before on the late flight from Paris. It had been too late to go home, and it was too early to call a meeting of his staff. Even if he was the Secretary of State, he didn't think it would be fitting to muster his troops at 4:00 A.M.

Mac's bald head gleamed in the bright bathroom light, and even though he hated to agree, he did look somewhat like Robert Conrad, TV's Frank Cannon, without the mustache. He smiled as he thought of the resemblance, but the clock on the wall reminded him of the meeting he was having in thirty minutes. The recent communication from Shiek Jofur Armani was making it necessary for him to call on Taggat Delaney once again. However, this time, the need for Steve Hardesty would last over an extended period of time; possibly eight to ten months. Mac slipped into a freshly starched white dress shirt, pulled on his suspendered trousers, and tied the cranberry silk tie into a half-Windsor knot. Slipping on his vest and closing the front buttons, he carried his dress coat into the front office. He wanted to review the information on Operation Pipeline before his staff arrived.

Mac eased into his familiar leather chair and pulled up to the desk. He took a deep breath, put on his reading glasses, and opened the EYES ONLY folder. The first page in the pamphlet was a directive from the President.

*"Recent deterioration of the Middle East situation continues. The continued conflict between Iran and Iraq has no peaceable solution in sight. The only thing the two countries can agree on is to continued gouging the West with their oil quotas and price fixing. This, in combination with the diminished flow of crude through the Straits of Hormuz and the inability to assure the safety of the world's tanker fleet, makes it necessary for the United States to consider further alternate sources of oil. At present we are unable to increase the flow from the North Slope of Alaska because of potential environmental risks. Therefore, we have turned elsewhere.*

*Recent developements in Saudi Arabia have placed Shiek Jofur Armani as the head of the country's Council for Oil Exportation. His "cartel" consists of four other members, but the decisions made by Armani are generally agreed upon by the group. Shiek Armani is a "friend" of our government. His assistance in past aircraft sales to Saudi Arabia has been instrumental in the consummation of those contracts.*

*We wish to obtain a secure, unimpeded flow of oil from Saudi Arabia without using the Persian Gulf and feel Shiek Armani would be instrumental in this procurement. Consider alternatives and use whatever peaceful means necessary to accomplish this goal."*

It had taken four months of constant travel to the Middle East, but Mac was very close to an agreement that would fulfill his directive. The Saudi and Egyptian governments, with assistance from U.S. engineers, were about to agree to construct a series of pipelines between Port Said, Egypt, and Magna, Saudi Arabia. This maneuver would permit tanker access to Saudi crude from a Mediterranean site. Concomitantly, it would improve the economy of both Egypt and Saudi Arabia while the U.S.

could guarantee the port's safety with its Mediterranean fleet. While the possibility of terrorism along the pipeline was an agreed drawback, both countries would try to minimize the problem by patrolling the length of the conduits with their own troops and those of the United Nations. However, Armani insisted that no U. S. military personnel be used, for he did not want it to appear the United States controlled the flow of oil through the pipeline. Mac also knew it would take much persuasion to convince the other countries bordering the Mediterranean that the environment would not be endangered.

Steve Hardesty had assisted in the courting of Sheik Armani on his initial visits to the United States, and judging from the letter Mac had received from Armani, he had done a damned good job. Mac smiled as he reread the letter.

> *Dear Mr. Secretary of State,*
>
> *Our recent tour of your most gracious country was greatly appreciated. We especially enjoyed the views of your magnificient Southwest. I cannot begin to tell you how friendly your citizens can be. We feel Mr. Hardesty would be an asset in our upcoming travels in Europe. His physical presence offers security to our group unlike one of our own pilots. If you could be so kind as to arrange his services, we would like to begin our negotiations as soon as possible. I'm sure you are anxious to begin the task of construction. I foresee a great future in the establishment of increased flow of oil into the Mediterranean market.*
>
> *We are prepared to compensate Mr. Hardesty for his services. Since we predict it will take at least eight to nine months to make the arrangements for this undertaking, we will gladly pay Mr. Hardesty one million dollars (U. S. currency) for his time. I hope he will consent to join us as soon as possible.*
>
> *Your servant,*
> *Shiek Jofur Armani*

Armani's request was going to make Mac's job harder. He felt Hardesty would not agree to assist if asked directly, and he didn't have an edge with Steve. But he knew he could pressure Taggat to help because of Taggat's past clandestine dealings with the Soviets. Fifteen years prior, Taggat had been under investigation for secretive deals with a black marketeer, Dimitri Constantine, in Baku, Azerbaijan, U.S.S.R. The federal government had not prosecuted because Taggat and his contact agreed to make it possible for the C. I. A. to secure military secrets from bases in that area of the U.S.S.R., and they agreed not to expose Dimitri's United States connection.

Mac leaned back in his chair and tapped the desk with his pen. He had been Secretary of State since the start of the present administration. His credentials included his decorations for valor at Normandy during the Second World War, his reputable corporate law practice, his past experiences in foreign affairs with the U. S. diplomatic service, and his gifted golden tongue. After law school, Mac had joined Taggat in establishing a law firm affiliated with Seth MacKenzie's Planter Bank. Mac's role was in the legalities of bank diversification. He traveled throughout the Eastern United States and Europe establishing business associations that proved favorable for the Bank, and later for him in the State Department.

Mac and his family had been quite satisfied with their lives before he was offered the position of Secretary of State, but Mac jumped at the opportunity. He relished the idea of the power that the position bestowed. The present situation was an excellent example, for right now, at this moment, Mac had the power to assure the President re-election. He knew it, and he loved it.

Mac continued to peck his pen on the desk. "Well, if they want Hardesty, by damned, they'll have him…Alice! You here yet?" Mac yelled through the partially opened door. He hated intercoms.

Alice McCafferty, Mac's secretary, had no problem hearing the ex-Army captain's booming voice. "I didn't know you were here. What can I do for you?"

"Get Taggat Delaney on the line, please."

"Yes, sir. Right away." Alice picked up her phone and called Taggat's New York office.

Milliseconds later the phone in Taggat's office rang.

Mae Stevens, Taggat's private secretary, picked up the headset. "Good morning, Taggat Delaney's office. May I help you?"

"Taggat Delaney, please. The Secretary of State calling."

"One moment, please." Mae fingered the intercom. "Mr. Delaney, Mac Orberson on line one."

Taggat punched the appropriate button on his phone set. "Hello, Mac?"

"One moment please." Alice connected Taggat.

"What can I do for you, Mac? I'm sure this isn't a social call this early in the morning."

"Taggat, I hate to do this to you, but I need another favor. This one is bigger than the last."

"That's a tall order, Mac. What's in it for me?"

"You had better wait until you hear what I'm going to ask."

"You know I'll help if I can."

"I know, and I appreciate all you've done and all you're about to do. Taggat, I've just received a request from Armani."

"What's he need? More women?" Taggat laughed.

"No, he wants Steve Hardesty."

"What's that supposed to mean?"

"He wants Steve to be his private pilot while the Saudi oil council travel about the Mediterranean trying to strike up interest in our pipeline project. Taggat, they'll need him for eight months."

"Hell, Mac! I can't obligate Steve for eight months' overseas duty without discussing it first. Ask him yourself."

"He wouldn't do it for me, but he'll consider it if it comes from you. I realize it's a difficult thing to do, but I need some answers, and I need them soon. Armani wants him bad."

"How 'bad'?"

"One million dollars 'bad'. That 'bad' enough?"

Taggat whistled. "Damn, that is 'bad'."

"I'll say. Can you help? Taggat, I think I can sew up this pipeline deal if we can use Hardesty."

"I don't know, Mac. Eight months is a long time."

"Look, Taggat, I wasn't going to mention this, but you can benefit from this, also."

"How's that? Hell, I'm losing a business partner and pilot for almost a year. I'll lose money, and you know it."

"You're a business man. Right?"

"Right."

"If you help me with this deal, I promise I'll give you first stab at handling the legalities and the finances for the pipeline."

"Wait a minute, Mac. You can't promise that. Only a Senate subcommittee can appoint legal counsel handling such a delicate matter."

"Yeah. So?"

"So…Oh! I catch your drift. You name the members of the subcommittee. Right?"

"You're a very perceptive man, Taggat. Now. How about Hardesty?"

"Bump the price, and you've got him."

"Bump the price! Taggat, you son-of-a-…"

"Wait a minute, Mac. What's the big deal? These guys are rolling in it. Make it a million, six, and you've got your man, your pipeline, and your fame. What the hell?"

"All right, if the Saudi's won't do it, I'll make up the difference myself. But, Taggat, I've got to have Hardesty, now. Understand?"

"How shall we do it?" Taggat drummed his fingers on the desk. He knew he was in trouble, but the figures kept whirling around in his head.

"I'm sending Paul Peterson down to Kennedy to pick up Hardesty."

"Hold on, Mac. Steve's not there now."

"Damn! When is he going to be back?"

"I expect him Thursday."

"All right, I'll have Paul there then. He'll escort Hardesty to Andrews Air Force Base for indoctrination. We'll have him on our first Trans-Atlantic flight."

"Wait a minute. Steve won't fly any of your commercial junk."

"Junk?"

"Yes, junk. Steve will insist on flying his own aircraft. I suggest you humor him."

"I don't care if he rows over in a goddamned boat, just have him at Andrews by next Thursday. And Taggat?"

"What else? I'm in deep shit already."

"Say your good-bye's. Steve will have a communication blackout for the duration of the project. Until the story breaks about the success of the pipeline construction, there won't be a mention of anyone's working on such a thing."

"Oh, damn. That's going to be a hard one, especially if my god-daughter and Steve have mended any fences over the past day or two."

"That's not my problem."

"No, but you're managing to make it mine."

"I'm sure you'll find a way to smooth it over."

"I'm sure."

"Taggat, you stand a lot to gain from this. Don't let me down."

"I'll hold up my end, Mac. Don't worry. Steve will be there Thursday. You have your boy here, and Steve will go. But you do me a favor."

"More money?"

Taggat laughed. "No. Make it look like it was all your idea. Don't make me the patsy. Steve will have an easier time believing in an obligation to his country a lot quicker than he'll feel obligated to me."

"I'll try, Taggat. Thanks. Goodbye…Oh, Taggat?"

"Yeah?"

"Remember, this is for your ears only. If none of this comes about, no one is to ever know what we've been doing. Understood?"

"Understood. Goodbye."

Mac hung up the phone and asked Alice to have Paul Peterson come into his office. Mac walked to the door and greeted Paul as he entered.

"Good morning, Mr. Secretary. Glad to see you're back safe and sound." The thin blonde haired Paul Peterson entered the Secretary's office and shook Mac's hand.

"Good morning, Paul. Have a seat." Mac sat down in his chair and waited for Paul to get comfortable. "Paul, I'm sending you back to Riyadh."

"So soon?"

"Yes. I've gotten Delaney to agree to give us Hardesty as Armani requested."

Paul's eyes widened, "Does Hardesty know about this?"

"Not yet. Why?"

Paul stood and walked to the front of Mac's desk. "I spent a lot of time with Hardesty during the Saudi's last visit. He'll do it, but he'll be pissed. I hope there won't be any repercussions."

"What kind of repercussions?"

"I'm not sure, Mr. Secretary, but if we don't handle Steve properly, he can explode. He has quite a volatile personality."

"He won't endanger this mission, will he?"

"No. No. Nothing like that. That's the one thing about him I like. If he has a job to do, he'll do it. He is quite an honorable person. Could I make a suggestion?"

"Certainly. I appreciate your input, and you know it."

"I think we should reactivate Steve's military rank."

"But Armani specifically said no military. I don't know, Paul."

"We won't have him wearing a uniform, but I think Steve will feel more obligation if we have a small hold over him with military rank. Honor…Duty…and all that, you know?"

"That's an excellent idea, Paul. Handle it, and be ready to move on this Thursday. I want you and Hardesty in Riyadh by next Monday."

"Where am I to meet him?"

"Kennedy Airport, Thursday afternoon, 1:00 P.M. You'll take him to Andrews for a quick indoctrination, then on to Ramstein, Cairo, and Riyadh."

"How are we flying?"

"Hardesty will be permitted to take his personal jet. He has a Lear C-21A. I believe you're familiar with the plane."

"You mean they have it back together?" Paul grinned. "You wouldn't believe the party those Arabs had in that jet on the way back from Vegas. Whoo!"

"I don't care if they were naked and in a pile." Mac grinned and pointed his finger at Paul. "We're going to get this pipeline, Paul. I know it."

"You might just be right. Jofur likes Hardesty, and I think he wants this deal to go through."

"Good! Let's capitalize on their relationship. Keep me informed on the progress on a weekly basis. You will communicate with me and me only. No other communication will be permitted with Hardesty or any one else involved with the project. Have a safe trip." Mac stood and shook Paul's hand. "And, Paul."

"Yes, Sir?"

"Try to keep Taggat's involvement out of this as much as possible."

"Yes, Mr. Secretary. I'm good at being the fall guy." Paul had lived in Saudi Arabia during his childhood. His father was an engineer with Shell Oil and had developed oil refineries in the country during their fledgling stages. Paul had grown up by his father's side always exposed to the people of the country. He was educated in the finest schools and received his college degree from Cambridge. When the Saudis nationalized the oil industry in their country and Paul's parents moved back to the United States, Paul returned to America and worked for the United Nations. Mac knew Paul through his acquaintance with Paul's father, and when Mac asked Paul to be the assistant secretary to Middle East affairs, Paul accepted the position without hesitation. Now, Paul had a chance to be part of a major political breakthrough, and he didn't want to do anything to jeopardize his position. He had a job, and he would do it.

\* \* \*

Mae walked into Taggat's office and placed a stack of papers in front of him. "Steve's not going to like what you've just done." Mae Stevens was forty six years old, six years younger than Taggat. She had worked for him for the past ten years, and their relationship was purely professional, much to Mae's chagrin. She loved Taggat, but she dreaded the possible lack of reciprocity. Therefore, she never revealed her desire.

Mae kept herself in excellent shape. However, her appearance, while being neat, was never fashionable or alluring. The other ladies in the office had recommended a change in her overall appearance, but Mae never felt it would help. Taggat never seemed to notice her, any way. She kept her long brown hair pulled into a tight bun and wore very little make-up. Her black rimmed glasses were too large for her face, while her business suits weren't eye appealing. One could have never guessed her age accurately, for she always looked to be at least…well, older.

"Steve won't mind what I've done. I did it for him, afterall. He'll be getting a million six."

"Don't get in a huff at me, Taggat Delaney. You did the talking. Explain it to Steve, not me."

"Don't remind me. If Steve and Sabrina manage to get closer during the next two days, he'll be fit to be tied when I tell him he has to leave the country for the next nine months. Anyway, how do you know about this? Were you listening? I could fire you for that."

"You won't."

"You're right. Besides being a good secretary, you're damned good to look at."

May tried to let the compliment go over her head, but it flustered her somewhat.

"Could I make a suggestion?"

"Sure. I'm open for anything."

"Don't tell Steve."

"What?"

"Well, If I were you, I'd let Mr. Peterson do the explaining."

"What do you mean?"

"Well, Mr. Orberson said Mr. Peterson was going to meet Steve at the airport. Didn't he?"

"Yes, but what does that have to do with not telling Steve."

"How were you to know what Mac had in store for Steve? You have no control over the matter. Tell Steve you have a rush transport to Andrews Air Force Base, and the passenger is waiting at Kennedy. Why should you know anymore about the matter?"

Taggat thought about the suggestion for a moment, then grinned. "Mae, you're wonderful. I knew I had you around here for a reason. Not only are you good looking, but you're smart, too."

Mae heard Taggat's remark about her intelligence, but his second compliment on her appearance impressed her the most. "Anything to help the boss," Mae managed to say even though Taggat's compliments had almost left her speechless.

"But when Steve finds out, he'll be royally pissed." Taggat scratched his chin and thought about facing Steve after the truth was out.

May handed Taggat a pen to start signing the papers. "Well, a million six can soothe a lot of wounds."

Taggat started signing the forms and smiled. "So true, Mae. So true."

# 9

Steve tossed his flight bag and Sabrina's briefcase into the storage compartment of the Corvette. He helped Sabrina into her seat, closed the door, and walked to the driver's side. Taking a quick look around the garage, he assured himself nothing had been left behind; then he got into the car and started the engine.

"Turn on the air conditioning...Quick!" Sabrina gasped and fanned her blouse. "I can't believe it's this humid already."

"At your service, my lady." Steve adjusted the air conditioning temperature to its lowest setting, put the car in reverse and backed out into the parking area located on the leeward side of the house. He looked over at Sabrina and noted her forlorn stare. "Something wrong?"

"No, nothing's wrong. I've always hated leaving the island. Now, I hate it more than ever." Sabrina touched her ring making sure it was still real.

"After these past three days, it's special to me, too. I didn't think I would ever be here with you again."

Sabrina smiled, leaned over to Steve, and kissed him on the cheek. "I really don't think you ever believed that."

"I always hoped it wasn't true. Now, I'm sure." Steve smiled, put the Vette in Drive, and headed down the driveway. "What do you think Cathy will say about our engagement?"

"I know exactly what she'll say. 'Dammit, Sabrina! You've jumped out of the frying pan and into the fire. You never know when you're well off'."

Steve laughed. "I'm sure that's right . I'm not sure what the folks at work will think. They'll be amazed, but I don't think they'll be surprised. After all, I did have orders to do this." Steve grinned as he negotiated the twisting road through the sand dunes.

"Oh, yes! Charlie's orders. I'll have to thank him when we get back to Kennedy. But you know, it doesn't make any difference what anyone thinks." Sabrina leaned across the console. "I've got the only man for me. I hope I can keep him."

"Keep me? You would have to kill me to get rid of me!"

Sabrina's eyes widened, and she retreated into the corner of her seat. "Don't say that! Don't ever say that! I don't want you to ever talk about dying."

"Easy, Brina. Just a figure of speech. I didn't mean it literally."

Sabrina didn't answer.

"Sabrina, are you all right? I've been worried about you since your fainting episode."

"Uh, yes, I'm okay. I just don't like to think about losing anyone ever again. I'm not sure I'd be able to handle it. I would rather die than lose another person close to me."

"All right. I promise I'll never leave you, at least not without checking with you first." Steve watched to see if Sabrina seemed to be getting back to normal. "Are you sure you're feeling well? I heard you in the bathroom this morning, and you sounded sick."

"I think it was something I ate last night. If it's still bothering me later today, I'll see a doctor while I'm in the city."

"Promise?"

"Promise."

"If you feel better by this evening, maybe we can go to dinner."

"I'd love to. Where?"

"Oh, I have a place in mind. Let's make it a surprise."

"Let's don't. I have to know what to wear. I'd love to go shopping for a special evening with you."

Steve laughed, "I never knew you to need an excuse for shopping."

"Are you going to tell me, or not?"

"Yes…yes. I thought we'd fly down to Boston and go to Julio's."

Sabrina gasped. "Really? I haven't been there since…"

"I left for Vietnam."

"Yes, that's right. Since the night before you left for the war. I remember it well."

"So do I. You looked like an angel. I carried the picture they took of us that night with me the whole time I was in 'Nam. I had it inside my flight helmet on every mission. It helped me remember what I was fighting for."

Sabrina grinned. "You're crazy." She thought back to that night. Her parents knew how much she cared for Steve and how Steve felt about her. They had been impressed with the way both had handled the relationship up to that point, and they couldn't deny their daughter the chance to see Steve before he left for his tour of duty. So they gave them a night to remember at Julio's. Sabrina kept her eyes closed as she savored the memory. After a few pensive moments, Sabrina took a deep breath, looked out the window of the car, and came back to the present. "The Island won't be the same until you and I can share it together. The house won't be the same until you're there with me."

"Your housemate might have a few things to say about that arrangement."

"Cathy? No. She knew I'd marry someday. She has contingency plans to build farther down the beach. She was going to start pretty soon anyway. The house will be ours. It's ours already." Sabrina quickly looked at Steve and became defensive. "That is, if you want to live here. I know you have your business, and I don't want to presume anything. I didn't mean to imply that I was trying to control your life."

"Whoa, Sabrina. It's all right. I know how you feel about the island. I'd love to live here. It wouldn't take much to shuttle to New York. Hell, I'm only at Kennedy three or four days out of the month anyway. It's as easy to fly back here as it is to Kennedy. Easier, in fact."

"I'm glad you feel that way. This place means so much to me."

"I know, and I'm willing to make certain concessions to be with you."

Sabrina became silent. The reality of the pregnancy began to wedge its way into her conscience. "Steve, what would you have done if I had married Kent?"

The smile disappeared from Steve's face. "I don't know, Sabrina. I know I would have left New York."

"Left New York! Why?"

"I wouldn't have been able to see you, and I couldn't stand knowing you belonged to another. And I especially couldn't have ever faced you if you were to have a baby that wasn't mine."

A deathly wave rolled through Sabrina's body. "What do you mean?"

"I'm not sure. I would be naive not to think you and Kent haven't had intimate moments, and I can and will live with that just as you know I've been in bed with other women. It makes no difference now that I have you, and I hope it makes no difference to you."

"It doesn't. I have you now, and no other woman will ever take you away. At least not while I draw breath. But how would a pregnancy make a difference if I were married?"

"I don't know. It just would. If I had to watch you have another man's baby, I wouldn't be able to handle it. It would infuriate me. Sabrina, I love you that much. So, to prevent that anxiety, I would have sold Taggat my share of the business and moved as far away as possible." Steve hesitated and allowed the flush to drain from his cheeks. He nervously laughed. "Hey, what's the difference? I've got you. You've got me. Let's talk about something else."

"Absolutely," she said, but she thought about how she was dying inside. Dying because she knew the only way she would ever keep Steve would be to proceed with the deception she had plotted on the beach. Sabrina leaned across the console and put her head on Steve's shoulder. She lightly stroked the hair of his right forearm, leaned close to his ear, and whispered, "I love you, and I'm sorry."

"Sorry?"

"Yes, sorry. Sorry for being so stupid. If I had known our lives would turn out this way, I would never have let anything happen between Kent and me."

"Don't do this, Sabrina. I told you. It doesn't make any difference."

"It does to me."

"Why? I don't love you any less. Why should it make a difference."

"It just does. That's all. It does to me. You weren't the first."

"Is that all?" Steve almost laughed, but he knew better.

"Is that all?. It's important to me."

"Don't worry," Steve grinned. "I may not be first, but I'm the best."

Sabrina sat up and hit Steve lightly on the arm. "You egomaniac." She smiled. "You're right, though," she said without looking at him. Sabrina leaned back in her seat and remained silent for the rest of the trip to the airport.

\* \* \*

Steve stopped the Corvette in front of the terminal door. "Why don't you go ahead and check in the car. I'll have one of the ground crew bring in the keys and make sure the Lear is ready. After I get her preflighted, I'll pull in front of the terminal."

"Fine, I'll use the time wisely," Sabrina slowly walked toward the terminal. "Well, Sabrina. You wondered how he might take the news. Now you know." Pulling the terminal door open she subconsciously handed the clerk the rapid check in slip and headed for the bathroom where she proceeded to vomit up her breakfast into the nearest commode. As a light sweat broke out over her forehead, all Sabrina could say was, "Damn!"

Steve pulled the car into a slot, took the keys and walked to the hanger where he singled out the familiar mechanic. "Jerry! How did it go?"

"No problem, Mr. Hardesty. I love working on these babies. I truly enjoyed having her company for the last three days."

"Ever think about leaving this place, Jerry?"

"Oh yeah! Millions of times, but my wife's family is here. So, I'm pretty well stuck."

"Well, if things change, and they often can without our control, you'll always have a job in New York." Steve handed Jerry the car keys which he had neatly wrapped in three one hundred dollar bills. "Have someone take those keys in would you?"

"Sure," Jerry handed Steve the money back, "but this isn't necessary. You'll get my bill."

"I know. Let's call this an 'extra' for your assistance. If you feel guilty about taking it, throw a party for your crew…on me. I'm not taking them back. It was worth the extra to have her looked after by the best."

"Thanks for the vote of confidence. I might look you up someday about the job."

"It's not an idle promise, Jerry. Mechanics with savvy are hard to find. Thanks again." After Steve shook Jerry's hand, her turned and climbed the entry steps situating himself. All the systems had been checked, and Jerry had left a note on the inside of the windscreen.

*Expected you. Tanks are topped. Systems checked out. She's ready to go.*

Ordinarily, Steve would have had harsh words to any ground crew member that had taken the liberty to preflight the Lear, but today things were going too well. He quickly rechecked the list, adjusted his voice activated headset, and gently eased the throttles forward. He pulled in front of the terminal, throttled down, and waited for the wheels to be chocked. He opened the door and waved for Sabrina to come onto the plane.

Sabrina ran from the terminal, up the steps, and kissed Steve. "I'm ready now."

After they took their places in the cockpit, Steve picked up the phone and verified his flight plan with Kennedy. "Why don't you call Taggat and tell him we're running late. We should arrive downtown by one-thirty. Then call Julio's and make dinner reservations."

"I should be finished with Taggat by four. How does eight-thirty sound?"

"Sounds fine." Steve turned on his headset. "MacKenzie Traffic, DHJ-003 requesting clearance for taxi and take off. Over."

"Roger, DHJ-003. You're clear to taxi and take off runway 14. Wind 175 degrees at 10 knots. No traffic reported in the area. MacKenzie, out."

"Roger, MacKenzie. DHJ-003, out." Steve throttle up and rolled to the entrance of the runway. No traffic was visible. He rolled onto the threshold and pushed forward on the throttle. The Lear responded smoothly, and they were airborne within seconds.

* * *

"DHJ-003, Kennedy Tower. You're free to land Runway 22R. Wind 045 degrees at 15 knots. Tower, out."

"Understood, Kennedy. DHJ-003, out." Steve followed the glideslope and touched down on schedule. He taxied to the private hangers of Delaney and Hardesty Flight Service, rolled the Lear in front of Hanger One, and brought the engines to idle. As Charlie chocked the wheels, Steve and Sabrina prepared to leave the plane. While they stood in the small aisle, Sabrina set down her briefcase, threw her arms around Steve's neck, and kissed him passionately. Then she looked up at him coyly when she sensed he wasn't going to pursue matters further. She whispered, "Are we finished?"

"For now." Steve said as he looked up and down Sabrina's body.

"I'm sorry to hear that," Sabrina said as she began unbuttoning her blouse. "Why don't we make them wait for a few more minutes?" She continued to loosen her buttons looking into Steve's eyes. "I'd love to make love on the Lear."

"Sabrina! They're outside waiting," Steve halfheartedly said as he gently touched the top of Sabrina's breasts through her bra. He could feel the firmness of her nipples through the fabric.

Sabrina closed her eyes and shuddered. "Let them wait," she whispered as she pushed her body against Steve's.

"Sabrina," Steve slowly moaned. "Believe me, I'd love to have a romantic interlude, but we'd have trouble explaining it to Charlie and the rest of the crew."

"Who," Sabrina purred as she allowed the sensation of Steve's touch to continue to take effect.

"Right!" Steve backed away and nervously laughed. "Come on, Sabrina. If we keep this up, I'll have to find a cold shower before I get off the plane."

Sabrina tried to calm herself as she slowly buttoned her blouse. "Okay, but you don't know what you're missing."

"Oh, yes, I do. Or, have you forgotten the past three days."

"I'll never forget them." Sabrina finished straightening her blouse and readjusted her hair. "Am I presentable?" She turned around in front of Steve. Sabrina was wearing a plain white cotton blouse, a navy blue skirt, brown tone stockings, low heeled navy blue shoes, and gold jewelry: necklace, bracelet, watch, and engagement ring.

"You look good enough to eat."

"You missed your chance."

"Don't remind me. I'm having trouble walking straight as it is."

Sabrina laughed as she patted the firmness in Steve's crotch. "Put him to bed. We'll have to see if he works later tonight."

"Promise?" Steve grinned.

"Promise."

Steve opened the hatch and allowed Sabrina to exit before him. As he walked out the portal, he noticed all the men staring at her. "All right, guys. Put your eyes back in your heads, and act like she has some clothes on. You're ogling my future wife." Steve held up Sabrina's left hand and showed the ring to the crowd.

"All right!" Charlie yelled. "It's about damned time. Congratulations! Hey, Sabrina! What did you do? I didn't think this guy would ever realize what he was missing by letting you get away. Of course, you know I talked him into asking you to marry him."

"Charlie!" The rest of the crew chimed.

"Well, I had a little help."

Sabrina was smiling at the group. She put her arms around Steve and started down the steps. "Regardless of who did it, I appreciate the message you sent." Sabrina walked over to Charlie and kissed his cheek. "Thanks."

Charlie brushed his cheek, blushed, and looked at Steve. "Hey, Steve. Taggat wanted you to phone him as soon as you landed, and there's an official looking fellow waiting for you in the office. He's been here since noon. The car that delivered him had government plates, and he introduced himself as Paul Peterson."

"Uh, oh. Paul's with the State Department." Steve turned to Sabrina. "I have to use the phone, Brina. We're going to take the Ranger into the city. It's ready in front of Hanger Five. I'll meet you there in ten minutes."

"Okay. I'll meet you there. Don't be late." Sabrina smiled and winked at Steve. Then, she turned to Charlie. "Charlie, is there anything cool to drink around here?"

"Sure, 'bout anything you'd want." Charlie took Sabrina by the arm and walked her to the office in Hanger Five.

Sabrina looked over her shoulder and watched Steve as he disappeared into his office. She had an uneasy feeling about the phone call, and wished she knew exactly who Paul Peterson was.

Steve entered his office and attempted to muster a smile. "Paul!" Steve shook Paul's hand. "How are you?"

"Fine, Steve. Didn't think I would be seeing you so soon. Have you recovered from last week?"

"Barely." Steve smiled and looked toward his private office. "Paul, I've got to call Taggat. Be right back."

"But…" Paul tried to stop Steve, but Steve walked into the back room and closed the door.

Steve called Taggat's office, and Mae placed him on hold. "Mr. Delaney, Steve's on line one. Remember, you don't know anything."

Taggat drummed the receiver for a few seconds, took a deep breath, and punched the light. "Steve! Glad to see you're back safely. Got any news?"

"Such as?"

"You know what I'm talking about."

"Oh?," Steve hesitated. "You mean about Sabrina and me. "

"Of course, dammit. What's happening between you two? Did Sabrina dump that turkey?"

"Sabrina's fine, and we're getting married. What the hell does Paul Peterson want with me?"

"I need to talk to you about…Wait a damned minute. Did you say you and Sabrina were getting married?"

"Right! A whirlwind courtship. What does Paul need, Taggat?"

"This is great, Steve. It's better than I would have hoped for. What happened to Pooley?"

"Sabrina dumped him about a week ago. We can talk about this later, Taggat. What about Peterson? I'm wanting to bring Sabrina in to meet you."

*Shit*, Taggat thought. *I'm in a real pickle.* "When's the wedding?"

"Taggat, you're not listening to me. We haven't set a date. Now, why is Paul in my outer office dancing around like a chicken on a hot rock?"

Taggat nervously took a breath and tried to relax. "Paul needs a lift to Andrews Air Force Base…*mucho pronto*. He came in on an unscheduled flight from London, and none of his State Department buddies were around to fly him to Washington. He tried to pick up a direct flight, but none were available. So, he called me. I was going to let Johnny take him, but when I told him you would be in at noon, he opted to wait. You have clearance into the Air Force base, so…," Taggat gulped. "I volunteered your services."

"Dammit, Taggat. Sabrina and I have dinner reservations for tonight. I like Paul, but Sabrina's a hell of a lot prettier."

"Steve, I didn't know you would be engaged when you came back from MacKenzie. You think I would have sent you if I had known this?" Taggat winced as he lied.

"I guess not, but I hate leaving Sabrina. We had a nice evening planned."

"I'm sorry, but Paul requested you take him. He almost demanded it. I don't know why he has such a bee under his bonnet."

"All right, I'll do it, but after this, don't make plans without checking with me first."

"All right. Sorry. Tell Sabrina I'll meet her on the roof heliport."

"Okay, Johnny will be bringing her in the Ranger."

"Fine, and Steve?"

"Yeah, Taggat."

"Be careful."

"Always."

"I mean it, Steve. Be careful. I'll see you when you get back. I'll take care of Sabrina."

"Taggat?"

"Yes?"

"You're going crazy. I'm just going to Andrews, for heaven's sake. I'll see you later tonight."

"Right. Right! Silly me. Goodbye, Steve."

Steve looked at the phone. "Goodbye?" Steve shrugged off Taggat's comments and headed for his outer office.

* * *

Taggat hung up the phone and pulled the lower right drawer open. "Mae, bring me a glass of water." He extracted the fifth of Makers Mark from the desk and waited.

May walked into the room and handed Taggat the glass.

"Care to join me? I need to drown a little guilt. By the way, Steve and Sabrina are going to be married."

"That's wonderful. It's about time those two got together."

"Wonderful? How can it be wonderful? I'm sending Steve away for nine months, and it's wonderful!"

"You're not sending him away. Mac Orberson is. Don't you think they would have gotten Steve if they wanted him regardless of your participation. If you hadn't helped, they would have done something else. You know they have their ways of doing things. Don't take this so hard. You were an innocent bystander they decided to use."

"I'm not so innocent, but that's an innocent way to look at it."

"It's the only way."

Taggat took a long drink from the bottle and chased it with water.

Mae winced. "How in the hell do you drink that stuff straight from the bottle?"

"Hell," Taggat held up the glass and looked at the remaining brown liquid, "this is smooth as silk."

* * *

Paul Peterson stood as Steve reentered the outer office, but Steve held up his hand once again.

"I've got to talk to the Hanger crew, Paul. Then we'll discuss our trip."

Paul smiled and sat back down.

Steve touched his intercom. "Charlie, you there?"

"Yeah, boss."

"Sabrina with you?"

"Nope, she's gone outside. I believe she's talking to Johnny."

"Good. Charlie, top off the Lear's tanks. I've got to make a short trip to Washington."

"When you gotta leave?"

Steve looked at Paul. "When?"

"Immediately," Paul smiled.

"Now, Charlie."

"Okay, Steve. I'll get her ready."

Paul stood, picked up his briefcase, and headed for the hanger.

"Wait a minute, Paul. What's this all about? I'm ready to talk."

"I think we should discuss this on the way to Andrews. I'm behind schedule as it is."

"Fair enough. I'll tell my fiancée, and be ready to go in fifteen minutes. The ground crew is refueling the jet. I'll meet you on board in ten minutes."

"Fine, I'll arrange clearance." Paul turned, frowned, and thought, "Fiancée! Oh, shit!"

"Please do that from here. I don't like anyone bothering my instruments."

Paul turned and faced Steve. "I've flown airplanes before."

"You haven't flown mine." Steve smiled while excusing himself. He quickly covered the distance between his office and the tarmac outside Hanger Five. He tried to put on his best face, but he knew his disappointment and anger were showing. He walked up to Sabrina and kissed her on the cheek. "Sabrina, I won't be…"

"What's wrong, Steve? You look as if you could chew nails."

"Dammit, I could. Taggat volunteered me for a job, and I'm pissed."

"What kind of job?" Sabrina tried not to let her disappointment show.

"I have to take a State Department official to Washington…immediately. I'm going to ask Johnny to take you in to meet Taggat."

Sabrina took Steve's hands in hers and looked him in the eye. "Don't be upset. I understand. I'll be waiting for you when you get back." Sabrina winked trying to break the tension. "Anyway, we have a big night ahead of us. Don't we?"

"You're unbelievable. I could shoot Taggat, and you take it in stride."

"Oh, I'll have a few choice words for Taggat, but I understand your position. You have your work, just as I have mine. I guess we'll miss dinner?"

"I'm afraid so, Sabrina. I'm sorry."

"Hey," Sabrina traced Steve's frown with her finger. "Wipe that frown away. I'll have Johnny bring me back to your place. We'll have a nice evening when you get back. We can go to Julio's anytime."

"Mmm, sounds nice. I'll hurry home."

Steve turned and looked at Johnny McKay, one of his senior pilots. "Johnny, would you take Sabrina into the Planter's Bank? Taggat's waiting for her."

"Sure, Steve. No problem."

"Take good care of her. She the future Mrs. Hardesty."

"I know. She told me. Congratulations!" Johnny climbed into the helicopter, situated himself, and began checking out the systems.

"I'll make it up to you, Sabrina. You know I wouldn't have planned this for the world."

"Stop apologizing. I knew I'd have to give you back to your job sooner or later. It just happened sooner than I thought."

"Thanks for understanding. I love you, and I'll be back as soon as I can."

"I'll make it worth the wait."

"I'll hold you to it…I have to go. This guy is in one big hurry for some reason." Steve hugged Sabrina and kissed her on the lips. He was about to release her, but Sabrina held on tighter.

"Hold me just a moment longer. I'm afraid to let you go. I love you so much, Steve. I need you. Please come back." Sabrina had gotten a cold chill down her spine just as Steve was about to release her. She searched for reassurance in his touch.

"It won't be for long. I really have to be moving so I can get back."

Sabrina let go, stepped back, and wiped the tears from her eyes. "Go ahead. Don't worry. I'll be waiting for you tonight."

"Are you feeling all right?"

"I'm okay. Bye."

The whine of the Bell's engine start up caused Sabrina to jerk.

Steve smiled. "I guess Johnny's ready, and I really have to go."

"Guess so. Don't worry." Sabrina turned and got into the helicopter.

Johnny handed Sabrina a headset and waited for her to position it on her head. "You ready?"

Sabrina nodded her head affirmatively, held up her right thumb, and sniffed. "Let's go."

The Bell Ranger rotated off the ground, flew vertical for fifty feet, and nosed over making a direct line for downtown Manhattan. Sabrina crooked her neck and looked back to see if she could see Steve's outline, but she couldn't find him among the ground activity. She looked forward, and fixed her gaze on the approaching skyline. "I'll give Taggat a piece of my mind when I get downtown," she mumbled.

"Did you say something?" Johnny asked as they pulled farther away from the airport.

"Just rehearsing my lines." Sabrina said through gritted teeth.

"For what?"

"For a heart to heart with my godfather!"

* * *

Steve stepped on board the Lear and looked over to Paul who was busy making himself comfortable in the aft cabin. "You won't believe how fast I can get you to Andrews," Steve commented as he passed Paul's seat.

"No hurry. We have a long trip in front of us."

Steve looked at Paul and grinned. "Right!" *I believe every one but me is going crazy*, Steve thought as he fastened his harness and adjusted his headset.

# 10

Taggat slowly sipped his third double from the Waterford crystal tumbler as he nervously awaited Sabrina's arrival. There hadn't been many occasions in his fifty-two years which compelled him to drink straight bourbon, but the anxiety associated with his rapidly approaching confrontation with Sabrina seemed adequate reason. He held the glass up and peered into one of the many facets. Light from his office windows danced inside the mass of Irish crystal until his own reflection bounced from one of the rounded surfaces.

"You don't look like such a bad fellow, Taggat Delaney. So why do you feel so terrible?...Why? Because you have done some stupid things in your life, but this one gets the prize. If Steve discovers your involvement in this plan, he'll never speak to you again. And, Sabrina?..." Hell, Sabrina might not speak to you for a week after she gets here." Taggat swirled the brown liquid around the bottom of his glass observing more than consuming.

He didn't look up from his study of the drink as Mae reentered his office, walked to his desk, refilled the empty water pitcher, and turned to leave. From her huffs, Taggat could tell she was exasperated with his behavior. "What's wrong, Mae? Haven't you ever seen anyone drink before? I needed this." Taggat held up the glass tipping it towards Mae.

"No you don't ! No one ever needs it. They just think they do." Mae looked at Taggat and her exasperation melted to compassion. "Get yourself together, Taggat. Sabrina will be here soon."

"Could you meet her up on the heliport, Mae? I need a few minutes to straighten up." Taggat asked in a pathetic fashion with a boyish grin.

"Please do! I'll bring you some coffee. You're going to need it."

"Wait a minute, Mae. I want to ask you something. Sit down." Taggat pointed to the black leather couch in front of his desk. He looked up and smiled at Mae's surprised look. "Please?"

Mae sat on the edge of the pleated cushion. She tugged on the hem of her gray skirt and nervously straightened her blouse. Mae had never experienced love for any one other than her parents, and she had always wondered if she would know what it would be like to fall in love with a man. How could she tell she was in love? She still wasn't sure, but she knew she wanted to protect Taggat from his hurt. She didn't know how, but she was determined to help him through this dilemma.

"How long have you worked here, Mae?"

"Ten years."

"That long? Damn! How have I let a good looking woman work around me for ten years without making a pass at her?"

"Are you making one now?"

"Possibly, but that's not why I asked you to sit down," Taggat slyly smiled.

Mae fidgeted in her seat. "Then, why did you ask me?"

"Mae, it has been a long time since I've felt so bad about something I've done." Taggat leaned forward and put his head in his hands. "Do you think Steve and Sabrina will ever forgive me?"

Mae stood, walked over to Taggat's chair, and removed the whiskey bottle from the desk. She recapped the Maker's Mark putting the bottle back into the lower right hand drawer and turned Taggat's chair to face her. Without changing emotion, she straightened his collar, buttoned his shirt's top button, and slid his tie back into position. She walked back to the couch, sat down, took a deep breath, and looked straight into Taggat's bewildered face. "Taggat, I tend to speak my mind, and, if I get out of line, stop me." Mae waited for a few moments, but when no response came from Taggat, she took a breath and started. "Mac has overstepped his limit this time, and you have done exactly what you had to do. Mac didn't give you a choice. He made you think you had one, but you didn't. Mac has alternative methods for getting Steve to work for him without your assistance. Look, Steve doesn't have to find out you're involved, and if he does, he'll understand. Steve's dealt with the government before. He knows how they work. As for Sabrina, she won't understand at first, and she'll be hurt, but she'll get over it and forgive you." Mae looked down at her watch. "I'm going upstairs to meet Sabrina. Straighten yourself up and get presentable."

Taggat stood and straightened his jacket. "I hope you're right. It would break my heart if I lost Sabrina's love."

"I'm right. Wait and see." Mae turned for the door, took a deep breath, smiled, and headed for the heliport. She was now more determined than ever to prevent a confrontation between Taggat and Sabrina.

Taggat walked into his private bathroom, washed his face, brushed his teeth, and overdosed with Scope. He tried to mask the bourbon, but he knew Sabrina would pick up on it right away. She seemed to have the nose of a teenager's mother. He returned to his desk, sat down, and crossed his hands on the top of the desk. He peered at his office door awaiting Sabrina's arrival feeling like a defendant waiting for the return of the jury.

* * *

The Manhattan skyline grew larger in the windscreen of the Ranger as the helicopter raced for downtown New York. What were once blurred forms became buildings. Each building took on its own distinctive shape until Sabrina finally recognized the Planter's Bank Building with its familiar brass encircled rice shock logo on the upper facade. The black pyramidal forty story tower stood on the corner of a section of smaller structures making the addition of a heliport feasible. The landing pad was cantilevered off the back of the northwest face of the pyramid. Johnny MacKay, and the other pilots flying into the city, were appreciative of this method of construction for it diminished the testy crosswinds that made rooftop landings so hazardous.

The helicopter flew a straight line toward the building until its top filled Sabrina's view. Johnny swung the aircraft around to the back of the structure and nestled the ship onto the H-marked pad. He kept the blades turning until the attendants rushed out and anchored the skids. Then, he bottomed the throttle and allowed the engine to wind down to idle.

"Okay, Sabrina. You can get out. Shall I wait for you?"

"No, but could you come back and pick me up around six ?"

"No problem. Watch the rotor."

"Okay, Johnny, and thanks." Sabrina looked toward the elevator enclosure, but Taggat was conspicuous in his absence.

Sabrina gave Johnny the thumbs up, gathered her things, and headed for the elevator. As she approached the small anteroom around the elevator doors, the call light announced the arrival of the car. Sabrina was ready to pounce on Taggat as soon as the doors opened, but she was caught by surprise when she saw Mae.

Mae walked over to Sabrina and gave her a big hug. "Sabrina, you look wonderful, but you always do. You get more beautiful every time I see you. How do you feel?"

Sabrina looked at Mae wondering what she meant. She looked down at her abdomen and checked to see if she was letting her belly pooch, but she wasn't. She wasn't showing any signs of pregnancy, but perhaps women knew some special sign that Sabrina wasn't privy to yet. "What do you mean, Mae? I feel fine."

"You know. About getting engaged. This is the greatest thing that's happened around here in a while. We didn't like Kent. He was a pompous ass." Mae showed no sign of regret in her statement.

"I'm glad to see you're as outspoken as ever," Sabrina replied with some perturbation.

"Thank you. I take that as a compliment." Mae grinned, escorted Sabrina into the elevator and pushed the floor button.

Sabrina smiled at Mae's confession but wondered why she had been assigned as the welcoming party. "Mae, I'm thrilled to death about my engagement, but right now, I've got a few things to say to Taggat. Why didn't he meet me?"

"He's busy," Mae nonchalantly replied as she watched the floors count off.

"I'll bet. He was afraid to come up here and face me, wasn't he?"

"Why should he be afraid to see you, Sabrina?"

"Because he shipped Steve off on one of his errands. He knew we hadn't seen each other for the past six months. You'd think he would have checked with Steve before he sent him on this trip."

"Well, you know Taggat. He's not one to ask for permission when it comes to work. Anyway, he didn't know you two were engaged, and Mac really didn't give him any choice. You know how Mac can be."

"Yeah, just like Taggat. Bullheaded. Well, I'm going to give him a piece of my mind anyway." Sabrina headed out the door as it swung open into the reception area of the law firm.

Mae rushed behind Sabrina and grabbed her arm. "No, Sabrina. You're not going to do that."

Sabrina swung around and looked at Mae with amazement. She coyly cocked her head, grinned, and squinted her eyes. "What? Mae, what in the world are you saying?"

"Sabrina, I don't want to make a scene, and I apologize for grabbing your arm. Would you come with me? Please?" Mae escorted Sabrina through the maze of hallways in the thirtieth floor office. Finally, she stopped and directed Sabrina into one of the many conference rooms. "Have a seat, Sabrina. We have something to discuss before you see Taggat."

"Mae. What's with the suspense?"

"Please?" Mae pulled out one of the padded chairs. "Have a seat. I won't keep you long."

Sabrina sat, poured herself a glass of water from the chrome pitcher located in the center of the round oak table, and looked at Mae. "I'm all yours."

"I'm sorry I'm acting so peculiar," Mae started as she sat in the chair across from Sabrina. "But I wanted to speak to you, woman to woman, about Taggat. I think you need to understand a few things before you see him."

"Did Taggat put you up to this?" Sabrina started to rise from her chair.

"No! He doesn't know we're here."

"What's going on, Mae? Is Taggat all right? Is he sick or something?"

"No, Taggat's not sick." Mae fidgeted in her seat. "Sabrina, I've worked for Taggat for ten years, and I've been in love with him for about the same amount of time. He doesn't know it, but I would do anything in the world for him."

Sabrina smiled and reached across the table and took Mae's hands in hers. "Mae, I think this is wonderful, but why are you telling me? You should be telling him." Sabrina released her grip and leaned back in her chair. "You're not making this confession for my benefit, are you? You're trying to break something to me easy about Taggat or Steve. Right?" Sabrina leaned closer to Mae.

"Okay, Mae. What is it?"

"Sabrina, Taggat loves you very much. He loves you as if you were his own daughter. You've got to believe he would never do anything to hurt you."

"Mae, what does this have to do with Steve?" Sabrina started to rise.

"Sit down, Sabrina. We've just started."

"Then get to the point, or I'm going to march into Taggat's office and get to the bottom of this."

"All right, Sabrina. Two days before you and Steve were scheduled to return from the Island, Mac contacted Taggat. He pressured Taggat to assure Steve's services for the job he is about to undertake. I know you and Steve are under the impression the job involves flying to Washington, but what you both don't know is that Steve won't be coming back today, tonight, or next week."

"What!" Sabrina jumped from her seat. The chair did a back roll onto the floor and up against the wall. Sabrina stood so quickly she became dizzy. She steadied herself against the table and leaned forward resting on her palms. She blinked her eyes a few times, took a deep breath, and looked into Mae's concerned face.

"Sabrina, are you all right?"

"I'm fine! Exactly when will Steve be back?"

"Sabrina, I know this will be hard, but Steve might not be back for six to eight months."

"Months!"

Mae rose from her chair, walked around the table, and picked up the chair. "Sit down, Sabrina. That's not all."

Sabrina eased halfway into her chair, but stopped mid position as Mae finished. "Not all? What else could there be?"

"Sit down, and we'll talk." Mae sat down and motioned for Sabrina to do the same.

"I can't sit. Didn't anyone consider Steve's feelings in all this? It's as if his wishes didn't matter." Sabrina's smile melted. "So, what else is there? You said we hadn't covered all of it." Sabrina sat silently pondering Steve's abrupt absence from her life. She would miss Steve horribly, but this unscheduled interlude would prevent Steve's premature discovery of her pregnancy. And it would make her plan for her and the baby's future more plausible. *Maybe this won't be such a bad thing*, she thought as May watched on with interest.

"Sabrina, Steve has been recruited by the State Department to be the personal pilot for a very important group of Saudi Arabians. He will be ferrying them around the Middle East and Mediterranean for the next eight months, and, we hope an important arrangement concerning oil will come out of their efforts. Mac cooked up the whole plan. Taggat didn't want to help, but Mac threatened Taggat with closure of the bank." Mae knew she had told a little white lie, but she didn't want Sabrina thinking Taggat was looking at monetary gain when it came to a decision about Steve.

"Threatened? That doesn't sound like Mac."

"People do strange things when they have the power to manipulate people. Mac assured Taggat that if he didn't help, he would have the bank shut down and audited by the Federal Reserve Board. Mac's a sly fox, but Taggat doesn't usually let him get the best of him. So, there must be more to it that just idle threats."

"Why should he be threatened? The bank has withstood audits before."

"I'm not sure, Sabrina. I know Taggat feels he has betrayed you and Steve. It tore me apart to see him agonizing with this, and I had to explain it to you before you spoke to him. I'm not meaning to step out of line, but I don't think Taggat would have ever explained all of it to YOU."

Sabrina reached over and clasped Mae's hands. "Thanks, Mae. I think I can see Taggat now."

Mae stood and started out the door.

"When do you think I can contact Steve?"

"Well," May hesitated at the door, "I'm afraid that presents another problem."

"You mean there's more?"

"Yes, unfortunately. Taggat was told there was a communication black out over the project. Nothing in, nothing out. Security reasons. And you're not to mention this to anyone. Otherwise, I think we all could get into a great deal of trouble."

"You mean I can't speak to Steve. At all? I don't believe this!"

"No, not at all, but remember, none of these decisions were Taggat's."

"I know. I know, but it doesn't make it any easier."

They walked from the conference room to Mae's office. Mae looked at Sabrina with eyes searching for understanding for the man she loved. "Remember, he loves you."

Sabrina squeezed May's hands. "I'll be nice." Sabrina turned and walked through Taggat's opened door. Her silent steps across the beige carpet didn't arouse Taggat from his thoughts. "Don't you have the courtesy to welcome me to New York. I missed you on the roof."

Taggat looked up, quickly rose from his chair without wavering, and walked toward Sabrina with his arms outstretched. "Sabrina! How's my favorite girl?"

Sabrina met Taggat kissing him on the cheek while hugging him around the neck. "I prefer the smell of Maker's to Scope."

Taggat backed away, grinned, and leaned on the edge of his desk. "Never could fool you, could I? Are you angry with me, Sabrina?"

"Why should I be angry, Taggat? I know you take a little nip every now and then."

"I don't mean about the liquor."

"Then what are you talking about?"

"I'm talking about Steve. That's what I'm talking about."

"Steve's fine. He just took off for Washington. He'll be back tonight. We have a dinner date." Sabrina nonchalantly walked over to the couch and sat down. She began opening her briefcase acting as if she were ready to transact business as usual.

"Oh, damn! I thought perhaps Mae had told you. You were so late coming down from the heliport."

"Told me what?"

Taggat walked behind his desk, sat down, and opened the drawer containing the Makers Mark. "Sabrina," Taggat picked up the bottle, put it on his desk, looked at the level of the liquid, and placed it back in its hiding place. "Oh, what the hell. I can't feel any worse than I already do." Taggat slid the drawer shut.

Sabrina had silently walked over to Taggat's desk as he was fidgeting with the bottle. She was standing beside him when he looked up. "Taggat, I know about Steve's assignment. Mae told me. I was trying to be difficult. I think I understand what has happened." Sabrina hugged Taggat's neck. "I still love you, you old poop."

Tears filled Taggat's eyes, and he had difficulty clearing the lump from his throat. "I love you, Sabrina. I would rather have gone myself than to put a blemish on your new life."

"We'll survive. We survived this past six months. Surely, we'll survive this." Sabrina tightened her hold on his neck. "You haven't hurt our relationship. My love for you has no conditions."

Taggat tried to clear his throat as he spoke. "If Steve hadn't been such good company to those fellows for the past few weeks, we wouldn't be in such a pickle. The Saudis don't trust their own pilots. They look for experience, and they can afford it. Steve's to be paid over a million dollars for his time."

"We don't need the money. That's not important. But don't fret, Taggat; I'll get through this. I might even be able to use Steve's absence to my advantage." Sabrina released her hold on Taggat's neck and walked back to the couch.

"Your advantage?" Taggat's surprise was only overcome by his curiosity.

"Calm down, Taggat. We'll get to that later." Sabrina sat on the couch. "Wanna know a secret?"

"I'm all ears."

"Mae tells me she has a thing for you. I'm not supposed to tell, but she really cares about you. I was ready to tear you apart today, but Mae set me straight. She's a good lady."

Taggat blushed. "Why are you telling me this? Why doesn't Mae?"

"Taggat, I swear! Mae's not going to do that, and you know it. You're her boss, for heaven's sake. Anyway, it's your place to make the moves, not hers."

"Why do men always have to be the ones to make the moves?"

"They aren't. Women make a lot of advances, but we make the man feel like it's his idea. It's all a part of the game."

"Game? What game?"

"Love, Taggat. Love. Are you immune to the feeling?"

"Not when it comes to you."

"I'm different. I'm talking about the love between a man and a woman."

"You're a woman, aren't you?" Taggat grinned.

"Taggat!"

"All right. I'm sorry. Tell me more. I thought May would have lots of other men in her life. She's a good looking woman—a bit plain, but good looking."

"You better put your glasses on, Taggat. She's been in love with you for the past few years, and you haven't caught the signals."

"I'm not good at sending or catching, Sabrina. Women make me nervous. What the hell would she want with an old dog like me, anyway?"

"Well, give her a try and find out. That's all I'm saying. If Mae finds out I'm the one that told you, she'll kill me." Sabrina looked at Taggat who was looking past the door into Mae's office. "Mae tells me Mac has something on you. I've never known you to let Mac get the upper hand. You want to tell me about it?"

"Sabrina, sometimes we do things we live to regret. At the time they seem right, but we regret them for the rest of our lives."

Sabrina grinned, thought about the pregnancy, and shrugged her shoulders. "I can certainly relate to that."

"The Government permitted me to slip by with something I shouldn't have done in the past. I can't discuss the particulars, but suffice it to say the deed was underhanded enough to put me in jail for a long time. Mac could have used it against me, but instead, I went along with his wishes. I would have done the same thing if I were in his shoes, but it's still a bad way to do business."

"I agree. Who's the lucky person breaking this news to Steve?"

"Paul Peterson is the government's representative. He's going to break the news to Steve when they touch down at Andrews. Mac is supposed to meet them there, and put the icing on the cake. I hope I'm not around when Steve comes home."

Sabrina smiled and winked. "I hope I am. Taggat, don't underestimate Steve's loyalty to you and to his job. He'll be angry, but he won't let personal feelings interfere with duty. However, I wish there were a way to contact him. The communications blackout is the hardest part."

"It's for your protection. Sounds like Mae filled you in completely."

"She keeps her finger on the pulse of the office."

"Sounds like she keeps her ear to the phone."

"Remember, she did this in your interest and not for any personal gain."

"I remember. I'm not going to fire her." Taggat leaned back in his chair and smiled. "That's for sure! But enough of all this. Let's talk about something else."

"What did you have in mind?" Sabrina flashed the engagement ring at Taggat. "You mean this?"

"Exactly! What else could I have meant? When did it happen?"

"The first night we spent on the Island. I was shocked. I never dreamed this would happen. At least not this fast."

"I'm not surprised, and I'm sorry it took this long."

"Me too." Sabrina looked at the ring instantly recalling the night Steve had given it to her.

"Why so solemn, Sabrina?"

"Just thinking."

"Penny for your thoughts?"

Sabrina looked up and smiled. "They won't cost you anything." Sabrina thought for a moment knowing she had to get the big news out immediately.

"Taggat, I'm pregnant." She looked up at Taggat, a tear in her eye. "Now you know what I have done and will regret for the rest of my life."

Taggat walked over and sat beside Sabrina. "It's Pooley's?"

"Who else?" Sabrina wiped her tears and looked surprised.

"You know what I mean."

"I know. I know. I'm upset. How could I have blown this? How could I have been so stupid?"

Taggat tried to comfort Sabrina. "Hold on, Sabrina. I'm sure there's a solution here some place."

Sabrina continued to cry. "I know you're disappointed in me, but I thought…"

"Hush that foolishness right now. I could never be disappointed in you. Does Steve know?"

Sabrina shook her head negatively. "I couldn't tell him. There never was a right time."

"Sabrina do you love Steve, I mean really love him? Don't misunderstand my question. It's important."

"Taggat, I love Steve with ever fiber of my body. I was going to tell him, but Steve scared me when we were talking about my relationship with Kent. If he knew I was pregnant and Kent was the father, I think he would kill Kent."

"Sabrina. You are to never tell Steve any of this. He WOULD kill Pooley."

"You think so, too?"

"I know so." Taggat stood and paced in front of the couch. After a few minutes of thought, he turned to Sabrina. "Sabrina, we're going to let Steve think this is his child. It's going to have to be that way. There is no other solution. Are you willing to go along with me on this? It could work easily or blow up in our faces."

"If it will allow me to keep this baby and have Steve too, it's worth the risk. As a matter of fact, that's exactly what I had planned. I would do anything to insure my child a father."

"When's the baby due?"

"Christmas."

"Good. Steve probably won't be back until after the first of the year."

"So?" Sabrina could hear Taggat's wheels turning.

"So, I think we can swing it. Obviously, you and Steve have had some intimate moments, and without the benefit of contraceptives, I hope."

"Do we really need to get into that?"

"Well? You have, haven't you?"

"Taggat, I'm no saint. I love Steve."

"Fine! That's all I need to know. Sabrina, from this day forward, you must think of your child as Steve's. You must talk of it as Steve's, and most important you must believe it! Pooley is history. Anyway, Steve loves kids. He wouldn't care if you had six or seven."

"God forbid!"

Taggat smiled. "You know what I mean. You two are meant to be together. I won't let this destroy your chance for happiness. Have you seen a doctor?"

"Not formally. I had a pregnancy test performed at one of the local laboratories."

"When?"

"About six weeks ago."

"Damn." Taggat scratched his cheeks and thought. "No problem. Give me the name of the doctor and laboratory where the test was performed. I'll take care of it."

"Take care of what?" Sabrina handed Taggat the papers he requested.

"Don't ask. Who else knows about the pregnancy?"

"Cathy, Kent, Kent's parents, and you."

"That's all?"

"Yes…No, wait. A lady that works in "The Bakery" on the island knows, but I doubt she would remember me. We spoke for a few moments the morning Steve arrived."

"What's her name?"

"Taggat! I don't remember! No…wait a moment." Sabrina envisioned the name tag the lady wore on her white uniform. "Her name is…Rosa! That's it! Rosa. Why is it important?"

"Could be, but don't worry about any of this, Sabrina. I'll take care of everything. Think only of the baby's belonging to Steve. You must keep that thought in your mind so you'll not make any mistakes."

"Mistakes?"

"Yes, mistakes. Anytime you talk of your baby, you must use Steve's name as the father. I'll handle the rest."

"I wish I knew what the devil you're talking about, but I know better than to ask."

"You're right. We'll have to handle this so Steve won't suspect a thing. It might be a bit underhanded, but it's the only way I can assure your happiness. I'll chance anything for that."

Sabrina rubbed her temples. "Okay…"

"Want to take a break?"

"I'd love something to drink…non-alcoholic."

Taggat fingered the intercom. "Mae, bring Sabrina something to drink. How about lemonade for three?"

"Three?"

"Sure! You'll join us won't you?"

"Are you speaking to me, Mr. Delaney?"

"Of course I'm speaking to you. Anyone else out there?"

"No, sir."

"Well, stop the 'sir' stuff, grab some lemonade and come on in here. We have some celebrating to do."

\* \* \*

Sabrina rose from the couch and walked to the picture window occupying the west wall of Taggat's office. She looked at the skyline through the afternoon haze. The sun was setting behind the distant buildings, and the golden halo around each skyscraper gave it lifelike characteristics. The buildings breathed in the force of the city and exhaled the energy of their inhabitants. The hustle and bustle of the throngs moving beneath her made Sabrina wish, but only for a moment, she was living in New York. She turned back toward Taggat. "Taggat, I need to change my will."

"That's the least of our problems. Do you have your changes written."

"Yes." Sabrina went to her briefcase and removed a legal size sheet of paper. She looked at the notes, and then at Taggat. "I want Cathy Winston named as godmother and guardian for my child. She has agreed."

"That's no problem, but you'll have to amend your will after you and Steve are married."

"I'll amend it, but for now, I want it so stated."

"I'll take care of the changes. What else?"

"I want to set up a trust fund for my daughter."

"Daughter?"

"Mother's intuition."

"Oh," Taggat grinned. "Just wondered."

Sabrina smiled, but her smile quickly melted to a thoughtful frown. "If I die before my daughter becomes of legal age…" Sabrina's frown began to quiver on each end, and her eyes filled with tears.

"Sabrina? Are you all right?" Taggat rose from his chair, walked to where she was standing, and led her to the couch where they both sat down. "Now, stop all this will bullshit and tell me what's really bothering you."

"Taggat, I'm frightened. I know it's silly…"

"Wait a minute. What are you frightened of? I told you I would take care of things."

"I know you will. I not afraid about those things."

Sabrina wrung her hands, reached for Taggat's, and grasped them as tightly as she could. "I'm afraid I'm going to die before my baby's born."

Taggat grinned. "Oh, hell…"

"No, Taggat. I'm serious." Tears came to Sabrina's eyes, and she began to shake. "I don't know what's wrong with me. Cathy says it's the pregnancy, and my hormones are all messed up. I'm not sure, but I know I'm scared."

"Sabrina, I'm sorry I laughed. If you're this frightened, let's talk about it. What's got you feeling this way, and I'm not going to blame it on the pregnancy."

Sabrina smiled.

"There. That's better."

"Thanks." Sabrina leaned against Taggat's shoulder. She wiped the tears from her eyes while sniffing back a few more. "I don't know, Taggat. Lately I've been thinking more and more of Mom and Dad. I've had flashbacks of my childhood, and they're coming more frequently. This happened with alarming repetition just after their death, and I thought it was over. But now they're back, and I can't shake them. I can't help but think this is a warning."

"What kind of warning?"

"A warning that it will soon be my turn."

"Your turn? Your turn to do what?"

Sabrina sat upright and looked at Taggat with surprise. "Why, my turn to die!"

"To die! Bullshit, Sabrina. Don't get me wrong. I'm not making fun of your feelings, but this is a normal reaction to the stress you've been under lately."

"How can stress do this to me?"

"I don't know, Sabrina. I leave that up to the shrinks, but I know I went through some of the same things when my father died."

"You? Surely not!"

"Why not? I'm no different than any one else. We all experience grief differently."

"Grief? My grief is over."

"It's never over, Sabrina. You just learn to cope with it better as time goes by. Your dreams are trips to more pleasant times, times when your parents could give you all the answers. You're wanting your Mom and Dad to take over and solve your problems."

"What are you, a psychiatrist or a lawyer?"

"From what I've paid in the past for therapy, a little bit of both."

Sabrina laughed. "So you don't think these dreams mean I'm going to die."

"Nah. They help you cope, that's all. And, unless you allow them to rule your life, they're healthy. The mind needs an outlet. You keep on dreaming. Believe me. It's cheaper than Psychiatry."

Sabrina smiled, leaned her head back on Taggat's shoulder, and hugged his neck. "Well, from now on, if I want someone to answer my questions and take care of my problems, I'll know where to come. And it won't be in my dreams. I love you, Taggat."

"I'm always here, Sabrina."

Sabrina squeezed Taggat's arm tighter. "Come on. Let's do some baby shopping. Maybe this little girl's grandfather would like to buy her a present."

"I'd love to."

They both cleared the tears from their eyes and walked out of the room arm in arm.

"Bloomingdales is only a few blocks down the street, isn't it? They have nice things there." Sabrina grinned.

"For whom, the baby or her mother?"

"Both!" Sabrina winked at Mae as she led Taggat out the door, confident he could solve all her problems. "Be back afterwhile, Mae. Then you can have him."

Mae and Taggat both blushed.

# 11

Takeoff from Kennedy had been on time, and the new navigational computer Jerry had installed functioned perfectly. When Steve achieved the assigned altitude and vectored to Andrews, he engaged the Lear's autopilot. He cycled through the flight plan in his on board computer, and if he remained on schedule, his plan to land at Kennedy at 5:15 P.M. would put him home forty five minutes before Sabrina returned. Then, they could have a comfortable evening at his apartment.

The clear weather and his cruising altitude of twenty-five thousand feet, enabled Steve to observe the ground patterns as they passed quickly beneath the nose of the Lear. His flight plan took them down the Delaware River, across the neck of the DelMarVa Pennisula and into the upper tributaries of the Chesapeake. As MacKenzie Island passed a mere two hundred miles south of his present position, Steve's thoughts turned to the three days he had spent with Sabrina. He was shocked she had so quickly agreed to marry him, but he wasn't about to question fate. He finally felt as if his life was acquiring some semblance of order.

As the Western Shore of the Bay slipped beneath his windscreen, Steve disengaged the autopilot and took manual control of the Lear. He could see the faint outline of Cape St. Claire on the edge of the Bay and the bigger outline of Annapolis just over his nose. He was fifty miles from the Andrews VOR station according to his DME. As he leisurely looked down to recheck his communication radio's tuned frequency, the sudden voice in his headset caused his head to snap to the view through the windscreen.

"Attention Unidentified Aircraft; heading 225; flight level 250. This is Andrews Air Force Base Control Tower. You are entering restricted airspace. Please identify. Over."

"Roger, Andrews. Lear DHJ-003. Flight level 250; heading 225; airspeed 375. Special flight for assistant Secretary Peterson. Landing instructions requested. Over."

"One moment DHJ-003. Uh?…003, we have no approval for your flight. Please divert. Over."

Steve edged around in his seat and yelled through the opened cockpit door. "Hey, Paul. Get up here on the double and talk to these fellows before we're history…

Hold on, Andrews. Keep the big guns on the ground. I've got Mr. Peterson coming to the radio. Over."

"Please divert 003. We have visual of your aircraft. If you do not divert within thirty seconds, we must instruct our fighters to destroy you."

"Come on, Paul! These boys usually mean what they say." Steve knew two jet jockeys were on his tail, and he was sure one of them had a heat seeking missile locked on one of his fuselage engines. "This plane's gonna heat up quick if you don't say the right words to these fellows."

Paul slowly eased into the co-pilot seat and put on his headset. "Andrew's Tower, this is Assistant Secretary of State, Paul Peterson. Special flight plan code 11345. Please check your data file. Acknowledge."

The temporary communication delay made Steve nervous. He looked to the left and right, but the Lear's windscreen made visual identification of anything to the rear virtually impossible. However, Steve knew they were there.

"Captain Hardesty and I are expected by Secretary of State Orberson. Over."

Steve looked at Paul and questioned the use of his ex-Navy rank. "What's this 'Captain' crap?"

Paul smiled. "We'll talk about that later."

"Roger, Lear DHJ-003, we have your flight plan, and it is confirmed. over."

"Leahr Oh-Oh-Three, come to a headin' of 270, descend to Angels five, maintain airspeed of 350 knots. Ovuh."

The strange Southern drawl interrupted the silence of their headsets. The communication came from one of the fighter pilots, but Steve still couldn't see him.

"270, five thousand feet, 350 knots, understood." Steve grinned, trimmed the aircraft, and mischievously looked at Paul. "Let's just see how slow he can fly that damned jet."

"What the hell are you doing?"

"Oh, hell. Sit back and enjoy. They know who we are now. Let's have a little fun. I want to see what the boy's are flying today."

"You goddamn jet jockeys are all alike!" Paul cinched himself tighter into the seat.

Steve changed heading, cut power, and allowed the Lear to slowly settle to five thousand feet. At altitude he powered up to maintain cruise at 200 knots. "They can't remain at this speed without my seeing them soon." He added a little power and began weaving back and forth in a slow sissors maneuver. "This will bring them in closer."

"Closer!" Paul tried to pull the harness strap tighter, but he had already cinched it as tight as it would go.

"Leahr Oh-Oh-Three, remain on your present heading. We're not plannin' to splash you, Cap'n. This is Majuh Ted Conolley. I'm the leaduh of a flight of two Falcons at your six o'clock high. I will identify visually." Ted Conolley powered up the F-16 and pulled along side the Lear's left front windscreen. He held his position fifty feet off the Lear's left wingtip.

Paul looked out his right window and then to his left. The nose of the F-16 surprised him. "Look out! He's going to hit us!"

Steve looked to his left and saw the pointed nose of the F-16 ease up even with the Lear. "Nah, he's just trying to get our attention."

Paul squirmed in his seat. "Well, he certainly got mine!"

Steve fired a salute to the F-16 pilot, and it was returned. "Good to see you, Major. I was wondering where you were hiding. This Lear isn't quite as easy to see out of as a F-4. Where's your wingman?"

"Understood, Captain. See you on the ground." The F-16 suddenly raised the nose and rolled left. Steve knew the wingman had his plane missle-locked the entire time his lead was along side. The F-16 pilot would keep them in his sights until the Lear touched down. These fellows took no chances even when a flight plan had been filed. They never knew when some fanatic might try and fly a plane-load of TNT or similar explosive into the center of the base trying to reenact the Kamikaze routine of late World War II.

"Lear 003, come left to 180, intercept glidepath at 15 miles. Then turn left to 090. Tower, out."

"Roger, Tower, understood." Steve followed the instructions and intercepted the glideslope. He traced the electronic path onto the runway and set the Lear down with expertise. As he applied his wheelbrakes, he looked up and saw the underside of the F-16 pass no more than fifty feet overhead. "Nice flying, Major."

Steve got no reply...as expected.

"Taxi to Hanger 43 and roll the Lear inside. She has to be refitted for our trans-Atlantic flight." Paul instructed Steve without looking up from his notes. "Mr. Orberson informed me he would meet us there."

"Wait a damned minute. This Lear is heading back for New York. What in the hell are you talking about? And, what is all this talk about me being a Captain?"

"I think we better complete this discussion in Mr. Orberson's presence."

"Well, someone better do some explaining fast. I'm planning to take off for Kennedy as soon as I can have the tanks topped off."

"Please, pull into the hanger. We'll talk about it."

Steve followed instructions and brought the Lear to rest in Hanger 43. The engines wound down, and Air Force ground crewmen surrounded the plane to chock the wheels.

"Follow me, Steve," Paul said as he picked up his briefcase and headed for the door.

Steve opened the door allowing Paul to deplane and followed him down the steps. As they stepped off the plane, ground crewmen headed up the gangway.

"Hold on, fellows." Steve held out his arm to halt the progress of the first Air Force man up the steps. "Unless your planning to sweep up the place, I'd prefer you stayed out of my jet."

Paul stepped between Steve and the Air Force Sergeant. He grasped Steve's arm and attempted to press it down. However, Steve's strength wouldn't permit success. "Calm down, Steve. These guys are only doing their job. I'll explain all of this as soon as we get to someplace more private."

Steve's building anger began to ebb. Reluctantly, he lowered his arm and allowed the men to enter his plane. "Paul, this better be good, or you and I are going to go 'round and 'round." Steve quickly turned and huffed his way across the hanger. As he and Paul walked across the concrete, Steve observed the line of fuel trucks and flight engineers readying for the attack on his Lear. "I'm getting negative vibes about all this Paul. Now, what the hell is going on?"

"It will all be clear momentarily."

Steve and Paul entered the small office at the end of the hanger where Mac was waiting for their arrival. Mac approached Paul as they came through the door. "Paul! Better late than never." Mac Orberson motioned for Paul and Steve to have a seat at the table. "Steve, I've not seen you for a while. How are you?"

"I'm fine, Mac. I mean, Mr. Secretary. What the hell is going on here?"

"Paul, doesn't Steve know what we're doing here?"

"Not as yet, Mr. Secretary," Paul sheepishly replied.

"Mac smiled at Steve. "Excuse us for a moment, Steve...Paul, join me outside."

As Mac closed the door, he looked into Paul's surprised face.

"I thought we were assuming all the blame. I was leaving the briefing up to you...us. I'm sorry if I misunderstood." Paul quickly attempted to clarify his understanding as to Steve's briefing status.

"Take it easy, Paul. Follow my lead. I think this will turn out better. Come on. Let's get back inside before our pilot gets upset."

"Yes, let's. I've seen Steve upset, and it's not a pretty picture."

Mac and Paul reentered the conference room. "Sorry for the delay, Steve. Now, where were we? Oh, yes. Steve, I had hoped Taggat would have filled you in on the particulars of your new job."

"Just a damned minute." Steve interrupted. "What's Taggat got to do with this? Maybe someone should start from the beginning. And, I assume there will be no return flight to Kennedy. Right?"

Mac didn't speak. Instead, he opened his briefcase and handed a envelope to Steve. "Open the envelope and look over its contents."

"Mac, what the hell's happening?"

"Look at the contents, Steve. Then we'll talk."

Steve opened the envelope and removed several photographs. The photos were old, but Steve could readily identify Taggat and a heavy-set gentleman seated at an outdoor cafe. Taggat was passing a briefcase to the gentleman in the next photo and an obvious exchange of briefcases took place during the session. The last photo was of Taggat entering the Swiss Bank of Lucerne.

"These are pretty old, aren't they?"

Mac looked sternly at Steve. "Age makes no difference, Steve. The photos you are looking at are of your business partner and a known Russian black marketeer, Dimitri Constantine. Taggat sold computer chips to the Russians in that exchange. According to the deposit he made in his Swiss account, the exchange netted him two million dollars. The C.I.A. followed Taggat during that trip and made these photos. They knew he was about to make the exchange and elected not to intervene. As it turns out, the chips weren't state of the art and were two major upgrades behind existing technology. However, the Russians were in need of those chips to maintain their missle development."

"In other words, the U.S. approved the sell."

"Somewhat. However, the government reprimanded Taggat and struck a deal. In exchange for dismissal of charges and return of funds, Taggat gave the C.I.A. names of his Russian contacts. However, he never returned the funds. Recent philosophical changes in administration permitted reopening of the case. I proposed the possibilities to Taggat, and he agreed to help us in this endeavor."

"Help you? How?"

"By giving you to us…your services, that is."

"I don't understand. Exactly what have I been volunteered for?"

"The group of Arab sheiks you chauffeured for the past couple of weeks, specifically Armani, have requested you to be their pilot for the next series of negotiations in connection with development of an important oil pipeline in the Middle East."

Steve looked down at the photos. He knew Taggat had been put in a difficult situation, and he knew the government could do a number of things to force Taggat to see things their way. He understood Taggat's submission to Mac, but he wished he had been made privy to the situation. Hell, he would have said yes. He loved this stuff. If it weren't for his engagement with Sabrina, he would gladly leave. A change of scenery was always good. "What do I have to do?"

"The job involves six to nine months of flying the oil shieks around the Mediterranean. The majority of the trips would be between Riyadh and Cairo, but over the next months you will visit all the Common Market capitals. Evidently, you impressed these gentlemen with your level of entertainment. They want you and only you for the job."

"Well, I don't want to spend the next six months being an entertainer or a pimp for the Arabs. Hell, that's all I did. I just tried to show them a good time. That's what Taggat told me to do." Steve smiled. "Those fellows can really party."

"We aren't asking you to entertain them. What we're looking for is security. We want to make sure they get where they are going and make the deals they need to make for the development of this project. That's your job. You are our assurance of safe travel for the Saudis. Armani is very perceptive in his refusal of a Saudi national for their pilot. They are too easily bribed into being at the wrong place at the right time. Access to the plane, or the ambassadors would be simple for Iraqi or Iranian terrorists. They wouldn't last three months. Any questions?"

"What are you fellows prepared to do to Taggat if I refuse. I'm sure there are numerous pilots you trust who can do the job proficiently."

"You're the only ONE Armani will agree to. He has placed a ban on our use of military pilots."

"And, if I don't agree, what? I've had a major change in my life since Taggat agreed to this tour for me."

Mac looked at Steve, reopened his briefcase, and handed Steve a small group of letters. The envelopes were addressed to Taggat Delaney, Planter's Bank, and the Flight Service. "The Federal Reserve and the I.R.S. are prepared to close your businesses tomorrow. Taggat will be charged with treason, and Planter's Bank would be temporarily closed pending an audit and investigation for the possibility of laundering Taggat's illicit earnings from the sale of the computer chips."

"You said a deal had been made? How can you do this? Especially to Taggat."

"This was the only way I could be assured I had you. It's business, Steve."

Steve could handle the closing of the flight service, and he knew Taggat could beat the Attorney General if given enough time. However, he didn't want Sabrina to live through the humiliation of closure of the bank. He couldn't put her into that compromise. "You're a bunch of real nice guys. You know most of this would never stick."

"Maybe, but we could make it pure hell for Taggat, Captain."

"And, what's with this Captain crap?"

"Paul?" Mac turned to Paul Peterson and furrowed his brow. "Doesn't the Captain know about his re-enlistment?"

"Re-enlistment, HELL!" Steve leaned against the table. "I'm tired of taking orders."

Paul handed Steve the envelope he had picked up from the Pentagon. "Steve, by executive order from the President and the Department of the Navy you have been reinstated into the military at the Naval rank of Captain."

Steve read the letter and laid the papers down on the table in front of him. "Okay, I'll do it. Not for you, not for the U.S., not for Taggat, but I'll do it for Sabrina."

"Excellent! We'll prepare for your departure." Mac turned toward Paul and lifted his hand in the direction of the door. "Paul, go assure that preparation is underway. I would like for you two to be in Riyadh by tomorrow evening, Washington time."

Paul closed his briefcase, stood up, and headed out the door. He turned back and looked at Steve's scornful gaze. "Steve, I'm sorry things had to be done this way, truly sorry."

"I'm sure. Oh, by the way, Paul."

"Yes?" Paul looked back at Steve hoping for forgiveness. "Don't bother my jet!"

"Sure." Paul shrugged his shoulders, turned and walked from the room. He wasn't sure how Mac continued to tolerate the things that had to be done to accomplish the work.

"Don't chastise Paul." Mac Orberson was closing his briefcase and preparing to rise. "He's following my orders. I'm the dirty rotten scoundrel in this scenario. Any animosity may be sent in my direction. I've become very thick skinned."

"Hold on a moment, Mac. You and I aren't finished."

"Steve, I have some pending appointments. I must get back to the State Department. Paul will fill in any details. I'm sorry, but I must leave. Have a good trip, and be careful. There're a lot of people in this world that would like to see your assignment fail."

Steve jumped from his seat and physically placed his body between Mac and the door. "You're going to listen to me for a minute. I've put up with your bullshit, told you I would do the job, and taken my re-enlistment rather well. The least you could do is sit down for a moment and listen to me."

Mac let out a long sigh. He looked a his watch, turned around and sat back down at the table. "You're absolutely right. Sometimes I forget I'm a person."

Steve sat caddie-corner to Mac and looked him in the eye. "I'm going to do this for one reason, Mac…Sabrina. I can't see her hurt, and you and I both know that if you closed the bank, it would kill her. Sabrina and I are engaged."

Mac melted a few degrees, thought about the upcoming marriage of his own daughter, and shook Steve's hand. "Congratulations, Steve. I didn't know." Mac thought for a moment.

"What is it, Mac?" Steve thought he had heard all the bad news he could stand. He prepared for some more.

"Steve, the President has placed a communications blackout on all participants in this project." Before Steve could reply, Mac decided to give him a rundown of the facts of the mission. "You are taking part in a project that could prove to be the final hurdle to the United States in freeing itself from dependency on oil shipments through the Persian Gulf. If Armani can swing the deals, a series of oil pipelines will stream into the

Mediterranean from Saudi Arabia. The U.S. will be able to tank all its oil from the Med straight to the East Coast and bypass the Gulf. Not only will we secure a steady flow of "safe oil" for the United States, but we'll also lock up a re-election for the present administration."

"I don't give one big damn about your administration's re-election, but I do care about Sabrina and Taggat. I don't like the communications blackout. They never work, but I'll live with it. What I do want is your word that those files on Taggat will be lost…permanently, and that topic will never come up again. Otherwise, I'll fly your little Arab buddies straight into the Red Sea. Understand?"

"You're bluffing! You know I can't destroy government files."

"I've warned you. If I don't get confirmation in your agreement to do this by the time we land in Saudi Arabia, your oil shieks won't live a month. I mean it, Mac."

Mac got up, walked to the door, and turned back to Steve. "I'll think about it, Steve. That's all I can do."

"You've got," Steve looked at his watch, "…thirty-six hours."

Mac walked out, closed the door, and smiled. He had Steve and Taggat where he wanted them. For the same price, he had won the reluctant assistance of them both.

Steve rose from the table and followed Mac through the door. He reentered the hanger, passed the busy ground crew, and walked outside. He looked back towards the direction of New York City. "I love you, Sabrina." He stood there momentarily, took a deep breath, and did an about face. He walked back into the hanger and found the head ground mechanic. "Now, show me just what the hell you're doing to my aircraft."

The mechanic looked up at Steve. He recognized him from the briefing the Secretary of State and Base Commander had with the crew. "Yes Sir, Captain." The sergeant fired Steve a salute.

The rush Steve got with the salute was inexplicable. *I can't help it, but I do love it,* he thought as he reviewed the particulars of the refitting.

# 12

"Does everything seem in order?" Taggat looked across his desk to where Sabrina sat on the couch. Her long black hair flowed over her left shoulder and fell close to the documents she was reading. She wore a white cotton skirt and a light blue silk blouse. A thin black leather belt wrapped her trim waist. Sabrina's right leg was over her left in a ladylike fashion, and the plain leather high heel shoe dangled off the tip of her toes. She rhythmically kicked her foot and chewed on the erasure end of a pencil as she read the new will.

Sabrina finished the last page of the document and tossed it beside her on the couch. She took a long drink from the glass of orange juice before placing it back on the coffee table in front of her. Then, she looked at Taggat noticing a smile his face. "What are you thinking about?"

"The pregnancy becomes you, Sabrina. I've never seen you looking better."

Sabrina flipped her hair behind her back, took a deep breath, and settled back on the couch. "Thanks, but it's a front. I'm tired. I slept well, but I must not have gotten my nap out." She took a few deep breaths while massaging the middle of her sternum. "I'm glad I'm seeing the doctor next week. I want to make sure this tiredness and shortness of breath are just effects of the pregnancy." Sabrina gestured toward the new will. "When did you get a chance to work on this? I'm impressed!"

"I'm glad you're seeing him next week, too. He'll alleviate some of your anxieties." Taggat put on his reading glasses and looked down at the document. "After I dropped you off at the house last evening, Mae and I came back to the office."

"You were supposed to take her out for drinks. Won't you ever learn?" Sabrina gave Taggat a look of exasperation.

Taggat peered over his glasses at Sabrina's furrowed brow and pursed lips. "I'm learning, but we did have work to do."

"All work and no play makes Taggat a dull boy." Sabrina smiled.

"Don't worry, Taggat still knows how to play." He readjusted his reading glasses. "Mae assigned two of the paralegals to stay on last night and begin work on the will. We wrapped up around two a.m.

"I think we've covered all the bases. Would you agree?" Taggat removed his glasses, and looked at Sabrina. "By the way, I took Mae home last night. Then we had drinks."

"Well, good for you. Did you give her a kiss goodnight?"

"Oh, hush. I do good work, but I don't work that fast."

Sabrina picked the papers off the couch and tapped the lead point of her pencil on its first page. "It's perfect. I'm ready to sign." She looked up from the packet of papers. "When's Johnny arriving?"

"He should be here in thirty minutes." Taggat called Mae and two of the other secretaries to come into his office. They completed signing the documents, and Taggat gave them to Mae for her notary. "We'll pick up Sabrina's copy on the way out, Mae."

"Fine, I'll have it ready." Mae gathered the papers and returned to her desk.

Taggat rose from his chair, walked to the couch, and sat down beside Sabrina. He took her hands in his and held tightly. "I was worried about you last night. Any more dreams?"

Sabrina squeezed Taggat's strong hands, and looked him in the eye. She always felt secure in his presence. "No dreams." She looked down at their intermeshed hands. "I think I'm worse when I'm alone. I need to have someone close to me." She looked back at Taggat. "Someone I love." Sabrina leaned over and kissed Taggat's cheek. "And Taggat, I do love you."

"I love you, Sabrina. As long as I'm alive, you'll never be alone." Taggat hugged Sabrina. He leaned back and wiped a small tear from Sabrina's right eye. "We all face problems in our life. No one gets out of this existence without a little adversity. Hell, if they did, there wouldn't have to be attorneys."

Sabrina laughed. "I've never thought of it quite like that. I guess you're right."

"There! You look better when you smile. I know you have a lot on your mind. Let me handle this thing about Kent, and I'll, somehow, get in touch with Steve. I promise. Don't add that to your worry list. Deal?"

"Okay, I'll try. No promises, but I'll try."

"Good enough." Taggat's phone beeped. He got up and walked over to his desk, and punched the intercom key on the phone set. "Yes, Mae?"

"The helicopter is on approach. Johnny should be landing within the next four or five minutes."

"Thanks." Taggat released the key, and looked back at Sabrina.

Sabrina closed her briefcase, stood up, and straightened her skirt. "I guess it's time to go," she sighed. "I've GOT to get back to work!"

"Sabrina, don't be such a stranger. I'd almost forgot how much I liked you being around." Taggat picked up Sabrina's briefcase. "I'll carry this."

They stopped in Mae's office, and Taggat placed the notarized copy of the new will in Sabrina's briefcase. He looked at Mae. "Well, aren't you coming?"

"Me?" Mae stood quickly before Taggat could change his mind. "Yes, I'd love to."

Sabrina grinned, but not so Taggat could see her. "Come on you two! Johnny will be waiting."

They silently rode the elevator to the roof, each wondering what the events of the past few days would mean to their future. The car glided to a stop with a pneumatic whoosh, and the door opened. The helicopter was waiting on the pad.

Sabrina took the briefcase, grasped Taggat's hand, and kissed his cheek. "It won't be so long between visits, I promise. Why don't you both wait inside? I don't like mushy good-byes." Sabrina turned to go out the door, but something made her turn and walk back to Taggat. She gave him another hug and kiss. "I love you, Taggat. I've never felt closer to you than I do now. Thanks for your help and advice." She turned and walked away before Taggat could speak. Sabrina quickly covered the distance to the helicopter, and got in. She looked back to the elevator enclosure and saw Taggat place his right arm around Mae's shoulder. *All right, Taggat!,* she thought as she buckled her harness. She turned to Johnny and gave him the thumbs up sign for departure.

Johnny increased throttle and pulled up on the collective. The Bell seemed to leap into the air. He kicked in right pedal, and the nose of the Jet Ranger rotated to his command. He eased the cyclic forward, and the nose headed for Kennedy. Johnny motioned for Sabrina to put on her headset. "I have the Beechcraft ready for departure. When we get back to Kennedy, you can go ahead and board while I clear up any glitches with the flight plan."

Sabrina nodded her head affirmatively, but her thoughts drifted out over the Atlantic in search of Steve. She had faith Taggat would make things right. But how? How could he erase Kent's paternity. Too many knew of it! She took a deep breath but felt as if she wasn't getting enough air. She disregarded her shortness of breath as anxiety and smiled. "I'll just have to be like Scarlet O'Hara and think about that tomorrow."

The helicopter put down in front of Hardesty and Delaney Hanger Five. Johnny secured the craft, opened his door, and looked at Sabrina. "You okay?"

"Just a little tired. It's been an eventful two days."

"I can imagine. The Beech is over in Hanger Six. I'll be there in a few minutes."

Sabrina picked up her briefcase and walked across the tarmac to the hanger. She climbed aboard the Beechcraft Model 99 airliner. The outside of the plane was painted in the same motif as the Lear, and the cabin was fitted with the same amenities. The passenger area had been refurbished with comfortable swivel chairs. The forward area had a small game table, refrigerator, television, and VCR. The carpet was a cream color, and the furniture shown in matching maroon leather. Sabrina took a 7-Up from the refrigerator, and after drinking about half the soda, discarded the rest. She eased into one of the recliner chairs, locked the back in the reclining position, fastened her seat belt, closed her eyes, and was asleep by the time Johnny returned to the plane.

\* \* \*

"Sabrina, wake up! It's time to get ready for school." Linda MacKenzie's voice carried up the stairs of the Boston townhouse and into Sabrina's bedroom.

The seventeen year old, black haired girl sat up in bed, looked over at her clock radio, frowned and lay back down. "I'm not going! I'm never going back to that school for as long as I live." Sabrina pulled the covers over her head.

"Well, you better die quickly because by the time I get upstairs you are to be out of bed, dressed, and ready to go." Linda waltzed into Sabrina's room, opened the curtains, went to the head of Sabrina's bed, and jerked back the covers. Sabrina lay nude, exposed to the world. "Sabrina! What have I told you about sleeping in the nude?"

The morning sun beamed through the panes and focused on Sabrina's face. "Mother! Close those curtains! Now! You know I hate light this early in the morning, and please no more lectures about my sleep attire. I'm comfortable." Sabrina blindly searched for her sheet.

Linda kept the sheet from Sabrina's reach. "Why aren't you feeling like school today?"

Sabrina tried to wind herself in her blanket. When she saw it was a losing battle, she sat up and looked her mother in the eye. "I'm not going because you won't let Steve take me to the Prom. I even told some of my friends he was coming. I can't show my face, now. I'm so embarrassed."

"Well, Sabrina, it sounds as if you dug your own little hole, and you'll have to figure your own way out. But let's not complicate things by getting into trouble at school." Linda walked behind Sabrina's sitting body. She leaned over and lightly slapped Sabrina's butt. "So, let's go!"

Sabrina jumped up and pouted off to the bathroom. She looked back at her mother as she rubbed her assaulted cheek. "How juvenile!"

"You know, Sabrina. It's hard enough to live in reality. Don't complicate your life by telling lies. You won't forget the truth, but the lies you tell will haunt YOU."

Sabrina had been mouthing the well-recognized speech her mother had dictated for the past ump-teen years. "Please, Mother! Not the lie sermon. I've heard it too many times, all ready."

"It must not have sunken into that pretty head."

Sabrina lowered her voice, and tried to sound solicitous. "I know how to settle all my problems."

"How's that? I'm all ears."

Sabrina leaned so that her head would be visible through the bathroom door. "You and Daddy could let Steve take me. I've asked a million times. I think he likes me, and, anyway he's a hunk."

Linda threw a towel at Sabrina's head. "Take your shower, young lady. You know your Father and I have discussed this matter, and we feel Steve is much too old for you."

"He's only seven years older." Sabrina looked back through the door. "Daddy's eight years older than you." She grinned and stuck out her tongue.

Linda's aim was better with the second towel. When Sabrina's tongue was stuck out and her eyes closed, the cotton projectile hit her in the face. "That's different. Later in your life, those years won't seem as significant as they are now. Anyway, we're the bosses; so no dating Steve. That's final!"

"Oh, pooh! If you let me go with Steve, I'll go look at that private school in Atlanta like you want me too. Otherwise, I'm staying right herel."

"You'll go anyway, if I say so."

"Will not!"

"Sabrina, get ready for school. We'll talk about the school in Atlanta later…Honestly!"

"If you don't let me go with Steve, I'll be the laughing stock of the junior class, and it will be all your fault."

"My fault? It's of your own doing." Linda walked into the bathroom and gave Sabrina's nude body a hug. "Remember, we love you, and we're trying to do the best things we can for you. I know you have trouble realizing that now, but someday, when you have a daughter of your own, you will."

"How can I have a daughter? YOU won't let me date any neat men."

"Hush! You're not supposed to talk about such things."

"Oh, Mother! Get real!"

"I'll show you 'real'! Now, quit trying to put off the inevitable and get ready!"

Sabrina shrugged her shoulders, stepped into the shower, and turned on the hot water. The steam condensed quickly on the cool shower enclosure.

Linda walked into the bathroom and looked at Sabrina through the door. "Your father might drop by this morning on his way back from the airport. Steve will probably be with him. They should be here before you leave for school."

Sabrina had just started washing her hair. "Mother! Why didn't you tell me sooner? I'm going to be a mess when he gets here. My hair will still be wet. Really!"

"What's the matter with that? Your father has seen you with wet hair. Don't worry." Linda smiled.

"Don't be funny." Sabrina called out from the shower. She could barely make out her mother's form on the other side of the door. "You know why I'm upset."

"I know. I was just kidding. By the way, your father thinks it will be all right if Steve takes you flying this weekend, but if you think you'll be too busy with the prom, I guess Steve will understand."

"I don't believe this! You let me get in the shower and then start telling me all this. May I really go flying? Really? I thought you and Daddy didn't want me to go. When can I go? Will Steve know about that this morning?" Sabrina was looking through the door and trying to see her Mother. Her form was becoming more difficult to make out. She turned off the shower and wiped the mist from the glass door. She still couldn't see her. She tried to open the door, but it wouldn't budge.

"Mother?! Where are you?" Sabrina called out. The mist kept accumulating even though the shower was off.

"I'm here, Sabrina. I'll always be here when you need me. Come to me and I'll make things better. Everything will be all right if you come to me."

Sabrina was frightened, her heart seemed to skip a beat while the mist made it difficult to breathe. "I can't come. Not now. I have too many things to do. I'm going to have a baby. I'm going to marry Steve. I don't want to die. I don't want to die."

"We love you very much, Sabrina. We'll be here when you're r...e...a...d...y." The voice became fainter.

"Mother, where are you? I'm frightened!" Sabrina tried to free herself from the shower, but now she couldn't find the door. She wasn't even sure she was in the shower any longer. The mist thickened, and she ran toward where she thought the door should be. "Help me, mother! Help me! I don't know what to do. I'm so alone. I need you. Help me!"

The mist engulfed her, and her feet were suddenly caught in a soft mire that was previously the tiled shower floor. She began to sink…deeper and deeper. She sank to her neck and stopped. Suddenly, the mire turned to sand and the smell of salt water filled the air. Waves began breaking around her head. They rushed toward her, engulfed her head, and just before she felt she would drown, they receded permitting her to breathe. When she could breathe, she used every ounce of strength to yell for help.

\* \* \*

Johnny left the pilot seat after adjusting the auto pilot. He thought he had heard Sabrina yelling. He was shocked to find her motionless in the chair. She was breathing, but her color was poor. He checked her pulse. It was fast. "Sabrina! Are you all right?" Johnny placed the emergency oxygen mask over Sabrina's face, set her upright in the chair, and continued to stimulate her by slapping the backs of her hands. "Sabrina? Please wake up. Please." He rechecked her pulse…one hundred and fifty.

\* \* \*

Suddenly, Sabrina felt as if she had been hit in the head with a mallet. There was something on her face. She wanted it off, but it seemed to keep the water out and helped her breathe. She saw someone through the water. It was a man, and he was holding her hand.

"Daddy? Is that you?"

\* \* \*

"Sabrina! Talk to me. It's Johnny. What's wrong?"

Sabrina opened her eyes. She was awake. The surroundings of the plane slowly became familiar. She blinked her eyes, and smiled at Johnny from behind the mask.

"Sabrina, you've scared me to death. What's wrong?"

She could barely breathe, much less speak. Her chest hurt terribly. "Hospital. Quick. My heart!"

Johnny left the oxygen running at the full flow rate. He placed a blanket over Sabrina's lower body, left her in the sitting position, and pulled the harness tightly around her. He ran to the cockpit and quickly settled back into his seat.

"Norfolk Control! Norfolk Control! This is Beechcraft DHP-002. I am fifty miles to your northeast on a heading of 220. Flight level 180. I am declaring an emergency. I need a straight in approach. Over."

"Roger, Beech DHP-002. Squawk 1600. What is the nature of your emergency?"

"Norfolk Control. I have a medical emergency on board. Twenty five year old woman with a history of heart trouble. She's had a fainting episode, and is now having trouble breathing. I need an ambulance standing by. Over."

"Roger, DHP-002. We have you on radar . There will be no need for further transmission. We will have a medical team standing by. Vector 225 for Runway 27. Skies are 2000 feet overcast; temperature seventy-two degrees; wind is 15 knots from 250; there's a slight drizzle. You will make an ILS approach to Runway 27. ILS VOR is 117.4. You're fifty miles from touchdown. Pick up the glideslope at fifteen miles at 3000 feet. Over."

"Roger, Control. Vectoring to 225. Descending to flight level 30. Tuning to 117.4." Johnny turned and looked back at Sabrina. Her color seemed better. "I'll have us down in ten minutes."

Sabrina could barely bring her hand up, but she managed to give Johnny the thumbs up.

"DHP-002, you have cleared the outer marker. On glidepath. Ten miles from touchdown."

Johnny couldn't watch Sabrina any longer. He had to give his undivided attention to the instruments. He prayed she'd be all right.

"Three miles to touchdown. On glidepath. The ambulance will be at the end of 27. We have two paramedics and a doctor from Norfolk General waiting. Exit runway to your right. Access area will be two hundred feet to the left. One mile. On glidepath. You should have runway in sight. Good luck DHP-002. Over."

"Roger, Control. Thanks!" Johnny could see the runway. He was at full flaps, and holding a little left rudder against the left to right quartering crosswind. The twin engine Beechcraft touched down on center line and rolled to the end of the runway. Johnny could see the ambulance off to his right, and he guided the plane to within fifty feet of the vehicle. He idled down, and the paramedics chocked the wheels. Johnny feathered the props and jumped from his seat to pop the hatch. The doctor and the paramedics were in the plane before the ladder hit the ground.

The apparent leader of the trio looked up at a bewildered Johnny. "What do we have?"

"I'm not sure? I couldn't arouse her after hearing her call for help. She has a heart problem. That's all I know. Uh…and…and when she was breathing it sounded like she was congested, so I set her up and gave her oxygen. Please help her."

They wired Sabrina to their EKG and switched her over to their own oxygen supply. The doctor listened to Sabrina's lungs and looked back at Johnny.

"Good thinking to sit her up. You probably saved her life."

Johnny was so nervous he had continued to back from the scene until he sat down in one of the chairs. He almost cried in relief when he saw that Sabrina was doing better.

Dr. Sam Shepherd, a second year resident in Internal Medicine, had been making emergency calls with the EMT's for the past three weeks. The call to the airport had been yet another welcomed diversion from the routine of hospital work. He ordered the paramedics to start an I.V. in Sabrina's left hand while he prepared medication. Sam looked directly into Sabrina's eyes. "You're an awfully young lady to have something like this happen. What heart problems do you have? I know you have a murmur, but I didn't spend much time checking. You're in heart failure!"

Sabrina looked at the blond haired physician through a clouded haze. All she could muster was a gurgled whisper. "Rheumatic Fever."

"Oh!" Sam reached over and picked up a vial of Lasix, a potent diuretic. He stuck it into the I.V. line.

Sabina could barely move her arm, but she managed to grab Dr. Shepherd's forearm before he injected the medication.

Sam looked up from his attention to the syringe. "Don't be frightened. This will help get the excess fluid off your lungs."

"I'm pregnant." Sabrina managed to gasp.

"It makes no difference. The heart failure is worse for the baby than these medications. We have to take the lesser of the evils. Your life is the most important thing right now."

Sabrina nodded her understanding and released his arm. The I.V. was running slowly as Sam administered twenty milligrams of Lasix I.V. "When we get you in the ambulance, I'll have to put a catheter in your bladder." He pushed six milligrams of Morphine Sulphate and 0.5 milligrams of Digoxin into the I.V. The paramedics had brought the stretcher into the cabin while Dr. Shepherd attended Sabrina. They placed her on the stretcher, carried her down the steps, and placed her in the ambulance. Sam, after quickly acquiring some final information from Johnny, jumped into the back of the emergency vehicle, which screamed off into the overcast afternoon.

Johnny watched the ambulance's tail lights until he could no longer see the tiny red dots. He ran back to the Beechcraft, taxied to the nearest service area, and hunted for a phone to call Taggat.

* * *

The emergency vehicle swayed in and out of traffic on its rapid transit to Norfolk General, but the movement didn't seem to affect Sabrina. She was becoming more comfortable as each minute ticked by. She was embarrassed by the placement of the catheter into her bladder, but the relief she received was worth the loss of modesty. A small canula supplied her with oxygen and ran into her nose, so she could speak. The pain in her chest wasn't as bothersome, and she could breathe much better. She looked over at the doctor and tried to say, "thanks", but the words wouldn't come out because of the dryness in her mouth.

"Only ten minutes from the hospital. Sabrina, do you have a doctor here in Norfolk?" Sam Shepherd continued to scan the EKG monitor as he spoke.

"I have an appointment next week with Dr. Robert Vance." Sabrina labored the information through the cotton that had formed in her mouth.

"Call the hospital. Get Dr. Vance on the line. Also, notify Dr. Tims we have a case for CCU." Sam barked orders to the paramedics then looked back at Sabrina. "Don't worry. Everything's going to be fine." He spoke to Sabrina, but didn't seem to be looking at her.

Pete Claven, the EMT driving the ambulance, handed the radio to Sam. "Doctor Vance is coming on the line."

Sam took the phone with his right hand while he adjusted the I.V. solution rate with his left. "Doctor Vance." Sam winked at Sabrina. "I have a good looking,"

Sabrina felt as if she blushed.

"…twenty five year old white female who is approximately…" Sam covered the phone, and looked at Sabrina. "How far pregnant?"

"About three months, I think."

"…twelve weeks pregnant. She has a history of rheumatic fever and a murmur of mitral stenosis. While flying home, she developed congestive heart failure. An emergency landing brought her to us. She has an appointment to see you next week. I have also alerted Dr. Tims to meet us at the CCU. She's received Lasix, M.S., and Digoxin. She looks much better already…Okay, I'll see you in about three minutes." Sam handed the radio back to the driver. "Dr. Vance will meet us at the hospital. Is there anyone we should be contacting?"

"No, Johnny, the pilot, will take care of that." Sabrina knew that everyone on the Eastern Seaboard would have been notified by now as soon as Johnny had powered up the plane. "What's happened to me? I remember hearing something about heart failure." Sabrina took a deep breath. "I feel so tired."

"Try not to talk too much. Breathe normally through your nose. The oxygen will make your respiration easier. The more you talk, the more you'll tire. Your heart has been taxed to its limit by the pregnancy. The heart muscle got too tired to work properly; so it began working ineffectively. That allowed the blood to back up in your lungs. You were drowning in your own blood, so to speak."

"Yuck! What a way to put it."

"Remember, breathe, don't talk. The pregnancy and the rheumatic fever made a loosing combination. I've used some special medication to strengthen your heart."

"What will this do to my baby?"

"I can't give you all the particulars. I'll have to bow to the specialists, but if you were my wife, I'd have to think twice about letting you have this baby."

"Sam, we're here! Get ready to roll."

"Sorry, we'll have to continue this discussion later. I have to secure things for transfer."

"But…" Sabrina tried to get more information. The possibility of damage to her baby frightened her more than the risk of her own health.

"Remember, breathe, don't talk." Sam rechecked the I.V. lines, the oxygen tubing, and the catheter. Sabrina looked up at the young blond doctor as he worked diligently to take her into the hospital. "Think twice about having my baby! What does he mean? There's no way they are going to make me abort this pregnancy. No way!" Sabrina's thoughts were running into one another. She had difficulty understanding her condition, and the medicine clouded her mind.

The back door of the ambulance swung open. "Let's go!" Dr. Shepherd pushed the stretcher toward the paramedics. The expanding X-frame sprang down at the ground, putting Sabrina at waist level. As she was whisked through the Emergency Room, she saw white cloaked, blood splotched doctors running to and fro yelling for nurses running to and fro looking for doctors. Patients walked aimlessly looking for both. The trip through the confusion was a wisp in her memory, and before it fully registered, she was inside an elevator and on her way to CCU.

Sam noticed Sabrina's attention to the E. R. confusion. "Don't pay attention to the E.R. That's not the real world."

The elevator door opened, and Sabrina's stretcher rolled through a small maze of corridors. Finally, her platform stopped inside a small room that appeared as well equipped as N.A.S.A.'s Mission Control. She was transferred to a different bed, and a nurse appeared at her side. She had introduced herself, but Sabrina couldn't remember her name. The nurse had Sabrina stripped and a hospital gown around her before she knew what had happened. Sabrina wanted to remind the nurse to be careful with her new clothes, but it was too late. They were all rolled up and put into a plain brown plastic bag right before her eyes. Sabrina winced as the nurse stuffed them into the bottom of the Hefty.

"Don't worry dear, we'll take good care of these. They won't get lost."

Sabrina smiled, flipped her eyebrows toward the ceiling, and thought, *Right, just cram them in. I love the wrinkled look!*

Attendants fixed electrocardiograph leads to her chest; they also raised the bed so her head was elevated, and a lab technician pounced on her to take blood specimens. Sabrina watched intently as the tech searched diligently for a blue river in her white forearm. After drawing Sabrina's blood from the discovered vein, he stored it in the appropriate tubes. She cringed as he prepared yet another syringe.

"You mean that's not all?"

"Only one more test. This will be painless." The tech drew up a clear liquid from a small vial into the syringe. He squinted as he squirted the excess material into the air. As he turned toward Sabrina, his face reminded her of a mad professor in one of the old horror flicks.

The "painless" specimen involved Dr. Frankenstein, as Sabrina would forever call him, skewering her wrist with a two inch needle and dancing the tip around on the wrist bone until a pulsatile red stream erupted into the barrel of his weapon. Sabrina gritted her teeth and groaned.

"Got it," he marveled as beads of sweat broke out on his forehead.

"Good!" Sabrina winced. "I'm sure glad that was painless."

"Sorry." The tech said as he pushed his glasses back upon his nose. He was no longer looking at Sabrina. All he could admire was his precious bounty-arterial blood for blood gas analysis. He placed the loot in an ice filled plastic cup and headed for the lab.

As her assailant withdrew, Sabrina noticed a tall, thin dirty-blonde headed man talking to Dr. Shepherd. He was smiling. "He had a nice smile," she thought. He was wearing a purple Polo shirt, khaki slacks, and Weejuns, WITHOUT SOCKS!. "Oh my God, I've gotten a Preppie for a Doctor!" Sabrina knew she was feeling better; her mind was becoming sharper, and her thoughts more cutting. She tried to edge up in her bed as she noticed the tall "preppie" walk toward her suite.

Bob Vance was trained in Chicago. He deplored northern Illinois weather. So, after graduating from Northwestern University and completing his Obstetrics and Gynecology residency at Michael Reese, he vowed to move to a warmer climate. His search for a hospital-based practice had brought him to Norfolk General. He enjoyed the proximity of the beach, the eastern Virginia climate, the fishing and hunting, and, most of all, the resident coverage of his patients that allowed him more free time.

Bob had received Sam's message as he completed a final set of tennis with his English friend, Richard Tims, the cardiology specialist who had also been called in on the case. He had quickly showered and thrown on the closest articles of clothing. He slipped on his most comfortable shoes as he headed out the door, but he had forgotten his socks. His tender feet were reminding him of that fact as he eased through the sliding door into

Miss Sabrina MacKenzie's CCU cubicle. Bob scanned all the monitoring devices and rejoiced that his specialty was Obstetrics.

"Hello, Miss MacKenzie. I'm Doctor Robert Vance. It appears as if they don't want you to get away from that spot." Bob motioned to the I.V. line attached to Sabrinals arm, the E.K.G. lead wires running up both sleeves of her gown, the oxygen line running to a nasal cannula strapped around her head, the catheter attached to her leg, and a pulse oximeter clipped over her left index finger.

"Apparently not." Sabrina tried to maneuver in the bed, but her tethers restricted her motion.

"Try not to move around too much; it might tire you."

"I feel much better. Dr. Shepherd was on the ball. He seems to have fixed me up." Sabrina didn't want to give Dr. Vance the idea she was feeling too ill.

"You're far from being fixed up, Miss MacKenzie."

"Please call me, Sabrina."

"Thank you, I will. I've always enjoyed calling beautiful women by their first names."

"Dr. Vance, you're embarrassing me."

"I doubt it. I'm sure you've heard that before."

"Well, yes, but not from someone that was sockless." Sabrina motioned to his feet.

"Oh, that. Sorry. The page caught me in the shower. I grabbed the closest things I could lay my hands on. It seems I forgot my socks, and my feet are killing me."

"That's a relief."

"Excuse me?"

"Oh, nothing. Just thinking out loud." Sabrina smiled and seemed relieved. *This fellow won't be half bad,* she thought.

"Sabrina, Dr. Tims will be caring for you during this hospital stay. I'm coming along for the ride this time. I have the information you gave the resident in the ambulance. I believe he's covered most of the bases, but, since his specialty is also to be cardiology, we need to establish a base of information for the pregnancy. When was you last menstrual period?"

"March eighteenth."

Bob Vance removed a gestational calculator from his hip pocket. He rotated the plastic disk and looked up at Sabrina. "That makes your due date December twenty-fifth, and you're fourteen weeks. I'll have an ultrasound done to confirm your dates." He picked up a small black device from the table, placed some of the EKG gel on a probe attached to the device, and placed the probe on a small area of Sabrina's lower abdomen he had exposed. "Whoosh, whoosh, whoosh...." Bob's face lit up. He looked at his watch, and then at Sabrina. "That's your baby's heart beat. It's pulse is one hundred and forty."

"That's my baby?"

"That's it! Nothing can make that sound except a baby's heart."

Sabrina began to cry tears of joy. "I don't believe it. It already has a heartbeat, and everything?"

"Not everything, not yet. It won't be ready for a few more weeks." Bob reached over and dried the tears from Sabrina's eyes. As he wiped the moisture from her cheeks, he empathized with Sabrina's condition. *So young and so sick*, he thought.

"You've made my day, Dr. Vance. I'll go through anything to keep this baby. I can't believe it! May I hear it again?"

Bob found the heartbeat with the ultrasonic doppler and let Sabrina listen for a few seconds.

As Sabrina relished the moment of hearing her baby's heartbeat for the first time, she thought about the resident's comment in the ambulance. "What did Dr. Shepherd mean when he said he'd have to think twice about me having this baby if I were his wife?"

Bob placed the doppler back on table beside the head of the bed. He leaned on the bed rail, reached over and lightly touched Sabrina's right hand. "Sabrina, you have a very serious condition, especially when associated with pregnancy. This set of circumstances places you at very high risk.

Until we know the severity of your heart disease, we can't make recommendations, but its very unusual for heart failure to occur this early in the pregnancy unless the heart is severely diseased. I'll be able to make a better prognosis after your assessment by Dr. Tims and further lab testing."

"I'll not have this baby aborted, Dr. Vance." She tried to muster as serious a tone as possible.

Bob looked at Sabrina's face. He thought about her reaction when he had found the baby's heartbeat. "No, I suppose you wouldn't, but let's cross that bridge when we come to it."

"How long do you think I'll be in the hospital?"

"Until you're well, I guess." Bob smiled at Sabrina and shrugged his shoulders. "Sorry, but I couldn't let that opportunity go by. I'm not sure when you'll be able to go home, Sabrina. I'm sure it will be at least three days before we have all our tests completed. We'll let you go when we've obtained a therapeutic level of heart medication, see no evidence of impending heart failure, and feel confident you have no other problems."

"I'm going to be fine, I assure you. I will have this baby."

"With that positive attitude, half of our job is already done." Bob lightly grasped Sabrina's palm, and squeezed with reassurance. "It will be a long battle, but we can do it!"

Sabrina looked into Bob Vance's eyes and immediately felt a confidence she hadn't felt before. She was happy she had Dr. Robert Vance for her Obstetrician.

"Dr. Tims will be in shortly, Sabrina. I need to give him a brief rundown of what's going on. He's very good at what he does. You and I will talk more after some of the test results are back." Bob released Sabrina's hand and started out the door.

"Dr. Vance?"

"Yes, Sabrina."

"Thank you."

"I haven't done much."

"More than you know. Thanks." Sabrina tried to get up on her elbows.

"You're welcome. Lie back down and get some rest."

Sabrina eased back on the bed confident Dr. Vance would help her pull through this temporary setback. With that assurance, she closed her eyes and drifted off into a light sleep.

# 13

Rodger Chesworth, the sixty-one year old ex-General Motor's executive, sat in his brown leather arm chair at the head of the dark oak conference table. Tank, as the other executives in the room affectionately called him because of his solid six-foot five inch, two hundred sixty-five pound build, looked up from the MacKenzie-Winston proposal and scanned the faces as each board member completed his review of the prepared pamphlet.

Tank had paid particular attention to Cathy Winston, the firm's representative, since she had arrived in his corporate office four days ago. She was a looker, but he had long passed the stage where he allowed looks to influence his impression of an individual's business savvy. Ms. Winston had gone about her business in a professional manner with her written proposal being impeccable. It covered all the points he had requested during their first meeting, and he liked it. However, today was showdown-the day when all the cards went on the table, and the board would vote for acceptance or refusal.

As Tank chewed on the earpiece of his glasses and thought more about this beautiful woman who had entered into their world, he noted the last head rise from the booklet. "Has everyone completed a review of the material?" A uniform affirmative nod was returned from all present. "Excellent! Before we vote, I have asked Ms. Winston to give a brief presentation to the board. I want to see exactly how solid this beautiful lady is before we entrust her firm with thirty-five million dollars. Agreed?"

The board members looked at each other, nodded their heads, and looked back to Tank.

"Good!" Tank pressed the direct line to his secretary. She had been instructed to have Ms. Winston come in at the signal. Within seconds Cathy entered the board room. She walked to the opposite end of the table, placed her briefcase beside her chair, and sat down. All the board members stood as she entered, and waited for her recognition.

"Please be seated, gentlemen," Cathy motioned around the room with her eyes.

Tank made particular notice of Cathy's attire. Her dark blue linen suit, white silk blouse, dark stockings and black heels conveyed her conservative thoughts. Her gold earrings, necklace, and bracelet were not ostentatious. Her hair was lightly permed, and she didn't overwhelm the room with perfume. *Good*, Tank thought. *She wants us to see Ms. Winston the business person, not Cathy, the beautiful woman. But how in the hell couldn't you notice those assets.* He grinned at his own thoughts, put on his glasses, and stood. "Ms. Winston, I've asked you here to review briefly your company's proposal. The members of the board have read your prepared booklet, and we have had adequate opportunity to assess your figures. We could vote on the question now, but I would like for you to tell us exactly why we should switch to your company for our employee's retirement plan. Maybe you could offer us added incentive."

Cathy stood, motioned for the other board members not to rise, and walked to the head of the table. She flipped a switch on the wall, and as a screen dropped from the ceiling at the opposite end of the room, the lights dimmed. Cathy touched the remote switch, and a picture of the facade of Chesworth Motors' corporate headquarters illuminated the screen. She walked to the screen and stood beside the picture.

"Gentlemen, I appreciate this opportunity to present my firm's position, and I hope, with what has been stated in the proposal, I won't have to change many of your minds." Cathy paused, took a sip of water, and proceeded. "Ten years ago Chesworth Motors was founded by Rodger Chesworth and five other General Motor executives with the idea to mass produce a safe, economical, aesthetically pleasing, and affordable vehicle. With its recent introduction of the…" Cathy flipped the second slide into view, and a picture of a bright red Ocelot, Chesworth's newest entry into the car market, hit the screen. It was the same promotional photo that had been approved by the board. A blonde headed young lady dressed in a cream-colored, red trimmed jogging suit, and a red head band stood behind the car. The slogan, *Ocelot..a purr-fect car for the times* blazed across the bottom of the picture. "…Ocelot, years of planning, progressive engineering and imaginative financing have culminated in one of the best vehicles to make an impact on the American market since the introduction of the Corvette." Cathy noted the smile on Rodger Chesworth's face. It was the first she had seen since she arrived. "Advance orders have already exceeded marketing predictions." Cathy flipped up pictures of bar graphs illustrating predictions of sales and actual sales. She pressed the remote, and a slide showing a construction area came into view. "With increased sales, plant expansion is underway, and by summer of next year, a production of eight thousand units per month is predicted. Research and development have recently improved gas mileage by twenty-two percent, without decreasing acceleration, and the only limitation on growth seems to be in the number of cars produced." Cathy turned up the lights. She placed an overhead projector on the end of the table and flipped on the switch. "Recent manpower requirements by Chesworth remain steady, but with expansion the number of employees is expected to increase by four hundred percent. Chesworth's payroll will increase four-fold making its retirement benefit contribution quadruple. Last year the net earnings in the retirement plan was a meager five point three percent."

Cathy looked up from the graph she was using to show employee increase. "Gentlemen, I need not tell you, that's deplorable." Without waiting for agreement, Cathy looked back at the sheet on the projector. "Last year, at MacKenzie-Winston, an eighteen percent increase was recognized by all accounts." Cathy turned off the projector. She picked up her briefcase, set it on the table, opened the top, and took out a set of computer printouts and passed them around the table. She gave each person a chance to look over the first page before continuing. "Last year, your company paid a one and one-half percent maintenance fee for your retirement package. That cut your growth to three point eight percent. According to employment records, your average worker remains with the company for four years, but there are a large number of employees that resign, quit, or are released after their second year. Your figures show four hundred thousand dollars was returned to the corporation at plan year end due to employees failure to qualify for benefits. That sum is then reinvested into the balance of the accounts, but the reinvestment fees are one and one-half percent once again. Therefore, you're losing money on the reinvestment accounts. I'm prepared to offer you a package that will charge a one-percent fee, give maximum growth potential, and take the worry out of your hands. In exchange, MacKenzie-Winston asks only two things: first, a seven year contract, and second, re-negotiation of fees after the first two years. Also, MacKenzie-Winston will guarantee in writing never to exceed a one point three percent fee for the length of the contract." Cathy placed the papers back into her case, closed the clasps, set the case on the floor, and looked Tank Chesworth in the eye. "Are there any questions, gentlemen?"

"I believe you have covered all our questions, Ms. Winston. If you will excuse us, the board will vote on the question."

Cathy picked up her briefcase and confidently walked out the door.

"Excuse me, Ms. Winston?" Tank's secretary looked up from her desk.

"Yes," Cathy answered, confident she had the account.

"There's a phone call holding for you. It's a Mr. Taggat Delaney."

Cathy's heart sank as she picked up the headset. "Hello, Taggat?"

"Thank, God, I've found you! Cathy, Sabrina's in the hospital."

"Hospital?" Cathy wavered slightly. "Where? Why? What's happened? Is she all right?"

"Sabrina's going to be fine. I've just left her. She's in Norfolk General. She developed heart failure during the flight back to the Island yesterday. Johnny McKay had to divert to Norfolk, and she was taken to the hospital from the airport."

"Johnny? Why wasn't Steve with her?"

"It's a long story. Too long for the phone. Sabrina is lucky to have gotten to the hospital so quickly. Dr. Vance, her obstetrician, was very helpful in making me understand what was going on, but she has also been seen by a cardiologist, Dr. Richard Tims. He has Sabrina bent out of shape."

"Why? Didn't he hold her hand right?" Cathy grinned.

"I wish it were that easy. He wants Sabrina to abort her pregnancy."

"Oh, you know about that?"

Tank Chesworth's secretary looked up at Cathy. "They would like for you to come back into the board room, Ms. Winston."

Cathy covered the mouthpiece. "All right, I'll be just a moment." She lifted her hand from the phone. "Taggat, I have to get back to a meeting. I'll leave for Norfolk as soon as I'm finished here."

"Good! Sabrina's torn up over that damned heart specialist. She ran me off and wouldn't speak to anyone. That's why I called you. You both seem to be on the same wavelength."

"I'll leave immediately."

"Great! Thanks, Cathy."

"Don't worry, Taggat. We'll figure out something. Good-by."

"Good-by."

Cathy hung up the phone, turned, and walked into the board room.

As she entered, the board members were milling around with drinks in their hands. Tank Chesworth walked over to her and extended his hand. "Congratulations, Ms. Winston. You now have the business of Chesworth Motors. The board voted unanimously to accept your proposal. Your contracts are signed, and we are looking forward to MacKenzie-Winston, Inc.'s association with our company."

Cathy mustered a smile. "Thank you, Mr. Chesworth."

"Please, call me Tank. We have reason to be a little less formal," Tank took a drink of his bourbon and water. "'bout thirty five million of them."

"Thank you, Tank. I'm sorry I don't seem elated. I assure you I am, but I've just learned that my business associate has been put in the hospital in Norfolk. I must leave immediately. Please don't let me put a damper on the party, but I have to go."

"I'm sorry to hear that, Ms. Winston. I hope it's nothing serious."

"So do I, and please, call me Cathy."

"I'd consider it a honor, Cathy. I hope your partner gets to feeling better. Is there anything we can do to help?"

"No, just don't think me impolite by leaving. I'm afraid I wouldn't be much fun at a party under these circumstances."

"I understand. By the way, Cathy, that was a bang up presentation. You knew you had the account, didn't you?"

Cathy gathered the contracts and looked up at Tank. "Tank, I knew I had the account the first time I looked through your files." She grinned and headed out the room.

"Cathy?" Tank waited for Cathy to turn back toward him. His face was very serious.

"Yes?"

"Never take too much for granted. When you deal with people, unpredictability is the rule, not the exception." Tank tipped his glass toward Cathy, and turned back to the remaining board members. "Gentlemen, may I have your attention?" He waited for the room to quieten. "Ms. Winston will not be able to join us for dinner. She has to leave for

Norfolk. I suppose she has other pockets to fleece." Tank looked at Cathy and smiled. "Cathy, we all wish you a safe trip."

All the men tipped their drinks toward Cathy's direction. "Here, here!"

"Thank you. I appreciate your confidence in our firm, and I assure you MacKenzie-Winston will work diligently to maintain your loyalty." Cathy walked through the door, picked up her briefcase, placed a copy of the contract into an appropriate slot, and asked Tank's secretary to mail the original to the company.

"I'll take care of it immediately," the secretary replied. "I've asked the security guard to bring your car up from the garage. It should be waiting for you."

"Thank you. That will help." Cathy headed for the door.

"Ms. Winston?"

Cathy turned and looked back at the secretary. "Yes?"

"I've enjoyed being around you this week. I've learned a great deal."

"THANK YOU!" Cathy walked back and shook her hand. "That's the best compliment I could have received." Cathy looked the secretary in the eye for a moment and made her realize she was sincere in her thanks. Then she turned and hurried for the lobby.

As Cathy turned the corner into the lobby, she saw the security officer standing by the door with her keys. Unfortunately, she didn't see the car. She quickly walked to the officer thinking he didn't have time to bring the car up to the entrance, but the look on his face began telling her something different.

"I'm sorry, Ms. Winston, but your car wouldn't start."

"Please be kidding! I don't have time for this, not today!"

"No, Mam, I'm not kidding. Don't worry, I've already called the BMW garage, and they're on their way with a wrecker. Fortunately, the dealership is only two miles away. They should be here any..." The guard noted a truck pulling into the covered drive. "...Here they are, now!"

"Great! Maybe, it'll just be the battery or something simple."

"No, I don't think so," the guard said, but he noticed how Cathy's spirit seemed to drop when he spoke. "Well, I don't know much about those foreign cars. Maybe it will be something simple."

The black and grey wrecker pulled in front of the building, and a young man dressed in white coveralls jumped from the cab. The security officer started out the door, but Cathy put her hand up in front of his path.

"Thanks anyway, but let me handle this. I'm in a terrific hurry."

"Okay, Ms. Winston. Good luck!"

Cathy pushed through the revolving door and met the service man as he circled the front of the truck.

"You the one with the bum BMW?" The freckled redhead approached Cathy with both hands in his pockets.

"Yes! The car's in the garage. Please take a look at it quickly. My friend has been put in the hospital in Norfolk, and I have to get there as soon as possible."

"Okay, but I don't know much about these cars unless it's just the battery. Otherwise, we'll have to tow her in to the garage."

"Fine, whatever it takes. Just hurry!"

The redhead helped Cathy into the wrecker and they found Sabrina's BMW. The attendant quickly checked the car and decided it wasn't the battery. "Gotta tow her in. Hop in the cab, and I'll be ready to go in a jiff."

Cathy resolved to tolerate the delay as much as possible, but she vowed to get a new car as soon as she had time to shop. "This is the last time I'll rely on Sabrina's "Classic", she thought as the freckled face man jumped into his seat. "That was fast."

"Yes, Mam. I aim to please."

They weaved their way to the dealership. As they pulled into the car lot, Cathy noticed that the dealership sold not only BMW, but also Porsche. Reggie, as the serviceman had introduced himself, busied himself with unloading the BMW, but Cathy headed for the showroom. "I'll be in the showroom. Come and get me when the car's ready."

"All right, Ms. Winston. I'll have someone look at it right away."

"I may as well enjoy the scenery while they look at the car," she thought as she headed for the display floor. She rounded the curved glass wall into the showroom, and stopped in her tracks. Cathy walked slowly into the showroom. Her pace slowed as she eyed it. The hand that wasn't holding onto her briefcase reached out for it. Suddenly, she was upon it. It sat there in all its gleaming glory. She had looked at one when she was first out of business school but couldn't afford it. When she moved to the island, she didn't need the transportation. But, now, she could afford it, and she definitely needed the transportation. She walked over to the white 911 Turbo-Carrera and began running her fingers over the sleek skin. The brown leather interior beckoned her. She tried to suppress the urge, but her hand went to the doorlatch automatically. The handle lifted up as if another force had taken over her body. She slid into the bucket seat and viewed the dials with a hypnotic gaze. The price sticker was lying in the passenger seat. Her right hand picked up the paper, and her mind scanned the figures. $74,000.00.

Suddenly, out of no where, a set of keys dangled in front of her face.

"Would you like to take her for a ride?"

Cathy looked up at the black haired salesman. He was about twenty five years old, six foot tall and very thin. His smile would melt ice. Cathy's right hand involuntarily reached up, grabbed the keys, and placed them into the ignition. "I'd love to."

"Just a moment, I'll get the door."

Somewhere in Cathy's memory, she did take the car for a test drive, and she did ask the salesman his name. However, all she could really remember saying was "I'll take it." No bargaining took place. After a few signatures, a few phone calls, and a fifteen percent down payment, Cathy was ready to leave for Norfolk.

Reggie waited for Cathy to finish signing all the necessary forms, and as she stood and turned to leave the salesman's office, he stopped her. "I see you got White Beauty."

"What?"

"That's what I've been calling the 911, White Beauty."

"Oh, yes. I can't believe I bought it."

"It's just as well you did, the BMW is out of commission for a few days. We have to order a part. It won't be in for a week."

Cathy searched through her purse, took out a hundred dollar bill,, handed it to Reggie, and wrote down the address of the ferry landing to MacKenzie Island. "Reggie, I have to go Norfolk immediately. Would you see that the BMW gets delivered to this address when the repairs are completed? Have the dealership bill us for the charges, and keep this for yourself. You've been a dear." Cathy gave him a peck on the cheek.

Reggie rubbed the spot on his cheek, and looked down at the bill Cathy had placed in his hand. He immediately recognized Ben Franklin's face. "Yes, Ma'am! I'll take care of it."

Cathy turned and looked back into the salesman's office. He still appeared to be relishing the sale. "Are we finished?"

"Yes, Ms. Winston. I've contacted the insurance company and your bank. There's no problem. They're sending us the balance of payment tomorrow. Enjoy!"

"Thanks! I certainly will."

"The tank's full and she's ready to go. Don't baby her. She likes to run."

Cathy tossed the keys up into the air and caught them in her right hand. "Don't worry. I'll give her plenty of exercise."

* * *

The distance from Durham, North Carolina, to Norfolk, Virginia, is one hundred and ninety five miles. Interstate-85 from Durham travels northeast to the La Crosse interchange in southern Virginia and then turns north to Richmond. From the LaCrosse exit, Highway 58 East is the quickest route into Norfolk. Unfortunately, Route 58 snakes its way through the Virginia countryside, and its length rarely includes four lane travel. The Porsche Turbo-Carrera was constructed for that type of highway.

Cathy blurred past the Suffolk bypass interchange on her approach into Norfolk. As she slipped the transmission from fourth into fifth and let the Porsche have its head, the speedometer needle crept past one hundred and five miles per hour. Cathy had forgotten how much she loved speed. She could command it with the touch of her foot and control it with the touch of her hand. She loved it!

The I-64 interchange came up quickly, and Cathy exited to the right following the hospital logo signs. She passed Norfolk International Airport and made the first off-ramp into the hospital area. As she pulled into the parking lot, she thanked the North Carolina and Virginia Highway Patrol for looking the other way this evening. She locked the doors to her new baby, and searched for the main entrance. The clock over the reception desk said 9:30. She had left Durham at 7:00 P.M. She walked over to the desk and waited for the pink smocked lady to recognize her presence.

"May I help you?"

"I'm looking for Sabrina MacKenzie. She was brought in as an emergency yesterday."

"My, my! There's been a flurry of people around that young lady today." The volunteer looked at the computer screen. "She's in CCU cubicle five, but there's no visiting at this time of night."

"I'm her sister. She'll see me."

"I'm afraid it's not up to the patient."

"Can't I go upstairs and wait? Maybe they'll let me in." Cathy mustered a few tears. "I don't know what to do. They said she was awfully sick, and I just have to see her." Cathy searched through her purse for a Kleenex.

"Well," the volunteer picked up a tissue from her box and handed it to Cathy. "I don't suppose that would hurt. Here, put this on your jacket."

The pink lady affixed a sticky tag to Cathy's coat. It branded her as a visitor.

"Thank you," Cathy said as she wiped the counterfeit tears from her cheeks.

The elevator ride to CCU ended in a waiting area outside the nursing station. Cathy rushed to the window and pecked on the glass. The duty nurse rolled the divider back, looked at Cathy, and then at the tag on her coat.

"Yes, Ms. MacKenzie? How may I help you?"

"I would like to see my sister, Sabrina. I was out of town when she was brought into the hospital."

"It is after visiting hours, and we have explicit orders from her doctor for no visitors...except family." The nurse looked at Sabrina's records. "Strange? She doesn't indicate she has a sister. Maybe I should check with the patient...in the morning!"

"You can do whatever you like, but I'm seeing my sister tonight. If you plan on stopping me, you had better call security." Cathy looked the nurse in the eye, tightened her jaw and furrowed her brow. "We can do this easy, or we can go about it the hard way. Which shall it be?"

The nurse felt Cathy's determination through the glass. She didn't want any disruption to the floor. The other patients' comfort came as her first priority. "I suppose a short visit will be permissible. I was just in Ms. MacKenzie's room, and she was awake. Enter the door to your right. Sabrina's in Cubicle Five."

Cathy went through the automatic doors, and saw the colored arrows leading to the various cubicles. Five's arrow was blue. She stood outside the cubicle for a few moments, geared up for what she might see, and then walked through the door. She saw Sabrina lying in bed with her eyes closed. Wires ran to various machines, and a small tube ran to her nose. There seemed to be three or four different rhythmic tones in the background. Cathy took a step closer to Sabrina's bed, and Sabrina suddenly opened her eyes.

As soon as Sabrina made eye contact with Cathy, she began crying. "Oh, my God! I'm so glad you're here. They want to take my baby. I can't do it, Cath. I just can't do it! Help me. Please help me."

Cathy rushed to the side of the bed and took Sabrina's extended right hand into hers. It seemed so cool. She leaned over the bed and gave Sabrina a hug, at least as much of a hug as she could. She kissed her on the cheek and smoothed her hair. "Settle down, Sabrina. They might run me off if you get...."

The nurse rushed into the room. "Is everything all right? Ms. MacKenzie's heart rate went up drastically. I'm afraid I'll have to ask you to leave, sister or not."

"I'm all right," Sabrina intejected. "I need to see my sister." Sabrina squeezed Cathy's hand. "Everything will be okay. I promise."

"All right," the nurse reluctantly submitted, and looked at Cathy. "Don't stay too long." The nurse checked the I.V. lines then ran her hand up Sabrina's arm. "Try and keep calm and maintain your breathing at a normal rate."

Sabrina tried to relax. "What can I do, Cathy? I have to convince Dr. Tims that I will not abort this baby. Dr. Vance is willing to help, but Dr. Tims just looks over his nose and in his British accent tells me I shouldn't even think about having a baby. I must terminate this pregnancy, or I'll die; no ifs, ands, or buts." Sabrina grasped Cathy's hand tighter. "You know I'll do anything to keep this child. Please help. Please?"

Cathy looked into Sabrina's wide beseeching eyes. Not long ago in high school, the roles were reversed, and Sabrina was there for Cathy. "I'll do everything I can to change his mind, Sabrina. I promise."

Sabrina tried to get up on her elbows, but Cathy wouldn't let her. "You'll help even if he says I'll die having the baby?"

Cathy couldn't force herself to answer yes. She looked into Sabrina's face and tried to make the words come out, but she couldn't.

"Promise me! I'll try and get out of bed if you don't!"

"Okay, I promise I will try to change Dr. Tims mind no matter what it takes, up to and including threats of murder. Okay?"

Sabrina relaxed. "Okay." As she eased back onto the pillow, the beeps emanating from the monitor seemed to slow down. She wiped the tears from her eyes and looked at Cathy. The fear once in Cathy's face was now replaced by concern. Sabrina smiled hoping to relieve Cathy's anxiety. "What's new in the world of Cathy Winston?"

The tension melted in Cathy's grip on Sabrina's right hand, and she almost cried. "How can you ask such a question?"

"Well, you said you would handle things, and I have the utmost faith in your ability."

"Don't be facetious."

"Not trying to be." Sabrina winced and reached to her chest with her left hand.

"What's wrong?" Cathy released her grip on Sabrina's right hand and reached for her left.

"What the hell is that?" Cathy fingered the engagement ring on Sabrina's third finger.

Sabrina relaxed and held her hand up to the light. "What? This little ole' thing? You didn't know? I thought Taggat talked to you."

"He talked to me, but I didn't give him a chance to say much. I was in a meeting at Chesworth."

"That's right! How did it go?"

"Oh, no you don't. You're not changing the subject that easily. What about this rock?"

"Cathy, Steve and I are engaged."

"Engaged?" Cathy gave Sabrina another abortive attempt at a hug. "If you're engaged, then why in the hell was Johnny bringing you back to the Island. And don't give me the trash about it being a long story. Taggat has already cut me off with that line."

Sabrina closed her eyes and recounted the days at Gull Haven with Steve. She then told Cathy the whole story: Steve's arrival and the instrument problem, Steve's proposal, their intimacy, their trip back to New York, Steve's assignment to Saudi Arabia, and her fateful trip, as much as she could remember, from New York to Norfolk. "I wish you could have been there when Steve was at the house."

Cathy laughed. "I bet you do."

Sabrina blushed. "Well, not for all of it, but I wanted to be able to share the excitement with someone besides Steve." Sabrina quietened and thought for a moment. She looked up and smiled. "How's Precious?"

Cathy's smile turned to a scowl. "Precious? Hell, Sabrina, why do you insist in giving that car a name? Precious is in the garage in Durham. I think she blew a gasket, or something."

"Poor dear. She's been so good to me. Is she going to be all right?"

"Yes, she...Oh, hell! You've got me talking about that damned car like it was a person. Your BMW is going to be repaired, and the garage will return it to the Island. I've made all the necessary arrangements."

Sabrina let out a sigh of relief. "If Precious is hurt, how did you get here?"

"I bought a car." Cathy puffed up and hoped Sabrina would ask about her new Porsche.

"Oh, my goodness. Cathy Winston has finally made a statement for her personal freedom. She's bought a car. What did you get? No, wait. I bet," Sabrina hesitated and thought for a moment. "I bet you bought a Nissan; you're so frugal."

"Nope! I bought a Porsche."

"A Porsche! I don't believe it. How much did you spend? This is not the Cathy Winston I know."

"I don't know what happened to me. The car made me do it. All of a sudden I was saying, I'd take it. Circumstances were beyond my control. I had just landed the deal with Chesworth..."

"You did!? We have Chesworth Motors? I don't believe it!"

"Why not? You said you wanted it. I thought that was why I went there."

"It was, but I didn't think Tank Chesworth would ever switch to our firm. He has always been a solid Chase Manhattan man."

"I changed his mind, but I don't want to talk about it right now. I want to tell you about my car. It's a 911..."

"What did you have do to get the account? Go to bed with the board?" Sabrina winked and laughed.

"I don't use those tactics." Cathy smacked Sabrina's hand. "I made him an offer he couldn't refuse. Now, about my car. It's a 911 Turbo-Carr…"

"What kind of deal? I bet it's going to cost us."

"Dammit, Sabrina. If you don't stop interrupting me, I…I'm going to turn off something." Cathy looked around at the monitors. "Well, I wouldn't know what to turn off anyway. I'm going to say this once and only once. Then I want to talk about my car. I told Tank we would handle his accounts with a maintenance fee of one percent. After…"

"One percent! That's barely our margin. What about.."

Cathy turned and started to walk out of the room.

"Wait! Where are you going?" Sabrina raised up on her elbows with a look of desperation on her face.

Cathy turned and gave Sabrina a scowl. "I told you not to interrupt me. I'm leaving until you learn a little etiquette."

"All right, I won't interrupt anymore. Please don't go."

Cathy walked back over to the bed. "You promise? You know I mean what I say."

"I know. Please don't go. I promise I won't interrupt. It's, just, you're giving me a lot of news, and I'm having trouble sorting it all out."

Cathy laughed. "I'm giving you too much news? What about me? I get a phone call telling me my best friend is in the hospital. I find out she's engaged to be married. Then, she tells me her fiancé has been whisked away on some secretive mission for the government, and she can't talk to him for a year. She's worried about a doctor that wants her to abort her pregnancy. Now, she tells me, I'M the one giving HER too much information."

"Sorry, I never thought about it that way." Sabrina eased back into the bed. "I'll be quiet."

"That's doubtful, but I'll try this one more time." Cathy took a deep breath. "Chesworth Motors is paying a one percent maintenance fee for the FIRST TWO years. From that time forward, they'll pay us a guaranteed one point three percent of the total account for the balance of a seven year contract. Sabrina, they're shifting thirty-five million to our firm-the whole damned account. I figured we could stand a slight discount to get that size account. I had finished the presentation when I heard about your predicament. After Tank Chesworth and his board voted to go with us, I rushed to the car only to find a wrecker was on its way to pick up both of us. That's when I fell in love with my..." Cathy held up her hand at Sabrina. "If you say one word before I'm finished, I'll eliminate the need for this monitoring equipment. That's when I fell in love with my 911 Porsche Turbo-Carrera. It's white with brown leather interior, and I love it. There, I've said it. You may speak." Cathy dropped her hand.

"I'm excited for you, Cathy." Sabrina yawned.

"I can tell." They both laughed.

Cathy's face lengthened, and the smile left her mouth. She traced the ring on Sabrina's hand. "That's some ring, Sabrina."

"Probably Cubic Zirconia." Sabrina smiled, but Cathy didn't respond.

"Does Steve know about the baby?"

Sabrina looked away from Cathy's face as if she were ashamed of what she was about to say, but before she spoke, she faced Cathy. "After Steve proposed to me, and we made love for the first, second, third, and fourth times..." Sabrina winked at Cathy and smiled.

"Hush about that. I don't want to hear about your love affair. Get serious!"

"The next morning I spent some time on the beach alone. My thoughts were racing, and my heart was torn between telling the truth and losing Steve, or lying and keeping him. Of course I didn't tell him, Cathy. Steve would kill Kent if he knew Kent was the baby's father. I decided then I would keep the pregnancy quiet and eventually tell Steve it was his child." Sabrina pulled Cathy's hand to her face. "Please don't think terribly of me, Cathy. I love Steve more than anything, and I don't want to lose him."

"I don't think terribly of you, Sabrina. I'll back anything you do because I know you have considered the alternatives, but you must be able to live with your decision." Cathy leaned closer to Sabrina. "I love you, Sabrina. Nothing will ever change that." Cathy stood up, straightened her clothes, walked to the window, and turned back facing Sabrina's bed. "Actually, I think it's a pretty good idea."

"You do?"

"Sure! There's a problem, however. Other people know about the pregnancy and that Kent's the father. Something will have to be done about that."

"That's what Taggat said."

"Did he recommend a solution?"

"No, but he did say he would take care of it. What do you think?"

"I think Taggat will take care of it. Has he ever let you down?"

"Never."

"Well, stop worrying about it."

The curtains rustled and the nurse walked in. "I hate to disturb this little party, but Ms. MacKenzie has to take her medication now, and she must get some rest." The nurse looked at Cathy. "The hospital maintains an adjacent motel with very reasonably priced rooms. I could arrange one for you, if you'd like."

"That would be nice. Thank you."

"Do you have to go?" Sabrina reached out for Cathy's hand, and looked at her with a frightened stare.

"I think I had better leave, Sabrina." Cathy bent over and whispered in her ear. "I have to do some homework on Dr. Tims, but I'll be back early in the morning." Cathy gave Sabrina a wink, turned, and walked out the door.

The nurse looked down at Sabrina. "You two must be very close." She handed Sabrina her medication and a small cup of water.

Sabrina took the tablets and looked at the door. The curtains were still moving from Cathy's exit. "Yes, we are. Very close." She relaxed back into the bed, and closed her eyes.

# 14

Cathy pushed the curtains aside with her hand and walked into Sabrina's cubicle. She pulled up a chair close to the head of the bed, and sat down. "So, how has your day been?"

"Where have you been? I expected you this morning, but you didn't show. Then I thought you would be here after lunch. Now it's 2:00 P.M., and you whisk in looking like a model out of Vogue."

Cathy gave Sabrina a hard look. "I didn't know I had a caretaker."

Sabrina leaned back from her supported position. "I'm sorry. I've missed you. It's been a rough day."

"Oh, how's that?" Cathy sneaked a small bag from her purse, opened the top, took out a few small brown bits, and quickly popped them in her mouth.

"Well, I've been stuck with needles, scanned with an ultrasound, echoed with some other apparatus, wheeled all over this hospital, and I still don't know what they have found out. I know I'm pregnant, but I knew that before I came here. I know I've had heart failure, but I'm better. What else do they need? I'm getting out of here before they start talking about aborting my baby again."

"You look much better this morning. Hey, you're off the oxygen."

"Yeah," Sabrina smiled. "You better be careful, you're sitting close to a digitalized woman."

"Whoo! Is that dangerous? You won't give off rays or anything harmful, will you?" Cathy laughed.

"What do you have in your little sack?" Sabrina sat up in the bed, crossed her legs, and eyed Cathy's purse. "I saw you sneaking some chocolate out of it just a minute ago."

"You noticed?"

"Of course, I'm not blind."

Cathy took the sack from her purse and handed it to Sabrina. "Are you sure you can have these?"

"I don't know, but I'm going to eat them anyway. I'm starved." Sabrina took the sack and opened it. "Chocolate covered raisins, mmmm." She took a handful, and picked them up, one by one, before popping them into her mouth. "Delicious. I haven't had anything sweet since I've been here. Why are you so dressed up?"

"Are you sure it's okay to have those?"

"Well, they haven't told me not to have them. Why the pretty clothes?"

"It's a long story."

"I've got all the time in the world." Sabrina motioned at the EKG lead attached to her and to the machine. "I'm going nowhere."

"What do you know about Dr. Tims?"

"He's a real horse's ass. Why?"

"Why do you say that?"

"Well, he's the only one wanting me to abort the pregnancy. There's no decision, no discussion, no alternatives. He marched in here, talked to me about my problem, drew some pictures on a couple of pieces of paper, stood up and announced I was going to be scheduled for a therapeutic abortion. The pompous ass stood right there," Sabrina pointed to a spot in the room near to where Cathy was sitting. "I told him I wouldn't agree to an abortion, and you know what he had the audacity to tell me?" Sabrina popped a few more chocolate delights into her mouth.

Cathy shook her head negatively.

"He said that if I had a death wish, I could try and carry the pregnancy."

"Ms. MacKenzie," he said, "if you don't abort this pregnancy, you will bloody well die. If you abort the pregnancy, you will live. There are no alternatives." Sabrina snatched a handful of raisins, and stuffed them in her mouth. "He's such an ass. Whoever heard of a doctor talking to a patient like that?"

"I don't know, Sabrina. Perhaps we should pay him some heed. He has an excellent reputation. Do you want to hear about his background?"

"I'd love to. I've been wondering what makes him tick."

Cathy got up from her chair, reached over and captured the sack from Sabrina's lap. "I believe you've had enough."

"Oh, pooh." Sabrina stuck out her lower lip and crossed her hands. "Is there anything in here to drink?"

Cathy poured Sabrina a drink of water, sat back down in the chair, took a notebook from her purse, and looked up.

Sabrina was still looking at the water. She pointed to the glass. "That's the best you can do?"

"Yes."

"You'd think you could bring a body something better than water. After all, you've been gone all morning."

"Sabrina! Do you want to hear this, or not? I swear, ever since you've been pregnant, all you've done is eat and sleep."

"And puke!" Sabrina said in a mocking tone.

"That too, but I didn't want to bring that up."

"Ha, ha. Very funny."

"Sit back and listen. I've worked hard gathering this information." Cathy waited for Sabrina to settle down, but she continued to bounce up and down on her behind in the bed. Cathy threw her the sack of raisins. "Here! Maybe this will keep you quiet."

Sabrina opened the sack and devoured a few more candies. "Thanks."

"Dr. Richard Tims was born in Norfolk County, England. He attended Cambridge University and graduated Magna Cum Laude. He was fifth in his medical school class at Johns Hopkins. His cardiology residency was in Atlanta at Grady Memorial. After residency, he did cardiac research at Massachusetts General and was subsequently lured here by one of his ex-professors to take over the cardiology service. He enjoys research and rarely takes on private patients. It seems he and Dr. Vance are very good friends. Otherwise, Dr. Tims would never have accepted your case."

"I wish he hadn't. He's a pain. Come on. Haven't you got anything good on him? You know, something we can use to talk him out of recommending an abortion."

"I'm afraid not. It seems he has no weak spots, but I'm giving it one last try."

"What do you mean?"

"I have an appointment with Dr. Tims in one hour."

"Oh, Cathy. Don't do that. Not for me."

"Why not? Is he an ogre?"

"On the contrary, he's a doll, but that's not the reason."

"Then why?" Cathy scooted to the edge of her chair.

"He's…he's…. so…British!"

Cathy laughed. "Whatever do you mean?"

"He has absolutely no sense of humor, and he's always so serious."

"So?" Cathy put away her notebook. "Why do you think he continues to recommend termination of the pregnancy? You look great."

"I don't know." Sabrina reached for the pad of paper setting on the bedside table. "Look at this. Maybe you can make heads or tails of it. You took some of this stuff in college."

Cathy walked over to the bed, and peered down on a yellow legal pad. An outline of the heart was drawn on the first sheet of lined paper.

Sabrina pointed to the page. "Dr. Tims told me this valve, the mitral valve, between the left atrium and left ventricle was scarred. When my heart pumps blood, the blood has a difficult time getting from the lungs out to the rest of my body. It also pushes blood back into the vessels of my lungs, congesting them. The pregnancy demands extra work, and all this extra has overloaded the capability of my heart to function normally. So, as Dr. Tims puts it, the big pump failed. The medicine I'm taking helps, but eventually the medicines aren't going to be enough."

"It seems to be working at the moment. Why won't it continue?"

"I don't know. He says it won't be enough, that's all. He told me if I tried to carry the pregnancy to term, I would have to stay in bed and live close to the hospital. And even at that, I might die."

"Well, what's wrong with that?" Cathy gasped. "Not about the dying, Sabrina. You know what I mean. What's so wrong about staying at bedrest. If I had the right man, I could do it for eight months."

"I know what you meant about dying and the right man, but I swear I don't know why he won't consider any alternatives. I told you. The man says no, and he expects me to accept his word as gospel."

"I'll have to see about this. Something seems inconsistent."

A lady in white carried a tray of food into the room, set it down on the bedside table, uncovered the tray, and left.

Cathy looked over the food on the tray and turned up her nose. "I think it's time for me to leave."

"I don't blame you." Sabrina sighed looking at the tray as Cathy headed for the door. "Oh, Cathy?"

"Yes?" Cathy turned.

"Let me know something as soon as you can."

"You'll be the first." Cathy smiled and left the cubicle.

* * *

"I'm sorry, Miss Winston, but the Doctor will be unable to see you today." Chris Jarvis, the male receptionist stood behind the desk and shook his head. "I apologize, but the the lady here this morning didn't understand our appointment book. She's double scheduled Dr. Tims for the entire afternoon. We were able to contact everyone except you."

"I have to see Dr. Tims. It's a matter of life and death. He's taking care of my sister, and she's in the hospital right now. I must speak to him."

Chris looked at Cathy's pleading face. "I tell you what. Have a seat, and I'll see what I can do. No promises, but I'll try. It all depends on the next group of appointments." Chris looked down at his book, but a beeping tone in the background alerted him. "Excuse me, I have to reload the dictation equipment." Chris turned and headed for a small room behind his desk.

Cathy looked over the desk top at the appointment book. She couldn't read the information well, upside down, but she thought the next three hours were blanked out, and Exec Phys was penciled into the slots. She settled her feet back onto the floor from her teetering position just as Chris came back to the desk. "If you don't mind, I have to step out for a moment. Please see if Dr. Tims can see me. I'll be back shortly."

"That might work out better. I will check. Thank you for being so understanding."

Cathy wasn't understanding at all. She knew control in the face of the enemy, and Chris was presently the enemy. She stepped outside the door and looked at her watch. 1:15 P.M. The appointment schedule had the executive physicals beginning at 1:30. Cathy watched the elevator door intently. Finally, the door opened, and a group of three well dressed gentlemen approached Dr. Tims' suite. As the group came closer, Cathy turned and acted as if she had just closed the door to the office. She waited until they were close to her, stood up, turned, and walked into the middle gentleman. "Oh, I'm sorry."

"Excuse me," the gentleman said as he grabbed Cathy by the arms. The other two looked on with envy. "Are you all right, Miss?"

"I'm fine. Upset, but fine." Cathy pointed her finger to Dr. Tims' name plate. "I don't know why these doctors won't call when they are going to be out of the office. I've had an appointment for two weeks, and now, I'm informed Dr. Tims won't be in for the rest of the day, some kind of emergency. I bet he wanted to go fishing." Cathy looked around at the faces to see if she had been convincing, walked down the hall, around the corner, and stopped. She looked back to see what the three men were going to do.

The men looked at each other and grinned. "Okay, Fred. Tee time in thirty minutes." The men did an about face and took off in the other direction. "Damn, I'm glad I don't have to have my prostate examined today!" They all laughed. "First time I'm going to be paid to play golf," said another. As they entered the elevator, Cathy could see relief on their faces.

Cathy walked back to the office, entered and sat down opposite the reception desk. She crossed her legs and picked up a magazine. She unbuttoned the top button of her white silk blouse and blew some cool air down between her breasts. The waiting room seemed hot. As she looked at the magazine, she thought about the three gentlemen once again and smiled.

Richard Tims walked by the waiting room entrance and looked across the reception desk into the lobby. In his direct line of vision was one of the prettiest women he had seen since coming to America. He stood in place and admired the blond reading the magazine. He stopped Chris by the sleeve of his shirt. "Who is that?"

Chris looked into the waiting area and saw Cathy. "She's waiting to see if you'll have time to discuss a hospital patient with her."

"She's not a patient?"

"No, doctor. Why?"

"She's beautiful. I might have a hard time keeping my mind on business." Richard smiled at Chris. "Oh, I forgot. You're immune to such."

Chris smiled and walked back to his desk. "Yes, I am. Thankfully."

A few minutes ticked by and Richard couldn't wait any longer. "Chris, show the lady back to my office. If the other patients arrive, I'll see them."

"I don't understand, Dr. Tims. I called and verified those appointments myself. Dow Chemical executives are always on time. I guess they couldn't make it this afternoon. I'll show her back. If the other gentlemen don't show, could I have the rest of the day off?"

"I think that's a capital idea." Richard looked back at Cathy. She had tossed her shoulder length hair back and was fanning cool air down the front of her blouse with a magazine. As she stood to walk back to his office with Chris, Richard could appreciate her full figure. Richard turned and went to his office arriving prior to Chris and Cathy.

Cathy followed Chris into Dr. Tims' office. As she entered, Richard rose from behind his desk. She was taken aback somewhat by his youthful appearance. She knew he was thirty-four years old, but she had expected someone not quite so good looking. He stood six foot tall with brown hair and blue eyes and appeared to weigh about one hundred and seventy five pounds. He wore a white, starched, long sleeved dress shirt, brown slacks, and a brown, white, and crimson striped tie.

"Dr. Tims, this is Cathy Winston." Chris had started the amenities, and Cathy walked toward the desk. She stopped just shy of the front. "Ms. Winston would like to discuss one of the patients you have in the hospital, a Ms. Sabrina MacKenzie. Here's her chart." Chris laid the chart on Dr. Tims' desk and left the office.

"Won't you sit down, Ms. Winston?"

Cathy stepped over to a black leather chair and sat down. "Dr. Tims, you have a friend of mine in the hospital, and I wondered if I could get some information?" Cathy could feel a flush in her cheeks.

"Why are you blushing, Ms. Winston? Is it too warm in here?"

Cathy fanned her blouse. "It is a little stuffy."

Richard got up to readjust the thermostat. "I'll lower the temp."

"That won't be necessary if you're comfortable. I'm sure it will cool down in a moment."

"That's fine. It's no problem." Richard sat down and looked at Cathy. She was more beautiful close up. Her eyes were blue, and her hair appeared to be naturally blonde. Her skin was silky and didn't have a blemish on it. "What is it you need to know about Ms. MacKenzie?…You know, you're a very beautiful woman."

"Excuse me?"

"I asked what you needed to know about Ms. MacKenzie."

"That's not what you said." Cathy fidgeted in her seat.

"I said you were a very attractive woman. Are you married?"

"Excuse me, Dr. Tims?"

"Please, call me, Richard."

"Pardon me?"

"Call me 'Richard'. Do you have problems with your hearing?"

Cathy smiled. "Please. Dr. Tims…Richard. You're not letting me finish my train of thought. I would like to ask you about my friend. She's very upset with your present recommendations that she abort her pregnancy. I would like to discuss some matters I feel pertinent to her case."

"You never answered my question."

"What question?"

"Are you married?"

"What's that got to do with Sabrina? No, I'm not."

"Thank you." Richard nodded graciously at Cathy.

"For what?" Cathy nervously grinned. "This is getting ridiculous."

"Thank you for calling me Richard, and thank you for not being married." Richard smiled.

"Am I missing something here?"

"Whatever do you mean? I thought we were getting along wonderfully."

"I thought we were talking about my friend."

"No, you're talking about your friend. I can't. Any information about my patients is privileged. Since I can't talk about Sabrina, I would like to talk about the nicest looking woman I've seen in quite a while."

"Do you make passes at women in your office very often?"

"No, you're the first." Richard smiled and hesitated. He wanted Cathy to think about his answer for a moment. "I tell you. You get permission from your friend for us to discuss her case, and I'll talk until I'm blue, but only on one condition."

"What might that be? I won't have to disrobe, will I? I shouldn't because you've already undressed me with your eyes several times."

Richard was taken aback by Cathy's frankness. "No, no. Nothing like that at all. Let's be serious."

"Oh, you CAN be serious?"

"I can be very serious, Ms. Winston. I assure you."

"Okay. What's the condition?"

"You must have dinner with me."

"When?"

"Tonight."

"Fine, but remember, this is business. I expect you to be a perfect gentleman."

"True to my British heritage. Cross my heart."

"I'll bet," Cathy mumbled to herself.

"Excuse me," Richard leaned forward on his desk. "Did you say something?"

"Nothing important, just talking to myself."

"Has that been going on long?"

"What?"

"Whispering to yourself. It's a sign of senility. Especially, when you don't remember what you've said."

Cathy looked at Richard with amazement. "You're crazy. Where shall I meet you?"

"Meet me here. Say, around six thirty?"

"Six thirty sounds fine."

Richard stood from behind his desk. "Very good, Ms. Winston!" He snapped his heels together and gave a mock salute.

Cathy rose from her chair, headed for the door, and turned quickly, looking Richard in the eye. "I felt that, Dr. Tims."

Richard blushed slightly. "Felt what?"

"Oh, nothing. I just wanted to see if the temperature was as hot in here for you as it was for me." Cathy turned, smiled, and walked out the door.

Richard watched Cathy leave. He wondered how she knew he was sizing up her backside. "Until tonight, Cathy Winston. Until tonight." Richard smiled.

* * *

"You know, Richard," Cathy said as she sat down her Kahlua and coffee. "You're a self-centered, egotistical pompous ass."

"Thank you! That's what makes me so appealing."

"Oh! How's that?"

"It's expected, and it helps me get what I want."

"Really!" Cathy leaned forward on the table to show Richard she was interested in what he was saying. "How?"

"It intimidates others. You should know about that."

"What do you mean by that little remark?"

"Isn't intimidation how you got your information about me? At least, that's what the administrative secretaries told me." Richard took another drink of his brandy. He seemed unmoved by Cathy's tactics.

"Caught! But what I learned was public information."

"True." Richard leaned back in his chair. "What do you want to know about Sabrina? I'm ready to talk. Ask me anything."

"What makes you tick, Dr. Tims?"

"I thought we were talking about Sabrina."

"We are, but maybe these answers will help me understand why you're acting the way you are with Sabrina."

"Is this for a book or something?"

"No, it's for Cathy Winston." The warmth of the evening was closing in on Cathy. She leaned forward on the table, and supported her chin in her hands.

"I didn't come tonight to give my life history. I thought we came on business."

"Really? Who made this date, me or you?"

"I did, why?"

"What was the reason you asked me out?" Cathy traced the top of her cup with her right index finger. She looked down at her coffee, then back at Richard. "Business or pleasure?"

Richard stared across the table. Cathy was leaning forward on her left elbow. Her black crepe dress was v-cut in the front, and enough flesh was exposed to arouse Richard's thoughts as to whether she was wearing a bra or not. She was tracing the top of her coffee cup with her right index finger, and the look on her face was quite provocative.

"Well, I'm waiting for an answer."

"Hmm. Well, I must admit I wanted get to know you better, and Sabrina gave us something in common. Are you trying to make a pass at me?"

"Moi?" Cathy straightened up in her chair. "Whatever gave you that idea? You must have more of an inflated ego than I thought." Cathy stood up, straightened her dress, and picked up her purse. "I have to excuse myself for a moment. Would you order me another drink?"

Richard laughed and stood as Cathy got up from the table. "Certainly." Richard again stood and assisted Cathy with her chair when she returned. Her Kahlua and coffee was waiting at her place. She looked up at Richard as he finished pushing in her chair. "Thank you."

Richard sat down, and tried to get back to the subject of Sabrina. He was uncomfortable talking about himself. "Well, are you ready to hear about Sabrina's condition?"

"Yes. I'm all ears." Cathy resumed her previous posture.

Richard grinned. "You Americans. You have some funny sayings. I'd say your ears weren't your biggest asset."

"Is there a sexual innuendo hidden in that comment, Dr. Tims?"

"No! There's a compliment though."

"All right. Compliment accepted. May we talk about Sabrina's problem? I'm having a difficult time keeping my defenses up."

"Oh, do I put you on the defensive?"

"Only when you speak." They both laughed.

"All right," Richard situated himself in his chair. "I guess we can talk shop." Richard motioned for the waiter, ordered another brandy, and looked at Cathy. "Your friend-and I gather this goes beyond simple friend-ship-has a true dilemma. Her problem stems from a bout with rheumatic fever when she was a child. Sabrina suffered damage to two heart valves."

"Yes, I understand. She explained some of this from a diagram you left. I have a minor in physiology and can appreciate the significance of the damage."

"Ah, physiology. I'm glad to see you didn't spend all your time in the business world." Richard smiled at Cathy.

"Yes, I thought I would try to become a well rounded individual. If I hadn't made it in business, I had hopes of becoming a vet."

"Really?"

"Yes," Cathy smiled. She picked up her steak knife, held it in her right hand, and twirled the point against her left index finger. Her eyes bore a hole through the table in the direction of Richard's genitals. "I've always thought I would get enjoyment from neutering male animals."

Richard swallowed hard and secretly reached for his groin. Fortunately, the table cloth hid his actions.

"Just kidding," Cathy laughed. "Did you think I was serious?"

Richard gulped. "Yes."

Cathy reached over and touched his exposed hand. "You're cute." She withdrew her hand and laid down the knife. "Okay, you may continue your discussion about Sabrina. I'll try to be serious."

"I thought you already had been." Richard took a drink of brandy. "Do you find men doing that when they're around you?"

"Doing what?"

"Holding their groin."

Cathy, amused and shocked, almost spit out the drink of coffee she was taking. "You are crazy."

"Yes, well. Better crazy, than castrated."

"Oh, shut up. Tell me about Sabrina."

Richard took out his pen, picked up a cloth napkin, and began drawing on the fabric. "We performed an echocardiogram on Sabrina today, and it revealed that both the mitral and aortic valve have been scarred enough to produce real problems.

The mitral valve controls the blood flow from the left atria into the left ventricle. The left atria receives the blood from the lungs after it has been oxygenated. Then, the blood travels into the left ventricle and out to the rest of the body through the aortic valve.

When the left ventricle contracts, the pressure created closes the mitral valve keeping blood from flowing in reverse into the atria and the lung. As the pressure in the ventricle rises above the aortic pressure, the aortic valve opens and the blood is ejected from the heart into the aorta and out to the rest of the body. After the ventricle has emptied, the pressure falls, and the aortic valve closes. This prevents the blood that has just been pumped from backflowing into the heart. Once completed, the cycle restarts. Quite a miraculous process, don't you think?" Richard looked up from his drawing. "Clear thus far?"

Cathy watched Richard intently. He was oblivious to the rest of the clientele in the restaurant as he drew on the napkin. "You should have been a teacher."

"Excuse me?"

"Nothing. Everything is clear so far. I'll stop you if the water gets muddy."

"Pardon me?"

"You know if something isn't clear. How long have you been in the States?"

"Obviously not long enough to learn about muddying someone's water."

"Don't worry about it. It's just a figure of speech."

"Oh, I'll not pay any attention to it then, all right?"

"Fine." Cathy smiled and shook her head in amazement.

Richard looked back to his drawing. "Sabrina's mitral valve is insufficient and stenotic as is the aortic valve. That means, it opens as the ventricle is pumping and allows some of the blood to be pumped backwards. Since the aortic valve is stenotic, it requires higher pressure to get the blood out. Therefore, more blood is required to achieve the normal effects throughout the rest of Sabrina's body. If enough blood isn't pumped, then an adequate oxygen supply is not provided to the tissues. Pregnancy places a major demand on the heart. It requires an increase of twenty percent in the cardiac work just to fulfill the requirements of the pregnancy. Normal women have that and more in reserve, Cathy." Richard looked up from his drawing. "Sabrina doesn't have it! She's already demonstrated that by going into heart failure. Her heart couldn't meet the demand. Hopefully, we can support her heart pharmacologically until she can have the abortion."

"Richard," Cathy reached across the table and took Richard's hands in hers. "Sabrina won't have the abortion."

"Then she could die. You must explain that to her and help us make her understand the need for the abortion."

"Oh, no! You're not going to lay that on me. I've promised Sabrina I would try and talk you into helping her through the pregnancy. Look, Richard. Every doctor in the hospital could see her and tell her your story. I believe the good Lord, Himself, could intervene and tell her she would die if she had the baby, but Sabrina's response would be the same in every case. She's going to have her baby. Isn't there anyway in your power to reconsider and help her through this?"

Richard looked into Cathy's eyes. "You might be helping Sabrina sign her own death certificate." Richard shook his head. "I don't understand you women."

"No, I think you understand women, quite well." Cathy squeezed Richard's hands harder. "You don't understand motherhood. Having a baby means different things to different people. I've had an abortion, and I know what it's like to give that up. I know it was best for me, but it still bothers me. To have a part of you become a child is beyond description…to feel life within you…to see the product of your love for another culminate into life, I can't explain it. A man has no means of comparison. None! No woman has ever wanted a child more than Sabrina wants her child. I know Sabrina told you about her parents' death? She has been virtually on her own since she was seventeen, but she has found someone she's deeply in love with, and she wants his child. He doesn't even know she's pregnant."

"You mean the father of the child doesn't know she's pregnant?"

"No, and what's worse, he'll be out of the country until February on assignment with the Government. Please understand me, Richard. I wouldn't ask this if I thought Sabrina would die, but surely there must be alternatives. If she moved to Norfolk, stayed at rest, took her medicine, saw you every week...Surely, you could see your way to try...try for Sabrina's sake, my sake. I'm begging you."

Richard had a difficult time understanding the concern Cathy demonstrated for Sabrina, but he could see the desperation in her eyes. He considered the possibilities, the alternatives, and the potential consequences. He looked down at the napkin for a moment and then up at Cathy. "All right, all right. I'll discuss it with Bob Vance. I'll work with him throughtout the pregnancy and see if we can get Sabrina close enough to term to deliver."

Cathy jumped from her chair and walked behind Richard. She grabbed him around the neck and hugged him tightly. "Thank you, Richard. Thank you. You won't be sorry, I promise."

"Take it easy. Your assets are choking me. Remember we're in a public place."

"I don't care. You've made me very happy. Sabrina will be ecstatic."

"Cathy?"

"Yes, Richard." Cathy had sat back down in her chair.

"You must promise me. If Sabrina shows any sign of further decompensation, you will support me in my recommendation for termination of the pregnancy. Otherwise, no deal."

"I promise. As long as you're willing to give her a chance, I promise."

"Fine." Richard looked around the restaurant. "It seems we're the last two here. Perhaps we should leave." After Richard paid the check, he helped Cathy from her chair and retrieved her coat from the cloakroom. As he slipped her arms into the three-quarter length, white silk brocade jacket, he looked her in the eyes. "Who are you, Cathy Winston?"

"What do you mean?"

"I mean, who are you? Do you give a damn about Richard Tims, or are you using him to get what you want for Sabrina MacKenzie?"

"Richard, what you see, and what you perceive to be me, is me. I put on airs for no one. I lie only if it's to protect a loved one. I tell people what I think. There is no sugar coating. If I like you, I like you. If I don't like you, I avoid you. If you upset me, I don't pout. I cuss and fight back. If you please me, I'm gracious. If you don't please me, I get even. That's me in a nutshell." She took Richard's right arm and put it around her waist. She put her arms around his neck and gave him a kiss. She looked into his surprised eyes. "I think we had better be going, don't you?"

Richard recovered from the shock but agreed to Cathy's suggestion with a nod of his head.

\* \* \*

"If you'll drop me off by my car, I'll pick up a few things before going to my room." Cathy leaned back in the passenger seat of Richard's Mercedes 190 E. "I'm bushed."

"Where are you staying?"

"In the hospital's motel room. It's cramped, but it's home." Cathy mustered a smile. "I hate living out of a suitcase."

Richard looked at Cathy's stretched out form. "You appear to be weathering it rather well."

"Huh. What I'd give for a nice long comfortable bath."

"What would you give?"

Cathy sat up in her seat. "What are you driving at? As if I didn't know."

"Whatever do you mean, Ms. Winston? You must have more of an inflated ego than I thought." Richard looked over at Cathy and smiled.

"Touche, Dr. Tims. Touche." She laughed. "What did you have in mind?"

"I live alone in the country, and I have a splendid guest house. It has its own bath, with Jacuzzi, and it's very quiet. You're welcome to spend the night if you'd like...no strings attached."

"Sounds inviting...I'll take it." Cathy didn't want Richard to change his mind. "Especially, if there's no strings attached." Cathy reached over and ran her hand up Richard's right arm to his neck. She traced the outline of his jaw and moved across the outline of his ear to the back of his neck. "How do you suppose we might unattach them?"

Richard was having a difficult time keeping his eyes on the road. "Unattach what?"

Cathy moved her hand over to her dress and traced the line of the spaghetti straps on her shoulder. She looked up at Richard. "Why, the strings, of course."

"I'm sure we'll find a way, as long as you left the steak knife back in the restaurant." They both laughed; Cathy's sound was more relaxed than Richard's.

"I told you I was kidding."

"I know, but it's going to take me a while to shake that one off."

The 190 Mercedes eased into the parking structure. Cathy directed Richard to a parking space close to her car. Richard opened his door and looked at a blue Mazda 323 parked in the next slot. Cathy opened her door and walked around to the back of the Mercedes.

"What are you looking at, Richard?"

"Your car. What do you need?"

"That's not my car. This is my car." Cathy pointed to the slot directly behind Richard's Mercedes.

Richard turned and looked toward the indicated space. "My goodness."

"Careful, doctor, you look like you're about to hyperventilate."

"You own…" Richard looked up at Cathy. "But, of course you do. You own a 911 Turbo. It's a beast of a car." Richard walked over and began tracing the outline of the Porsche. He looked up and smiled. "A car befitting the personality of its owner. How long have you had it?"

Cathy looked at her watch. "Oh, about forty hours. It's still a virgin for anything over one hundred and ten. What do you mean, 'befitting my personality'? Should I be offended?"

"NO! Absolutely not," Richard quickly responded. He walked around the entire length of the Porsche, then looked back at Cathy. "A clean, pure, unblemished skin of beauty covering a soft, plush, classy interior wrapped around a subtle, but hot, engine. She's nice to those who know how to handle her but can terrorize those who go lightly on the control and heavy on the accelerator."

"Oh, quit fantasizing over the car."

Richard walked to Cathy and put both hands around her trim waist. "I wasn't talking about the car."

Cathy pushed him away. "Hush, Richard. We can take the Porsche and leave your car here if you'd like."

"I thought you'd never ask," Richard said as he took the key from Cathy and opened the door. He helped Cathy into the car, walked around to the driver's side, and slid into the brown leather bucket seat. He leaned back and placed both hands on the steering wheel.

Cathy looked over at him and smiled. "Porsche…there is no substitute."

"Where have I heard that before?"

"Oh, it's from a Tom Cruise movie. I'm a movie nut. It just came to mind as I watched you get into the car." Cathy sighed. "Let's go, I'm tired."

Richard slipped the key into the ignition, depressed the clutch, and turned the key over. The turbocharged six came to life. He just sat there listening to the idle.

Cathy watched the boyish expression come over Richard's face. "Be careful, you might get spoiled."

Richard grinned. "What a way to go?"

"BEEP.... BEEP.... BEEP...BEEP...Dr. Tims call CCU stat. Dr. Tims call CCU stat."

"Damn. I'll use the phone in my car." Richard turned off the ignition.

"You don't suppose it could be about Sabrina, do you?"

"I wouldn't think so. It's probably some other patient. Dr. Shepherd is covering for me tonight. It shouldn't take long."

Cathy watched Richard go to his car, pick up the cellular phone, and talk to the hospital. He put down the phone, turned contemplative, and walked back to the Porsche. He leaned down and talked to Cathy through the opened driver's window. "It was about Sabrina. Doesn't seem serious, but I think I had better go see her. Sam said she has developed P.A.T. That's a term meaning her heart is beating too fast. We have to get her back to a regular rate. I'll have to take a raincheck on the rest of the evening. I'll have one of the residents escort you to your motel room."

"That'll be fine. I need some sleep."

Richard escorted Cathy to CCU. As they walked off the elevator, Sam Shepherd was standing in the hallway. Cathy saw Sam waiting for Richard, and she grasped Richard's arm tightly. Richard covered her hand with his.

"She's all right, Cathy. Sam's waiting to give me an update. I asked him to meet me here when I spoke to him on the telephone."

"Thank goodness," Cathy said as she relaxed her hold on Richard's forearm. "I thought he was going to give us bad news."

"Don't be melodramatic. She's not in that bad of shape."

Cathy quickly removed her hands from Richard's arm. "I wasn't being melodramatic. I'm concerned."

"I know. I'm sorry. I didn't mean to be flippant. I have a hard time remembering that patients, friends and family aren't versed in the habits of doctors and hospitals. Forgive me?"

"I forgive you." Cathy recaptured Richard's reassuring hand.

"How's she doing, Sam?" Richard asked as they approached the white clad resident.

"I was going to call you back, but I knew you were on your way up. She converted with the first dose of Isoptin. She's doing fine, regular sinus rhythm since." Sam shrugged his shoulders. "I guess I yelled 'wolf' too soon."

"You did exactly what you were ordered to do. Don't ever apologize for that. Remember, don't ever apologize to other doctors or families if you treat too quickly, only if you treat too slowly." Richard's tutorial side was coming out in his discussion with Sam. As soon as he recognized the obsession, he backed off. "Sorry, I get on my soap box a little too often."

Sam looked at Richard in amazement. "Excuse me?"

"I said I get on my soap box too often." Richard looked at Cathy. "Sam, I would like to introduce Cathy Winston. Cathy, this is Dr. Sam Shepherd. He's the doctor that rode in from the airport with Sabrina. If it weren't for Sam, Sabrina might not be in as good a shape as she is now. "

"Pleased to meet you, Ms. Winston." Sam stretched out his hand to Cathy.

"Please, call me Cathy." Cathy shook Sam's hand, held on for a moment, and released the grip slowly.

"Thank you. I'd consider it an honor. I've always liked calling beautiful women by their first names."

"You Virginia boys sure like to ooze with the charm." Cathy smiled as she looked Sam in the eye.

"I hate to interrupt your attempt to pick up my date, Dr. Shepherd, but I have a job for you."

Sam smiled at Cathy and then turned to face Richard. "What's that?"

Richard looked at Cathy. "I'm sorry this evening didn't turn out as we wished, but I feel I should stay with Sabrina for a while. I might give her some mild sedation, and I want to watch her monitor."

"I'm sorry too, Richard." Cathy pulled herself up to Richard's ear. "There'll be others. I promise." She kissed him on the cheek.

"Sam, would you show Cathy to her motel room? She'd like to get some rest."

"Gladly!" Sam took Cathy's arm, and they walked down the hall toward the exit.

"What did you do to him tonight?" Sam asked Cathy when they were out of Richard's range of hearing.

"What do you mean?" Cathy looked up into Sam's eyes.

"Dr. Tims has never said sorry to anyone, particularly a lowly resident."

Cathy smiled, leaned against Sam's arm and paced with him down the hall.

Richard watched Sam place his arm around Cathy's waist. "Hey, Sam. Remember, I hold the outcome of your residency in the palm of my hand; so watch out what you put in the palm of yours."

Sam escorted Cathy to the exit. As they turned left toward the resident rooms, Richard's eyes widened. "Sam! I said her motel room, not the 'on call' room!"

Sam turned and grinned. "Oh, yeah! I forgot." He smiled and directed Cathy to exit.

Richard smiled, turned, and strolled through the automatic doors of CCU. He stopped at the nurse's station and watched Sabrina's tracing for five minutes. Then he made his way to her cubicle.

Sabrina looked up as he entered. "Mmmm, don't you look dapper."

"New dress code for evening rounds," Richard replied flatly as he continued to watch the monitor.

"Oh, no. Your attire has Cathy written all over it." Sabrina sniffed. "And, I can smell Cathy's Shalimar."

"Quite perceptive. I understand your heart was trying to do a dance this evening."

Sabrina's smile gave way to concern. She looked at the monitor and then at Richard. "What does all this mean?"

"Oh, this doesn't mean much, but we'll have to follow you very closely throughout the rest of the pregnancy to make sure it doesn't try any more tricks." Richard continued to watch the monitor. "You'll have to stay on a mild fluid tablet called Lasix, a potassium supplement, and your digitalis during the entire gestation. I'll have to see you everytime Dr. Vance sees you. Can you accept that responsibility?" Richard looked down at Sabrina. He didn't change his facial expression; victory nor defeat showed in his face.

Sabrina looked at Richard in amazement. "What do you mean, 'throughout the pregnancy'? I thought you wanted me to have an abortion."

Richard smiled at Sabrina for the first time. "Let's just say I had some polite arm twisting and gentle eye opening on the joys of motherhood. I think we can give it a go for a while longer. What do you say?"

Sabrina jumped from the supine position so quickly it caught Richard off guard. She reached out with her arms and grasped him around the neck. He started backing up in surprise, but if he backed too far, it would extract Sabrina from her bed.

"Dr. Tims! You've made me the happiest woman on Earth. I'll be good. You'll see. I'll do everything you say."

"If you do, you'll be the first." Richard eased Sabrina's neck hold and settled her back into the bed. "Sabrina, if you are to survive this and have a healthy baby, you must restrict your activity to a minimum. I would keep you right here the entire time, but that's not practical. I think you should move closer to this area, take a leave of absense from your business, and REST!"

Sabrina lay nervously in the bed, wringing her hands and listened to Dr. Tims' every word. "I can keep both you and Dr. Vance for my doctors?"

"Absolutely, I wouldn't have it any other way."

"I'll rest, I'll take my medicine, and I'll do everything you want me to do. I promise."

"I won't hold you to that." Richard continued to watch Sabrina's regular cardiac rhythm. "I think we've done about enough watching and talking." Richard looked down at Sabrina's smiling face. "What do you think about going home tomorrow?"

Sabrina's mouth fell opened. "You mean it?"

"I wouldn't have said it otherwise. You get some rest." Richard pushed four milligrams of Valium into Sabrina's I.V. "We'll get things ready to go tomorrow."

"O...," Sabrina yawned. "kay. Whoo, what have you given me?"

"Something to help you rest."

"It sure wo.r..k...s.....f....a.....s......t." Sabrina closed her eyes and let out a deep sigh.

"Yes, it sure does." Richard looked down at Sabrina's sleeping form and whispered. "I hope you haven't promised the bloody impossible, Richard ole boy." Richard returned to the nurse's station and told the staff the dose of medication he had given Sabrina so it could be properly charted. "I'll be in the resident quarters for the evening, ladies. Goodnight."

"Goodnight, Dr. Tims." The three nurses on-duty responded.

* * *

Sabrina was anxious to leave the hospital. She had already had her hour long instruction session with Dr. Vance and Dr. Tims. The nurses had given her all the necessary education on the home telemetry unit. She was to check in twice daily with the CCU, and they would interpret a tracing Sabrina transmitted by phone. The dietitian had explained her diet. She was ready, beyond ready to check out, but **NO** Cathy.

"Where in the devil is she?" Sabrina thought as she watched out the window. She patted her foot and looked down at her watch for the fifth time in so many minutes.

Suddenly the door burst open, and Cathy breezed in carrying enough sacks to obliterate the surface of the bed. "Sabrina," Cathy took a deep breath. "You'll never guess where I've been and what I've done. It's been such a wild morning that I don't know where to begin."

"How about getting me out of here first and then tellihg me about it. I want to go home, wherever that is going to be."

"Don't get in such a hurry." Cathy picked up a yellow and blue box and tossed it to Sabrina. "Put this on. You've worn those clothes forever and a day."

Sabrina opened the box. "It's lovely." She picked up the yellow and white jumper from the box.

"I thought it would cover your expanding belly as the baby grew."

Sabrina went into the bathroom and changed clothes. When she returned, Cathy had a folder of information to give Sabrina.

"Sabrina, don't get upset. I know you think I get a little impulsive on occasion, but this seemed to be the right thing to do and the right time to do it."

"Cathy, what on Earth have you done now?"

"Hush, and listen. You owe me for last night. I was invited to Richard's house, but you had to have your little fit."

"Whoa! Do you mean you were going to spend the night at Richard's last night?"

"What's the matter? You think you're the only one that can go out and have fun?"

"I didn't mean it like that."

"I know. I'm kidding. Does digitalization mean the loss of humor?"

"*NO!* I thought you had sworn off the male species."

"I had until I met him. He's an old stuffed shirt, but he's a cute one."

"Do you think this could be serious?"

"I hope so." Cathy winked at Sabrina and laughed. "I should have further opportunities to find out. They did recommend we move to Norfolk."

"We?"

"Of course. You didn't think I would let you move here and live by yourself, did you?"

"Well, I wasn't sure."

"You'll never learn, will you?" Cathy handed the packet of information to Sabrina. "I love you as if you were my sister. I won't let anything happen to you that I have the power to prevent. If it required twenty-four hour a day vigilance, I would do it. Look at the papers. That's the other surprise I have for you." Cathy was excited. She walked around Sabrina and tried to hurry her through the forms. "That's why I was late this morning. I've bought us a condo!"

"A condo!" Sabrina leafed through the sales contracts. "These have both our names on them."

"Of course they do. I knew you'd love the place. It has a big living room, dining room, a huge kitchen, and three bedrooms. Each bedroom has its own bath, and each bath has its own Jacuzzi. Two of the bedrooms are big enough to include a sitting area. Behind the condo is a private garden area. See..." Cathy flipped through the pictures that Sabrina was trying to hold.

"Cathy, this is beautiful, but I shouldn't own part of it. You put your money down and signed the papers."

"Don't hurt my feelings. what's mine is yours. You can pay me half if you like it. If you don't, I'll worry about it later. If you do buy half, I don't want to have to do all the paper work again." Cathy continued to dance around Sabrina. "The best part is we're two streets over from the beach, and only ten minutes away from the hospital. The fresh air will be good for you and the baby. You had better say yes because they're delivering the furniture today."

"Furniture?"

"Sure. You didn't think we were going to move all that stuff from the island, did you?"

"No, but I'd like a few things so it will feel like home."

"I'm having the personal things shipped tomorrow. I've made the arrangements. They're even going to bring your car."

"Precious?"

"Oh, hell." Cathy smiled at Sabrina. "So, what do you say?"

Sabrina looked at the papers, looked at Cathy, and gave her a big hug. "I say, let's go home to..." Sabrina looked at the address. "...1100 Ocean Boulevard." She looked back to Cathy and smiled.

"Great! You have to go down in a wheelchair, silly hospital policy or something. I'll go get one, and we're off." Cathy hustled out the door, rounded up a wheelchair, and went back to get Sabrina.

She was excited beyond explanation. Finally, she was going to be able to do something for Sabrina that was important, really important.

As she rolled Sabrina down the hall, she couldn't quit talking. "I've found a grocery store that will deliver. What's so neat, Sabrina, is that they let you shop on your VCR. You pick out your groceries from their weekly videotape, hit a code, call the store, transmit your codes, and boom. Your groceries are delivered within two hours. Neat, huh?"

"Marvelous. What has come over you?"

"I don't know. I feel like I'm doing something for you, finally, I guess."

"Cathy, you always do things for me. Look at the deal you just landed with Chesworth. I still can't believe that."

"That's business. I mean, well, with this, I'm helping you achieve something you really want. I'm helping you to obtain a dream, like you did for me. You don't think I've gone overboard, do you?"

"Overboard? Oh, I don't know. What would you call buying a new seventy thousand dollar car, finding a new man, buying a two hundred thousand dollar condo and a house full of furniture?"

Cathy laughed. "I see what you mean."

As they passed through the lobby, Richard greeted them. Cathy looked at Richard, and her gaze widened. "Hi, I didn't expect to see you."

"I wanted to see my expectant mother off."

"That's all?" Cathy pouted.

"No, that's not all." Richard leaned over and kissed Cathy on her cheek.

"Thanks. We're moving into a new home today."

"Really? Both of you? Cathy, you are a true friend, indeed."

"I told you I was, and I don't say anything I don't mean."

"I'm beginning to realize that. Take good care of her. Sabrina"

"Oh, you remembered my name?"

Richard laughed. "You know, you're both quite alike."

Cathy and Sabrina looked at each other. "Us? Nah!"

Richard grinned. "Sabrina, I'll see you soon, and, Cathy, I'd like to see more of you, sooner."

"Oooooh, I'd like that," Cathy squirmed like a teenager.

"Okay, you two, we're gathering an audience, and I want to go home!" Sabrina crooked her neck to see the activity happening behind her back.

"Okay, okay! Good-by, Richard. I'll see you tomorrow."

"Good-by." Richard walked away from the lobby toward CCU. It would take more than a few days to absorb the changes that had come into his life.

Cathy watched Richard until he rounded the corner to the elevators.

Sabrina patted her foot, locked the wheels to the wheelchair, and got up. She started out the door. "Hey, you coming with me?"

Cathy looked down at the empty wheelchair and started to laugh. She picked up her sacks from the space behind the chair, and caught up with Sabrina. "Sorry. Let's go home."

"Thanks! That's the best three words I've heard since I arrived at this place." Sabrina looked around at the lobby of the hospital. She knew she would reluctantly come to know it much better.

# 15

Transcaucasia, the area of the Soviet Union bordered on the East by the Caspian Sea, the West by the Black Sea, and the North and South by the Great and Little Caucasus Mountains, respectively, encompasses three regions: Georgian S.S.R., Armenian S.S.R., and Azerbaijan S.S.R. The Azerbaijan region is the easternmost of the three "states", and Baku, its capital, because of its guarded position on the southeastern shore of the Apsheron Peninsula, boasts one of the best harbors on the Caspian. This area is rich with oil deposits, and the countryside surrounding Baku is freckled with oil derricks and oil storage facilities. In spite of these modern "developments", the city has maintained its ancient beauty. The wide boulevard extending down the middle of town to the harbor is dotted with cafes and small shops uncommon to typical Russian cities. On warm days these cafes come alive with the people of the city and exude an ambiance unexpected in a communistic state.

While Baku, located in northern Azerbaijan, depends on its endowment of oil deposits, Lenkoran, the southern social center, flourishes on a more agrarian culture. The land around Lenkoran produces a great percentage of the Soviet Union's winter produce, and near Lenkoran, on the coast of the Caspian, sprawls the largest Coastal wildlife preservation in the U.S.S.R.

The people of the Baku region, the Turkic Azerbaijanis, comprise seventy-five percent of the population. The rest are Russians. The Turkic Azerbaijani's ties are with their Turkish ancestors while the people of Lenkoran, the Talishi, are of Iranian descent. With the advent of Communism, the literacy of these groups increased to nearly one hundred percent, and with the development of the Azerbaijan Institute of Petroleum and Chemistry, a center for higher education expanded close to the homes of those that qualified for that privilege.

Tallia Maransk, a thirty year old Talishi, was one of those grateful for the presence of the Institute. Otherwise, she would have completed her final education in research chemisty in one of the northern universities. Tallia, a tall, thin, black haired, olive skinned, well-proportioned woman grew up in the outskirts of Lenkoran. Her habits, beliefs, and religious values were strongly linked to her Iranian ancestors, but her political ties revealed the presence of the Supreme Soviet. Even though she had heard the terrible stories of the Revolution and the viciousness of the KGB, her devotion was to the U.S.S.R. Her father, the overseer of the wildlife preserve on the Caspian Coast, was also a loyal Marxist who enjoyed many freedoms not enjoyed by others. One of his liberties, which Tallia enjoyed most, was his possession of a firearm. Tallia's tomboyish desire to learn to fire the weapon frightened her mother, but made her the envy of her friends. Her father cherished the moments he and Tallia spent outdoors as she became proficient in her use of his smuggled 9mm Beretta, too proficient for his ego's liking. Even though he didn't like Tallia's superior expertise, one of his saddest days came when Tallia put down the gun and made more time in her life for boys.

As Tallia grew, she developed into an extremely intelligent and beautiful woman though she was quite shy. The boys, intimidated by her intellect, stopped asking her for dates, and the girls, mistaking her shyness for snobbiness, kept their distance. Tallia's beauty alienated her peers. So, Tallia directed her energies to her studies. She qualified for higher education at the Institute and surpassed many of those who had previouly scorned her. After her graduate training, she was assigned a position in Baku as a research chemist. Her life settled into a routine of work and caring for her parents who had moved to the city after her father became too old to work at the preserve. Until recently, Tallia accepted that routine as her lot, at least until her parents passed away. Then, she would be alone, a future she was in no hurry to welcome and very desirous to alter.

* * *

As Tallia watched the second hand slowly creep around the large white face of her laboratory clock, she thought of how her life was about to change. *How can this be?* She pondered as her monotone assistant droned calculations from a recent experiment into her left ear. She had met Christian only a few short months before, but it seemed she had known him all her life. As she thought about Christian, she reminisced about their first encounter. She could still see him as he walked up to her table at the cafe. She was enjoying her lunch and the noon-day sun, when the bronze-skinned stranger approached and introduced himself as Christian Sandobol. He asked to join her, and she readily agreed. He told her he was an Afghani, working for the Soviet government and assigned to investigate the movement of black market arms through Baku to Krasnovodsk and on to the Afghanistan frontier. The arms were making their way into the hands of Afghan rebels and being used to harass Russian troops along their disputed borders. He questioned Tallia about empty containers marked with her laboratory's insignia found discarded around the rebel camps. They had to have been used to conceal smuggled arms. Tallia listened to Christian's questions because she didn't want to be implicated in such a plot against her government, but Christian's questions floated in and out of her mind as she fantasized making love with this stranger. She blushed when he caught her at her daydream. When she returned to reality, she assured Christian she knew nothing about the use of her lab's containers, and furthermore, she had nothing to do with packing or shipping of products from her lab. Her job concentrated on developing new distillation techniques for crude oil. Christian seemed to accept her confession, but instead of excusing himself, he asked if he could join her for lunch. Captivated by his good looks, she readily agreed.

Tallia and Christian's relationship flowered from that first meeting. She became rapt in the blinding mist of first love. Christian was the first man who seemed to really care for her. Aside from his attentiveness and concern, his lovemaking was so gentle, so fulfilling, that when Christian told her he loved her, Tallia truly believed him. He took her places she had never been before, both physically and emotionally. The once boring city of Baku became alive. Their discussions of the city and the surrounding countryside put new life into Tallia's desire to raise a family near where she had grown up.

Finally her hopes had turned into something real. On one of their trips into the Baku countryside, Christian had asked Tallia to marry him. She had quickly agreed. He told her they would have to move closer to Afghanistan for a while, but someday they would be able to return to Baku. It made no difference to Tallia. She would go anywhere to be with Christian.

Christian was to call and finalize their travel plans before 5:00 P.M., but the hour was about to arrive and there had been no phone message. Tallia was worried. Suppose something had happened to him. Suppose he didn't love her. Suppose she didn't do the right things when they made love. Afterall, she had no experience. Suppose…

"Tallia!" The assistant tried to get Tallia's attention, but she seemed in a trance. "Tallia!"

"Yes?" Tallia shook her head and looked at the assistant in frustration. "What do you want?"

"Telephone." The assistant pointed to the wall mounted telephone; its receiver conspicuously hanging down to the side. "I answered for you. You seemed to be thinking of other things."

Tallia gulped, jumped from her stool, and raced to the phone. "Hello, Tallia Maransk," she panted into the mouthpiece.

"Tallia, my love."

"Christian, it is you. I thought…"

"You thought I had forgotten. No?"

"No!…I mean, yes. I thought you had forgotten me. I was so worried. I thought I would never see you again."

"Never? Never would I forget the woman that has made my life worth living. Are you prepared to come with me? I need you so."

"Yes, Christian. I'm ready to go. You're all I've ever cared for-all I've ever loved. Say when and where, and I will come."

"You are sure? You are prepared to leave your parents? Your work?"

"Yes! My parents want my happiness. That is all they have ever wanted. They understand, and they are happy I'm ready to love a man and have a family. I'm happy, also."

"Good, good, Tallia. I am happy, too. Very happy. I love you very much."

"I love you, Christian. Are we leaving tonight?"

"Yes. Meet me on Pier Fifteen at 10:00 P.M. We will leave from there. I have all your papers. Go straight home and get your things. You should tell your parents what time you are leaving and from where. That way they will not worry. Please be on time. Our Captain is not a patient man."

"If I tell them, they will want to come and see me off. I don't know if I could stand that."

"You must not permit that." Christian blurted out the answer quicker than he had wanted.

"Why? Why, not?"

"I do not wish them to go home unattended. That's all. It's to be a moon-less night, and it might be dangerous for them to be walking around unescorted. Say your good-bys at home. If everything works out in Afghanistan, we'll be back very soon. Perhaps we will live in Baku someday."

"You mean it? There might be a chance? My parents will be very happy."

"I didn't want to mention it until I was sure, but my commanding offi-cer confirmed my assignment in the security office of the petroleum plant."

"Oh, I'm truly happy. I was happy before, Christian, but I'm ecstatic, now."

"I'd hoped that would make your leaving easier to accept."

"It does…Oh, it does. I might even be able to work at my job again."

"You didn't resign, did you?"

"No, I just took a leave of absence, like you recommended."

"Very good. It seems as if we're set to go."

"Yes, it will be a more comfortable departure, now. Thank you. I love you. See you at ten. I do love you, Christian." Tallia embraced the phone relishing the news Christian had given her. She loved him and would follow him anywhere, but knowing she would be back "home" someday relieved her gnawing anxiety about losing contact with her parents and homeland.

"Until then my love, until then, I will count the minutes." Christian Sandobol hung up the phone and looked at his cohort. "It is almost set, Yakim. Almost set." He rubbed his black mustache and beard in thought.

"I knew you could do it, my friend. I knew Yassar Akazian could arrange the biggest insult to the Russian oil industry in our fight for recognition. At least this oil will not be used to supply the Russian dogs that continue to harass our brothers in Afghanistan. Perhaps the Communists will yield to our Highest One's wishes to buy oil from our Homeland." Yakim Haffar smiled and patted Yassar on the shoulder.

"It makes no difference. If this plan works, the destruction of this area will make them concentrate their efforts on rebuilding for a number of years giving us the chance to infiltrate the region with our operatives. Then someday all our people will be under one flag, and this land will once again be under the watchful eye of the Ayatollah." Yassar smiled and smacked Yakim's back. "And the best part is the Russians will think one of their own created the problem. Now come, there is much to do. Let's not wallow in our glory too quickly."

Yassar Akazian and Yakim Haffar, two of the most hunted terrorists in the Middle East, had infiltrated Russia from northern Iran four months previously. Their methods were ruthless and their techniques impeccable. They had learned their trade in one of the many terrorists' camps located in the Lebanese foothills. Death to them meant nothing and killing even less. They had regard for no other individual, only their own ultimate gain and potential glory. One of them was better than the other only because of his intelligence and capability of manipulating human emotions. That was Yassar. He had shown his qualities and gained his reputation by performing many of the terrorist bombings in London and Israel. He had also assisted in hijackings and some of the hostage kidnappings, but none of these compared to the magnitude of this night's mission. If everything went as anticipated, eighty percent of the oil stored in Baku would be destroyed, the primary refinery would be incapacitated, and the movement of all vessels in and out of the harbor would be stalled for the next month. The Soviets would have to withdraw its border troops in order to maintain order in the region. At least, that was Yassar and his director's calculated intentions.

Over the past two months, Yakim had smuggled C-4 plastic explosive into Baku from a secret base in Rasht. Rasht was in northern Iran, and it had been very easy to bring in small vessels under the Russian surface radar capabilities. After all, why should the Russians expect trouble from the sea in this area. Their expensive radar dealt exclusively with air attacks. Much of the mission, especially their escape, relied on the poor quality of the Russian surface radar and the ineptness with which it was used. With the help of information indirectly obtained from Tallia, Yakim and his cohorts had been able to disseminate the explosives into various storage areas. They had also learned of two major ship departures out of Baku

Harbor this very evening. Their escape and Tallia's kidnapping would have to occur tonight. It had been difficult, but they had managed to attach magnetic mines to the underside of both of the departing vessels. One, or both would go down in the harbor channel. They had timed all charges to detonate within minutes of 10:30 P.M. If Tallia was late, she would die, along with anyone on or near Pier Fifteen.

Yassar stood alone on the dock. He looked at his watch. 10:10. Tallia was late. Yakim had warned him that they would need at least ten minutes to get out of range of the concussion from the explosions. His watch was synchronized with the timers on the charges. He knew of Yakim's abilities. The charges would work and on time. Yassar checked his watch once again. 10:15. He turned and headed for the craft.

"Christian…. Christian…. I'm here…"

Yassar turned and saw Tallia walking down the pier toward him. He ran to her side, grabbed her bag, grasped her arm, and rushed for the boat.

"What's your hurry?" Tallia attempted to pull her arm from his tight grip.

"We must leave immediately. There is much danger…There…there is to be an arrest of black marketeers by the KGB. I…I don't know when, and I don't want you to be involved…Quickly, we must go…hurry!"

Tallia was forcefully escorted to the boat. She balked when she saw the thirty foot inboard. "This is a bit small to take on the Caspian, don't you think? There is a storm brewing."

"Get aboard quickly…quickly!" Yassar threw her bag to Yakim. He then helped Tallia onto the deck.

Yakim escorted Tallia forward to a small cabin. "Get in, and don't come out!" He closed the door and locked the latch from the outside. There was barely enough room in the cabin to crouch. Tallia sqeezed forward and lay down on a small bench seat in the forward part of the cabin. The boat lurched from its berth.

"Heyl!! What's going on here?" Tallia yelled, but she was thrown off the bench and rolled against the door by the quick acceleration of the twin engines. She heard the high pitch revving of the engines and sensed the speed of their exit from the harbor. The boat continued to bounce until it planed on the smooth surface of the jettyed portion of the Harbor. She straightened herself from her position on the floor, regained her balance, and started to crawl to the bench, but her balance was rocked again as the boat hit the uneven surface of a sea disturbed by a distant storm. She corrected her stance, but was again shaken by some of the strangest sounds she had ever heard. They were distant, but their effect was great. The boat felt as if it were about to come out of the water, but the engines continued to rev at maximum. Tallia crawled to the door, and began beating on the hatch. Before she finished her second volley against the wooden door, the hatch opened and Yassar appeared.

"Come! See what you have enabled us to do." Yassar grabbed Tallia's left arm and hastily escorted her to the deck.

Tallia stood on the pitching deck, wiped the spray from her eyes, and looked back toward Baku. She was taken back by the sight. Flames appeared to surround the city, and two large tankers were floundering in the harbor. Fire had erupted on one of their decks, and oil was leaking into the water of the basin. She looked at Christian and then at his friend. Their faces were illuminated by an eerie orange glow from the distant explosions. She could see their pleasure at the sight.

"What has happened, Christian? What have I enabled you to do?"

Yassar looked at Tallia. "Tallia, my name is Yassar Akazian. I tell you this because you will live with me and never tell a soul, or you will not live at all. Do you understand?"

Tallia shook her head. She did not understand, but she was unable to speak.

"I have dealt a blow for my people against your government. Your oil will no longer supply your military along the Afghan border, and your country will have to purchase its fuel supply from my brothers in Iran."

"You...you're not Christian Sandobol? You...you don't love me? Then why? Why have you...you son-of-a-bitch. You've used me."

"Yes, woman, and I will keep using you or kill you." Yassar brushed Tallia's hair aside and stroked her skin down to her cleavage.

Tallia slapped his hand away. "Do not touch me, you...you are camel dung. I spit on you."

Yassar pulled a 9mm Beretta and stroked Tallia's cleavage with the muzzle. "You will do as I say! There will be no choice, except death." He slapped her across her face with the back of his left hand.

Tallia fell to her knees on the deck, looked at the gun in Yassar's right hand, and decided to submit for the moment. "I will find a way to get you, you will see. When I do, I will kill you. I promise you that. Then, I will return to my country."

"I would advise against it!" Yassar laughed aloud.

"Why is that?" Tallia asked as she rose from the deck and rubbed her left cheek.

"I have left certain clues behind in Baku that will implicate you with the explosions. There will be wire found that originated from your lab. Certain bank accounts will be found by the KGB with inappropriate amounts of money for a lab scientist to earn. Partially burned letters addressed from you to your parents explaining how you had grown bitter with the treatment of your Iranian brothers will be found. If I were you, I wouldn't plan on going back to Baku for quite some time."

Standing became increasingly more difficult as the pitch of the waves increased. Tallia's gaze was still transfixed on the leaping orange flames in the distance. Her imagination couldn't fathom the ramifications of the night. All she could think of was finding a way to vindicate herself and to kill Yassar and Yakim. "I'm going to be sick." Tallia hung her head over the gunwale and regurgitated her supper.

"I think it best if Tallia took a nap. Don't you, Yakim?" Yassar grabbed Tallia around the upper arms and Yakim straightened out her right forearm. Yakim deftly threaded a needled syringe into an antecubital vein and pushed a clear liquid into her circulatory system. Tallia immediately felt a numbness spread over her body, and she lost consciousness.

"Put her back in the cabin, Yakim. Do you think she will sleep until we arrive at the coast?"

"Most assuredly! I will supplement the dose of diazepam I just gave her with another injection once we have her in bed. She will be asleep for at least eight hours."

"Excellent! We will be home in three hours. Check the radar, but only for one sweep. See if any vessels followed us out of the harbor."

Yakim pulsed the radar and checked the screen. "All activity is heading for the fires in the harbor. There are no following vessels."

"As anticipated, Yakim. As anticipated." Yassar looked back toward the lights on the horizon, once again. "I hope we have not kicked the Bear too hard," he remarked quietly.

"What is it, Yassar?" Yakim asked as he still watched the radar scope.

"Nothing, Yakim, nothing. Don't overuse the radar. There could be patrol boats vectoring this way."

Yakim switched off the radar and corrected his course for the coast of Iran.

* * *

Yakim eased the boat into its covered berth in the Bandar-e Anzali harbor. The threatening storm was whipping up a light rain as Yassar finished tying the lines. The last five miles of the trip had been tense in such a small vessel. Waves were now peaking at three to five feet, and the whitecaps had filled the aft area with six inches of water. Even though the storm showed no signs of abating, Yassar could see Igor Rafstini waiting on the dock. As Yassar stepped onto the pier, Igor approached.

"Yassar, welcome home. I assume your mission was a success?"

"I'm sure you know already. I believe you would not welcome us if it had not been." Yassar didn't trust Igor. Igor had learned the ropes as an active terrorist, like Yassar, but now he made his living as an "arranger". Igor was the buffer. He protected the terrorist from being identified by his employer, and vice versa.

Igor laughed his deep gutteral laugh and patted Yassar on the back. "You are right, my friend. It was a huge success. The fires still burn. My contacts say the city is in turmoil. I think we have finally impressed our Communist friends. Do you not?" Igor watched with interest as Yakim left the boat. Tallia's limp body was draped over his shoulder, and Yakim's right hand had pushed Tallia's skirt well above her lower right buttock. "A spoil of war, eh Yassar?"

Yassar smiled. "A very nice comfort on cold nights, such as this." Yassar watched Yakim put Tallia in the back seat of the black Mercedes. Yakim closed the door and waited for Yassar to join him. "To what do we owe this honor? Usually, Igor Rafstini only welcomes home the defeated." Yassar patted Igor's shoulder holster. "Usually with hot lead or cold steel."

"You are the perceptive one, Yassar. Quite perceptive I must speak to you of another mission, right away."

"I can't think of other duties, Igor. Not tonight! Might we discuss this tomorrow? The trip across the Caspian was very tiring."

"I'm afraid not. Come !" Igor directed Yassar to an old shack close to the slip As he passed the automobile, he motioned for Yakim to join them. They entered the small building, and the trio sat at a small table lit only by a dirty kerosene lantern. Igor removed a flat flask from his inner coat pocket and offered them brandy. They both heartily accepted. "I hope the brandy will warm your bodies and spirits for I have a great undertaking for you…" Igor waited for a few moments and poured Yassar and Yakim another glass.

"While you have been busy in Russia, much has happened. Our neighbors across the Gulf have begun a great endeavor. Along with the Americans, our Saudi enemies are trying to get the Mediterranean community to construct a series of pipelines from Saudi Arabia to Eqypt."

Yassar suddenly became very sober. "If they do that, they can dry up the Gulf. Saudi Arabia can corner the world's oil market, and that would leave us…"

"Penniless after a few years, my friend, unless we submitted to the Saudi's price controls and sales quotas."

"They could never hope to complete construction. There are too many opportunities for sabotage," Yakim said as he became deeply interested in the conversation.

"Possibly, possibly, but..." Igor was about to explain, but Yassar interrupted him.

"If they had enough interest from the surrounding countries, and the proper deals were struck, they could patrol the pipeline from one end to the other. It could be made impossible to approach without discovery."

"Exactly," Igor said. "The only thing to do is to stop the idea before it starts. To do that, we must take Armani and his oil council hostage."

"How might we go about that? Surely, they aren't traveling together."

"Yassar, I love you," Igor smiled. "You think like me, but fortunately for us, the Saudi's do not. They are traveling together, and they aren't carrying military escort."

"No fighter coverage?"

"Nothing!"

"Fools...They are asking for trouble."

"Maybe, but the Americans are afraid to show force because they don't want to make the European Market aware of their influence. Also, U.S. military presence in Europe is not as desirous as it once was." Igor pulled out a plan of the Cairo airport. "We have a man in the ground crew at the Cairo Airport. He will arrange to work on Armani's plane during its next visits. He will win the confidence of the pilot..."

"Who is the pilot?" Yassar asked.

"We're not sure as yet, but as soon as we find out, I will let you know...We do know they have requested an American. If it is the same pilot they used in their last trip to the U.S., his name is Steven Hardesty. He is a Vietnam War ace, but we're not sure."

"Will we use our base here for the hostages?" Yassar asked as he sipped on his third glass of brandy. The Caspian's chill was finally leaving him.

"Yes, it's the safest spot. We are far away from the reaches of the Naval Carrier Groups. We risk little chance for reprisals."

"Unless…" Yassar said.

"Unless, what?"

"Unless, we have stung the bear too hard tonight."

"What do you mean, Yassar?" Yakim asked.

"I mean, the Soviets could possibly offer assistance in making reprisals."

"Never," Igor said. "If, we hear from our Northern neighbors, we will hear before that. Their vengeance is usually swift and hard. And, if you've done you're job right, it will be some time before the KGB sifts through all of your false evidence. Does the girl carry any weight with the Soviet government?"

"We've done our job correctly, Igor. You may be assured. But, the KGB is very good at what they do. Fortunately, the girl is just a worker. She is only the scapegoat."

Igor grinned. "Good, then she is worth nothing."

"Only to me, Igor. Only to me." Yassar replied.

"Ah yes, it could be a cold winter." Igor looked back to the map. "May I tell the Ayatollah you will do this thing?"

Yassar and Yakim looked at each other. This was the first time a direct request had been made.

"He wanted me to let you both know this was his personal request. A successful mission carries his thanks and rewards." Igor grinned as he touched the map with his hand.

"Tell the Ayatollah we will do it, and we will succeed!"

"Very good! I will take my leave and relay the message. I will get back with you very soon, and finalize the dates. Unfortunately, we will probably be able to give you only twenty four hours notice on the mission."

"We will be ready, Igor. I promise."

Igor touched Yassar on the shoulder. "I trust you will, my friend."

Igor stood and walked out. Yassar and Yakim remained seated until they heard his car drive away. They both sat silently and let the complexity of the new mission sink into their thoughts.

"Let's go to the base. I am very tired." Yakim said.

"Yes, we have much to do."

"Much."

They left the hut and got into the car. Yassar looked into the back floorboard. Tallia was still asleep.

"She is beautiful, isn't she, Yakim?"

"Very."

"It is a shame she's expendable."

"The other men will want to share her beauty. You know that."

"Tell them she is my woman. If they abuse her, they must answer to me. Make them understand. If you cannot, I will!"

"I will, Yassar. She will be left alone, I assure you."

"Very well, let's go home."

\* \* \*

## WASHINGTON, D.C. (FOUR WEEKS LATER)

Mac Orberson walked into the Situation Room at the State Department, performed a silent head count, nodded to the Air Force Major he had requested to attend, and sat down at the head of the long conference table. "All right ladies and gentlemen, let's get started. We have some very interesting things to discuss this morning." Coffee cups clattered, pastry laden forks clanked against china plates, and throats were cleared, but finally Mac gained everyone's attention. "Before we start this morning, I want to introduce Major Kelly Blanford of the U.S. Air Force. Major Blanford is the Commanding Officer of Air Force Intelligence at Andrew's Air Force Base. I've asked him to make a few comments on some recent data we have obtained from one of our surveillance satellites. Major Blanford."

The Major stood and requested that the screen be lowered behind Mac's seat. "Thank you, Mr. Secretary. Ladies and Gentlemen." The Major flashed a picture of a satellite on the screen. "Skybird III, one of our reconnaissance satellites, is presently on an orbit passing over the Caspian Sea area. As you can see," The next slide flashed onto the screen. "normal infrared for industrial areas is blue-green as you see here in the Baku region, and brown for agriculture depicted here surrounding Lenkoran." The next slide fell into the projector from the Kodak carousel. "Four weeks ago Skybird made a pass of the same area and transmitted the picture you are seeing now. This photo was taken at 3 A.M. local time. The striking difference, as I'm sure you've noticed, is the marked thermal increase in this region of the Apsheron Peninsula. Ladies and Gentlemen," The Major turned toward the group. "The bright red color indicates that Baku, the capital of this region and one of the biggest oil refinement areas in the Soviet Union, is one solid blaze." The lights came back up, and the projector cut off. "Our operatives in the Baku area have confirmed a group of explosions, both on land and in the Baku harbor. Photographic evidence revealed that seventy-five percent of the oil derricks and storage facilities in the area were destroyed. The largest refinery has been knocked out of commission, and two of the Soviet's largest tankers were destroyed in the harbor blocking the entrance for a minimum of six weeks. Apparently, this was an act of terrorism aimed at the Soviets in retaliation for their refusal to accepts offers to purchase Iranian oil, and the increase in the Russian military probing of northern Iran. Information from reliable sources indicates an increase in subversive activity along the Russian-Iranian border and an increase in small craft activity on the Caspian prior to the explosions.

The KGB has attempted to place blame on one of the petroleum plant's research chemists, but our information indicates it's the work of Yassar Akazian and his group of terrorists. For three months prior to this assault on the Soviet people, our men have seen him and his chief flunky Yakim

Haffar frequenting many of the usual hangouts in the area." The Major turned to Mac. "That's all I have Mr. Secretary."

Mac readjusted his chair from the vantage point he used to view the slides. "Thank you, Major. We appreciate your coming in from Andrew's to discuss this matter."

"My pleasure, Mr. Secretary." The Major gathered his slides and left. Mac waited until the door closed behind Major Blanford. He looked around the table at the bewildered faces. "Why have we had our review course in infrared space photography? I'll tell you why. Two days ago, the President was contacted by the Soviet Premier. The U.S. has been asked to assist in medical relief to this area." Mac watched as the mouths dropped open. "It's hard to believe, I agree, but the Russians are wanting our help. The explosions and fires have disrupted normal electrical and water service into the area. Recent heavy rains have swollen the rivers and streams leaving large areas of flooding. Cases of typhoid, dysentery, and cholera have increased drastically. An early snow season in the Caucasus's has closed the passes preventing rapid deployment of local medical aide. The Medical Relief Corps of the Soviet Army doesn't have adequate indigenous supplies or all the air lift capability of getting what's needed into the area very fast. So, they have asked for our help."

"Any restrictions in our assistance?" Phil Markey, a recent transfer from Army logistics, chimed into the conversation. "Excuse me, I didn't mean to interrupt."

Mac smiled and looked at his notes. "Good question. We have been given the go ahead by the President to commit a medical team to the area. We will be given a "safe" flight corridor into Baku, but at no time will we be permitted to bring in any military hardware. Okay, we're going to help, but how? I'm open for suggestions, and the President wants an answer by 4 P.M."

A long silence fell across the table. The faces of the assistants looked like schoolchildren caught without their homework.

"Well, I'm waiting." Mac barked from the head of the table.

Phil Markey cleared his throat and raised his pencil into the air.
"Phil."

Philip Markey had spent many months planning and executing, on paper, such scenarios. His fluency in Russian, and his understanding of the Russian people had made him a perfect choice for the recently developed Department For Study of Soviet Behavior. In high school, his slimness, dark-rimmed glasses, and greasy hair had labeled him as a "nerd". However, his youth had given way to a medium built, nice-looking man who no longer used glasses but relied on contact lenses for refractory correction.

Phil answered Mac's recognition by standing slowly. "Mr. Secretary, I've spent the past two years in Germany studying deployment and supply in the event of Russian invasion of our NATO allies. We could have a work-ing compound in Baku within sixty hours if the Russians will comply."

"How in the hell could we do that, Phil? We can't seem to get anything accomplished right here in Washington within three weeks."

Phil did not respond to Mac's joke. Instead he walked toward Mac and pointed to the screen. "May I use the map?"

"Certainly!" Mac slid sideways as Phil pulled down the set of maps illustrating Europe and the Middle East. "Using detachments of various air wings and the army medical corps, a fully equipped Mobile Army Surgical Hospital could be ready for transfer across the frontier from Bitlis, Turkey, to Baku within the next thirty-six hours. The U.S., with Soviet assistance, could have a functional compound in sixty hours." Phil looked at Mac. "If we're permitted to resupply this base, we can immunize and treat every case within a one hundred mile radius of Baku. And with Soviet military assistance, any cases withing five hundred miles could be airlifted into the area for immediate care."

"When could we start on this, Phil?"

"Immediately, Mr. Secretary. Mobilization could be complete in eight hours."

Mac looked around the table. "How does everyone feel about this?"

No opposition was voiced, and Mac looked back to Phil. "Okay, Phil. I'm going to speak to the President and the NSC, immediately. You begin coordinating the move with the White House Chiefs, and we'll have something organized to give to the President this afternoon."

"Yes sir, Mr. Secretary." Phil began gathering up his papers and prepared to leave the room.

"Not so fast, Phil." Mac waited for him to be seated. "I've saved the best for last." Mac hesitated as he scanned the eyes that had suddenly turned his way. "I want each of you to prepare an announcement for your individual departments signaling the beginning of the Saudi-Egypto Pipeline."

Smiles crept over the group.

"Early this morning I was contacted by Paul Peterson. He had just left a crucial meeting between Shiek Armani and the Egyptian cabinet. It seems the Egyptians have accepted the final group of requests proposed by the Saudi's. As soon as Armani gets approval from his government, the construction phase can begin. Hopefully, we can make the announcement before Christmas."

All present stood and began clapping their hands. "Bravo, Mr. Secretary. Bravo."

"Wait…Wait a minute." Mac retrieved everyone's attention. "It's not over yet, people. We have a long way to go. Remember to keep the lid on this so we won't be sorry later. We're embarking on a very exciting time for this administration. If we handle this situation in Baku properly, and cap it with the Pipeline announcement, we may seal this administration's re-election. What's even more important, we will assure freedom from Persian Gulf oil delivery. Thanks! This meeting's adjourned." Mac watched as everyone filed out to their separate duties. As he watched the final person exit through the door, he knew he was a part of history in the making, and it gave him a greater sense of power than he had ever felt. Mac loved the sensation.

# 16

Taggat listened intently as his phone call to Sabrina's condominium rang for the fourth time. He did, and didn't want to talk to Sabrina, but the sooner he gave her the bad news the better. He was about to hang up when a breathless answer came from the other end of the line.

"Hello," Sabrina answered between gasps.

"Sabrina!. I thought I had missed you."

"Oh." Sabrina said without enthusiasm. "Hello, Taggat."

"My, don't you sound enthusiastic."

"I'm sorry. I was about to go out the door. I have a doctor's appointment, and I'm late."

"Sabrina, I met with Mac yesterday."

Sabrina sat on the edge of the couch and grasped the phone with both hands. "And?" She held her breath hoping Taggat would tell her Steve was coming home.

"I'm afraid I don't have any good news. Mac is still adamant; no communication with Steve."

"I expected as much." Sabrina halfheartedly relaxed her grip on the phone. "When does he think Steve might be home?"

"He's not sure, but it could be mid-February." Taggat held the phone away from his ear preparing for the scream.

"Mid-February? That's five more months. The baby will be two months old. Steve doesn't even know I'm pregnant. In order for our plan to work, he has to have some warning about the pregnancy."

"I'm working on it, Sabrina, but these things take time. I did find out Steve will be in Cairo over the next five or six days. I'm trying to reach him through different channels, but I'm afraid I won't be able to swing it."

"I know. I know, and I guess I understand. I'm just getting depressed. This is a hard time for me." Sabrina sighed into the phone. "I guess it's a combination of being fat and tired and not having a solution to this problem. I hate problems with no solutions."

"They don't exist, Sabrina."

"What?"

"All problems have solutions. We just haven't found it yet, that's all."

"I hope we find it soon. I've really been down lately. I'm not eating well, and my doctor is getting on my case."

"Is the baby all right?"

"The baby seems fine, and I'm doing better than expected. I'm going to have an ultrasound today to see how she's growing. At my last checkup, Dr. Vance thought the baby was a little small, but I don't see how she could be because I'm huge."

"If the baby's doing well, why are you so down?"

Sabrina paused for a few moments, and let out a deep breath. "It's a combination of everything, I guess. I sit here at home and watch the world go by. Cathy's sharing her time with Richard, and I'm stuck in the house sharing my time with a computer terminal and television."

"Cathy's still seeing Dr. Tims?"

"Oh, yes. They're quite a number. However, Richard threw her a curve yesterday."

"What's that? Don't tell me he's married and has a family in England."

"Almost as bad. It seems he's been offered a research grant back in London. I think he's going to accept, and so does Cathy. He'll be leaving in January, and Cathy thinks he might ask her to marry him."

"What do you think Cathy will do?"

"I'm not sure, anymore." Sabrina hoped Cathy would stay, but she would never say so. "She's fallen pretty hard for the man, but you know Cathy."

"No, I don't! I don't think anyone knows Cathy, except maybe you. It would surprise me if she ever got married."

"What makes you say that?"

"Come on, Sabrina. You and I both know Cathy will never submit to the confinements of marriage. She's a free spirit and has to have her own way about everything. However, I've been wrong before, and I could be wrong now. I believe I'll hold judgment on that couple for a few more months. We'll have to see how things are as January approaches."

Sabrina didn't respond for a few seconds. "Taggat? I'm still worried Steve's going to find out that this is Kent's baby, and…"

"I told you not to worry, and you're to stop thinking that way. I've taken care of most of the problem, and I may be putting the icing on the cake today. Besides, if Steve finds out you're pregnant, what's to keep him from thinking it isn't his."

"Nothing, I guess."

"Correct!"

"What did you mean about putting icing on the cake?"

"I'm meeting with Brian Pooley this afternoon."

"Why?!"

"You'll have to trust me with this, Sabrina. I'm winging it myself. I can tell you, Brian contacted me last week. It seems he and his wife are now separated."

"I'm not surprised."

"Evidently, the scene with Brian, Kent, and Beth Pooley was quite strained. To make a long story short, Brian left in a fit of rage barely avoiding an all out fistfight with Kent."

"Why does Brian want to meet with you? Surely, you wouldn't handle his divorce proceedings."

"Well, I've dealt with Brian on previous real estate negotiations, and he knows my reputation in civil matters." Taggat scratched his chin. "I might find a way for the firm to take the case. A great deal of money is involved, and I see no conflict of interest as long as I don't handle the case directly."

Sabrina grinned. "Taggat, you're a scoundrel."

Taggat smiled. "I know, but business is business."

Sabrina looked at her watch. "Oh, Taggat! I'm late. I've got to go. Call me after your meeting with Brian. Please?"

"I will and don't worry!"

"I can't help it. It's a pregnant woman's prerogative. And, Taggat?."

"Yes?"

"I love you."

"I love you, too."

"Say hello to Mae."

"Who?"

Sabrina laughed. "Good-bye" She eased the phone back down onto its cradle, gathered her keys from the table, and hurried out the door.

Taggat looked at the phone, smiled, and put the receiver down. He picked it up quickly. "How was that, Mae?"

Mae opened the door to Taggat's office, walked over to his desk, and placed the morning mail in front of him. "I saw you were finished with the phone call. Here's the mail. Was Sabrina upset about not being able to contact Steve?"

"You tell me." Taggat peered over his reading glasses. "I wasn't listening." Mae said defensively.

"I stand corrected. Excuse me if I accused you wrongly."

Mae smiled. "You tell Sabrina hello from me, too." Mae spun and left before Taggat could respond.

"Women!"

\* \* \*

"It seems the ocean air is agreeing with you, Sabrina." Bob Vance slid Sabrina's chart away from him onto the desk. He always tried to place Sabrina's appointment in his last morning slot so they could sit and discuss any unusual problems. Bob knew Sabrina was depressed. Her weight was not increasing appropriately, she had dark circles under her eyes which she tried to mask, and she didn't seem to take the same care with her attire as she did earlier in the pregnancy.

Sabrina looked down into her lap. She spoke, but her thoughts were elsewhere. "Yes, Cathy and I love our place here. It's convenient to the hospital, and I've eliminated most of my worries by being in Norfolk. You and Dr. Tims were certainly right about that."

"Most of your worries? What's bothering you? The pregnancy is going well, though I do have a few things we need to discuss."

Sabrina looked up from her lap and across the desk. "What's wrong? Is something wrong with the baby?"

"No, no. I didn't mean to alarm you. I want to review a few things, that's all."

"She looked fine on the ultrasound."

"Yes she did, didn't she?" Bob pulled the chart back and opened to the scan results. "Sabrina, you're presently at thirty-two weeks. You've got eight weeks until term. However, your baby, by the ultrasound measurements, is only twenty-eight weeks size. That doesn't mean she's due later, but it does mean she's going to be a small. I predict she'll only weigh four and one-half pounds."

"That's awfully small, isn't it? She'll be premature."

"No, the weight has nothing to do with maturity. As long as you make it past the thirty-sixth week, your baby won't be premature. Your baby is small because there's evidence of I.U.G.R."

"I.U.G.R? I haven't seen that term in the literature you've given me."

"I.U.G.R. stands for Intrauterine Growth Retardation."

Sabrina grabbed her abdomen in a protective fashion. "My baby's going to be retarded?"

"NO! It doesn't mean that at all. IUGR refers to a discrepancy in length of gestation and fetal size. In your situation, the heart problem is an insult to the normally growing pregnancy. Since the insult has occurred through-out the pregnancy, the baby is small. It's not a problem as long as it's recognized and treated appropriately."

"How is it treated?" Sabrina slowly released her grasp on her abdomen.

"With more of what you're doing. Rest, rest, and more rest. Beginning next week, I'm going to start performing some special heart beat testing on the baby. The tests are called Non-Stress Testing."

"You don't have to stick a needle into my baby do you?"

"No. Whatever gave you that idea?"

"I saw it in a book. They were testing to see if a baby was ready to deliver, and they stuck a needle into this lady's abdomen.... an amnio-cen..t...I'm not sure what it was called."

"Amniocentesis, but the baby isn't stuck, and you might have to have that performed, too. If it is done, I will do it, and your little girl won't be the wiser."

"How do you do the heart beat testing? You don't have to give me any more medicine, do you?" Sabrina stuck out her tongue as if she were sick.

Bob smiled. He liked, Sabrina. She was a pretty lady enduring a diffi-cult pregnancy, and apparently weathering the situation with a wonderful sense of humor. "No more medicine."

"Good! If I poke one more pill down my throat, I think my stomach will retaliate."

"The heart beat test can be done here in the office. We attach a monitor to your abdomen, and record the baby's heart beat over a length of time until we observe fetal movement with acceleration of the heartbeat on three separate occasions. If we don't see evidence of fetal movement then we perform a contraction stress test. I will discuss that later if it's necessary. We'll also measure the amount of fluid around the baby each week. There are certain well-studied parameters that must be met. If not, then we'll prepare to deliver your little girl. I know you will, but try not to worry. These are routine tests done in these situations all the time. I want to make sure your baby remains healthy."

Sabrina patted her belly. "We do, too. I'm sure you'll do what you think is best. I need this little one. She means the world to me." Sabrina looked back into her lap and started to think about Steve. "I just wish…" She stopped in mid sentence and longingly looked away from Dr. Vance's stare. Then, she looked up at Bob and smiled. "Sorry, I promised myself I wouldn't do this. Anyway, you don't want to hear about my problems."

"On the contrary, I do, if you feel like discussing them."

Sabrina twirled the strings of her waist band between her fingers, held back a few tears, looked up at Bob and smiled. "I try hard not to cry, but sometimes I get lonely and start thinking. I wish I had someone to share this with." She pointed to her protruding abdomen. "I thought I would be strong and could make it on my own, but I know differently, now. I need someone-someone to lean on-someone special."

"Someone like your pilot?"

"How did you know? We haven't discussed Steve before."

"Richard has a big mouth. It seems he heard you mention something about your friend after he had given you some medication in C.C.U."

"Fiance.."

"Fiance?"

"Yes, fiance, and he doesn't know I'm pregnant."

"You haven't told him?"

"I can't."

"Can't!?"

"No, it's a peculiar situation."

"How peculiar? I can't imagine."

Sabrina scooted to the edge of her chair, trying to get as close to Bob as possible. "Dr. Vance, I'm engaged to a man who is presently working for the government. He is on a State Department assignment in Europe and the Middle East." Sabrina saw Bob become more interested in her story at the mention of the State Department. "For security purposes, the State Department won't release his location, but I've learned by way of my attorney, and god-father that Steve will be in Cairo over the next six days. I was hoping to contact him with news of the pregnancy while he was there, but my attempts have been stifled by the Secretary of State. The only news I have is not to expect him home until February." Sabrina leaned on the desk and put her head onto her crossed arms. She tried to hold back her tears, but the flow had been stanched too many times. She began to cry. "My baby will be two months old before her father sees her. I'm sorry, I really didn't mean to do this."

Bob rose and walked to Sabrina's side. He sat down on the arm of the chair and placed his hand on Sabrina's back. "I think you've needed this cry for a long time. Don't you?"

Sabrina lifted her head from the desk and looked into Bob's eyes. She wiped her tears on his lab coat leaving some of her mascara trailing across the white field. "I've tried to be strong, but this has just about done me in."

Bob sat for a moment, then handed Sabrina a Kleenex from the box on his desk. He walked back to his chair, sat down, and thumbed through his Rolodex. "Sabrina, I can't promise anything, but I might be able to contact your fiance."

Sabrina wiped her tears, sniffed into the Kleenex, and looked quizzically at Dr. Vance. "How? I've tried everything. My godfather is a personal friend of the Secretary of State, and he won't help."

"I know, I know. I have a friend in the State Department, and he owes me a few favors. I might be able to do a little arm twisting and get in touch with your flyboy. As long as it doesn't cause a breech in security, I'm sure he would do it for me."

"Do you really think it might be possible?" Sabrina straightened in her chair. Her tears seemed to dry magically. "To hear from Steve would be wonderful. I'd settle for anything. I need some reassurance. I need to know he still loves me."

Bob handed Sabrina a pad of paper and pen. "Write his full name down for me, and I'll see what I can do. I can't promise anything for sure."

"I don't care. At least you're trying." Sabrina was so nervous she could hardly write Steve's name. She shook as she handed the pad back to Bob. "I could kiss you."

"I haven't had any better offers, but save it for later." Bob took the pad from Sabrina's shaking hand. He walked around the desk and took Sabrina's hands in his. "You go home, get some rest, and I'll call you as soon as I hear something. I promise."

Sabrina stood up and kissed Bob on the cheek. She noticed the flush coming to his face. "I'm sorry, I didn't mean to embarrass you, but you've made me very happy."

"I hope I'm not building false hope," Bob quickly replied.

"I know, and I'll try not to get too excited, but I do appreciate your attempt to help." Sabrina walked out of the office with a new sense of hope. She tried not to rely on Dr. Vance's contact, but something reinforced her belief she would hear from Steve. Somehow. Some way.

Bob stood until Sabrina left. He sat down and rotated the Rolodex to Paul Peterson's name. He touched in the number and waited.

"Good morning, Deputy Secretary Peterson's office. May I help you?"

"Good morning, this is Dr. Bob Vance, Mr. Peterson's wife's doctor. Could I speak to Mr. Peterson?"

"I'm sorry. Mr. Peterson is out of town. Would you care to leave a message?"

"No, thank you. I'm trying to reach him about some important health information concerning his wife. It's very important." Bob winced a little.

"What was your name again, please?"

"Dr. Robert Vance of Norfolk, Virginia. License number 22340. Graduate of Johns Hopkins Medical School. I'm sure it will be in the security check you're calling up on your CRT. The Secretary's wife's name is Coleen."

"Thank you for waiting, Dr. Vance. The Secretary can be reached at our Cairo Embassy. The number is, Overseas Operator 56, number 121-345-6698. I hope the Secretary's wife is not in poor health."

"No, nothing serious, but I'm not at liberty to give out that information to anyone except Paul. Thank you." Bob hung up quickly. "Whew," he thought. "I hate doing that, but it's for a good reason." He dialed the international number.

"Good evening, United States Embassy, Cairo. Sharon Leigh speaking. How may I help you?"

"Good evening, this is Dr. Robert Vance of Norfolk, Virginia. I'm trying to reach Paul Peterson. It's concerning his wife."

"Just a moment. I'll ring his office." The line sounded as if it went dead.

"Hello, hello. Is anyone there?" Bob looked at the receiver. "Damn!"

"Hold please," the phone leaped to life. "I had to page Deputy Secretary Peterson. He'll be on the line momentarily."

"Hello, Bob? What kind of lies are you telling my secretary. Coleen doesn't have another ectopic pregnancy, does she?"

"No, nothing like that. The last time I saw Coleen, she was healthier than you or I. I did stretch the truth a bit, but I needed to speak to you, Paul."

"What can I do for you? I'm sure you didn't call Cairo to chit-chat."

"Paul, I need a favor...a big favor."

"How big?"

"Paul, I have a patient who's pregnant."

"Aren't they all?"

Bob laughed. "Just about. No, seriously. Her fiance has some connection with the State Department in the Middle East. At present, he's a pilot on special assignment, and he's supposed to be in Cairo."

"Steve Hardesty?"

"Yes, that's his name. Do you know him?"

"We've met. How do you know about Hardesty? There's a communication blackout on this project...Wait a minute. Did you say his fiance was pregnant?"

"That's correct. She's also been quite ill. Don't scare the man to death, because she's all right now. She want's to get a message to him, and hopes for a reply. Is there any way possible?"

"I think I could clear it, as long as I can reach him while he's here in Cairo. What's the message?"

"Ask him to send a message to Sabrina. She's pregnant and having some complications, but doing well, now. She loves him, and misses him very much. Her address is 1100 Ocean Boulevard, Norfolk, Virginia."

"I'll do what I can, Bob. I don't believe there will be a problem."

"Thanks, Paul. I owe you."

"No problem. I owe you my wife's life." Paul hung up the phone, drafted a message, and gave it to Sharon. "Sharon, put this in the proper security envelopes and have it delivered to Captain Hardesty when he arrives in the morning. I'll verify clearance."

"Yes, Mr. Peterson."

* * *

Sabrina nervously sat beside the phone anticipating news from Dr. Vance. With each caller her temperament had become so short that on the last ring she had almost bitten a man's head off over the phone line when he had tried to solicit a donation. Her tolerance for daytime television had reached capacity, but for the moment, she had become interested in a passionate love scene between a man resembling Steve and a blonde, blue-eyed woman. She closed her eyes and tried to imagine herself in such a situation. In the midst of the TV couple's heavy petting, a phone rang. Sabrina sighed hoping she and Steve would never be interrupted by the phone, but suddenly she realized the phone wasn't on television. It was hers!

She jerked the receiver off its cradle, dropped it on the floor, reached over her protruding belly, and picked it up. "Hello."

"You sound out of breath. I told you to get some rest."

"I am resting. Is this Dr. Vance?"

"None other, and I've got good news."

Sabrina immediately muted the television and grasped the phone until her knuckles were white. "You talked to him. You talked to Steve?"

"No, not to him, but I was able to get my friend to deliver a message. Hopefully, you'll receive an answer as soon as Steve arrives in Cairo."

"You don't mean it! I can't believe it. How? How did you do it?"

"I told you. I have friends in high places. Plus, I have a few markers I can call on occasion."

"Where is Steve?"

"I don't know, Sabrina. Now you know they wouldn't give me that information."

"I know. I know. I'm just excited. I don't know how to thank you, Dr. Vance."

"Your exuberance is thanks enough. If I can get you out of that well you've been climbing down, I'll be happy."

"What did you tell him?"

"Only what we discussed, nothing else.,,

"Oh, Dr. Vance, if you only knew what this means to me. You've certainly made my day...month...year!"

"I'm happy for you, Sabrina. You deserve some good news. Good-by."

"Good-by, Doctor. I'll see you next week." Sabrina was off the couch and at Cathy's bedroom door before the phone stopped rattling in its cradle. She burst through the door and caught Cathy standing in front of the dresser mirror in her bra and panties. She was holding two different dresses in front of her.

"Which one of these should I wear?" Cathy turned and asked before Sabrina had a chance to open her mouth.

"I've got the best news, Cathy. Guess what?"

"You're going to hear from Steve. Now, which dress should I wear?"

Sabrina deflated before Cathy's eyes, looked at the dresses, and pointed to the one Cathy held in her right hand. "That one, I guess."

"I thought so. It shows the most breast. Richard's a boob man, no question."

"Well, you've got enough to show."

"Tut, tut. No jealousy now."

Sabrina held her upper arms tight against her chest and attempted to make her breasts appear larger. "I've got my own, thank you."

Cathy looked at Sabrina, and they both laughed.

"How did you know?" Sabrina let out the breath she was holding.

"Know what?" Cathy threw the dress she held in her left hand down on the bed and started slithering into the yellow cotton dress Sabrina had selected.

Sabrina walked over, sat down on the bed, and started fingering the navy blue outfit Cathy discarded looking up as Cathy wiggled into the last bit of the V-neck, wide waisted, above the knee dress. "You know. About Steve?"

"Hell, Sabrina. That's all you've talked about since you've gotten home from the doctor. Steve this, Steve that, Steve all the time. I would think you wouldn't want to hear from him." Cathy turned nonchalantly and started putting on her make-up.

Sabrina looked up from the bed. "Why would you think that?"

Cathy quickly turned from the mirror. "Well, if I were trying to keep something from someone, I wouldn't want to hear from him. I think the surprise when he gets home would be enough to contend with."

"I've thought about that. I need some reassurance, that's all. Don't you understand?" Sabrina looked back down at the navy outfit. "I miss him, Cathy. I see you going out with Richard. I hear you talk about the good times you have. I listen to your stories about your intimacy."

Cathy turned from the mirror. "Hold on, girl. I haven't given away any secrets. You know I don't talk about my sex life."

Sabrina grinned. "I thought that might get your attention."

Cathy threw a cotton ball over to Sabrina. "Here, use this if you think you're about to cry."

"Ooooo! You have no sympathy at all."

Cathy walked to the bed and sat down next to Sabrina. She put her arms around her and gave her a hug. "I'm happy for you, Sabrina. I really am. I guess I'm too practical. I don't want you to be hurt. We're going to have a tough enough time carrying out this deception when Steve gets back. I don't want to compound it by giving away too many facts for Steve to mull over while he's over there."

"Taggat said he was going to take care of it. As a matter of fact, he's meeting with Brian Pooley today."

Cathy released her hold on Sabrina. She rose and walked to the mirror and continued to primp. She put on her lipstick and looked back over at Sabrina. "Why is he meeting with Brian Pooley?"

"I forgot to tell you." Sabrina scooted around in the bed until she faced Cathy. "You were right about Brian. He and Beth are separated, and he's in New York now."

"New York?"

"Yes, Taggat said he and Brian were going to meet, but he wouldn't tell me what they were going to discuss."

"How long is Brian going to be in New York?"

"Forever, I guess. I don't know. Why are you so interested in Brian Pooley."

"Oh, just asking." Cathy remembered the impression she had of Brian. Brian represented power, pure, undisputed power. If they could win him to their side in this game of deception, Steve wouldn't stand of chance of finding out about the baby's true father. "I might have to go to New York and see Brian one of these days."

"Why? You're seeing Richard."

"Hey, Richard doesn't have a ring in my nose."

"Well, excuuuuuse me."

Cathy laughed. "Sorry. I didn't mean to jump down your throat." Cathy began brushing her hair. "Men are all alike anyway."

"Well, that's a generalization if I've ever heard one. Would you care to expand?"

"No!" Cathy took a deep breath as she finished her face. She looked at Sabrina's reflection in the mirror. "I guess this move Richard is contemplating is bothering me more than I thought. He's trying to pin me down." Cathy turned to Sabrina and pointed her finger. "No smart remarks about the Freudian slip." They both smiled and laughed. "You know I can't stand to be pressured."

"How's Richard pressuring you?"

"Oh, you know." Cathy turned back to mirror, straightened her dress, and turned back to Sabrina. "How do I look?"

"Ravishing. How's Richard pressuring you?"

Cathy walked to her closet and selected a light cream colored knee length coat. "He's wanting a decision from me about going with him to England. That's all he has on his mind except a few other little personal things." Cathy lightly pinched Sabrina's arm and winked.

Sabrina smiled, looked down at her folded hands, and inwardly wished Cathy wouldn't go to England. "What did you tell him?"

"I told him to back off and that I wasn't going anywhere until we had this baby. That's what I told him."

Sabrina smiled and felt relief, but she didn't want Cathy to see. She continued looking at her hands.

"And, I told him I didn't like someone asking so damned many questions." Cathy looked at her watch. "I've got to go. Richard wants me to meet him at his office, and then we're driving to Washington to eat at some hotsy-totsy restaurant. I think he wants to drive my car more than he wants to see me."

"Okay, I get the hint. I'll stop asking so many questions. I know I'm selfish, but I really want you to be happy. That's all I've ever wanted. Believe me?" Sabrina started for the living room.

Cathy caught Sabrina, gave her a hug and pecked her on the cheek. "I know, and you know me well enough to know I'll do what I damned well please. See you later. I'm glad you're going to hear from Steve. I hope it's soon. 'Night. Don't wait up."

"Don't worry. Have a good time." Sabrina followed Cathy out of the bedroom, into the living area, and to the front door.

Cathy turned and looked at Sabrina. "Any further instructions, mother?"

"Did you take your pill today?" Sabrina smiled.

"Oh, hush." Cathy left through the partially opened door.

Sabrina closed the door and watched Cathy walk down the sidewalk. She got into her car and pulled away into the evening sun. Sabrina locked the door, switched the mute button off, and tried to become interested in the late afternoon programming. However, her mind continued to wonder when she might hear from Steve. As she watched Wheel of Fortune, her eyes became quite heavy, and she drifted off into a light sleep.

## CAIRO, EGYPT

"Excuse me, Captain Hardesty?"

Steve looked up from the Miller Lite beer he was enjoying in the bar of the Cairo Hilton. "That's me, all over. Who's asking?" Steve had had about all of the shuttle piloting he could take. He hadn't talked to anyone except the Saudi's and Paul Peterson for the past five months. When they were in any country other than Saudi Arabia, Steve was confined to either the plane or the local U.S. Embassy. They had even assigned a Marine guard to him. The nights were long, and he wanted to see Sabrina. He had to find a way home.

"Captain Hardesty. I'm a courier from the State Department. I have a message from Mr. Peterson."

"Wonderful. What does the tyrant want now? I've made so damned many trips for these guys, you wouldn't believe it. Hell, last week I had to take the Arabs to Amsterdam. One of those guys heard that women sold themselves in store windows. Crazy bastard thought he could buy them and bring them home with him." Steve grinned and held the envelope up to the light. "What's in here?"

The courier had a difficult time not laughing at Steve's story about the Saudi's. "I'm sure I don't know the contents of the message. I was requested to wait for a reply."

Steve opened the envelope and unfolded the message.

CAPT. STEVEN HARDESTY
FROM:PAUL PETERSON
  STEVE, SABRINA WISHES TO HEAR FROM YOU. I HAVE PERMITTED THIS COURIER TO ACCEPT A WRITTEN MESSAGE. OBVIOUSLY, YOU ARE TO CONVEY NO INDICATIONS AS TO YOUR LOCATION OR FLIGHT PLANS.
  NORMALLY THIS CONTACT WOULD NOT BE PERMITTED, BUT A FRIEND TELLS ME YOU'RE GOING TO BE A FATHER. YES, SABRINA'S PREGNANT. CONGRATULATIONS.
PAUL

Steve read the message three times. Pregnant? Steve looked up at the courier. "I'm going to be a father." He jumped from his chair and grabbed the courier's shoulders. "I'm going to be a father." He looked around. No one, including the courier, seemed to be moved by his exuberance. "What does this mean? A friend?"

"I don't know, sir. I have no knowledge of the message or the facts contained in it."

"Of course, you don't." Steve sat down and fingered the message. "I'll be damned. I don't believe it. This is a little fast, don't you think, Sabrina? Don't worry. I'll get home. I promise. Somehow, I'll get home...Soon!"

"Excuse me, sir. Do you wish to send a reply?"

"Huh? Oh, yes excuse me." Steve thought for a few seconds, wrote his reply and handed it to the courier. "When will she get this?"

"Figuring the time difference, she'll probably get it late tonight."

"Great, that should work out perfectly."

"If you say so, sir." The courier took the message, placed it into his briefcase, and left the bar.

The daily parade at the Hilton moved about Steve without recognition. He was deep in his own thoughts. "Hell, I can be home in two days, no sweat. We'll be in Jiddah by early morning. I'll make the necessary arrangements with a fill in pilot, and take off for London. Leave London by late tomorrow afternoon, and I'll be in New York five hours later. Let's see, with the time differential, that makes me home by the evening of day after tomorrow." He lifted his beer and toasted his promise of desertion if necessary, but he would be going home-home to Sabrina and their baby.

# 17

The scimitar sliver of moon cast little light on the perimeter of Cairo International Airport. The two black clad figures lying outside the barriers of concertina wire would have gone unnoticed to the casual eye, but Yassar Akazian knew they would be discovered unless their contact showed momentarily. Everything had gone as planned thus far. Prior to his and Yakim's entry into Egypt, Yassar had been notified of the successful preparation of the secret airfield, and the Rasht headquarters was ready for the arrival of new hostages. They were all set, but where was the damned operative. Yassar prepared to withdraw from his position when a low whistle came from the darkness on the far side of the fences. Shortly, a brief flash of red light appeared.

Yassar hooded his red lensed flashlight and returned two quick flashes. Since his eyes had grown accustomed to the darkness, Yassar quickly spied the half-crouched form snaking through the inky shadows of the barriers. The quickness of the approaching shadow reassured Yassar the path had been rehearsed. Yassar had not been consulted on the decision for the operatives at the airport. Igor had made those choices, and that part of the plan made Yassar uneasy. However, the stealthness of the approaching form renewed his confidence for success.

The silent shape elevated the last circle of wire and crawled closer to Yassar. "Commander Akazian, I am Jamal. Follow me! Quickly! Stay in my footsteps. This area is heavily mined." As quickly as Jamal had approached, he departed. He did not look back during his renegotiation of the path.

Yassar and Yakim followed Jamal through the maze of barbed wire, trip flares, and claymore mines. After they cleared the last fence, the trio sprinted to the closest hanger. Once inside, Jamal removed a portion of his dark clothing and placed the turtleneck in the false bottom compartment of his foot locker. He removed a long black duffle from a closet hidden behind a wall hanging, and hefted its weight onto the metal table in the center of the room where they stood. "Welcome to Cairo, Commander." Jamal bowed slightly from the waist.

"Very good, Jamal. We thought you had been discovered. Is there enough time to prepare?" Yassar spoke as he watched Jamal empty the contents of the duffle on to the table top.

"Yes, there will be plenty of time, but the schedule has been moved up. Armani and the council have notified the controller of a midnight departure. I must move you into the plane very shortly. I have prepared a place on the craft where you will be undetected." Jamal opened a small plan of the plane's interior. "There will be two small containment areas in the aft hold. This portion of the plane is only partially pressurized during flight. I have a wrist altimeter for both of you. Oxygen is in the areas. Use it if the plane flies above twelve thousand feet." Jamal picked a rifle up from the milieu of weapons he had removed from the duffel and handed it to Yakim. "Here is the AK-47 you desired, and a ban-doleer of ten, forty shot clips." Jamal picked up the nine millimeter pis-tol and gave it to Yassar. "Nine-millimeter Beretta, sixteen shot clip, silencer, four additional clips, four antipersonnel grenades, and adhesive tape. Is that everything you requested?"

"Everything! Jamal, you have done well."

"You both must realize a gun shot at the altitudes you're traveling will depressurize the cabin, and a grenade blast will disintegrate the airplane."

"If necessary, it will be done." Yassar said while never looking up from is study of the Beretta.

Jamal handed them tan jumpsuits. "Put these on. They're always worn by the ground crew." Jamal looked at his watch. "We have two hours. Come, I have something for you to eat."

"Have you received any information about the pilot? We have heard nothing."

"Not much. He's a Navy Captain who served in the Vietnam War and was heavily decorated. He takes his job seriously, and that could present a problem."

"How?" Yassar asked as he drank the warm tea Jamal had prepared.

"He dislikes ground crew interference in checking his instruments. He always preflights the jet himself. However, I think I have finally won his confidence. The last time they were here, he permitted me to start the engines and have the radios set to their proper frequencies."

"I hope he permits you the same liberties tonight, Jamal, or our trip could be very short." Yassar watched Jamal's expression as he spoke.

"Don't fear, Commander. I'm sure I have won his trust."

Yassar set down his tea, picked up the Beretta, and chambered a round. Jamal's head jerked toward the sound, but the only sight he confronted was the nine millimeter's muzzle inches from his nose. "For your sake, Jamal, I certainly hope so." Yassar smiled and slowly lowered the hammer on the pistol.

"I understand, Commander."

"Does the American have a family?"

"None known to us."

Yassar rubbed his beard and looked at Yakim who was field-stripping the AK-47 and assuring its proper function. "Yakim, we will have to deal with the American as the situation demands. He will not try to disrupt our plans while we're airborne. However, once we're in Rasht, we won't have to afford him that luxury. He is expendable. Yakim, I know you hate the Saudis, but you must restrain yourself and your weapon. We must keep Armani and his apostles alive. Understand?"

"Understood." Yakim looked up from his weapon check procedure and acknowledged Yassar with the appropriate eye contact.

Yassar unzipped his tan jumpsuit, picked up the adhesive tape, and wrapped four revolutions of the tape around his undershirt just below the nipple line. Then, using great precision, he taped the four antipersonnel grenades to his chest. He interconnected each of the pull pins with monofiliament line, and brought the line through a small hole he cut above the left breast pocket. He took a two inch long safety pin from the box of supplies provided by Jamal and connected the line to the safety pin. Now, all he would have to do to activate all four grenades would be to pull the safety pin with force. He took a second safety pin and attached the first to his jumpsuit creating protection from inadvertently pulling them while confined in the storage hold. Yassar looked up from his work and saw Jamal watching him closely. "Come, Jamal. Sit back down, and we will give you news of our homeland."

Jamal listened eagerly to their discussion of Rasht until his digital wrist-watch beeped and brought him out of the trance created by Yakim and Yassar. "Come, we must go. Your coveralls are fitted with special slots for weapons and supplies. Store them until needed. The guards around the plane will not examine you." Jamal looked again at his watch. "Follow me, we must leave now."

The coveralled trio left the hanger and casually walked to the light encircled cream and maroon Lear jet. The plane was being fueled, and four men with fire extinguishers dressed in similar coveralls stood at strategic locations around the plane. Other men in coveralls moved in and out of the stairway. Jamal handed Yassar a small tool box and gave Yakim a hand held vacuum. "Follow me into the plane and give the first two men you see these articles." Jamal turned and began up the steps.

The Egyptian guard from the left rear of the aircraft approached them as they started into the plane. "Jamal, who are these men? I don't think I've seem them before."

"Oh, yes. They have been with me since last week. I always use them on special jobs such as this."

The guard walked to within three feet of Yassar. He looked very closely at their clothing and backed away. "I was off last week. I guess I could have missed them. Okay, proceed." The guard turned and walked back to his sentry position.

Jamal, Yassar, and Yakim slowly entered the plane. Two men with the same build and body stature as Yassar and Yakim took their equipment and waited for instructions from Jamal. "Remain in the plane for ten more minutes." Jamal handed them each a navy colored ball-cap. "Put these on. After ten minutes, leave the plane making sure the guard at sentry post three sees you. Wave to him if necessary, but be certain he sees you. Understand?"

"Yes, Jamal. It is understood." The larger of the two replied while the smaller, Yakim's stand in, shook his head affirmatively.

Jamal directed Yassar and Yakim to the aft storage area. He carefully lifted the carpet from the hold's floor and opened two doors. The compartments were each six feet long and two feet wide. They had been lined with foam rubber for comfort and fleece for warmth. The green oxygen tanks and attached masks were conveniently stored at the head of each position. "I have concealed these areas so they will go undetected." Jamal lay down in the right hand compartment. His feet were directed to the door and his head to the rear of the aircraft. "You should lie in these areas, thusly. This way, if you are detected, you can open the covers from the middle and come out fighting." Jamal demonstrated the inner latch release. Jamal rose out of the slot and close the cover. "After you are both in the compartments, I will seal the edges of the doors with a caulk. I do not believe there will be any question on the part of the pilot about leaks, particularly while we're on the ground." Jamal reached into his coverall's inner pocket and handed Yassar a slip of paper. "Here's the information you requested of our radio operator. You should be over the Red Sea after twenty minutes of flight. Good luck. Until I can assist you again, I am your servant."

Jamal looked at his watch. "If you have no questions, I will seal you into your compartments."

Yassar looked at the places prepared in the cargo's floor. "Yakim, it appears we are destined to rest in our coffins before we die." Yassar scratched his beard and looked at Jamal. "I don't like the uncertainties of the American. I would like to kill him while we're flying to Rasht, but it is too dangerous in such a small plane. Watch him closely as you prepare for takeoff, Jamal. If you notice anything of use to us, radio the frequency I am writing down." Yassar pulled a ballpoint pen from the upper outer right hand pocket of his suit and wrote a radio frequency on a small piece of paper. He handed it to Jamal.

Yakim stepped into his compartment. "Surely, the American would not attempt anything. It would mean death to the Arabs and himself."

"Perhaps he doesn't fear death, Yakim. Remember, he has won medals for his bravery. His actions will depend on what's going on in his life. Right now! Tonight! We must rely on the unknown." Yassar stepped into the fleece lined compartment and sat down.

"I do not fear death, either. If the American makes the wrong decision, I will kill everyone." Yakim sat down next to Yassar, balled his fist, relaxed and lay down in his cocoon.

"I don't fear his actions or the thought of death, Yakim." Yassar replied as he relaxed into the foam. "However, we both know it will not serve our purpose if we kill Armani. I feel the American may prove to be too unpredictable to keep alive for long. He could present a problem after we have arrived in Rasht. If he gives us any trouble, we must exterminate him, but we would have to keep it quiet, at least until the Saudis agree to our terms. Nothing must keep us from succeeding in our mission. Nothing!" Yassar reached over and patted Yakim's shoulder. He looked up into Jamal's face. "Okay, cover us. We are ready."

Jamal closed the doors over Yassar and Yakim sealing the edges of the panel with silver colored caulk. He placed appropriately cut and matched carpet sections back over the flooring and looked down on the area to verify adequate concealment before he walked out the compartment door. Before closing the door, he peered into the dark hold and silently wished his comrades good luck.

Jamal left the plane and continued to observe the movement of the men, making sure entrances and exits were adequate to keep the guards confused. He purposly went by sentry position three and spoke to the guard. They both agreed the two new men weren't very good and should be sent back to their old jobs. As Jamal spoke to the guard, two black Mercedes rounded the corner of the hanger. They stopped short of the ring of lights encircling the plane. Jamal recognized Steve Hardesty climbing out of the back seat of the first car. He was carrying a large stuffed animal of some sort. Along with him were Armani and one other member of the oil council. The other three Arabs got out from the rear car.

\* \* \*

Steve had sat in bewilderment after the courier left the bar. "Sabrina, pregnant? I can't believe it." He studied the head on his beer and pleasantly thought of fatherhood.

"Ah, here you are, Steve Hardesty. We must leave for Jiddah, immediately." Jofur Armani, had silently approached Steve's chair and pleasantly smiled.

Steve looked up from his beer. "Hey, Jof. what's the rush?"

"Please to call me, Jofur. Your need for informality shocks me. Don't you Americans take anything seriously?"

"Hey, Jof. Lighten up. Always Mr. Pomp and Circumstance. Sit down." Steve got up and pulled out a chair for the straight backed Saudi. "Have a beer and drink a toast with me. I'm going to be a daddy."

Armani looked at him quizzically. "You? You're not married. How can you be a father?"

"Come on, Jof. This is the nineties. Have a beer with me."

"I cannot. Please, no more beer. We must depart for Jiddah, immediately."

Steve coaxed Armani down into the chair. "Look. No one has given me the time of day since I've started on this little Mediterranean jaunt with you well dressed oil pumpers. I'm not going anyplace until you have a drink and toast my parenthood." Steve held Armani firmly in his seat by the top of his shoulders.

Armani had seen Steve handle three or four men, at one time, in a few unplanned "situations" over the past five months, and he wasn't about to rain on this man's parade. "Well, maybe I will have one drink."

"Good!" Steve released his grip and sat back in his seat. "Why are we leaving so soon?" Steve motioned for the waitress. She walked over, and Steve looked at Jofur. "What will it be, Jof?"

"I'd like champagne, Bollinger '73." Armani looked at Steve. "My treat. It's not everyday one finds out he is to be a father." Jofur Armani appreciated the finer things in life. His education in England had whetted his appetite for life's finest, and his money enabled him to afford it. He had picked up some of the English mannerisms, but his loyalty was to his country. Like most of the Saudis, his interest was in improving the quality of life for his people. He had no need for further monetary gain.

"You're all class, Jofur. Hey, listen. You know I'm just ribbing when I call you, Jof. I have the deepest respect for you fellows. What you're trying to do is outstanding. I hope this all goes through. I really do. Do you have any children?"

"Twelve."

"TWELVE! Hell, I should be toasting you!"

"I have six wives." Armani said with a straight face as the waitress opened the champagne and poured two glasses.

"Will there be anything else, gentlemen?"

"No, thank you." Armani smiled at the buxom brunette and looked back at Steve."

"Six wives?"

"Yes, I don't have time for more than six."

Steve grinned and shook his head. He lifted his glass and touched Armani's. "Here's to Fatherhood."

"Of course. May your firstborn be strong and courageous, like his father." Armani touched Steve's glass, drank, and sat his stemware back on the table. "Now, we must go. Our cars are waiting, and I promised my government we would be back in Riyadh by noon tomorrow. Tonight we have finalized the plans, Steve Hardesty. Hopefully, we will have you home by Christmas."

Steve finished his glass, picked up the bottle, shoved the cork deeper into the neck, and looked over at Armani. "Well, let's go, Jof. I've got a pregnant woman back home I've got to hurry up and marry. Got to make that boy legal."

"What if it's a girl?" Armani rose from his chair.

"She wouldn't dare." Steve smiled.

They walked down the hall past the hotel's gift shop.

Inside Steve spotted a stuffed giraffe. "Wait a minute. I've got to get that for Sabrina and the baby." Steve hurriedly purchased the giraffe and rejoined Armani.

They exited the front of the hotel, entered one of the two black Mercedes 560 SEL'S, and sped off into the night.

\* \* \*

Steve climbed from the Mercedes and walked to the Lear with Armani. "Get your group settled, and I'll make preparations to take-off." Steve headed for the plane as Armani walked toward the other members of his group. As he approached the Lear, Steve saw Jamal walking toward him. "Hey, Jamal, what's happening? You got this baby ready?"

"She is about ready. All we have to do is go through the final checklist."

Steve handed his flight bag to Jamal. "Put this in the cockpit. I'm going to store the giraffe in the aft storage hold." Steve started up the steps before Jamal could stop him.

"But I can do that." Jamal headed for Steve with his right arm stretched out hoping to receive the stuffed animal.

"You go up front. I'll be there in a moment." Steve entered the plane and walked to the aft hold. He opened the door, turned on the light and pushed the giraffe to the back of the storage area. He secured the toy to the side of the plane with elastic straps and as he turned to leave, his right foot scuffed up the edge of the carpet, almost causing him to trip. He reached down and noticed a glue like substance under the disturbed corner of floor cover. He tapped the intercom, "Jamal, come back here, please."

Jamal almost jumped through the windscreen when the intercom came to life. "Yes, sir. I'll be right there." Jamal slowly made his way back through the entering Arabs to the aft hold. He opened the door and stopped in his tracks. He watched as Steve began stripping up the carpet over the compartments.

Steve looked up at Jamal. "What the hell has happened in here?"

"Oh, a thousand pardons, Captain Hardesty. I hoped you wouldn't have noticed my handy work. One of my workmen spilled some oil on the carpet. I cut the horrible stain out and repaired the area with a swatch of matching material. I guess I didn't do such a good job after all."

Steve stopped his inspection of the area, stood up, walked over to Jamal, and lightly grasped his shoulder. "I appreciate your repair attempts, but from now on tell me everything there is to know about this aircraft, no matter how insignificant you might think it to be. Do you understand?"

"Most assuredly, Captain. I won't forget."

"Fine. Finish putting the carpet back, and come forward." Steve turned and walked to the door. "Jamal?"

Jamal's heart skipped another beat as he looked up from his position kneeling over the carpet. "Yes, Captain?"

"That's a good match on the carpet. Thanks for taking the pains to be precise."

"You are welcome."

Within their places of concealment, Yassar and Yakim slowly returned their weapons to safe.

Steve threaded his way through the buckled in Arabs, and situated himself into his seat. He tuned to the special preinstructed military frequency and place the David Clark headset over his ears. "Cairo Control, this is Covey-One. Come in."

"Roger, Covey-One. I read you loud and clear."

"Control, I need immediate clearance for departure and vectors, over."

"One moment, Covey-One. Roger One. We can clear you for taxi and take-off on Runway Two-Five. You will be vectored to the Gulf of Suez; proceed to twenty four degrees north longitude, and then vector to Jiddah. I have relayed your flight coordinates to coastal defenses and our early warning radar aircraft. Do not deviate from your approved flight plan or you could be considered hostile and fired upon."

Steve had heard the same speech many times. At first he liked to play around with the military aircraft, but the Lear didn't have the necessary moves. Lately, he just fed the coordinates into the autopilot and relaxed until final descent."

Jamal reentered the cockpit, and he and Steve completed the final checklist. "Thanks, Jamal. You better get off. We're ready to roll."

"Very good. I look forward to your next arrival." Jamal smiled at Steve knowing he would probably never see this American again, not in this life anyway.

Steve looked at Jamal and smiled. "I look forward to it, Jamal. You've been very helpful." Steve knew he wouldn't see Jamal again, but why get

into the particulars. He was ready to leave and anxious to make prepara-
tions to depart for New York. The plan was formulated in his head, and
he would expedite it as soon as he arrived in Jiddah. When Steve saw
Jamal had exited the plane, he powered up the Lear and rolled to Runway
Two-Five. Once he was on the threshold, he contacted the tower. "Cairo
Control, Covey-One ready for take-off. Over."

"Roger One, you are cleared for take-off. Over."

Steve pushed the throttles forward and the Lear gathered speed. At one
hundred and eighty knots, Steve rotated off the ground and retracted the
gear. With a steady climb and speed increasing, he decreased flaps.

"Covey One, vector 075 degrees, and maintain flight level 05. Over."

"Roger Tower, 075 degrees, 5000 feet." Steve reached the assigned altitude and contacted radar fire control on the East Bank. He then contacted
the circling AWAC.

"Roger, Covey-One. We have you on scope. Come right to 145
degrees, climb to flight level 15."

"Roger, Mother-One, 145 degrees, fifteen thousand feet." Steve
adjusted his altitude and course. He entered his coordinates into the flight
computer, activated the auto pilot, and relaxed. His thoughts turned to
Sabrina and the baby.

As the Lear pierced the night with the autopilot directing its moves,
Steve was left to his thoughts interrupted only by his freqent scan of his
instruments. On one scan he noted a slight decrease in cabin pressure, and
was about to rise from his seat to see if a problem had occurred in the passenger cabin. However, a call from the AWAC kept him seated.

"Roger, Mother-One, I read you loud and clear. I'm preparing to vector 115 degrees for Jiddah. Out."

"Covey-One, climb to flight level 25. You have traffic on intercept your
quadrant. Over."

"Roger, Mother-One. Climbing to 25,000 feet. Out."

Steve leveled off at 25,000 feet and turned to a heading of 115. He
noticed the pressure bleed had stopped, but he was going to check it any-

way. As he prepared to rise from his seat, he felt a cold round object against his right temple. As he reached and turned to see what was irritating him, he was confronted by the business end of a silenced nine millimeter Beretta. "What the hell is going on?" Steve reached for the weapon.

"Say nothing, American." Yassar said as he pushed Steve back down into his seat. "Do not use your radio. I am Yassar Akazian of the Free Peoples Iranian Army. You will do as I say or we will all die." Yassar unzipped the top of his coveralls so Steve could see the hand grenade arrangement. "I'm prepared to die for my country. Do not underestimate my determination. My comrade has your friends covered with an automatic weapon in the back. They are tying each other up as sheep should be. They will be safe as long as you do as I say. Agreed?"

"What makes you think we're going anywhere you want?"

"Shut up, American! You will do as I say. Don't endanger your passengers with silly American heroics."

Steve considered his options. He had none. "It appears I have no choice." He leaned over and peered through the connecting door. He saw three of the five Saudis tied and gagged around the table. The other Iranian was sitting opposite the group holding a Russian AK-47. "If you fire those weapons, this plane will decompress and we'll all be dead."

"You are right, Captain. So, don't do anything foolish and make me use them."

Steve looked at Yassar wondering how he knew about his military rank. "What else do you know about me?"

"I do my homework, Captain Hardesty." Yassar sat down in the co-pilot seat and strapped himself in. He held the Beretta on Steve's face the entire time. "Descend to two thousand feet. Head inland at Yanbu, and follow the railroad across the desert. We will refuel at Ash Shaqro. There is an airfield at these coordinates. We will be expected." Yassar tore off part of the paper he had been given by Jamal and handed it to Steve. "Pay attention, Captain. Your inland approach is coming up."

"I see you know something about navigational equipment."

"I've flown before." Yassar smiled.

Steve made course and altitude corrections. "Listen, Yassar, or whatever your name is. I'm not worth anything to you. You can do much better. My government's not in the habit of dealing with terrorists."

"Don't flatter yourself. The five men in the back are worth enough to buy your entire Navy. They are my hostages. You mean nothing."

"Covey-One, you have deviated from your designated flight path. Please acknowledge. Mother-One, out."

Yassar clicked off the communication module. "Let them eat dead air."

"They'll start looking for us. As you said, the men in the back are worth something to these fellows flying around baby-sitting them."

"They will be too late. Proceed on course. When you make landfall, drop to five hundred feet. They will lose you in ground return."

Steve crossed the coast and dropped to five hundred feet. On Yassar's instructions, he increased throttle and the Lear's speed climbed to four hundred knots.

"Now, drop to two hundred feet." Yassar watched Steve and the instruments intently.

"Wait just a damned minute. I don't have a terrain avoidance radar on this buggy. You want us to auger into the desert?"

"Do you want me to fly it?" Yassar smiled at Steve.

"If you'll let me hold the gun." Steve smiled back.

"If I fly, Captain, it will mean you're dead. What option do you choose?"

"I'll fly." Steve descended to two hundred feet, and kept the railroad track under the nose of the Lear. The Lear fought the thermal draft changes as they traversed the Al Hijaaz-Asir Mountains. Steve knew they would be reported overdue in Jiddah, and the AWAC would signal their course change. It was a matter of time before a group of F-15's would vector to their last transmission site. He kept the throttles just below maximum making as hot a thermal print as possible.

"Okay, Captain. Come left to 075 degrees." Yassar commanded as he set the radio to 143.5 Mghz.

"We better find that gas station…fast." Steve watched as the red low fuel light flashed its warning.

Yassar adjusted the head mike. He keyed the mike with three short bursts and two long. A voice replied. "101.4, Yassar smiled, and set the Instrument Landing System's radio to 101.4. Immediately the DME illuminated placing them seventy miles from the station. "Follow the signal into the strip."

"Wait a minute. We're seventy miles from something, but what?"

"Just fly, Captain." Yassar watched the DME. At ten miles he looked at Steve. "Drop your airspeed to two hundred knots. Keep the nose up and drop flaps at five miles, then, drop gear at two."

"If I drop below two hundred knots, she'll stall."

"Stall speed of the Lear with almost empty tanks and full flaps is 180 knots."

"Yassar, you continue to amaze me." Steve dropped the gear as instructed. He could see a small building in the distance.

"The runway begins to the right of the building."

Steve adjusted his flightpath while allowing the plane to continue its descent. He spied the makeshift runway lights and centered the plane between the points of illumination. The plane touched down on what felt to be a firm surface, and Steve brought the Lear to a halt.

"Circle around and stop the jet in front of the building."

Steve followed orders and stopped the Lear where indicated. Suddenly a group of people encircled the plane, chocked the wheels, and placed camouflage netting over the entire frame.

"Very good, Captain. I may have a use for you, yet. Come with me." Yassar escorted Steve off the plane and placed him in the tent with the five Saudis. "We will be here for a short time. The plane is to be refueled, and then we'll depart."

"What is the meaning of this?" Armani stood and walked toward Yassar.

Yakim jabbed the butt of the AK-47 into Armani's abdomen as he neared them. Jofur fell to the floor in a crumpled heap gasping for breath.

Steve rushed to him, knelt, and looked at Yakim with hatred. "You fuckers are awfully brave when your enemy is defenseless."

"Shut up, American! I'll shoot you like a rat in the street and think no more of it." Yakim started to raise his weapon.

"Easy, Yakim." Yassar pushed the muzzle down toward the ground.

"What do you intend to do with us?" Armani managed to choke out as his breath returned.

Steve looked down at Armani's reddened face and around the tent into the frightened faces of the other Saudis. "Gentlemen, they intend to hold us for ransom."

"You can't hold us prisoner in our own country." Armani tried to rise, but Steve held him on the floor."

Yassar smiled. "I believe we are doing just that, Sheik Armani."

"Don't worry, Jof. We won't be here long, I'd imagine we're heading for Iran." Steve looked up into Yassar's eyes. "Right, Yassar?"

"Shut up!" Yakim snapped.

"Hold it, Yakim. Let him talk. It will pass the time. A caged animal can do no harm."

Steve smiled at Yassar. "Thanks, Yaz. I assume we'll be held until a ransom is paid or agreement fulfilled."

Yassar and Yakim laughed at Steve's remark and exited through the tent flap.

Steve and the Saudis settled themselves around the sides of the tent accepting their temporary fate. As the Iranians busied themselves with their refueling tasks, Steve wondered how his life fit into Yassar's scheme. He realized immediately that his life was virtually insignificant. The Saudis were Yassar's hold card. They would probably eliminate him when they got to their destination. Soon, he became too tired to think and drifted off into a light sleep.

\* \* \*

"Get up, quickly! Get up! Get up!" Yakim jumped around the tent punching the hostages in the ribs with the muzzle of his rifle.

Steve rolled over and looked up into Yassar's face. "Whew, you're a rough sight to wake to."

Yassar grinned. "Your ability for humor amazes me." Yassar handed Steve his flight jacket. "Put this on. We must leave immediately."

"All right, already. What's the rush?" Steve shoved his arms into the sleeves and hurried to keep out of reach of Yakim's prodding.

Steve and Yassar assumed their previous positions in the cockpit. The engines were running.

"Let's go. Everything is in perfect condition." Yassar looked out the windscreen and then back at Steve. "Now!"

Steve pushed the throttle levers forward, did a sharp left turn around, and released both brakes. The Lear gathered speed more slowly across the packed sand runway, but the take-off was smooth.

"Hold 095 degrees and remain at five hundred feet." Yassar barked commands as he watched out the windscreen to his right.

"Expecting company?"

"Possibly. It's of no importance now we're off the ground. No one will touch us while we're airborne. Maintain your airspeed, and we'll be over the coast in thirty minutes. After crossing the coast, turn to a heading of 010 degrees."

Suddenly a voice burst into their headphones.

"Unidentified aircraft on heading 080. This is Commander Najran of the Royal Saudi Air Force. Identify or be shot down."

Steve looked over at Yassar who was showing no emotion. "Okay, Yassar. The joke's over. What do you want me to do?"

Yassar put the tip of the silencer over Steve's right nostril. "You fly this damned plane. I'll take care of those fools." Yassar keyed his mike. "Saudi Commander. This is Yassar Akazian of the Free People's Army. We have commandeered this jet and are flying to Iran."

"That will not be permitted," the Iranian F-15 commander replied.

"You will permit it! We have Captain Steven Hardesty of the United States Navy, Jofur Armani, and four other oil ministers hostage." Yassar watched the windscreen hoping the coast would appear. He knew he had the upper hand, but he never tried to predict the itchy trigger finger of a jet jockey.

"I must have confirmation of their presence." Commander Najran pulled his F-15 Eagle along side the Lear.

Steve looked out his left window over at the gray ghost of an airplane that had emerged from the darkness. The reddish glow of the pilot's instuments illuminated the Commander's helmeted head making it appear as if he was suspended in mid air.

"Tell him," Yassar motioned to the mike and punched Steve's right arm with the Beretta.

Steve looked out the window at the suspended pilot. "Commander, this is Captain Steve Hardesty of the U. S. Navy. This joker's correct. He has six of us hostage, and we are headed for Iran. He has an explosive device attached to his body, and he's holding a weapon on me. His buddy has the others tied up in the back. I'm sure he wouldn't mind blowing all of us out of the sky if need be. Let's not anger him too much. Okay?"

"Roger, Captain. I'll get back with you."

Steve waited as the fighter pilot radioed for fire orders. Steve looked at Yassar. "You had better hope a diplomat and not a military man is giving this guy advice." Steve lifted his brows, shrugged his shoulders, and hoped for a reprieve, also.

"Captain Hardesty?"

"Roger."

"We will escort you to the coast; then you'll be released."

Yassar grinned. "I told you, Captain. Your soft American ideals have rubbed off on the Saudis. They give Armani too much worth. That's good for me, bad for you."

"Captain Hardesty, maintain your heading and speed. You will be picked up by two F-14 Tomcats at the coast. They are from the *USS Carl*

*Vinson.* Keep your frequency set to 132.4. If you alter course, I've been given fire orders to destroy your aircraft." Commander Najran eased back on the F-15's throttles and settled to a fire position on Steve's tail.

"Roger, Commander."

Several tense minutes passed as the Saudi northeastern coast crept beneath the Lear.

"Captain Hardesty, you are passing over Al Qatif. I will leave you, now. I have been instructed to inform your captors their private runway and comrades have been destroyed. There are no survivors. A combined air and land assault was carried out at 0400 hours. Good luck. Out."

"Roger, Commander. Thanks."

Yassar, still showing no emotion, looked at Steve. "Turn left to 010. We're forty-five minutes from touchdown."

"I guess we're traveling farther into Iran than I anticipated." Steve readjusted his seating.

"All the way to Tehran." Yassar began readjusting the Nav Computer to the preset frequencies.

"Cuvey-One, this is Lieutenant Zeke Rafferty of the United States Navy. I'm at your six o'clock high and have missle lock."

"Roger that Lieutenant. Where are you from?"

Yassar tapped Steve on the arm with his pistol. "Cut the chatter."

"Knoxville, Tennessee, Cap'n. Is there anyway we can help the situation prior to Iranian airspace penetration? Over."

"No way in hell, Lieutenant. Ease up on that trigger finger."

"Roger, Cap'n. I'll get back with you in a moment." Lieutenant Rafferty radioed the *Vinson* that the situation was grave. He received escort orders only. The com center deep in the bowels of the Nimitz class nuclear carrier radioed Ramstein Air Base in West Germany. "Put the Blackbird up. Bogey's present heading 010, speed 450 knots, destination probably Tehran or coastal city in northern Iran. ETA: one hour."

At Mach three, the Blackbird surveillance spy aircraft could be passing over northern Iran as the Lear touched down. It's cameras, with luck, could pinpoint the destination of the hostages.

"Captain Hardesty, we have no fire orders. We're breaking off, now. Good luck."

"Thanks, Lieutenant."

"See, Captain Hardesty. I told you we would be fine." Yassar watched the southern Iranian coast pass under the jet.

"You're in my homeland, now." Yassar leaned back in the co-pilot seat and activated the auto-pilot. The jet climbed to fifteen thousand feet and smoothed off at 400 knots. "Why do you Americans place such a value on life? It creates such an easy target. Don't you realize there is no greater honor than to die for your leader?"

"We don't hesitate to die for our beliefs. God knows how many were lost in past wars. But there's no honor in using religion as an excuse for murder, thievery, and torture. Hell, Yassar, I know how easy it is to blot out a life. I've seen men die. They had ideals like you and I, and they wanted to live as much as I want to live. They died gloriously, but they're just as dead. What did they gain? Honor? Glory? Hell no! They did it because they were trying to protect the World from people like you."

"Shut up, Captain. Your silly ideals sicken me." Yassar pointed the gun at Steve's forehead. "I'm your god, now, and this is my lightning bolt. I control your life or death in my hands. Does your God have that power? Will your faith prevent this bullet from piercing your brain and killing you instantly? NO! I control your destiny by my will, and my will is determined by my beliefs. Don't you Americans understand? You can't change our beliefs. You must learn to live with them and not try to alter them to fit your molds." Yassar smiled and pulled the hammer back on the Beretta. "Prepare to meet your God, Captain." He put his finger in the trigger guard and pulled. The hammer fell forward with a loud snap. Yassar laughed. "See, Captain. You are alive. I willed you not to die at this time. I am truly your god."

"You silly son-of-a-bitch," Steve had not flinched during Yassar's little show.

"Commander Esfahan calling Commander Akazian."

"Ah, Esfahan, your voice is a welcome sound. We have the cargo as anticipated."

"Roger. We will escort you to the preassigned coordinates."

Yassar reactivated the auto-pilot after programming in their new coordinates. The plane swung around to a heading of 008.

"We have you visually and will follow you in," Esfahan radioed.

For the next thirty minutes, Yassar didn't look from his watch out the windscreen. "Our destination is Rasht. There's an old military base fifty kilometers west of town. The town is twenty kilometers inland from the Caspian. There will be no escape for you or your friends. You will be released if all our demands are met, but don't tempt me. You're the least needed of the lot."

"You know your demands will never be met."

"Then you won't have a future to worry about, Captain."

"There, to the right, the lights of Rasht. Make a wide turn right, then left. Come in over the town on a heading of 270. Pass directly over the strobe on the tower you see to your left. After crossing the tower, drop to one thousand feet. You'll be on course with the runway and four miles out."

Steve strained to see the landmarks.

"Full flaps, now." Yassar keyed the mike. "Light two seven."

Steve saw the runway come to life. He was on line and apparently on the correct glideslope. "Gear down." The jet settled onto the end of the runway. Steve reversed engines and braked the Lear to a stop. "Where to, coach?"

Yassar smiled and looked at Steve with wide eyes. "I think I will have to keep you around for a while, Captain. You humor me. We will have to talk again, soon."

"Hey, Yassar?"

"Yes, Captain?"

"Let me give you something to think about."

"What's that, Captain Hardesty?"

"You know that little act you did with the pistol?"

"Yes?"

"How do you know is wasn't my god that made you keep the chamber empty?" Steve didn't smile or wait for an answer. He powered up the engines and turned the Lear back towards the hangers.

Yassar directed Steve to the right hand hanger as they rolled off the runway onto the tarmac. After the engines were shut down, Yakim and Yassar escorted Steve and the Arabs into the building. When they entered the wide doors, Steve could see the interior of the hanger had been converted into a prison block. There were six individually constructed concrete cells at the north end of the space. The walls were concrete block and the entrances were steel bar doors. Steve assumed they would be escorted to the toilets because they weren't provided in the locked areas. He had also noted a French built Draussalt Mirage parked on the tarmac opposite their hanger. He hoped it was stationed here permanently because it could provide a quick way out of this place if the situation made itself available.

"This is your cell, American dog." Yakim shoved Steve into the cell and shut the door. "Consider this your last living place." Yakim laughed.

Steve spun around and pointed his finger at Yakim. "Bang, you're dead. I'll get you someday you little shit."

Yakim pulled the bolt back on the AK-47. He aimed at Steve's forehead and placed his finger in the trigger guard.

Steve was convinced Yakim would have fired if Yassar hadn't walked up at that moment.

"Yakim, don't fire! I have a few more things to say to the Captain."

Yakim lowered his weapon and placed it on safe. "One day, American, no one will be around to save your ass."

Steve diverted his attention from the rifle to Yassar. "Thanks, Yaz...Hey! Who is this?" Steve motioned to the black haired beauty Yassar had his arm around. She didn't seem to be enjoying his company, but Yassar clasped her closer anyway.

"Captain, this is my woman, Tallia. She will be responsible for your meals."

"My pleasure, Tallia. I hope we can sit down and talk sometime." Steve thought he detected a smile on Tallia's face.

Yassar jerked Tallia closer. "She is permitted to talk to no one but me." Yassar turned to Tallia. "Come woman, I need comfort after our long flight."

Steve watched Yassar pull Tallia across the floor of the hanger, and they disappeared through the door on the opposite side. Steve looked around the perimeter of the eight by eight foot cell, kicked the walls to assure their solidity, and sat on the edge of the provided cot. "I'll make it through this, Sabrina," Steve thought. "I'll get home."

# 18

"So, has your afternoon been interesting?" Richard meekly asked as he removed his coat and placed it on one of the empty chairs at their dining table in Chowning's Restaurant. He sat opposite Cathy and waited for her reply.

"I guess so if you call walking my legs off while waiting for you 'interesting' ". Cathy had been waiting for Richard for the past long hour in the restaurant. She had driven from Norfolk to Colonial Williamsburg earlier that day and had walked the full length of Glouchester Avenue, twice, working up an appetite. After window shopping at a few of the craft stores, Cathy arrived at the restaurant thirty minutes prior to their reserved time. Richard had promised to arrive by 6:00 P.M., and by seven, Cathy had consumed all the bread and bubbling cider the waiter had to offer. Just as she was preparing to leave, Richard arrived. "Richard! Where have you been? I thought I was getting stood up!"

"I am sorry, Cathy. I had an unexpected admission to Coronary Care. The patient is one of the cardiology resident's father. He asked me to take care of him, and I felt I had to stay until he was stable. I came as soon as I could, but I'm not sure I'll be able to stay. I gave the Coronary Care Unit this number. I hope you don't mind."

"Me? Mind? Why should I mind? It's not like we've been waiting for this time away from Norfolk for a month." Cathy's obvious frustration with the situation was beginning to gather glances from the tables in their vicinity.

"I know I should have called, but by the time I finished getting the patient admitted and stabilized, I was already late. I drove as fast as I safely could, but I don't have a Porsche, you know." Richard smiled. He hoped injecting a little levity would soften Cathy's crust. "Shall we order?"

Cathy had hoped Richard would show remorse for keeping her waiting, and she was glad he did. She tried to understand his position, but it was hard being second, especially to something you couldn't fight. "I accept your apology, and I'll stop pouting. But please call me when you're going to be late. I was beginning to worry."

"About me, or your stomach?"

"Stomach first, you second." Cathy smiled and reached over to grasp Richard's hand. She looked up and noticed a gentleman approaching their table. "Don't look now, but you've been found." Cathy withdrew her hand and slumped back in her chair.

A man in a three cornered hat walked to Richard's left side, leaned over slightly from the waist, and spoke. "Excuse me, are you Dr. Tims."

Richard watched as Cathy retreated into her chair and peered out the window. It wasn't going to be a night to remember. "Yes, I am," he replied to the head waiter.

"There's a phone call for you, Doctor. You may take it over here, please."

"Excuse me, Cathy." Richard waited for a reply, but all he received was Cathy's arm waving to the phone. "I'll be back in a moment."

"Humph." Cathy shrugged. She watched Richard disappear into a small hallway. He reappeared almost as quickly. He walked slowly back to the table, pulled out his chair, and sat down. Cathy perked up from her scowl. "What was the phone call about? Medication?"

Richard looked at Cathy and frowned. "No, I have to leave. My patient has developed some complications. We're going to have to cath him tonight, and he may possibly have to have bypass surgery. I'll probably be up all night with him. I have to go, Cathy. I'm sorry. Do you want me to follow you back?"

"Hell no! I'm having something to eat! I didn't wait around here all day to go home without supper. You go ahead and do what you have to do. I'll be fine. I did just fine before Dr. Tims came into my life." Cathy motioned for the waiter to come over to the table.

"I'm truly sorry. I'd hoped the evening would have turned out better." Richard stood up and put on his coat. "Drive carefully, a light rain started as I pulled into the parking lot." Richard turned to leave.

"Richard?" Cathy looked up from the menu.

"Yes?" Richard turned to see one of the few smiles Cathy had mustered this evening.

"I'm sorry I'm acting like a baby, but we don't get away from Norfolk often, and I wanted tonight to be special. I've let my disappointment cloud my attempt to understand your profession. I do understand, but I can't help being upset and a little jealous. Forgive me?" The response was so out of character for Cathy she winced as she talked.

Richard walked over to Cathy and gave her a kiss. "Of course, I forgive you, but I'm the one pleading for mercy. Do you think I might get some?"

"What?" Cathy grinned. "Mercy?"

Richard laughed. "Of course, what kind of gentleman do you think I am."

"Oh, I think we've already established that on previous encounters, but you'll refresh my memory soon, won't you?" Cathy kissed Richard lightly on the lips. "Drive carefully. I'll leave shortly, but I've got to have a cup of coffee and some of the yummy apple pie I've seen them carrying around for the past forty-five minutes."

Richard smiled. "You do have a weakness for sweets, don't you? I'll call in the morning. I love you."

"Me too," Cathy whispered. She knew her response wasn't exactly what Richard would have liked to hear, but this was the most she could give the relationship for the moment.

Richard smiled hoping to receive more of an admission of love from Cathy, but he could tell she was in no mood for emotional confessions. So, he buttoned up his coat while giving Cathy a good-bye smile and departed the restaurant.

Cathy watched as Richard departed. She waited a few moments before summonsing a waiter and ordering apple pie and coffee. While she waited for her order, she watched the rain splatter against the window, and her thoughts turned to Richard and their relationship. Given time, their relationship might materialize into something with future 'possibilities'. But at the present, she had too many priorities. She knew she would stay with Sabrina until the baby was born, and she wanted to be close when Sabrina faced Steve. After those critical situations were resolved, she could direct her energy to her own relationship. Cathy's feelings for Richard seemed sincere, but the rapture of her physical attraction to him was clouding the issue. She needed more time-more time to allow the cloud to pass and for their true relationship to solidify. However, Richard's acceptance of the research grant in London had pressured him to ask Cathy to marry him, and he had requested, no, demanded, a decision on his proposal by Christmas. Cathy had yet to reveal to Sabrina the fact of Richard's proposal because she knew it would upset Sabrina. Therefore, she had procrastinated in her answer for the past month, but now Richard was beginning to pressure her for a yes or no. She had begged off as long as possible, but with Thanksgiving coming in one week, she knew Richard would demand an answer soon.

Cathy hated demands. "Hell, I'm not sure I even love him," Cathy spoke to the splatter of raindrops on the windowsill.

"Excuse me? Did you say something?" The waiter questioned as he set down Cathy's pie and coffee."

Cathy looked up and smiled. "No, nothing important." Then, she looked down at the huge dessert. "Mmm, looks yummy."

"I hope you enjoy it. I gave you a large portion. I know you've been waiting for a while and missed your supper."

"Don't worry, I won't let it go to waste." As she scooped the first mouthful, she heard the rain hit harder against the window.

\* \* \*

Interstate Sixty-Four runs southeast from Williamsburg through Hampton, Virginia, across the mouth of the James River via the Hampton Bridge and Tunnel, and on to Norfolk. Virginia Highwaypatrolman Sergeant Bill Hartsfield had been assigned to traffic control for the past three days and was working the stretch of Interstate between Patrick Henry International Airport and Hampton. He had eased his patrol car into the median along side a group of pine trees, aimed his *Vascar* radar unit at the south bound traffic lane setting the upper limit at seventy-five, and opened his thermos. He eased back in his seat, closed his eyes and listened to the soothing beat of the rain on the roof of his five liter Mustang. As he sipped on his first cup of coffee, a burst from the radar gun alerted him to a speeding violator, but when he looked at the readout, the LED illuminated 76. "Hell, I'm not getting out in this rain for one mile over my limit." He reset the unit and eased back into his reclining seat. Suddenly the tone aroused his attention once again. He opened his eyes and looked at the LED. "Shit, that's got to be a mistake." He reset the gun, and the alarm resounded immediately. "SHIT!" He peered at the LED-134 mph. As he stared at the LED, a white automobile flashed by his patrol car. "Son-of-a-bitch!" He started the engine, did a one hundred and eighty degree turn into the southbound lane and hit his lights and siren. He picked up his radio and keyed the microphone. "Unit twenty one in pursuit of white sportscar Southbound 64. Speed in excess of one hundred and twenty miles per hour."

"Roger, twenty one. What's your twenty?"

"Mile marker ninety-four, Control."

"Roger, twenty one. Please advise when tag numbers are available."

"Hell! I might not be able to catch the damned thing. It was clocked at one hundred and thirty four on my radar as it passed. You better alert thirty-three it's headed his way."

"Roger, twenty-one. Will advise. Over."

Every ounce of Bill's body was directed into the accelerator. The Mustang was straining to pass one hundred and ten, and Bill hadn't seen a hint of the white sportscar. As he flashed by the rest stop at mile marker one hundred, he thought he caught a glimpse of a white sportscar sitting in a slot in front of the rest rooms. "That son-of-a-bitch isn't going to out-smart me!" He let up on the accelerator, slipped the transmission into second, waited for the car to decelerate to fifty, checked the rear view mirror, locked the tires, and did a one hundred and eighty degree spin. He let up on the brakes, hit the accelerator, and sped for the exit lane of the rest stop. As he approached the lane, he slowed down and weaved between the traffic pulled to the side in recognition of his lights. He eased down the line of parked vehicles until he saw it. "There that son-of-a-bitch is. I've got his ass but good." Bill pulled the patrol car behind the white Porsche and stopped. He put on his hat, holstered his Smith and Wesson .357 Magnum, and cautiously opened his door. He got out and eased around the back of his car peering through the back window of the 911 Turbo Carrera. "No one inside," he thought. He leaned over and felt the exhaust. "Still hot. This has to be the car." Bill walked back to his patrol car and picked up the radio. "Dispatch, TwentyOne. Over."

"Roger, Twenty-One. Go ahead."

"I have a white Porsche. Plate number: EMD-CW. What the hell kind of plate designation is that?"

"Roger, Twenty-One. Hold…Vehicle registered to one Cathy, with a C, Winston. Present address: Gull Haven, MacKenzie Island, Virginia. No wants or warrants. Over."

"Roger, dispatch. Over."

Bill laid down the radio and looked back at the Porsche. "What a car," he thought. "Hell, that thing would cost me two year's salary." Bill got out of the patrol car and walked over to the Porsche. As he rubbed his hand along the "whale tail" spoiler he looked up and saw one of the most beautiful women he had ever seen walking down the sidewalk from the convenience area. He eased up the path a short distance to get a better look at the blonde as she approached. He stopped as she passed. "Evening, Mam."

"Good evening, Officer," Cathy said as she walked past the Highway Patrolman. Cathy kept her face down against the wind as she passed the policeman. She pulled out her keys and looked up to see her exit blocked by a Highway Patrol Car with its lights flashing. *Damn, I hope he didn't get a good look at the car as I passed*, she thought as she turned to the patrol-man. "Excuse me, Officer."

Bill turned to the voice and saw Cathy standing next to the white Porsche. His mouth dropped open.

"Do you think you could move your car? I need to get out." Cathy looked down at the door and inserted her key.

Bill Hartsfield walked up behind the blonde, put his hand on the butt of his weapon, and tapped her on the shoulder. "This your car, Mam?"

"Why yes, is there a problem?" Cathy looked at the officer with her blue eyes and put on her innocent face.

Bill laughed. "Yes, Mam. I believe there is."

"Please, my name is Winston, Cathy Winston."

"Well, Ms. Winston. I clocked you at 134 miles per hour as you passed me approximately ten minutes ago. That's a bit fast, don't you think."

"I'm afraid you're mistaken, Officer.." Cathy looked at the Patrolman's name tag. "Hartsfield. I've been at this rest stop for the past fifteen minutes. I was returning from Williamsburg this evening, and I must have eaten something that didn't agree with me. I felt ill and pulled over. I remember distinctly. It was eight forty-five when I pulled into the parking place. That was five minutes before you said you saw me pass you. Tell me, how could I do that?"

"Do you have any witnesses, Ms. Winston?"

"Why," Cathy looked around at the parking spaces. "I did, but I guess they've left. There was a young couple parked here in a blue Pontiac Grand-Am."

Bill remembered the Pontiac. He had eased around it before he spotted the Porsche.

"Couldn't we please hurry." Cathy anxiously looked at Bill. "I have a friend in Norfolk, and she's been ill. I told her I would try to get to her place by nine-thirty. If you don't let me get going, I might have to speed." Cathy let her arms down to her side in exasperation. Her white Cashmere coat fell opened revealing her lavender dress. It was cut low in the front, originally for Richard's benefit, but having it available to divert the policeman's attention didn't hurt. Cathy watched the patrolman's eyes wander down the front of her body.

"I guess I can't hold you…I mean, keep you here, Ms. Winston. I'll have to take your word about the times. I'm sorry if I've inconvenienced you. Drive carefully." Bill turned and headed for the patrol car. He turned back to Cathy. "By the way, Ms. Winston."

"Yes, officer?"

"What does your plate, EMD-CW, stand for?"

"Eat My Dust, Cathy Winston." Cathy smiled, unlocked her door, got in, and started the car. She let out the breath she had been holding, and waited for the Patrolman to move his car.

Bill grinned at Cathy's explanation about her license tag, slowly walked to the Mustang, shut off the lights, and pulled forward. He heard the Porsche's exhaust reverberating as it pulled out into the exit lane. Bill backed into the Porsche's slot, pulled into traffic behind the Turbo-Carrera, and followed Eat My Dust, Cathy Winston back to the Langley

Air Force Base exit before turning around. As he watched the red tail lights disappear into the distance, he knew the lady had lied to him, but their meeting had been so enjoyable, he didn't mind. He would remember the sight of the beautiful blonde in the lavender dress beside the white Porsche for a long time to come.

As the headlights of the Highway Patrol car split from her direction of travel, Cathy eased the accelerator down, and the Porsche slid past sixty-five settling at ninety. For the first time in thirty minutes, Cathy breathed easier. She knew she would have been arrested by the policeman if she hadn't lied and flirted her way out of the predicament. From now on she vowed to hold her speed at least below one hundred.

The remainder of the trip into Norfolk was uneventful, and Cathy arrived home by nine-thirty. Her apple pie and coffee was gone, and the excitement of the return trip had

prepared her for some serious snacking. She picked up the newspaper from the front step, opened the door, entered the condo's front hall, hung her coat in the closet, and started into the living room. "I'm home!" To her surprise, Sabrina was sitting on the couch holding a crumpled piece of paper. Her swollen red eyes were the first thing Cathy noticed as Sabrina looked up. She rushed to Sabrina's side. "What's wrong? Has something happened?" Cathy laid the paper down beside Sabrina and took her hands in hers.

Sabrina continued to sniffle, but she managed a smile. "I finally got a message from Steve."

"My goodness. What did he do? Dump you?" Cathy peeled the paper from Sabrina's grip. She opened the telegram and smoothed the wrinkles.

FROM:CAPT. STEVE HARDESTY, U.S.N., CAIRO, EGYPT
TO:SABRINA MACKENZIE; OCEAN BOULEVARD; NORFOLK, VIRGINIA
DEAR SABRINA,

I DON'T HAVE MUCH TIME TO WRITE WHAT I REALLY FEEL. I LOVE YOU VERY MUCH AND CAN'T BELIEVE I'M GOING TO BE A FATHER. YOU HAVE

MADE ME THE HAPPIEST MAN ON EARTH. I HOPE
EVERYTHING IS GOING WELL. I WISH I WERE THERE,
AND I WILL BE THERE FOR THE BIRTH OF OUR
CHILD. I HOPE TO WORKOUT A PLAN TO SEE YOU
WITHIN THE WEEK.

LOVE, STEVE.

"This is great news, Sabrina. Why such a long face, and all the tears?"

"I'm happy, but I'm so scared. I'm happy Steve's planning to come home, but frightened about the possibility of him discovering the truth about the pregnancy."

"This is what you've planned to happen, isn't it? Steve would come home and find out you're pregnant. You break the news it's his baby, and you didn't want to worry him while he was gone. You get married and live happily ever after. Right?"

"Yes, but I'm still upset and feel so guilty."

"Guilt? About what?"

"Steve might have changed his mind and not want to marry me, but with the pregnancy, he could feel an obligation."

"Hell, Sabrina!. He's tickled to deathl Can't you read?" Cathy thrust the note under Sabrina's nose. "Steve asked you to marry him before he left. He didn't know you were pregnant. Right?"

"I guess you're right." Sabrina wiped a few tears from her cheek.

"Why in heaven's name would you even suspect he wouldn't want to marry you? The man's had the hots for you since he first met you, hasn't he?"

"I don't know!"

"You know. You don't want to admit it, but you know."

Sabrina dried her eyes, looked at Cathy, and smiled. "I've always wished."

Cathy put her hands around Sabrina's. "Steve loves you. He has loved you since he first met you. Otherwise, he wouldn't have been around when you finally realized Kent was an egotistical asshole. Do you think a man that didn't love you would have proposed the first chance you were back together."

"I suppose not." Sabrina looked at Cathy's eyes. "I can still worry, can't I?"

"No. You're not permitted. Doctor's orders."

Sabrina collected the note from Cathy's hand, folded it, and put it in her robe pocket. "I want to save this. What brings you home so early? I didn't expect you back until the morning."

"It's a long story. Richard had to return to the hospital before we had a chance to order. I've not had anything to eat except pie and coffee, and what's worse, I almost got picked up for speeding. Scared the devil out of me."

"That's doubtful! How fast were you going?"

"Oh, a little over a hundred."

"How little?"

"I buzzed by a State Boy doing a hundred and thirty five."

"ONE HUNDRED AND THIRTY FIVE! They would have locked you up and thrown away the key. How did you get out of that?"

"I lied, that's how. I buzzed off the Interstate as soon as my radar detector went off. I knew he had me, but it was dark and rainy. I hoped he hadn't seen the car close enough to ID me. I bluffed, showed a little boob, and escaped the long arm of the law." Cathy grinned and raised her eyebrows.

"You never cease to amaze me, Cathy Winston."

Cathy stood up, stretched, and headed for the kitchen. "I'm starved. Let's pig out and watch a little television." She began rummaging through the refrigerator shelves and cabinets.

"Your goodies are hidden on the cabinet shelf above the stove." Sabrina knew Cathy was right about Steve's love, but she continued to think about the baby and her future even as she lived the deception. If she wanted her life to be as she had always wished and dreamed, there was no option. She would have to continue to take the chance and live with the fear of discovery. For her baby, it was worth the risk.

"Hey, Sabrina? How about some popcorn? I won't put any butter or salt on it. Yech! Sounds awful, doesn't it, but I'll sacrifice to have a binge partner."

"I don't guess one night of indiscretionary poking will hurt, but I'll have to pass on chocolate."

Cathy picked up a sack of M & M's, opened the top, and put a hand-ful in her mouth. "Me too," she said in a muffled tone with the colored candies dancing around on her tongue. Cathy looked into the eight ounce bag of candy coated snacks. "You little rascals aren't long for this world." She put the popcorn in the air popper, and headed for the bedroom. She quickly pulled off her clothes, grabbed her favorite terry cloth robe and slippers, and headed back to the kitchen.

Sabrina was in the kitchen when Cathy returned.

"Sit down, turn on the tube to Channel Eight, and I'll bring in the goodies."

"Oh, no! Are we going to have watch horror movies?"

Cathy put her hands on her hips and gave Sabrina a look of exaspera-tion. "Of course! Chocolate and popcorn aren't chocolate and popcorn unless you're watching a scary movie."

They settled in front of the television set. Sabrina picked her way through the bowl of popcorn and slipped a M & M for an occasional dessert. Cathy opened the paper, scanned the headlines, subconsciously munched on popcorn, and waited for the first horror movie to begin. "Sabrina, what was the doctor's name that performed your pregnancy test."

Sabrina continued to sneak the chocolates while Cathy had the paper in front of her face. "I don't remember. Johnston or Johnstone? I'm not sure. I can go get the slip if it's important. Why?"

"Listen to this. Dr. Robert C. Johnstone of Gloucester Point, Virginia, reported his office was vandalized over the weekend. 'Apparently, the van-dals were looking for drugs', the doctor was quoted as saying, 'because no records were missing'. Dr. Johnstone advised officials he kept no con-trolled substances in his office since the majority of his practice was

Obstetrics. Now, that wouldn't be so unusual, but right below that article is this. Kleinsmith Laboratories reported a major computer malfunction over the weekend. Their experts say a knowledgeable computer operator had acquired access to their files and searched the records. At this time, they don't feel any of the records were disturbed, but a more thorough search is underway."

"Put the paper down! The first movie is starting. Who cares about that stuff?"

"I don't know. It seems unusual is all."

"What seems unusual?" Sabrina stuffed a few more M & M's into her mouth.

Cathy snatched the bag away. "Hey! Don't eat all the chocolate. I thought you weren't going to have any."

"I lied."

Cathy peeked back into the black sack. "I see you did!" Cathy put a few more candies in her mouth and mumbled. "I just find it unusual that the doctor doing your pregnancy test, and the lab performing the procedure were both vandalized, that's all."

"What? I didn't understand you." Sabrina turned her attention from the set to Cathy.

"Forget it."

"Good. Gimme some more candy." Sabrina reached behind her back, but didn't receive any more candy. She kept wiggling her fingers hoping to get a prize. "Hey, where's the chocolate." Sabrina turned to Cathy and gave her a nasty look.

Cathy rattled the empty bag over Sabrina's hand and grinned. "All gone."

"No problem," Sabrina rolled to her left, opened the bottom of the side table, and removed a two pounder bag of M & M's from her stash. She ate a few and tossed them to Cathy. "Here. Enjoy."

"You rat. You're not supposed to be eating this stuff."

"Doctor Vance told me to gain weight. I thought I'd oblige." Sabrina turned and sheepishly smiled.

They stayed up most of the night watching television and eating. They laughed and talked. Each having her own worries, concerns, fears, and loves, but not discussing any of them. Tonight was for fun. Tomorrow could be for worry. Both fell asleep halfway into the third horror flick; side by side enjoying one night of decadence.

* * *

"Cathy! Wake upl Quick!" Sabrina frantically yelled as she shook Cathy by her shoulders.

"Wha…What's going on?" Cathy tried to push herself up with her hands from the position her body had assumed during the night. "Oh, damn! My hand's asleep. I must have slept on it."

"Hush!" Sabrina pointed to the television set. "Look!" Sabrina was still in a frenzy.

"Look at what? I can hardly see. Lord, what a taste in my mouth. What did we eat?" Cathy rubbed her face with her hands and began to stretch.

"Open your eyes, and look at the television. Quick! When I woke up, I saw him. He's on television. I can't believe it!" Sabrina walked toward the television and pointed to the man on the screen. "It's Steve!"

Cathy finally focused on the picture and yawned. "Damned if it isn't! What's he doing on the tube?" She stretched until her robe came opened, and she realized she didn't have on any clothes. "I've got to go to the bathroom. What's for breakfast, M & M's?"

"Oh, gross. Wait a minute. Let's see what's this is all about."

The picture of Steve faded from the screen, and Tom Brokaw appeared. Behind him was a map of Iran with the logo of an airplane superimposed. Hijacked was printed above the logo. "Ladies and Gentlemen. What you have just seen is a videotape submitted to our Middle East Bureau. The tape was delivered to our correspondents yesterday. It is reported to be a tape of the American and Saudi Arabian hostages from a recent hijacking."

"Oh my God, Steve's been taken…" Sabrina brought her hands to her mouth.

"Hush! Let's hear what they have to say." Cathy grabbed Sabrina by the shoulders, and they both sat down on a stool four feet from the television.

"The individuals you have seen are members of the Council for Petroleum Exports for the Saudi Arabian Government. It has been rumored they have been visiting Cairo and other Mediterranean capitals testing the idea of a network of Saudi pipelines into the Eastern Mediterranean area. The names of the committee members are being withheld for security reasons. However, the American hostage seen on the tape has been identified as Captain Steven Hardesty of New York City. Captain Hardesty, a Vietnam War Naval Ace and recipient of the Distinguished Flying Cross, was recently re-enlisted by the Navy to serve as a private pilot for the Saudi officials. The hijacking occurred at two a.m., Cairo time, as the plane was on a return flight from Cairo to Jiddah."

"I don't believe this." Sabrina half cried. "I don't believe it. I was celebrating his return and he was already a hostage." Sabrina turned to Cathy. "What are we going to do? I have to help him! I don't know what to do."

Cathy leaned back and looked Sabrina square in the eye. "Sabrina, get yourself together. First of all, let's try and get some more facts. Second, calm down! You're no help to anyone in your present condition. Third, what the hell can we do?" They turned back to the screen.

"According to the kidnappers, these hostages will be held until the Saudi government halts all present negotiations with Egypt, or any other country for construction of the pipelines. Also, they are seeking twenty five billion dollars in retribution for damages brought upon Iran for price fixing of crude oil. At the moment, we have no information concerning the location of the hostages, but in all probability, they are being held somewhere in Tehran. For the moment, the United States Department of State has withheld comment. Secretary of State MacCauley Orberson is apparently enroute from New York to Washington, and is expected to fly to Ridyah later tonight. A full report will follow this evening. Thank you, and Good Day."

"Quick, turn to CBS." Cathy ordered from her perch.

Sabrina aimed the remote and clicked in the appropriate channel. Dan Rather appeared on the screen. "According to our contacts in Iran, what you are about to see is footage of an interview with the American pilot, Captain Steven Hardesty. Supposedly, he has been the private pilot for the Saudi officials since August. His assignment was made by the Secretary of State at the request of the Saudi Government. Captain Hardesty is a honorably discharged Naval officer whose service attachment was reactivated. Presently, Captain Hardesty owns and operates an elite flying service with his partner, Taggat Delaney. Mr. Delaney is not available for interview at this time. We have been informed that Mr. Delaney, a prominent New York attorney,

and long time friend of Captain Hardesty, has been rushed to the White House for consultation…"

"That's how we can help Steve!" Sabrina jumped from the stool. "We'll get a hold of Taggat and figure out a way."

"…and now, we'll go to the tape." The picture switched to the videotape.

Sabrina sat back down on the stool and stared at the screen.

The tape began by panning a small brownish grey walled room. In the center of the room was a grey square table. Behind the table was one metal folding chair. The camera then panned to a door in the back right portion of the picture. Steve entered through this door. His hands were tied in front of him, and a guard was walking closely behind. The guard's face was obscured by a black wrap mask, and he was armed with a Russian AK-47 assault rifle. He directed Steve to be seated in the folding chair and stood behind and to Steve's left. He placed the muzzle of the weapon within six inches of Steve's left temple, handed him a piece of paper, and directed him to read.

Steve looked at the paper. "I am an American pilot being held hostage by the Iranian Government. My crimes against this government are compounded daily…Wait a damned minute! I'm not reading this crap." Steve crumpled the paper and threw it into the guard's face. The picture suddenly went blank as the cameraman placed his hand over the lens. In the background, a scuffle between the guard and Steve could be heard.

The tape continued blank for a while, but quickly returned to show Steve bound to the chair. A second guard had assumed a position to his right. This masked guard held a pistol to Steve's head. A small trickle of blood oozed from the left side of Steve's mouth, and his left eye was reddened. The new guard instructed him to read.

"I will be held captive until the Saudi government pays twenty five billion dollars to the Iranian people. Also, the Saudi Government must cease all negotiations with Egypt concerning construction of an oil pipeline. If these demands aren't met within six weeks, the Saudi Arabian officials and I will be killed." They untied Steve from the chair, ordered him to stand, and escorted him from the room.

"Switch to ABC!"

Sabrina touched the remote and Peter Jennings popped onto the screen. "We will have followup reports as the news breaks. NIGHTLINE will cover the entire subject of hijackings and the present policy our government follows in these matters."

Sabrina turned to Cathy. "I know what we have to do."

"What's that? We going to raid Iran?" Cathy smiled.

"No, not us, but we can get someone who can."

"Who? Rambo?" Cathy giggled. "Sabrina, what in the world are you talking about?"

"We need to get in touch with Taggat. He has numerous contacts in the government and military. If any one can help us, he can. He'll know how to make something happen." Sabrina looked at Cathy and firmly put her hand on Cathy's knee. "Come on, let's make some phone calls and plan our next move. Taggat got Steve into this, and he can damned well get him out!"

"Wait a minute, Sabrina. You're not going anywhere. Remember? The baby! You can't take this. At least, not this late in the pregnancy. Complete rest are the words I remember from Dr. Vance. Besides, Taggat can't be contacted. He's on his way to Washington."

"That's it, Cathy! You're a genius. We'll have to go to Washington and meet with whoever's pulling the strings in this project. I believe we both know the culprit, and his name is Orberson."

"We can't go to Washington. That baby is too important, and you couldn't get into the executive bathroom in the State Department, much less a secret meeting." The phone rang and Cathy answered. "Hello, Cathy Winston…Yes, *it* was…Yes, she's okay. Thanks. See you tonight. Good-by."

Sabrina watched Cathy as she spoke. "Was that Richard?"

"Yes. He was wondering how you were. He saw the report while making rounds. He sat down in the bed with one of his female heart patients. She almost had a relapse when he did."

"If he calls again, tell him I'm better than fine because I know how we can get Steve out of Iran."

"Sabrina, let's talk about this logically. This country hasn't dealt with hijackers in a long time. There won't be any negotiations. I'm afraid it's going to be a waiting game."

"I not talking negotiations, I'm talking rescue."

"No way! They don't know where he is in Iran. It would be a plan destined for failure before it began."

"Don't be so sure. I'll bet they already know exactly where they are, but they won't publicize it. I'll find out."

"You do anything you want as long as you remain in this apartment. Promise?"

"Okay, I promise."

"I'm going to get ready and go to the grocery store. We need a few things. Will you try and take it easy while I'm gone?"

"Yes, mother. Lord, you'd think I was twelve years old." Sabrina picked up her things from the previous night's television marathon, and went into her bedroom. She took a warm shower, turned on her television to one of the local stations, and lay down on the bed. The idea of finding Taggat continued to circle in her head. The warm shower had relaxed her aching muscles, so she closed her eyes, and drifted back to sleep. In the background a local newswoman came onto the screen. Sabrina didn't hear the newscast, but Cathy watched while she cleaned the kitchen. The news cast was brief. "Today, the body of Rosa Pittman was found in her over-turned car in a marshpond on MacKenzie Island. For the alumni of Soames College, Mrs. Pittman will always be remembered as the friendly face in "The Bakery", a pastry shop located close to the Soames campus. Local authorities have ruled the drowning as accidental. Apparently, Mrs. Pittman was driving home when her car struck a slick portion of pavement, crashed through a guardrail, and overturned in the marshpond. The local sheriff believes Mrs. Pittman was knocked unconscious by the crash, and drowned after her car overturned in four feet of water. Now, for our local weather."

Cathy whisked by the television set, turned it off thinking that the incident was sad, but she didn't know Rosa Pittman. She tiptoed to Sabrina's door, glanced into her room, and saw she was asleep. She walked back through the living room, picked her keys up from the coffee table, and left through the front door. As she walked to her car, she looked out to the East. "Strange," she thought. "It looked like a storm moving this way. We rarely have bad weather from that direction at this time of year." She opened her car door, started the engine, and headed for the grocery.

Sabrina abruptly awoke from her nap knowing what she had to do. She located her briefcase and took out a small booklet containing phone numbers. One was marked, "Taggat(P)". She dialed the number and waited. Two rings later the phone was answered.

"Taggat Delaney's office," a strange voice answered.

"Who's this? Where's Mae?"

"Who's calling please?"

"This is Sabrina. I have to speak to Taggat immediately."

"I'm sorry, Mr. Delaney is on his way to Washington. I'm unable to reach him at the moment. Do you care to leave a message?"

"No, no message. Is Taggat flying on a governmental plane or one of the flying service's?"

"I can't give out that information. I might lose my job."

"Listen, I'm Mr. Delaney's god-daughter. I'm pregnant, and I think I'm in labor. If I have this baby, and he's not informed, you'll lose a lot more than your job."

"Yes, Mam, but…"

"No buts…OOOOH…God, this hurts."

"Okay, okay! I don't want any trouble. Mr. Delaney is being taken to Washington on one of the flight service's planes." She rifled through the Rolodex and gave Sabrina the number.

"Thank you. I'll be sure and tell Taggat you cooperated…OOH."

"Thank you, and good luck. I hope everything goes all right."

Sabrina didn't answer. She cycled the phone, and dialed the number she had been given. "Yes, operator. The number is 111-333-Victor-One-Tango 7788. Thank you, I'll hold."

The red light flashed on the instrument panel of the twin Beechcraft. John McKay switched the button to transmit. "Victor-One-Tango 7788. John McKay."

"Johnny, thank goodness I got you. I need to speak to Taggat."

"Sabrina, how are you?" Johnny looked at the secret service agent sitting next to him. The agent was preparing to terminate transmission. "An emergency? Okay, I understand. Hold on." Johnny covered his microphone. "It's Mr. Delaney's god-daughter. Something about an emergency."

The agent activated his head mike. "Mam, this is Special Agent Gulley of the U.S. Secret Service. This number is cleared for emergency transmissions only. I'll have to ask you to terminate the call."

"Please," Sabrina grunted. "I'm in labor and the baby is in trouble. I have to talk to Taggat. OOOOH…Please!"

"Wait a moment. I'll get him on the line."

Agent Gulley moved to the passenger cabin and approached the table where Mac and Taggat were discussing the hijacking. "Excuse me, Mr. Secretary. Mr. Delaney has a phone call. It's his god-daughter. She states she's in labor."

Taggat jumped from his seat. "Mac, I have to take the call."

"Sure, but be careful saying anything about what you've seen so far."

"No problem." Taggat picked up the extension located in the back of the plane.

"Sabrina, are you okay? You're not supposed to be in labor, yet."

"Taggat. Shut up and listen. I'm not in labor. Everything's all right with the baby. I have to see you. We have to discuss Steve's situation."

"Okay, I'll do what I can." Taggat spoke as he watched Agent Gulley appear to read his lips.

"What? Oh, you're being watched?"

"That's correct."

"All right, I'm leaving for Washington…" Sabrina looked at her watch. "…in fifteen minutes. Will it be possible for us to get together?"

"I'll try to do that as soon as I can."

"Meet me tomorrow. I'm checking into the Hyatt on the Mall. I'll expect you at 3:00 P.M."

"Very well, I'll try. Sabrina, I have to go. Tell the doctor to take good care of you. Love you, goodby."

"Goodby."

Taggat made his way back to his seat. "Mac, do you think I'll be able to see Sabrina while she's in the hospital?"

"Absolutely not! You've already seen some very delicate information, and what you're about to hear is top secret."

Taggat looked out the window and became pensive. "All right, but I'm going to have one very upset god-daughter."

"That's better than one very dead god-daughter." Mac peered at Taggat over his glasses. He hoped he had impressed him with the importance of strict silence.

Sabrina quickly gathered a few clothes and stuffed them into her small Hartman suitcase. She went to the kitchen, picked up a Post-it pad, and jotted Cathy a note:

CATHY,

DON'T TRY TO FIND ME. I HAVE TO HELP STEVE. I'LL BE ALL RIGHT. I WON'T BE ABLE TO TALK TO YOU UNTIL I'VE MADE SURE STEVE IS SAFE. DON'T WORRY, I KNOW WHERE THERE'S A GOOD DOCTOR. LOVE YA, SABRINA

She stuck the note to the refrigerator, picked up her bag and rushed out the door. As she turned the corner and headed for the Interstate, Cathy's white Porsche rounded the opposite corner and slid into the driveway.

# 19

"Sabrina, how are you?" Taggat's voice resounded over the hotel room's telephone.

"Taggat! I've been worried sick. I've been in Washington for three days and haven't heard a word from you. You were supposed to have met me the night I arrived."

"Sabrina, settle down and let me explain." Taggat waited for a few moments, sensing Sabrina's exasperation.

Sabrina sat down on the edge of one of the beds in her two bedroom suite located on the top floor of the Hyatt. She squeezed the phone receiver, took a deep breath, and answered. "All right, I've settled down. Now, what's going on?"

"I need to see you this evening, Sabrina. I'm leaving town tomorrow, and what I wish to discuss can't be said over the phone. When will it be convenient?" Taggat looked over at Pete Gulley, the Secret Service agent who was assigned to his security and listening on a second phone. With a nod of Pete's head Taggat received the okay to continue.

Sabrina looked at her watch. "Leaving town? Where are you going?"

"Let's discuss it tonight."

"All right." Sabrina pouted hoping Taggat would sense her frustration. "How about seven?"

"Seven will be fine."

"Can't you tell me anything? I've been a wreck since you didn't show up the first night. Now, you call and tell me you're leaving town and there has been absolutely nothing about Steve in the papers or on the news."

"There's a reason. I'll try to cover everything tonight."

"Well, I've already waited for three days. I guess a few more hours won't matter."

"How's the baby?"

"She seems active enough, but I'm worried about her growth. My stomach hasn't gotten much larger over the past two weeks. I've made an appointment to see an obstetrician at George Washington University this afternoon."

"George Washington? Why don't you go back and see your own doctor?"

"I don't want Cathy to know where I am. She'll make me come back to Norfolk. I have to be close to where I can find out about Steve."

"I understand, and I'm sure you and the baby are going to be fine. I'll see you at seven. I love you, Sabrina."

"I love you, Taggat. I'm not very happy with you, but I love you. I'll order supper."

"Better make it for three."

"Why?"

"Order enough food for three. You'll understand when we arrive. Good-by."

"Good-by." Taggat's remarks bewildered Sabrina. "Supper for three? Leaving town? What's he talking about? It damned well better have something to do with Steve. Well, I don't have time to worry about that now.

I'll worry about it later." Sabrina gathered her purse and coat and headed out the door. The service elevator at the end of the hall opened directly in to the lower parking level. It was the quickest route to her parking place. "Taggat seemed awfully reserved on the phone," she thought as she started Precious and pulled out into a bright November afternoon.

The drive to the University Hospital was relatively quick in the light traffic. As she entered the parking lot, a guard house and white barricade prevented her further progress. A broad shouldered black gentleman leaned over to her window and waited for Sabrina to lower the glass.

"Excuse me, Mam. May I help you?"

"I have an appointment in the obstetrics clinic in thirty minutes."

"Yes, Mam. I need your name and birthdate."

"That seems a bit drastic to park my car." Sabrina looked quizzically at the guard.

"Yes, Mam, but I have to confirm your appointment before I permit you to enter. We've had a problem with vandalism in the parking structure. It's a new rule, but it's for your protection. Sorry for the inconvenience."

Sabrina handed him her driver's license.

The guard typed the necessary information into the computer terminal, and a printout was generated. The guard inspected the sheet, tore the paper from the printer, and handed the printout to Sabrina along with her license and a plastic card. "Okay, Ms. MacKenzie, you may pass. Park on level six, use the hospital entry from that level by inserting this encoded card, and follow the directions on the back of this sheet. Please leave the card at this parking enclosure when you leave."

"Thank you," Sabrina said as she laid the papers on the passenger seat and pulled away. "Goodness! I feel like I'm trying to get into a prison instead of a hospital." Sabrina followed the printed directions, and found the obstetrics clinic without difficulty. Thirty minutes later, after she had been weighed, blood pressure taken, blood drawn, and urine specimen requested, Sabrina was taken to an exam room. She read a recent issue of *Time* magazine until the door opened and a lady who appeared to be in her mid twenties entered. She was wearing a blue blouse, white skirt, white Reeboks, and a white lab coat. She had short brown Dorothy Hammill hair, brown eyes, and a pleasant smooth skinned face. Various objects, whose use Sabrina was in no hurry to see demonstrated, projected from her pocket.

"Good afternoon, Ms. MacKenzie. I'm Dr. Saunders." Geri Saunders was a third year obstetrical resident at George Washington University Hospital. Three down, one to go, was Geri's attitude, especially after her badgering at the Patient Treatment Conference prior to her walk to the clinic. She was emotionally spent, and she hoped her first case of the afternoon wouldn't be too complicated. When she opened the door to Sabrina's exam room, she encountered a well dressed, nice looking lady who appeared to at least be able to read. Geri also noted the patient's choice of reading material. *Time* magazine certainly said more about the patient's intellect than the usually encountered *Batman* Comic book or some similar literary challenge being attacked by her typical gum chewing teenage patients.

Sabrina sat the *Time* on the counter beside her chair. "Good afternoon, Doctor."

Geri sat in the chair facing Sabrina and placed the chart on the desk. "I believe this is your first visit to see us?"

"Yes, doctor, it is. I've been seeing a physician overseas. My fiance and I were waiting to be married here in the States, but I requested to come home and seek medical help because of complications with the pregnancy." Sabrina looked through her purse. "Here's a summary of my pregnancy thus far." Sabrina handed Dr. Saunders a packet of papers she had collected from Bob Vance's receptionist under the guise of scrapbook favors. She had deleted his name from each of the forms. "I have a bad heart from rheumatic fever, and I've had heart failure early in the pregnancy. I'm on Digoxin .25 milligrams, Lasix 20 milligrams, and Potassium supplement. At my last visit before leaving Saudi Arabia, my doctor told me the baby may have IUGR, or something of that nature."

Geri Saunders let out a long sigh. "So much for a simple patient," she thought. "Well, Ms. MacKenzie, you and I are in for a long afternoon. Why don't we start at the beginning."

Geri skillfully guided Sabrina through the pregnancy and found the information Sabrina gave her to be correct medically. After Geri completed the history, reviewed the papers Sabrina had provided, and completed a physical exam, she reviewed the problems that might arise with labor and delivery. The speech sounded similar to the discussions Sabrina had had with Dr. Vance. After Geri excused herself, Sabrina was shuttled around the various departments, having an EKG, Ultrasound, ECHO cardiography, and Non-Stress Test.

After completing the testing procedures, Sabrina returned to the same exam room. It was 5:00 P.M., and Sabrina was tired. She had told Taggat to meet her at seven, so she nervously awaited the test results watching the clock sweep away the time.

Dr. Saunders reentered the room with a chart twice as thick as before. "Well, Ms. MacKenzie…"

"Call me, Sabrina. I feel we've gotten to know each other this afternoon. Do you keep everyone this long?" Sabrina smiled, and looked at her watch again.

"No, Sabrina, I don't keep everyone this long. Only my favorite patients are permitted this much time."

"Thank you. Was that a compliment?"

"Yes, it was intended to be." Geri closed the chart, put her doctor face on, and looked into Sabrina's eyes.

"Sabrina, you're a very lucky lady. I can't imagine the physician in Saudi Arabia permitting you to travel."

"I gave him no choice."

"Well, it makes no difference. You're here, and you're doing remarkably well."

"I think I hear a 'but' coming."

"You're very perceptive."

"Not really, just used to doctors."

Geri couldn't hold back the smile. "Excuse me, I don't mean to be disrespectful."

"On the contrary, I'm glad to know you have a sense of humor." Sabrina grinned.

"Sabrina, you're in your thirty-sixth week of pregnancy. Your heart is doing well, and your EKG is normal except for the effect of the medication you're taking. The baby is active with a normal Non-Stress Test. However, the estimated weight of your baby is only four pounds. That's definitely evidence of IUGR. Your pelvic exam revealed your cervix to be dilated two centimeters and about fifty percent thinned out. In other words, you're very close to being inducible. I noted a diminished amount of amniotic fluid around the baby on the ultrasound. Therefore, with all the evidence pointing to time for delivery, I recommend we induce labor within the next week or ten days. Between now and then, I will see you every three or four days for special heart beat testing."

"But my due date isn't until December the Twenty-fifth."

"It makes no difference. The baby will be ready. Your little girl will be better off out than in, and so will you."

"Well, I can't have the baby in the next ten days. That's impossible. I have to contact my fiance. I wanted him to be here when I had the baby. He won't be back until the end of December."

"I recommend you not wait that long, Sabrina. Your baby's health is dependent on delivery at an optimal time, and that's very soon. To postpone the delivery permits too many parameters to change."

"I understand and appreciate your concern, Doctor, but I must try and contact my fiancee."

Geri sensed the urgency in Sabrina's voice. "Okay, Sabrina. I don't know why you won't agree to this in your baby's interest, but I'll make a deal with you."

"I'm listening."

"The reactive Non-Stress Test gives us no more than three to five days to play with. I'll reserve a spot on the induction schedule in ten days. You go home, contact your fiancee, and meet me here Friday. We'll do another test, see how the baby is doing, and then decide when we'll induce labor. You should, and WILL have the baby within the next ten days. Continue to rest and I'll see you Friday."

Sabrina didn't want to take the time to argue the point with Dr. Saunders. "Okay, I'll contact my fiancé, and see you then. Surely I can reach him by then. I'll be a good girl and take it easy."

"I'll accept that decision."

"Thank you, Doctor Saunders. You've helped me a lot."

"Goodby, Sabrina." Geri Saunders walked from the exam room and stopped outside the physician's lounge and dictation cubicles. She watched Sabrina walk up the hall, leave her slip with the secretary, pay her bill in cash, and leave the clinic. "She won't be back," Geri thought as she stepped into the cubicle, completed her dictation on Sabrina's chart, and went to see her last patient of the afternoon. When she returned to the lounge, Phil Jenkins, a second year resident, was leafing through Sabrina's chart.

"Anything of interest, Phil?" Geri didn't like junior residents reviewing her work.

"Did you see this lady?" Phil asked as he sipped on a *Tab*. He handed the can to Geri. "Care for some?" As he asked, he handed her a fresh unopened can from behind his back.

Geri momentarily turned up her nose until Phil pulled the can from its hidden position. "Thanks. I need it." Geri opened the can, took a few sips of the cold liquid, and looked at Sabrina's chart with Phil. "I saw her. She's supposed to be back for a visit Friday, but I'm not sure she'll show up. She paid the receptionist cash as she checked out of the clinic."

"She's wanted."

"What? What in the devil are you talking about?"

"Yeah, she's a wanted woman." Phil took a piece of paper from his back pocket. "I found this so interesting, I made a copy and put it in my pocket. A doctor in Norfolk, Virginia has circulated a "Wanted Poster" to the hospitals in this area of the State looking for his patient. Sabrina MacKenzie's the patient! I'm surprised you haven't seen the flyer."

Geri took the sheet from Phil. She read in amazement. "I'll be damned if I've ever seen anything like this." She looked up the hall of the clinic as if Sabrina were still present. "She said she had been in Saudi Arabia and had just gotten back in the area." Geri walked to the phone and called the office number of Dr. Robert Vance. "Busy! Come on, Phil! We have to make rounds. I'll call Dr. Vance as soon as I can and give him her address. I doubt if it's correct, but I'll give it to him, anyway."

Sabrina dropped the encoded card at the guard house. It was 6:00 P.M. She patted her abdomen, smiled, and pulled into traffic. "Hang on little girl. You don't have much longer to wait. Once I make sure your future Daddy is all right, we'll head back for Virginia."

* * *

"Sabrina, dinner was excellent." Taggat eased back in his chair and looked over at Pete Gulley. "It beats the hell out of the State Department's galley, doesn't it, Pete?"

"Yes, sir! It certainly does." Pete Gulley, Mac Orberson's top security officer, wiped the last remnants of dessert from his mouth. "Thank you for supper, Mam."

Sabrina nudged Taggat and whispered. "Why did you have to bring him?"

"For security purposes, Ms. MacKenzie." Pete smiled and leaned back in his chair. "I have very good hearing."

"Pete doesn't approve of us meeting tonight, Sabrina. He thinks I'm going to slip up and tell some important national secrets."

Sabrina's flush of embarrassment from being overheard had passed. "Do you know any?"

"Nah!"

"Taggat, I've been very patient this evening. We've talked about everything from the weather to money, but you've managed to avoid the subject." Sabrina looked over at Pete. "Are we going to discuss Steve, or not? I've been waiting for three days since his capture was announced, and I want to find out something."

"You're right. I've procrastinated long enough, but, before I begin, Pete has something he has to say." Taggat turned to Pete and prompted him to talk.

Pete stood and faced Sabrina. "I've already advised Taggat we shouldn't be having this conversation. It could endanger your life, and the lives of the hostages. However, since you're Captain Hardesty's fiance, and pregnant with his child, I guess you deserve to know what's happening. The President and Secretary of State have agreed to this meeting, but only on certain conditions. Before we proceed, you must agree to those stipulations."

"Go ahead. You're both scaring me to death. I couldn't stand not to know, now."

"What Taggat's about to tell you must be held in the strictest confidence. After you've been made privy to this information, you will be required to remain under governmental protective custody, and have a personal companion until December Twenty-Sixth."

"Whoa, I'm due to have this baby by Christmas, possibly before!"

"If you go into labor, you will be cared for in a local facility." Pete watched Sabrina's response. "Possibly, George Washington Hospital."

"What if I don't agree to go to George Washington?"

Pete looked at Sabrina and grinned. "I believe you have a doctor at George Washington University, don't you?"

"What do you mean?"

"Didn't you go to George Washington Hospital today and see Dr. Geri Saunders?"

"I did, but for consultation. I intend to have my baby in Norfolk."

"Didn't Dr. Saunders advise you to return Friday for an appointment?"

"How did you get your information?"

"Don't bother with that, Sabrina." Taggat interjected. "That damned State Department ID carries a lot of clout.

Go ahead and agree with his terms, and let's get on with this." Taggat was showing the stress of the past week.

"All right, I agree. As long as you agree for me to have the baby here in Washington with Dr. Saunders or in Norfolk with Dr. Vance." Sabrina looked at Pete with a glare. "How long have you been watching me?"

"Since you checked into the hotel." Pete glared back and grinned. "I'll agree to those terms. Taggat, I'll be in the other room. Let me know when you're finished. I'm expecting Miss Cummings at 11 p.m." Pete walked into the bedroom, turned on the television, and sat down.

"He's real sweet, isn't he?" Sabrina said with a scowl.

"He's only doing his job, Sabrina. We've gotten into something deeper than we wished." Taggat ushered Sabrina to the couch, sat down, and took her hands in his. "Sabrina, the reason I haven't contacted you over the past few days is because we've developed a plan to rescue the hostages from Iran."

Sabrina jerked her hands from Taggat's. "You know where Steve is? He's safe?"

"He's safe, and, from all indications, he's not been moved. The President has approved a rescue mission. It's scheduled for sometime around Christmas."

"Wait a minute, Taggat. Back up a few steps. You said WE intend to get him out. What part do you play in this?"

Taggat got up, walked over to the dinner cart, poured a glass of wine, and took a few sips. "Sabrina, I'm going with the rescue party."

"Like hell you are!" Sabrina got up, walked to Taggat, grabbed his hands, and looked into his eyes. "Isn't having one of you over there enough? I can't face having you both go. Taggat, I've lost more than my share of loved ones. I couldn't stand to think about losing you or Steve."

"I have to go, Sabrina. I owe it to Steve. I have to make sure there's at least one person looking out for his interest. Hell, they can't hurt a tough old dog, like me. Besides, there are certain arrangements that only I can make." Taggat puffed up and smiled.

Sabrina knew Taggat had made up his mind, and his determination showed in his demeanor. "I love you, Taggat Delaney. You better not try anything foolish, and get yourself killed. I'd never forgive you." Sabrina tried to manage a smile. She straightened Taggat's tie and sniffed back a few tears. "I've grown accustomed to my new Father."

Taggat smiled and took Sabrina into his arms. She rested her head on his chest. "Sabrina, I've loved you like my own since you were born. I've watched you grow, and, now I see you before me about to become a mother. Through the years I've seen you fall in and out of love, but when Steve came into your life, I knew he was the one. It broke my heart when it appeared you two had broken up, and I rejoiced when your love for Steve persevered. God willing, I might have a chance for those feelings some day, and I look forward to that time. But I must do this because I am partially the cause of Steve's presence in Iran. I want to be there when we get him out."

Sabrina cried on Taggat's suit. "Sorry, but this isn't exactly how I planned for this pregnancy to end. I won't have anyone with me when I have my baby. I'd hoped to have Steve, and he's gone. I'd hoped to have Cathy, and I've deserted her looking for you. Now, I'm not going to have you because you feel obligated to help Steve. Life's not fair, Taggat. It's just not fair. I'm afraid I'm going to lose both of you, and if I did, I wouldn't have any reason to live."

"You'll have the baby!"

"I know, but I'll be alone. I don't want to be alone. Ever!"

"Sabrina, Steve and I will be fine. The men who are working on this have it down to a fine science. We'll have Steve out before they miss him, and we'll be home by New Year's Day. You'll see."

"You'd better. How would I ever explain all of this," Sabrina pointed to her abdomen. "...to Steve, if you weren't here."

"You already know how! I've told you." Taggat waited for Sabrina to look at him. "I've taken care of everything. Sabrina, I wasn't going to tell you this, but since there is a slim chance I might not..."

Sabrina placed her hand over Taggat's mouth. "Don't **say** it!"

"It won't keep it from happening."

"It might; you never know."

"All right, I won't say it. Remember when I told you I met with Brian Pooley?"

"Yes, and I've had the strength not to ask what you discussed."

Taggat grinned. "I know, and I imagine it has killed you. Brian begged me to ask you for visitation privileges with the child."

"I know, but I don't see..."

"How?"

Sabrina nodded affirmatively.

"Sabrina, Brian agreed to relate a message to Beth and Kent in return for consideration of visitation privileges."

"What kind of message? What could you have him tell Beth worth that price? Anyway, who the hell gave you permission to permit visitation to any one? How would I explain Brian Pooley to Steve?"

"Hold your horses. First things first. Brian agreed to tell Beth he had learned you miscarried. You and I both know Beth will tell Kent."

"Yeah," Sabrina shrugged. "They probably had a party."

"Now, Beth and Kent have no way of knowing the baby is to be born. They're out of your hair forever. As far as I know, Steve doesn't know Brian Pooley from Adam. All Brian has to do is pose as a past friend of the family, and his wish is fulfilled. Easy?"

"What about the doctor who did my pregnancy test? Wait a minute..." Sabrina released her hold on Taggat, and walked over to the serving cart. She picked up a small remnant of a croissant, took a bite, and turned facing Taggat. She pointed the tip of the roll in his direction. "Taggat Delaney, what did you do to that doctor's office and the laboratory, and what about the lady in "The Bakery"?"

"Sabrina, don't ask. I've made certain arrangements with certain individuals, and I know better than to ask any questions of their techniques. That's all I can tell you."

Pete Gulley wandered in from the bedroom. "Taggat, we better wrap this up soon. Valerie should be here shortly, and you have an early plane to catch."

"All right, Pete. I won't be but a few more minutes."

The door bell rang and Pete answered. "Hello, Val. You're right on time."

"Whew, I thought I was going to be late. The traffic around the hotel was awful." Valerie Cummings had worked for the State Department for the past ten years. She enjoyed "baby sitting" security risks. She stayed in the best places, ate the best food, and enjoyed the niceties of life. The present arrangement with Sabrina seemed no different than the rest.

Pete and Valerie walked over to Taggat and Sabrina.

"Sabrina MacKenzie, I would like to introduce Valerie Cummings. Valerie…Sabrina."

"Its a pleasure to meet you, Sabrina. I'm sure we'll get to know each other much better over the next few weeks."

"I wish it were under more pleasant circumstances." Sabrina grinned, but she didn't like Ms. Cummings. Her thin face, unkempt hair, and poor attire made Sabrina uneasy about her dedication to her work. Besides, she resembled Beth Pooley.

"I understand, but this won't be too bad. I'll try to make you as comfortable as possible." Valerie turned to Pete. "May we have a few moments alone?"

"Certainly." Pete turned to Taggat. "Taggat, we must be going. Five minutes." Pete held up five fingers for emphasis.

"Okay. We're about finished with our good-byes."

Sabrina held on tightly to Taggat's arm. "No, we're not!"

Taggat poured two glasses of wine. He handed Sabrina one then held his glass to hers. "Here's to you, my daughter, and to your unborn child.

I'll see you both, as time goes by, either in this life, or in the one granted us by the good Lord hereafter."

Tears returned to Sabrina's eyes as she sipped the wine. She noted the tear in Taggat's eye, also. "Taggat, I won't think about you not coming back to us. You're not going to get out of being a grandfather that easily."

Sabrina tiptoed up and kissed Taggat's cheek. "Go on! Do what you have to do!"

Taggat kissed Sabrina's cheek and squeezed her tight for a few extra seconds. "I love you, Sabrina." Taggat wiped the tears from his eyes and walked past Pete and Valerie. "Come on Pete! You're holding up the show." Taggat continued to the door, but stopped before turning the knob. He turned, winked at Sabrina, and held up both hands.

"Oh, oh. Here comes his old Irish blessing," Sabrina thought as she remembered Taggat's exits at many of their previous gatherings.

"Now, let those who love us, love us. And those that don't love us, may God turn their hearts. If he does not turn their hearts, may he turn their ankles so we will know them by their limp. Goodnight, Sabrina MacKenzie. I'll see you next year."

Sabrina threw a napkin at Taggat, but it fell short of its mark. "Get out of here you old poop." Sabrina turned, wiped the tears from her eyes, and retreated to the bedroom. She needed to be alone for a while.

# 20

December 22nd....

Captain Arch McConnell looked over the faces of his twelve man Special Ops team. They were ready, and Arch knew it. They had been training for the past five weeks on this particular operation, but their training over the past year had been designed for hostage rescue.

Arch was thirty-seven years old and had been in the Army since he was nineteen. He had dropped out of college after his first year making him easy prey for the eager draft boards of the Vietnam War era. He was sent to Fort Knox, Kentucky for boot camp, and in his first assignment to Germany, the Army taught him to drive tanks. Arch was in heaven, but after two months, he was pulled out of his tank position and trained on the M-60, .30 caliber machine gun. From that moment on, Arch knew he was destined for Vietnam. After serving his required tour of one year in

Vietnam, Arch eagerly volunteered for two more. During his extended tours, he attained the rank of sergeant.

After Vietnam Arch applied for Ranger training and was accepted to the special camp at Fort Benning, Georgia. The training had been a true test of his stamina and endurance, but he made it. His savvy for field situations, understanding of tactics and weapons, and lust for victory inspired those around him. He advanced to the rank of Captain and assumed a training role in the Rangers. His assignment as Ground Operations Commander in Operation Silent Night came as no surprise.

For five weeks, the men had trained on rapid deployment. Their training camp had been mocked up to resemble the air field and quarters in Rasht, Iran. Arch's team had honed their insertion time down to a brisk one hundred seconds. However, they were pitted against the clock and pop up silhouettes, not live targets. Arch was the only man in his group that had ever fired at a live target, but he knew his men would perform. He had removed ambivalence from their minds and nailed the unbiased sense of self-survival in its place. They wouldn't hesitate to kill when the chips were down. He saw it in their faces. His men followed his command to the letter. As Arch scrutinized each member's face, he knew they would succeed. If they could get to their objective, they would save the hostages.

However, there was one deterrent for success, and that deterrent in the form of Taggat Delaney sat across the Galaxy C-5B cargo bay from Arch. Taggat was completely out of place among the camouflaged soldiers and weapons. Oh, Arch knew why Taggat was here, and he was under orders to assist Taggat in his duties, but he didn't like it. *Well, I had better make the most of it*, Arch thought as he released the harness from his six foot two inch frame, picked up a woolen blanket, and walked across the cargo bay to Taggat's shivering body. "Here, try this. It might help." Arch unfolded the blanket and tossed it across Taggat's lap.

If there were two things Taggat hated, it was being cold and being cramped. In his present situation, he was both. "Thanks, Captain. I'll put it to good use." Taggat wrapped the blanket around his shoulders.

"What in the hell are we taking with us?" Taggat pointed to a shrouded object which consumed the width of the bay. It had wheels, and that was all Taggat could see. The security officers wouldn't permit him to touch the canvas.

"I'm not permitted to discuss our cargo, Mr. Delaney, but I can tell you it will be put to good use."

"When are we going to get off this flying icebox?" Taggat attempted to shrink into the blanket. Suddenly, a red light came on over his head.

"Looks as if we're getting ready to land, now."

"Finally." Taggat buckled his harness belt, and the giant aircraft settled down onto the runway.

As the front bay doors opened and the gangway settled onto the tarmac, Taggat watched a tall thin figure walk up the ramp and approach Arch.

"Did you take care of my baby?" The figure asked.

"With kid gloves," Arch motioned for Taggat to come over to where they were talking. "Hoot, I'd like you to meet Taggat Delaney."

"Welcome to Turkey, Mr. Delaney. I understand you've helped make this trip possible." Hoot reached over and shook Taggat's hand.

"Taggat, the mountain of canvas belongs to Hoot," Arch informed Taggat to further explain Colonel Gibson's presence.

"It's a pleasure to meet you, Colonel. I've been wondering what the hell we've carted around. I know it's a plane, but what kind?" Taggat pointed to the shrouded behemoth. "And as for the trip, my contact is the only help I can hope to give."

"Well, we all have our duties." Hoot walked toward the canvas mountain. "Taggat, how would you like to see my baby?" The tall, sparsely haired, thin mustached Colonel looked over to Arch for the okay.

"It's all right. Taggat has clearance for this project."

Arch McConnell's team helped Colonel Gibson remove the canvas cover.

While he waited, Taggat walked to the gangway. He noticed the ground crew had directed the pilot to taxi to the entrance of a large hanger.

Through the opened doors, Taggat could see a myriad of electronic equipment and a beehive of activity.

Colonel Gibson walked up behind Taggat waiting a few seconds before he spoke. "Admiring the view, Mr. Delaney?"

"Please, call me Taggat, and yes, I am. It appears this hanger is ready for something like a space launch rather than the arrival of a cargo plane."

"What it's ready for is this." Hoot turned and directed Taggat's view to the uncovered aircraft.

"What the hell is that?" Taggat's mouth gaped as he turned and stared at the cargo bay's revealed contents.

"Taggat, *that* is the latest development in stealth technology. It's barely discernible on radar and provides the capability for 'silent' bombing missions into enemy territory. The construction design and materials make it almost 'invisible' to enemy radar. If you'll excuse me, I have to see that Baby is moved into her new home." Taggat walked with Hoot to the nose of the sleek black jet. The skin of the airplane hardly reflected the lights of the cargo bay.

The transfer truck rolled into the cargo bay and connected its tow-bar to the front gear of the F-111 Stealth aircraft. At the last minute the connecting cables were released and the jet was eased down the gangway into the hanger. It was placed in the middle of the hanger floor with its wheels covering three previously designated points. Immediately, white jump-suited men attached electrical cables and computer hookups to spots on the fuselage of the jet.

Taggat looked over at Arch as they both watched the Colonel flit about the airplane. "It looks like the Colonel means business."

"Always," Arch said. "Why don't you give Baby the once over while I brief Hoot."

Taggat started for the plane, but turned back to Arch. "By the way, why do you call him Hoot?"

Arch smiled. "It comes from his training days. Being from Dallas, he was the cowboy of his group. His instructors began calling him Hoot after the cowboy in the movie serials-Hoot Gibson. The nickname stuck, but don't let his light nature fool you. Hoot is the best of the best. He helped develop Baby. You'll have to excuse me, Taggat." Arch turned and headed for a small room located on the opposite side of the hanger.

Taggat walked over to the jet. He had never seen anything like it. The plane was approximately sixty feet long, thirty feet from wingtip to wingtip, and stood about fifteen feet high at the level of the cockpit. The jet exhausts were channeled through slats above the trailing edge of the aircraft, and the wing's leading edges were encased in a ceramic material. Taggat slowly ascended the ladder to the cockpit. The control panel was futuristic. Only the most essential engine information was displayed by needle gauges. The remaining information showed up on one of three display screens. Taggat descended the ladder, walked to the hanger door, and looked to the East. "It won't be long now, Steve."

* * *

"Hoot, we've been restricted to high probability military targets only, but you have been released to pilot discretion. Before I can proceed from Baku, I have to have those surface to air missle locations destroyed." Arch outlined the probable SAM sites around Rasht and along the Northern Iranian coast.

"I'll take care of it." Hoot responded casually as he looked over the map Arch had opened. He traced the line from Incirlik, Turkey, their present location, to Baku.

"How in the hell did the Air Force get the Russkies to agree to this?"

"Hell, Hoot. You know about as much as I do. It seems the Air Force has been flying medical aide into the Baku area over the past three months. The Iranians caused the Russian's problems, and Ivan wants to get even. They have permitted us to bring a rescue team into the Baku area. That's to be our staging point. The only drawback is the Russians won't permit us to bring all of our military supplies on the plane. Why? I don't know. That's why we need Delaney. He has a contact in Baku providing us with additional hardware. We had to bring him along because the Russian contact wants the security of his presence."

"You know a hell of a lot more than me, that's for sure." Hoot smiled at Arch.

"I guess I knew more than I thought, but we're still the delivery team. The politics of all this crap has already been arranged. I hope Ivan doesn't have any surprises for us." Arch removed an envelope from his sleeve pocket. "Here's your official orders. After you review them, let's talk."

"Fine." Hoot took the orders, turned and walked to the aircraft. He ascended the ladder to the cockpit, slid into the custom molded seat, and turned on the electronics. He called up his navigational computer, tactical maps, and opened the envelope.

TO: COLONEL CHARLES GIBSON USAF SN 05302234
FROM: COLONEL CLINTON SMITH, CHIEF OF STAFF USAF
REFERENCE: SILENT NIGHT
　　　AT YOUR DISCRETION, BUT IN COORDINATION WITH CAPT. ARCH MCCONNELL, YOU ARE TO DEPART INCIRLIK, TURKEY, 25 DEC PROCEEDING FOR AIR REFUEL AT VAN, EASTERN TURKEY. AFTER REFUEL, YOU'RE TO PROCEED INTO IRANIAN AIRSPACE AND DESTROY SAM SITES AND AIRFIELD IN WESTERN TEHRAN. THEN YOU ARE TO PROCEED TO RASHT, IRAN AND DESTROY SAM SITES AND AIRFIELD. COORDINATES ARE STORED ON YOUR STRIKE PROGRAM. YOU ARE TO DESTROY ANY AIRCRAFT CAPABLE OF HELICOPTER PURSUIT, AND THEN WITHDRAW FROM IRAN. RETURN COURSE TO EASTERN TURKEY IS AT YOUR DISCRETION. COORDINATE MISSION TO

COINCIDE 0600 AIRSTRIKE TEHRAN BY SIX A-6
INTRUDER BOMBERS. FLIGHT OF TWO F-14 TOM-
CATS PROVIDING CAP. RESCUE 0630 RASHT. RUSS-
IAN IL-76 MAINSTAY RECONNAISSANCE AIRCRAFT
MANNED BY U.S. AND RUSSIAN TECHS WILL PRO-
VIDE RADAR DATA.
GOOD LUCK
GOD SPEED

Hoot reviewed his maps and double-checked the coordinates that had been previously programmed into the Inertial Navigation Computer. The tactical computer chip for the area was installed. Once he was satisfied with the set up, he exited the aircraft. After destroying the orders in the shredder, he returned to the briefing room, poured himself a cup of coffee, and reviewed the map with Arch.

\* \* \*

"Taggat, let's saddle up. We've a date to keep." Arch yelled to Taggat from his vantage point in the hanger door.

Taggat looked up from his observation of a Staff Sergeant's radar test program, thanked the sergeant for his tolerance, and headed for Arch.

The Special Ops team had been off-loaded and transferred into two other C5-B Galaxy aircraft. The fuselages of the airplanes were marked with a red cross designating the craft as medical relief; however, within the belly of one was two Bell Ranger Gunships, and in the other, two UH-LN Hueys. Arch and Taggat, along with the twelve members of the team, flew in the plane with the Hueys.

Arch walked up the plane's gangway, turned to Hoot, and saluted. Hoot returned the salute and gave Arch the thumbs up. Arch walked to a seat close to the cockpit and picked up a radio headset. "We're to cross the border at Artushat. Two Mig-25's will escort us to the base in Baku."

"Roger, Captain. We'll coordinate the crossing with the E3. We'll be flying the same corridor as all the other relief planes. I've been instructed to join up with the other craft over Kagizman prior to Soviet airspace penetration."

"Okay, let's do it!"

* * *

"Hummer, this is Red Dog Three. Radio check on one-three-niner."

"Roger, Red Dog Three. Read you, five by five. Hummer out."

"Do you have us on scope, Hummer?"

"That's a roger, Red Dog Three."

"I make us at 44 degrees, 40 minutes east; 39 degrees, 32 minutes north."

"Roger Red Dog Three. You are entering Soviet Air Space. I have two positives heading your way. By their signature, they're Mig-25's. Heading 250 degrees, six hundred knots closure. They're over Lake Sevan."

"That's our welcoming committee. Thanks Hummer. Red Dog Three, out." Captain Bill Conyers reset the Galaxy's radio to the assigned frequency. "Soviet Aircraft, this is U.S. C5-B Galaxy, Mission Mercy. We're transponding on our preassigned frequency. Flight level 330, airspeed 275, heading 094 degrees. Four ship complement. I'm lead. Over."

"Roger C5-B, we have you on scope. This is Colonel Yuri Gogol of Western Defense. We are eighty kilometers from you. Maintain speed and heading."

"Roger, Colonel. C5-B, out."

The Mig-25 Foxbats streaked above the four Galaxy cargo crafts. Colonel Gogol and his wingman rolled their craft to the left and performed a wide descent to the Galaxy's flight level. Then, they merged onto the C5-B's wingtip.

"Galaxy C5-B, come left to heading 079 degrees.

Maintain speed 275 knots. Baku airbase has been alerted to your arrival. Runway 09. Wind 15 knots, 225 degrees. Out."

"Understood, Colonel. Thanks." Bill Conyers activated his intercom. "Captain McConnell, we'll be landing in forty five minutes."

Arch shook his head in confirmation. "Thanks, Captain." Arch punched Taggat's arm. "We'll be landing in forty five minutes. I hope your contact is ready."

Taggat shivered. "He'll be ready. Dimitri's always ready to make a dollar. He's got nothing to lose on this deal. We buy his ordinance. We use the equipment, and give back what's left. Dimitri sells the equipment again. What could be better?" Taggat tried to smile, but his teeth were chattering. "Why do you keep it so damned cold in here?"

Arch smiled. "The avionics work better."

"Then, the damned things should work excellently!"

Arch activated his intercom. "Bill, how have the Soviets been treating you?"

"They've been very helpful, Arch. The buzz around the airport has been different lately. I think they're expecting something to happen, but they're not sure what."

"I hope not. We wouldn't want to blow our cover before we have a chance to use it."

"Excuse me, Arch, I have a radio call from the Migs."

"Galaxy C5-B, approach Baku 015 degrees. ILS has been activated. Pick up glideslope on 104.5 at twenty kilometers distance, 1300 meters elevation."

"Understood."

The Galaxies landed as directed and taxied to a group of large hangers where the previous supplies had been dropped. The aircraft transporting Taggat and the Special Ops team rolled to the hanger doors and opened its cargo bay. Arch could see two Hueys in the hanger. Boxes of equipment lay stacked around the helicopters. "Keep the men aboard until Taggat and I make initial contact," Arch directed Sergeant Ramirez, his squad leader.

"Yes, sir."

"Come on, Taggat. It's time for you to earn your keep." Arch and Taggat walked down the gangway into the hanger. "Can we trust your friend, Taggat?"

"Without reservation." Taggat looked into the hanger for a familiar form. He immediately recognized a face he hadn't seen in twenty years.

"Dimitri, you old dog!" Taggat walked briskly to a short, rotund, bald headed gentleman looking ten years his elder.

"Ah, Taggat. It is you." Dimitri smiled and embraced his old comrade. "For a while I was afraid the K.G.B. had lied to me." Dimitri waved his hand across the equipment. "As you can see, I have brought all you requested. The officials don't seem to be asking as many questions as usual."

"We've made a good deal, Dimitri. My government has assured your immunity." Taggat leaned closer to Dimitri. "I wouldn't hang around long after it's over, however."

"My thoughts exactly, my friend." Dimitri grinned. "What you do with all this, Taggat? I ask no questions usually, but you have emptied my store house."

"Better not to know, but if we do the job, and don't ruin the helicopters, you'll get all the remaining equipment back with your money."

"I like your deals, Taggat. You make me a rich man like old times, eh?"

Taggat smiled, but inwardly he regretted the deal he had made in the past. It had cost him much. "Sure Dimitri, just like old times."

Dimitri looked through the stack of equipment. "You Americans are very wasteful. Very wasteful, indeed." He turned and faced Taggat. "All this equipment. Helicopters. Weapons. Ammunition. Night-vision goggles. Hundreds of thousands of dollars worth of equipment…left on the ground in Vietnam. So wasteful!"

"We value our people more than our material, Dimitri. It seems your leaders are coming around to some of those same ideals."

"I hope so, Taggat. I hope so. My people have been filled with much hope since Mr. Gorbachev became Premier. If it would only continue, I might come and visit you next."

"Hopefully for different reasons!"

Dimitri laughed. "Most assuredly. I want to see the Yankees."

"If you make it to New York, I'll personally take you." Taggat patted Dimitri's shoulders.

Taggat went over the check list with Dimitri, and walked back to Arch. "Arch, everything checks out."

Arch looked back into the entrails of the cargo plane. "Okay, Sergeant. Let's check it out." Arch circled his right hand in the air.

The men filed out of the Galaxy and fanned out toward the equipment.

Dimitri watched the soldiers descend on the boxes. "Merry Christmas, gentlemen. Merry Christmas."

# 21

Cathy looked out Richard's bedroom window at the countless number of stars poking holes in the blackness of a moonless night. Sabrina had been missing for almost four weeks, and Cathy had looked everywhere. She knew Sabrina had to be in Washington, and she thought she had found her after a search of hotel check-ins had placed Sabrina in the Hyatt. However, Sabrina had checked out one week later, and absolutely no one knew where she had gone. It was as if she had vanished from the Earth. With such a large area to cover, Cathy had to remain content and hope that Bob Vance's inquiries to the surrounding hospitals would give them a lead. "Where are you, Sabrina?" Cathy thought as her eyes traced the outline of the treeline behind Richard's house.

"What's wrong, Cathy? Can't sleep?" Richard rolled to his left side and supported his head on his left elbow. "Come back to bed. I'm cold."

Cathy turned and smiled. She wrapped the white satin robe loosely around her, but left the belt untied. She walked to the side of the bed, took off her robe, and slid in between the sheets. She snuggled up to Richard, smiled, and kissed him on the cheek. "You weren't so cold earlier this evening as I recall." Cathy adjusted her position in the bed so her hips rested against Richard's naked pelvis.

"What were you thinking about? Sabrina?"

"Yes, why?"

"I'd hoped you were thinking about us."

"Richard, I can't think about us. At least, not now." Cathy worked her hips closer and rolled her head toward him.

"And when do you suppose you'll be able to devote some time to us, Cathy? I've got some deadlines looking me in the face. They want me in London by the fifth of January. I'll have to go, but I don't want to go without you. I love you. I want to marry you."

"Hush," Cathy said as she covered Richard's mouth. "I can't discuss marriage. I have to know Sabrina's all right before I can think of anything else. When I know Sabrina and the baby are fine, I'll be able to devote my undivided attention to us." Cathy moved her hand down to Richard's left thigh and slowly slid her fingertips closer to his groin.

"You're trying to change the subject, Cathy." Richard reached over and gently placed his right hand over Cathy's left breast. The nipple hardened against his palm.

"I don't seem to be getting any opposition." Cathy rolled on top of Richard and kissed him. Her tongue searched the inside of his mouth. She felt him harden against her left thigh. She supported herself on her palms and let her breasts lightly trace the outline of Richard's chest.

Richard eased down in bed, cupped Cathy's breasts in his hands, and placed both nipples in his mouth. He gently teased the hardened nipples until Cathy began to moan with excitement.

She pulled away from his teasing and knelt between his legs. She kissed the inside of both thighs and gently stroked the base of his penis. She held its base in her right hand and lightly traced the outline of the head with her tongue.

"I can't stand that. You're killing me."

Cathy straddled Richard's groin and leaned over placing her lips beside his ear. "Well, put it somewhere it will do you some good," she whispered.

Richard reached behind Cathy and grabbed her hips with is hands. He eased her down onto his groin until he was deep within her. Her warmth overcame his ability to hold on.

Cathy slowly sat up placing her entire weight on his groin. She moved back and forth in a sliding motion against his pelvis. The pace quickened until both exploded in waves of ecstasy.

Cathy eased her sweaty body slowly down on Richard and rolled to his side. She curled against his motionless form leaving her left leg across his thighs, closed her eyes, placed her hand on his chest, and slept.

The tone of her breathing clued Richard that Cathy was asleep. He loved making love to Cathy, and he knew she enjoyed it, also. But Cathy used sex as a tool. A tool to manipulate him. A tool to keep him quiet when she wished. He enjoyed the manipulation, for now. But he knew it would eventually eat away at him until he couldn't tolerate it any longer. He remained silent for now because he knew that's what Cathy wanted. Soon, however, he would have to demand an answer. Sabrina, or no Sabrina, Richard would have to pressure Cathy to say yes or no to his question of marriage. Afterall, it was only fair to him. He had to know where he stood in Cathy's life. At this point in their relationship, he was afraid of her answer. But soon, he would have to demand a response. Cathy would have to make a choice.

\* \* \*

The phone awakened both of them. Richard groped for the receiver while Cathy pulled the covers and a pillow over her head. "Hello, this is Dr. Tims."

"Hello, Richard. Bob Vance."

"Bob. What can I do for you?"

"Richard, I found Sabrina."

"Sabrina?!"

Cathy immediately threw the pillow and covers off her head and sat up in the bed. She leaned toward Richard hoping to hear something over the phone.

Richard reached over and pulled the sheet up over Cathy's upper body, winked, and covered the mouthpiece. "I didn't want to be tempted. Bob's found Sabrina...Where is she, Bob?"

"She's still in Washington. Sabrina saw an Ob-Gyn resident at George Washington University Hospital. The doctor called me last night. She didn't know I was looking for Sabrina until one of her junior residents showed her the flyer we had distributed. She tried calling me a couple of weeks ago, but my line was busy, and she forgot about it until Sabrina came into their Ob clinic again today. She saw Sabrina for the first time three and a half weeks ago and has been seeing her since. Somehow, the State Department has become involved and convinced the doctor to delay delivery until after Christmas. Since her first visit, Sabrina has been escorted to the clinic by a woman who seems to be a bodyguard. Dr. Saunders was told by the Feds not to discuss Sabrina's case with anyone, but after remembering the poster, she elected to contact me."

"Did she have any idea where Sabrina was staying in Washington?"

"No, but it had to be close to the hospital. Sabrina told Dr. Saunders it only took fifteen minutes to drive to her appointment."

"Why are the Feds involved, Bob? Did she have any idea?"

"No, she didn't, but you can bet your sweet British butt it has a lot to do with Steve Hardesty. I think Sabrina went to Washington, stirred up some news about the hijacking, and got herself into some hot water with the government. They probably have her under wraps somewhere. Could you pass along the information to Cathy. I can't seem to locate her." Bob smiled to himself.

"I believe I might know where she is. Good-by Bob, and thanks." Richard hung up the phone and looked into Cathy's wide eyes. "Cathy, Bob has located Sabrina."

"Where, Richard? Where?"

"Washington, and it seems the Feds have been keeping her under protective custody or arrest. Who knows? I guess that puts it out of your hands. Eh?"

Cathy jumped from the bed. "I knew she still had to be there. I knew it!" She put on her robe and headed for the bathroom.

"Wait! Where are you going?"

"Washington, of course." Cathy said it as if she needed not to explain."

"We can't head off to Washington. We don't have a clue where she is in D.C. And didn't you hear me? The Government has her."

"I heard you, and we don't need a clue. All we need to do is make a visit to the State Department. This is the break I've been waiting for. Don't you see, Richard? They'll have to tell us where she is."

"Whatever do you mean?"

"The State Department knows where she is. I've suspected that all along, but now that I have proof, I can pressure them to tell me where she is."

"You think they're going to tell you? All we have to do is to go to Washington, walk up to the information desk at the State Department, and ask them to tell us where they're keeping Sabrina MacKenzie. I can see it now. Why yes, Miss Winston, we have Miss MacKenzie in a townhouse in Georgetown. Here's the key. Do you need a car? They aren't going to tell us where she is, Cathy."

"Don't be so sarcastic, it doesn't become you. When we go to the State Department, we'll threaten them. We'll tell them we know why Sabrina's in Washington, and we're going to break it to the press unless they permit us to visit her. We know enough to wing it a little, and with luck we might get a lead on Sabrina's location. If we keep the pressure on, I think we will at least get to see her."

"Unless they decide to keep us, also! Cathy, I can't afford to get mixed up with the government. I'm not a citizen. They can ship my ass out of here, pronto."

"Well, you're leaving in January, anyway, aren't you? They couldn't decide what to do with you in that short a time."

"I'm glad you care so much."

"Richard!" Cathy tried to calm herself. She didn't want to scare Richard away. She needed him, at least for now. "Look, we can keep ourselves out of trouble, and they aren't going to keep us. We'll tell them we've given a press release to the *Washington Post*, and if the reporter hasn't heard from us within twelve hours, he'll release the story."

"Where do you get these ideas? You act as if you're comfortable with this situation."

"You worry too much, Richard. It's obvious you haven't had to bluff your way through any difficult situations. If you had gotten into some of the things I have, you would understand better."

"I don't think I want to understand. Surprise me, but not too much." Richard rolled over in the bed and stretched.

"Well?" Cathy said in exasperation.

"Well, what," Richard yawned.

Cathy threw his underwear at him. "Why aren't you getting dressed?"

"You mean we're going today? I thought we'd spend Christmas Eve together."

"We are!"

"Alone!" Richard motioned for Cathy to join him in the bed.

"I haven't got time. Come onl We're wasting the time we have."

"Oh, all right, but I'm going under protest."

"I don't give a damn how you go, but let's go!"

Richard leisurely climbed out of bed and stretched his arms toward the ceiling.

"Would you please get dressed. I'm begging."

"Only if you take a shower with me."

"All right, for Pete's sake."

"Who's Pete?"

"Hell, Richard! I don't know who Pete is. It's just a saying. Come on!" Cathy led Richard to the shower, turned on the water, adjusted the temperature, and they got under the spray.

"Wash me, slave." Richard said as he closed his eyes to the water and leaned against the back wall of the shower enclosure.

Cathy threw a cold wet washcloth at Richard hitting him in the groin. "Wash yourself. You might be minus a few parts if I mess with you right now."

"I'll take my chances." Richard moved behind Cathy, lathered his hands, and began slowly washing Cathy's breasts.

"Get away! RICHARD!! I have my mind on too many other things right now. I'd love to make love to you in the shower, but now is not the time. I'm done." Cathy opened the shower door, stepped out, and began to dry off. She leaned over and looked back into the mist. "Richard, please hurry. I have to do this for Sabrina."

"I understand, but what am I going to do with this?" Richard pointed down to his erection.

Cathy looked down. "Oh, that? Just a minute. I've got just the thing," Cathy said in a sexy tone.

"OOooh," this might be better than I thought," Richard said to himself.

"Are you ready?" Cathy asked from outside the shower.

"I'm always ready for you." Richard reached out expecting Cathy to step in. Suddenly, from around the edge of the opened door, Cathy's hand appeared holding a large glass of ice water."

"Here! I think this will take care of that problem.', She threw the water at Richard, and hit her mark...dead center.

"Whewwwww!" Richard gasped. "I think you've taken care of it forever," he cried out in a mock high pitched tone.

"I doubt it," Cathy said as she laughed her way to the closet.

"I owe you one, Cathy." Richard yelled from the shower as he finished washing.

"Promises, promises." Cathy walked back into the bathroom and pitched Richard a towel. "Now, would you please finish so we can leave? Or, shall I get another cup of water."

Richard held up in hands in surrender. "I'm hurrying. I promise."

* * *

"Listen to me, young lady," Cathy stood within inches of the State Department's Information Desk's secretary's face. "If you don't want to get into a lot of trouble, you'll tell me who's in charge of the Iran hostage situation, and you'll tell me quick!"

"I'm sorry," the secretary cowered away from Cathy's intimidation. "I don't know who's in charge. I'm filling in for the full time secretary. She's sick." The secretary regained some courage. "I'm not sure I could give you that information, any way."

Cathy leaned farther toward the secretary. She was about to go onto her tiptoes, but Richard pulled her to the side. "I told you we should have stayed in bed. Don't get us in trouble, please. Now, I'm begging."

"You're begging for some more ice water, that's what you're begging for. Don't worry, Richard, we'll get some action."

Cathy walked back to the receptionist. "Excuse my boyfriend, he gets a little zealous at times. Now, where were we?"

"I've called the Chief of Security, Mam. He'll be down in a moment. I really can't help you any further." The receptionist looked away trying to avoid any discussion with Cathy.

"You've helped me immensely. That's who I wanted to see!" Cathy turned from the desk and walked back to Richard. "I told you we would get some action. The Security Chief will be down in a moment."

"What? He's probably coming down to run us out of the building or arrest us." Richard looked around the lobby expecting to see a group of armed guards enter at any moment. "Come on, Cathy. Let's go." Richard reached for Cathy's arms.

Cathy jerked her arm from Richard's reach. "Go? Not a chance. We're getting results. Let's run with it for a while."

Richard was getting very nervous. "I'm still not sure we should be doing this, Cathy. I'll bet the water can get very hot in here."

Cathy took Richard's hands. "Don't worry, Richard. What are they going to do? All they can say is no!"

"What if they do say no?"

"Then you'll really see me get angry."

"That's what I was afraid of."

The elevator doors opened and a man walked toward Cathy and Richard. He extended his hand to Richard as he approached. "Good morning, I'm Pete Gulley, Chief of Security. Is there a problem?" Pete Gulley had been paged when the hostage situation had been mentioned by the forceful couple in the forum of the State Department.

"Good morning, I'm Doctor Richard Tims of Norfolk. This is my fiance, Cathy Winston."

Cathy looked at Richard queerly. "Wait a minute. I've not agreed to marry you…yet." She looked at Pete. "You bet your sweet buns there's a problem. Can we go somewhere a little less conspicuous to discuss the matter?"

"I think that would be better. My office is on the fifth floor. Follow me." They took the elevator to the fifth floor, and Pete led them to his office. They walked through an outer office and into a larger room. A desk sat against the far wall in front of a bank of bookcases, and a small rectangular oak table sat three feet in front of the desk. Around the table was two wing-back chairs and a love seat. "Won't you sit down," Pete directed Richard and Cathy to the love seat. He sat in the wing-back chair to their left. "Comfortable?"

"Enough," Cathy quickly replied. "May we get down to business?"

"Certainly. What can I do for you?"

Cathy leaned closer to Pete and looked him in the eye. "I'm here to inquire about Sabrina MacKenzie. You might know her because of her association with Steve Hardesty, the American being held hostage in Iran."

"I'm familiar with the Hardesty situation, but I've not heard of this MacKenzie woman."

"Of course, you haven't." Cathy grinned. "How far up the chain of command are you?"

"Far enough to know I don't need to discuss these matters with the two of you. Perhaps we should terminate this discussion before you both get into trouble."

Richard started to rise. "I think that's a good…"

Cathy halted him by placing her hand on his thigh. "Don't try to intimidate me, Mr. Gulley. I don't scare easily. I have a feeling you know more about this than you care to demonstrate. Why don't you tell me where Sabrina is, and we won't have to get messy."

"Messy? What do mean, 'messy'? You should be the one worrying. You're openly discussing matters that could be construed as dangerous to national security."

"Oh hell! National Security be damned. What do you think is going to happen to your little charade when we release this information to the press."

"Just what do you think you know?"

"I'll tell you what we know, Mr. Gulley. You're holding a woman who's term pregnant…possibly against her will. Her unborn child is jeopardized every day by her potentially poor health. She comes to Washington to innocently discuss Steve Hardesty's situation, and, all of a sudden, she isn't heard from by her physicians or friend. Ironically, she's seen by a doctor in the George Washington Obstectrical Clinic, and this doctor says she's chaperoned by a woman from the State Department. The papers love this stuff. Shall I go on?"

"Surely, you don't have total disregard of what a story like that could do to any attempt to free Hardesty. I don't believe you would take a chance."

Cathy stood up and faced Pete. "Try me!"

Pete looked at Cathy. He could see determination in her face, but he needed to get a feel for her commitment. "I could have you both placed into protective custody."

Richard squirmed in his seat.

"Don't worry, Richard. Mr. Gulley's blowing a little smoke." Cathy tunred toward Pete. "Consider this scenario, Mr. Gulley. Sabrina MacKenzie is a pregnant lady who could get very sick very fast. Her personal physician stands in this room ready to testify to the fact. You deny access to his patient. She gets ill and dies before you get her to the hospital. Her baby dies. You were warned about this dreadful possibility, but you elected to disregard the warning as a bluff. You're just as guilty of killing that woman and child as if you held a gun to their heads and pulled the trigger. No matter what happens to the hostages, you're in deep trouble with no way out."

Pete nervously fidgeted in his chair. "Is this true, Doctor?"

"I'm afraid so, Mr. Gulley. Sabrina's condition could decompensate quickly. She had been treated for congestive heart failure during the pregnancy. If she has any further deterioration, she could die quickly. Her lungs would fill with fluid, and she would drown."

Pete considered all the risks and possibilities. "Excuse me for a moment." He walked to the outer office and phoned the White House.

"Way to go, Richard. You did well."

"All I did was tell the truth. That's more than I can say for you."

"It's getting us what we want."

"NO, Cathy. It's getting YOU what YOU want. I want to get out of here. Sabrina's a big girl. She can bloody well take care of herself."

"Settle down, Richard. He's coming back. I think we've won."

"Don't you listen to anything I say?"

Cathy quickly looked to Richard and grinned. "What?"

Richard smiled and shrugged his shoulders as Pete reentered the room.

"I've been authorized to take both of you to see Miss MacKenzie in the morning. We cannot release her because she knows information crucial to the hostage's security. We have made arrangements for her to be delivered at George Washington Hospital. She has a physician in that facility, but, since Dr. Tims is here, he will be permitted to conduct an exam of the patient to assure her well being. Once the examination is made, both of you will leave Washington and not return until Miss MacKenzie has her child, or you hear directly from her. Is that acceptable?"

Cathy looked at Richard. "Agreed. Where is she?"

Pete smiled. "Meet me in the lobby of the Hyatt on the Mall at 7:00 A. M. We'll have breakfast on Uncle Sam, and then we'll go see Miss MacKenzie. Ms. Winston, I congratulate you on your techniques. Of course, you knew we wouldn't take a chance with Sabrina's health. If the Doctor hadn't been here, I would have sent you packing. Now, if you'll excuse me, I have to make some preparations for tomorrow." Pete stood silently at his desk.

Richard stood and held out his hand for Cathy.

Cathy stood but didn't take Richard's hand. "Wait a moment. I have a few more questions."

"Not now, Cathy! We've accomplished a bloody lot already. Let's not push it, shall we?"

Cathy could sense the tenseness in Richard's voice. "Okay, I guess they can wait until we see Sabrina."

"Good," Richard sighed.

They both left the office, took the elevator to the front lobby, and walked out.

As Richard passed the receptionist, he thanked her for the help she had provided, but Cathy offered no words of recognition. As Richard eased into the driver's seat, he let out a long gasp. "I'm glad that's over. Where do you want to spend the evening?"

Cathy scooted around in her seat and looked seriously at Richard. "You know we'll have to take her with us in the morning, don't you?"

Richard's head jerked back in amazement. "What?"

"I mean, we'll have to get her out of where ever she's being kept."

Richard laughed. "I've never heard so much rubbish. I'm not getting mixed up with the State Department. I've been willing to go along with you up until now. I understand your devotion to Sabrina, but you're carrying this a bit far, don't you think?"

"No! I don't think I'm carrying it too far at all."

"Cathy, we can't fight the government in this. That's crazy. I'm not jeapordizing my future by taking any more chances. We could get arrested for what you're thinking."

Cathy glared. "Richard, I'm taking Sabrina home with me to Norfolk. She wants to have her baby with the people she loves around her, not strange governmental officials. If you don't want to do it, that's fine. I'll take care of it myself. Now, drive me to the Hyatt. I want to check the place out before tomorrow morning. We can stay there if you'd like."

Richard shrugged his shoulders, started the car, and headed for the hotel.

\* \* \*

"Richard, stop! Stop the car!" Cathy bolted from her seat. "Quick, park here!"

"But, the lobby entrance is up a level," Richard said as he scanned the parking places and maneuvered the Porsche into the next available bay. He switched off the ignition and heard the door open as Cathy prepared to exit the automobile. Richard reached out and grabbed Cathy's sleeve.

"Wait a minute. What's going on?"

"I'm not sure, but I think I saw Sabrina's car. It was hidden in the corner slot we passed. I caught a glimpse as we rounded the last turn." Cathy brushed Richard's hand away and got out of the car. "Let's go. I have to check."

Richard picked up the small travel bag from the back seat, locked the doors, and activated the alarm system. He looked up and saw Cathy rounding the corner into the other section of the Hyatt's basement garage. As he walked around the corner, he saw Cathy inspecting a red BMW. The car had been concealed in a dark corner space under a meshwork of heating and air conditioning ducts. A black canvas had been thrown over the car, but a corner had slipped exposing the license plate; MAC-ONE.

"It's her car, Richard. No question." Cathy pointed to the tag. "She's here. I know it."

"How can you be so sure? She might have been here at first and taken to a different location by the State Department."

"Why would they do that? They don't have any reason to expect someone to be looking for Sabrina. Taggat's the only relative, and he's working with them. Steve's a hostage, so who's to care?"

"I guess they didn't figure on you getting involved. Otherwise, they would have put her on the moon."

"Exactly, and that gives me an advantage."

"Cathy, they know about you now. We better cool it, okay? We can see Sabrina in the morning and be on our way. Come on Cathy; playing around with the State Department makes me nervous. I'll make sure she's all right when we see her tomorrow."

"No way, Richard. They don't expect me until tomorrow. I've got this afternoon and tonight to figure out a way to help Sabrina out of this."

"I was afraid you'd feel that way. Okay, let's suppose she is here. I think we should wait until tomorrow and see her. Remember, it's Christmas Eve and..."

Cathy's eyes pierced Richard's. "I know what day it is! I plan on finding Sabrina and being out of here by tomorrow morning."

"Wait a bloody damned minute! You're talking treason, and it could be dangerous. Those fellows have firearms. Why can't we spend some time together, see Sabrina in the morning, assure ourselves she'll be fine, and let this thing end as it should...peacefully."

"Oh hell, Richard. I have to get Sabrina out of this mess so we can be together when she has the baby, don't you understand?"

"Dammit, Cathy! You act as if it's your goddamned baby. What the hell is going through your head?"

Cathy snapped the bag from Richard's hand. "It is my goddamned baby! Now, are you going to help, or not?" Cathy headed for the elevator, punched the button marked L, and entered the car when the door opened. She held the "Door Open" button, and looked at Richard. "You coming?"

Richard shook his head in amazement and rode with Cathy to the Lobby.

"I'm going to check around and see if I can find out anything about Sabrina. Why don't you see if there are any rooms available."

"Yes, Mam." Richard said as he walked to the registration desk. He filled out the registration papers and went to find Cathy to tell her of their good fortune in securing a room on Christmas Eve. He was astonished to find her engaged in a conversation with the Bell Captain. The man was of Spanish descent, about five feet ten inches tall and medium build. Richard walked up behind Cathy and lightly grasped her upper right arm. "Come on, Cathy. Let's go to our room."

Cathy jerked her arm away. "Just a minute!" She snarled at Richard, but replaced her smile when she turned to the Bell Captain. "I want to talk to this gentleman for a few more minutes."

"I think you've asked enough questions for the day," Richard said while smiling at the Bell Captain. "It's all right. We talk to each other like this...a lot."

Cathy turned quickly and gave Richard another icy stare. "I'll decide when I have or have not asked enough questions, and I'll have you know I wasn't finished!"

"Excuse the hell out of me. Cathy, I've put up with this crap long enough. Who the hell do you think you are?" Cathy had Richard at the limit of his patience. Not only had she assumed all the initiative, which was fine with him, but she had shown total disregard for the potential consequences to his career. Now, she was bordering on having total disregard for his presence. Richard wasn't about to tolerate that!

"Richard, if you don't like the way things are going, then LEAVE!" Cathy turned her smile and attention to the bell man.

Richard again encircled her arm with his hand and spun her around. "Cathy, what the hell is going on? I think we've taken this far enough. Don't you? Look, we have an opportunity to see Sabrina. Let's not blow it!"

"I'm not blowing anything! If you can't stand the heat, then get out of the kitchen! Now, leave me the hell alone! I'm busy! I'll take care of you later." Cathy jerked her arm away from Richard's grasp.

"Take care of me? Take care of me! Cathy, you're such a bitch, an impersonal bitch!" Richard looked at the bell captain. "Excuse me, but I've just realized I'm involved with a woman who doesn't give a good goddamn about anything except herself and another woman. I think the bitch goes both ways, what do you think?"

Cathy smiled at Richard. "Are you finished?"

Richard huffed. "With what?"

"With your little demonstration in frustration."

"You go to hell! I'm leaving."

"Fine, it will be one less thing for me to worry about."

"That does it!...You know, Cathy, you have a problem with priorities. Obviously, Sabrina is your priority, top priority. Everyone else runs a distant second."

"Hey, Juan. Give the man a cigar. He's getting smarter all the time."

The Bell Captain tried to melt into the floor and pretend none of this was happening.

"Okay, Cathy. I've had enough. I think I better go back to Norfolk."

"Good, you'll be better off there. Secure in your own little world."

"I'll catch a cab. Here's your goddamned keys and the room key." Richard pitched the keys to Cathy. They flew past her outstretched hand and hit the wall beside Juan. Juan picked up the keys and handed them to Cathy.

"Richard, there's no need to take a taxi." Cathy's tone had settled down, and she sounded almost placative.

Richard turned hoping Cathy had changed her mind. As he turned, the Porsche keys hit him in the chest.

"Take my car. I'll drive Sabrina's car home." Cathy turned and restarted her conversation with Juan.

Richard bent over, picked up the leather shrouded key ring, walked back to Cathy, took her by the shoulders, turned her around, and looked her in the eye. "Don't I mean anything to you? Don't WE mean anything to you?"

"Richard, I think you had better leave. We've put on quite a show for the lobby. You're embarrassing me." Cathy turned back to the bell captain. "Juan, let's see, where were we?"

Richard stood in amazement. "Cathy Winston, I...I.."

Cathy turned, looked at Richard, and waited. "Well, spit it out. You what? Come on, Richard. I can't stand someone who won't speak their mind."

"I'm too bloody angry to speak. Good-by!"

"Good-by, Richard."

Richard shrugged his shoulders, spun around and headed for the garage. As he slid into the car seat, he wondered what his relationship with Cathy would be after their first big tiff. At the moment he was so angry, he could chew nails. However, he loved Cathy and was willing to try to rectify their differences...just not now. As he unharnessed the Porsche's horses and ate up the miles between Washington and Norfolk, Richard tried to forget Cathy's harsh words. He knew she was stressed because of Sabrina's situation. *I'll love her up when she comes home. That will bring her around.* Richard thought as he pushed a little harder on the accelerator.

\* \* \*

"Sorry about the little show, Juan. I don't know what got into him. He's usually not that explosive. I'll love him up a little. He'll be all right."

Juan shrugged his shoulders. "No problem."

"Juan, I need some help. My sister checked into this hotel a few weeks ago, and I was supposed to meet her. I'm a few days late, and no one seems to know anything about her. I know she was here. She told me she was going to be staying at the Hyatt on the Mall. Do you think you might be able to help me?" Cathy eased a fifty dollar bill toward Juan.

Juan quickly picked up the bill. "I'm not sure, what's her name?"

"Just a minute." Cathy rifled through her purse and produced a picture of Sabrina. "Here's something better. Here's her picture. Her full name is Sabrina MacKenzie."

Juan looked at the picture. "I'm not sure. She looks familiar, but it has been more than a few days since I've seen her."

"Well, maybe it has been longer that a few days, but can't you be more specific?" Cathy slid another fifty in Juan's direction.

Juan deftly pocketed the second bill. "What did you say her name was?"

"MacKenzie. Sabrina MacKenzie."

"One moment." Juan disappeared into a small room adjacent to his stand. Cathy waited for what seemed to be an eternity. After five minutes, Juan came back with a computer printout under his right arm. "Sorry it took a few minutes, but I had to wait until I was sure I was the only one accessing this particular file. I think I might have something here that will interest you."

"How interested do I have to be?"

"Oh, I think this could be worth about five."

"And I could report you to your supervisor."

"Oh, I don't think you would want to do that, not if you really want to find your sister."

"Well, Juan, it looks like this is your lucky day."

Cathy took five one hundred dollar bills from her purse and held them in front of Juan. He quickly reached for the money as before, but Cathy snatched them from his grasp. "Whoa, Juan, not until I see the information."

"Oh no. If you see it first, you won't have to pay."

"I can get it from anyone that can get into the computer."

"No, no. Not this information. I have to access it off a private file known only to me. I know a lot about computers. Usually the hotel cancels their files after fifteen days, but I save them for just such occasions. You never know when some important people might need some special information in this town."

"All right, you have me where you want me." Cathy took the money and placed it in a neat stack. She gently picked up the bills and held them for Juan to grab. As he reached, Cathy quickly tore the bills in half."

"Aiye! Why you do such a thing?"

Cathy handed Juan half the stack. "Half now, the other half after I've seen your information. It's still good money, but if you try to stiff me and it's not good information, it won't do either of us any good."

"Fine, I have plenty of tape." Juan opened the paper. He leafed through a few of the pages until he came to a specific date. "Here, Here it is! Notice the registration at 13:40 on November eighteenth."

Cathy looked at the printout. She saw the name Sabrina MacKenzie, Suite 811. "Now, we're getting somewhere." Cathy handed Juan two of the bill halves.

"The computer shows her to have checked out one week later, but there was no housekeeping order for the suite on the daily log. Also, no one else has checked into the suite since the day of her registration. Besides, things on the eighth floor have gotten pretty secretive. I've seen a lot of different caterers going in and out of that floor, but no guests have come through the lobby."

"You keep your finger on the pulse of things around here, don't you Juan?"

"Yes, I do. You can never tell when it might be profitable."

Cathy gave Juan the other three bill halves. "Thanks for the help."

"Thank you!" Juan waved the bills at Cathy and smiled.

Cathy took the elevator to the eighth floor. The door opened and a huge man in a gray business suit confronted her. "Excuse me," Cathy said. "Wrong floor. My husband told me the eighth floor, but I see my paper says seventh. Sorry."

"No problem," the man said as he withdrew his hand from inside his jacket.

The door closed, and Cathy went back to the lobby. She walked over to Juan. "You still open for business?"

"Sure. What can I do for you?"

"Who gets past the gray gorilla on eighth?"

"Only the caterers."

"Don't they order from the hotel dining room?"

"No. They bring the food from an outside kitchen."

"Why? What do you think is going on up there?"

"I don't think," Juan smiled. "It doesn't pay. I report what I see, that's all."

"Look, Juan. I'm into you for six hundred dollars. I think I deserve a few of your thoughts."

"Okay. I think your sister is being held under protective custody by some governmental agency. I've seen it before. They keep witnesses here on occasion. It usually works this way."

Cathy knew Juan was right, but for the wrong reasons. "Do you think you might be able to get me past the goons?"

Juan thought for a moment. "Maybe. Come with me."

Cathy followed Juan into a small room behind his stand.

"This is how I get my friends around this place." He held out his hand and passed it over a full line of clothes hangers. "Every service uniform known to this hotel is here. It should guarantee entrance to the floor, but not to the room. You're on your own for that." Juan reached out and removed a brown dress with red trim. Capital Caterers was written in red script across the back. "These are the folks that are scheduled to deliver dinner tonight. I believe this is your size. When they arrive, you could mix with the group. You might get lucky."

"Thanks, Juan. How much for this one?"

"On the house."

"Ooo, be careful. You might loose your reputation." Cathy leaned forward and kissed Juan on the cheek. She took the dress, rolled it into a small ball, and placed it in her bag. She left Juan's cache and took the elevator to the seventh floor. She found her room, sat down on the edge of the bed, kicked off her shoes, and took out the Yellow Pages. She knew exactly what she was going to do, but she had only a few hours to accomplish her task.

After finding the addresses she needed, Cathy opened her travel bag and took out a pair of jeans and sweatshirt. She opened the door to the room, looked up and down the hall, and, without being seen, dragged one of the small planters into the room. She took the planter into the bathroom, placed her jeans and sweatshirt on the floor, and sprinkled the dirt from the planter over the clothes. She stomped the dirt into the clothing, scooped up the excess, refilled the planter, and placed it back into the hall. She removed a razor blade from Richard's shaving kit, and without a thought about Richard put the kit back into her suitcase. She made several erratic slits in the sweatshirt and pants, and frayed the material as much as possible hoping the aging process would be adequate for her purposes. She put on the clothes, took her raincoat from her bag, and put it on. She straightened up the room and headed for the lobby.

Cathy left the hotel at 3:30 p.m. The address she had obtained from the Yellow Pages was about one mile away. Approximately one half mile from the hotel, she passed a liquor store and entered.

"What'll be, Miss?" A robust voice came from a cherry cheeked man behind the counter.

"You look like Santa Claus." Cathy was amazed at the resemblance of the proprietor and Clement Moore's bright jolly old elf.

"Thanks. I hope the kids think so. I'm playing Santa when I get home. What can I get for you?"

"Half pint of Jack Daniels."

"Sure. That'll be all?"

"That's all."

"Not enough to celebrate with. What else can I get you?"

"Enough for one."

"Gotcha…Sorry."

"How late are you open?"

"I'm closing at eight. The kids want me home early."

"Merry Christmas," Cathy said as she paid the gentleman. "Hope your kids have a nice Christmas."

"You too, young lady." He turned and began humming "Jingle Bells".

Cathy left the store and walked another quarter mile. She entered an alley between two tenement buildings, opened the bottle of Jack Daniels, sipped a small amount, swished it around, and spat it out. "Yuck! How in the hell does any one drink this stuff straight?" She sprinkled some of the bourbon on her clothing and poured the rest into a nearby trashcan. She place the bottle in her pocket, tossed her hair into a ratty nest, tied a scarf over her head, wiped some of the collected soot from the buildings onto her pants and shirt, and left the alley feeling, looking and smelling the part of a street person. By the time she finished her trip's last leg it was four thirty.

Cathy looked at the sign; Free Clinic-OPEN. "Now to put my plan into action," she thought. She tucked her raincoat under the stoop leading up to the front entrance hoping it would be there when she returned. She walked up the flight of steps to the clinic, took a deep breath, and walked into the waiting room expecting to encounter a thong of people. Instead, she was confronted by an empty room. She walked over to the reception window and surprised a young nurse and physician in the throes of an embrace. Cathy coughed, "Excuse me, young people. Reckon I could see the doctor?"

The couple jumped apart. The nurse smiled at Cathy as she straightened her uniform. "Certainly. We'll be with you in a moment." She handed Cathy a sheet of paper. "Would you fill this out, please?"

"I'll do it!" Cathy said with a Kentucky drawl.

The doctor wiped the lipstick from his mouth as he disappeared through a connecting door.

Cathy handed the form back to the nurse.

"Thank you." The nurse turned the form around so she could read the name. "The doctor will see you momentarily, Mrs. Muffett."

"That's Muff-ette," Cathy said.

"Excuse me?"

"I said, the name is 'Muff-ette', not 'Muffit'."

"Oh, excuse me." The nurse rolled her eyes in exasperation. The buxom brunette nurse walked to the back hallway. She approached the tall lean black haired medical resident. "I have a good one for you. She reeks of alcohol, and looks like hell." She handed the doctor the clipboard. "Don't take too long," she purred. "We still have a date after we close, don't we?" She ran her fingers thorough his hair, leaned forward, being sure to press her breasts against his chest, and planted a kiss on the tip of his nose.

The resident took a deep breath. "Most certainly. I'll be sure to dispense with this problem quickly." He held the clipboard up in the air.

"Good! You won't be sorry." She winked. "I'll show the woman back to the exam room." The nurse returned to the window and summoned Cathy.

Cathy eased back to the small room and sat down in a folding metal chair beside a small desk. The doctor entered the room immediately.

"Now, Mrs. Muff-ette. What can I do for you?"

Cathy immediately began sobbing. "Well, you see, Doc, it's like this." Cathy sniffed and wiped her eyes with the dirty cuff of her sweatshirt. "I lost my family on Christmas Eve 'nigh on to three yar ago. Every time Christmas comes 'round, I just go to pieces. I cain't sleep unless I drink, and I don't like to drink unless I cain't sleep. You know what I mean?"

The Doctor shook his head affirmatively. "Have you ever been hospitalized?"

"Oh, my heavens, yes! I was in a looney bin for three months after I lost my precious Ralph and baby girls."

"How old were your children?"

"Three and...and..." Cathy sniffed and began to cry.

The doctor leaned over and gently touched Cathy's shoulder. "I'm sorry. I didn't mean to make you relive your tragedy." He looked at her with sympathetic and caring eyes.

Cathy gained her composure. "I'm all right. I jest need something to help me through this time of year. Could you please help me?" Cathy placed her grubby hands across the doctor's.

The resident winced. "Have you taken anything before?"

Cathy looked down at the floor. "I tried to kill myself after my family died. I blamed myself for their loss. You see, I was gone that night." Cathy looked up into the resident's eyes. "Working. Trying to make enough money to give my babies a Christmas. A fire started when one of them electric heaters got too hot. The trailer went up in a flash. Well, when I came home and saw all those firemen spraying my house, I didn't know what to do.." Cathy intended to give the doctor a play by play description of her fabricated story hoping the temptation of the nurse's voluptuous body would wear the physician's patience thin.

The doctor interrupted Cathy's recap. "What medicine have you used?"

"Well, after they watched me for a few days in one of them psychic houses, I was sent home. I had to stay with a friend or have a family member stay with me before they'd let me go. They were afraid I'd try to kill myself again. Well, honey, I wasn't going to try that again...Nearly scared myself to death...Thought I was going to die.." Cathy smiled and winked at the resident.

The doctor grinned. "Did they prescribe any medication when you went home?"

"Just a sleeping pill."

"What kind of pill did they give you?"

"I'm not sure. It was long and red. It started with an N...The doctor said they give it to older folks cause it weren't too strong."

"That sounds like Noctec. Chloral hydrate is the generic name."

"Yep...that's it. That's the one. I don't know what the generals call it, but that's the one. Could you give me a few of them pills? I sure would appreciate it. Otherwise, I have to drown my woes in this." Cathy pulled the bourbon bottle from her pocket, looked at its empty contents, and tossed it into the waste basket. "Another fine soldier bites the dust."

"You know this medicine shouldn't be mixed with alcohol. It greatly potentiates its affects."

"You don't mean it!" Cathy gasped. "Why, I wouldn't need Jack, if I had the medicine. I've done well with it before, Doc. Couldn't you see your way clear to give me a few. Just enough to last me through the New Year?"

"Do you have any place to stay?"

"I'm staying at the mission on Thirty-fourth." Cathy remembered the address from the phone book.

The resident pulled a prescription blank from his pocket. "I guess I could give you a few." He wrote the prescription as he gave Cathy the instructions. "Chloral Hydrate 500 mg. Capsule. Take one capsule at night when needed for sleep. I'm giving you 25 capsules, and there won't be any refills." He handed the prescription to Cathy. "This should get you through the season."

"It'll be plenty. Don't you worry. I'll be okay. Now, you and that cute little nurse go have a good time." Cathy sobbed. "Me and my Ralph used to really live it up on Christmas Eve. After we got the kids into bed, we used to lie under the Christmas tree and make love." Cathy looked at the resident and winked. He was blushing. "I don't mean to embarrass you, honey. You two go have a good time, and I thank ya." Cathy stood up and started to walk out.

"Just a minute, you forgot your prescription." The resident handed Cathy the slip of paper.

"Sorry. I guess I was thinking about my Ralph, and I plumb forgot it." She took the paper from the doctor and patted him on the cheek. "Thanks again, and you have a Merry Christmas."

"You, too, Mrs. Muff-ette. Be careful with that medicine."

"I will." Cathy left the clinic after thanking the nurse. She relocated her rain coat and headed for the nearest service station. She used the restroom to clean herself as much as possible prior to her next visit to a pharmacist. She found an open store, had the prescription filled by an anxious pharmacist who could talk about nothing except getting home, and headed for the nearest liquor dispensary.

The young woman clerking the Congressional Liquor Store was shocked by Cathy's appearance when she entered. "What may I get for you?"

Cathy looked around the shelves. "I'd like a bottle of the Courvoisier V.O.C. in the Baccarat crystal." Cathy pointed to the top of the locked cabinet.

"That bottle costs four hundred dollars! Don't you think you might..."

Cathy counted out five one hundred dollar bills and laid them on the counter. "If you get it down in less than thirty seconds, you can have the extra one."

The clerk scurried to the top of the cabinet and extracted the case from its position. She dusted off the box, put it in a thick shopping bag, and handed it to Cathy. She quickly rang up the sell and pocketed the extra hundred before Cathy changed her mind. "Thank you, very much, and Merry Christmas."

Cathy smiled, picked up the sack, and departed the store. "Merry Christmas to you," Cathy said over her shoulder as she left. Cathy arrived back at the hotel at six thirty, and made it to her room without being noticed. She removed her clothing discarding the articles in the nearest trash container. Then, she showered, washed her hair, and dressed in the uniform Juan had provided.

Cathy carefully removed the seal from the bottle of Courvoisier and poured the caramel colored, sweet smelling liquid into one of the hotel's glasses. She then dissolved all of the Noctec capsules in the brandy and carefully replaced the liquid into the bottle. Cathy repositioned the seal so entry could only be discovered by the closest scrutiny and shook the bottle so the mixture would disperse evenly.

The phone rang, as Cathy prepared to close the box, almost causing her to drop the package on the floor. "Damn! Who the hell is calling this room?" She picked up the phone.

"Hello!"

"Hey, momma!" Juan's voice resounded from the headset. "I thought you would like to know the caterer's have arrived."

"Juan! It's you. You nearly scared me to death. They're here! Already?"

"Already? It's seven-fifteen. They're late."

"Okay. Thanks."

"Good luck, good looking."

Cathy smiled. "Thanks again, Juan."

"If you're ever back in town, look me up. You're good for business."

Cathy hung up the receiver, grabbed the package, and headed for the service elevator. When the elevator door opened, she was confronted by a group dressed in the same uniform.

"Well, come on!" A voice from the back of the elevator gruffly said. "Let's get this over so we can go home. I'm missing Christmas Eve with my kids."

Cathy held up the brandy box. "Sorry, I forgot this." She squeezed into the elevator, and the crew proceeded to the eighth floor. Cathy held her breath as the door opened. The gray gorilla stood aside as the groups pushed their carts into Suite 811. Cathy held her breath as she looked around the room. Sabrina wasn't there. "Damn," she muttered to herself.

A young woman walked into the sitting area from a bedroom. She was drying her hair. "Oh, supper. Good! I'm starved."

The guard directed the crew to put the food on a table in the center of the sitting area. After they finished, they were expected to leave.

Valerie Cummins looked over the table. "Looks delicious." She walked to the other bedroom door. "Sabrina,"

Cathy's attention immediately turned to the bedroom entrance.

"Supper's here." Valerie called and turned back to the table.

"I'm not hungry. I don't feel well. You go ahead and eat. I'll be in after while."

"Okay," Valerie replied. "Suit yourself."

Cathy quickly walked to the bedroom door. The guard promptly stood between her and the opening. Cathy spoke around the guard into the opened doorway. "I have a special package from Taggat Delaney for Miss MacKenzie."

"We'll take the package," the guard reached out to Cathy.

"This is to be delivered to Miss MacKenzie, and Miss MacKenzie, only!" Cathy held the package closer.

"I said…"

Sabrina appeared behind the guard. She had recognized the familiar voice. "It's all right. I'll take the package." Sabrina wormed her way around the goliath and stood in front of Cathy.

Cathy almost cried, but bit her lip and held the package out to Sabrina. "Mr. Delaney wanted you to share this with your friends. He knows you aren't drinking, so he asked me to give you a hug." Cathy gently negotiated Sabrina's abdomen. "Be ready to leave around midnight. I love you."

Sabrina looked at Cathy through her tears of joy. "I think I'm in early labor."

"Damn, Sabrina. You're always complicating things. Okay, hold your legs together or something. Just be ready to leave. You'll know when it's time." Cathy winked.

"Come on, Sabrina. Let's eat. I'm in a hurry to have some of that present." Valerie eyed the brandy box as the guards escorted the caterers out of the room.

Cathy managed to be the last to enter the elevator. As the guard turned his back and headed for the suite, Cathy quickly jumped out of the elevator and into the hall. She turned and looked at the amazed faces. "Go ahead, I forgot to give the lady her card." Cathy headed for the Suite, but she ducked into a linen closet instead. She cracked the door enough to obtain a view of the hallway.

"All clear," one of the guards said after looking back towards the service elevator.

"Made it," Cathy sighed with relief.

The wait was unbearable, but finally Cathy saw Valerie come into the hall and offer the guards some brandy.

"I'm sorry, Miss Cummings. No drinking on duty."

"Oh, for heaven's sake. It's Christmas Eve. This is delicious. I'm on my second."

The guard eyed the glass.

"Go on! Take it!" Cathy yelled to herself.

"Well, maybe this once. It is Christmas, and that smells delicious." The guard took the glass.

"All right!" Cathy silently rejoiced.

The guard drank the large glass, and after fifteen minutes, Cathy watched as he slowly melted down the wall and went to sleep. She waited ten more minutes and carefully eased the closet door open. She snaked along the wall and peeked around the corner. The guard in front of the suite was sitting in front of a planter sleeping like a baby. One of the fake palm fronds dangled in front of his face. Cathy carefully entered the Suite.

Sabrina was standing over Valerie. She looked at Cathy and laughed. "What did you put in that stuff? She stopped talking in mid sentence."

Cathy rushed to Sabrina and hugged her neck. "I'm so glad I found you. I thought I had lost you to Uncle Sam."

"Never," Sabrina winced. "I really think I'm in labor, Cathy."

"All right, we'll have our reunion later. Get your things, and be sure you have your keys. I found your car."

"How are we going to get out of here? They might have some one watching the garage."

"No! I've checked it out. Come on." Cathy pulled up the edge of the long white tablecloth covering the catering table. "Crawl under."

"Crawl under? I'm term pregnant, and you want me to crawl under?"

"Look, labor or not, get your butt under this table so we can get out of here. otherwise, you're going to have your baby in Washington D.C., and you'll have to visit me in Leavenworth."

Sabrina slowly crawled under the cart. "Not so bad," she grunted.

Cathy snickered as she pushed the cart through the door and headed for the service elevator. She pushed the call button, and as the door opened, Cathy gasped to see Juan standing in the car. "What the hell are you doing here?"

Juan winked. "Did you get what you came for?"

"Who wants to know?"

Juan looked into the hall. He grinned as he saw the guards sleeping. "Come on. I've cleared the other buttons. The lower garage has been closed off for the past thirty minutes."

Cathy smiled. "Thanks, Juan."

"Yeah! Thanks, Juan, or whoever you are," Sabrina's muffled voice emanated from under the cart.

Juan smiled. "Clever."

Juan escorted them to the parking garage. After walking into the garage area and assuring it was empty, he motioned for Cathy to bring the cart out of the elevator."

Sabrina moaned and groaned as she negotiated her way from under the cart, and slowly stood up. "Whew, that was fun. Let's do it again," she laughed , and then winced with another labor pain. "Cathy we better go. These contractions are closer."

Cathy walked over to Juan. "Thanks, Juan. I don't know how to repay you." She leaned closer and kissed him on the cheek.

"Don't worry. No problem. I enjoy the riskier things in life. Now, go on before they discover she's gone." Juan handed Cathy her bag. "Here, I got this from your room. I figured you'd need some clothes before morning."

Cathy started to speak.

"Don't say anything else. GO!" Juan turned and pushed the cart on the elevator. He didn't look back.

"Nice guy," Sabrina winced.

"Yeah. Aren't they all?" Cathy looked at Sabrina's sweaty brow. "Come on, let's get you to Norfolk."

Cathy situated Sabrina in the back seat, started the reluctant BMW, and weaved her way out of the garage. "I'm glad Precious decided to start this time."

"Me too. Turn on the air conditioner. I don't feel so well."

"Hell, Sabrina. It's twenty above zero outside." Cathy looked into the back seat. Sabrina had just vomited into one of the floormats. "Okay, you want air conditioning, you've got air conditioning." Cathy stopped at the gate and handed the attendant the ticket from the car's dashboard.

The lot attendant punched the ticket, looked at the car, and then at Cathy. "This ticket is six weeks old. I'm not sure how to charge for that. I'll have to call the front desk."

"I don't think that will be necessary," Cathy said as she handed the woman three one hundred dollar bills.

"I don't think so either," the lady said as she eyed Ben Franklin's portrait. "Maybe we could put it on the room charge."

Cathy smiled. "I think that's an excellent idea." Cathy quickly pulled out of the garage and headed for I-95.

"How's it going?" Cathy asked Sabrina as she headed up the ramp onto the Interstate.

"I'm not going to make it to Norfolk. I feel terrible. I can't seem to get enough air to breathe, and the baby's not moving much."

"Where can we stop? I don't know any doctors. Do you?"

"How far is it to Clifton Forge?"

"Fifty miles. Why?"

"Stop there. I've heard Dr. Vance talk about one of the doctors there. His name is John Chadwick. Drop me off at the Emergency Exit, and I'll go to labor hall by myself. Stay in the car for a while, then come up to the floor."

"Why do all that?"

"We don't need a scene in the E.R. You know how you can be."

"All right! But I'm coming up before you have that baby. I don't want you to be alone."

Sabrina reached forward and grasped Cathy's shoulder. "I know, and I don't want to be alone."

Cathy wheeled off the Interstate and made her way to Greene Memorial Hospital. She pulled in front of the E.R. Entrance and stopped. Sabrina picked up her coat and purse and slowly slid out of the back seat. She didn't look at Cathy as she spoke. "I love you, Cathy. I'll never forget what you've done for me tonight."

"Oh, shut up and go have a baby. Sabrina?"

"Yes?"

"I love you, too."

"I know." Sabrina stood up and walked toward the electric doors entering the E.R.

Cathy watched Sabrina disappear into the lights of the Emergency Room. Then, she pulled away and parked in a dark area of the lot, retrieved a blanket from the trunk, and laid down in the front seat. She noticed the clock on the dash; 2:00 A.M., Christmas Day. She tried to sleep, but rest wasn't going to come easily.

# 22

## DECEMBER 24; U.S.S. CARL VINSON; PERSIAN GULF

As Kent watched the wake slip under the fantail of the *Vinson*, his thoughts turned to yesterday's briefing for the Christmas morning mission. He was assigned to fly top cover for a live bombing mission, and he was nervously excited. Practice and simulation was over. Tomorrow was real. Tomorrow he would be flying against real targets manned by unpredictable human beings, not ghostly computers. He wanted the mission to proceed perfectly, but most of all he hoped he would live through his first real test as a pilot.

"Lieutenant Pooley, Captain Jacobs requests your presence in Ops Room Three." The Marine Corporal snapped to attention behind Kent's vigil on the stern of the ship.

"Thank you, Corporal." Kent weaved his way through the passageways of the *Vinson* until he found the familiar door of Operation Room

Number Three. Upon entering, he eased into the seat next to his Radar Intercept Officer, Mookie Brandonovich. "Sorry I'm late, Mook. Been doing some thinking."

"Me too, and lots of praying." The dark headed Polish immigrant's son smiled at Kent and flashed one of his patented thirty two teeth grins.

"I hear you!" Kent couldn't help but smile.

Captain Frank Jacobs, Commander of the Air Group, or CAG, walked to the front of the room and turned on the projector. The sandy haired Vietnam ace flipped up the first slide, a picture of the Persian Gulf. "The *Vinson* has come to station at a point five miles off the coast of Kuwait. We don't like it in these cramped quarters, and we're here only as a show of strength in support of Saudi Arabia in this hostage situation. However, in view of these escalating sorties we are about to begin, the *Vinson* will be pulling out of the Gulf after recovery of our planes tomorrow. After what has been planned, we'll probably have to fight our way out." Frank paused and looked around at all the sober faces. "At zero hundred hours, December 25, the *Vinson* will proceed to a point fifteen miles off the coast of Kuwait into International waters. From this point at approximately 0400 hours, we will turn into the wind and launch a strike mission against the southern coast of Iran. The first group to launch will be a group of six Intruders, two Prowlers, and four Tomcats. The Tomcats will fly top cover for the Bombers while the Prowlers will make it very difficult for the shore batteries to know what the hell is going on. The Intruders will seek out and destroy SAM sites, airfields, and targets of opportunity around the following cities; Abadan, Ahvaz, and Masjed Soleyman. Jake, you and Kent will follow up Torrey and Moose. Your callsign will be Bird Dog Two. Torrey and Moose-Bird Dog One. At 0430, a second flight of four A-6's and one E6-M Prowler will take off to clean up any targets in this area, extending no further than one hundred klicks inland. The coastal emplacements must be neutralized before the second launch can commit. You fellows will have to hit them hard, but don't take any unnecessary risks. We're here to put on a show and make some noise. The purpose of this mission is to create a diversion for a rescue mission directed at Rasht."

Kent inwardly grinned. He had been following the circumstances around Steve Hardesty's hijacking, and he wondered if Hardesty and Sabrina had ever gotten back together. It seemed ironic that he, of all people, was involved in a potential rescue of Sabrina's former boyfriend.

"The F-14's will be equipped with the Hughes AIM 54 Phoenix missile. Gentlemen, it costs the taxpayers one million dollars every time you pull the trigger on one of these babies, so shoot straight and pinpoint your targets. After launch, the *Vinson* will sail to this point two hundred miles from the Iranian coast. We don't want any Exocet's within range of the ship. This mission will be a success. If it is not, it won't be because of a failure of any crew from the *Vinson*. Understood?"

"Aye, Aye, Sir!"

Kent looked over at Mookie and smiled. "Looks like the real thing, Mook. Let's go look over our ship and review the information down in Intelligence."

"Do you think we'll see any action?" Mookie nervously asked.

"Nah, the A-6 jockeys will have all the fun." Kent headed out of the room.

"Fun?" Mookie grinned an anxious smile. "Fun? What the hell do you call fun?"

Kent turned. "Come on. This will be a cakewalk. Hell, we've had harder days back in Norfolk."

## RASHT, IRAN; DECEMBER 24, 1600H

Steve sat on the hard bunk of his eight foot square cell. Across the floor of the hanger, directly in front of his cage, he could see the rear mess entrance of the troop barracks. He had been a hostage for sixty-three days. Not long, by past hostage experiences, but long enough for Steve. He knew his days were numbered, and he wasn't sure why he had been allowed to live this long. Perhaps the rapport he developed with Yassar during the flight had served in part of his salvation. Steve disliked Yassar's ideals and methods, but he respected the thoroughness of his technique. However, Yakim was another story. Steve knew Yakim didn't need a reason to kill. All Yakim needed was opportunity.

On the abbreviated exercise walks the hostages were permitted, Steve made mental sketches of the compound. He could close his eyes and see the layout perfectly. The runways were oriented East to West and Southeast to Northwest. It was fifty paces across the tarmac to the pilot ready room. He had observed Yassar enter and exit the building fully suited for recon flights in the Mirage. Steve knew he had to reach the ready room and take off before they discovered he was missing. He couldn't afford the luxury of a pressure suit because he couldn't take the time to look for one. Hopefully, it wouldn't require a lot of aerobatics to escape to the north. His plan was to fly straight into Soviet airspace and surrender to the first interceptor he aroused. If he timed it right, he would be out of his cell, across the tarmac and have the jet started within two or two and one-half minutes. He had counted at least thirty ground troops including Yassar and Yakim, and he had to get out of the complex before they were aroused. The jet had taken off at all times of day, so he hoped the startup routine would not raise suspicion. He hoped to execute his plan in the morning, Christmas Day, before daylight, and he hoped everyone remained tardy in their work details as they had for the past month.

Steve felt that everything about his plan was feasible. However, the one variable was Tallia. Tallia, Yassar's beautiful consort had to be convinced to help him. He had had many talks with Tallia over the past months, and he had grown very close to her. He felt that the feeling was mutual. However, he had not approached her about so severe a request. He wasn't sure how he was going to do it, but he must persuade her to leave his cell unlocked after she took up the trays from the evening meal. He had rehearsed a way in his mind to approach her throughout the day, but when he noticed the door into the troop's mess opening, he knew rehearsal was over. It was show time.

Tallia pushed a small cart across the hanger floor. She appeared unusually tired. Her long black hair was disheveled, and she seemed more intolerant of Yakim's persistent badgerings. Steve noted how she slapped at the rifle muzzle as Yakim nudged her across the hanger with the tip of his AK-47. Steve hoped he could stuff Yakim's weapon down his throat one day, but his attention today was to Tallia. She must be recruited, NOW!

Steve began rubbing his right ankle in preparation for execution of his plan. After Tallia finished passing the Arabs their trays, she rolled her cart to a halt in front of Steve's cell. She picked up the tin tray, placed it on the concrete floor, and pushed it under the bars.

Steve looked up from his ankle manipulation. "Would you mind bringing the plate in tonight? I've injured my ankle, and I don't think I can get up from the bunk."

Yakim shoved himself in front of Tallia leveling the rifle at Steve's chest. "Get up, or I'll shoot you where you sit."

"I'll try," Steve angrily retorted. "But I haven't been able to stand on my foot this afternoon."

"Get up, American. You'll get up or not eat for the next week!" Yakim motioned to the plate with the tip of his weapon.

Tallia looked at Yakim with exasperation and started to push her way toward the cell. "Move, Yakim. I'll get the plate. Can't you see he's hurt his foot?"

"Stand back, bitch! Let the American get it for himself."

Steve put both feet on the floor and stood up.

"See!" Yakim grinned and looked at Tallia. "I told you he could walk."

Steve took a step forward, yelled with pain, and fell to the floor hitting the concrete harder than intended.

Yakim leaped forward with fire in his eyes. "Come on, American. I'm tired of this act. You want me to come in there and help?"

Steve looked up at Yakim and grimaced. "Fuck you, pig!"

Yakim became livid. He pulled back the bolt of the AK-47, chambered a live round, and leveled the gun in the direction of Steve's head. "Don't mock me, you flea. I must now do what I've intended to do all along. Prepare to die, American." Yakim took the gun off safety.

Tallia stepped in front of Yakim and placed her hand over the muzzle. "Put the gun down, Yakim. Yassar would be very upset if you killed the American. He left explicit instructions to keep him alive until after Christmas." Tallia knew she was pushing her limits with Yakim and Yassar, but she no longer cared. Death would be welcomed if it were her only means of escape. "You know Yassar will give you your way with the American in a few more days."

Yakim eased the safety on and lowered the gun. "You're right." He smiled and looked into the cell. "Mend your ankle, American. I wouldn't want you to limp to the firing squad I'll prepare after tomorrow." Yakim turned toward Tallia. "Feed him, woman. I'm going over to the other side of the hanger. The stench over here gags me."

Tallia entered the cell and leaned over to help Steve onto his bunk. "You really shouldn't tempt Yakim, Steve Hardesty. He will kill you some-day, and neither Yassar nor I will be able to prevent it from happening."

"Screw Yakim!" Steve permitted Tallia's assistance, but as he sat down on the bunk, he leaned closer to her head. "Tallia, help me. I must try and escape."

Tallia jerked her head away and looked at Steve in amazement.

"Don't look at my face. Look at my ankle and act as if you're trying to see if something's wrong."

Tallia turned her attention to Steve's left ankle.

"The other one."

"Oh." Tallia grinned, but her smile quickly melted to a face of despair. "How can I help you? I'm a prisoner myself."

"Leave my cell door open when you come back to pick up the plates tonight. I'll do the rest."

Tallia was shocked. "I don't have a key. Only Yassar and Yakim have the keys to the cells. I cannot do it!"

Steve leaned forward and grasped Tallia's small soft right wrist. "You must! They'll kill me in two or three days. I'd rather die trying to get away than be killed like a caged animal."

Tallia turned her head and looked into Steve's eyes. "If I do this, and they find out, I'll be killed. Believe me! Yassar would kill me in a moment if he thought I interfered in any way in his plan."

Steve knew she was telling the truth. "If you do this for me, I'll take you with me. That's all I have, Tallia. That's all I can promise."

"Hurry, Tallia!" Yakim yelled from across the hanger. "The American doesn't need all that help!" Yakim had finished his cigarette and began to slowly walk across the hanger floor.

"I'm hurrying, but you want him in good shape for his execution, don't you?"

Yakim stopped, shrugged his shoulders, and lit another cigarette.

"Thanks for the vote of confidence," Steve jeered.

Tallia turned her face to Steve. Instead of smiling at his last remark, she had tears in her eyes. "Steve, I have no place to go. Yassar made sure of that when he took me from my home in Baku. I'm destined to remain a slave forever. I don't see how I can help."

"Look, Tallia. I'm going to try with or without you. I don't have time to explain, but I promise I can fix any problem you might have with your government. I have friends in the right places. Please believe me. You're my only hope."

"I must think, Steve Hardesty."

"Please think about it quickly. Our time is running out."

"If I do what you've asked, you must not only take me with you. You must promise me one other thing."

"Anything." Steve looked up and saw Yakim stamping out his cigarette. "Quickly."

"You must kill Yassar. I cannot leave knowing he will continue to treat people like he has treated me."

"Tallia, I dislike the man as much as you, but the opportunity may not present itself. Meet me in the pilot ready area at five thirty A.M. This could be the shortest plane ride you've ever had."

Tallia grinned, leaned over, and placed the plate on the bunk. "I've never had a plane ride. You're ankle looks fine."

Yakim stood at the cell door. "Come on, Tallia. I think we've fooled with the dog long enough."

Tallia nervously hurried out of the cell. She didn't look back as she pushed the cart across the hanger and back into the troop's mess area.

Steve trusted his impression of Tallia's despair, and he prayed her hatred of Yassar was greater than her will to live. He knew their chances of success were slim—damned slim. However, he had made a self-commitment—succeed or die. Steve finished what he could stand to eat, put the plate on the floor, and pushed it as far as possible without getting out of the bed. He anxiously watched the entrance into the troop's quarters. An hour went by, but Tallia didn't return. Suddenly, the door opened, and Steve began to breathe easier. However, it was Yassar, not Tallia, who walked through the entrance. He came straight to Steve's cell, bent over, picked up the plate, looked at its contents, looked at Steve, and smiled.

"Good trip?" Steve grinned at Yassar.

Yassar smiled in return. "I understand Yakim tried to end your life once again tonight?"

"Oh, you know Yakim. He's a million laughs. Tallia cooled him down. She's one cold lady."

"Talking of women is beneath me, Hardesty. Yakim is a valiant soldier. You must never put him in a situation like you did tonight. Understand?"

"Yes, but you see, Yassar, my ankle…"

"I do not care if your ankle is injured or if you're playing a little game. I will no longer be able to protect you from Yakim."

"Protect me?"

"Yes, Hardesty. A soldier should die a soldier's death in the heat of battle. You don't deserve to die the death I've had to promise Yakim. You've injured his pride, and I had to give you to him. He will be able to do to you as he pleases after tomorrow. I have saved you through your Christmas, but to heal Yakim's pride I have promised him the privilege of ending your life. I hope you can understand our ways."

Steve looked at Yassar with an icy stare. "I'll never understand your ways, Yassar, but I appreciate your attempts to keep me alive as long as possible." *You're one cold son-of-a-bitch*, Steve thought as he motioned to the plate. "I thought Tallia was picking up the plates?"

Tallia won't be back tonight. I have plans for her. I've been too long without a woman. Good night, Steven Hardesty."

Steve fell back on his cot, looked up at the ceiling and sighed. "Dammit!"

\* \* \*

A light breeze across his face aroused Steve. He slowly opened his eyes and looked around. He saw Tallia kneeling beside his bunk. She had a blanket wrapped around her waist and a shawl over her shoulders. Her eyes were reddened, and she smelled of Yassar.

"I didn't expect you," Steve whispered.

"Shh," Tallia held her finger to her pursed lips. "The cell is unlocked. I must go."

Steve reached and grabbed Tallia's arm. Her shawl came loose revealing her naked upper body. She quickly pulled the shawl closed.

"Five thirty, remember!" Steve noticed Tallia's smooth skin, and her ample breasts, but his mind was busy with other plans.

Tallia leaned over and kissed Steve on the cheek. "It will be worth whatever it takes to rid myself of Yassar. He sickens me. I'm nothing but an object. We should have known one another in better times, Steve Hardesty. I could love a man such as you." Tallia smiled, flicked a small lock of Steve's hair across his forehead, turned and slinked across the hanger floor finding her way back to Yassar's bed. She sighed as she realized he had not aroused. As she eased into the bed beside his naked body, her revulsion almost caused her to retch. "That was the last time, dog.

One way or another, the last time." A smile came across her face as she thought of going home. Either the wings of a plane or an angel would take Tallia Maransk home. She didn't care which.

## BUKHARA, EASTERN TURKMEN, S.S.R. 25 DECEMBER 0230

It was scheduled as a routine flight of two TU-95D Bear Bombers from Bukhara, Turkmen, S.S.R. to Yerevan, Armenia, S.S.R. At an altitude of eight thousand meters and seven hundred kilometers per hour, the flight time was estimated to be three hours and ten minutes. However, when the live ordinance began to load into the bays, Colonel Yuri Andrevi knew his crew of twelve would begin to discuss other possible destinations. Yuri had known about the mission for the past four days. A briefing with high command had filled him in on the particulars.

As the four Kuznetsov NK-12MV turboprop engines were being started and brought up to power by the co-pilot, Major Gregor Isimovich, Colonel Andrevi activated the intercom. "Attention, attention, this is Colonel Andrevi. I'm sure you've been watching with interest the onloading of our live contact bombs. The ground crew has loaded a full bay of one thousand pound bombs which will be dropped over an enemy target. Since some of you are from the Azerbaijan Region, I'm sure you're aware of the atrocities inflicted upon Baku a few months ago. Our intelligence agency has determined, beyond a shadow of a doubt, the attack was perpetrated by an Iranian terrorist. The story of the lone attack by a disgruntled worker has been overplayed as a cover for our mission." Yuri switched off the intercom.

"Ready, Major?"

"Ready, Colonel. All engines running and up to operational power and temperatures."

"Okay, Gregor. Prepare to take her out."

"Bukhara Control, Bear One ready for takeoff."

"Roger, Bear One. Bear Two, Tower."

"Roger, Tower. Ready for takeoff." Colonel Alexander Similovski, the pilot of the second bomber promptly replied.

Colonel Andrevi adjusted his harness. "All crew members, prepare for takeoff." Yuri pushed the throttles forward slowly to full. The Bear lumbered down the runway and picked up speed to takeoff velocity.

Gregor watched the ground speed climb. "Three hundred kilometers...Now!"

Yuri eased the yoke back and the giant Bomber slowly gave up her earthly bonds. The plane gradually achieved altitude and leveled off at eight thousand meters. "It's your aircraft, Gregor."

"My aircraft," Gregor replied as he took control.

Yuri switched on the intercom. "Pilot to crew. We have attained altitude of eight thousand meters. Our mission will take us to the west as our original flight plan had indicated. However, after passing over Krasnovodsk, we will change course for Tehran. Our flight time to Tehran will be one hour from our change in direction. Our wing bomber will deviate from his course shortly afterwards making best time to his target, Tabriz. We are to cluster bomb oil storage facilites and an airbase. We will enter Iranian airspace with fighter coverage provided by two USA Tomcat fighters approaching from the South. However, we must employ all countermeasures to assure our success. We don't know how good the Yankees are, and we can't be sure they'll make it. Tonight we are to strike an important blow for our country. The U.S.S.R. will never be tolerant of attacks on its homeland by another country or renegades. That is all."

All Peter Minsk, the young corporal who manned the right rear tail gun could say was, "Oh, S...h...i...t!"

## INCIRLIK AIR BASE, ADANA, TURKEY 25 DECEMBER 0230

"Colonel, Gibson," the communication sergeant snapped to attention.

"Yes, Sergeant?"

"Ugent dispatch from Ismir." The sergeant held out the brown envelope to Hoot.

"Thank you, Sergeant." Hoot took the dispatch and walked to the
Ready Room. He closed and locked the door, slit the top of the envelope,
and removed the deciphered message.

TO: COLONEL CHARLES GIBSON USAF SN 05302234
FROM: COL. CLINTON SMITH, CHIEF OF STAFF USAF
RE: OPERATION SILENT NIGHT
  AS OF 0300H 25 DECEMBER, OPERATION SILENT
NIGHT IS A GO!DISREGARD PREVIOUS ORDERS. PRI-
MARY TARGET, TEHRAN, CANCELLED. CHANGE PRI-
MARY TARGET TO RASHT. SECONDARY TARGET
BANDAR-E ANZALI SAM SITE.
  GOOD LUCK AND GOD SPEED.

Hoot shredded the papers and left the ready room. As he opened the
door, a red jump suited man snapped to attention.

"Colonel Gibson, here're the ordinance requests. They are loaded.
The refueling coordinates are on the last page." The sergeant handed
Hoot a clipboard.

Hoot leafed through the lists. The F-111 was equipped with four fully
enclosed ordinance bays. Each bay had a limited amount of pylons. "Let's
see. 1900 pounds of extra fuel, check. Four AIM-9M Sidewinder, heat-
seaking missles, check. Two AGM-65D Maverick missles, check. Six
Durandal Antirunway Bombs, check." Hoot signed the papers, took the
coordinates, and handed the clipboard back to the ordinance officer.
"Everything seems in order, Sergeant."

"Yes, sir. Thank you, sir."

"Carry on, Sergeant."

"Yes, sir."

Hoot was fully suited, and ready for takeoff. He looked at his wrist
watch. 0255H. "Time," he thought. He looked at Baby. She sat low to the
ground like a black cat ready to pounce on its prey. "Okay, Baby.

Showtime!" Hoot climbed the ladder and eased into the cockpit. He strapped in, adjusted his helmet, verified his oxygen and G-suit connections, and called up his flight plan. He made the appropriate changes and wiggled further into his seat. He looked up, spied his flight prep attendant, and gave the thumbs up. Hoot was given the ready sign for start up. He checked to assure the engine exhaust ports were clear from personnel and started the two F-404 General Electric turbofan engines.

The flight officer hooked into the plane's intercom. "How's she feel, Colonel?"

"Both engines running smooth. Diagnostics...clear. Tactical...clear. Weapons...clear. Fire control, damage control, navigational, all appear operational. Baby's ready!"

"Roger, remember flight recorder is voice activated. All you have to do is talk into the helmet mic, and we'll have you recorded for posterity."

"I'd prefer you wouldn't put that quite so bluntly, Sergeant."

"Roger, Colonel. Sorry. Breaking off transmission. Give 'em hell!"

"That's a given." Hoot smiled and checked his communications radio. "Incirlik Tower, Widowmaker ready for takeoff."

"Roger, Widowmaker. Read you five by five. You're cleared for takeoff, Runway 13. Winds from 30 degress at 15 knots. We have takeoff confirmation of the KC-135 Stratotanker from Ankara. Refueling coordinates as indicated. You're scheduled for refueling at 0400 and 0600. Tanker assigned to station for thirty minutes. Good hunting."

"Roger, Tower. Widowmaker confirms. Time 0314." Hoot pushed the throttle forward until Baby eased out of the Hanger. He rolled to the runway threshold and rechecked his systems. Everything seemed in perfect order.

If you didn't know the plane was about to take off, you wouldn't have known it was sitting on the runway. The tower crew squinted to see the jet. Air Traffic Radar wasn't able to pick up an exact signature, but they knew it was there, sitting, waiting...waiting to begin a mission testing the capabilities of man and machine.

"Flaps full, all systems functional." Hoot checked the Heads Up Display and fixed his focus on the runway centerline. "Widowmaker, ready for takeoff."

"Widowmaker, cleared."

Hoot pushed the throttle slowly to full. The sleek black stilleto cut into the moonless Turkish night. One hundred and fifty knots rapidly reeled past the speed indicator on the left side of the Heads Up Display, or HUD, and Hoot eased back on the stick. The F-111 slipped into the sky. "Gear retracted." Hoot held a slow ascent until the airspeed crept to 300 knots. Then, he climbed to altitude leveling the jet at ten thousand feet. "Setting autopilot for rendevous with KC-135. Autopilot engaged. Instruments all operational. Tactical set up to pick up relay from E-3 AWAC on station fifty miles from the Iranian border. Airspeed, 450 knots. ETA Tanker, thirty-five minutes."

\* \* \*

Captain Joe Ewalt, a native Californian, had lifted the KC-135 Stratotanker off the runway in Ankara one hour previously. He was flying a lazy eight around the refueling coordinates for the past ten minutes. He took a look at his digital wristwatch. 0410. "Our boy's going to be late for his date if he doesn't show up soon." Joe pointed to his watch as he spoke to Lieutenant Jim Ferrell, his co-pilot. Joe triggered his intercom. "Freddy?"

Sgt. Frederick Peabody, refueling boom operator acknowledged. "Roger, Cap'n?"

"Freddy? Any sign of our hookup?"

"No sir, but it might help if somebody told me what I'm looking for."

"You know as much as I do. I'm where I'm supposed to be, when I'm supposed to be. That's all I can do. We're coming up on coordinates again. Take a hard look. He has to make it this time or he'll scrub."

Freddy strained his eyes into the darkness. "Nothing but black, Cap'n. Might as well have my head stuck in a bottle of ink."

"Jack, you have anything?"

Jack Spruance, radar operator, peered at his scope. "No sir, I picked up some weird activity to our stern about ten minutes ago, but I think it must be a moisture ladened cloud.

\* \* \*

The capabilities of the F-111 never ceased to amaze Hoot. He had been following the Tanker for two minutes. He was five hundred feet below its tail, and he had been matching the three hundred seventy five knot speed for the entire time. He looked at his on board digital clock..0411.24. "I better give Gasman a wakeup call."

Hoot activated his communications radio. "Widowmaker to Gasman. Hey, you guys going to fly around all day. I've got a hungry Baby down here. Drop me a nipple!"

\* \* \*

Jim Ferrell spilled his coffee as he jerked forward in his seat. "What the hell!"

Joe Ewalt smiled and switched to transmit. "Widowmaker, this is Gasman. Read you loud and clear. You shook us up a little. Where the hell are you?"

"I'm following your track at your six oclock low." Hoot smiled at the calm voice.

"Uh, we can hear you, Widowmaker, but we can't see you. Permission to use lights."

"Persmission granted." Hoot called up the refuel grid on the right hand CRT. By centering the middle crosshairs on the boom and matching airspeed, Hoot could assure easy hookup with the refueling boom.

"Hit the lights, Freddy. I don't know what's down there, but keep your power low. We don't want to blind him."

Freddy turned his location lights to fifty percent. "Holy, Shit! What the hell is that thing?"

"I was hoping you could tell us." Joe Ewalt maintained his speed and heading so refueling could commence.

"Whew! That's one good looking aircraft, Widowmaker. Boom extending. Pull on in."

"Roger, Gasman." Hoot eased the F-111 forward, centered the crosshairs, and Freddy flew the boom into the refuel receptacle. "I've got a green light, Gasman."

"That's a roger, Widowmaker. Starting transfer, Now!" After a few tense moments, the refueling operation was completed. "Break away confirmed, Widowmaker. You're free to navigate." Freddy retracted the boom and turned off the lights and video camera.

"Roger, Gasman. Don't forget our 0600 date. My Baby will need another feeding or she'll be upset." Hoot powered back, fell away from the tanker and slipped into the low altitude cloak of weather, land forms, and radiant heat.

"All right, Freddy. What the hell did we refuel? My radar didn't show a damned thing. For all I know, you pumped jet fuel into a bird." Jack Spruance continued to strain his eyes into the electronic abyss of his radar scope.

"I'd rather leave it to the tape, fellows. It was one strange bird."

"Okay, gentlemen, let's go home. At least the next crew will be able to see what's hooking up with them." Joe turned the tanker toward Ankara. His job was done. He looked forward to a good cup of coffee and seeing Freddy's mystery guest.

\* \* \*

Hoot checked his clock, 04:16:00. He called up the tactical map. The computer was receiving the information from the E-3. The AWAC's call sign was Ferret. "Flight level 400 feet. Ground avoidance doppler warning set at 100. Air speed 425 knots. Don't want to be late. I'm crossing the Iranian border…mark. Well fellows, we've just invaded a foreign country. Ferret reports launch of two Mig 29's from Tabriz. Heading 270 degrees, airspeed 550 knots. Looks like they're the early border watch. They should be no threat. Their nose radars will be opposite my track. Three hundred miles to Rasht. Time 04:25:00. ETA 05:15:00. I should hit the SAM site at Bandar-e Anzali five minutes before the choppers are in range. Can't spend any extra time over target, or it will be close."

## READY ROOM THREE, FLIGHT DECK LEVEL, U.S.S. CARL VINSON, FIFTY MILES EAST KUWAIT CITY, 25 DECEMBER 0330H

"Okay, gentlemen. Take your seats. We have a lot to cover." Frank Jacobs waited for the pilots and crews to quieten down. "I know you've got some tight stomachs, but listen up. There have been some flight assignment changes. All flights will launch simultaneously. All target hits are to be coordinated. Hit fast and get the hell out. We'll be hitting both military and non-military targets. There will, in all probability, be civilian losses on the part of the enemy. Those losses must be acceptable in your minds. Any hesitancy in carrying out orders could endanger the lives of your crew and your ship. If this presents a problem with any of you, speak now." Frank looked around the room at the expected absence of hands. "Very good. We'll hit targets along the coast and for distances fifty miles inland. You will be broken into the same two groups as previously briefed. Group callsigns will be—Covey One and Covey Two. First launch in thirty minutes. Any questions?" Again, no hands were shot into the air. "Jake, I want to see you and Kent immediately after the briefing."

They both acknowledged with nods of their heads.

"No questions? Okay, let's do it!"

The pilots filed out of the room as they would on any other day, but today was different, and they knew it. At least their stomachs knew it.

"Jake, you and Kent will fly CAP for Covey One. At least that's what we want every one to think. After you're launched, I'm sending the ready alert aircraft on your track. They'll join you before Covey One makes its run. As you cross the coast beyond Kharg Island, you are to enter the

Zagros Mountains and fly to the Northern Coast of Iran. Maintain a low profile to target, but once you've arrived, you'll fly cover for a Soviet Bear Bomber making a bombing run on Tehran. The Bear's call sign is Phantom. Here are your coordinates. It's imperative you arrive by 0500, because the Bear will penetrate Iranian airspace at that time. The Soviets aren't flying cover because they're afraid it will arouse suspicions. It seems the Russian's penetrate the northern coast of Iran frequently without any CAP. Your call sign for the hook up with the Russians will be Shadow One and Two. After the bomber makes its run, you'll be refueled by a KC-135 from Bitlis. After refueling, you'll proceed to Incirlik and then return to the Carrier. It's going to be hairy. That's why I've selected two of my best."

"Yes, sir!"

"Okay! Stay low to rendezvous, and good luck."

## BAKU, AZERBAIJAN S.S.R. 25 DECEMBER 0300H

The two JetRanger Gunships and two Huey slicks sat on the tarmac outside the Baku Airport Hanger where Taggat and Dimitri had held their reunion. The pilot of Huey number two, Saviour Two, was getting accquainted with his new ship. Fortunately, Dimitri had supplied supplemental transportation, because the original gunship was found to have a broken rotor shaft when it was off loaded from the Galaxy, and there hadn't been enough time to make appropriate repairs. Saviour One, Three, and Four were functioning normally. The Special Ops team was gathering in the hanger. All members had been supplied their weapons, nightvision goggles, and radios. When Taggat refused to stay in Baku, Arch reluctantly assigned him to one of the slicks. He was instructed on use of the M-60 .30 caliber machine gun and told to remain in his seat until the target was secured. Arch didn't want a civilian on this trip, but Taggat's determination to help with Steve's extraction convinced him otherwise.

The team was split into two groups. One would attack the troop quarters in force while the other freed the hostages. If the timing was right, it would work. Arch knew it would. He had no doubt!

"Okay, gather around." Arch looked into the twenty four eyes staring from the twelve camouflaged faces. The flush of anxiety was well hidden beneath the greasepaint. "Men, this is why we're here. I'm damned proud of each and every one of you. As you know, I'm not much for speeches, but I know you'll do the job. We've come a long way, and we're not going home empty handed. Right?"

"RIGHT!"

"Okay! Mount Up!"

They split into their respective groups and boarded the choppers. Each man knew his job. There were no thoughts of defeat, because each knew Arch didn't condone thoughts of failure.

Arch watched like a mother hen as the teams loaded. As the last men entered the choppers, the Soviet guard snapped a salute. Arch fired a return, looked around the aircraft, held his right hand into the air, and circled his index finger three times.

The pilots knew the signal. The gunships lifted off first, then the slicks. The four helicopters headed due south maintaining an altitude of 400 feet and an airspeed of 110 knots.

Arch strapped in next to Taggat and noticed Taggat's paleness. "ETA 0545, Taggat."

All Taggat could do was shake his head. He felt as if he were in the bowels of an angry cement mixer.

Arch took out a map and showed their route to Taggat, hoping he could suppress Taggat's fear for a few moments longer. "Our course will take us over the Caspian to this point." He showed Taggat a point just to the south of Baku. "We'll insert into Iran at Bandar-e Anzali. They have a SAM site there, so, if our early morning caller doesn't take care of it, we might have a short trip. When we hit the airfield, you keep that M-60 trained on the troop barracks and keep firing until I say stop. The gunships will prep the area with machine gun fire and rockets. We'll circle the airfield and come in from the south over the hanger. I'm putting this ship down in the door of that hanger. We're going to be on the ground one hundred and twenty seconds, MAX! You'll stay in this Huey. Do you understand?"

"You'll have no problem with me. I'm shaking so damned much, I'm not sure I can stand up."

"You'll do fine. Settle back and leave the driving to us." Arch looked over the pilot's instruments. "Saviour One to flock. Maintain present heading and speed. Remember, our rendezvous and refuel point will be Lenkoran. If any of you are split from the group, make it to Lenkoran. We'll return to Baku from there."

## KHARG ISLAND, IRAN 25 DECEMBER 0415

"Okay, Lonewolf." Jake Tanner radioed Kent his instructions. "The Ready Alert fighters are on station. Break away and descend to five hundred feet on three. Three...Two...One...Break!"

Jake and Kent broke from the A-6 squadron and headed for the Iranian coast. They had topped their inboard tanks after launch and were carrying centerline drop tanks which they would eject once they had coupled with the Bear.

"Okay, Mookie, here we go. Hummer, Foxtrot One and Two are feet dry."

"Foxtrot Two, Foxtrot One, over."

"Roger, Foxtrot One." Kent keyed his mic, checked his instruments, and verified his arming switch was off.

"Okay, let's do what we're paid for."

The F-14's slid into Iranian airspace and stalked their way along the valleys of the Zagros Mountains. They darted from the last cover of the peaks north of Shareza and slithered across the southern flats of the Dasht-e Kavir desert. After avoiding the more populated areas to the north of their position, they headed for Tehran. They avoided radar stations using the new tac plan scope on the Tomcat. It brought up on the central CRT the terrain, the radar station, and types of radar in use, pulse or continuous doppler. Then, it would plot a proposed best route through the area to avoid recognition.

"Foxtrot Two, turn left to 280 degrees on my mark. Let's move West of Theran under cover of the Elburz Mountains. Exit North between Karaj and Qazvin. Prepare to execute turn…Now. Activate COM frequency with the IL-76 and see if we can pick up his downlink. What about it, Frosty?"

"I've got 'em, Cowboy. They show the Bears moving West from Krasnovodsk. One is breaking South for the coast. That'll be our Bear. Heading 035 for intercept. Bear heading 195 at fifteen thousand feet, airspeed 400 knots. ETA for intercept, three minutes. Got him, Mookie?"

"Copy that, Frosty."

"Okay, Foxtrot Two. Feet wet. Let's get altitude. Climbing to fifteen thousand for intercept." Jake 'Cowboy' Tanner pushed the throttle forward and eased the stick back for a gradual twenty degree climb."

The swept wings of the Tomcat moved back along its fuselage like a skier bringing his arms into his body for aerodynamic efficiency.

"Fifty miles to intercept, Lonewolf." Mookie tried to swallow, but the cotton in his mouth wouldn't budge.

"Roger, Mook. I've got it on forward camera. That's one big airplane."

"Decrease airspeed to 475 knots. We'll move in on their six." Jake had been carefully watching the Bear's intent since it appeared on camera. He didn't like working with the Russians since his entire training had dealt with destroying them.

\* \* \*

"Colonel Andrevi, I have the two American fighters in sight," Peter Minsk spoke into the intercom. "They have come along our right side, and are saluting me. What should I do?"

"Salute them back." Yuri Andrevi had been getting feed back from his radar officer. He knew the Tomcats were close, but their prompt appearance on his tail made him happy they were friendly. "Shadow One and Two, this is Phantom." Yuri smiled at his co-pilot. "I love these little names, don't you, Gregor?"

Gregor Isimovich smiled and nodded affirmatively.

"Roger, Phantom. We're at your service. You've got two angry Tomcats at your nine o'clock, and they're ready to prowl."

"Very good. Expect activity when we break thrity kilometers of the coast. Our probing flights are usually challenged at that point. Your air challenges should be along the corridors from Tehran, Rey, or Tarish."

"Roger, Phantom. We'll climb to twenty thousand so we can get a jump on any one coming our way. Good hunting." Jake checked his fuel. Main tanks full, drop tanks empty. "Dropping tanks. Climb to twenty thousand on my lead." Jake looked over at the diminutive figure in the tail gunner position of the Bear, and fired a second salute. This time it was answered. Jake dropped his accessory tanks and pushed the throttle forward.

Kent followed Jake's lead, and they raced past the nose of the Bear into the dim glow of a Christmas dawn. Kent pulled back on the stick until an altitude of twenty thousand feet was obtained. He followed Jake through a wide right turn until they came back to the same track of the Bear. They regained visual on the Bear, but remained above and behind his track. Kent checked his stores: four Sidewinder All Aspect Heat seeking air to air missiles and two AMRAAMS, medium range radar guidance air to air missiles.

"Shadow One and Two, this is Sable. We've got two bogies. Heading 355, Angels Ten, One hundred miles, Eight hundred knots closure."

"Roger, Sable." 'Frosty' Williams, Jake Tanner's RIO, confirmed transmission to the IL-76 early warning radar plane and glued his eyeballs on the scope. "Cowboy, vector 195 for the bogies."

"That's a Roger, Frosty. Breaking right for the bogies. Ok, Lonewolf let's get them quick."

\* \* \*

As the Tupelov-95 Bear Bomber flew on into the pink glow of dawn, Colonel Andrevi knew he was at the mercy of two American fighter pilots and the hopeful lack of attention of the Iranian SAM operators. "Seventy five miles to target. Let's acitvate our jammers and prepare to dispense decoys." Yuri tightened his muscles into the harness, closed his eyes, and said a brief prayer.

\* \* \*

"I've got them, Kent. I've got them. They're at ten thousand feet, 400 knots, and heading 045 for the Bear." Mookie kept his eye on the radar screen as he plotted the intercept. "They're running some kind of search pattern. I think they are treating this like an exercise."

"Okay, Lonewolf. Let's take them while they're not looking. We'll pass them high and hot, go inverted, and come up on their six. Be ready to fire as soon as your radar has locked. What about it, Frosty."

"They still haven't made us, Cowboy. There's no time like the present."

Jake pushed the throttle to full military power, and the F-14 streaked over the track of the Migs. When radar downlink from Sable showed them one mile beyond target, Jake went inverted, pulled back on the throttle, and hit his speed brake. He eased back on the stick nosing the F-14 toward the ground. As the F-14 rolled back to level flight, Jake retracted the brake and pushed forward on the throttle. Now, he was on the same track as the Mig, but three miles behind his unsuspecting target. Jake activated the Hughes targeting radar. Immediately the information hit his Heads Up Display, and the missile lock tone sounded in his headset. "Keep your eye on that trailer, Kent. I've got missile lock on the lead." The diamond pipper enlarged to fill the targeting box. "Firing...NOW!"

As the solid fuel AMRAAM missile ignited, night turned to day and suddenly back to night again. The missile tracked perfectly and the Mig began jinking, trying to get away from the deadly phantom emerging from no where. However, it was too late. The missile found its mark and obliterated the entire tail section of the Mig. The remaining front segment spiraled toward Earth.

"Chute at three o'clock low."

"Roger." Jake checked his three o'clock and saw the billowing chute swaying back and forth to the ground. "He can't blow a Bear away with a parachute. Where's that trailer?"

"I've got him," Kent promptly called out. "He ducked behind the hill at our ten o'clock. Breaking left, now. I'm it."

"I'm at your four o'clock low. Go get him." Jake pulled comfortably close to Kent's right wing and followed his lead.

"Okay...okay...I've still got him." Kent kept the Mig 21 in his HUD, armed a Sidewinder, and headed for the deck. He rolled the F-14 inverted and pulled the nose to the Mig keeping lag pursuit on the bandit. When he reached the same altitude as the Mig, Kent rolled back to level flight. He maintained fifty knots closure and aimed the nose of his Tomcat at a point just behind the tail of the Mig 21. As the ranging bar on the right of his HUD began to descend, the arming pipper tracked the target with its intermittent tone perking in Kent's headset. Kent pulled the nose of the Tomcat in front of the Mig and eased forward on the throttle. As he and Mookie pulled a two and one-half G turn into the MIG, the pipper hit its mark. "Missile lock...Firing!"

The Sidewinder ignited and blistered a path to the exhaust of the MIG. The MIG driver anticipated the shot, dropped a flare and pulled up immediately. The Sidewinder shot through the flare and exploded into a faraway hillside.

"Shit...A miss!" Kent saw the MIG driver heading for altitude possibly to gain the advantage. "Oh, no you don't." Kent pushed the throttle to full and into first stage of afterburner. "Hold on, Mook. We're going supersonic."

The MIG 21 rolled inverted and pulled back to the deck.

"Kent, he's headed back to the deck. I just saw him flip inverted and pull his nose down."

"Hold on and grunt hard." Kent rolled inverted, pulled back on the throttle, hit the speed brake, and pulled the nose over. As soon as he rolled back to a canopy up power descent, he armed the second Sidewinder. The computer picked up the target. The Mig made a hard right turn and started back up. "Mook, that silly bastard is pulling up into our track. Switching to guns..." As Kent marveled at his good luck, the MIG headed for an intersect of their tracks only one thousand yards out. The target circle revealing the supposed impact of the Vulcan's 20 mm projectiles crossed the nose of the MIG as Kent touched the trigger. The six thousand round per minute cannon spewed two hundred rounds of white hot metal in the direction of the MIG, and in a flash of silent white light, the left wing blew off the MIG's fuselage. Kent pulled hard left to avoid the debris.

"Good kill, good kill! Damn, that was a sweet move." Jake fidgeted in his seat looking for more targets.

"If you two are quite finished, I suggest we get back on station." Frosty Williams calmly keyed the mic and spoke as he watched the silhouettes in his scope.

"Right," Kent and Jake calmly replied, regrouped their thoughts, and shut off their targeting radars.

"Vector 095 for the Bear. Altitude eight thousand feet, speed four hundred.... Holy Shit! What is all that?" Frosty William's scope lit up with multiple white dots in the vicinity of the Bear Bomber."

"Frosty, that must be the decoy weapon Intelligence suspected Ivan of having. I've never seen anything like this before." Mookie watched in disbelief.

"Give me a best fix on the Bear's last position, Mook. I don't give a tin-ker's damn about any of that trash." Kent disregarded the clutter on his screen.

"Okay, Lonewolf. Vector 095. Fifty miles."

## 200 MILES WEST OF RASHT, IRAN; FLIGHT LEVEL 400 FT., 0450H, 25 DECEMBER

"Two hundred miles to target. ETA Rasht...20 minutes. I've switched tac-tical computer to receive downlink from Sable. Two MIG 21's have been splashed by fighter cover coming in with the Bear. Now, I know why I was kept out of Tehran. Thank you, Clint."

Hoot kept the F-111 hugging the terrain. His electromagnetic emit-tance would remain low until he dashed to Rasht. "Well, this should keep some heat off the Bear. I've cleared the mountains. Fifty miles to Rasht. I might wake up a few folks on the coast, now." Hoot slowed the F-111 to four hundred knots. The Mavericks had to have time to arm, once they were fired, so Hoot eased the F-111 above five hundred feet. Now, he became visible to ground radar units. "Coming up on Rasht! Hot Damn, the lazy bastards don't have the radar unit on. Fish in a bar-rel...Forward Looking Infrared Camera of the Maverick scanning target. I've locked the Maverick onto the SAM radar dish. I'm in range...open-ing bay doors...firing. Maverick away...closing bay doors. Maverick run-ning hot and true. Taking Baby to one thousand feet...arming Durandals...rolling inverted and back to level flight...targeting runway intersection ...steady...opening bay doors...dropping Durandals... switching to rear cameras. Durandals have now ignited and just slammed into the runway. Damn...Concrete is flying every where. Hope everyone had their heads down...well at least the important everyones. The radar dish just blew into a million pieces. Maverick hit its mark. Hey, these fel-lows have some aircraft. There's a Mirage, a civilian plane, and a SeaCobra on the tarmac. That Mirage could catch my butt, but quick."

Hoot gained altitude to 2000 feet, pulled a hard right turn, and came back over the airfield from the west. He armed his Vulcan and straffed the tarmac across the Mirage's and Lear's location. As the 20 mm projectiles cut through the bodies of both planes, the partially filled tanks of the Mirage erupted and demolished the aircraft sending flying debris through an adjacent building. Hoot pushed the throttle to max, performed a wide turn, and came back across the tarmac spitting the Vulcan at the SeaCobra ending its useful existence. "Well, they won't follow me out of here. Next stop, Bandar-e Anzali."

He quickly dropped the F-111 back to 500 feet, but the pulse radar of the SAM station in Bandar-e Anzali had his signature. Hoot's defense screen lit up with an indication for a radar guided missile launch. Hoot released a decoy, jinked left, dropped to 200 hundred feet, and activated his forward targeting camera. The SAM passed behind the F-111 and exploded in the decoy's proximity. The radar dish at Bandar-e Anzali locked into range of the Maverick. "Coming to five hundred feet...opening bay doors...pickling target...firing...Closing bay doors." The Maverick ran true to target, and the radar dish disintegrated into a collective heap of scrap metal. "I'm out of here. Mission accomplished." Hoot pushed the throttle to max, dropped to two hundred feet, and headed for the mountains.

"Widowmaker, this is Sable. We have a launch of two MIG-29's from Tabriz. Heading 270, 600 knots."

Hoot checked his tactical display. "Okay, Sable. I've got them. They're heading for the border hoping to hop me as I cross, but they don't know what they're looking for." Hoot adjusted course and lagged behind the Migs. "Hell! I might as well let them run interference for me." The Migs slowed to five hundred knots and remained on a 270 degree heading. The F-111 followed behind and below their path. As the Migs headed across Lake Urmia, they broke right to a heading of 010 degrees. They remained on that heading for a moment, then turned back to a heading of 090 degrees hoping to pick up the perpetrator of the raid on Rasht and

Bandar-e Anzali before he or they crossed the border. As they turned to the 090 heading, Hoot slid Baby behind their radar track and across the border into Turkey. He reset his NAV computer for his refueling rendezvous. "Okay, men. I've softened them up. Go get 'em."

## BANDAR-E ANZALI, IRAN, 0510H, 25 DECEMBER

"Damn, I thought we were going to take on that SAM site without help." Arch McConnell watched the explosion of the radar site with relief. The four helicopters passed two miles West of the site one hundred feet off the deck making a bee line for the Rasht complex. "Saviour One to Saviour Three and Four. Break off and head on in. Soften them up. We'll be hot on your tail. After you hit the troop complex and pilot ready area, concentrate your fire on the tarmac, but keep the area in front of the hostage hanger clear. Understood?"

"Loud and clear, Sir. Saviour Three, out."

"Understood! Saviour Four, out."

"Okay! Now, what the hell you waiting for, a goddamned invitation from the Iranians?" Arch barked into the mic.

The two JetRanger gunships raced ahead of the Hueys toward their target remaining fifty feet off the deck.

"All right, team. Prepare to disembark. Lock and load." Arch's face assumed rock hardness. He was ready. His team was ready. "Showtime!"

The Gunships approached from the North. The pilots had rehearsed this scene until they could do it in their sleep. As they closed to target, they increased altitude to two hundred feet. Saviour Three targeted the troop complex while Saviour Four zeroed in on the pilot ready area.

Simultaneously, they began firing the flare fin rockets. Each helicopter was equipped with two-twenty rocket cannisters, and both choppers delivered their full payload. Then they crisscrossed the area with the death chatter of their .30 caliber chain guns.

"Saviour Three to Saviour One. Target prepped. Green Smoke dropped in landing zone."

"Roger, Saviour Three. Watch our ass. We don't want to be downed by any friendly fire." Arch signaled to the pilot. "Go! Go! Go!"

## HANGER COMPLEX, RASHT, IRAN...0510H, 25 DECEMBER

Steve was shaken from his thoughts of escape by the explosion and shattering of the hanger as football size pieces of concrete were hurled through the tin walls. He jumped from his bunk and looked around. "What the hell!"

The door from the troop complex flew opened, and Yakim raced across the floor. "Get up, get up! We must move you Saudi dogs." Yakim turned his weapon toward Steve. "American, it's time to die." Yakim raced toward Steve's cell. The AK-47 was leveled toward the center of Steve's cage. As Yakim approached the cell, he looked quickly down to assure a live round was chambered, but as he looked up the second explosion hit. The front of the hanger was showered with flying debris from the explosion of the radar unit causing Yakim to briefly look in that direction. When he looked back toward Steve's cell, he was surprised to see the cell door open. Yakim attempted to stop, but Steve had stepped forward to meet him, grabbed the muzzle of the AK-47 and lifted his knee into Yakim's groin. Yakim fell to the floor in a writhing clump.

Steve relieved Yakim of the AK-47, turned the muzzle in the direction of the fallen Iranian, and, at point blank range, pumped five rounds of .30 caliber ammunition into Yakim's chest. "Hope that didn't hurt your pride, you son-of-a-bitch!" Steve removed and slung Yakim's ammo bandolier, grabbed the cell keys from the dead body, and opened the other cells. "Jof, keep your group here. I'll try to find us a way out."

Steve looked outside the hanger. The concrete powder and smoke from the explosion on the runway had the air thick. He unslung the weapon and switched to full automatic. He checked the clip, and it appeared full save the five spent on Yakim. As he looked up, three Iranians rounded the corner of the hanger. They didn't know what hit them as Steve emptied the clip across their unsuspecting bodies. All three fell dead in their tracks. "Get their weapons and keep the other Iranians out of here."

Steve sprinted low to the ground across the tarmac. He didn't look up, but as he crossed, he heard the high pitched sound of a jet engine. As he dove through the door of the ready area, a giant ball of flame erupted behind him accompanied by a loud explosion. Half the room was in shambles, and, when Steve looked outside, he saw his only means of escape going up in smoke. The Mirage and the Lear were gone! He quickly looked to the helicopter. The SeaCobra appeared functional. "I'll have to learn to fly that egg beater real…." Before he could finish his thought, the SeaCobra burst into a ball of flame. "What the hell is going on!?" As he heard another high pitched whine, he caught movement out of the corner of his right eye. The door to the locker room opened. Steve leveled the AK-47 at the upper half of the door. The person coming through the door didn't appear friendly, so Steve placed two rounds from the rifle into the gapping mouth of the surprised Iranian. It wasn't until he went over to the body that he recognized Yassar.

"Getting ready for a little night flight, were we? Well, neither of us is flying out of here."

Steve walked to the door to survey the damage. He looked up into the fire lit sky. "You're one good shot who ever you are." A shadow filtered across the wall to Steve's left. He immediately dropped to his knees and aimed the rifle in that direction.

"Steve Hardesty, it's me." Tallia crouched low and entered the gaping hole where a door once existed. "What's happen…" Tallia saw Yassar's body. "Is he dead?"

"As four o'clock."

Tallia looked at Steve in bewilderment.

"Yes, he's quite dead."

Tallia walked over to the body. She leaned over and withdrew Yassar's 9mm Beretta from its holster. She stepped back from the body and shot Yassar's head with three rounds from the Beretta. She then spat on its near unrecognizable face. "Rot in hell, you bastard!" She looked back at Steve. "I guess we're stuck here, afterall."

Steve was amazed by Tallia's calmness. "Let's try to get back to the hanger. We'll stand a better chance in there." Steve squinted across the tarmac. It was becoming difficult to see with the burning wreckage of the aircraft generating thick black smoke. "Let's try and make a break back to the hanger, now." Steve started to bolt for the hanger when he spotted two men running for the building. He quickly unslung his weapon and brought it to his shoulder.

CRACK...CRACK...CRACK.... The sound of the Beretta reported above Steve's head. The running figures he had in his sights hit the ground. He looked up to see Tallia putting the weapon back on safe.

She smiled. "My father taught me to shoot."

"Well, he did a damned good job. I'm glad you're on my side." Steve tilted his head as a familiar sound resounded over the crackling of the fire. "No, it couldn't be," he thought. Yet, the sound was still there. "Come on, Tallia. If this is what I think it is, we have to get back to the hanger. NOW!" Steve grabbed Tallia's right hand with his left, and they sprinted across the tarmac. With twenty yards to go, the pilot ready room and troop quarters began receiving rocket fire from the helicopters. Steve and Tallia ran through the remnants of the hanger door as debris from the explosions filled the tarmac.

Steve waved the Arabs down and pulled Tallia to the floor of the hanger behind a mound of concrete and steel. "Everyone, stay down!" Steve headed for the door to see if he could identify any markings on the helicopters. He noticed Tallia had followed him to the door. "Tallia, get back behind the concrete. I don't know who these people are, and, until we do, you have to stay behind some cover."

"No, Steve! If I'm to die, I will die fighting beside you." Tallia looked into Steve's eyes. She felt safe beside Steve—secure, warm, needed. She knew she could rely on him, and he could rely on her.

Steve quickly looked outside the hanger, but he couldn't identify any markings through the smoke. He heard the chain guns chatter. "Dammit, Tallia! Don't give me any trouble. Not now!" Steve turned and saw the determination in Tallia's face. He knew she would stay with him regardless of what he said. "Okay, I don't have time to argue." Together, they ducked behind a pile of concrete fragments and watched as the JetRangers make mincemeat of the compound. The .30 caliber machine guns made short work of keeping the tarmac devoid of any living personnel. The gunship made a run past the hanger door at low level, stopped, hovered, pointed its nose toward the hanger, and hung in mid air while a small cannister fell from the door and began emanating green smoke. The smoke swirled until the gunship pulled away. The JetRangers continued to perform low passing circles of the distant remains of the pilot-ready area, frequent bursts of automatic fire resounding from their weapons.

Steve began to relax as the automatic fire slackened, but his stomach muscles tensed as he heard a familiar sound. At first it was faint and barely distinguishable, then the characteristic whump, whump of a Huey slick crossed the roof of the hanger. Steve could feel the vibration from the blades as the chopper passed above them. As he looked back through the door, two Hueys sat down on the tarmac. The door gunners began peppering the surrounding buildings with their machine guns as ten black clad men carrying automatic weapons dispersed from the bays. Steve knew their job had been rehearsed by the efficiency of their actions. "Drop your weapons," Steve yelled. "Don't let them mistake you for Iranians."

Six members of the Special Ops team rushed into the hanger. Four systematically searched through the hanger while two approached the group. One of the two flipped up his black sleeve exposing an emblem of the American flag.

"Hot damn! I'm glad to see you guys." Steve jumped from behind the concrete and waved for the group of hostages to gather. "This is all of us. Everyone else is the enemy. Let's get the hell out of here."

Tallia jumped up from her hiding place, grabbed Steve, and kissed him. "I'm ready to leave. I'm so happy."

Arch McConnell walked over to the group. "Good to see you have things under control, Captain. I'm Captain McConnell, Special Ops. Everything all right?"

"Is now!"

"Who's the good looking lady?"

Steve pulled Tallia closer. "She's a Russian national who has been held hostage for the past seven months. If it weren't for her, we would all be dead. I told her she could go with us if we got out of this mess."

Tallia tensed.

Steve gave her a reassuring squeeze.

Arch looked around at the hostage group. "That's no problem, Captain. Let's saddle up. There's someone in the chopper wanting to see you." Arch activated his shoulder mounted radio. "Okay, mop it up and move back to the choppers. All the chicks are A-OK. LET'S MOVE OUT!"

Steve and Tallia walked to the chopper. Steve assisted Tallia into a spot and sat down beside her. He looked at the back of the man still firing the machine gun into the troop hanger. "Hey..Hey…. HEY! You can stop shooting. It's over!" Steve noticed the gunner couldn't speak. Steve stood up and walked beside the man still shooting the weapon. "Taggat! What the hell are you doing here?"

"Shooting this goddamned machine gun. What the hell does it look like?"

"You can stop. It's over." Steve grinned.

"I can't stop. My hands won't let go! Too damned scared to quit."

Steve helped Taggat ease his grip on the trigger. The gun stopped firing, and Taggat turned to Steve. He put his arms around Steve's shoulders and hugged him tightly. A tear formed in his right eye. He pulled away, sniffed, and dried the tear on the cuff of his shirt. "It's sure good to see you, Steve." Taggat shook Steve by the shoulders. "Especially in one piece."

Steve smiled. "Glad you could make it. Now, what the hell are you doing here?"

"They couldn't get along without me."

"You know I'm pissed at you, but right now all I care about is getting the hell out of here. Taggat, how's Sabrina? I'm dying to find out about her and the baby."

Tallia jerked her head in Steve's direction. "Baby? Who's having a baby?" Her thoughts began to race.

Taggat looked at the floor, thought for a moment, and looked up at Steve. "The last time I saw Sabrina she was fine. The baby seemed to be doing well, but that's all I know. Hopefully, we'll make contact once we get back to Turkey. Until then, that's all I can tell you."

"That's better than nothing. I guess I'll have to wait."

Taggat grinned. "Damn! It's good to see you." Taggat hugged Steve, and their past differences melted.

Four members of the team and Arch jumped into the helicopter. Arch picked up the mic. "All Saviours, all Saviours. Circle up and head home. Out!"

Steve sat down next to Tallia, put his arm around her shoulders, and pulled her close to his side.

Tallia looked at Steve and smiled. "You said you were going to give me my first plane ride." She closed her eyes and leaned against Steve's shoulder. A smile returned to her face.

## 15000 FEET OVER TEHRAN, IRAN. 0545 25 DECEMBER

"Okay, Anatol. It's your airplane." Colonel Andrevi released control of the Bear to his bombardier.

Anatol Yakov took control via the bombsight. Through the lens of the bombsight, he centered the crosshairs on a cluster of fuel storage tanks on the northern side of Tehran. As he released half his bombload, the Bear raised slightly in the sky. "Bombs away." Anatol turned the sight and brought the Bear over an airport in the northeast section of the city. He released the remaining cannisters of destruction. "Bombs away. It's your airplane, Colonel."

Yuri turned the Bear north, gained altitude, and headed for the open water of the Caspian.

Anatol watched the bombs fall to target. Suddenly, the ground erupted with the red billowing mushrooms of destruction and death. The city appeared to light up before his eyes. Anatol grinned with his great accomplishment, and announced direct hits to the rest of the crew. They celebrated as they flew out over the Caspian not comprehending the quantity of sorrow, hardship, and life long incapacity they had delivered.

As the Bear passed fifty kilometers from the coast, Yuri activated the communication radio. "Thank you, American pilots, Shadow One and Two. Someday, I hope we meet where I can give you personal thanks."

Peter Minsk saluted with sincerity as the two Tomcats pulled away into the morning sky.

\* \* \*

"Kent, let's find that KC-135. I've got one thirsty Tomcat."

"Roger, Cowboy. Hey, Cowboy?"

"Roger, Lonewolf?"

"You're one hell of a wingman."

"That's a ditto, Lonewolf. That's a ditto."

"Hey, you arrogant sons of bitches. What about us?" Mookie yelled from his back seat.

"What do you think, Cowboy?" Kent smiled behind the oxygen mask.

"These two RIO's?" Jake grinned. "They're the best."

Kent laughed. "You've got that rig...." BEEEEEP BEEEEP BEEEEP The proximity klaxxon sounded in Kent's ear. Kent looked around quickly, popped two cannisters of chaff, and hit the throttle. "Jake, get the hell out of here. I'm in trouble!" Kent rolled the F-14 inverted and started to pull the nose over, but a sudden flash to his left ripped off the wingtip of the Tomcat. Kent felt a sudden searing pain in his left chest that took his breath away. "Mookie, you…al…right?"

"Yeah, Kent. What's happened? We've lost the port engine, and power is bleeding from the right."

"I'm..loos.ing h.er, Mo..ook. Eject..E.ject..E.j.ect"

"I'm not going without you, Kent."

"Dammit, Mook. Eject! I've got to hold her level so you can get out. I'll be right behind you."

Mookie pulled the canopy release, reached over his head and pulled the ejection rings. After he activated the ejection chair, he didn't remember anything until he was dangling beneath the orange and white chute floating down toward the cold waters of the Caspian.

Jake Tanner headed for the deck while Frosty radioed their position to the AWACS. He didn't know what had happened to Kent and Mookie, but he knew it wasn't good. Jake circled his Tomcat back to the point of last contact and spotted the flaming debris hit the water and explode. He and Frosty checked for chutes, but only identified one. He hung around until the chute hit the water, and the strobe began transmitting. Jake had to abort any further cover because his low fuel lights were blinking, and he didn't want to miss his hookup with the KC-135.

"What do you think, Frosty?"

"Shit, Cowboy. We've lost one of them. I don't know which one, but one went in with the plane."

"You're right, Ted. Let's get some fuel. We don't want to join them." Jake tried to shake the sudden empty feeling, and turned to business at hand, getting his plane and crew home safely.

# 23

After the brief introductions, John walked across the labor room floor, pulled a chair up beside Sabrina's bed, and sat down. Up close, he could sense Sabrina's labored breathing and some mild cyanosis of her lips and fingers. "The Nurse tells me today is your due date. Is that correct?" Before Sabrina answered, John turned to Maggie. "Start oxygen per nasal prongs...six liters per minute and have the lab come back to repeat her gases after she's been on 0-2 for thirty minutes." John turned to Sabrina. "This will help your breathing."

"I understand. Do what ever is best for my baby." Sabrina grimaced. "I believe this little girl thinks it's about time to come into the world."

"Little girl?"

"Yes, by ultrasound."

"Oh." John motioned for Maggie to come to the bedside. "I'm going to examine you, Sabrina. Let's see how far away we are from delivery." John put on a glove and instructed Sabrina to bring her legs up. "You're five centimeters dilated. The baby is head first and descending into the pelvis. Maggie, hand me an amnihook." John ruptured the membranes noting that the amniotic fluid was clear. He applied an internal heart monitor and an intrauterine pressure catheter to measure the quality of Sabrina's contractions. "Have you been seeing a doctor during this pregnancy?"

"Yes, Dr. Robert Vance. His office is in Norfolk. I have a copy of my records in my purse." Sabrina waved her hand toward the closet. "I believe the nurse put it in there."

Maggie retrieved Sabrina's purse and handed it to her.

Sabrina removed the copies of her record and handed it to John.

"How did you and Bob Vance get acquainted? MacKenzie Island is an hour from Norfolk."

"You might say fate brought us together. I was visiting a friend in New York. On the way home, I developed heart failure. My pilot made an emergency landing in Norfolk, and I was taken to Norfolk General. Dr. Vance and Dr. Tims took care of me while I was there. I've been seeing them since. I was on my way back to Norfolk tonight, but the baby didn't want to wait."

"Back? Where have you been? If you were my patient, you wouldn't have been traveling."

"I wasn't suppose to be, but I've been a bad girl. I had to go to Washington. Personal reasons. I started into labor, tried to make it home, but was afraid I couldn't make it. So, here I am."

"I'm glad you stopped." John turned to Maggie. "Ask Madarsk to come up. We need an epidural…Sabrina, I'm asking the anesthesiologist to administer an epidural anesthetic. It will alleviate the pain of the contractions and decrease some of the load on your heart."

"Sounds good to me. I'm ready for some relief."

Manjim Buxjani, the anesthesiologist, responded quickly to the labor hall. He had worked in Greene Memorial for three years. After training in England and working in a large northern medical center, Manjim enjoyed the pace of this small Virginia hospital. Even though his parents lived in

India, his family was settled into the "American" way of life. His desire to return to India had been canceled many times by his family's will to remain in the United States. Manjim stopped at the labor hall door and shook the sleep cobwebs from his brain. He enjoyed obstetrics, but some of the words coming from a laboring woman still shocked his formal English education. He pushed the door open and walked into the labor room. "Ah, good morning."

"Dr. Buxjani. I'm glad you're here." John stood and motioned for Manjim to walk closer to the bed. "Sabrina, this is Dr. Buxjani. He's the anesthesiologist I mentioned."

"Glad to see you. I understand you can help me with this malady called labor."

"Yes, yes. I'm so glad to see you have a good sense of humor. It always helps when I'm about to stick a needle into someone's back."

"Manjim, this is Sabrina MacKenzie. She prefers, Sabrina."

"So happy to meet you, Sabrina." He nodded their acquaintance as Sabrina fidgeted through another contraction. "The anesthetic I'm going to give you, Sabrina, is placed in the lower part of your back. The needle is used to guide a small catheter into the epidural space. It remains until we have no further use of anesthesia or analgesia. The medicine reduces your pain, and may make your legs weak, but they should not become paralyzed."

"What do I need to do?"

"I would like for you to roll to your left side, curl into a slight ball, and stick your back out as much as possible. I know you have a baby in there, but do the best you can. I will numb the area where I'm going to be inserting the catheter. Are you allergic to any medication?"

"None that I know."

John walked around to the opposite side of the bed. "Sabrina, why don't you lie over this way, and I'll ask you a few more questions while Dr. Buxjani is putting in the anesthetic." John helped Sabrina roll to her side and curl as requested.

"I'm cleaning a small area on your back with antiseptic." Manjim talked to Sabrina as if they were in a world of their own.

"Go ahead. I'm doing fine." Sabrina smiled at John. "Does he always enjoy his work?"

"Who, Manjim?…Always. He'll come anytime of day or night. I think there's the blood of an obstetrician in his veins."

Sabrina giggled.

"You must hold still. I'm preparing to place the catheter."

"Okay, sorry." Sabrina felt the prick and the tingle of medicine as the local anesthesia infiltrated her skin.

John noticed Sabrina wince, so he tried to divert her attention. "How long has it been since you were evaluated by your cardiologist?"

"It been quite some time, but I had a full evaluation three weeks ago at George Washington Hospital."

"Why George Washington?"

"It's a long story. I'd rather not get into it, but the doctor said my heart was doing as well as expected. She recommended induction at thirty eight weeks, but I couldn't at the time."

"You couldn't? Why not? It seems it would have been ideal."

"Well, let's say I was preoccupied. My Uncle had other plans for me."

"You're uncle? I didn't think you had any living relatives." John looked at Sabrina quizzically.

"I really can't talk about this any further. I've been requested not to discuss the circumstances of my visit in Washington."

"I'm inserting the needle into your back," Manjim continued his discourse. "You'll feel some pressure as the needle passes through the spinal ligaments." Manjim felt his way into the epidural space with the Toohey needle. He carefully watched as a small drop of saline he had placed on the luer tip of the needle was sucked into the barrel of the needle indicating proper placement. Then, he passed the curved tipped catheter into the needle directing it toward the base of Sabrina's spine. "I'm withdrawing the needle, now." He removed the needle from the site, slid it off the catheter, taped the catheter to Sabrina's back, and injected a test dose of the Fentanyl mixture. "I want you to tell me if you feel any relief from this medicine. If it works properly, I will place a constant infusion pump on the catheter."

"My last contraction was much better. Is that the way it should be?"

"Yes, yes. Very good. I will start the medication by infusion pump, now. The pump will keep the level of anesthesia constant. We'll observe your blood pressure very closely, and I'm going to place a device on your right index finger which will measure the amount of oxygen in your bloodstream." Manjim motioned for Maggie to apply the pulse oximeter.

"I feel as if I'm going to the moon. When do I get my next set of wires?" Sabrina asked hoping she had fulfilled her need for attachments.

"Right now!" Maggie smiled as she attached the EKG electrodes.

"This is the way to have a baby." Sabrina smiled at John. "I hope it doesn't sour our relationship, Dr. Chadwick, but I simply can't discuss my Washington trip."

"No, no! Don't worry. I'm a big boy."

"John, the catheter seems secure. I'm going into the lounge and read. Call me if you need anything."

"Thanks, Manjim."

Sabrina winked at Dr. Buxjani. "Yes, thank you very much."

John reexamined Sabrina's lungs. She was still exhibiting some congestion in the bases. "Maggie, let's put in a catheter and administer forty milligrams of Lasix intravenously. Sabrina, I'm going to have the nurse give you some medicine to help remove some of the excess fluid in your lungs. She's also going to put a catheter into your bladder. I don't think it will be uncomfortable because of the epidural."

Maggie inserted the catheter and gave the medication. She continued to monitor and record vital signs, IV fluid rates, rates of oxygen delivery, and readings of the fetal monitor. Things continued normally for a short while, but fifteen minutes after administration of the epidural, Maggie noticed the first late deceleration, a sign of deterioration of the fetal status. She rapidly called John's attention to the tracing.

John closely watched the monitor for the next fifteen minutes and clearly saw evidence of late decelerations with each contraction. "Maggie, let's do a scalp pH."

Maggie headed for the storage locker to retrieve the required equipment.

KNOCK..KNOCK..KNOCK..KNOCK A loud rap persisted on the door.

John looked up from his scrutiny of the fetal monitor. "Who the hell?" John looked rapidly at Sabrina. She was smiling. "Excuse me? I apologize for the slip of the tongue, but we're busy in here. Maggie! Take care of that, would you?"

Maggie opened the door and was confronted by Wanda Knight, the LPN working on the postpartum floor. "What is it, Wanda?"

"May I speak to you, Ms. Quince?"

Maggie stepped outside and shut the door. "What do you need. We're awfully busy."

"Ms. Quince, I..I..I don't know what to do with this person. I don't know what to tell her. I've told her no visitors are permitted in the labor hall without the doctor's permission, but she insists on coming back here and seeing her sister."

"Slow down, Wanda. Who are you talking about?"

Wanda took a deep breath and exhaled. "There's a woman outside the labor hall doors. She insists on seeing Ms. MacKenzie. She says she's her sister. I've tried to make her wait, but she's determined to get back here. I don't know what else to do."

"It's all right, Wanda. Have her come back, and I'll speak to her."

"Thank you!" Wanda left quickly. She held the labor hall door open and motioned for the visitor to enter.

Cathy strutted through the door. "Well, thank the Lord!" She walked to within inches of Maggie and looked her in the eye. "Are you the nurse I have to speak to in order to see my sister?"

"I am," Maggie backed away from Cathy.

"Well, where is she?" Cathy lifted her head and yelled over Maggie's shoulder. "Yoo Hoo, Sabrina. I'm here honey. Don't worry. Everything is going to be fine, now."

"You'll have to quieten down, Miss."

"That's Mrs. Winston, thank you! Why do I have to be quiet? Got some sickies back here, honey?"

"Mrs. Winston. Your sister is ill, and the doctor is with her at this moment. So I would appreciate it if you quieted down."

"Ill? How ill is she?" Cathy continued to keep her voice below yelling. She wanted Sabrina to hear.

"If you don't quieten down, I'll have to…"

Cathy gave Maggie a cold stare. "You'll have to what?"

Maggie stepped closer to Cathy. "I'll have Security pull your butt off this floor! That's exactly what I'll do. Understand?"

Cathy sized up Maggie's determination. She sensed her dedication, and she didn't want to keep the nurse from Sabrina's side any longer. Cathy stepped back and lowered her voice. "I would appreciate it if I could see Sabrina. I'm worried to death about her. I'm sorry I've come on strong, but it's because I'm concerned. Please accept my apology."

"Thank you. If you'll wait a moment, I'll check with the doctor and see if it's all right."

As Maggie turned to the labor hall door, John exited with a blood specimen in his hand. "Maggie, I'm going to run this pH, but I think we're going to have to do a section. The baby is continuing to show evidence of distress, and she's not deliverable."

"I'll get her ready…And, John?"

"Yes?"

"This is Sabrina's sister. May she see her for a moment."

"Fine, but I want her out of there before we start surgery." John turned and headed for the blood gas analyzer.

"Thank you, doctor." Cathy headed for the labor room door.

"Just a moment." Maggie handed Cathy a yellow disposable gown. "Put this over your clothing."

Cathy entered the room. She was shocked by the number of cables leading to and from Sabrina. She rushed to her side and took her hand. "What in heaven's name is going on? You look like an overstuffed pin cushion."

Sabrina smiled at Cathy. "It's okay, I'm in good hands. I'm glad you came in. I thought you might sleep through the delivery."

"The doctor said something about a C-section. What's happening?"

"The baby is having some problems. Dr. Chadwick just tested some of the baby's blood. If it shows the baby needs to come out right now, he will have to do a section."

"How in the hell did he do a blood test on the baby?"

"He stuck this god-awful thing into my vagina and took it out of the baby's head."

"Yuck! Did it hurt?"

"Nah! I'm not even embarrassed. Too late, now." Sabrina smiled.

John ran the specimen through the blood gas analyzer. The results displayed a brilliant red 7.14 on the pH meter. "Damn," he mutter as he headed for the Doctor's lounge. He knocked and opened the door. "Manjim, we're going to have to do a section. The baby's in a little trouble."

The sleepy eyed anesthesiologist looked up from his reading. "No problem. We'll use the same anesthetic. I'll have to boost the dose, but it should do fine."

"Good! Let's do it!" John walked into the labor room and looked at Maggie. "Prep her for a section." He turned to Sabrina. "Sabrina, I'm going to have to deliver your baby by section. The scalp blood sample indicated the baby might not be getting enough oxygen. We're moving you into the operating room right away. I'm afraid your sister will have to wait outside."

Sabrina grabbed for Cathy's arm. "No! Please, Dr. Chadwick. Let Cathy come into the operating room with me. I know I'll do much better if she's there."

"Okay, I don't have time to argue." John looked at Cathy. "If you feel yourself getting sick just sit down on the floor. We won't have time to fool with two patients in the OR."

"I'll be fine. Is the baby going to be all right?"

"We'll know for sure when we get her out. Okay, everyone. Let's go! Maggie, call the ER and tell Larry to come up to the OR…stat!"

"It's already done." Maggie attached the oxygen tank to Sabrina's mask, and, with Wanda's assistance, moved the bed into the O.R.

Sabrina, along with her monitors, was placed on the operating table, and Dr. Buxjani's masked face magically appeared up side down over her head.

"Sabrina, I'm placing some additional medicine into the catheter. We'll be ready to go in a moment."

Sabrina turned her head as Cathy came through the door. She was wearing a light green scrub suit, fluffy hat, and mask. Sabrina snickered. "Don't you look cosmopolitan?"

"Shut up! You're not exactly making a fashion statement."

"Sit down here." Manjim directed Cathy to the chair at the side of the head of the table.

"Hello, Ms. MacKenzie," A strange voice came from behind a masked individual that had entered the room. "I'm Dr. Goodenau, the pediatrician. I'm here to take care of your baby."

John walked in with his hands scrubbed.

"Tell me everything you're doing so I won't be afraid. Okay?" Sabrina anxiously asked as she watched Dr. Chadwick dry his hands.

"I will, Sabrina. Try to relax. I know it's difficult, but it's best for your baby." John donned his gown while looking to the head of the table. "Are we ready, Manjim?"

"Yes, she tests to T-4 after I gave her the boost."

"All right, Sabrina. I'm going to put a drape over your abdomen. It's big and sticky, but I don't think you'll feel it." John opened the 3-M Ioban drape, peeled the protective back from the iodine impregnated sticky operating field, and place it on Sabrina's abdomen. He unfolded the large upper and lower sheets and assured the circular opening was ready to catch the fluid and blood from the surgery. John leaned over the top of the drape and peered down at Sabrina's face. Her anxiety was increasing, but she appeared to be doing well with her breathing. "The drapes won't cover your face, but the screen will keep you from seeing the actual operation."

"That's fine with me. I don't want to see you cut me. I just want to see my baby."

"It won't take too long." John marked the incision site with a purple pen, looked at Madarsk, got the non-verbal nod to start, and made the incision. "Sabrina, I'm making the incision now. Do you feel anything?"

"No, I just feel a little pressure. Is that normal?"

"Yes, that's normal." John proceeded with the operation. "I'm through the skin and the subcutaneous fat. Now, I'm incising the fascia. That's the tough supporting layer outside the muscles. Now, I'm lifting the facia from the muscles. The buzzing you're hearing is the coagulation instrument. It stops bleeding. Now, I'm entering the abdominal cavity. I have to push the bladder down before I make the incision into the uterus. Still doing okay?"

"Still doing fine," Sabrina managed a reply. She held on tightly to Cathy's hand.

"Okay, Sabrina, we're about to have a baby."

"You mean it?" Tears came to Sabrina's eyes. "My baby is about to be born?" Sabrina looked at Cathy and squeezed her hand harder. "Cathy, I'm about to have my baby. I made it! Maybe those dreams were silly."

"I told you, Sabrina. I told you." Cathy peered over the drape and was confronted with a field of bright red and the head of a new born baby. "Oh, shit. What a mess!" Cathy quickly sat down and took some deep breaths.

"What's wrong, Cathy? Is there something…"

"No, Sabrina. Every thing is fine. Having babies is a messy business." John reassured Sabrina as he completed delivering the baby. "It's a girl, Sabrina. She has a lot of black hair." John suctioned the baby while the scrub nurse cross clamped and cut the cord. He lifted the crying baby over the draped barrier, showed her to Sabrina, and handed her to Larry.

"I've got her," Larry said as he accepted the baby and placed her in the warmer. He quickly dried her off, suctioned her mouth and nose, and checked her heart rate and respirations. "She looks good, Sabrina. She's small, but healthy."

Sabrina absorbed the sight of her baby. She couldn't believe she had delivered. She had completely divorced the idea of having the baby from her recent activities in Washington. Now, those days seemed like another life. Now, her sole responsibility lay in the warmer. "Please come back to me, Steve. I need you so." She thought as she continued to cry.

"Are you feeling okay, Sabrina?" Manjim looked down and dried Sabrina's eyes with a guaze.

"I'm perfect. I couldn't feel better." Sabrina glued her eyes to the pink person in the warmer.

Larry looked over from his exam of the baby. "We're going to take her to the nursery, Sabrina." He wrapped the baby in a warm blanket and carried her to Sabrina. "You can touch her. She won't break."

Sabrina released Cathy's hand and reached out to the baby. She touched her on the forehead and traced the outline of her nose and mouth. "You're so small Stephanie Kathleen."

Cathy's tears turned to sobs. "That's a beautiful name, Sabrina. When did you decide?"

"During our midnight ride. She had to be named for you and her daddy."

Larry looked at Cathy. "Why don't you go with us to the nursery. Then you can come back to the recovery room and tell Sabrina how much she weighs."

Cathy threw a questioning look to Sabrina. "Is that okay?"

"It's okay. I'm all right, but hurry back."

"We're about to finish," John interjected. "I'm closing the skin. We're going to watch you in the recovery room for a while, Sabrina. Dr. Buxjani will be leaving the catheter in your back for a few days. It will help alleviate your pain post op, and reduce the stress on your heart. The baby will be able to see you after Dr. Goodenau checks her over and is assured everything is all right."

"What time was she born?" Sabrina asked as she watched Cathy and Dr. Goodenau exit with the baby.

Maggie checked her records. "5:34 A. M., Sabrina. Merry Christmas."

"Thank you. Thank every one of you. This is the happiest day of my life." Sabrina continued to cry.

"Hold still, Sabrina. I'm having trouble hitting a moving target."

"I'm sorry." But Sabrina continued to choke on her tears.

John finished applying the skin clips, and helped Maggie and Manjim move Sabrina to a bed.

Sabrina was rolled to the recovery room. She seemed to have even more wires connected to her body. However, all the different beeps and tones didn't phase her. She had her girl. She was small, but she was here. She remembered Dr. Buxjani telling her she might get sleepy, and she heard Maggie say her baby weighed four pounds and ten ounces. Then she slept.

John completed the paper work, dictated the operative summary, leaned back in his chair, closed his eyes and relaxed. "What a day," he exclaimed as he exhaled slowly.

Maggie returned from giving report, quietly walked behind John, and started giving him a neck and shoulder massage.

"Oooo, that's nice," John sighed as he opened his eyes and looked into Maggie's. "You can stop in about two years."

"I thought we might continue at your place. I missed the party. Remember?"

"I remember. Maggie, I've been thinking. You've been chasing me for the past year, and I think it's about time we got married. What do you think?"

Maggie stopped the massage and slapped John on the shoulder. "Chasing you? mar...mar...married? Are you joking? And just what if I said yes?"

John shrugged his shoulders and smiled. "Dunno? Try it."

Maggie tilted her head and looked at John with a smile. "Ask me again, and I might."

"Margaret Quince, will you make me the happiest man in the world, and marry me?" John again smiled.

"John Chadwick. You're a devil. Are you serious or is this another one of your pranks?"

"Excuse me a moment, Maggie. I have to go to the bathroom." John snickered, stood up, and headed for the lounge.

Maggie blocked the door. "Not so fast. You didn't answer me."

John lifted Maggie by the shoulders and sat her to the side. "My bladder's about to pop, Maggie. You're the one procrastinating. What else can I say?" John ducked into the lounge. He changed his clothes, opened the door, and walked into the hall. Maggie was still dressed in her scrubs and waiting.

"Yes, John. I'll marry you. Now. What do you say to that?"

John reached out with his left hand and grabbed Maggie's left hand as he slipped his right hand into his right pant pocket. As he slid the two carat diamond ring onto Maggie's fourth finger, he looked into her eyes. "I'm glad we've settled the question. I love you, Margaret Quince."

Maggie's knees buckled as she looked at the ring. "You mean you meant it? We're...we're engaged?"

John pulled her close, kissed her, and looked into her misty eyes. "Most definitely!"

Maggie continued to feel the ring as she looked at John. "Let's go home? I have some celebrating to do."

"They didn't leave much food."

"We won't need it." Maggie winked, gave John a kiss, and headed for the locker room.

John went back into the recovery room and walked over to Sabrina. She was still dozing. He listened to her heart and lungs. Her heart was beating regularly, and her lungs were clear. He checked out with the Recovery

Nurses and headed to the labor hall. Maggie was standing in the hall holding her left hand with her right when he arrived.

"When I came out, and you were gone, I thought I had dreamed this."

John embraced her. "It's no dream, Maggie. I want you to be my wife.
More than I've wanted anything else in my life. That ring has burned a
hole in my pocket for the past month. Last night at the party I knew I
had to give it to you today. I need you Margaret Quine. I need you to be
my wife."

Maggie kissed John's earlobe and whispered, "How fast can we get home?"

# 24

Brian had agreed to go along with Taggat's fabrication of Sabrina miscarrying the pregnancy because it would absolve Kent of any connection with the baby. Hopefully, Beth would be appeased, and when divorce proceedings began, she would be less vindictive. As partial payment for Brian's involvement in the contrivance, Taggat had assured him he would be able to see and maintain contact with the child. However, Brian didn't completely trust Taggat. So, he decided to take out a little insurance. In order to see the baby, Brian knew he mustn't loose contact with Sabrina. After leaving Taggat's office on the day they completed their discussions, Brian firmed up his employment of a private investigator to observe Cathy and Sabrina until the baby was born.

As Brian eased his 560 SEC Mercedes alongside the Navy blue Ford in the parking lot of Greene Memorial Hospital, he knew he had done the right thing. He waited, and in a few moments, a brown cashmere cloaked, gray hair, middle aged man opened the door and slid into the passenger's seat.

"Afternoon, Mr. Pooley. The party you've waited so long to see is in the nursery of this hospital." The man's porcelain capped front teeth gleamed in the eerie glow of the afternoon sun as it filtered through the car's tinted windows.

"Thank you, Mr. Phelps. You've done an excellent job, as usual." Brian handed the gentleman a signed check. "I believe this fulfills our agreement. I'll take it from here."

Gregory Phelps folded the check, tucked it into his inside coat pocket, and handed Brian a sheet of information on the birth of Stephanie Kathleen. "Thank you, Mr. Pooley. If I can be of further assistance, please don't hesitate to call."

"I have your number," Brian quickly responded as he patted the car's telephone.

Greg Phelps opened the door and exited the Mercedes. He slid back into his Ford, started the engine, and pulled off into the red afternoon sky. "Easiest ten grand I've ever made," he said to himself as he patted the folded piece of paper just placed in his pocket.

Brian eased back into his seat, and wrapped the blue wool topcoat tightly around his middle. "Better wait a few hours before I see Sabrina. I don't want to seem too anxious." Brian closed his eyes and thought of his next move. He needed to be part of Sabrina's life in order to have contact with the child. Without Steve, it would have been simple. However, with Steve as part of the picture, Brian needed something or someone else to wedge him into Sabrina's daily thoughts. He needed Cathy.

From the detective's reports, Brian knew about Cathy's recent Washington confrontation with her doctor-lover. Maybe he could capitalize on their tiff, but he had to be careful. Careful, because he had all ready become infatuated with Cathy's beauty. He mustn't, if possible, let his feelings overshadow his ultimate goal. His mind continued to click among the various possibilities as the sun peeked from behind a large cloud and filled the parking lot with its warming rays.

\* \* \*

"See, Cathy. She has ten fingers and ten toes…just like she's supposed to. Dr. Goodenau said she was normal in every way…small, but normal." Sabrina's eyes were focused on the baby as she spoke to an interested but distant Cathy. "What do you think she'll be when she grows up?"

"Rotten! That little girl doesn't stand a chance. With you and Steve spoiling her, and me giving her what you don't, she just doesn't have a chance."

"What do you mean? I thought you were headed for England." Sabrina didn't look at Cathy as she spoke because she knew her anxiety over Cathy's potential departure would show.

"Nah. Those plans have changed…permanently." Cathy flipped her response with no emotion as she walked closer to Sabrina and the baby.

"What happened? I thought you and Richard were about to take the plunge."

Cathy lightly touched Stephanie's nose and mouth. "We had potential, but Richard turned out to be such a wimp. His priorities are all screwed up."

"Don't you think that's something you two could resolve?"

"No!" Cathy's voice was stern. She calmed down before continuing. "What happened, has happened for the best. Let's let bygones be bygones." Cathy tickled the baby's abdomen. "You know? She is precious. Maybe I'll have one just like her some day."

"I'm sure you will. Someday you'll find the right man, and everything will fall into place." Sabrina knew Cathy was troubled, deeper than she showed. But she also knew to stay clear of Cathy's emotions when she was told to do so.

"I appreciate your wishes, Sabrina, but I've given up on men. They're all a bunch of pubescent teenagers with their minds in their shorts. I'm going to look for an older man, someone who can give me what I want."

Cathy stood and walked to the window. The midday sun was yielding to a low group of gray clouds marching in from the northwest.

"And what is it Cathy Winston wants?" Sabrina stopped in mid Pamper change.

Cathy turned from the window and faced Sabrina. "From now on, my relationship with a man will revolve around what I can get out of it. Love, sex, nor desire will enter the picture." Cathy clenched her right fist. "I want power, Sabrina. The power only money can buy." Cathy pointed her finger at Sabrina. "Not the money I have, but the kind of money you or the Pooley's have. That's power. If I had that, we wouldn't have gone through all this past difficulty. If I had that power, I would be dangerous."

"Careful, Cathy. Sometimes we get what we wish for, and remember, power breeds contempt. Besides, I don't like to hear you talk like that. Sometimes I think I don't know you when you rattle on like this."

"I mean it, Sabrina. I'm fed up with my choices in men so far. Why keep tormenting myself?"

"I don't have your answer, but money isn't the solution. Money can create powerful people, but only for those who know how to use it. People must respect you before you're powerful."

"Or fear you!"

"That's true, but fear leads to enemies, and you…we need all the friends we can get."

"Hell, Sabrina. If I had the power, I wouldn't need friends. All I need is you. Don't you see? I'd do anything in the world for you because I know you would do the same. We have the relationship I'm searching for."

Sabrina put the baby in the basinette, walked over to Cathy, and held her hands. "Cathy, I don't want to sound like a mother, but I seem to qualify, now. What you want is not attainable with a man. Our relationship has been molded over the past ten years. We've fussed, cussed, cried, and celebrated over each other's ups and downs, and we have a beautiful friendship. But it's taken those ten years to get to where we are. You're not going to do that in six months, a year, or even two years with a man. It takes time!"

"Why? You've done it with Steve."

"No I haven't. Not yet. I love Steve, and I know we'll have our bad times." Sabrina looked over at her baby. "Perhaps sooner that I want to think."

"Then why do you want to get married? If Steve can't give you the same devotion I give you, how can you love him?"

"You know how!" Sabrina smiled and winked.

"Oh no! You're not getting off that easily. You're brain isn't in your pants. I know you too well."

"You're right. That's not the only reason. Steve makes me feel good about myself. He makes me feel warm inside. He gives, I take. I give, he takes. It's a two way street. It will take us years to get to where you and I are, but he's the only man I want. Keep searching for that man, Cathy. You'll never be sorry."

"I'll take your points into consideration." Cathy smiled. "You do sound like a mother. Does giving birth affect your brain?"

Sabrina laughed. "No. At least I hope not."

A knock at the door caused both their heads to turn. The nursery nurse waddled her four-foot ten-inch frame through the door and across the floor to the basinette.

"Excuse me. I've come to get the baby. I hate to do it, but we wouldn't want this little darlin' to get cold." She gathered the basinette and headed out the door, but stopped midway through her exit. "By the way, honey. There's a very distinguished gentleman waiting to see you. He's good looking, too." The nurse winked. "I've had him wait until I got the baby. I'll show him in as I leave."

"Who in the world?" Sabrina questioned Cathy as the door closed. "No one knows where we are."

"I guess we'll know in a moment. I just hope he isn't with the government, whoever it is."

"You're crazy," Sabrina giggled while pinching the fleshy part of Cathy's upper arm.

Cathy's frown didn't change to a smile. "I'm serious." She looked at Sabrina who was still giggling. "Sabrina! Quit! I am serious."

The door opened a few inches, and a white handkerchief appeared. "Might an interested party come in for a visit?" Brian asked as he waved the cloth in surrender.

"My God," Sabrina quietly exclaimed as she grabbed Cathy's arm. "It's Brian Pooley. What should we do?"

"I guess we'll have him come in."

"Come in, Brian." Sabrina raised her voice.

The door opened, and in walked Brian. He was wearing a red Pendleton sport coat, white shirt, green tartan neck tie, and khaki slacks. "Merry Christmas, ladies. Sabrina, I've seen Stephanie, and she's beautiful." Brian walked to Sabrina and kissed her on the cheek. "She looks just like her Mother. Thank heavens!"

They laughed.

"No welcome for me?" Cathy queried.

Brian walked to Cathy and shook her hand with both of his. "Nice to see your beautiful face once again, Ms. Winston."

"Please call me, Cathy. How come she gets a kiss, and I only get a handshake?"

"Cause she had the baby." Brian looked at Sabrina. "You look pale, Sabrina. Aren't they feeding you?"

"Not yet. I just got out of bed. The baby had to be delivered by Cesarean."

"I'm sorry to hear that. I know you must have been frightened. You were all alone."

Cathy puffed. "I was with her."

Brian held up his hands in mock surrender and grinned. "No offense...No offense."

"None taken," Cathy quickly replied.

"Brian, how in the devil did you find us? No one knew I had stopped here to have the baby."

"Let's just say I'm fortunate to have friends in high places and leave it at that. Okay?"

"See what I told you, Sabrina." Cathy winked at Sabrina.

Sabrina discounted Cathy's remark and turned back to Brian. "Well, no matter how you found us, I'm glad you did."

Sabrina hugged Brian the best she could since she still had her I.V. in her left arm."

Cathy shrugged her shoulders. "You're always welcome, Brian, as long as you didn't bring any FBI or CIA agents with you."

Sabrina laughed.

Brian tried to act surprised, but he knew the reason for Cathy's caution. "Something I should know about?"

"Definitely not!" Cathy blurted.

"How long can you visit, Brian?"

"As long as you two can stand me. I'm a free spirit. Beth and I have separated, but I guess Taggat has already told you the sordid details."

"Separated?" Cathy tried to appear surprised. "I'm sorry to hear that. I know Beth didn't care for either of us, but I would have never wished this to happen."

"Water under the bridge, Cathy, but let's not talk about it. I want to talk about the baby. I'm living in New York, now, and I want to make sure I get to see that little girl whenever I possibly can…as long as it's okay with her mother." Brian looked at Sabrina.

"Brian, I appreciate what you've done about Kent and the baby, but I'm not sure how the arrangement is going to work out with Steve."

"I heard you two were serious." Brian tried to cover up his investigation with another lie. "Taggat mentioned it to me. He has a big mouth."

"Don't I know." Sabrina smiled.

"Sabrina, I know it will be difficult, but please try to think about what I've asked. I need that little girl."

"I'll think about it, but I can't make any promises. Not yet. Not until Steve gets back. Or when Steve gets back. Damn! I hope he gets back." Sabrina held back a tear.

"Now don't you worry. Steve's going to get back." Brian noticed Sabrina begin to get depressed. "Best thing you could do is get yourself some rest. Things always look better after a good nap."

Sabrina yawned and sat on the edge of the bed. "Maybe you're right. I'm feeling a bit tired."

"You do look a little weak." Cathy walked to Sabrina and sat. "You feel all right?"

Brian watched Cathy as she walked to Sabrina. Cathy looked magnificent. Her blonde hair seemed more radiant than ever.

"I'm fine, Cathy. I need a little sleep. That's all. Why don't you and Brian go out to dinner while I get some rest. That is, if Brian doesn't mind."

"I'd be honored."

Cathy looked up and smiled. She turned to Sabrina. "You think he's safe?"

"I'm not sure, but I guess dinner will be safe enough."

Brian walked over, took Cathy's hand, and assisted her from the edge of the bed. Cathy gathered her things, and she and Brian headed out the door. As they were leaving, the Presidential Seal appeared on the television.

"Ladies and Gentlemen, the President of the United States."

Cathy and Brian turned and walked back to the bedside.

"Why in the world would he be coming on the television on Christmas Day?" Cathy asked as she sat down beside Sabrina.

Sabrina shrugged her shoulders. "Peace on Earth, Good Will toward Men, I guess."

"I think it's more than that," Brian sat in the bedside chair and intently watched the set.

"My fellow Americans.." The President was seated at his desk in the Oval Office. "I hope you have had a Merry Christmas."

"Oh, no. It's just a well wisher…" Sabrina stirred in the bed.

"Shhhh!" Cathy shot Sabrina a frown.

"Well, excuse me!" Sabrina pouted.

"Shhhh!" Cathy furrowed her brow and put her finger to her pursed lips.

"Oh, hell!" Sabrina sat up in bed and sighed.

The President picked up a stack of notes. "I have just addressed a joint session of Congress informing them of a successful rescue mission of the hostages in Iran."

"Oh, my God! Steve's been rescued." Sabrina began fidgeting with the sheets.

"Sabrina, slow your breathing down. It'll make you dizzy." Cathy ordered without looking at Sabrina.

"At 5:30 A. M., Teheran time, a joint mission of the United States and Soviet military launched attacks on known military and terrorist targets within the borders of Iran. During these attacks, a rescue mission originating from inside the Soviet Union, but manned by U. S. military personnel, was carried out against a base near Rasht, Iran, the location of our hostages. The mission was a complete success without the loss of one hostage."

"Thank, goodness." Cathy commented.

Sabrina was still biting her sheet, too nervous to cry, too excited to scream, and too happy to laugh.

"Multiple sorties were flown against the Iranian Southern coast by squadrons from the *U. S. S. Carl Vinson.*"

Brian's interest increased.

"Brian, wasn't Kent assigned to the *Carl Vinson?*" Sabrina let loose of her sheet long enough to ask.

"Yes, he was. I hope he's all right."

"We have been informed of some loss of American lives, but the details have failed to reach us at this time. My deepest sympathy goes out to those families."

Cathy reached for Brian's hand. "I hope Kent is all right, Brian. I mean that."

"Thanks," Brian said as he firmly grasped Cathy's hand. "I hope so, too."

"Our hostage, Captain Steven Hardesty, will be flown to Ismir, Turkey. He will then be taken to Ramstein, West Germany, where he will undergo debriefing. We hope he'll be home by New Years.

I will address a session of the U.N. Security Council tomorrow. We feel we have done what was necessary, and we know the price was worth the message we delivered. We can not continue to live at the whim of terrorist groups. The message of our forefathers, "Don't Tread on Me", must be rekindled. We will continue to deliver that same message to all who attempt to hold us ransom. Today, we sent the message special delivery to the homeland of those who held us at gunpoint. We will deliver the same message over and over again until it's clearly understood.

I hope you've had a safe and pleasant day, and I wish you a very Happy New Year. Goodnight."

Sabrina eased her grip on the sheet. "I hope Taggat is all right. The silly fool went with them."

Brian jerked his head around to Sabrina.

Sabrina saw his surprise and shrugged her shoulders. "It was something he had to do. What can I say?"

Brian smiled. "If he had his mind made up, you're right. There was nothing you could say."

Cathy stood up and straightened her dress. "Okay, people. I'm happy they've been rescued, and I'm sure they'll all be all right, but I'm hungry. Brian, I thought I had a dinner date. How about it?"

Brian stood, looked at Sabrina and smiled. "Sure you'll be okay?"

"I'm great, now. You two go on and have a good time. I'll be able to rest better, now that I know Steve's coming home."

Cathy sat down on the bed, put her arm around Sabrina's shoulder, and looked at Brian. "She's fine. I'm the one that should be worried. All this celebration is coming up, and I'm included. It's enough to make a person sick." Cathy kissed Sabrina's temple. "See you later, Momma."

Sabrina watched Brian and Cathy depart. She knew they would hit it off well. After all, they were too much alike not to. The only struggle they would have would be seeing who got whose way first. She smiled, and it felt nice. Finally, she had the pressure of the pregnancy and Steve's capture over. She had a healthy baby girl, and she was fulfilling her life's dream: a loving husband, a healthy child, and good friends…a family once again, her family. Sabrina leaned back on the bed, closed her eyes, and slept.

*She was standing alone in an airport, but she didn't know where. It was foggy, and snow was floating down past the terminal windows. People were moving to and fro, but she didn't recognize anyone. In the background, flights were being called, but there were no destinations. She was frightened, and when she tried to move, she found her feet were glued to the floor.*

*Suddenly, from across the terminal, two forms moved steadily toward her, but stopped before she could recognize them.*

*"Sabrina, come with us. It's almost time. We can all be together, now."*

*"Mother, is that you?" Sabrina squinted against the thickening mist.*

*"Yes, Sabrina. Your father and I have come for you."*

*"Come for me? I can't go anywhere. I've got a new baby. It's a girl."*

*"We know, and we're so proud. Your baby will be fine. We've come for you." They walked toward her with their arms outstretched.*

*"Noooooooo! I can't go. I won't go. Not, now!" Sabrina tried moving her feet, but they remained fixed. Suddenly, a wave of cold air moved through her body and caused her to gasp. She felt so strange, and she thought she was floating. She looked down and saw herself standing in the mist. However, before she could comprehend exactly what was happening, a heavy hand hit her in the chest.*

"Ms. MacKenzie…Ms. MacKenzie! Wake up! You're having a bad dream."

"What?" Sabrina jumped up in the bed before she was fully awake. Her heart was pounding, and beads of sweat glistened on her brow. "What's happening?"

"Calm down. You're okay. You're just having a bad dream."

Sabrina slowly brought herself to consciousness. It was a dream. Thank the Lord! Sabrina moved her feet and wiggled her arms. She felt fine, but the dream seemed so real.

The nurse grinned but was disturbed by Sabrina's irregular pulse. She decided to call Dr. Chadwick.

* * *

"I'm sorry we had to drive into Richmond to find a place to eat." Brian commented as he watched Cathy finger the rim of her brandy snifter.

"Oh, I don't mind." Cathy looked up and smiled. "Sorry I haven't been the best company. I'm a bit tired myself. My nervous energy is beginning to wane. Actually, I enjoyed the drive up. It gave us some time to get better acquainted. I'm afraid I didn't leave such a good impression at our last meeting."

Brian laughed, but suddenly became serious. "I'm glad you were there. You know, you're the one that gave me the push to rid myself of Beth."

Cathy sat up in her chair. "How so? I tried to keep my mouth shut, but Beth is someone who brings out the worst in me. I told Sabrina she wasn't meant for you."

"What gave you that idea?"

"Oh, I just had a feeling." Cathy yawned. "What exactly happened to the two of you?"

"Well, it's a long story that goes back many years. I'm sure you don't want to hear all the details."

"Yes I would! Any way, it might do you some good to get it out in the open." Cathy wrapped her hand around the brandy glass and leaned forward to listen.

Brian looked over Cathy's shoulder into the distance. As he evoked memories he had long tried to forget, he wondered what was compelling him to tell Cathy any of this. But the longer he looked at her, he knew. Her interest was the impetus, and her beauty made talking easy. "Beth is quite a bit older than I."

"How much?"

"You leave no stone unturned, do you?"

"Nope." Cathy smiled.

"Ten years. I'm forty nine."

"You don't look forty nine…Oops, sorry. That's the brandy talking. I was thinking it, but I didn't mean to say it."

"That's all right, I appreciate the compliment." Brian smiled, took a long drink of his cooling coffee, put the cup down on its saucer, and continued. "Kent arrived late in Beth's life, and she dedicated her entire existence to his comforts." Brian noticed Cathy yawning. "Am I boring you with this?"

"No, I'm getting sleepy. I've been up for the past thirty-six hours. It's catching up with me."

"Why don't we leave so you can get some rest?"

"Well, I really don't have any place to go. I'd have to drive all the way to Norfolk to be home. I wouldn't make it."

"Why don't I get us two rooms here. Hyatt Hotels are usually accommodating."

Cathy laughed. "I know." She looked, but Brian didn't seem amused. "Private joke. Sorry."

Brian smiled and waved for the waiter.

Cathy reached over and grasped Brian's hand. "Promise me you'll finish your story when we get to the room…. rooms. Please?"

"I promise."

After stopping in the gift shop for sundry items, Brian and Cathy made their way to the fourth floor. The rooms were adjoining, and both had king size beds.

"Umm, the bed looks scrumptious." Cathy sat on the edge and smoothed the bedspread with her right hand. "Give me a few minutes to change and come back. All right?"

"All right, but I'm not sure you'll be awake for the rest."

"I'll make it. I'm interested in why that woman let a catch like you get away." Cathy put her hand to her mouth. "I did it again, didn't I?"

Brian laughed and headed for his room. "I'll be back in a moment."

"Don't close the door." Cathy quickly replied. "I like knowing someone's around."

"Okay. I promise I won't peek."

Cathy went into her bathroom and undressed. "Whew, that feels better already," she commented as she turned on the shower and adjusted the water temperature. She eased into the steaming spray and slowly washed the past thirty six hours from her body. After drying, she slipped on the robe she had purchased and spritzed on a fresh supply of Chanel No. 5. As she attempted to pull the robe together in the front and tie the sash, she wished small hadn't been the only size available. The warm shower was taking its toll on her state of consciousness as Cathy slid between the sheets and propped herself on two pillows. She wanted to talk to Brian, but she wasn't sure she'd make it through the next five minutes.

Brian had removed his sportcoat and tie before he headed back to Cathy's room. He had fixed himself a bourbon and water from the servibar, and opened a small bottle of Blue Nun for Cathy. He tapped on the door-jam before entering Cathy's room. "Are you ready to accept visitors?"

Cathy yawned. "Ready." As Brian rounded the entryway, Cathy spied the Blue Nun. "Oh, my favorite. A nice way to cap off the evening." Cathy pointed to a chair at the bedside. "Come over and have a seat. I want you to continue telling me about what's been happening in your life since we last met."

Brian handed Cathy the wine and eased into the chair. He could smell Cathy's perfume from his seat. The scent was very alluring, but Brian couldn't determine the brand. "Your perfume is unique. What is it?"

"Chanel. It's an old standby, but I love it."

"Ummm...I think it's my favorite, now." The combination of the perfume and the picture of Cathy sitting in the bed with her blonde hair just wet on the ends, her blue eyes glued to him, and her robe opened just enough to reveal her ample cleavage was very arousing.

"I'll have to remember that." Cathy winked. "Excuse me. I'm really letting the alcohol affect me."

Brian set his drink on the table. "Let's see. Where was I?"

"You had mentioned Beth was dedicated to Kent, and you had been left out of her life."

"Did I say that?"

"I'm not sure. I guess I assumed part of it."

"You're very perceptive."

Cathy smiled.

"For the past five years, because of the money I've made, I've been able to do about as I've pleased. Beth and I had been tied to the West Coast because of my business, but when I sold a large amount of land I had been holding in the Northwest, the profits gave us the freedom to do anything we wished. Kent was leaving for Annapolis, and I had hoped Beth and I could rediscover each other. I hope I'm not embarrassing you by talking about Beth."

"No, not at all. Go on."

"After Kent left for Annapolis, Beth didn't want to do anything. She seemed to live from day to day ,hoping to hear from Kent or planning trips East with the ulterior motive of visiting Kent. I refused to accompany her, and she became more and more distant. For the past three years we have been husband and wife in name only, and I mean name only…separate bedrooms, separate lives."

Cathy looked at Brian's well conditioned body. "What a waste." She blushed. "Don't pay any attention to me. I'm prone to do that."

"Do what?"

"Put my mouth in motion before I put my mind into gear. The wine must be talking." Cathy yawned. "Go ahead."

Brian cleared his throat and smiled. "Yes, well…Beth and I knew our time was counting down." Brian leaned forward, put his elbows on his knees, and looked down at the floor. "We continued to live together for Kent's sake. However, when this situation with Sabrina and the baby came to a head, it was the straw that broke the camel's back. Kent came home the week after you and Sabrina left. The scene wasn't pretty. Kent and I got into a scuff about his deception, and before I knew it, I was walking out of the house. I told Beth she could keep the California property, and I would live between New York and London where my company owns penthouses. Soon, our divorce will be final, and as far as I know, I may never see Beth again." Brian looked up at Cathy to see what kind of response he was getting. She was sleeping with the wine glass in her right hand. As her arms had relaxed, her robe had fallen open exposing part of her right breast. Brian gently eased her down in the bed and pulled the sheet up around her shoulders. "Sleep well, Cathy Winston. You're a beautiful lady."

Brian returned to his room and called Greene Memorial.

"Sabrina MacKenzie's room please."

"Hello," Sabrina said with a start.

"Sabrina, you okay?"

"Bad dream. Just trying to go back to sleep."

"Sorry I bothered you, but I wanted you to know Cathy and I won't be back until mid morning."

"Mid morning? What is Cathy up to?"

"Sleeping."

"Sleeping? Where are you two?"

"We had to drive into Richmond to find a decent place to eat. Cathy was very tired, and I suggested getting a couple of rooms here at the Hyatt. We're just off I-95, so we'll be back early tomorrow."

"Brian, don't take advantage of Cathy. She's been hurt recently."

"You don't have to worry about Cathy. She's safe with me."

"All right, Brian. Take care of her, okay?"

"Why? You going someplace?" Brian grinned.

"I hope not, Brian. I hope not. Good-by."

"Sabrin..." The phone clicked. "What the hell was that all about?"

Brian peeked into Cathy's room. She seemed to be resting comfortably. He returned to his bed, removed his clothes, and eased between the sheets. As he reached up to turn off the night light, Cathy walked through the adjoining doorway. She had a blanket wrapped around her. "I woke up, and you were gone."

"You were sleeping. I figured you'd be out until morning. I called Sabrina and told her everything was okay. She seemed strange."

Cathy yawned. "She's always strange. I don't want to be alone, Brian. Not tonight. Not ever. May I lie down beside you? I'll be a good girl. Promise." Cathy crossed her heart like a child.

Brian patted the bed beside him. "Okay, I'll keep my hands to myself, but I only make that promise for tonight."

Cathy grinned and crawled into the bed on top of the blanket. She curled into the fetal position with her butt toward Brian and quickly fell to sleep.

Brian softly touched her hair as her perfume floated into his nostrils. Who are you, Cathy, and what do you want? You don't seem to want anybody getting close, but you don't want to be alone. You're hard on the outside, but very fragile and easily hurt. Brian ached to be close to Cathy, and he hoped there would be other nights like this in their future.

\* \* \*

The windows in Brian's and Cathy's room faced southeast, and the blinds had not been completely pulled the night before. The vertical slit in the center permitted a shaft of light to transect the room, and as the sun ascended, the beam cut across Brian's face summoning him awake. He carefully rose from bed so he wouldn't arouse Cathy. Then he showered, shaved, and dressed. He left Cathy a note telling her he would be back in two or three hours. If she awakened, he didn't want her to worry.

\* \* \*

Cathy bolted awake. She slowly recognized the surroundings, and she read the note Brian had left. The two sleepless nights were still taking their toll. She rustled around in the bed, and realized she was in Brian's room.

"Oh, no! I've done it again." She sat up in the bed and almost cried. "No. Wait a minute. Surely I would remember that." She rolled over in the bed not even trying to keep her robe closed and ordered breakfast. "Yes, room service. Cathy Winston in 403. I would like an order of whole wheat toast, fresh squeezed orange juice...large, coffee, and three extra-strength Tylenol." As she finished ordering breakfast, the door to the room opened. Brian walked in with four bags in his hands.

"Ah, she awaketh."

Cathy smiled. "Yes, and she feeleth awful."

"Why?"

"I didn't do anything stupid last night, did I?"

"Like what?"

"You know what! I woke up in your room with this skimpy robe on...partly on. My body is hanging out everywhere."

"Quite beautifully, I might add."

Cathy smiled but offered no thanks. "I do some silly things when I drink, but I didn't think I had too much last night, did I?"

"Calm down, Cathy. You were a good girl last night."

"Thank goodness."

Brian handed her two of the sacks he was carrying. "Here. Merry day after Christmas. Thanks for last night."

Cathy reached for the sacks but stopped before grasping the shopping bag handles. "Wait a minute. I thought you said I was a good girl."

"You were. Very good." Brian raised his eyebrows and smiled.

"Oh, no..."

"Oh, open them. You didn't do anything wrong last night. I figured you didn't want to wear the same clothes back to the hospital."

Cathy opened the first package. "It's beautiful, but you shouldn't have." She lifted the dark navy wool dress from the box. It was plain, but the cut was elegant. There was a shallow V-cut in the front, long sleeves, full back, and mid calf length. The second box contained all the accessories; bra, pants, slip, stockings, shoes, purse and a white Cashmere coat. "Ooooo, I love it, but how did you know my sizes?"

"I snooped around a bit this morning. Hope you don't mind?"

"Not a bit," Cathy said as she retreated into the bathroom. After showering, she arranged her anatomy into the black pants and bra, slithered into her panty hose, and applied a spray of perfume to her cleavage and other pulse points. After slinking into her slip and dress, she applied what little make up she had and walked back into the room.

"Would you fasten this…," she stopped when she looked up and saw Brian staring at her. "What's the matter?"

"Cathy Winston, you're the most beautiful woman I've ever seen."

"Thanks. I needed that."

"I meant it." Brian walked over to Cathy and handed her another small box. "I enjoyed this so much, I thought I would get you a fresh supply so you would always have some available.

Cathy opened the new bottle of Chanel. "Thanks. I was running a little low."

The knock at the door ended their eye embrace.

"Uh…" Brian looked over at the door. "I'll get it."

He opened the door and permitted the waiter to place Cathy's breakfast on the table near the window. Brian tipped the waiter noting that the young man never took his eyes off Cathy as Brian handed him the money. "Will that be sufficient?"

"Yes sir. That's very nice." The waiter still hadn't looked at Brian.

"Excuse me, Thomas." Brian read his name from his tag.

"Yes sir."

"Thomas?"

The waiter finally looked at Brian. "Yes sir?"

"That'll be all. Thanks." Brian grinned.

"Yes, sir. Thank you, sir. Ring and ask for me if you need anything."

"We're fine. Thanks again."

As the waiter backed out of the room, Brian couldn't help laughing. "Do you have that effect on all men?"

"No," Cathy smiled. "Sabrina's fiance says that most men cover their crotch when they're around me."

Brian's eyes opened wide. "That's an interesting observation. I think I'll leave that one alone until I get to know you better."

"Let's eat. I'm starved." Cathy opened the blinds permitting the warmth of the morning sun to flow into the room. She stood for a moment in the sunlight and basked in the effect. "I hate winter. If it weren't for the business, I'd live in Florida or somewhere it was warm year around."

"Like California?"

Cathy spun around. "Yes, even California." She sat down at the table. "Would you like something?"

"I'll share some coffee and your company if you don't mind?"

Cathy looked up from buttering her toast. She smiled and let out an exasperated breath. "Do I look like I'd mind? I'm wearing your gifts and looking forward to our next dinner together."

Brian sat down, poured a cup of coffee, added a little Half and Half, and stirred. He looked over at Cathy as she delicately flipped her hair behind her ear and ate her toast.

"Look at the front page of the paper." Cathy motioned with her head.

Brian picked up the rolled newspaper from its spot on the tray. He unrolled the front page and noted the headlines: "Iranian Hostages Freed". "What about it? It's what we heard on the news last night."

"Not the headlines. The picture. That's Sabrina's fiance. That's Steve Hardesty." Cathy pointed to the picture of Steve that was patched into the upper right corner of a map that showed the routes of rescue.

Brian let Steve's image soak in for a moment. "Do you think Sabrina is going to marry the guy?"

"Do you think the sun's going to rise in the morning?"

"That sure, huh?"

"Sabrina's loved Steve since she was seventeen."

"So, what was Kent? A rebounder?" Brian was mildly offended.

"Look, Brian. Sabrina thought the relationship with Steve was over before she met Kent. She fell in love, or at least what she thought was love, with Kent before she ever permitted any intimacy to happen. Believe me, she would have never permitted Kent to make love to her unless she thought it was real. Sabrina is not a woman of the world when it comes to men."

"And, is Cathy Winston?" Brian smiled as he peered over the rim of his coffee cup.

"Let's just say I've been hurt by men. Fortunately, I've seen the basic flaw in the male personality, and I've about decided to give up on the species." Cathy looked up from her second piece of toast and slyly grinned. "That is, unless someone changes my mind."

"What would someone have to do to change your mind?"

"Who's asking?"

"For now, let's just say an interested party."

"I want a man who's no longer a boy. I'm tired of the antics and games men play."

"Well, I don't know who you've been with before, but I guarantee that when you're around me, you'll feel like a woman."

"That's sometimes the problem, Brian. Most men want a woman for one thing…an object of their selfish passion. After that, they're treated like subservient creatures. I can't accept that, and never will."

"Cathy! Look at yourself. You'd bring out the animal in a man."

"I'm more than this body, Brian. I'm a functioning, intelligent, feeling human being."

"I know that, and I respect you for what you are. Don't ask me how, but I know what you and Sabrina have been through over these past months."

Cathy looked askew at Brian and raised her brows. "How in the hell would you know?"

"I asked you not to ask. Someday, I'll tell you all about it."

"Maybe after dinner, huh?"

Brian smiled. "Yes, maybe after dinner. Look, Cathy. Everything we do is for a reason. We all try to get things from someone else. It's the way we're conditioned. Last night you showed me how to have a good time once again…a good time that didn't have a planned sexual ending." Brian stopped and looked into Cathy's eyes. "Why don't you give me a chance to show you how a man appreciates a woman. Come to New York and spend a few weeks. We'll do the town. Then, you tell me if I'm just a big boy, or maybe you could include me in your list of the right men."

"I can't go to New York!" Cathy snapped, but she quickly withdrew from her hard line stance, reached over, and grasped Brian's hand. "Sabrina needs me, Brian. But your offer is inviting. I could use a rest after this past four months."

"I understand your bond with Sabrina, and I respect it. But…" Brian's head jerked toward the ringing telephone. "Damn!"

Brian sighed, stood, walked over to the phone, and picked up the earpiece. "Hello, 403." He held his hand over the mouthpiece and spoke to Cathy. "Sorry, I left my number with my answering service."

Cathy smiled, looked out the window, and sipped on her coffee. "Whew," she thought. "I'm glad the phone rang. Things were getting a little hot."

"Cathy, it's for you. Dr. Chadwick at the hospital." Brian shrugged his shoulders, not knowing what the doctor wanted.

Cathy gasped. "Oh, my God."

"Easy, Cathy. It's not always bad news."

Cathy slowly walked over to the phone, took the earpiece, and grabbed Brian's arm as he was about to walk away. "Stay close?"

Brian shook his head affirmatively and watched Cathy's face as she answered and listened.

"Okay, we'll be there right away." Cathy shook as she hung up the phone. "It's Sabrina. She's developed a bad problem. She's in ICU.

They…" Cathy began shaking uncontrollably and slowly sat down on the bed.

Brian eased down beside her, put his arm around her shoulders, and held her hand. "What is it, Cathy? For God's sake, tell me! Is Sabrina all right?"

Cathy looked up at Brian and leaned her head on his chest. "My God, Brian. Dr. Chadwick thinks Sabrina's dying."

"Dying!? What happened?"

"They think she had a blood clot go to her lung and possibly her brain. They want us to get there right away."

Cathy sat dumbfounded on the bed as Brian made sure everything was taken care of in the room. He helped Cathy up, put on her coat, and supported her as they headed for the car. As they passed the door, Brian picked up the other sacks with his free hand. As they walked down the hall, the stuffed elephant's head and trunk swayed to and fro from the top of the bag.

# 25

A suddden heaviness in her chest awoke Sabrina. She was having difficulty breathing. Each breath was labored, and the crushing pain was becoming unbearable. She reached for the call bell and rang for the nurse.

"Yes, Ms. MacKenzie. May I help you?"

"I'm having difficulty breathing." Sabrina gasped for air. "I think it's my heart…please hurry. I feel so stran…"

"Ms. MacKenzie?…Ms. MacKenzie? I'm coming. I'll be right there." Mary Lenox dropped what she was doing and responded to Sabrina's call. As she entered the room, Mary immediately noticed Sabrina's grave condition. She promptly started oxygen, grabbed her stethoscope, and listened to Sabrina's chest. The breath sounds were distant, the heart had a gallop rhythm, and there was evidence of pulmonary congestion. Mary elevated the head of the bed and lowered the foot. "Breathe deeply, Sabrina. You'll feel better. I'll be right back. I've got to get you to I.C.U. and talk to Dr. Chadwick." Mary headed for the nurse's station and requested assistance from the night supervisor. She paged Dr. Chadwick to come to the I.C.U. immediately and rounded up the necessities to get an intravenous started. As Mary started back to the room, the phone rang. "Hello, Obstetrics."

"Mary, what the hell is going on?" John leaned across Maggie's sleeping body and spoke quietly on the phone.

"Dr. Chadwick, I need you immediately. Sabrina's in trouble. I think she could have thrown an embolus or something worse. Regardless, she's gone into heart failure. I've started oxygen, and I've put in a call to Dr. Rafstani."

"Good thinking, Mary. I'll be right there. Give her forty milligrams of Lasix I.V., get stat blood gases, administer ten milligrams of Morphine, and head for the Unit. While we're waiting for Jorge, have one of the cardiology residents consult."

"What if Dr. Raf isn't on call."

"Find him, any way. We need him, stat! I'll be there in twenty minutes."

"Yes sir! I'll have the operator work on it right away."

Sabrina felt relieved with the oxygen flowing, but she knew she would be much better if she could only go to the bathroom. *If I could just get rid of this gas, I'd feel much better*, she thought. She knew she might not make it to the bathroom without help, but she had to try. She pulled off the oxygen mask, got out of bed, and headed for the lavatory. "Not so bad," she said to herself as she negotiated the short distance. As she entered the bathroom, a severe pain hit her in the left chest. Suddenly, she couldn't breathe. She tried calling for help, but nothing came out. Sweat popped out on her forehead, and she felt sick. Her vision faded as if she had entered a dark tunnel. Her balance was difficult to maintain. She began falling, but it didn't seem for real. She reached out and tried to catch herself, and, for a moment, she thought she had caught a rope that would support her. However, the rope she caught turned out to be the emergency cord attached to the nurse call bell.

* * *

As Mary Lenox reentered Sabrina's room, the emergency call light buzzed over the door. Mary charged into the room. "Oh, my God," she exclaimed as she almost fell over Sabrina's feet. Mary leaned down and checked Sabrina's pulse and respirations; heart rate 140, respirations 50 and shallow. "Someone help me...Quick!" Mary yelled at the impersonal intercom. The aide arrived quickly, and she and Mary managed to move Sabrina onto a stretcher, restart oxygen, restart an I.V., and head for the Intensive Care Unit.

Russ Willis, a second year cardiology resident, was close on their heels as they moved Sabrina into unit five. "Damn!" He exclaimed as the E.K.G. leads were reattached. "We've got V-tach. What's the story, Mary? Give me 50mg of Lidocaine, Stat!"

Mary opened Sabrina's chart. "Twenty seven year old lady with history of Rheumatic Heart Disease. Delivered by section yesterday. Appeared fine until a few minutes ago. Complained of chest pain then fainted. She's been in failure previously. I think she's thrown an embolus."

"Good observation...50mg Lidocaine push...Now. Mark time... Okay." Russ continued to observe the tracing. "Okay, she's converted to sinus rhythm. Maybe it wasn't a big embolus. Heparin 5000 units I.V. now, and set up a pump to deliver 1000 units per hour...Damn, she's back in V-tach. Gimme another 50 mg. of Lidocaine and set up a drip. Do we have a good airway?"

"I've got a good airway," Jim Hopper, the anesthesiology resident, responded. "She seems to be breathing on her own, but she's not responsive. What's her pressure?"

"60/40"

"Looks like were back in sinus rhythm." Russ exhaled. "Let's get a set of blood gases. Give me a heparinized syringe." Russ palpated Sabrina's right groin, found her femoral pulse, and sank the needle into the pulsation. The bright red fluid pushed the glass plunger up the barrel of the syringe. He turned and handed the syringe to one of the crash team nurses. "We needed these a minute ago."

"Right!" The nurse turned and sprinted for the lab.

"Russ! She's gone into V-fib. I'm going to intubate her." Jim Hopper grabbed a laryngoscope and endotracheal tube. He place the scope, deftly threaded the tube into the trachea, and started 100 percent oxygen by ambu.

"Damn! The embolus must be larger than we thought. Give me the paddles!"

The nurse handling the crash cart handed Russ the electroconversion paddle. "200 joules on my mark...Now!"

"Clear."

Everyone dealing with the code stepped back momentarily to avoid possible shock.

Russ placed the discs on Sabrina's chest; one in the middle of her sternum, and one just below the left breast. He pressed the discharge buttons.

"T.... H...U...M...P!" Sabrina's body jerked upwards and then fell back onto the bed.

Russ watched the monitor. "We've still got V-fib. Give me 240 on the paddles."

"She's on 100 percent 0-2, Russ. I've got a good airway."

"Okay, Jim."

"240 joules, Dr. Willis."

"Clear!" Russ discharged the paddles once again.

"THUMP!"

Russ intently watched the monitor. He immediately saw the sinus rhythm when the interference from the shock cleared. "Okay! We've got sinus rhythm. What's her pressure?"

"60/40"

"All right. Let's start a dopamine drip."

The head nurse of the team prepared the drip and attached it to the fluids that were slipping into Sabrina's veins.

"That should get her pressure up." Russ went to the head of the bed. He looked down into Sabrina's eyes. "Come on, Sabrina. Come back to us. You can do it!"

"Doctor, the gases are here."

"Read them out!"

"pO2 75, pCO2 55, pH 7.31, base excess 23."

"Okay, give he an amp of bicarb, set up the ventilator, and repeat the gases in five minutes. What's her pressure?"

"90/60..pulse 78 and regular."

"All right!" Russ went to the head of the table. "Sabrina," he yelled. "Sabrina! Open your eyes!"

No response.

Russ lifted Sabrina's lids and looked into her eyes. "Come on, Sabrina. I know you're in there." He used a small pen light and checked for pupillary response. The pupils were widely dilated and responded sluggishly to the light. "Come on, Sabrina. Come on back to us. Please!"

John Chadwick and Jorge Rafstani entered the I. C. U. cubicle simultaneously. Jorge Rafstani, the staff chief cardiologist took a quick look around. "Okay, some of you people clear out. Russ, give me a quick assessment."

"I've just electroconverted this young lady from V-fib. It took two shocks, but she seems to be in sinus rhythm, now. I'm using a dopamine drip to keep her pressure up, and a lidocaine drip to decrease her cardiac irritability. Her gases aren't great, but she could have an underlying pulmonary embolus. We've started heparin at 1000 units per hour after a 5000 unit bolus. She's has underlying rheumatic heart disease and delivered a baby at term by uncomplicated Section yesterday. That's about all I have. I can't explain the deep obtundation because we were on top of her when she went into V-fib. I guess there's a possibility of cerebral embolism since she was in fib and converted." Russ looked up at Dr. Rafstani for the first time. His focus had been fixed on Sabrina during his entire discussion.

As Russ and Dr. Rafstani discussed the case, John walked over to the bed and grasped Sabrina's cool hand. "What happened to you, Sabrina?" He thought. "You have everything to live for, now. Don't leave us. My God. Don't leave us." A tear welled up in John's eye. The bond he had created with Sabrina seemed unusual. The vibrancy he had seen in Sabrina's eyes, and the devotion she had exhibited to her child had made him feel closer than he had ever felt to any other patient. John turned from his position and looked at Jorge. "What do you think, Raf?"

"Dammit, John. I don't know for sure, but I'll bet she had a P.E., went into rapid failure, then into V-tach, and V-fib. She could have formed a clot the ventricle when she was in fib and flipped it to the brain when she converted. That's the only way I can explain her profound cerebral deficit. We need to get a CAT scan as soon as we can move her, and we'll need an EEG."

John turned back to Sabrina. Her vibrant smile was obstructed by an endotracheal tube. Her flowing black hair was pulled back and tucked inside a loose fitting surgical cap. Her body was violated by tubes into her badder, nose, and rectum. John removed the surgical cap and placed her hair on the pillow. He leaned close to her ear. "Please come back, Sabrina. Fight hard for your new baby. I know you can do it." John placed Sabrina's limp hand on the bed, walked to the nurse's desk, and called his house.

Maggie reluctantly picked up the ringing phone. "Hello. Dr. Chadwick's residence.

"Maggie, come to the hospital. I.C.U. I need you."

"What's wrong, John? Is it Sabrina?"

"Yes. She's bad. I'm not sure she'll make it. She's flipped a massive pulmonary embolus, cerebral embolus, or both. The keys to the Suburban are hanging in the kitchen. I have to find Cathy."

"I'll be right there. John, I love you."

"I love you, Maggie. Please hurry."

* * *

Cathy leaned against Brian's side as they stood in front of the nursery window. Cathy's gaze was fixed on Stephanie, but her thoughts were on Sabrina. "It doesn't seem possible."

"What's that?" Brian questioned as he dried a new tear from Cathy's cheek.

"How can everything seem so perfect one minute and then blow up in your face the next?"

"I've never questioned divine providence, Cathy, but I assure you, there is a reason."

"How can you believe that? What possible reason is there in Sabrina's illness? She has a new baby to take care of. Surely, a gracious God wouldn't take her away from her daughter."

Brian turned to Cathy. "Cathy, I can't convince you, now. I know that. But I assure you, there is a God, and he's here with us. I believe that with all my heart, and you have to keep the faith that whatever happens will be for the best. That faith has kept me going for a long time without letting me down. I don't expect it will now."

"I hope you're right, Brian, but I've only had faith in myself so far. Unfortunately, I have no control over what's happening." Cathy fell forward on Brian's chest. "I feel so helpless. Surely, you can do something." Cathy looked into Brian's eyes. "Please?"

"It's out of my power. We'll just have to wait."

"What will I do if Sabrina doesn't make it? I'm not a mother."

"What do you mean?"

"If Sabrina dies, I'm to be the guardian. I'll be the baby's "mother". I'm no mother."

"We'll have to do whatever we'll have to do. Time will tell us. You're strong, and you have plenty of friends."

"I don't have friends. I only have Sabrina."

"You're wrong, Cathy. You're dead wrong."

"CODE BLUE, I. C. U...CODE BLUE, I. C. U...CODE BLUE, I. C. U." The hospital intercom blared out its call over Brian and Cathy's heads.

Cathy grasped Brian tighter. She knew what Code Blue meant, and she was afraid it meant Sabrina was closer to death.

"Come on, Cathy. Let's go downstairs and see what's happening." Brian led Cathy to the elevator, and they slowly entered the arriving car.

They patiently sat outside I.C.U., and after what seemed an eternity, John Chadwick and Maggie came into the waiting room.

"What's happened, Dr. Chadwick. How's Sabrina?" Cathy nervously wrung her hands as Brian sat steadfast by her side.

John walked toward Cathy. He could see the terror in her eyes. If Maggie had not been with him, he wasn't sure he would have had the strength to talk. John pulled up two chairs, and he and Maggie sat opposite Cathy and Brian.

"She's dead, isn't she? I knew it! Oh, my God." Cathy fell against Brian's side.

"Cathy," John reached out and grabbed Cathy's hands. "Cathy, get hold of yourself. She's not dead, but we've had another episode where her heart stopped. It started immediately with external massage and a small amount of medication, but…"

Cathy's eyes shot open. "But, what? What!?"

"But, we're still not getting any response from her.

Sabrina isn't coming around like she should. I don't know how long her heart can continue to hold out, and I'm not sure why she's in such a deep coma."

Cathy slumped, but Brian quickly supported her.

"Is there any hope, Doctor?" Brian held on tightly to Cathy's collapsing body.

"There's always hope, Mr. Pooley. Presently we have Sabrina's heart stable, but I'm not sure for how long. We're not sure how large an embolus she threw to her lung. Because of her condition, we can't move her to X-ray and do the usual work up. Our biggest problem is determining the amount of brain damage that has occurred. We have a neurologist on the way. After the E.E.G., we should know something. I hate keeping you hanging, but that's all I know for now."

"I appreciate what you're doing, Dr. Chadwick." Cathy opened her eyes and smiled. "It's just that…. Sabrina's all I have, and I can't stand the thought of losing her." Cathy closed her eyes and began a muffled cry into the fabric of Brian's coat.

"What do you think the E.E.G. will show?" Brian grasped Cathy tighter as he posed the question to John.

"I'm afraid it will be bad news. The way Sabrina looks now, I'm afraid there won't be any brain activity."

Cathy looked at John. "You mean, I might never speak to Sabrina again?"

"It's a possibility, Cathy. I'm sorry."

"Please make her better. She doesn't deserve this! It should be me in there, not her. Please make her better."

John leaned closer to Cathy. "Don't do this to yourself, Cathy. You have no blame. You didn't give Sabrina rheumatic fever, and you didn't force Sabrina to have the baby. Sabrina couldn't prevent the first, and she wouldn't have changed a thing about having her baby. You and I both know that. Sabrina has lived her life as she wanted. You have to be content with that fact. If you were the one lying in that bed, Sabrina would be wishing the same thing."

"But, you don't understand," Cathy whimpered. "Sabrina wouldn't hurt a fly. She's kind and gentle, and she would never utter a bad word about any one. I'm the one who should be punished. I'm the one who should be in there. Don't you see?"

John paused while Cathy worked through her sorrow. He had a difficult time dealing with the question Cathy posed.

Maggie felt John's uneasiness and took his left hand with her right. "Cathy, we all have our own crosses to bear. Some different than others. No one is being punished. It doesn't work that way. Things happen, and we have no control over them. We do the best with what we have. If it's

God's will for Sabrina to come back to us, then so be it. If not, we'll have to accept that also. You know that's what Sabrina would tell you."

Cathy didn't respond. She fixed her eyes on the I.C.U. doors hoping Sabrina would walk through, but knowing she would never see Sabrina alive again.

\* \* \*

*Sabrina walked the halls of the hospital, but no one seemed to notice her. She saw Cathy and Brian, and they appeared sad. She told them not to worry. She was all right, but they didn't seem to hear. She could hear everyone around her, but she couldn't tell exactly what they were saying.*

*At first she was in a small room where everyone was working on a patient. She left the room because she felt she didn't belong. She didn't want to interfere with the doctors and nurses. When she left the room, she was suddenly outside the nursery. Stephanie was sleeping. Sabrina tried to get the nurse's attention, but no one noticed her presence. Sabrina turned from the window, and without taking the elevator, she was back on the floor where Cathy and Brian were sitting. They were talking to Dr. Chadwick and Maggie. Cathy looked terrible. Sabrina tried to get closer, but the more she walked the farther away they seemed to get.*

*Suddenly, Sabrina was drawn into I.C.U. She stared into the room marked Unit Five where doctors were working with a patient. The patient looked like her, but that couldn't be possible. She was…here, or was she? Sabrina became frightened. She turned to run from the room, but as she turned, she was confronted by her…Mother.*

*"Mother! Why are you here?" Sabrina was no longer afraid. She was warmed by her Mother's presence.*

*"I've been sent to help you, Sabrina. I've come to welcome you into our arms again. It's time to join us."*

*"You mean…I'm dying?" Sabrina turned to look at the patient once again, but the room was no longer there.*

*"Yes, Sabrina, but don't be afraid."*

*"I'm not afraid. You're here. But what about Stephanie and Cathy? I don't want to leave them."*

*"They will be fine. They have each other, and Cathy has found someone who cares for her and the child. The man loves them very much. Now, you must come. We're no longer a part of their world."*

*Sabrina held her Mother's hand, and they walked the misty corridor toward a bright door. Sabrina was no longer tired. There was no pain. She felt new strength surge through her. As they passed through the door, Sabrina looked back.*

*"Don't look back, Sabrina," her Mother said as she grasped Sabrina's hand tighter. "What happens there is not of your concern. You are safe and with us, once again."*

*Sabrina turned and looked forward. They had passed through the door, and on the other side stood her father. As they approached her father's image, Sabrina reached out, and her father took her other hand. Together they walked into the blinding light.*

\* \* \*

"John. I'm afraid we've got ourselves a predicament."

Bill Megland, the examining neurologist, spoke to John as they sat at the I.C.U. nurses station.

"What's the problem?" John kept his head in his hands as he spoke.

"The E.E.G. is flat, but her heart is functioning well. Neurologically, she's dead."

"Any chance for recovery?"

"There's always a chance, John. We both know that. But we also know the chance is damned slim. It will only be through divine intervention that this lady will ever be among the living." Bill took a deep breath. "Sorry, but that's how I see it. I've begun some routine things, but the way the E.E.G. appears, I don't see much chance. I'll check back in an hour or two."

"Thanks, Bill. I don't know what I'll say to her friends."

"Want me to talk to them?"

"No, this is my job. I promised I would let them know as soon as I did."

Bill patted John on the back. "Good luck. This is the toughest part about being a doctor."

"You said it!" John closed his eyes and tried to envision the happy moments. He would always remember Sabrina MacKenzie; her joy, her smile, her tears. They would always haunt him. As tears came to his eyes, a sudden chill came across John's body. He looked around, but no one had approached. Suddenly, a faint voice seemed to come from inside his head...Sabrina's voice.

"Don't weep for me. I'm happy. Everything will be fine."

John shuddered and shook his head. "Who's there?"

"Who's where?" Maggie asked as she walked to John's side.

John stood and smiled. "I'm not sure. I thought I heard Sabrina."

Maggie reached out and embraced John. "Don't feel like you're losing your mind. I thought I heard her, too. I believe she is happy." Maggie cried softly into John's shoulder. Together they walked through the doors to face Cathy.

* * *

Cathy had closed her eyes for only a moment, or so she thought. She was caught in a dream, a dream of good times. She and Sabrina were sitting on their porch enjoying a cool leisurely lunch while the solitude of the bay whispered around them.

Sabrina calmly turned to Cathy. "Cathy, you must take care of Stephanie. You're all she has."

"Sabrina, what are you talking about. You're so silly."

"Cathy! Stephanie needs you. You're her mother, now. I'm leaving, and I'll not be back. At least, not as you know me. But I'll always be with you."

"Sabrina, don't talk in riddles. Where are you going?"

"I have to go with my mother and father, Cathy. They've come for me."

"Sabrina, are you dying?"

"Yes, Cathy. I must go."

Cathy began to cry. "Don't leave me, Sabrina. You're all I have. Please don't go."

"Don't cry, Cathy." Sabrina said as she seemed to drift away. "Be strong, like you always were for me. Be strong. You have someone that cares for you. You haven't known him for long, but he cares. He can give you all you've ever really wanted. Take care of Stephanie. I'll be in your heart forever. I...love...you." Sabrina reached out and touched Cathy's extended hand. The chill caused Cathy to jerk. As she opened her eyes, she saw Brian.

"You all right?" Brian asked with concerned eyes. "I'm all right, but Sabrina's dead, Brian. I know it."

"Don't give up, Cathy. It's too early."

"No, Brian. I know it. She spoke to me. She's gone."

"I believe she spoke to you, Cathy. But let's wait for the doctor. He should be out in a moment."

\* \* \*

"Doctor Chadwick, come quickly!" The nurse called from Unit Five.

John jumped from his seat and hurried into the cubicle. As he entered the room, he encountered the nurse pulling the crash cart from the storage area. He looked up and noted a straight line on the monitor.

"She was doing fine, but suddenly, her heart just quit beating. Shall we try epinephrine?"

John walked over to the bed, looked at Sabrina's shell, and then turned to the nurse. "We'll not be doing anything. I'm afraid Sabrina MacKenzie doesn't live in there anymore." John slowly walked over and turned off the respirator.

"But Doctor, she hasn't been listed as a no code. We must try."

"Dammit, Jean. She's dead. I can't put her through this any longer. Can't you see?" John looked up into the nurse's eyes. His right hand was clenched into a fist, but there were tears in his eyes.

Maggie walked over and grabbed John's hand.

He slowly released his fist.

"It's okay, Jean." Maggie reassured the nurse. "The neurologist listed her E.E.G. as flat. We're not going to try any heroics. Chart it exactly as you see it. Everything will be all right."

"Okay, Maggie, but I'll have to report this to the I.C.U. committee."

John quickly tightened his fist and turned for Jean Hartman, but Maggie stopped his progression.

"Report what you must, Jean. John is doing what he feels is right for this patient. He'll explain everything in the chart and to the committee. Ask her friends to come in to the Unit, please."

Jean promptly left the room.

John and Maggie carefully and respectfully removed all the wires and tubes from Sabrina's body. Maggie fixed Sabrina's hair neatly behind and beside her head. They straightened the sheets and covered Sabrina's face.

"She's no longer in pain, Maggie." John stood beside the bed and lightly touched the sheet over Sabrina's face.

Maggie walked to John's side and held him firmly about the waist.

A rustle at the door caused them both to turn. Cathy and Brian stood quietly.

"She's gone, Cathy." Maggie reached out with her other hand and beckoned for Cathy to join them.

Cathy and Brian walked over to their side, joined arms and silently stood in reverence.

"Can I see her?" Cathy shuddered.

"Of course." Maggie drew the sheet from Sabrina's face.

Cathy leaned forward, kissed Sabrina's cool cheek, and stood erect. "I love you, Sabrina. Help me through this, and, as time goes by, I'll see your face again." Cathy grabbed for Brian's hand. It was there.

* * *

Brian and Cathy sat silently in the hospital cafeteria. Cathy numbly stirred her coffee as Brian watched.

Occasionally, Cathy would look up, start to speak, but then return to her study of the cup. Brian was about to speak, but he noticed a gentleman approaching their table.

"Excuse me. Are you Brian Pooley?"

"Yes I am," Brian said as he and Cathy looked up from the table.

"I'm David Brock, the hospital administrator. There's a gentleman in my office that needs to speak to you. He says he's from the Department of the Navy. Evidently, he found you through your answering service."

Cathy and Brian rose from the table.

"I think he wanted to speak to Mr. Pooley privately." David said to Cathy.

"It's okay, Mr. Brock. She's a close friend."

"Suit yourself. Follow me please."

As they entered the administrator's office, a Naval captain promptly stood to attention. "Mr. Brian Pooley?"

Brian stopped, felt weak kneed, but was supported by Cathy's hold on his arm, and gathered strength to speak. "Yes."

"Mr. Pooley, I'm afraid I have some bad news."

"What's happened to Kent?"

"It's not the usual custom of the Navy to make these announcements in a public place, but since we were unable to contact you or your wife at your residence, the President requested I find you personally. I'm sorry to inform you that your son, Lieutenant Kent Pooley, was killed in action over hostile territory while on a recent air mission. He died at 0630 hours, Christmas Day. The President wishes to extend his condolences, and wishes to inform you your son will be awarded the Navy Cross, posthumously."

Brian was dumbfounded.

"A telegram has been sent to the address on the West Coast. A detachment from San Francisco will arrive tomorrow to make the announcement in person. We have still been unable to get any response from the house in Monterey."

"Uh...my wife is probably out with her friends. Are you sure about this?"

"I'm sorry, Mr. Pooley, but this has been confirmed. The body will be transported to Washington in five days. We will help in any way we can to assist in arrangements for the funeral. Your son has the right to be buried in Arlington."

"No...no. His mother wouldn't hear of it. We will make arrangements for him to be buried at home. Uh...Thank you, Captain." Brian's knees began to buckle, and Cathy helped him to a seat.

"Thank you, Captain. I'll take care of Mr. Pooley from here." Cathy looked up, gave the Captain a quick smile, and turned her attention to Brian. "Brian, I'm terribly sorry. It doesn't seem possible this can all be happening. What can I do to help?"

Brian reached up and grabbed Cathy's forearm. "No...You've got enough to do. I'll take care of this. I must get to the coast before the Navy arrives tomorrow."

"I'll call Johnny McKay and make arrangements. Don't worry. We'll get you there by morning." Cathy released her hold on Brian, asked to use the phone, and called the flying service.

Brian quickly turned in his seat to face Cathy. "Wait! I can't leave you."

"Brian, you must go. This is settled. Sabrina's gone. We won't have the service until Taggat comes home. I'll be here. Waiting for you. Together we'll make some sense out of all this. Together we'll find the happiness we have searched for. I want that. Do you?"

"Of course," Brian said without hesitation. "I just can't believe Kent's gone. I guess I won't believe it until I see him." Brian leaned forward, put his head in his hands, and prayed.

Cathy hung up the phone and knelt beside Brian. "It's all arranged. Johnny's coming to pick you up at the hospitals heliport. You'll be back in New York in four hours, and depart for the coast in six. You'll be in San Francisco in twelve hours."

Brian grasped Cathy's hand and looked at her through teary eyes. "Thanks, Cath. I'll be back as soon as I can. I promise."

"I know, Brian. I know."

# 26

Arch McConnell paced the hard concrete floor of the makeshift head-quarters he had established in the hanger of the Baku airport. The area was warmed by four large cast iron stoves the Russians had provided after they learned that the United States soldiers were to remain until the missing American pilot had been rescued or found. Arch patted his foot in disgust as he looked around at his huddled masses. They had to get out of Russia...out before their welcome waned.

Their flight into Lenkornan had been uneventful, but Saviour Two, one of the large Huey helicopters, had been diverted to assist in the search for the F-14 pilot. The Saudis, Taggat, Steve, Tallia, Arch, and the remain-der of the team had been ferried into Baku by the remaining helicopters. So far, the search team had rescued the Radar Intercept Officer from the *Vinson* based Tomcat, but the pilot was presumed dead. However, they had been unable to find a body. If nothing was found today, Arch had been ordered to discontinue the search and proceed with the team to Ismir, Turkey.

"Saviour Two to Base. Savior Two to Base. Over." The radio message broke into the cold stillness of the hanger.

"Roger, Saviour Two. Read you five by five. Over." Arch keyed the microphone to receive.

"The pilot's remains have been found. We are returning to base. ETA one hour. Over."

"Message understood, Saviour Two. Have you passed the information on to the E-2? Over."

"Roger that, Base. E-2 copied our data, and the information has been relayed to Ismir. Over."

"Did you get a verbal confirm on that transmission from one of our boys? Over."

"Uh…that's a roger, Base. Verbal confirm. over."

"Who was the pilot, Two? Over."

"A Lieutenant Kent Pooley. His R.I.O. said he and the pilot were flying CAP for a TU-95 Bear on a run into Teheran. I'd love to have seen the Russkie's faces when those fellows pulled along side. Over."

"What happened to them Two? Over."

"Seems it happened after the show was almost over. Pooley and his wingman had taken out two Migs and returned on station with the Bear. The bomber made its run and was heading home. The Tomcats had split off to link up with their tanker when a SAM popped out of nowhere and detonated along side their airplane. Pooley held the plane straight and level while the RIO punched out, but the lieutenant went down with the ship. All we could find was parts. Pretty messy. Over."

"They all are, Two. They all are. Over."

"Roger that, Base. Two, out."

"Hurry home, Two. We've got a light in the window. Base, out."

The name, Pooley, was not lost on Taggat's attentive ears. He slowly extracted himself from his sleeping bag, stood, and tried to shake the effects of Dimitri's vodka. He too was in a hurry to get home but not for the same reasons as Arch. Taggat wanted to find out about Sabrina, he wanted to see Mae, but most of all, he wanted to get Steve out of Russia and away from Tallia. She had not left Steve's side since the rescue, and Taggat had expected her to return with Steve after their trip to Tallia's home, but Steve had returned alone. However, he had been in one foul mood since returning and had not mentioned Sabrina one time. Taggat was smart enough to know the symptoms of infatuation and knew that the further Steve was from Tallia the better.

Taggat warmed his hands, fixed two cups of coffee, wrapped his sleeping bag around himself, and wandered over to Arch. "Coffee?" Taggat stretched the steaming porcelain mug out to Arch.

"Thanks." Arch took the cup and held it in both hands.

"I'm glad the Saudis left this afternoon. Those guys make me nervous." A shiver moved violently through Taggat's body. "Damn! It's cold! "I hate to be cold."

"Yeah, you've made that point clear many times." Arch laughed. "I'm glad they're gone, also. That's five fewer to worry about."

"Any news about when we might get out of here? This place is getting old…fast!" Taggat looked around the stark gray hanger. "The Ritz…it ain't."

Arch smiled. "Well, the chopper just called in. It seems they found the pilot's remains. They should arrive within the hour. After we get our act together, we should be able to clear out by dawn."

Taggat fidgeted. "Arch, I don't want to put you on the spot, but did I hear you mention the name…Pooley?"

Arch lifted his eyebrows. "Yes. Why?"

"I know a Kent Pooley. He's a F-14 pilot in the Navy, and he's stationed on the *U. S. S. Carl Vinson*, but I can't imagine his being this far North."

"Well, he was, Taggat. His remains have been positively identified, and confirmation has already been sent to the States. How do you know Pooley?"

"It's a long story, and I didn't know him well. He and my god-daughter were seeing each other for a while. He was full of himself, but I guess you military types have to be that way. You think of yourself as indestructible so you can become indestructible."

"Well, it seems Pooley and his wingman did their part to keep the Iranians busy while we were saving your friend's ass." Arch pointed to Steve. "They flew combat air patrol for a Russian bomber on its way to Teheran. They took out two Migs while the Russians laid their eggs. A surface to air missile got Pooley's plane. His RIO ejected, but Pooley must have never bailed out. He'll probably be up for the Navy Cross. Might even become a national hero after all this. Who knows?"

Taggat patted Arch on the back and waved around to all the rescue team. "Well, I know who the real heroes are, and I'll never forget it. But I guess Pooley's parents will receive some solace in the medal. He was an only child."

"Sad, very sad." Arch turned toward the hanger door. "Excuse me, Taggat. I have to rouse the team. We've got a lot of preparation before lift off." Arch walked to the other end of the hanger. He warmed his hands and began waking the sleeping men.

Taggat retreated to the welcomed heat of the wood stove. He hovered within its warm radius for a few minutes and then walked over to Steve's resting place.

* * *

*The fire's reflection danced across the windows of the small street level Baku apartment occupied by the Maransk's. The only break in the glow was created by the two bodies huddled close to the crackling warmth of the hissing logs. The small blanket that they shared was draped over their shoulders, and occasionally their arms would flex to their mouths as they sipped the ice cold thickened vodka.*

*Steve looked at Tallia through a vodka induced haze. The fire danced across her dark eyes and played tricks between her partially visible breasts. Steve* could tell that the alcohol hadn't had too much effect because he felt the stirrings of his prolonged abstinence between his legs. As Tallia placed her hand inside his left thigh, Steve, trying to hid his firmness, jumped as if shocked.

"I'm sorry. I just wanted to scoot a little closer. Have you hurt your leg?" Tallia turned to Steve and smiled. "Or are you trying to play tricks on me like you did Yakim?"

"No tricks. I just felt a stiffness coming on." Steve slightly chuckled at his own little joke.

"Oh, where? Shall I rub it? Massaging the stiffness will help. Remember?" Tallia replied with innocence since she had not caught the levity in Steve's remark.

"No!…No. I don't think rubbing would be wise." Steve downed another ounce of vodka and refilled his glass.

"Be careful, Steve. The vodka will hit you quick, and you'll be asleep before we can enjoy the fire."

"Tallia, sleeping might be the safest thing for me right now."

"And why is that, Steve Hardesty?" Tallia turned toward Steve so they were knees to knees. She looked into his eyes and wondered if he would ever feel about her like he did the woman he had talked about so much while he was a hostage. She glanced at the open top of his shirt. The hair of his chest was visible just above the first button. As her gaze traveled down his torso to his groin, she noticed the fullness extending along the inside of his right leg. "I'm glad you're enjoying the fire." Tallia smiled, but did not avert her gaze from Steve's groin.

"I'm sorry. A beautiful woman has this effect on me, and Tallia, you are beautiful. But, its just that you aren't…"

Tallia placed her finger to Steve's lips. "Don't say anything else. I understand your devotion to your fiancée. But remember this, Steven Hardesty. If things don't seem to work out like you thought, I will always be here. You're the only man I'll ever give myself to again."

"Oh, you don't mean that, Tallia. You know you'll find someone. You're too beautiful not to have the men chasing you and fighting for the chance to make you love them."

Tallia leaned forward grabbing Steve by the shoulders and pulled his face toward her. She kissed him passionately and for a moment had thoughts about unbuttoning his shirt, but her mind won control over her heart, and she resisted. As she pulled away from the kiss, Tallia looked deeply into Steve's eyes. She could feel his desire but knew he would never betray the woman he had left behind…the woman pregnant with his child. The thought almost turned her stomach. "Don't feel any guilt about my love for you, Steve. You cannot control what I feel, and I will never confess these feelings to any one but you. I wanted you to know how I felt, but I believe you already knew."

Steve backed away breaking Tallia's embrace. He slowly stood and faced the fire widening his stance as he fought a brief moment of alcohol induced dizziness. The warmth of the fire heated the front of his body while the draft from the fireplace kept his back cool. "I don't know how to respond, Tallia. I really don't. You know that if it weren't for Sabrina…"

Tallia quickly stood interposing her body between Steve and the fireplace. "Please don't say anything more. It's not necessary. I know all too well what your situation is, and I'm trying to understand. Don't ask any more of me than that, but I'm not sorry I have fallen in love with you, Steve. Let's not speak of this any further. After tomorrow, it will be of no consequence. I want us to enjoy our last night together."

"Last night?" Steve looked into Tallia's eyes searching for the meaning of her revelation. "I thought you were going to America."

"No. My place is here, at least for now. Perhaps, someday, I will come to America." Tallia turned placing her back to Steve, her hands searching for his until they were found. "Perhaps, someday, you will want me to come to America."

Steve's grasp of Tallia's hands loosened, but he didn't let go. "Perhaps."

Tallia's smile was lost but to herself. "I love you, Steven Hardesty."

*"And I you, Tallia Maransk." Steve closed his eyes and wondered how it was possible to have these feelings for two separate women. When he opened his eyes, Tallia was gone. The only face he saw was Taggat's.*

\* \* \*

"Wha…what is it?" Steve reluctantly gave up his memories of the previously night and looked up at Taggat. "Oh, it's you. What's happening?"

"Get up. We need to talk."

Steve eased up out of the sleeping bag and stretched. He wrapped himself in a wool blanket, gray with a red star embossed on the corner, and walked over beside Taggat's position by the stove. "Wooo, it's cold. Why did you get me out of my cocoon?"

"We're pulling out at daybreak."

"It's about damn time!"

"Do you mean that?"

"Mean what?"

"Do you mean that you're happy that we're leaving?"

"Of course I'm happy. Why shouldn't I be?"

"Well, I've been catching mixed signals about you and the Russian woman."

"Actually, she's Azerbaijani not Russian."

"Whatever." Taggat shrugged his shoulders. "I thought you and she were getting a little close."

"Well, Taggat. It really isn't any of your business, but for the record, Tallia and I are close, but she and I know where my heart is. So, we were adult enough to leave it at that. And I would appreciate it if we didn't discuss that relationship again."

"Consider the subject closed."

"Good." Steve headed back to get what little gear he had together.

"Are you going to tell Sabrina about her?" Taggat took a sip of his coffee.

"I don't see the immediate need to do so. Do you?" Steve didn't turn to face Taggat when he spoke.

"Nope," Taggat smiled. "Most certainly not."

"Good," Steve proceeded across the hanger floor to his nest. "Let's go home."

* * *

Mac Orberson's plane touched down at Ramstein Air Force Base at 1:30 P. M. He had landed only two hours prior to the arrival of the transports from Turkey. Mac had requested that Paul Peterson be on hand for the arrival because the news he had to convey to Taggat and Steve was going to be difficult, at best, and he wanted a familiar face to be around.

Mac stepped out of the Air Force jet into the clear cold day. He looked down the steps finding Paul at the foot ladder. Mac descended the steps while pulling his topcoat tighter around his neck and his hat firmly down over his bald head. As he stepped closer to Paul, he gave no indication of their six month separation. "Paul, we have to talk. Is there someplace private?"

Paul smiled while photographers snapped. "Certainly. I have a warm spot in the hanger. Follow me."

They dodged the interviewers and found their way to a converted ready room. Paul followed Mac into the room and closed the door. "I've set up a makeshift conference room. I thought you might want to talk to Taggat and Steve after they arrive."

Mac looked at the accommodations. "This will function nicely. Good to see you, Paul." Mac removed his coat and extended his hand. "Have a seat," he requested while motioning to one of the chairs.

"Problems?" Paul settled into the chair.

"Damn right. Hardesty's fiancée died after she gave birth to his child."

"Dammit!"

"Exactly. What do you think Hardesty is made of? You know what I mean. How will he handle this?"

Paul became pensive for a moment then looked at Mac. "I'd say from outward appearances he probably won't show much emotion, but he'll take it hard inside. You better not discuss this until after the initial festivities are over. If he finds out as soon as he arrives, he'll be looking for an airplane out of here before your final words are out."

"Good point. After the ceremony, let's have Taggat and Steve come in here, and we'll discuss the situation. Make arrangements to have my private jet ready for departure as soon as we finish." Mac rubbed his chin. "Taggat's going to take this hard…real hard."

A rap at the door diverted their thoughts. Paul opened the door and confronted a burly red headed Staff Sergeant.

"Transport's on final, Gentlemen."

"Thank you, Sergeant." Paul closed the door and turned to Mac. "Shall we?"

Mac stood, put on his coat, and followed Paul out the door.

\* \* \*

"All right, you mean mothers. Let's look sharp!" Arch McConnell walked up and down the rows of the Special Ops Team while barking orders, checking weapons, and straightening uniforms. "Team, Attention!" He looked up and down the ranks. "That's more like it! Troops, right face! Column of twos, march!"

As the dark camouflaged troops marched down the ramp of the C5 Galaxy and onto the red carpet, the Air Force band began playing "The Stars and Stripes Forever." As soon as the first note played, the men brought their shoulders further back and lifted their heads higher. They marched onto the tarmac and stopped in front of the reviewing stand.

"Parade, rest!" Arch did a stiff about-face. "Troops ready for inspection, Sir!"

Taggat viewed the scene from the head of the loading ramp. He and Steve watched as Mac reviewed the men. Taggat started down the ramp motioning for Steve to join him. "Come on. Let's join the fun. After all, Steve, you're the reason for all this."

Steve held Taggat by the arm. "Hold on, Taggat. Let's let them bask in the limelight for a while. They took the majority of the risk."

"Like hell!" Taggat shot back. "You had the opposition well controlled by the time they hit the pavement.

"It makes no difference, Taggat. When you put on that uniform, you are prepared to die, and that deserves recognition."

"All right, I'll wait." Taggat reluctantly held up his progress down the ramp.

Mac stepped up behind the podium, and silence fell over the crowd. "Today, we celebrate a special occasion. We have gathered here to welcome home a countryman who has been held hostage in a foreign land. His captors flaunted his abduction over world television nine short weeks ago. Now, we'll profess his freedom in the same fashion."

Cheers went up from the crowd.

Mac cleared his throat. "Even though we deeply thank the other nations involved; Germany, Turkey, Saudi Arabia, and the Soviet Union, we owe our deepest thanks to our military." Mac waved his hand along the line of the team. "These men, as all our armed servicemen and women, were ready to lay down their lives for the rescue of a single American. Think about it, a mission to rescue six men, and only one of them an American. With cooperation from all our armed services, we have successfully dealt a blow to his captors. We will continue to show the world, with the help of men and women such as these, that the United States will never accede to the threats of any country at any time." A tremendous applause erupted from the stands.

"Mac could always put a good speech together," Taggat commented from his stand at the head of the gangway.

As the applause diminished, Mac looked over the troops and reviewing stands. He still got a high when speaking in public. The rush never diminished. He knew that the successful initiation of the pipeline's construction and the safe return of the hostages would seal the President's bid for reelection. Mac also knew he would be in line for President in four short years.

Mac stepped closer to the microphone and cleared his throat. "Ladies and Gentlemen. I have been authorized by the President to award a special campaign ribbon to the troops. Also, I have been assigned to award a field commission to Captain McConnell."

Mac left the podium and walked along the line of men awarding each their appropriate ribbon. He stopped in front of Arch, reached inside his coat pocket, and retrieved a small black box. He opened the box and pinned the oak leaf clusters on Arch's shoulder epaulets. "Congratulations, Major. Well done!"

Arch saluted. "Thank you, Mr. Secretary."

Mac returned to the podium, looked over at the transport, and saw Taggat and Steve standing at the head of the gangway. "Now, we would like to welcome Captain Hardesty back to friendly soil."

Steve took his cue, straightened up, and proceeded off the plane. He looked back at Taggat. "You coming?"

"Oh, I can come?" Taggat grinned and walked beside Steve down the gangway.

"By the way, Taggat. Thanks for coming." Steve said out of the corner of his mouth.

Taggat just smiled.

A thunderous ovation welcomed Steve and Taggat's arrival on the podium. As they stood behind the microphone, a flight of four F-16's flew in tight formation five hundred feet overhead. The band struck up "The Star Spangled Banner," and the troops came to attention.

Mac welcomed Taggat and Steve. "Welcome home, Captain. The American personnel of Ramstein Air Force Base and our German allies extend their warmest greetings. We're glad to have you home." Another round of applause went up from the stands.

Steve walked up to the microphone, cleared his throat, and spoke. "Thank you, Mr. Secretary. Seventy five days ago I wouldn't have expected to set foot on free soil again. The best I could except was to see it from six feet under." Steve smiled.

A muffled laugh murmured through the crowd.

"Don't be shy about laughing. I can laugh about it. Now!"

Another roll of laughter moved through the gathered troops.

"I owe my life, not only to the men standing before you, but also to a woman who is not here with us today. She's a Soviet citizen who had also been taken hostage by the same madmen as I. Her belief in freedom, and her willingness to risk her life for me, made my road to safety possible. Her name is Tallia Maransk, and someday, I hope she also will set her feet on free soil." Steve cleared his throat. "No one can understand the pride I have in calling myself an American."

The crowd went wild.

As mist came to his eyes, Steve absorbed the applause. He waited for a minute as the applause subsided. "A few years ago, I served in Vietnam flying jets from the deck of an aircraft carrier. I have flown numerous flights over hostile territory threatened by death or capture, but I was always the one, or at least thought I was the one who controlled my destiny. Until you live through a situation where you are a captured animal, you will never know what freedom really means. Now, it means more than ever. On Christmas morning when the other hostages and I were huddled in the shambles of a blown up hanger watching our only means of escape burn before our eyes, we wrote ourselves off as dead. We knew we would never see our homelands again. We armed ourselves and prepared to return as many of our captors to Allah, as we could before we were killed." Steve wiped the mist from his eyes.

Mac looked at Paul and whispered. "Not emotional, huh? This guy could be a shoo-in for public office."

"Who'd figure?" Paul shrugged.

"Then we heard the sound of helicopters...our helicopters. When we saw the Hueys come in over our position, land, and release this thundering herd of men from its doors, we knew we were safe. Nothing would hamper our return to the United States. Nothing would keep us from being free once again." Steve looked for something to wipe a tear from his eye. As he searched his pockets, he came upon a piece of paper in his flight jacket. He pulled it out and looked at the writing. It was Tallia's. He placed it back into the pocket while wiping his eyes with his opposite jacket sleeve.

Mac walked back over to Steve and smiled to the crowd. "Steve," he spoke softly through his smile. "We have to talk after this hullabaloo settles down." Mac dropped his arms, straightened his coat, and stepped closer to the microphone. "We want to thank everyone for braving the cold. There will be a base reception at 14:00 hours in Hanger B. Thank you."

As the stands cleared, Mac escorted Taggat and Steve to the conference room. The welcomed warmth allowed them to peel out of one of their layers of clothing, and after the three of them were seated at the conference table, Mac pulled some files from the briefcase. He hoped there would be an answer to the unpleasant task before him, but as he pursed his lips and furrowed his brows, he knew there was no easy way to relate his information.

"Mac, what the hell is going on? You look as if you lost your best friend. I thought we were supposed to be happy." Taggat looked at Mac and then inquisitively at Steve.

Mac squirmed in his seat, fidgeted with the folder, and loosened his collar. "Look. There's no easy way to tell the both of you this. So, I'm going to shoot straight from the hip. While we were busy with our jobs over here, there was a lot happening at home. Steve, Sabrina's had the baby."

"All ready?" Steve began counting the months. "She's only six months pregnant."

Mac looked quizzically at Steve. "Steve, Sabrina did have the baby, but she had complications after the birth of the child."

"What kind..."

"Just a minute, Steve. It gets worse. Sabrina's dead."

"Dead!" Taggat and Steve blurted.

"Dead?" Steve fell back in his seat. "How…How could she be dead?" Steve looked over at Taggat. "I thought she was only having some minor complications. Oh, my God." Steve hung his head in thought.

Mac interrupted before Taggat could respond. "I don't know where you got your information, but Sabrina's medical problems, according to my experts in the States, were quite severe. They feel she was lucky to have gotten to term and deliver. At least the baby's all right. She's…It was a girl. She's small, but she's okay."

"Term?" Steve looked at Taggat. "Isn't term nine months?"

Taggat trying to skirt the issue stood and began pacing the room. "I need a drink. Dammit, Mac! Get us something in here to drink. Now!"

Mac rang a small buzzer beside his position, and an Air Force Sergeant entered the door.

"Sergeant, bring us some bourbon."

"Yes Sir, Mr. Secretary."

Taggat walked over to the table and leaned close to Mac's face. "You sure about this, Mac?"

"Taggat, it has been confirmed."

Taggat slumped down in the nearest chair, leaned forward hanging his head in his hands. "How can this be? Did the Doctors at Bethesda say how it happened?"

Steve looked up from his thoughts about the length of a term pregnancy and queried, "Bethesda? I thought she was going to deliver in Norfolk."

"She wasn't at either place. She delivered in a small hospital in Clifton Forge."

"Where the hell is Clifton Forge?" Taggat mumbled.

"It's off the Interstate South of Washington between Richmond and Williamsburg."

"What the hell was she doing there? I thought she was in your team's protective custody and had planned to deliver in Washington." Taggat still didn't look up.

"What the hell is going on here?" Steve leaned forward in his chair. "I thought she was in Norfolk."

Mac looked at Taggat's bowed head and into Steve's questioning face. "Steve, Sabrina had come to Washington trying to find out more about your situation. When we filled her in on this operation, we felt it best she remain in Washington and deliver in a government facility. Evidently, her friend, Cathy Winston, didn't think we could do the job. She drugged our team with chloralhydrate laced brandy and extracted Sabrina from us. Evidently Sabrina was in labor, and they stopped in Clifton Forge. Sabrina had the baby on Christmas Morning. The little girl weighed just over four pounds. The doctors say she's doing all right, and she does appear to be full term."

Steve's head shook negatively. "Impossible," he murmured.

"Sabrina had a severe complication on the first day after her delivery. She apparently threw a blood clot to the brain and died."

"You said the baby was at term?" Steve questioned, not responding to the news of the cause of Sabrina's death.

"Yes. That's the information we received from the records. The pediatrician that evaluated the baby at birth seems to be well qualified."

Steve looked at Taggat. Taggat had not raised his head. He continued to sit, sob, and rock. "That's impossible, isn't it, Taggat? Sabrina and I have only been back together for the past six months. The first time I made love to Sabrina was six months ago. There's no way the baby could have been full term. Right?...Dammit, Taggat! Look at me and tell me what you know about this."

Taggat looked up and tried to focus on Steve through his reddened eyes. "Know about what?" He sniffed.

"You heard, goddammit! The baby...Sabrina's baby. Mac said the baby was full term."

"The doctors made a mistake. We'll look into it when we get home. It's not important. My daughter's dead. That's what's important."

"Wait a minute here." Mac flushed and looked at Steve and Taggat. "Is there something I should know? We've got a hero going home to a dead fiancée. A baby that is supposedly his. A woman who has drugged my men. And a situation that could blow up in our face if the facts aren't straight. Taggat, what DO you know about this? This could be a political bombshell."

"Yes, Taggat. I'm interested, also." Steve stood and leaned forward against the table supporting his weight with his hands. "Sabrina and I were together in July. I've been gone since. She should have only been six months pregnant at Christmas. Now, Mac tells me she delivered a term baby. Something's rotten here, and I think you know about it."

"Yes, Taggat. Let's get this all out now. We don't want to have any unanswered questions when we face the President."

"Fuck the President, and fuck the both of you! My daughter's dead, and the two of you don't give a good god-damn. Steve, I thought you loved Sabrina. I guess I was wrong."

"I did love her, Taggat. But I've got to know the truth. Was she having my baby?" Steve leaned closer to Taggat.

"Yes, Taggat. Please enlighten us about this before we make asses of ourselves when we get home. You know this could kill us politically if there is a scandal." Mac leaned against the table and pecked his pen against the hard surface.

"I don't believe the two of you. What in the hell are you really worried about? Never mind. Don't answer that. I don't want to know the answer." Taggat stood and mustered his inner strength. "All right, I'll tell you the truth. Steve, the baby wasn't yours. There. You're out. So, get the hell out of my sight. I don't give a damn if I ever see you again."

"Whoa. Wait a minute…Taggat…Steve. Let's not say a bunch of things we'll be sorry for. Let's try and be civilized about this. Remember, you've both lost someone very important to you. Taggat, let's hear your side of the story. Just calm down and tell us what was going on."

"Where's that goddamned bourbon?" Taggat yelled.

"I'm sure it'll be here in a moment," Mac's face flushed, but his temperament remained level.

Taggat calmed down for a moment and began to formulate the story. "All right. I'll tell you everything, but it's going to hurt. I don't see why I need to drag this out. Sabrina's dea…" Taggat slumped back into his seat and began to cry. "Oh, my God. I can't believe I'll never see her again."

Steve was exasperated, and his patience was wearing thin. "Oh hell, Taggat. Straighten up and tell us."

Taggat looked up and burned a hole into Steve's forehead with his gaze. "You're one cold son-of-a-bitch. You know that?"

"You don't know the half of it, Taggat. I just want to know what I was about to get myself into. Hell, it sounds as if I was lucky to have been sent over here. You and Sabrina were sitting home pretty damn proud of yourselves, weren't you. You had found a patsy father for her bastard child."

"Goddamn you, Steve!" Taggat jumped from his chair and swung a Steve's face.

Steve reacted, feinted the punch, grabbed Taggat's arm slamming him head first onto the table. He pinned Taggat's arm sharply to the table and leaned down closer to his ear. "You try that one more time, asshole, and I'll kill you before you blink. You know I can do it."

"Gentlemen! Gentlemen!" Mac stood and nervously laughed.

The guard entered the room with a 9mm Beretta in one hand and a bottle of Jack Daniels in the other. "What the hell is going on in here?"

"Everything is fine, Sergeant." Mac held up both hands. "Put the bourbon on the table, and holster that weapon before someone in here gets the bright idea to use it. I think we need some attitude adjustment."

Steve released his hold on Taggat as the Sergeant put the bourbon on the table.

Taggat and Mac drank a long triple bourbon while Steve tensely stood in the same spot where he had just released Taggat.

After a few moments, Taggat looked up from his drink. "The baby belongs to Kent Pooley."

Mac choked. "The pilot that was killed? Oh shit!" Mac tilted his head back and closed his eyes.

"That goddamn, no good, son-of-a-bitch! If that little fucker wasn't already dead, I'd kill him." Steve slammed his fist into the table.

"Exactly!" Taggat yelled. "That's exactly what I told Sabrina you would do, and that's why she was afraid to tell you. She didn't want you to get into trouble. It was my idea not to tell you about the baby, Steve. Not Sabrina's."

"But she continued the charade. She continued to cover up the truth. How long, Taggat? How long would she have let it continue?"

"She would have told you, Steve. Sabrina would have told you before you were married. Don't hate her for this. She knew she was taking a big chance having the baby. Sabrina loved you so much, it was easy to convince her that concealing the pregnancy was for the best."

"I'm sorry, Taggat, but I can't accept this. I know you thought it was the best for Sabrina, but I can't believe you would have let me taken the fall for Pooley's baby. I can't believe it!"

Taggat shrugged his shoulders. "I would have done whatever was best for Sabrina. I was blinded by my love for her, and I had hoped you would feel the same."

"I understand that, but why didn't she tell me. Why didn't she tell me when we were at the beach. She took me for the perfect fool. Here she was pregnant with one man's child while she was being proposed to by another. What could have been more prefect?"

"We're not getting anywhere with this. Are we? If you can't accept what has happened and forgive Sabrina, then I'm happy she never had to face your sarcasm. Someday you'll realize what you've missed. Then you might forgive." Taggat turned to Mac. "When can we get away from here. I need to get home. I have to be at Sabrina's funeral."

Steve turned, threw up his hands, and walked toward the door. "I'm out of here. I've had all of this I can stand."

"Just a minute. Hold on!" Mac shuffled his papers and stuffed them into his briefcase. "We have to make travel arrangements. Steve, you're expected in Washington tomorrow. They have you scheduled to go on national television with the President. We have to leave…"

"I'm not going back to the States. Not quite yet. Has my money been deposited into my Swiss account from the deal with the Saudis?"

"No. Not yet." Mac closed his briefcase. "Why?"

"Well, see to it. Now! I expect it in there within twenty four hours. Understand?"

"Hold on! You aren't giving orders around here. I am."

"No, Mac. Not this time. If you don't take care of this immediately, I swear I'll break this whole damned story to the press. I don't think this administration wants that mess, and I don't thing the Saudis would like it either. I'll be staying in Europe for a while. I have some unfinished business." Steve looked at Taggat. "When you get home, draw up the papers to sell me your share of the flying service. I'm buying you out for two million dollars."

"Just a damned minute." Taggat puffed. "It's worth a hell of a lot more than that."

"It may be, but you're selling if you don't want Sabrina's name plastered all over the newspapers."

"You wouldn't do that?"

"Try me." Steve glared into Taggat's eyes.

"Hell, you've got it. I don't want anything to do with the business anyway. I only held onto my share to humor Sabrina." Taggat again sat down and began to weep at his mention of Sabrina's name.

"Look, Steve. You have no room to threaten. I've got the government on my side, and we could make your life miserable if we chose to do so." Mac edged between Steve and Taggat.

Taggat raised his hand. "Hold on, Mac. Steve's right. We don't want him in the States. It will be a much better story to confess Pooley as the father of the child. The nation will still have a hero...at least the daughter of a hero. It will be much better press than the alternative."

Steve smiled at the comment. "Fine by me. Mr. Orberson, I want you to arrange safe passage on your next transport to Baku. Then I want you to have a new Lear waiting for me at this base in three days. I'm sure the government wants to replace my lost property. You both have a good trip home. Taggat, I'll see you in two weeks." Steve turned, opened the door, and headed out into the hanger. Once he was into the open area of the hanger, he stopped and took a deep breath. In frustration, he slammed his fists into the pockets of his flight jacket, and he once again encountered the crumpled piece of paper. He pulled it from his pocket and read.

*Steve,*

*If you ever have a moment when life is getting you down, and you feel that no one is on your side, read this note and remember our moments in front of the fire that cold December night. I will always love you.*

*Tallia*

Steve carefully folded the note and replaced it into the inner pocket of his flight jacket. He proceeded across the hanger floor and onto the tarmac. As he rounded the corner of the hanger he encountered an airman walking toward the hanger entrance. "Excuse me, Airman. Which hanger is used for staging the medical relief to the Soviet Union.

"Hanger 15 at the other end of the taxiway, Sir."

"Thank you, Airman." Steve fired the Airman a salute and started his journey back to Baku.

# 27

Beth Pooley sat in the oversized leather chair looking out over the Pacific Coastline. Brian had worked his way through many problems from this chair, but Beth didn't need any more work on her's. She had found her solution.

On the desk in front of her was a half empty quart bottle of bourbon that had been full two hours ago. Around her chair, over the surface of the desk, and brimming out the top of the wastebasket were crumpled pieces of her stationery. She always had trouble getting the written word exactly as she liked. However, after the twentieth or thirtieth attempt, she wasn't sure which, she finally had the note to Brian like she wanted. She picked the final draft up from the desk and read;

> *Dear Brian,*
>
> *Our life together was always what I had imagined marriage to be. I felt loved. I may not have been, but I felt as if I were, and that's what was important to me. Our love produced a*

*child…my Kent. I need not tell you that my life and breath was Kent. How can I explain the feelings a mother has for a child? You would never understand. Kent's life became my life. I know I was possessive and protective, but that was my lot. No one decided that for me. Now, they have taken away my life. I breathe, I eat, I see, I feel, I hear, but I'm not alive. With Kent's death, my life has ended. All I'm doing is ending my body's existence, for the life in it is gone. I'm going to give you your freedom and find Kent. We'll be happy.*

*Brian, dear Brian, don't mourn me, for my heart will no longer be broken. I still love you. Don't begrudge me this action.*

*Beth*

Beth folded the note and placed it into an envelope. She licked the seal and placed it in the center of the desk where she had cleared a spot with the swipe of her arm. She spun the chair around and looked into the setting sun. The sinking globe sent out dancing orange rays as Beth reached into her robe pocket and extracted a folded sheet of yellow paper. She unfolded the paper and read the message from the Department of the Navy for the hundredth time.

*Dear Mr. and Mrs. Pooley,*

*We regret to inform you that your son, Lieutenant Kent Pooley, USN 45332341, was killed in action over hostile territory at 0645h 25 December. He performed in the highest tradition of our armed forces. His action not only saved the life of his co-pilot, but also was instrumental in saving the lives of his fellow countrymen. He has been recommended to receive the Navy Cross. A special ceremony…*

Beth quit reading and let the note drop among the clutter, but the words of the Naval officer delivering the note, and the reality of the telegram burned their harsh imprint on her mind. She turned the chair back around and opened the top right drawer of the desk. From the back of the drawer, she removed a small oak box, set it in front of her, and slowly lifted the top. Inside was the Colt 9mm automatic pistol Brian had given her. She smiled as she remembered his concern for her safety while he was away on his many business trips. It had made her feel secure, and now she was happy she could put it to good use.

Beth picked up the steel blue instrument and laid it on the desk top. She removed the clip from the weapon's handle, reached into the drawer, and retrieved one round of ammunition from a full box of fifty. She deftly placed the 100 grain hollow-point round into the clip and slid the clip back into the handle until it locked into place. She poured another three fingers of Wild Turkey, put the gun in her lap, grasped the glass, and turned her chair back to the Pacific Panorama.

As she let the empty glass slip from her hand, Beth closed her eyes and tried to imagine the days when she and her young son would go down to the sea and play in the surf. She had always enjoyed watching Kent discover new things in the ocean. Her mind returned to the warm summer afternoons when they would picnic on the shore and watch the sailboats tack across the choppy waters of the bay. Their bright sails would always excite Kent. Beth smiled and opened her eyes. Through her tears and against the backdrop of the setting sun, Beth could see young Kent running toward the ocean's edge. Suddenly, as if he were real, he turned and beckoned.

"Come on, Mommy. Come on. I'm waiting for you. If you don't hurry, we'll miss the pretty sailboats." Again he turned and headed for the pounding surf.

Beth reached out with her right hand. "Wait, Kent. Wait, baby. Mommy's coming. Don't leave me…not again."

Kent's specter turned and smiled. "I'll never leave you, Mommy. You're all I have."

Beth began crying. The vision began to fade. She reached into her lap, picked up the gun, slid back and released the slide loading the round into the chamber. She clicked the safety button off and looked back into Kent's fading image.

"Hurry, Mommy. Hurry! I miss you."

"I miss you, baby. I'm coming." Beth placed the gun to her right temple. "God, forgive me." She pulled the trigger...

* * *

Brian floored the accelerator of the rented Lincoln Continental and hoped he had arrived home ahead of the telegram announcing Kent's death. He didn't want Beth to face the news alone. He had decided to tell Beth about the baby being alive hoping the fact would give her a piece of Kent to hold onto. If she could accept the fact that the child was a part of Kent, her life would continue to have purpose. As he rounded the last turn in the driveway, he noticed a number of vehicles randomly parked in front of the house. It took a few seconds for it to register they were police cars, marked and unmarked. An ambulance was also parked near the garden entrance. Brian pulled the Lincoln into the closest spot, got out, and headed for the front door.

"Excuse me," a uniformed policeman stopped Brian as he crossed the pavement. "Are you a relative of Mrs. Pooley?"

"I'm her husband. What's wrong?"

"Excuse me, Sir. Would you please come with me, Mr. Pooley? Captain Reynolds would like to speak to you." The officer led Brian up the walk, through the garden, and into the front hallway.

A group of men were standing at the far end of the hall in front of the study door. They stopped talking and looked up as Brian and the officer entered.

"Wait here for a moment, Mr. Pooley." The officer held his hand and pointed to the spot where Brian had stopped. The uniformed policeman slowly approached the group and selected a tall, thin, gray-haired gentleman with his back to Brian.

Brian didn't hear what was said, but the uniformed officer and Captain, Brian assumed, walked his direction.

"Mr. Pooley, this is Captain Reynolds. Now, if you'll excuse me."

"Thanks, Pete. Mr. Pooley, I'm Captain Mark Reynolds of the Monterey Police Department."

"What's going on, Captain? What's the matter. Has there been a break-in or something?" Brian began looking around for signs of Beth. "Where's my wife? Is she here?"

"Mr. Pooley, I'm afraid I have some bad news. Perhaps you would like to sit down."

"No, I don't need to sit. What's going on here? I have a right..."

"Mr. Pooley, your wife is dead. I'm terribly sorry."

"Dead? How?" Brian wavered slightly, and the Captain grabbed his arm.

"Why don't we sit down over here in the living room?"

"Thank you, Captain. I believe I better."

Captain Reynolds led Brian over to the couch. The leather squeaked as they sat down in unison.

"How did this happen, Captain. Was there a robbery?"

"No, sir. It appears your wife has committed suicide...single 9mm projectile to the head."

"That's impossible. She didn't have any reason to..." Brian stopped mid sentence. "Had she found out about our son?"

"Apparently that is the reason. We found this telegram on the floor beside her." Mark handed Brian the yellow piece of paper. "This note was on the desk. It's addressed to you. You may read it, but don't destroy it. We need it for evidence."

Brian read the impersonal telegram, opened the envelope, and read the note. As he read, tears came to his eyes. He handed the notes back to Captain Reynolds. "Thank you for allowing me to read these first. When did this happen?"

"The coroner thinks it happened around 7:00 P. M. last evening. The cleaning lady found her this morning. She's the one that called the police. She informed us you and your wife were separated. We had tried to contact you, but your answering service forwarded us to a hospital in Virginia. Now, I know why we couldn't find you."

"Can I see her?"

"I wouldn't advise it, Mr. Pooley. We're taking pictures now. The coroner will be finished in thirty minutes. Would you like anything to drink?"

Brian thought it strange to be offered hospitality in his own home. "No, I'll fix something for myself in a moment. I need a few minutes to let this sink in."

"I understand, Mr. Pooley. We only have a few more questions, and then, we'll be leaving." Captain Reynolds got up and returned to the group of detectives in the hall.

Brian sat stoically for a few moments, rose, went to the dry bar, fixed a double scotch, pulled a book of photographs from the adjacent shelf, and returned to the couch. As he sat and sipped, he traced the family history through the photographs. In recent photos only Beth and Kent were included. Brian was conspicuously absent. "I guess that's the way it's been for a long time. Now, they're together again."

"Excuse me?" Detective Reynolds asked as he sat down next to Brian.

"Just thinking out loud, Captain."

"I realize this seems like a bother, Mr. Pooley, but we will have to have a coroner's inquest concerning the death of your wife."

"I understand. When will that be?"

"We'll set the date tomorrow. I'll notify you. Will you be remaining at the house?"

Brian looked at the Captain with surprise. "I...guess so. Why?"

"Well, I wasn't sure, and I didn't want to imply any disrespect, but some folks have trouble staying near a place where someone has died."

"Captain, I've been so near death for the past few days, I don't think this will matter." Brian noticed the Captain's puzzlement. "You won't believe this, but I have to go back to the East Coast to attend a funeral. Do you think an inquest will be necessary?"

"If all the evidence points to suicide, the inquest could be waived. As I said, I should be able to let you know by tomorrow."

"Brian leaned forward and put his head in his hands. "I thought I could beat the Naval Detachment. I didn't think they would send a telegram."

"I believe it's protocol."

"Of course, but I didn't think. I guess that's been my problem lately. I haven't been thinking. I should have been here."

"Mr. Pooley, I don't think you should try to blame yourself. Believe me, I've seen a great number of suicides, and if a person has decided to end their life, they will do it no matter who's around. You have to accept her decision. We'll never know what was going through her mind."

"Oh," Brian grasped the photo book tightly. "I know what was going through her mind. Beth was devoted to our son. She didn't want, nor care, for an existence that didn't include Kent. When she found out he had died, she died that very instant. What you found was her answer to joining our son." Brian choked. "You see, she never wanted Kent to have to go anywhere alone." Brian began crying but got a hold on himself before the Captain reached for his shoulder.

"Would you like for me to have the doctor prescribe something for you?"

"No. I don't think I'll need anything. I'll be all right."

"Are you sure, Mr. Pooley?"

"I'm not sure right now, Captain, but, as time goes by, I will be."

Mark Reynolds rose as they rolled the stretcher through the living room and out the door.

Brian looked up just enough to see a white sheet stretched over the black rubberized body bag. It flashed into Brian's mind that Kent would have been brought home in the same fashion.

"We're leaving now, Mr. Pooley. I'll have a man drive by later this evening and check on you, if that's okay."

"That's fine, Captain. I appreciate it."

"We've closed off the study. Please stay out of there for tonight. We'll be back early in the morning to complete our work."

"I'll have no need to go in there. Thank you." Brian reached into his pocket and pulled out his key ring. He removed one of his extra house keys and handed it to the Captain. "I might not be here early in the morning. Have your men let themselves in and lock up on their way out."

"Yes sir. I'll see to it myself. Good day, Mr. Pooley. I'm sorry we had to meet under these circumstances."

"Me too, Captain." Brian mustered the best smile he had.

Brian closed the door as the last officer departed. As he turned and looked down the long hall, he couldn't imagine not hearing Kent's or Beth's voices ever again. The bright yellow police tape jumped out at him as he passed the study, and he couldn't bring himself to go into Beth's bedroom. He slowly opened the door to his room. Everything was in the same condition as when he had left. He lay down to rest, but a million thoughts raced through his head making sleep impossible. Returning to the living room, he poured a second glass of Scotch and sat in one of the side chairs. He slowly sipped the drink and fingered through the photo book once again. The feeling the pictures created was too depressing, so Brian leaned back and closed his eyes. "If you can hear me, I want you to know I loved both of you very much. I know I wasn't the best father, but I tried to do the best I could. I'll miss you both very much. Kent, Sabrina gave you a beautiful daughter, but she paid the ultimate price...her life. Beth, I wanted you to know about the baby, but I was too late. I'm truly sorry. I'll take care of our grand-daughter, Beth. This I promise you. Please forgive me. May God bless you both and grant you eternal peace." The prayer gave him peace, and Brian slept.

The phone beside the couch almost lept off its cradle. Brian jerked, shook off some of the scotch, and looked around the room. The sun was setting in the panorama of the picture window behind him. He reached for the phone noticing his watch—7 P.M. *Probably about the time Beth killed herself last night,* Brian thought.

"Hello," Brian yawned.

"Thank goodness it's you. I was afraid I would have to hang up if Beth answered."

"Cathy, is that you?"

"Yes. You sound funny. Are you okay?"

"I was dozing. Cathy?"

"Yes, Brian?"

"Beth's dead."

Cathy slumped back on the living room sofa. "This all has to be a nightmare. I can't believe it. What happened?"

"She committed suicide."

"Suicide! Why? Did she learn about Kent before you arrived?"

"Yes. Evidently, the Navy delivered the telegram the night before I arrived. The coroner thinks she killed herself last night. The house lady found her this morning. I arrived just after the police. It was terrible."

"Brian, I'm sorry. I'm truly sorry."

"Thanks. How are you? I hated leaving, and as it turned out, I guess my trip wasn't necessary since I didn't arrive soon enough." Brian choked. "I guess I've failed in a lot of things, lately."

"Don't punish yourself, Brian. You've done what you thought was best. That's all you could do." Cathy paused. "Brian, I'm having Sabrina's funeral in two days. The State Department called and advised me Taggat would be home tomorrow."

"What about Steve?"

"I don't know, Brian. The message was very strange. They told me Steve would be remaining in Europe to pursue further State Department activities. I'm not sure what has happened. I asked them if he knew Sabrina was dead and that the baby had been born."

"Well, what did they say?"

"The only comment I got was that Captain Hardesty had resigned his commission and was remaining in Europe. They gave me no further information."

"Taggat will know what's happened. You can get the information from him. I'll be there for the funeral. Then, I'll fly back for Beth and Kent's ceremony. I want to wait for Kent's body to arrive before I have the funerals. How's Stephanie?"

"She's fine. I'm leaving for the Island in the morning. I've got to have some time to think all this out. I'm so confused. The hospital has agreed to board the baby until I can make some plans...arrange a Nanny or something." Cathy began sobbing. "Brian, what am I going to do? I'm not a mother. Sabrina was supposed to be here for that. What am I going to do?"

"Hey...hey! This isn't the Cathy Winston I know. She can handle anything."

"Yes, anything adult! What in the hell am I going to do with a baby!"

"May I make a suggestion?"

"Please!"

"How about bringing Stephanie out here for a few weeks, or months, or whatever?"

"Whoa! Stephanie is my responsibility. I can't leave her in California."

"I don't want you to leave her. I want you to live here with her."

"But..."

"Wait a minute. I know we've only known each other for a few days, but what we've gone through is enough for a lifetime. It will do you a world of good to get away. I'll have Maria find us some more help. That way, you can have some experienced help being a new mother. How about it?"

"Brian, I'm..."

"Wait, don't answer that. How about coming out for a short while after Sabrina's funeral? I'll have a nursery fixed up while I'm there. It'll do us both some good. Therapy, or something like that. You know?"

"I couldn't do that. I have a business to get back together."

"I'm sure your business will be fine. You have good people helping. You know things can run themselves for a while. Think about it?"

"All right, I'll think about it, but what would the neighbors think?"

"Who gives a damn! We're both old enough not to care about that, and Stephanie won't mind."

"It does sound tempting and relaxing. I'll give it a great deal of thought. But, Brian?"

"Yes?"

"Don't toy with me. Don't pretend to care just to be near the baby. I can't deal with that."

"Cathy, I love Stephanie, and I would do anything to be near her. But I've given up deceit. I want you here because I want to be near you. I need you, Cathy Winston. Don't you understand?"

"No, no, no! Don't say any more! I don't want to be needed. Please, if I decide to come and spend some time, I want us to go slow. I mean real slow. Please?"

"All right. I understand."

"Good. I don't want us getting our emotions all tangled up when we are so vulnerable."

"Cathy?"

"Yes, Brian?"

"You will want to stay after you are here for a while. I know you will."

"How do you know that?"

"Because it is what Sabrina would have wanted."

"That may be, but let's get through this next week, and we'll see what happens." Cathy let out a long sigh. "Will you be coming back soon?"

"If you don't mind, I don't want to be alone for the next few days."

"I don't mind. There's plenty of room at the beachhouse. The airport on the Island can handle private jet traffic. Call me before you arrive, and I'll come pick you up."

"Fine, I'll wrap up a few things here tomorrow, and see you tomorrow evening. Goodnight."

"Goodnight, Brian." Cathy hung up the phone. She wandered around the condominium. What was a place of happiness a few short weeks ago had now turned to a collection of sad memories. Cathy retired to her bedroom and lay on the bed. She tried to think about her life, and what was to come, but she shut it from her mind. She hated to be alone. She hated to be a mother. "Yuck, I hate babies." She thought about Brian's offer, and the more she turned it over in her mind, the more it appealed to her. "Maybe I'll take him up on his offer. I need a rest. And Stephanie needs a daddy. After all, Brian Pooley probably thinks he loves me, and that wouldn't be so bad either. I could do a hell of a lot worse. Yes, maybe I will go to California and test the water there. After all, I still have to take care of myself. Right? Right!"

# 28

"Cathy, I'm leaving for England tomorrow, and I want you to come with me."

Cathy sat on the couch in the den of her home on Gull Haven. The same couch where not long ago she and Sabrina had planned out their trip to the west coast to visit Brian and Beth Pooley. Her black wool dress fitted smartly about her figure, but Cathy was immune to her surroundings this day...the day of Sabrina's funeral. She looked up at Richard and smiled. "Richard, I'm sorry for the show I put on in Washington, and I want you to know that I do care for you very much."

"But you don't love me. Correct?"

"Correct." Cathy twisted the handkerchief in her fingers. "I just..."

"Please, don't say anything else. Your message is quite clear. Let's just leave it at what it was and remember the good times we've had." Richard turned to leave the room, but was halted by Cathy's touch on his arm.

"Richard, you're such a little boy. You and I were fantastic together, and if things had been different, maybe I would be off to England with you. But Richard, I have responsibilities here that I can't sweep aside. I have a little girl that's going to grow up thinking of me as her mother…well not her mother, but you know what I mean." Cathy began to cry and fell against Richard's chest. "Richard, what am I going to do with a baby?"

"Cathy, I'm not sure what will happen, but I know you well enough, and I'm sure you'll come up with some plan to take care of yourself and the child. I only hoped you would have been able to do it with me. I too am sorry for our argument, and perhaps if I hadn't acted so quickly, you would be going home with me."

"I think that's the entire problem, Richard. You see, I am home, and I'll never think of anyplace besides this house as my home. I might live someplace else, but this will always be mine and Sabrina's and now Stephanie's home. Nothing or no one will ever change that." Cathy kissed Richard on the cheek. "Good-by, Richard. I'll always remember what we had together. No one can take away those memories."

Brian stepped through the door into the den and summoned Cathy. "It's time, Cathy. The limo has arrived."

Richard stepped back from Cathy and walked out of the room past Brian. He stopped for a moment looking at Brian. "Take care of our ladies, Brian. They'll always mean the world to me." Without waiting for a reply Richard turned and left through the front door.

"He's a very nice gentleman, Cathy. Are you sure you want to let him go?" Brian helped Cathy put on her coat.

"Jealous?" Cathy smiled through her tears.

"Yes, but I can cope."

Cathy smiled and buttoned up her coat. "Let's go."

Brian lightly grasped Cathy's right upper arm and escorted her out into the cold afternoon.

* * *

The snow flakes languidly drifted from the ashen sky. As they hit the jagged edges of recently turned earth, the symmetrical shapes crushed on impact sending their powdery substance spraying over the fresh spade cuts in the ground. However, the virgin white shroud couldn't disguise the harshness of the newly dug grave.

The Chesapeake was unusually still this day. The waves that usually smacked the shore and stole the loose sand chose to leisurely lap against the beach leaving the shore unchanged. The geese, who were generally anxious to erupt from the protective waters of the bay and search out their favorite eating spots, floated leisurely on the surface like corks. The whole world seemed to sense the solemn occasion about to occur.

The cemetery on MacKenzie Island was a small family plot telling the coming and going of the generations. Sabrina's was to be yet another head-stone in the saga. The grave site welcomed the rising sun of each new day and was surrounded by a small garden that celebrated the coming and going of each season.

Cathy knew the ceremony would be her hardest time. To say farewell to Sabrina seemed impossible. How could she say good-by to someone she loved? How could she let go of someone she held dear to her heart...forever?! She knew it would be a long time before these past eight months became reality. So many things had happened...so many. As she clutched Brian's hand, she hoped and prayed for better days ahead.

As the minister walked to the head of the grave site, Cathy looked around at those present: Taggat being supported by Mae; John Chadwick protectively holding Maggie against the building wind; Richard, dear Richard...The scene at the beach house yesterday wasn't pretty, and Cathy wasn't sure Richard would stay for the funeral after she had told him about Brian and her plans for the baby, but out of respect for Sabrina, he had come. Richard had also announced his impending depar-ture for London to continue his cardiovascular research.; Mac Orberson, who had advised Cathy that all the charges for her Christmas Eve festiv-ities had been dropped.

The tall gray hair minister cleared his throat signaling everyone he was ready to begin. "We have come to this hilltop to celebrate the passing of Sabrina MacKenzie. Yes my friends, celebrate, not mourn. Sabrina has cast off the burden of life to enjoy the tranquillity of eternity. She has joined those that have gone before her, and she is embraced by their presence. She lives on in the hearts of those she has left behind, and she will, therefore, live forever. Not a day will go by that she is not thought of, envisioned, or talked to in some fashion.

God grants us a special divine power, the capability of creating new life. Sabrina lives on with new life, her daughter, Stephanie. She is a living part of Sabrina's very existence. Though she is too young to have known her mother, she'll rejoice someday in being Sabrina's child." The minister turned and looked at Cathy. "Our lives never seem to turn out the way we plan them. There's never enough time to do all we want. We must remember why we're here, why God has put us on the Earth. Our existence is for enjoyment of life itself, to love our fellow man, and to make the lives that come after us easier than those before. Sometimes, the way seems to disappear from our sight. We have difficulty finding our true path down life's road. But, we should never fear, for all we have to do is reach out, and the way is illuminated. The way is given to us by God's hand. Trust in Him, and you'll never be lost." The minister returned his focus on the casket.

"Don't ask me to explain the ways of the Lord, for only he knows the divine plan. Be joyful in the knowledge that he is always here. Let us pray...Our Father, accept the soul of Sabrina MacKenzie with open arms. Help us understand the meaning of your ways. Help Stephanie grow and be mindful of Your and Sabrina's gift of life. Keep all of us in your watchful eye and forgiving heart. Amen."

The minister walked over to Cathy and leaned forward. "Be strong, Cathy. Sabrina has entrusted you her life's most prized possession, her child. A child Sabrina gave her very own life to create. Remember only that fact as the years ahead reveal their hardships and wonders. May God go with you."

"Thank you," Cathy choked.

Brian and Cathy remained at the graveside as the remaining mourners filed past the casket and dispersed to their respective cars. The snow, which began as a flurry, was now spitting as a brisk northwestern wind breathed life into it. In preparation for the cold evening, the geese were talking and preparing to fly inland to fill their bellies. Their gaggling was reaching takeoff pitch.

"Let's get back to the car," Brian shivered. "It's really getting cold."

Cathy released his hand and walked to the casket. "Good-by, Sabrina. I love you." Cathy briefly touched the surface of the casket. She knew Sabrina wasn't in there. Sabrina's essence would always be in Cathy's thoughts, her dreams, and her heart. Cathy turned, walked to Brian, and firmly grasped his hand. "I'm ready to go."

"Good. Let's go to the car."

Cathy pulled back on his hand. "No. Not to the car, not just yet."

"Then where, Cath. I'm getting cold. Aren't you?"

"Yes, I'm cold, but I want you to know I'm ready to go to California with you. Ready for Stephanie and I to be with you, forever." She grasped his waist and hugged tightly. "I need you. Is that enough?"

"For now, yes." Brian embraced Cathy, and tears began to re-form in his already reddened eyes. "Let's go get Stephanie. We have a new life, a better life ahead."

Cathy looked back over her shoulder. "I'll be back, Sabrina. I'll be back, and I'll bring your daughter when I come." She looked back at Brian. "Ok. Now, I'm ready to go to the car. I'm freezing."

As Brian and Cathy walked back to the limo with their heads bent against the driving snow, two figures walked from the shadows of the surrounding trees, approached the partially snow covered casket and stopped. The larger of the two brushed the soft white blanket from the bronze lid and let a gloved hand linger lightly on the cold steel. The smaller figure snuggled closer to the first waiting for the cue to leave. After a few solemn moments, they departed.

As the shadowy couple's car slowly passed the edge of the Bay below the cemetery, the flock of anxious geese seemed to jump off the surface. They circled low over the spot from where they erupted, and at first, seemed to lose their sense of direction in the spitting snow storm. Their squawking was loud enough to draw the mourners' attention from their partially sound-proofed limousines. As they watched the flock, it circled lower and lower until it seemed the birds would surely fly into the trees surrounding the cemetery. However, one of the older geese finally took up the lead position in the V-formation and instinctively led the flock to a safer altitude directing them inland to the feeding grounds. Each bird followed the older goose without question, forging ahead with a new confidence in the final destination.

THE BEGINNING

9 780595 000166